The Portable
Henry James

Edited with an Introduction by
JOHN AUCHARD

PENGUIN BOOKS

PENGUIN BOOKS

Published by the Penguin Group

Penguin Group (USA) Inc., 375 Hudson Street, New York, New York 10014, U.S.A.
Penguin Group (Canada), 90 Eglinton Avenue East, Suite 700, Toronto,
Ontario, Canada M4P 2Y3 (a division of Pearson Penguin Canada Inc.)
Penguin Books Ltd, 80 Strand, London WC2R 0RL, England
Penguin Ireland, 25 St Stephen's Green, Dublin 2, Ireland (a division of Penguin Books Ltd)
Penguin Group (Australia), 250 Camberwell Road, Camberwell,
Victoria 3124, Australia (a division of Pearson Australia Group Pty Ltd)
Penguin Books India Pvt Ltd, 11 Community Centre, Panchsheel Park, New Delhi – 110 017, India
Penguin Group (NZ), cnr Airborne and Rosedale Roads,
Albany, Auckland 1310, New Zealand (a division of Pearson New Zealand Ltd)
Penguin Books (South Africa) (Pty) Ltd, 24 Sturdee Avenue,
Rosebank, Johannesburg 2196, South Africa

Penguin Books Ltd, Registered Offices: 80 Strand, London WC2R 0RL, England

First published in Penguin Books 2004

5 7 9 10 8 6

Copyright © Penguin Group (USA) Inc., 2004
All rights reserved

Page 620 constitutes an extension of this copyright page.

LIBRARY OF CONGRESS CATALOGING-IN-PUBLICATION DATA
James, Henry, 1843–1916.
[Selections. 2003]
The portable Henry James / edited with an introduction by John Auchard.
p. cm.
Includes bibliographical references.
ISBN 0-14-243767-0
I. Auchard, John, II. Title.
PS2112.A3 2003
813'.4—dc21   2003048739

Printed in the United States of America
Set in Adobe Sabon

PENGUIN CLASSICS

THE PORTABLE HENRY JAMES

HENRY JAMES was born in 1843 on Washington Place in New York City, of Scottish and Irish ancestry. His father was a prominent theologian and philosopher, and his elder brother, William, was also famous as a philosopher. He attended schools in New York and later in London, Paris, and Geneva, entering the law school at Harvard in 1862. In 1865 he began to contribute reviews and short stories to American journals. In 1875, after two prior visits to Europe, he settled for a year in Paris, where he met Flaubert, Turgenev, and other literary figures. The next year he moved to London, where he became so popular in society that in the winter of 1878–79 he confessed to accepting 107 invitations. In 1898 he left London and went to live at Lamb House, Rye, Sussex. Henry James became a naturalized British citizen in 1915, was awarded the Order of Merit, and died in 1916.

In addition to many short stories, plays, and books of criticism, autobiography, and travel, he wrote some twenty novels, the first being *Roderick Hudson* (1875). This was followed by *The Europeans, Washington Square, The Portrait of a Lady, The Bostonians, The Princess Casamassima, The Tragic Muse, The Spoils of Poynton, The Awkward Age, The Wings of the Dove, The Ambassadors,* and *The Golden Bowl.*

JOHN AUCHARD is a professor of English at the University of Maryland, College Park. He has been a Fulbright lecturer at the Università degli Studi di Milano, a visiting professor at the Università di Messina, and has also taught at the University of North Carolina. Among his works on Henry James are *Silence in Henry James: The Heritage of Symbolism and Decadence* and the Penguin Classics edition of James's *Italian Hours.*

Contents

Introduction

I.

When H. G. Wells attacked Henry James's late fiction, he described "a magnificent but painful hippopotamus resolved at any cost, even at the cost of its dignity, on picking up a pea which has got into a corner of its den." Wells claimed, wickedly, that upon reaching the end of a James tale one generally discovered something terribly reduced, supremely portentous, and certainly peculiar—"on the altar, very reverently placed, intensely there, is a dead kitten, an egg-shell, a bit of string." A few years later E. M. Forster must have been happy with himself when he wrote that James's people recalled "the exquisite deformities who haunted Egyptian art in the reign of Akhenaton—huge heads and tiny legs, but nevertheless charming." Joseph Conrad revered the work of Henry James, but even he could only "imagine with pain the man in the street trying to read it. . . . One could almost see the globular lobes of his brain painfully revolving, and crushing and mangling the delicate thing." Even sympathetic magazine reviewers of the day had to admit that although the novels of Henry James might sometimes bleed, generally they did not bleed red.

Such generalizations enraged Ezra Pound: "I am tired of hearing pettiness talked about James's style. . . . I have heard no word of the major James, of the hater of tyranny; book after early book against oppression, against all the sordid petty personal crushing oppression, the domination of modern life. . . . The outbursts in *The Tragic Muse,* the whole of *The Turn of the Screw,* human liberty, personal liberty, the rights of the individual against all sorts of intangible bondage! The passion of it, the continual passion of it in this man who, fools said, didn't 'feel.' I have never yet found a man of emotion against whom idiots didn't raise this cry." Nor could Virginia Woolf tolerate complaints about a Byzantine syntax or an obsession with the niceties of upholstery: "For to be as subtle as Henry James one must also be as robust; to enjoy his power of exquisite selection one must have 'lived and loved and cursed and floundered and enjoyed and suffered,' and, with the appetite of a giant, have swallowed the whole." It is as if she would cast Mr. Henry James as Rodin's great statue of Balzac, looming high above the human comedy.

As the twentieth century kept reading Henry James, Jorge Luis Borges found him darker, more exotic, and heavier than anyone had suspected: "I have visited some literatures of the East and West; I have compiled an encyclopedic anthology of fantastic literature; I have translated Kafka, Melville, and Bloy; I know of no stranger work than that of Henry James. The writers I have enumerated are, from the first line, amazing; the universe postulated by their pages is almost professionally unreal; James, before revealing what he is, a resigned and ironic inhabitant of Hell, runs the risk of appearing to be no more than a mundane novelist, less colorful than others." And then it was Graham Greene who said that after "the death of Henry James a disaster overtook the English novel." Greene's final tribute is unequivocal: "He is as solitary in the history of the novel as Shakespeare in the history of poetry."

And so even today one begins an introduction to Henry James with some defensiveness, and a mulish desire to gather the troops, for the talk of the fussy, the bloodless, and the absurdly subtle never goes away. There is some truth in such talk, but not much truth.

II.

For example, André Maurois was mostly wrong when he called James "a great writer who spent his whole life wandering in a literary limbo between the paradise of European culture and the hell that was the Golden Age of America." The fact is that, even in the earliest tales, signs of stagnation trouble that European seduction. Rare lives may unfold on wonderfully manicured English lawns or they may shift about behind beautiful Left Bank façades, but for the most part in Henry James, Europe waits and waits for new blood. Although it was in 1920, four years after James's death, that Ezra Pound called Europe "an old bitch gone in the teeth," Pound had long judged it a "botched civilization" for which so many young would soon die. Back in 1907, when Picasso had sensed that European vitality was dying out after a 2,000-year run, his visionary *Les Demoiselles d'Avignon* thrust slashing African masks beside the languishing graces of Western high culture. For Picasso at least, if renewal was to come, it would have to come from the boundlessly raw.

Although admittedly milder than Picasso's explosion onto the European scene, the cheerfully barbaric American vitality of Henry James's fiction—"she's not, after all, a Comanche savage," someone says in defense of Daisy Miller—had been unsettling European culture for decades, and it had been offering its disruption in even the most casual gestures. When at the start of *The Portrait of a Lady* the American Isabel Archer walks out onto the lawn of a splendid English estate, a dog, "looking up and barking hard," runs straight at her "with great rapidity." Rather than cry out, as any young lady might do, she grabs up the quivering thing "without hesitation" and holds him up "face to face while he continued his quick chatter." The American energy concentrated in her outstretched hands is characteristic—bracing, fearless, somewhat thoughtless. The listless men look up from their teacups and they stare—"The ladies will save us," one of them has just said—and only then do they begin to move. When a Europeanized aunt soon reprimands the young woman from Albany that "Young girls here—in decent houses—don't sit alone with gentlemen late at night," Isabel asks to be told about all the things one should not do. "So as to do them?" asks her aunt. "So as to choose," says Isabel. Choice. It was to become a tremendous American word, and it still has power to make the world tremble.

Elegant, smart, universally admired, and far better adjusted to the European ways than was Daisy Miller, Isabel Archer nonetheless betrays a fierce disposition when she describes a vision of happiness that may seem shocking even today: "A swift carriage of a dark night, rattling with four horses over roads that one can't see—that's my idea of happiness." Even more reckless and unattached than Whitman on the open road—at least he dreams of a *camerado* moving along vaguely beside him—this superior nineteenth-century woman suggests a self-reliant resistance that will make her hard to hold: by society, by family, by husband, children, friends, tradition, by any demands from the outside whatever, by anyone or anything.

With his so-called "International Theme," James takes what is best in the American character—and his Americans can have remarkable vigor and freshness—and he attempts to merge it with the great European achievement. It is with such an ambition that James sweeps his generally appealing Americans over the sea, and then makes them—amiable people who love their liberty—squint hard into the complicating mists of history. That history generally reveals itself in a social aspect marked by manners, for an infinite past has taught James's Europeans that there is a good way of doing almost everything—a good way to begin an acquaintance or end one, a good way to speak or remain silent or prepare an *omelette soufflée,* or raise your daughter or accommodate an exigent parent or express thanks or sympathy or grief, or properly hide that grief, or end an affair or begin one, or enter a room or a box at the opera or prepare to die, or perhaps even to pick up an apricot.

If you agree to conform, European life can be good, for that life will be more artful, polished, layered, subtle, skilled, practiced, ordered, serene, thoughtful, graceful, cultivated, and, sometimes, intelligent. But Europe makes powerful demands, and it takes things away, and what it takes away can make you restless and bored, and it can make you stand oddly still. James's Venice, for example, may represent the ultimate European *polis* as social art, and yet in *Italian Hours* she is a stern mistress—the "fault of Venice is that, though she is easy to admire, she is not easy to live with"—for such beauty does not come without sacrifice. If you wish to live with her or recline in her shadow, you must study and learn to conform, for every inch of the city must look and act as Venice always has—or almost. So keep your raucous invention to yourself, and your tonic wildness too, and a good deal of your self-expression—at least as long as you linger in the lagoon where James suggests that something may have gone wrong, that the long bewitching, accumulated heaped-up beauty can sometimes feel like splendid dying: "Decay is in this extraordinary place golden in tint and misery *couleur de rose.*"

Then there are the Americans in their prototypical "terrible town" of New York, where, in 1907 in *The American Scene,* James already recognized "the power of the most extravagant of cities, rejoicing, as with the voice of the morning, in its might, its fortune, its unsurpassable conditions." Although breathing in a "thinner air" than in any European capital, James is nonetheless stirred by "the universal will to move—to move, move, move as an end in itself, an appetite at any price." His American city "grows and grows, flinging abroad its loose limbs even as some unmannered young giant at his 'larks,' and that the binding stitches must for ever fly further and faster and draw harder; the future complexity of the web, all under the sky and over the sea, becoming thus that of some colossal set of clockworks, some steel-souled machine room of brandished arms and hammering fists and opening and closing jaws." The wondrous, monstrous, rejoicing New World capital amazes and astounds Henry James, and it seethes with life, but the truth is that it never really works as a place for him.

And yet, still, he never forgets that magnificent Europe is a subtly damaged culture—or perhaps he merely discovers inevitable features of a mature one. In *The American,* Christopher Newman goes to Paris and in all innocence first mistakes a marquis for a butler, and then mistakes an aristocratic family's ruthlessness for merely stubborn manners. Yet it is unwise to make too much of Americans deceived by weary Europeans who have steeped so long in experience that their every move has become cautious, calculated, shrewd, and manipulative. James's Europeans have learned over time what his Americans do not yet know, that survival is never secure, that great care must always be taken, that bad air blankets the town every night, that a swift carriage of a dark night can smash into a wall, that it is not so easy to discover a mountain of gold, that one can never be sure of a lover, or in fact sure of anything. In *The Ambassadors* the charming Marie de Vionnet does not explain to Lambert Strether why she has decided to marry off her daughter in a loveless but advantageous—in her terms, surely, a suitable—match. She merely invokes an inflexible old wisdom, a *"vieille sagesse,"* as the foundation of her actions, and she leaves it at that. The shaken American stares into her exquisitely delivered revelation, suddenly aware that he is glimpsing something "ancient and cold in it—what he would have called the real thing."

Some Europeans might insist that American innocence in Henry James is less ignorance of evil than an inability to comprehend how insecure and dangerous life can be, and so James's daring, generous, sometimes lucky, optimistic, incurably young, and frequently rich Americans make big mistakes and often fare badly—even when Europeans have nothing to do with it. After ignoring their counsel, Daisy Miller walks into the miasmal Colosseum at midnight and then takes ill and dies. When experience gets redefined by James as intense awareness, and when tradition instructs that every perception and every action has a past, a present, and a future, the value of innocence becomes a tough call. The innocent eye that rakes the horizon may be as glorious as Emerson's transparent eyeball or as fresh as the eye of an American Adam who would extinguish prejudice and see the world as if for the first time. But then again it may only be an eye that offers a fearfully blank stare, and then blinks and forgets.

From the vantage of the early twenty-first century, the clash of civilizations that James considered can seem relatively mild, and yet his exploration remains sobering. If even between sibling cultures an abyss was discovered to have quietly ripped open—and in his fiction none of the marriages between the Old World and the New claim sure success—what chance does the West have to reconcile with the world of the real East, where stern authority has no desire to mask its will with exquisite charm? In Melville's book an island harpooner awakens out of Ramadan and then slides into bed beside his newly found American friend, but Queequeg and Ishmael drift through a woozy political idyll virtually impossible in or out of Henry James. The divide between a culture of individual freedom and a culture of tradition—H. G. Wells identified communities of will, and communities of faith and obedience—is a great divide, and it is a persistent and deep one in Henry James, as it should be, even though many Americans in the novels scarcely seem to notice. In the tales and novels it often is the exact place where things tear asunder, a place of broadly political crisis that stubbornly resists reconciliation—at least without the virtual annihilation of one side or the other.

In reference to that annihilation, the death of Daisy Miller is really only a little death, and soon some battles go to the Americans. In James's 1884 "Pandora," a German aristocrat on a New York–bound ocean liner sits on deck and reads a tale about a "forward little American girl, who plants herself in front of a young man in the garden of an hotel." Of course he is reading Henry James's *Daisy Miller.* After having dismissed Pandora Day as merely a "Daisy Miller *en herbe,*" Count Otto Vogelstein soon recognizes her more hard-boiled charm, and later in Washington he observes the young woman on a sofa beside the President of the United States: "He looked eminent, but he looked relaxed, and the lady beside him was making him laugh." Soon news comes that her unremarkable fiancé from Utica, New York, has been offered the post of minister to Holland. With "Pandora," James extends his consideration of the general American character, here as that of the "American Girl" defined by a simple fact: "You knew her by many different signs, but, chiefly, infallibly, by the appearance of her parents. It was her parents that told the story; you always saw that her parents could never have made her." She, this American girl, had invented herself. And by 1884 one already suspects that, unlike Daisy Miller, Miss Pandora Day—with her half-ominous, half-innocuous name—will be hard to kill.

But stray victories or not, for the most part in James's fiction, those Americans who would be free take great personal risks, and those societies that would be very free risk losing some of the most alluring and stabilizing features of civilization. James presents a cultural and moral interplay where there are always trade-offs. One way or another in his fiction, freedom—and it is heady freedom—figures as a wild ride into the night, even when a young lady merely stays up late with gentlemen, or chooses an ill-advised husband, or takes a quiet stroll around town after dark. When at the end of *Daisy Miller* the two rivals meet over the young woman's grave, her Italian escort sputters out his excuse: "For myself, I had no fear; and she wanted to go." When James revised the tale, he intensified the declaration: " 'For myself I had no fear; and *she*—she did what she liked.' Winterbourne's eyes attached themselves to the ground. 'She did what she liked!' "

To do what one likes. If it does not quite suggest the dark side of democracy, it nonetheless sounds a hint of brutality as obdurate as anything that motivates the aristocrats who work for themselves, for their families, for their heritage, for their own specific kind. And as much as James loves the Americans he creates—and that is almost always the case—he brings few of them close to happiness. Again and again as their personal paths trace the long bloody unfolding of human liberty, James shows their freedom as extraordinary—as a wondrous thing— and yet he never fails to present it as perilous, and as one of the most fragile inventions that has been brought out onto the face of the earth.

III.

Then there is the complaint that James is unfathomably slow and dull. And in fact after the great, astounding, and sometimes freakish works of Melville, Hawthorne, and Poe, the post–Civil War ambition for something called realism could seem woefully tame. William Dean Howells, James's early editor and then lifelong friend, was writing his own fiction with the expressed ambition of presenting "poor Real life," but the younger novelist soon grew tired of such humility, and in 1871 James would report to Grace Norton that, concerning his mentor, "Thro' thick and thin I continue to enjoy him—or rather thro' thin and thinner." But Howells, with his healthy democratic sense that there was "nothing insignificant," was on a good path, and in time that path would become quietly exciting and unquestionably important. As unengaging as the word "realism" may sound, it shouldered a genuinely monumental task as it addressed the radical question of what remained of interest and value once the gods had vanished and all the altars had been stripped bare. No longer encouraged to be remotely religious, dimly transcendental, or even, as in Edgar Allan Poe's tales, obscurely magical, literature found itself moving onto a potentially dispirited plain of bluntly materialized existence. Some writers, like Bret Harte, Hamlin Garland, and Mary Noailles Murfree, would develop a narrower focus than Howells and dress things up any way they could, throwing out lots of asides that were regional, colloquial, indigenous, or merely peculiar to the elders sitting in rush-bottomed chairs close to the walls. But although local color had diversity and much charm, even such keen observation would never carry the day. The realist revolution had to come from a different focus, and it did.

Although of course that revolution did not start with the fine entertainments that were the Sherlock Holmes tales, that violin-playing English genius understood just where to look. Peering down hard at absolutely pure matter, Arthur Conan Doyle's detective comprehended that, in order to see the reign of wonder that remained, you needed formidable attention and unflinching concentration, the likes of which had never been known. To find fascination in the divested modern condition, one had to pore over every bit of phenomena as if it were a matter of life and death. And only then might you discover the villain of the piece, the secret truth or the innocent son, and only then would your mind attain to full activity. You would scarcely move a muscle with all that tense watching—and thinking—but you would have your adventure; and so detective fiction, still furiously active today, suddenly began. Holmes's perceptions would make a baffled Dr. Watson think the solution was magic, but the correction had to come: the solution was nothing of the kind, dear Watson; it was only "Elementary." There was not one drop of anything occult about it, but merely great intensity and surpassing attention to pure phenomena—an oxymoronic miracle of realism to be sure, but the stuff of realism nonetheless.

Arthur Conan Doyle may have worried about dullness, and he may have known that to make people pay *that* much attention, at the outset at least you needed something sensational, and it had to be discovered on the blood-splattered carpet. Also, the rug would do well to be found in a really nice room of a duke's country house, or at least somewhere in the gloomier reaches of the vicarage. But the scenes to which

Henry James brought his observation were rarely the sort which intrigued Sherlock Holmes, and so his subjects could seem somewhat dim—until one noticed that they were tumultuous. For example, in "The Beast in the Jungle," the shape of the tale is the shape of a life in which absolutely nothing happens, and that is the point—although as it is finally extended, elaborated, and then comprehended, it is shocking and breathtaking. James himself knew he would never—or almost never—write of "murders, mysteries, islands of dreadful renown, hairbreadth escapes, miraculous coincidences and buried doubloons." Yet he would find tigers leaping from among the gentle English hills and catastrophe descending over tea.

Far from any muscular picaresque—and that is the habit that still marked the philosophical journey of *Moby-Dick* or the more purely moral one of *Huckleberry Finn*—his real vector was the inward turn. Only superficially social, less so in the late fiction when the cast of characters would generally diminish, James's movement was that of the mind and eye, and so it may be no surprise that he fared rather badly during the five long years when he wrote mostly for the stage. Finally in 1895, when he faced a torrent of catcalls on the opening night of *Guy Domville,* he fled from the theater "green with dismay." He declared that "you can't make a sow's ear out of a silk purse" and returned to the novel. In his effort to win some kind of popular success, he had been willing to rewrite both *Daisy Miller* and *The American* as comedies, but happy endings were not nearly enough for his restless audience, and all along he must have known that his great genius was contending with an ostentatious genre that, at least for his hypersensitive characters, could become a wild and fretting dumb show. When, with a long supersubtle look, a gentleman onstage turned to a lady and she looked back at him, all the two valiant actors could do was tense their muscles, stand eerily still, and hope that no one coughed. People always cough. Perhaps it is somewhat ironic that in the gigantizing medium of film James finally has some of the popular success he sought. Only now, as the camera looms in and the sound track swells, can the flicker of an eye show as the absolute cataclysm the playwright probably intended it to be.

Attention to the psychological, social, and moral close-up, as well as to the unattended impulses and vibrations that gather—strike—then race off in each life each day, had never known such luxury. Critics had long claimed that in Henry James time did creep, and it was nothing new when the subtitle of a 1903 review announced "Four Hundred Large Pages in Which Little Happens." But that was almost the point, for as James's novels offered more and still more attention to the multiplied phenomena of life, seconds swelled into eternities where in the half-space between stairway and door an intimacy could be sealed, a betrayal could be launched, a marriage might end, or, as a young woman slowly turned to the wall, she could precisely begin to die. When Graham Greene called Henry James the last of the religious writers, he probably did not mean to insist that James believed in God, but rather that James achieved a near-religious quality as the "last novelist" to whom everything was important and everything mattered—every thought, every half-thought, every hesitation, every evasion, every breath, all of it.

Yet intense attention to an infinite number of minor things—in Joyce, in Proust, in Virginia Woolf, and notoriously in Freud, among others—would more generally mark the modernist sense of what mattered. Even the once heedless Oscar Wilde would one day write from prison that in the end all things had been important: "I forgot that every little action of the common day makes or unmakes character." He adds up the pieces: "While I see that there is nothing wrong in what one does, I see that there is something wrong in what one becomes." It was strange that, like the great Cotton Mather worrying if the tiniest stumble revealed an offense against his Lord, the secular world had slowed all the way down and had once again begun to take infinite care with all the neglected bits of life.

But there was good reason for the heightened attention. In the eighth century the Venerable Bede described human life as a bird's flight through a warm hall in winter: "the bird swiftly sweeps through the great hall and goes out the other side." Even in an age of belief, the image must have been formidable, but in the purely secular moment of the late nineteenth century the flight had gained immensely in speed and terror. Writing in an age when God was surely dead, Walter Pater suggested how that flight must somehow be slowed and enriched, its doomed arrow's path made into a near-infinite and more complicated thing. In the conclusion of his 1873 *The Renaissance,* Pater recognized the absolutely demystified human span: "We are all under sentence of death but with a sort of indefinite reprieve." And he observed that "[o]ur one chance lies in expanding that interval, into getting as many pulsations as possible into the given time." Pater's sleight of hand with that briefly living interval might be no more than a clever substitute for the lost Eternity, but the enlargement—once it was glutted with what he called "the fruit of the multiplied consciousness"—might still serve. When Pater spoke of how the artistic consciousness could give a renewed "quickened sense of life," he said one must "burn with a hard gem-like flame." And so, as if yearning for the lost world's extinguished tongues of fire, he moved to make the enriching artist as good as a priest.

A few years after the death of Henry James, James Joyce—Borges's "near-infinite Irishman"—brought modernist expansion to its limit and, for some, beyond it. When he superimposed ten years out of Homer on an ordinary Dublin day, he immeasurably amplified an arbitrary eighteen-hour period and thereby managed to return at least some sublime richness to the dwindling moment of modern life. Borges judged that the accomplishment of *Ulysses,* in its "unrelenting examination of the tiniest details that constitute consciousness," in fact "stops the flow of time." Yet the fact is that in Henry James a similar enrichment and a similar temporal adjustment had been going on for decades.

In his 1884 essay "The Art of Fiction," James speaks of a writer envied for opportunities which allowed her to write about the "way of life of the French Protestant youth." James reports she had no special opportunities, but she merely had been gifted with a "genius" for static observation,

... having once, in Paris, as she ascended a staircase, passed an open door where, in the household of a *pasteur,* some of the young Protestants were seated at a table round a finished meal. The glimpse made a picture; it lasted only a moment, but that moment was experience. She had got her direct personal impression, and she turned out her type ... she was blessed with the faculty which when you give it an inch takes an ell, and which for the artist is a much greater source of strength than any accident of residence or of place in the social scale. The power to guess the unseen from the seen, to trace the implication of things, to judge the whole piece by the pattern, the condition of feeling life in general so completely that you are well on your way to knowing any particular corner of it—this cluster of gifts may almost be said to constitute experience, and they occur in country and in town, and in the most different stages of education. If experience consists of impressions, it may be said that impressions *are* experience, just as (have we not seen it?) they are the very air we breathe. Therefore, if I should certainly say to a novice, "Write from experience and experience only," I should feel that this was rather a tantalizing monition if I were not careful immediately to add, "Try to be one of the people on whom nothing is lost!"

"Try to be one of the people on whom nothing is lost"— Sherlock Holmes might have given the advice to his medical man friend. In the blink of an eye—"it lasted only a moment"—the man or woman of genius takes the fleeting impression and clicks on it and freezes it, and then expands it almost to infinity.

In *The Portrait of a Lady* Isabel Archer stands in a similar doorway and, with sudden intensity, sees a flash of life. Beyond "the threshold of the drawing room she stopped short"—and there, in the space of an instant, she perceives her husband with one of their old friends:

Madame Merle was there in her bonnet, and Gilbert Osmond was talking to her; for a minute they were unaware she had come in. Isabel had often seen that before, certainly; but what she had not seen, or at least had not noticed, was that their colloquy had for the moment converted itself into a sort of familiar silence, from which she instantly perceived that her entrance would startle them. Madame Merle was standing on the rug, a little way from the fire; Osmond was in a deep chair, leaning back and looking at her. Her head was erect, as usual, but her eyes were bent on his. What struck Isabel first was that he was sitting while Madame Merle stood; there was an anomaly in this that arrested her. Then she perceived that they had arrived at a desultory pause in their exchange of ideas and were musing, face to face, with the freedom of old friends who sometimes exchange ideas without uttering them. There was nothing to shock in this; they were old friends in fact. But the thing made an image, lasting only a moment, like a sudden flicker of light. Their relative positions, their absorbed mutual gaze, struck her as something detected. But it was over by the time she had finally seen it.

As if with a magnifying glass out of a detective story, something negligible yet powerful has been detected, and although the "thing" is over by the time it is seen, the perception is prodigious. Isabel Archer has perceived an unsuspected and concealed intimacy—and thereafter a dark secret ranges about in the shadows.

By 1905 Claude Bragdon had recognized that, "Like some microscopist whose instrument, focussed on a pellucid drop of water, reveals within its depths horrible monsters feeding on one another, Mr. James shows forth the baffled passion, fear, jealousy, and wounded pride, the high courage and self-sacrifice which may lurk beneath the fair and shining surface of modern life in its finest and most finished manifestations." Isabel Archer has become someone upon whom nothing is lost, and her adventure has become one of perception and heightened thought: "Isabel had often seen that before, certainly; but what she had not seen, or at least had not noticed. . . ." Such moments of static perception and intense consideration are particularly common and extended in the last three James novels, in *The Ambassadors, The Wings of the Dove,* and *The Golden Bowl.* At a climactic moment in that final novel, for example, Adam Verver asks his daughter an apparently mild question and his daughter responds, also mildly, in twenty words—but not before a narration of seven hundred tense words describes the extraordinary mutual consciousness that fills the seconds between uttered question and uttered response. Thought in James becomes a great player, and it is thought accreted, aestheticized, glorified, toyed with, poeticized, rarefied, refined, indulged, coaxed, venerated, and eventually haunted.

The first *New York Edition* preface describes the consequence of how complexity rages when such thought slowly unwraps experience: "Really, universally, relations stop nowhere, and the exquisite problem of the artist is eternally but to draw, by a geometry of his own, the circle within which they shall happily *appear* to do so." And in the final preface, "the whole conduct of life consists of things done, which do other things in their turn, just so our behaviour and its fruits are essentially one and continuous and persistent and unquenchable, so the act has its way of abiding and showing and testifying, and so, among our innumerable acts, are no arbitrary, no senseless separations." First and last, James emphasizes that nothing ever stops, that experience is "unquenchable," that no detail fades, that no action is discrete, that closure is fantasy, that there is always another side, and another turn of the screw, and therefore that some complicating beast—one probably unknown to the simpler convictions of only yesterday—is surely out there ready to be born. A century later the lesson remains forceful.

James relates how "the young embroiderer of the canvas of life soon began to work in terror, fairly, of the vast expanse of the surface, of the boundless number of its distinct perforations . . . ," and how that artist had to comprehend that "continuity is never, by the space of an instant or an inch, broken, and that, to do anything at all, he has at once intensely to consult and intensely to ignore it." Such metabolizing complication becomes the generalized condition of the late fiction, and therefore, in *The Golden Bowl*, Fanny Assingham must explain to her husband how the unfathomable complexity of each "case" means that one must always proceed with great caution:

He smoked a minute: then with a groan: "Lord, are there so many?"

"There's Maggie's and the Prince's, and there's the Prince's and Charlotte's."

"Oh yes; and then," the Colonel scoffed, "there's Charlotte's and the Prince's."

"There's Maggie's and Charlotte's," she went on—"and there's also Maggie's and mine. I think too that there's Charlotte's and mine. Yes," she mused, "Charlotte's and mine is certainly a case. In short, you see, there are plenty. But I mean," she said, "to keep my head."

But the consequent strain on moral judgment was as great as any artistic or psychological strain. Almost a century before Mrs. Assingham's explanation, Madame de Staël had contemplated all the possible causes and connections, and she had declared that to understand all is to forgive all—*"tout comprendre, tout pardonner."* She may have understood too much—or so it seemed, as with one neat declaration she eviscerated not only sin but the heart of blame and the guts of moral responsibility. So her 1807 *Corinne* betrays fear—or at the very least chic weariness—as to where the growing sophistication of her time was taking her and taking everyone. By the end of the nineteenth century, society had grown even more clever, and morality had become even more slippery. In his preface to the 1890 *The Picture of Dorian Gray,* Oscar Wilde declared, "There is no such thing as a moral or an immoral book. Books are well written, or badly written. That is all." Wilde was scandalous and few people troubled over his ethical decrees. Yet one stops and thinks when, in James's final novel, Mrs. Assingham asserts that "stupidity pushed to a certain point *is,* you know, immorality. Just so what is morality but high intelligence?" Here is a shocking, elitist morality to be sure, and yet her view addresses a suspicion of much of the modern world, that the bright ones are the better ones and that "intelligence" is, now, finally, the only supreme good.

Despite her imperious tone, Mrs. Assingham does not speak for Henry James. Or at least it is not that simple. Especially in the late fiction, great intelligence so complicates judgment that the consequent ethical ambiguity brings the best people close to crisis. The difficulty of James's style may in fact be a necessary expression of a moral sense that will never again know the sharp edges of any Hebraic decalogue or any other venerable righteousness. George Steiner has observed that since the late nineteenth century "difficulty" has moved to the center of the aesthetic experience, and there it insolently remains. "No themes," James explains in the preface to *What Maisie Knew,* "are so human as those that reflect for us out of the confusion of life, the close connection of bliss and bale, of things that help with things that hurt, so dangling before us for ever that bright hard metal, of so strange an alloy, one face of which is somebody's right and ease and the other somebody's pain and wrong." Consideration of "point of view" becomes a prime tool of an artistic intelligence that must always move, challenge, test itself, and then perhaps discover an unexpected story at the end. "He and his neighbors are watching the same show," writes James in the preface to *The Portrait of a Lady*, "but one seeing more where the other sees less, one seeing black where the other sees white, one seeing big where the other sees small, one seeing coarse where the other sees fine. And so on, and so on; there is fortunately no saying on what, for the particular pair of eyes, the window may *not* open."

James's preface to *What Maisie Knew* suggests the difficulty, in the increasingly intelligent, increasingly relativistic modern world, of "really keeping the torch of virtue alive in an air tending infinitely to smother it; really in short making confusion worse confounded by drawing some stray fragrance of an ideal across the scent of selfishness, by sowing on barren strands, through the mere fact of presence, the seed of the moral life." When R. P. Blackmur praised James's "pure intelligence," he offered a false congruence, for he blurred the moral/intellectual dilemma. Blackmur claimed that in Henry James, "intelligence is conscience, and the eloquence of conscience is heroic truth," but James's moral determination is never as tidy as that. It has been said that his was the tragedy of a man born between two worlds and at home in neither, and there is some truth in that. Yet equal strain came from a divide as troubling as any between the European and the American ideals. Beautifully raised by a noble father—"our father, caring for our spiritual decency unspeakably more than for anything else"—Henry James everywhere pursued the unwavering moral flame that was still just visible from out of the mists of the past. Yet at the same time he knew what was coming and he looked ahead to seek the fullest expression of human intelligence, which in fact may be the most restless fire that burns.

In 1918 T. S. Eliot called Henry James "the most intelligent man of his generation," a man with a "mind so fine that no idea could violate it." He was not being sarcastic. Eliot understood that when relations never stop, judgments rarely settle, and therefore James's sublimely open mind indeed might have been the best model of the best kind of thought. Of course, at the moment he made his judgment, Eliot was already seeking something other than such expansive liberality and perhaps something other than the best kind of thought, for amid the ashes of the war, Eliot believed that society would be rebuilt with the pillars of judgment and the stones of belief. And so he soon found comfort in the old orthodoxies of traditionalism, Anglo-Catholicism, and the Christian state. Yet his praise of James still seems sincere, even if his declaration hints at something ambiguous and troubling, perhaps that although "be one of the people on whom nothing is lost" may be a noble call, it sounds out a heartless rule, one impossible to fulfill and potentially paralyzing—politically, socially, even morally.

The purely modern intellect of Prince Hamlet discovered that the radically examined and interiorized life is not without grave risks, for the more one thinks about things, the harder action can become, and, yes, of course, there can be few philosopher kings. Dr. Watson, that most decent Polonius, never really gets it, but he moves easily about town and he seems happy, while it is Holmes, with his magnificent teeming brain, who settles in for the night and mainlines cocaine. Eliot suggests such psychological strain for the highly exercised intelligence when he says that James "makes the reader, as well as the personae, uneasily the victim of a merciless clairvoyance." Authorial omniscience once sounded godlike and smug, but if merciless clairvoyance is what guides the creative intelligence through the age of anxiety, the heightened consciousness will know more than it bargained for, more than it wanted to know. What it was to learn, especially about itself, would be terrifying.

James Agate said *The Turn of the Screw* could freeze the scalp of a man reading it on a sunny afternoon at the seaside with the band playing Gilbert and Sullivan. Years before that James had dismissed it as a "bogey-tale" and an *"amusette,"* and for decades most readers took him at his word, at least until 1924 and 1934 when Edna Kenton and then Edmund Wilson questioned the perceptions of a woman on whom nothing is lost—and not the vibration of a hair seems lost on the governess at Bly. In his 1884 "The Art of Fiction," James had offered the apotheosis that "impressions *are* experience," but almost fifteen years had passed when a young woman, one who admitted to a "terrible liability to impressions," was to see, or sense, the presence of two ghosts who, she is sure, wish to possess the children. What she discovers is cataclysmic, although her own homespun Dr. Watson—that most trustworthy housekeeper, Mrs. Grose—has never noticed a thing.

It is in fact a serious tale with broad implications. When it is understood that the ghosts may not be real, but instead that a clergyman's daughter may project the entire ghastly parade, then the grandeur of human perception and human intelligence gets thrown into grave doubt. Although *The Turn of the Screw* was written before Freud would up the sexual ante and finally annul any Enlightenment claim for a purely rational intelligence, back in 1873 Pater had already guessed what was coming: "Experience," he had written, "already reduced to a group of impressions, is ringed round for each one of us by the thick wall of personality. . . . Every one of those impressions is the impression of the individual in his isolation, each mind keeping as a solitary prisoner its own dream of a world."

With *The Turn of the Screw* it is hard to say what is the truth, and the tale does not say. Perhaps a sensitive and intelligent young woman saves an imperiled soul, or perhaps a very unstable young lady merely squints out from a chamber of consciousness that is just a fetid little room. And that room might be heaped with sexual repression and jammed to the rafters with all the lurid and unlovely things a person trails behind from the moment of birth. It is an extreme case here, but in principle it is a general one—that the idea of objectivity may be absurd, for although we may sincerely believe that demons walk the path, the truth may be that the only place they inhabit is the psychic landscape within. Then the little boy would have died for nothing, except to show how in 1898 a fresh psychology was rewriting the world, and showing it—a "real" world so close only a few years before—as farther away than anyone knew and as more uncanny and complex than anyone had ever guessed.

The terrors are countless in *The Turn of the Screw*, but above all there is the tremendous moral ambiguity, and then at the end there is the weight of the dead child, his forehead glistening with a perfect dew of sweat. But perhaps the real fear comes from the isolation the tale comprehends: that here is a life one can make with intelligence, that an attentive, thoughtful, and well-meaning person—even a person who reads Henry James with confidence and care—may in fact be a solitary prisoner in a dream or a nightmare of a world and may never suspect it for a moment.

IV.

The narrator of James's 1896 "The Figure in the Carpet" seeks the *"secret,* or latent intention" in the *oeuvre* of the novelist Hugh Vereker, but that secret remains hidden—if indeed there ever was one. In recent years a hunger for such a clue has focused on the sexuality of Henry James. Although this general introduction can pay scant attention to James's complex biography, it must note the related revolution that has come to the criticism, for although it was with trepidation that James's early biographers circled the ground around "latent homoerotic tendencies," recent biographers and recent critics have often identified homosexuality as the figure in the carpet.

Yet such considerations are not new. As early as 1902 J. P. Mowbray wrote, "In trying to form anything like a comprehensive estimate of Mr. James's mature work, the effeminacy of it has to be counted with. One cannot call it virile." When in Hemingway's 1926 *The Sun Also Rises* Bill Gorton advises Jake Barnes about the sexually debilitating injury he received in the war, he recommends, "That's what you ought to work up into a mystery. Like Henry's bicycle." The reference is to the injury that James reported in his 1914 autobiography *Notes of a Son and Brother*: "Jammed into the acute angle between two high fences . . . I had done myself . . . a horrid even if an obscure hurt." A legend soon grew concerning what James had described as "a private catastrophe or difficulty, bristling with embarrassments." Evidence suggests a back injury, but this is what that legend developed: the young Henry James had fallen from a high bicycle, or from a horse, onto a picket fence, and he had, in some way, been castrated. Some took his admission as an explanation of why he never served in the Civil War. Others said it accounted for his lifelong celibacy.

Some agreed with Blackmur's judgment that, "Like Abélard who, after his injury, raised the first chapel to the Holy Ghost," Henry James turned to art. Others hinted at less theological aspirations. By the time of Hemingway's novel, the "mystery" was so generally well known that the two easygoing fishermen could chat about "Henry" and Hemingway could expect his readers to get it. "It wasn't a bicycle," Jake corrects his friend:

> "He was riding horseback."
> "I heard it was a tricycle."
> "Well," I said. "A plane is sort of like a tricycle. The joystick works the same way."
> "But you don't pedal it."
> "No," I said, "I guess you don't pedal it."
> "Let's lay off that," Bill said.
> "All right. I was just standing up for the tricycle."
> "I think he's a good writer, too," Bill said.

Such oblique and suggestive wordplay—about a bicycle, a tricycle, a pedal, and a joystick—is uncharacteristic of Ernest Hemingway. The two men sense a lapse of decorum and they change the subject. The key to this strange passage is surely the fact that since at least the 1920s in France—and Jake Barnes and Bill Gorton are on their fishing trip in southern France— *une pédale* has been a common term for a male homosexual.

Hemingway went no further. Critics go much further today. Do more recent biographical considerations help explain why in the fiction the marriages generally fail, why isolation so often rules, why so much remains unspoken and passions dry up, why an old man urges a young one to live, why a strange spreading syntax shrouds the place, why a baffled little boy is sent home from school, or, why, facing another man in a graveyard, John Marcher repents the shape of his entire life? Yes and no. The reader is permitted and encouraged to ask any questions whatsoever. Yet back when tradition saw Emily Dickinson's poetry as a retreat from a botched love affair with a gentleman, Allen Tate offered a corrective which still seems sound now that Dickinson is discussed as a lesbian poet: "If we suppose—which is to suppose the improbable—that the love affair precipitated the seclusion, it was only a pretext: she would have found another."

Whatever the reason Emily Dickinson climbed the stairs and shut the door, James did nothing of the kind. For years he dined out almost every night, and then with friends he traveled through England, France, Italy, the United States, or visited those friends in their grand or middling homes, or wrote to them and they always wrote back—letters marked by devotion. When he turned seventy in 1913, almost three hundred of them pooled their money for a suitable gift, and when John Singer Sargent declined payment for the portrait that now hangs in the National Portrait Gallery, they used the fund to buy a golden bowl. When the next year a suffragette entered the Royal Academy and—with a meat cleaver—attacked the painting, 390 well-wishers sent letters of condolence to a friend who admitted he felt "scalped and disfigured." At the death of Henry James in 1916, Logan Pearsall Smith wrote of the loss of a great and remote man:

> I feel as if a great cathedral had disappeared from the skyline, a great country with all its civilization been wiped from the map, a planet lost to the solar system. Things will happen and he won't be there to tell them to, and the world will be a poorer and more meagre place. We shall all miss the charm and danger of our relationship with the dear elusive man, the affectionate and wonderful talks, the charming letters, the icy and sad intervals, the way he kept us all allured and aloof, and shone on us, and hid his light, like a great variable but constant moon.

And in spite of the long-standing affection of many friends, the response was startling when in 1900 Morton Fullerton apparently asked James about that figure in the carpet:

> I wish I could help you, for instance, by satisfying your desire to know from "what port," as you say, I set out. And yet, though the enquiry is, somehow, of so large a synthesis, I think I *can* in a manner answer. The port from which I set out was, I think, that of the *essential loneliness of my life*—and it seems to be the port also, in sooth to which my course again finally directs itself! This loneliness, (since I mention it!)—what is it still but the deepest thing about one? Deeper about *me*, at any rate, than anything else: deeper than my "genius," deeper than my "discipline,"

deeper than my pride, deeper, above all, than the deep counter-mining of art.

Finally one comes back to this gray lumbering thing that James claimed for himself and a little for everyone. It may have been that his loneliness—such persistent alienation, separation, and remoteness, whether at home or abroad, in his fiction or in his private life—was the fruit of a blighted sexuality that kept intimacy at bay while it let regrets mount and mount. But then again, Chekhov said that if you are afraid of loneliness, don't marry, and so perhaps the explanation should go further.

Perhaps the marginalization was idiosyncratic to a singular man born in 1843 into an uncommon family on Washington Place in New York City, with a kind mother named Mary and a one-legged philosopher-father who once saw a ghost hunch down in a room. That father—who had been a friend of both Emerson and Carlyle—so despised pedantry that he kept all five children constantly on the move, from one teacher to another and from one school to another, so that their minds would never fix on any "inhumanity of Method." Before he was twelve, Henry had gone through seven schools in New York alone, and years later he would recall how, during a particularly volatile stretch, he and his siblings "had been to my particular consciousness virtually in motion." But the father went further than that, and would move them from one town, from one country, from one continent and one language to another—"our rootless & accidental childhood," his sister would later complain—with transitory homes in New York, Albany, Boston, Newport, and Cambridge, but also in Geneva, London, Paris, Boulogne-sur-Mer, and Bonn. The James children got a deep experience of European organicism and European repose—but they got it odd, bit by bit, and always on the road. So William James may have known best when he said his brother was "a native of the James family, and has no other country."

But even William James was mostly wrong, for in fact his brother was above all an American, and he had deeply American habits—as when in youth he left his entire family behind and crossed the Atlantic to go it alone. It is useful to recall that when Alexis de Tocqueville came to the United States, he saw a distinguished future for a remarkable people, but he also suspected a somber potential beyond anything the founding fathers had conceived. Here was a people and here was a nation where every connection, every link, was being challenged, and where, as he wrote in 1840, the

> ... woof of time is every instant broken, and the track of generations effaced. Those who went before are soon forgotten; of those who will come after, no one has any idea. ... [The Americans] acquire the habit of always considering themselves as standing alone, and they are apt to imagine that their whole destiny is in their hands.
>
> Thus not only does democracy make every man forget his ancestors, but it hides his descendants and separates his contemporaries from him; it throws him back forever upon himself alone and threatens in the end to confine him entirely within the solitude of his own heart.

Therefore it may have been a blood and bone American isolation that was felt by the expatriate Henry James when he sat on the Riva degli Schiavoni or walked on the Rue de Rivoli. And it may also have been a doggedly American isolation that marks the fiction's independent, rather parentless, vaguely childless people who rarely stay home but keep on the move or at least remain strangely unsettled. Long before Henry James— even before Bartleby turned inward or Hawthorne's minister lowered his black veil—perhaps de Tocqueville was right after all when he wondered if American democracy might not be creating a new kind of human being.

V.

By the turn of the century, art had begun to look suspiciously like religion. Spiritual enough to satisfy languishing needs, it had an esoteric and holy vocabulary, an ancient tradition, a long novitiate, a priesthood jealous of its power, a rule of inspiration, and a pattern of grace. With its meditative isolation and its searching mystic moments, it knew it was vaguely larger than itself and it promised greater things. In our obscurely spir-

itual Western culture, it still does. Its cathedrals—the magnificent museums of New York, Philadelphia, Chicago, Cincinnati,
and James's own fictional "American City."—had suddenly
rent the surface of the earth and risen to cast sublime shadows,
and on Sundays the congregations always came. Although
James was not alone in turning to art for what might still give
life dignity, grace, and shape, he may have taken art's promise
further than anyone else. At the very least, as Blackmur recognized, James honored the "sacred rage of his art as the only
spirit he could fully serve."

He served it well and produced an impressive body of
work—thirty-five volumes in the most inclusive posthumous
edition of his fiction. "Nothing could be allowed to interfere
for long with the labour from which he never rested," his secretary eventually recalled, "except perhaps during sleep." But
the fiction itself was not enough and neither was it enough that
he revised the work of his youth and "matured" those books,
making them right, with countless touches that were fine, and
then finer. His sacred rage took him further than that and led
him to brood on all that he had done before, and then from
1907 to 1909, in the prefaces to his *New York Edition,* he described his own fiction and then the genre of fiction itself,
which he took more seriously than anyone ever had. He presented the novel—so often in his time considered a mere entertainment—as a genuine art form that could be as rich as
painting and as hard as marble. Convinced "that the Novel remains still, under the right persuasion, the most independent,
most elastic, most prodigious of literary forms," he avoided
talk of inspired magic, or of a poet who has drunk the milk of
paradise, and instead presented a mastery entirely unrelated to
any galvanizing glance of the Muse. The prefaces may seem like
tracts of a new theology, but above all they work—as the first
preface introduces his subject—at the demystification of art
and the clearing up of the "rich, ambiguous aesthetic air."

These prefaces discuss the practical problems the writer faces
in making a novel. They are about craft. They talk of the "novelist's process," his "system of observation," the "literary
arrangement," the "constructional game," the "steps taken
and obstacles mastered," the "thousand lures and deceits," the

"points of view," the tricks, mistakes, shortcuts, and inventions, and ultimately how the refining novelist must, hardheadedly, "boil down so many facts in the alembic, so that the distilled result, the produced appearance, should have intensity, lucidity, brevity, beauty." As James elucidates fiction's exacting requirements, he presents the novelist much like the painter who knows the laws of perspective: "I have ever failed," he writes, "to see how a coherent picture of anything is producible save by a complex of fine measurements." He judges his own fiction technically and artistically, which is to say aesthetically. And it is only incidental that, in the critical prefaces at least, James comments on anything political, psychological, biographical, or even moral. It is art and art alone that takes the field. It is art and art alone that sweeps the horizon.

Some said that for James the real world had been replaced by a highly artificial one, a fascinating and complex architectonic structure, but one that existed apart, and was far removed from the heat of the day. When H. G. Wells led the "painful hippopotamus" through his parody, he suggested as much, but then he turned mean: "And the elaborate copious emptiness of the whole Henry James exploit is only redeemed and made endurable by the elaborate copious wit." In a surprisingly courteous response, the seventy-two-year-old James defended his mix of art and life: "I live, live intensely and am fed by life, and my value, whatever it be, is in my kind of expression of that." Then Wells wrote back, churlishly, about his own "horror of dignity, finish and perfection. . . . To you literature like painting is an end, to me literature like architecture is a means, it has a use. . . . I had rather be called a journalist than an artist." At such apostasy James finally lost patience:

Meanwhile I absolutely dissent from the claim that there are any differences whatever in the amenability to art of forms of literature aesthetically determined, and hold your distinction between a form that is (like) painting and a form that is (like) architecture for wholly null and void. There is no sense in which architecture is aesthetically "for use" that doesn't leave any other art whatever exactly as much so; and so far as literature being irrelevant to the literary report upon life, and to its being made as interesting as possible, I regard it as relevant in a degree that leaves everything else behind. It is art that *makes* life, makes interest, makes importance, for our consideration and application of these things, and I know of no substitute whatever for the force and beauty of its process.

It is an astonishing claim. James does not suggest that art explores or deepens life, and neither does he say that art exists for its own sake. Art *makes* life and *makes* importance, and with such an assertion the ordinary way of the world—so rich and easy in its gorgeous formlessness—becomes a hazy, dubious, second-best thing. Here it is art and only art that might touch the world with a consecrated hand and make it live, while the world—as beautiful, languid, and as heavy as Michelangelo's Adam—just waits.

But James understood that when "life" moves onto a subordinate plain, there can be trouble—for the artist, for the writer, even for the reader—and so an elusive balance preoccupies the fiction. As far back as "The Madonna of the Future," an equivocating painter wastes both all his life and all his art, and in *Roderick Hudson* a beautiful woman lures a sculptor away from his sacred rage—and everything collapses. When, in "The Lesson of the Master," the acolyte asks if "the artist shouldn't marry," the Master says he "does so at his peril—he does so at his cost." But then the Master himself marries and the lesson becomes uncertain.

As he was about to grow old, James broadened the question and weighed the more general life of the mind against the more frankly active life, which in the late fiction often becomes the more frankly sexual life. Vaguely artistic but definitely contemplative people in *The Ambassadors*, in "The Beast in the Jungle," and in "The Jolly Corner" eventually ask if they have failed "to live," and late in life each has a moment of blasting regret. If, a year before he died and under biting attack from Wells, James denied any anxiety concerning the schism between art's "sacred hardness" and the scramble of "real" life, he had in fact often troubled over the disquieting split: "Life being all inclusion and confusion, and art being all discrimination and selection." When, in the 1892 "The Real Thing," a book illustrator of an *"édition de luxe"* uses a real gentleman and a real lady as models for images of the upper class, the sketches turn out "execrable." But when an Italian orangemonger and a vulgar Cockney named Miss Churm ("She couldn't spell, and she loved beer") pose as such grand people, the "alchemy of art" succeeds, and the illustrations turn out fine. The real thing, whatever that is.

Although there is no question about it—for Henry James art offered the best chance for some kind of supreme achievement—he would still question art itself. For centuries its myriad images had been dragged down every gleaming hall and then jammed up high on the altars right next to God, and so art had grown spoiled and soft. But things were different now and now art had to fight for its place. James provided his interrogation—in his fiction and in his criticism—just as the twentieth century was about to ask hard questions about art's value and art's claim to truth. James knew that if it was to remain important—and it may no longer be important today—art needed to be challenged and fostered, repelled and embraced, and made generally tougher, and that is what he did. Over a long career he grappled with it and tested it—aesthetically, morally, and pragmatically—with great intelligence and with something that became increasingly rare after his death: a complete lack of cant.

VI.

This introduction has been particularly misleading in one important way. In an attempt to fight the stereotype of a tottering mandarin who was fussy, prissy, prim, and panicked by even one drop of vulgarity, it has dragged Henry James onto the field of battle and has watched him contend with turbulent forces. There has been all of America versus all of Europe, then a deep moral sense confounded by obsessive modern intelligence, and finally art's chiseled perfection defied by the inconstant pulse of life. Those battlegrounds are in fact there, but such emphasis fails when it describes a writer who was a stranger to joy, for as much as anything else, one remembers the pleasure of the text. And then one recalls that years ago a professor told his students that Henry James was the funniest man who ever lived. Everyone blinked, but it did not take that long to get the joke.

Those who read Henry James—and there are more of them out there than is generally imagined—do so in part for the way he says things. He could do anything with a sentence except butcher it, and his friend A. C. Benson spoke with precision when he said that here was a style that could crack a walnut or pat an egg. James could be long-winded, extravagant, arch, polyglot, allusive, fierce, gentle, *recherché*, exquisite as hell, and then—at those gawky moments when he tried to be one of the boys—oddly slangy, indubitably so. Then he would "hang fire" all over the place, or describe a delicately dying heiress who would "pay a hundred percent—and even to the end, doubtless, through the nose." His was a hungering, inching, devious style that could trace the dusky path and then roam too far into the woods, and he knew it: "I wander wild," he notes after a particularly phantasmagoric aside near the end of *Italian Hours*. We read him on Matilde Serao's depiction of "love, at Naples and in Rome," and our lips part as we sound the mystic distinction of those two prepositions. He knew he was something called Jamesian, which most of all means that he was luridly loving of the byways of the sentence and scrupulous beyond the demands of any jealous god. Like anyone, he sometimes tired of his own ways, but most of the time he liked them. When a literary friend complained that Mrs. Thomas Carlyle had mastered "the art of mountaining molehills," James considered and replied, "Ah! but for that, where would *any of us* be?"

When the mature James read Shakespeare, he apparently cared little for the "meaning" of the text. He kept coming back to the words. A "ripe, amused genius," James's Shakespeare—and it is telling and daring that he calls Shakespeare by his own given name "the master"—would heap up words in the "incomparable splendor" of a supreme poetic gift. As his style matured—yes, Shakespeare's—it became "something that was to make of our poor world a great flat table for receiving the glitter and clink of outpoured treasure." Then, perhaps thinking of the mountaining elaborations of his own late works, James claims that such style can go anywhere: "Anything was a subject, always, that offered to sight an aperture of size enough for expression and its train to pass in and deploy themselves. If they filled up all the space, none the worse; they occupied it as nothing else could do." Less a brooding artist than a supreme virtuoso, James's Shakespeare is as careless of audience as he finally is of subject, and at the end he is a "divine musician who, alone in his room, preludes or improvises at the close of the day":

> He sits at the harpsichord, by the open window, in the summer dusk; his hands wander over the keys. They stray far, for his motive, but at last he finds and holds it; then lets himself go, embroidering and refining: it is the thing for the hour and his mood. The neighbors may gather in the garden, the nightingale be hushed on the bough; it is none the less a private occasion, a concert of one, both performer and auditor, who plays for his own ear, his own hand, his own innermost sense, and for the bliss and capacity of his instrument.

Style is different from the sacred rage of perfect art. It is more easy, self-indulgent, general, more generally happy and more promiscuous, and finally it is inescapable. For James it was the essential process by which the individual engages the universe—the very membrane of individual consciousness. It defines and "inevitably provides for Character"—"Every inch of it is personal tone, or in other words brooding expression raised to the highest energy." Shakespeare's powers of expression—"the greatest ever laid upon man"—could meet any part of that universe and work any subject, flicker, or *donnée*. Whatever Shakespeare touched with "the lucid stillness of his style," he changed and made it his, as his style achieved "some copious equivalent of thought for every grain of the grossness of reality." Here unconcerned with the question of any significant "truth," the modernist Henry James has no complaint that "the subjects of the Comedies are, without exception, old wives' tales," and that the "subjects of the Histories are no subjects at all." It is sufficient that "each is but a row of pegs for the hanging of the cloth of gold that is to muffle them."

When James affirmed the "absolute value of Style," he recognized that no matter what it addresses or describes, brilliant language can be irresistible. And his contemplation also suggests what Shakespeare surely knew, that poetic language is sly, and that it rides a conundrum. An agonized king stares into the void and comprehends that life is a petty, dusty, miserable tale told by an idiot, full of sound and fury, signifying nothing. And yet it is an undeniable fact that as unknown generations chant his searing empty lines until the end of time, they will do so, always, with helpless happy smiles upon their lips.

One admits a similar puzzle concerning the idiosyncratic language of Henry James, and that his language gives great pleasure, and that such pleasure is important—even in the postmodern world. Although as a young man James had produced confident works of art, over time his language evolved more than the language of most writers. He got, as Huck Finn might put it, more and more style. Colette spoke of the plays of Shakespeare as those before—and after—he knew he was Shakespeare, and that happened to Henry James. In 1873 a regular guy—"Harry," his family called him in their letters—rode a horse through the Italian *campagna*. When he spotted a tavern, he decided to "rein up and demand a bottle of their best." In 1907—and by then ferociously Jamesian—the Master records that while traveling at dusk through the same Italian countryside, he and his friends had "wished, stomachically, we had rather addressed ourselves of a tea basket." Hardly anything has changed—except the words. We smile at the inimitable locution and we shake our heads with fond delight. But although James is talking about nothing important, the change is monumental. For as he finally rides on into the night, he is moving about on a different planet.

NOTES TO THE INTRODUCTION

xi *"a magnificent but painful hippopotamus"*: Leon Edel and Gordon Ray, eds., *Henry James and H. G. Wells: A Record of Their Friendship, Their Debate on the Art of Fiction, and Their Quarrel* (London: Rupert Hart-Davis, 1959), 248.

xi *"the exquisite deformities"*: E. M. Forster, *Aspects of the Novel* (New York: Harcourt, Brace & World, 1927), 161.

xi *"imagine with pain"*: Roger Gard, ed., *Henry James: The Critical Heritage* (London: Routledge & Kegan Paul, 1968), 268.

xi *"I am tired of hearing pettiness"*: Ezra Pound, "Henry James," in *Literary Essays of Ezra Pound*, ed. T. S. Eliot (New York: New Directions, 1968), 296.

xii *"For to be as subtle as Henry James":* Virginia Woolf, *Collected Essays,* vol. I (New York: Harcourt, Brace & World, 1967), 284 (first published in 1920).

xii *"I have visited some literatures":* Jorge Luis Borges, "The Abasement of the Northmores," in *Selected Non-Fictions,* ed. Eliot Weinberger (New York: Penguin Putnam, 1999), 247–48 (first published in 1945).

xii *"the death of Henry James":* Graham Greene, "François Mauriac," in *Collected Essays* (New York: Penguin, 1951), 91 (first published in 1968).

xii *"He is as solitary":* Graham Greene, "Henry James: the Private Universe," in *Collected Essays* (New York: Penguin, 1951), 34 (first published in 1936).

xii *"a great writer":* André Maurois, preface to Georges Markow-Totevy, *Henry James,* trans. John Cumming (New York: Minerva Press, 1969), vii.

xiii a *"botched civilization":* Ezra Pound, *Hugh Selwyn Mauberley,* V.

xiv the *"fault of Venice":* "Venice" [1882], in *Italian Hours.*

xv *"Decay is in this extraordinary place":* "The Grand Canal" [1892], in *Italian Hours.*

xv *"the power of the most extravagant of cities":* "New York Revisited," in *The American Scene.*

xvi *"vieille sagesse":* *The Ambassadors,* Book Ninth, I.

xvi *communities of will, and communities of faith and obedience:* H. G. Wells, *The Outline of History* (Garden City, New York: Garden City Books, 1940), 735.

xix *it was only "Elementary":* Although iconic in film adaptations, "Elementary, my dear Watson" was never said, exactly, by Holmes in the Conan Doyle tales. But the following passage appears at the end of "The Crooked Man," and he is speaking to Dr. Watson: " 'Elementary,' said he. 'It is one of those instances where the reasoner can produce an effect which seems to his neighbour, because the latter has missed the one little point which is the basis of the deduction. . . .' "

xx *"murders, mysteries, islands of dreadful renown":* "The Art of Fiction."

xxi *"Four Hundred Large Pages":* "James's *The Ambassadors:* Four Hundred Large Pages in Which Little Happens," *Chicago Tribune,* 21 (November 1903): 13; reprinted in Kevin J. Hayes, ed., *Henry James: The Contemporary Reviews* (Cambridge: Cambridge University Press, 1996), 404.

xxi *Graham Greene:* In the essay "François Mauriac," noted earlier; see also Greene's essay, "Henry James: The Religious Aspect," in *Collected Essays*.

xxi *"I forgot that every little action":* Oscar Wilde, *De Profundis*.

xxii *"We are all under sentence of death":* The 1873 conclusion to Pater's *The Renaissance: Studies in Art and Poetry*.

xxii *"near-infinite Irishman":* "Flaubert and His Exemplary Destiny," in Jorge Luis Borges, *Selected Non-Fictions*, ed. Eliot Weinberger (New York: Penguin Putnam, 1999), 393.

xxii *"unrelenting examination":* "Joyce's *Ulysses*," In Weinberger, ed., *Selected Non-Fictions*, 13.

xxiii *"the threshold of the drawing room":* The Portrait of a Lady, chapter XL.

xxiv *"Like some microscopist":* Claude Bragdon, review of *The Golden Bowl, Critic* (January 1905), xlvi, 20.

xxiv *seven hundred tense words:* See *The Golden Bowl*, Book Second, XXXVII; the passage begins with Adam Verver's question, "But to what in the world?"

xxv *"Really, universally, relations stop nowhere":* New York Edition preface, *Roderick Hudson*.

xxv *"the whole conduct of life":* New York Edition preface, *The Golden Bowl*.

xxv *"He smoked a minute":* The Golden Bowl, Book First, IV.

xxvii *Blackmur . . . "pure intelligence":* R. P. Blackmur, "Henry James," in Robert E. Spiller, et al., *Literary History of the United States: History*, third revision (New York: Macmillan, 1963), 1048, 1063.

xxvii *"our father, caring for our spiritual decency".* Henry James, *A Small Boy and Others* (1913), in *Autobiography* (New York: Criterion Books, 1956), 126.

xxvii *"the most intelligent man of his generation":* T. S. Eliot, "In Memory" and "The Hawthorne Aspect," *Little Review* 5 (August 1918): 44–53.

xxx *homosexuality as the figure in the carpet:* The most comprehensive treatment of this issue is found in Hugh Stevens, *Henry James and Sexuality* (Cambridge: Cambridge University Press, 1998), with an extensive bibliography.

xxx *"In trying to form":* J. P. Mowbray, "The Apotheosis of Henry James," *Critic* 41 (November 1902); reprinted in Kevin J. Hayes, ed., *Henry James: The Contemporary Reviews* (Cambridge: Cambridge University Press, 1996), 381–82.

xxx *"Jammed into the acute angle":* Notes of a Son and Brother, chapter IX.

xxxi *"Like Abélard":* Blackmur, Op. cit, 1040.

xxxi *"If we suppose—which is to suppose the improbable":* Allen Tate, "Emily Dickinson," *Essays of Four Decades* (Wilmington, DE: ISI Books, 1999), 287 (first published in 1936).

xxxii *"I feel as if a great cathedral":* Edwin Tribble, ed., *A Chime of Words: The Letters of Logan Pearsall Smith* (New York: Ticknor & Fields, 1984), 46.

xxxiii *"I wish I could help you":* Leon Edel, ed., *Henry James Letters: 1895–1916,* IV (Cambridge: Harvard University Press, 1984), 169–70.

xxxiii *"inhumanity of Method":* Henry James, *A Small Boy and Others* (1913), in *Autobiography* (New York: Criterion Books, 1956), 124.

xxxiii *"virtually in motion":* Ibid., 122.

xxxiii *"our rootless & accidental childhood":* Ruth Bernard Yeazell, ed., *The Death and Letters of Alice James* (Berkeley: University of California Press, 1981), 148.

xxxiii *"a native of the James family":* Ignas K. Skrupskelis and Elizabeth M. Berkeley, eds., *The Correspondence of William James: 1885–1889,* vol. 6 (Charlottesville: University Press of Virginia, 1998), 517 (letter to his sister).

xxxiv *"woof of time is every instant broken":* "Of Individualism in Democratic Countries," in Alexis de Tocqueville, *Democracy in America,* vol. II, trans. Henry Reeve (New York: Knopf, 1989), 99.

xxxv *"sacred rage of his art":* Blackmur, Op. cit., 1040.

xxxv *"Nothing could be allowed":* Theodora Bosanquet, *Henry James at Work* (London: The Hogarth Press, 1924), 265.

xxxv *"that the Novel remains still":* The *New York Edition* preface, *The Ambassadors;* subsequent citations from the preface to *Roderick Hudson.*

xxxvi *"I live, live intensely":* Leon Edel, ed., *Henry James Letters: 1895–1916,* IV, 769–70.

xxxvii *"Life being all inclusion":* New York Edition preface, *The Spoils of Poynton.*

xxxix *crack a walnut:* A. C. Benson, *Memories and Friends* (London: John Murray, 1924), 197.

xxxix *"the art of mountaining molehills":* Desmond MacCarthy, *Portraits: I* (London and New York: Putnam, 1931), 152.

xl *"He sits at the harpsichord":* Leon Edel, ed., *Henry James: Literary Criticism: Essays on Literature, American Writers, English Writers* (New York: Library of America, 1984), 1210–11.

Chronology

1843 Henry James Jr. (the "Jr." retained until after the death of his father) is born April 15 just off Washington Square in New York City to father Henry James Sr. (1811–1882), a religious thinker with strong Swedenborgian interests and a substantial income from an inheritance, and mother Mary Robertson Walsh James (1810–1882). Brother William James, born the previous year (1842–1910), would become a distinguished philosopher and psychologist (*The Principles of Psychology*, 1890; *Varieties of Religious Experience*, 1902; *Pragmatism*, 1907). Thoreau visits the James home, and the two very young sons are taken to Europe.

1844 In England, life-changing "vastation" of Henry James Sr. takes place, caused by a "damnèd shape squatting invisible to me within the precincts of the room." Family travels to Paris.

1845–57 Returns to New York City, then spends two years in Albany. Three more siblings—Garth Wilkinson "Wilky" James (1845–1883), Robertson James (1846–1903), and Alice James (1848–1891)—are born. (Robertson's later life is plagued by alcoholism, and Alice is diagnosed in youth as a "neurasthenic.") Home is on 14th Street in New York, where Bronson Alcott, Horace Greeley, and Ralph Waldo Emerson—a good friend of Henry James Sr.—are frequent visitors. Family travels to Europe, with extended stays in Geneva, London, and Paris.

1858–62 Family returns to America and settles in Newport, Rhode Island. After trips to Geneva and Bonn, they return to Newport. Henry briefly studies art. Extinguishing a fire in 1861, he receives an "obscure hurt"; when drafted into the Civil War, he is excused for what is probably a related back injury. Spends a term at Harvard Law School. Brother "Wilky" is gravely wounded in battle.

1864 The unsigned "A Tragedy of Error," James's first published story, appears in the February *Continental Monthly*. Unsigned review of Nassau W. Senior's *Essays on Fiction* appears in the October *North American Review* (James's payment: $12.00).

1865 First signed publication, "The Story of a Year," appears in the *Atlantic;* first signed review appears in the *Nation*.

1866 Strong friendships develop with Oliver Wendell Holmes and William Dean Howells, and with acquaintances of his youth Thomas Sergeant Perry and painter John LaFarge. Meets Charles Dickens on his American tour. Travels to England; meets George Eliot, Dante Gabriel Rossetti, William Morris, Edward Burne-Jones, and Charles Darwin; dines with John Ruskin. Visits France, Switzerland, and Italy.

1870 Cousin Minnie Temple dies at age twenty-four ("radiant and rare, extinguished in her first youth"); years later dedicates lengthy section of autobiographical *Notes of a Son and Brother* to her and asserts that her death marked "the end of our youth."

1871 First novel, *Watch and Ward,* published (serialized in periodicals but not reprinted in book form until 1878). Visits Emerson at Concord.

1872–74 Accompanies aunt and sister Alice on European tour; writes regular travel essays for the *Nation*. Escorts Emerson through the Louvre ("His perception of art is not, I think, naturally keen"); meets Matthew Arnold in Rome. Revisits the United States.

1875–76 Publishes three books in three genres in one year—his first books: *A Passionate Pilgrim and Other Tales* (short stories), *Transatlantic Sketches* (travel essays), and *Roderick Hudson* (first novel in book form). Returns to Europe, where, except for visits to the United States, he will reside for the rest of his life. In Paris, develops close friendship with Ivan Turgenev ("the divine Turgénieff"), and an acquaintance with Gustave Flaubert. Meets Alphonse Daudet, Guy de Maupassant, Ernest Renan, Gustave Doré, and Émile Zola. Takes up residence in London on Bolton Street.

1877–78 Writes *The American. Daisy Miller* appears in *Cornhill Magazine*—a popular success (the greatest of his career) and soon pirated. Publishes first volume of critical essays, *French Poets and Novelists,* and *The Europeans.*

1879 *Confidence,* his weakest novel, earns popular approval and good royalties (one of several novels later excluded from the *New York Edition*). Has social success in London; meets Robert Browning, Tennyson, George Meredith, George du Maurier, Trollope, Edmund Gosse, T. H. Huxley, Robert Louis Stevenson, James McNeill Whistler, Holman Hunt, and Frederick Leighton.

1880–81 Writes *Washington Square.* In Italy, develops close friendship with Constance Fenimore Woolson; works on *The Portrait of a Lady* in Venice and Florence (published in 1881). Visits the United States.

1882 Mother dies during James's American visit ("She was patience, she was wisdom, she was exquisite maternity"). Returns to London and travels to France (*A Little Tour in France,* 1884); returns to United States on notice of father's illness, but father dies while James is in transit ("The house is so *empty*—I scarcely know myself"). Reinstates younger brother's inheritance ("Wilky" had been disinherited by James Sr. after he drained the family's resources).

1883–84 Wilky dies; Turgenev dies. James turns over income from his own inheritance to sister Alice. With her companion Katharine Loring, Alice moves to England and eventually settles in London near her brother. James publishes "The Art of Fiction" ("the chamber of consciousness") several months after brother William publishes on "consciousness a continuous stream." Publishes *Portraits of Places* (collection of previously published travel essays).

1886–89 Moves to London's De Vere Gardens. *The Bostonians* is criticized for satirizing reformer Elizabeth Palmer Peabody; brother William himself judges it "a pretty bad business." Writes *The Princess Casamassima,* "The Aspern Papers," and *The Reverberator*; essay collection, *Partial Portraits.* Alice James begins keeping diary.

1890–91 Publishes *The Tragic Muse.* Disappointed with fiction sales, turns attention to dramatic stage and rewrites *The American* as a play with a happy ending. *The American: A Comedy in Four Acts* opens to critical and popular success.

1892–94 Grieved by death of sister Alice ("I shall feel very lonely in England") and by Constance Fenimore Woolson's apparent suicide in Venice ("Before the horror and pity of it I have utterly collapsed"). Robert Louis Stevenson also dies ("that beautiful, bountiful being"). Katharine Loring publishes four copies of Alice James's diary; Henry eventually destroys his copy.

1895 Disastrous first night of *Guy Domville* ends excursion into the theater.

1896–98 Develops powerful friendship with Joseph Conrad ("a beautiful and generous mind"). Publishes *The Other House*, *The Spoils of Poynton*, and *What Maisie Knew*. Takes a twenty-one-year lease on Lamb House, Rye, East Sussex, where he writes *The Awkward Age* and subsequent novels. Begins dictating his work. Writes *The Turn of the Screw*. Begins friendships with H. G. Wells and Stephen Crane.

1899 Publishes *The Awkward Age*. In Rome, meets young Norwegian-American sculptor Hendrik C. Andersen and begins an emotionally charged friendship ("I wish I could go to Rome and put my hands on you"). Purchases Lamb House.

1900–1901 Begins work on *The Sense of the Past*, which experiments with time travel (it remains unfinished at his death and is published posthumously). Publishes *The Sacred Fount*. William James writes parts of *Varieties of Religious Experience* while staying at Lamb House.

1902 Publishes *The Wings of the Dove*, "The Beast in the Jungle." Travel essays are collected in *English Hours*.

1903 Publishes *The Ambassadors* and the commissioned biography *William Wetmore Story and His Friends*. Important friendship develops with Edith Wharton.

1904 Publishes *The Golden Bowl*. Returns to the United States, in spite of discouragement of brother William ("You are very dissuasive—even more than I expected"), after a twenty-year absence. Tours as far south as Florida, as far west as California; lectures on "The Lesson of Balzac" and "The Question of Our Speech"; American press notes the visit and publishes caricatures of his supposed stupefaction at American customs.

1905 Returns to England; begins work on *The Novels and Tales of Henry James*; publishes edition generally known as the *New York Edition*.

1906–9 Continues exhausting work on revisions and prefaces for the *New York Edition*. Publishes two travel volumes, *The American Scene* (1907), on his recent American tour, and *Italian Hours* (1909), collecting Italian essays written over thirty-five years. Writes "The Jolly Corner." Initial *New York Edition* royalties amount to just over £40. Friendship with young Hugh Walpole. Begins work on *The Ivory Tower* (published incomplete and posthumously). Experiences bouts of depression; burns most letters he has received over the years.

1910 James has a nervous breakdown ("My *nervous* condition—trepidation, agitation, general dreadfulness"); alcoholic younger brother Robertson dies alone in Concord; James revisits the United States, where brother William soon dies ("my best & wisest of friends"). Henry James is the last alive of the five siblings ("I feel stricken & old & ended").

1911 "Revises" *The Outcry*, written as a play in 1909, as a minor novel. Health improves; begins work on first autobiographical volume. Awarded honorary degree from Harvard. Wharton, Gosse, and Howells lobby unsuccessfully to have Nobel Prize awarded to him.

1912 Receives honorary doctorate from Oxford (*"fecundissimum et facundissimum scriptorem"*). Judging James's finances as precarious, Wharton secretly arranges to have $8,000 of her Scribner's royalties offered him as an "advance"; his spirits improved, returns to work on *The Ivory Tower*.

1913 James's seventieth birthday; distinguished John Singer Sargent portrait commissioned by almost three hundred friends. Publishes first autobiographical volume, *A Small Boy and Others*.

1914 Publishes second autobiographical volume, *Notes of a Son and Brother* (final volume, *The Middle Years*, is published posthumously in 1917). Health troubles continue ("desiccated antiquity"). Devastated by outbreak of war ("black and hideous to me is the tragedy that gathers"). Supports Britain at war; visits soldiers in London hospitals. Meets the forty-year-old Winston Churchill.

1915 H. G. Wells launches satirical attack on James in *Boon*. James destroys more letters and personal papers. In support of wartime England, and after forty years in that country, is naturalized as a British citizen ("Civis Britannicus Sum!"). Suffers first stroke in December ("So it has come at last—the Distinguished Thing").

1916 Receives the Order of Merit, January 1. Suffers final illness; dies February 28. Ashes are interred in James family plot in Cambridge, Massachusetts.

Acknowledgments

Deep thanks to Anne Drury Hall, who reads Henry James just as he would have wished to be read. To David Wyatt, with whom talk about James, as about most things, calls up all my powers. To Peter Mallios, who sleeps with Emerson under his pillow. To Elizabeth Anania Edwards, back then and now. To K. C. Summers and Craig Stolz, who let me think Jamesian thoughts while wandering around Cambodia, Mali, Bolivia, and India. To Jackie DeCesaris, for her mind and fine spirit. The care, generosity, and constant good will of Michael Millman, Barbara Campo, and Cathy Dexter—my editors at Penguin Putnam—helped make this project an uncommon pleasure. My warm thanks also go to friends and colleagues who have given help and support in ways they may not always recall: Sylvie Bouvier, Glen Schroeder, Zoé, Taï, and Hugo, Kerry Armstrong, Marlene Ellin, Phil Reed, Ted Leinwand, Richard Cross, Kent Cartwright, Claudio Filippone, Sandra Morrison, Richard Fletcher, Todd McDaniel, Massimo Giuliani, Elizabeth Loizeaux, Sharon Kozberg, Michael Teitelman, William C. Hunter of Tokyo and far-off Belize, Alessandra Angelini of Rome—and of course her matchless Jambo. And this year in particular, in a special way I thank my brother, Steve Auchard.

I

FICTION

In his lifetime Henry James published 114 tales and twenty novels. Two incomplete novels, *The Ivory Tower* and *The Sense of the Past,* were published posthumously. The present edition must be content to offer a sampling of the shorter fiction, since, for example, *The Portrait of a Lady* runs to almost ten times the length of the "nouvelle" *Daisy Miller* and generally comes in at over 500 pages. Although it was as a novelist that James had his most serious ambitions, there need be no apology for the achievement of his tales, and in fact the prefaces to the *New York Edition* provide serious, shrewd, tantalizing comment on all the following works—except for the late and potentially self-referential "The Jolly Corner," about which James does little more than note, uncharacteristically, that "there would be more to say than my space allows."

Daisy Miller: A Study

Cornhill Magazine, *June–July 1878. Rejected by the American* Lippincott Magazine *because of a perceived "outrage on American girlhood," as James notes in his* New York Edition *preface,* Daisy Miller *was published in England in Leslie Stephen's magazine. It created a sensation and made its thirty-five-year-old author a celebrity. James would never again write anything that would have such startling success. But neither would he be so casual with copyright issues, for two pirate editions deprived him of almost all revenue from the tale. One of the most powerful expressions of the incarnation that would become known as the American blonde, the young woman from Schenectady was soon so well known that in James's 1884 tale "Pandora" it was sufficient to refer to another young American as merely another "Daisy Miller."*

I.

At the little town of Vevey, in Switzerland, there is a particularly comfortable hotel. There are, indeed, many hotels; for the entertainment of tourists is the business of the place, which, as many travellers will remember, is seated upon the edge of a remarkably blue lake—a lake that it behoves every tourist to visit. The shore of the lake presents an unbroken array of establishments of this order, of every category, from the "grand hotel" of the newest fashion, with a chalk-white front, a hundred balconies, and a dozen flags flying from its roof, to the little Swiss *pension* of an elder day, with its name inscribed in German-looking lettering upon a pink or yellow wall, and an awkward summer-house in the angle of the garden. One of the hotels at Vevey, however, is famous, even classical, being distinguished from many of its upstart neighbours by an air both of luxury and of maturity. In this region, in the month of June, American travellers are extremely numerous; it may be said, indeed, that Vevey assumes at this period some of the characteristics of an American watering-place. There are sights and sounds which evoke a vision, an echo, of Newport and Saratoga. There is a flitting hither and thither of "stylish" young girls, a rustling of muslin flounces, a rattle of dance-music in the morning hours, a sound of high-pitched voices at all times. You receive an impression of these things at the excellent inn of the "Trois Couronnes," and are transported in fancy to the Ocean House or to Congress Hall. But at the "Trois Couronnes," it must be added, there are other features that are much at variance with these suggestions: neat German waiters, who look like secretaries of legation; Russian princesses sitting in the garden; little Polish boys walking about, held by the hand, with their governors; a view of the snowy crest of the Dent du Midi and the picturesque towers of the Castle of Chillon.

I hardly know whether it was the analogies or the differences that were uppermost in the mind of a young American, who, two or three years ago, sat in the garden of the "Trois Couronnes," looking about him, rather idly, at some of the graceful objects I have mentioned. It was a beautiful summer morning, and in whatever fashion the young American looked at things, they must have seemed to him charming. He had come from Geneva the day before, by the little steamer, to see his aunt, who was staying at the hotel—Geneva having been for a long time his place of residence. But his aunt had a headache—his aunt had almost always a headache—and now she was shut up in her room, smelling camphor, so that he was at liberty to wander about. He was some seven-and-twenty years of age; when his friends spoke of him, they usually said that he was at Geneva, "studying." When his enemies spoke of him they said—but, after all, he had no enemies; he was an extremely amiable fellow, and universally liked. What I should say is, simply, that when certain persons spoke of him they affirmed that the reason of his spending so much time at Geneva was that he was extremely devoted to a lady who lived there— a foreign lady—a person older than himself. Very few Americans—indeed I think none—had ever seen this lady, about whom there were some singular stories. But Winterbourne had an old attachment for the little metropolis of Calvinism; he had been put to school there as a boy, and he had afterwards gone to college there—circumstances which had led to his forming a great many youthful friendships. Many of these he had kept, and they were a source of great satisfaction to him.

After knocking at his aunt's door and learning that she was indisposed, he had taken a walk about the town, and then he had come in to his breakfast. He had now finished his breakfast, but he was drinking a small cup of coffee, which had been served to him on a little table in the garden by one of the waiters who looked like an *attaché*. At last he finished his coffee and lit a cigarette. Presently a small boy came walking along the path—an urchin of nine or ten. The child, who was diminutive for his years, had an aged expression of countenance, a pale complexion, and sharp little features. He was dressed in knickerbockers, with red stockings, which displayed his poor little spindleshanks; he also wore a brilliant red cravat. He carried in his hand a long alpenstock, the sharp point of which he thrust into everything that he approached—the flower-beds, the garden-benches, the trains of the ladies' dresses. In front of Winterbourne he paused, looking at him with a pair of bright, penetrating little eyes.

"Will you give me a lump of sugar?" he asked, in a sharp, hard little voice—a voice immature, and yet, somehow, not young.

Winterbourne glanced at the small table near him, on which his coffee-service rested, and saw that several morsels of sugar remained. "Yes, you may take one," he answered; "but I don't think sugar is good for little boys."

This little boy stepped forward and carefully selected three of the coveted fragments, two of which he buried in the pocket of his knickerbockers, depositing the other as promptly in another place. He poked his alpenstock, lance-fashion, into Winterbourne's bench, and tried to crack the lump of sugar with his teeth.

"Oh, blazes; it's har-r-d!" he exclaimed, pronouncing the adjective in a peculiar manner.

Winterbourne had immediately perceived that he might have the honour of claiming him as a fellow-countryman. "Take care you don't hurt your teeth," he said, paternally.

"I haven't got any teeth to hurt. They have all come out. I have only got seven teeth. My mother counted them last night, and one came out right afterwards. She said she'd slap me if any more came out. I can't help it. It's this old Europe. It's the climate that makes them come out. In America they didn't come out. It's these hotels."

Winterbourne was much amused. "If you eat three lumps of sugar, your mother will certainly slap you," he said.

"She's got to give me some candy, then," rejoined his young interlocutor. "I can't get any candy here—any American candy. American candy's the best candy."

"And are American little boys the best little boys?" asked Winterbourne.

"I don't know. I'm an American boy," said the child.

"I see you are one of the best!" laughed Winterbourne.

"Are you an American man?" pursued the vivacious infant. And then, on Winterbourne's affirmative reply—"American men are the best," he declared.

His companion thanked him for the compliment; and the child, who had now got astride of his alpenstock, stood looking at him, while he attacked a second lump of sugar. Winterbourne wondered if he himself had been like this in his infancy, for he had been brought to Europe at about this age.

"Here comes my sister!" cried the child, in a moment. "She's an American girl."

Winterbourne looked along the path and saw a beautiful young lady advancing. "American girls are the best girls," he said, cheerfully, to his young companion.

"My sister ain't the best!" the child declared. "She's always blowing at me."

"I imagine that is your fault, not hers," said Winterbourne.

The young lady meanwhile had drawn near. She was dressed in white muslin, with a hundred frills and flounces, and knots of pale-coloured ribbon. She was bare-headed; but she balanced in her hand a large parasol, with a deep border of embroidery; and she was strikingly, admirably pretty. "How pretty they are!" thought Winterbourne, straightening himself in his seat, as if he were prepared to rise.

The young lady paused in front of his bench, near the parapet of the garden, which overlooked the lake. The little boy had now converted his alpenstock into a vaulting-pole, by the aid of which he was springing about in the gravel, and kicking it up not a little.

"Randolph," said the young lady, "what *are* you doing?"

"I'm going up the Alps," replied Randolph. "This is the way!" And he gave another little jump, scattering the pebbles about Winterbourne's ears.

"That's the way they come down," said Winterbourne.

"He's an American man!" cried Randolph, in his little hard voice.

The young lady gave no heed to this announcement, but looked straight at her brother. "Well, I guess you had better be quiet," she simply observed.

It seemed to Winterbourne that he had been in a manner presented. He got up and stepped slowly towards the young girl, throwing away his cigarette. "This little boy and I have made acquaintance," he said, with great civility. In Geneva, as he had been perfectly aware, a young man was not at liberty to speak to a young unmarried lady except under certain rarely-occurring conditions; but here at Vevey, what conditions could be better than these?—a pretty American girl coming and standing in front of you in a garden. This pretty American girl, however, on hearing Winterbourne's observation, simply glanced at him; she then turned her head and looked over the parapet, at the lake and the opposite mountains. He wondered whether he had gone too far; but he decided that he must advance farther, rather than retreat. While he was thinking of something else to say, the young lady turned to the little boy again.

"I should like to know where you got that pole," she said.

"I bought it!" responded Randolph.

"You don't mean to say you're going to take it to Italy?"

"Yes, I am going to take it to Italy!" the child declared.

The young girl glanced over the front of her dress, and smoothed out a knot or two of ribbon. Then she rested her eyes upon the prospect again. "Well, I guess you had better leave it somewhere," she said, after a moment.

"Are you going to Italy?" Winterbourne inquired, in a tone of great respect.

The young lady glanced at him again.

"Yes, sir," she replied. And she said nothing more.

"Are you—a—going over the Simplon?" Winterbourne pursued, a little embarrassed.

"I don't know," she said. "I suppose it's some mountain. Randolph, what mountain are we going over?"

"Going where?" the child demanded.

"To Italy," Winterbourne explained.

"I don't know," said Randolph. "I don't want to go to Italy. I want to go to America."

"Oh, Italy is a beautiful place!" rejoined the young man.

"Can you get candy there?" Randolph loudly inquired.

"I hope not," said his sister. "I guess you have had enough candy, and mother thinks so too."

"I haven't had any for ever so long—for a hundred weeks!" cried the boy, still jumping about.

The young lady inspected her flounces and smoothed her ribbons again; and Winterbourne presently risked an observation upon the beauty of the view. He was ceasing to be embarrassed, for he had begun to perceive that she was not in the least embarrassed herself. There had not been the slightest alteration in her charming complexion; she was evidently neither offended nor fluttered. If she looked another way when he spoke to her, and seemed not particularly to hear him, this was simply her habit, her manner. Yet, as he talked a little more, and pointed out some of the objects of interest in the view, with which she appeared quite unacquainted, she gradually gave him more of the benefit of her glance; and then he saw that this glance was perfectly direct and unshrinking. It was not, however, what would have been called an immodest glance, for the young girl's eyes were singularly honest and fresh. They were wonderfully pretty eyes; and, indeed, Winterbourne had not seen for a long time anything prettier than his fair countrywoman's various features—her complexion, her nose, her ears, her teeth. He had a great relish for feminine beauty; he was addicted to observing and analysing it; and as regards this young lady's face he made several observations. It was not at all insipid, but it was not exactly expressive; and though it was eminently delicate Winterbourne mentally accused it—very forgivingly—of a want of finish. He thought it very possible that Master Randolph's sister was a coquette; he was sure she had a spirit of her own; but in her bright, sweet, superficial little visage there was no mockery, no irony. Before long it became obvious that she was much disposed towards conversation. She told him that they were going to Rome for the winter—she and her mother and Randolph. She asked him if he was a "real American"; she wouldn't have taken him for one; he seemed more like a German—this was said after a little hesitation, especially when he spoke. Winterbourne, laughing, answered that he had met Germans who spoke like Americans; but that he had not, so far as he remembered, met an American who spoke like a German. Then he asked her if she would not be more comfortable in sitting upon the bench which he had just quitted. She answered that she liked standing up and walking about; but she presently sat down. She told him she was from New York State—"if you know where that is." Winterbourne learned more about her by catching hold of her small, slippery brother and making him stand a few minutes by his side.

"Tell me your name, my boy," he said.

"Randolph C. Miller," said the boy, sharply. "And I'll tell you her name"; and he levelled his alpenstock at his sister.

"You had better wait till you are asked!" said this young lady, calmly.

"I should like very much to know your name," said Winterbourne.

"Her name is Daisy Miller!" cried the child. "But that isn't her real name; that isn't her name on her cards."

"It's a pity you haven't got one of my cards!" said Miss Miller.

"Her real name is Annie P. Miller," the boy went on.

"Ask him *his* name," said his sister, indicating Winterbourne.

But on this point Randolph seemed perfectly indifferent; he continued to supply information with regard to his own family. "My father's name is Ezra B. Miller," he announced. "My father ain't in Europe; my father's in a better place than Europe."

Winterbourne imagined for a moment that this was the manner in which the child had been taught to intimate that Mr. Miller had been removed to the sphere of celestial rewards. But Randolph immediately added, "My father's in Schenectady. He's got a big business. My father's rich, you bet."

"Well!" ejaculated Miss Miller, lowering her parasol and looking at the embroidered border. Winterbourne presently released the child, who departed, dragging his alpenstock along the path. "He doesn't like Europe," said the young girl. "He wants to go back."

"To Schenectady, you mean?"

"Yes; he wants to go right home. He hasn't got any boys here. There is one boy here, but he always goes round with a teacher; they won't let him play."

"And your brother hasn't any teacher?" Winterbourne inquired.

"Mother thought of getting him one, to travel round with us. There was a lady told her of a very good teacher; an American lady—perhaps you know her—Mrs. Sanders. I think she came from Boston. She told her of this teacher, and we thought of getting him to travel round with us. But Randolph said he didn't want a teacher travelling round with us. He said he wouldn't have lessons when he was in the cars. And we *are* in the cars about half the time. There was an English lady we met in the cars—I think her name was Miss Featherstone; perhaps you know her. She wanted to know why I didn't give Randolph lessons—give him 'instruction,' she called it. I guess he could give me more instruction than I could give him. He's very smart."

"Yes," said Winterbourne; "he seems very smart."

"Mother's going to get a teacher for him as soon as we get to Italy. Can you get good teachers in Italy?"

"Very good, I should think," said Winterbourne.

"Or else she's going to find some school. He ought to learn some more. He's only nine. He's going to college." And in this way Miss Miller continued to converse upon the affairs of her family, and upon other topics. She sat there with her extremely pretty hands, ornamented with very brilliant rings, folded in her lap, and with her pretty eyes now resting upon those of Winterbourne, now wandering over the garden, the people who passed by, and the beautiful view. She talked to Winterbourne as if she had known him a long time. He found it very pleasant. It was many years since he had heard a young girl talk so much. It might have been said of this unknown young lady, who had come and sat down beside him upon a bench, that she chattered. She was very quiet, she sat in a charming tranquil attitude; but her lips and her eyes were constantly moving. She had a soft, slender, agreeable voice, and her tone was decidedly sociable. She gave Winterbourne a history of her movements and intentions, and those of her mother and brother, in Europe, and enumerated, in particular, the various hotels at which they had stopped. "That English lady in the cars," she said—"Miss Featherstone—asked me if we didn't all live in hotels in America. I told her I had never been in so many hotels in my life as since I came to Europe. I have never seen so many—it's nothing but hotels." But Miss Miller did not make this remark with a querulous accent; she appeared to be in the best humour with everything. She declared that the hotels were very good, when once you got used to their ways, and that Europe was perfectly sweet. She was not disappointed—not a bit. Perhaps it was because she had heard so much about it before. She had ever so many intimate friends that had been there ever so many times. And then she had had ever so many dresses and things from Paris. Whenever she put on a Paris dress she felt as if she were in Europe.

"It was a kind of a wishing-cap," said Winterbourne.

"Yes," said Miss Miller, without examining this analogy; "it always made me wish I was here. But I needn't have done that for dresses. I am sure they send all the pretty ones to America; you see the most frightful things here. The only thing I don't like," she proceeded, "is the society. There isn't any society; or, if there is, I don't know where it keeps itself. Do you? I suppose there is some society somewhere, but I haven't seen anything of it. I'm very fond of society, and I have always had a great deal of it. I don't mean only in Schenectady, but in New York. I used to go to New York every winter. In New York I had lots of society. Last winter I had seventeen dinners given me; and three of them were by gentlemen," added Daisy Miller. "I have more friends in New York than in Schenectady—more gentlemen friends; and more young lady friends too," she resumed in a moment. She paused again for an instant; she was looking at Winterbourne with all her prettiness in her lively eyes and in her light, slightly monotonous smile. "I have always had," she said, "a great deal of gentlemen's society."

Poor Winterbourne was amused, perplexed, and decidedly charmed. He had never yet heard a young girl express herself in just this fashion; never, at least, save in cases where to say such things seemed a kind of demonstrative evidence of a certain laxity of deportment. And yet was he to accuse Miss Daisy Miller of actual or potential *inconduite,* as they said at Geneva? He felt that he had lived at Geneva so long that he had lost a good deal; he had become dishabituated to the American tone. Never, indeed, since he had grown old enough to appreciate things, had he encountered a young American girl of so pronounced a type as this. Certainly she was very charming; but how deucedly sociable! Was she simply a pretty girl from New York State—were they all like that, the pretty girls who had a good deal of gentlemen's society? Or was she also a designing, an audacious, an unscrupulous young person? Winterbourne had lost his instinct in this matter, and his reason could not help him. Miss Daisy Miller looked extremely innocent. Some people had told him that, after all, American girls were exceedingly innocent; and others had told him that, after all, they were not. He was inclined to think Miss Daisy Miller was a flirt—a pretty American flirt. He had never, as yet, had any relations with young ladies of this category. He had known, here in Europe, two or three women—persons older than Miss Daisy Miller, and provided, for respectability's sake, with husbands—who were great coquettes—dangerous, terrible women, with whom one's relations were liable to take a serious turn. But this young girl was not a coquette in that sense; she was very unsophisticated; she was only a pretty American flirt.

Winterbourne was almost grateful for having found the formula that applied to Miss Daisy Miller. He leaned back in his seat; he remarked to himself that she had the most charming nose he had ever seen; he wondered what were the regular conditions and limitations of one's intercourse with a pretty American flirt. It presently became apparent that he was on the way to learn.

"Have you been to that old castle?" asked the young girl, pointing with her parasol to the far-gleaming walls of the Château de Chillon.

"Yes, formerly, more than once," said Winterbourne. "You too, I suppose, have seen it?"

"No; we haven't been there. I want to go there dreadfully. Of course I mean to go there. I wouldn't go away from here without having seen that old castle."

"It's a very pretty excursion," said Winterbourne, "and very easy to make. You can drive, you know, or you can go by the little steamer."

"You can go in the cars," said Miss Miller.

"Yes; you can go in the cars," Winterbourne assented.

"Our courier says they take you right up to the castle," the young girl continued. "We were going last week; but my mother gave out. She suffers dreadfully from dyspepsia. She said she couldn't go. Randolph wouldn't go either; he says he doesn't think much of old castles. But I guess we'll go this week, if we can get Randolph."

"Your brother is not interested in ancient monuments?" Winterbourne inquired, smiling.

"He says he don't care much about old castles. He's only nine. He wants to stay at the hotel. Mother's afraid to leave him alone, and the courier won't stay with him; so we haven't been to many places. But it will be too bad if we don't go up there." And Miss Miller pointed again at the Château de Chillon.

"I should think it might be arranged," said Winterbourne. "Couldn't you get some one to stay—for the afternoon—with Randolph?"

Miss Miller looked at him a moment; and then, very placidly—"I wish *you* would stay with him!" she said.

Winterbourne hesitated a moment. "I would much rather go to Chillon with you."

"With me?" asked the young girl, with the same placidity.

She didn't rise, blushing, as a young girl at Geneva would have done; and yet Winterbourne, conscious that he had been very bold, thought it possible she was offended. "With your mother," he answered very respectfully.

But it seemed that both his audacity and his respect were lost upon Miss Daisy Miller. "I guess my mother won't go, after all," she said. "She don't like to ride round in the afternoon. But did you really mean what you said just now; that you would like to go up there?"

"Most earnestly," Winterbourne declared.

"Then we may arrange it. If mother will stay with Randolph, I guess Eugenio will."

"Eugenio?" the young man inquired.

"Eugenio's our courier. He doesn't like to stay with Randolph; he's the most fastidious man I ever saw. But he's a splendid courier. I guess he'll stay at home with Randolph if mother does, and then we can go to the castle."

Winterbourne reflected for an instant as lucidly as possible—"we" could only mean Miss Daisy Miller and himself. This programme seemed almost too agreeable for credence; he felt as if he ought to kiss the young lady's hand. Possibly he would have done so—and quite spoiled the project; but at this moment another person—presumably Eugenio—appeared. A tall, handsome man, with superb whiskers, wearing a velvet morning-coat and a brilliant watch-chain, approached Miss Miller, looking sharply at her companion. "Oh, Eugenio!" said Miss Miller, with the friendliest accent.

Eugenio had looked at Winterbourne from head to foot; he now bowed gravely to the young lady. "I have the honour to inform mademoiselle that luncheon is upon the table."

Miss Miller slowly rose. "See here, Eugenio," she said. "I'm going to that old castle, any way."

"To the Château de Chillon, mademoiselle?" the courier inquired. "Mademoiselle has made arrangements?" he added, in a tone which struck Winterbourne as very impertinent.

Eugenio's tone apparently threw, even to Miss Miller's own apprehension, a slightly ironical light upon the young girl's situation. She turned to Winterbourne, blushing a little—a very little. "You won't back out?" she said.

"I shall not be happy till we go!" he protested.

"And you are staying in this hotel?" she went on. "And you are really an American?"

The courier stood looking at Winterbourne, offensively. The young man, at least, thought his manner of looking an offence to Miss Miller; it conveyed an imputation that she "picked up" acquaintances. "I shall have the honour of presenting to you a person who will tell you all about me," he said smiling, and referring to his aunt.

"Oh, well, we'll go some day," said Miss Miller. And she gave him a smile and turned away. She put up her parasol and walked back to the inn beside Eugenio. Winterbourne stood looking after her; and as she moved away, drawing her muslin furbelows over the gravel, said to himself that she had the *tournure* of a princess.

II.

He had, however, engaged to do more than proved feasible, in promising to present his aunt, Mrs. Costello, to Miss Daisy Miller. As soon as the former lady had got better of her headache he waited upon her in her apartment; and, after the proper inquiries in regard to her health, he asked her if she had observed, in the hotel, an American family—a mamma, a daughter, and a little boy.

"And a courier?" said Mrs. Costello. "Oh, yes, I have observed them. Seen them—heard them—and kept out of their way." Mrs. Costello was a widow with a fortune; a person of much distinction, who frequently intimated that, if she were not so dreadfully liable to sick-headaches, she would probably have left a deeper impress upon her time. She had a long pale face, a high nose, and a great deal of very striking white hair, which she wore in large puffs and *rouleaux* over the top of her head. She had two sons married in New York, and another who was now in Europe. This young man was amusing himself at Homburg, and, though he was on his travels, was rarely perceived to visit any particular city at the moment selected by his mother for her own appearance there. Her nephew, who had come up to Vevey expressly to see her, was therefore more attentive than those who, as she said, were nearer to her. He had imbibed at Geneva the idea that one must always be attentive to one's aunt. Mrs. Costello had not seen him for many years, and she was greatly pleased with him, manifesting her approbation by initiating him into many of the secrets of that social sway which, as she gave him to understand, she exerted in the American capital. She admitted that she was very exclusive; but, if he were acquainted with New York, he would see that one had to be. And her picture of the minutely hierarchical constitution of the society of that city, which she presented to him in many different lights, was, to Winterbourne's imagination, almost oppressively striking.

He immediately perceived, from her tone, that Miss Daisy Miller's place in the social scale was low. "I am afraid you don't approve of them," he said.

"They are very common," Mrs. Costello declared. "They are the sort of Americans that one does one's duty by not—not accepting."

"Ah, you don't accept them?" said the young man.

"I can't, my dear Frederick. I would if I could, but I can't."

"The young girl is very pretty," said Winterbourne, in a moment.

"Of course she's pretty. But she is very common."

"I see what you mean, of course," said Winterbourne, after another pause.

"She has that charming look that they all have," his aunt resumed. "I can't think where they pick it up; and she dresses in perfection—no, you don't know how well she dresses. I can't think where they get their taste."

"But, my dear aunt, she is not, after all, a Comanche savage."

"She is a young lady," said Mrs. Costello, "who has an intimacy with her mamma's courier."

"An intimacy with the courier?" the young man demanded.

"Oh, the mother is just as bad! They treat the courier like a familiar friend—like a gentleman. I shouldn't wonder if he dines with them. Very likely they have never seen a man with such good manners, such fine clothes, so like a gentleman. He probably corresponds to the young lady's idea of a Count. He sits with them in the garden, in the evening. I think he smokes."

Winterbourne listened with interest to these disclosures; they helped him to make up his mind about Miss Daisy. Evidently she was rather wild. "Well," he said, "I am not a courier, and yet she was very charming to me."

"You had better have said at first," said Mrs. Costello with dignity, "that you had made her acquaintance."

"We simply met in the garden, and we talked a bit."

"*Tout bonnement!* And pray what did you say?"

"I said I should take the liberty of introducing her to my admirable aunt."

"I am much obliged to you."

"It was to guarantee my respectability," said Winterbourne.

"And pray who is to guarantee hers?"

"Ah, you are cruel!" said the young man. "She's a very nice girl."

"You don't say that as if you believed it," Mrs. Costello observed.

"She is completely uncultivated," Winterbourne went on. "But she is wonderfully pretty, and, in short, she is very nice. To prove that I believe it, I am going to take her to the Château de Chillon."

"You two are going off there together? I should say it proved just the contrary. How long had you known her, may I ask, when this interesting project was formed? You haven't been twenty-four hours in the house."

"I had known her half-an-hour!" said Winterbourne, smiling.

"Dear me!" cried Mrs. Costello. "What a dreadful girl!"

Her nephew was silent for some moments. "You really think, then," he began, earnestly, and with a desire for trustworthy information—"you really think that—" But he paused again.

"Think what, sir?" said his aunt.

"That she is the sort of young lady who expects a man—sooner or later—to carry her off?"

"I haven't the least idea what such young ladies expect a man to do. But I really think that you had better not meddle with little American girls that are uncultivated, as you call them. You have lived too long out of the country. You will be sure to make some great mistake. You are too innocent."

"My dear aunt, I am not so innocent," said Winterbourne, smiling and curling his moustache.

"You are too guilty, then!"

Winterbourne continued to curl his moustache, meditatively. "You won't let the poor girl know you then?" he asked at last.

"Is it literally true that she is going to the Château de Chillon with you?"

"I think that she fully intends it."

"Then, my dear Frederick," said Mrs. Costello, "I must decline the honour of her acquaintance. I am an old woman, but I am not too old—thank Heaven—to be shocked!"

"But don't they all do these things—the young girls in America?" Winterbourne inquired.

Mrs. Costello stared a moment. "I should like to see my granddaughters do them!" she declared, grimly.

This seemed to throw some light upon the matter, for Winterbourne remembered to have heard that his pretty cousins in New York were "tremendous flirts." If, therefore, Miss Daisy Miller exceeded the liberal license allowed to these young ladies, it was probable that anything might be expected of her. Winterbourne was impatient to see her again, and he was vexed with himself that, by instinct, he should not appreciate her justly.

Though he was impatient to see her, he hardly knew what he should say to her about his aunt's refusal to become acquainted with her; but he discovered, promptly enough, that with Miss Daisy Miller there was no great need of walking on tiptoe. He found her that evening in the garden, wandering about in the warm starlight, like an indolent sylph, and swinging to and fro the largest fan he had ever beheld. It was ten o'clock. He had dined with his aunt, had been sitting with her since dinner, and had just taken leave of her till the morrow. Miss Daisy Miller seemed very glad to see him; she declared it was the longest evening she had ever passed.

"Have you been all alone?" he asked.

"I have been walking round with mother. But mother gets tired walking round," she answered.

"Has she gone to bed?"

"No; she doesn't like to go to bed," said the young girl. "She doesn't sleep—not three hours. She says she doesn't know how she lives. She's dreadfully nervous. I guess she sleeps more than she thinks. She's gone somewhere after Randolph; she wants to try to get him to go to bed. He doesn't like to go to bed."

"Let us hope she will persuade him," observed Winterbourne.

"She will talk to him all she can; but he doesn't like her to talk to him," said Miss Daisy, opening her fan. "She's going to try to get Eugenio to talk to him. But he isn't afraid of Eugenio. Eugenio's a splendid courier, but he can't make much impression on Randolph! I don't believe he'll go to bed before eleven." It appeared that Randolph's vigil was in fact triumphantly prolonged, for Winterbourne strolled about with the young girl for some time without meeting her mother. "I have been looking round for that lady you want to introduce me to," his companion resumed. "She's your aunt." Then, on Winterbourne's admitting the fact, and expressing some curiosity as to how she had learned it, she said she had heard all about Mrs. Costello from the chambermaid. She was very quiet and very *comme il faut*; she wore white puffs; she spoke to no one, and she never dined at the *table d'hôte*. Every two days she had a headache. "I think that's a lovely description, headache and all!" said Miss Daisy, chattering along in her thin, gay voice. "I want to know her ever so much. I know just what *your* aunt would be; I know I should like her. She would be very exclusive. I like a lady to be exclusive; I'm dying to be exclusive myself. Well, we *are* exclusive, mother and I. We don't speak to every one—or they don't speak to us. I suppose it's about the same thing. Any way, I shall be ever so glad to know your aunt."

Winterbourne was embarrassed. "She would be most happy," he said; "but I'm afraid those headaches will interfere."

The young girl looked at him through the dusk. "But I suppose she doesn't have a headache every day," she said, sympathetically.

Winterbourne was silent a moment. "She tells me she does," he answered at last—not knowing what to say.

Miss Daisy Miller stopped and stood looking at him. Her prettiness was still visible in the darkness; she was opening and closing her enormous fan. "She doesn't want to know me!" she said, suddenly. "Why don't you say so? You needn't be afraid. I'm not afraid!" And she gave a little laugh.

Winterbourne fancied there was a tremor in her voice; he was touched, shocked, mortified by it. "My dear young lady," he protested, "she knows no one. It's her wretched health."

The young girl walked on a few steps, laughing still. "You needn't be afraid," she repeated. "Why should she want to know me?" Then she paused again; she was close to the parapet of the garden, and in front of her was the starlit lake. There was a vague sheen upon its surface, and in the distance were dimly-seen mountain forms. Daisy Miller looked out upon the mysterious prospect, and then she gave another little laugh. "Gracious! she *is* exclusive!" she said. Winterbourne wondered whether she was seriously wounded, and for a moment almost wished that her sense of injury might be such as to make it becoming in him to attempt to reassure and comfort her. He had a pleasant sense that she would be very approachable for consolatory purposes. He felt then, for the instant, quite ready to sacrifice his aunt, conversationally; to admit that she was a proud, rude woman, and to declare that they needn't mind her. But before he had time to commit himself to this perilous mixture of gallantry and impiety, the young lady, resuming her walk, gave an exclamation in quite another tone. "Well; here's mother! I guess she hasn't got Randolph to go to bed." The figure of a lady appeared, at a distance, very indistinct in the darkness, and advancing with a slow and wavering movement. Suddenly it seemed to pause.

"Are you sure it is your mother? Can you distinguish her in this thick dusk?" Winterbourne asked.

"Well!" cried Miss Daisy Miller, with a laugh, "I guess I

know my own mother. And when she has got on my shawl, too! She is always wearing my things."

The lady in question, ceasing to advance, hovered vaguely about the spot at which she had checked her steps.

"I am afraid your mother doesn't see you," said Winterbourne. "Or perhaps," he added—thinking, with Miss Miller, the joke permissible—"perhaps she feels guilty about your shawl."

"Oh, it's a fearful old thing!" the young girl replied, serenely. "I told her she could wear it. She won't come here, because she sees you."

"Ah, then," said Winterbourne. "I had better leave you."

"Oh no; come on!" urged Miss Daisy Miller.

"I'm afraid your mother doesn't approve of my walking with you."

Miss Miller gave him a serious glance. "It isn't for me; it's for you—that is, it's for *her*. Well; I don't know who it's for! But mother doesn't like any of my gentlemen friends. She's right down timid. She always makes a fuss if I introduce a gentleman. But I *do* introduce them—almost always. If I didn't introduce my gentlemen friends to mother," the young girl added, in her little soft, flat monotone, "I shouldn't think I was natural."

"To introduce me," said Winterbourne, "you must know my name." And he proceeded to pronounce it.

"Oh, dear; I can't say all that!" said his companion, with a laugh. But by this time they had come up to Mrs. Miller, who, as they drew near, walked to the parapet of the garden and leaned upon it, looking intently at the lake and turning her back upon them. "Mother!" said the young girl, in a tone of decision. Upon this the elder lady turned round. "Mr. Winterbourne," said Miss Daisy Miller, introducing the young man very frankly and prettily. "Common" she was, as Mrs. Costello had pronounced her; yet it was a wonder to Winterbourne that, with her commonness, she had a singularly delicate grace.

Her mother was a small, spare, light person, with a wandering eye, a very exiguous nose, and a large forehead, decorated with a certain amount of thin, much-frizzled hair. Like her daughter, Mrs. Miller was dressed with extreme elegance; she had enormous diamonds in her ears. So far as Winterbourne could observe, she gave him no greeting—she certainly was not looking at him. Daisy was near her, pulling her shawl straight. "What are you doing, poking round here?" this young lady inquired; but by no means with that harshness of accent which her choice of words may imply.

"I don't know," said her mother, turning towards the lake again.

"I shouldn't think you'd want that shawl!" Daisy exclaimed.

"Well—I do!" her mother answered, with a little laugh.

"Did you get Randolph to go to bed?" asked the young girl.

"No; I couldn't induce him," said Mrs. Miller, very gently. "He wants to talk to the waiter. He likes to talk to that waiter."

"I was telling Mr. Winterbourne," the young girl went on; and to the young man's ear her tone might have indicated that she had been uttering his name all her life.

"Oh, yes!" said Winterbourne; "I have the pleasure of knowing your son."

Randolph's mamma went silent; she turned her attention to the lake. But at last she spoke. "Well, I don't see how he lives!"

"Anyhow, it isn't so bad as it was at Dover," said Daisy Miller.

"And what occurred at Dover?" Winterbourne asked.

"He wouldn't go to bed at all. I guess he sat up all night—in the public parlour. He wasn't in bed at twelve o'clock: I know that."

"It was half-past twelve," declared Mrs. Miller, with mild emphasis.

"Does he sleep much during the day?" Winterbourne demanded.

"I guess he doesn't sleep much," Daisy rejoined.

"I wish he would!" said her mother. "It seems as if he couldn't."

"I think he's real tiresome," Daisy pursued.

Then, for some moments, there was silence. "Well, Daisy Miller," said the elder lady, presently, "I shouldn't think you'd want to talk against your own brother!"

"Well, he *is* tiresome, mother," said Daisy, quite without the asperity of a retort.

"He's only nine," urged Mrs. Miller.

"Well, he wouldn't go to that castle," said the young girl. "I'm going there with Mr. Winterbourne."

To this announcement, very placidly made, Daisy's mamma offered no response. Winterbourne took for granted that she deeply disapproved of the projected excursion; but he said to himself that she was a simple, easily-managed person, and that a few deferential protestations would take the edge from her displeasure. "Yes," he began; "your daughter has kindly allowed me the honour of being her guide."

Mrs. Miller's wandering eyes attached themselves, with a sort of appealing air, to Daisy, who, however, strolled a few steps farther, gently humming to herself. "I presume you will go in the cars," said her mother.

"Yes; or in the boat," said Winterbourne.

"Well, of course, I don't know," Mrs. Miller rejoined. "I have never been to that castle."

"It is a pity you shouldn't go," said Winterbourne, beginning to feel reassured as to her opposition. And yet he was quite prepared to find that, as a matter of course, she meant to accompany her daughter.

"We've been thinking ever so much about going," she pursued; "but it seems as if we couldn't. Of course Daisy—she wants to go round. But there's a lady here—I don't know her name—she says she shouldn't think we'd want to go to see castles *here*; she should think we'd want to wait till we got to Italy. It seems as if there would be so many there," continued Mrs. Miller, with an air of increasing confidence. "Of course, we only want to see the principal ones. We visited several in England," she presently added.

"Ah, yes! in England there are beautiful castles," said Winterbourne. "But Chillon, here, is very well worth seeing."

"Well, if Daisy feels up to it—," said Mrs. Miller, in a tone impregnated with a sense of the magnitude of the enterprise. "It seems as if there was nothing she wouldn't undertake."

"Oh, I think she'll enjoy it!" Winterbourne declared. And he desired more and more to make it a certainty that he was to have the privilege of a *tête-à-tête* with the young lady, who was still strolling along in front of them, softly vocalising. "You are not disposed, madam," he inquired, "to undertake it your-self?"

Daisy's mother looked at him, an instant, askance, and then walked forward in silence. Then—"I guess she had better go alone," she said, simply.

Winterbourne observed to himself that this was a very different type of maternity from that of the vigilant matrons who massed themselves in the forefront of social intercourse in the dark old city at the other end of the lake. But his meditations were interrupted by hearing his name very distinctly pronounced by Mrs. Miller's unprotected daughter.

"Mr. Winterbourne!" murmured Daisy.

"Mademoiselle!" said the young man.

"Don't you want to take me out in a boat?"

"At present?" he asked.

"Of course!" said Daisy.

"Well, Annie Miller!" exclaimed her mother.

"I beg you, madam, to let her go," said Winterbourne, ardently; for he had never yet enjoyed the sensation of guiding through the summer starlight a skiff freighted with a fresh and beautiful young girl.

"I shouldn't think she'd want to," said her mother. "I should think she'd rather go indoors."

"I'm sure Mr. Winterbourne wants to take me," Daisy declared. "He's so awfully devoted!"

"I will row you over to Chillon, in the starlight."

"I don't believe it!" said Daisy.

"Well!" ejaculated the elder lady again.

"You haven't spoken to me for half-an-hour," her daughter went on.

"I have been having some very pleasant conversation with your mother," said Winterbourne.

"Well; I want you to take me out in a boat!" Daisy repeated. They had all stopped, and she had turned round and was looking at Winterbourne. Her face wore a charming smile, her pretty eyes were gleaming, she was swinging her great fan about. No; it's impossible to be prettier than that, thought Winterbourne.

"There are half-a-dozen boats moored at that landing-place," he said, pointing to certain steps which descended from the garden to the lake. "If you will do me the honour to accept my arm, we will go and select one of them."

Daisy stood there smiling; she threw back her head and gave a little light laugh. "I like a gentleman to be formal!" she declared.

"I assure you it's a formal offer."

"I was bound I would make you say something," Daisy went on.

"You see it's not very difficult," said Winterbourne. "But I am afraid you are chaffing me."

"I think not, sir," remarked Mrs. Miller, very gently.

"Do, then, let me give you a row," he said to the young girl.

"It's quite lovely, the way you say that!" cried Daisy.

"It will be still more lovely to do it."

"Yes, it would be lovely!" said Daisy. But she made no movement to accompany him; she only stood there laughing.

"I should think you had better find out what time it is," interposed her mother.

"It is eleven o'clock, madam," said a voice, with a foreign accent, out of the neighbouring darkness; and Winterbourne, turning, perceived the florid personage who was in attendance upon the two ladies. He had apparently just approached.

"Oh, Eugenio," said Daisy, "I am going out in a boat!"

Eugenio bowed. "At eleven o'clock, mademoiselle?"

"I am going with Mr. Winterbourne. This very minute."

"Do tell her she can't," said Mrs. Miller to the courier.

"I think you had better not go out in a boat, mademoiselle," Eugenio declared.

Winterbourne wished to Heaven this pretty girl were not so familiar with her courier, but he said nothing.

"I suppose you don't think it's proper!" Daisy exclaimed. "Eugenio doesn't think anything's proper."

"I am at your service," said Winterbourne.

"Does mademoiselle propose to go alone?" asked Eugenio of Mrs. Miller.

"Oh, no; with this gentleman!" answered Daisy's mamma.

The courier looked for a moment at Winterbourne—the latter thought he was smiling—and then, solemnly, with a bow, "As mademoiselle pleases!" he said.

"Oh, I hoped you would make a fuss!" said Daisy. "I don't care to go now."

"I myself shall make a fuss if you don't go," said Winterbourne.

"That's all I want—a little fuss!" And the young girl began to laugh again.

"Mr. Randolph has gone to bed!" the courier announced, frigidly.

"Oh, Daisy; now we can go!" said Mrs. Miller.

Daisy turned away from Winterbourne, looking at him, smiling and fanning herself. "Good night," she said; "I hope you are disappointed, or disgusted, or something!"

He looked at her, taking the hand she offered him. "I am puzzled," he answered.

"Well; I hope it won't keep you awake!" she said, very smartly; and, under the escort of the privileged Eugenio, the two ladies passed towards the house.

Winterbourne stood looking after them; he was indeed puzzled. He lingered beside the lake for a quarter of an hour, turning over the mystery of the young girl's sudden familiarities and caprices. But the only very definite conclusion he came to was that he should enjoy deucedly "going off" with her somewhere.

Two days afterwards he went off with her to the Castle of Chillon. He waited for her in the large hall of the hotel, where the couriers, the servants, the foreign tourists were lounging about and staring. It was not the place he would have chosen, but she had appointed it. She came tripping downstairs, buttoning her long gloves, squeezing her folded parasol against her pretty figure, dressed in the perfection of a soberly elegant travelling-costume. Winterbourne was a man of imagination and, as our ancestors used to say, of sensibility; as he looked at her dress and, on the great staircase, her little rapid, confiding step, he felt as if there were something romantic going forward. He could have believed he was going to elope with her. He passed out with her among all the idle people that were assembled there; they were all looking at her very hard; she had be-

gun to chatter as soon as she joined him. Winterbourne's preference had been that they should be conveyed to Chillon in a
carriage; but she expressed a lively wish to go in the little
steamer; she declared that she had a passion for steamboats.
There was always such a lovely breeze upon the water, and you
saw such lots of people. The sail was not long, but Winterbourne's companion found time to say a great many things. To
the young man himself their little excursion was so much of an
escapade—an adventure—that, even allowing for her habitual
sense of freedom, he had some expectation of seeing her regard
it in the same way. But it must be confessed that, in this particular, he was disappointed. Daisy Miller was extremely animated, she was in charming spirits; but she was apparently not
at all excited; she was not fluttered; she avoided neither his eyes
nor those of any one else; she blushed neither when she looked
at him nor when she saw that people were looking at her. People continued to look at her a great deal, and Winterbourne
took much satisfaction in his pretty companion's distinguished
air. He had been a little afraid that she would talk loud, laugh
overmuch, and even, perhaps, desire to move about the boat a
good deal. But he quite forgot his fears; he sat smiling, with his
eyes upon her face, while, without moving from her place, she
delivered herself of a great number of original reflections. It
was the most charming garrulity he had ever heard. He had assented to the idea that she was "common"; but was she so, after all, or was he simply getting used to her commonness? Her
conversation was chiefly of what metaphysicians term the objective cast; but every now and then it took a subjective turn.

"What on *earth* are you so grave about?" she suddenly demanded, fixing her agreeable eyes upon Winterbourne's.

"Am I grave?" he asked. "I had an idea I was grinning from
ear to ear."

"You look as if you were taking me to a funeral. If that's a
grin, your ears are very near together."

"Should you like me to dance a hornpipe on the deck?"

"Pray do, and I'll carry round your hat. It will pay the ex-
penses of our journey."

"I never was better pleased in my life," murmured Winterbourne.

She looked at him a moment, and then burst into a little laugh. "I like to make you say those things! You're a queer mixture!"

In the castle, after they had landed, the subjective element decidedly prevailed. Daisy tripped about the vaulted chambers, rustled her skirts in the corkscrew staircases, flirted back with a pretty little cry and a shudder from the edge of the *oubliettes*, and turned a singularly well-shaped ear to everything that Winterbourne told her about the place. But he saw that she cared very little for feudal antiquities, and that the dusky traditions of Chillon made but a slight impression upon her. They had the good fortune to have been able to walk about without other companionship than that of the custodian; and Winterbourne arranged with this functionary that they should not be hurried—that they should linger and pause wherever they chose. The custodian interpreted the bargain generously—Winterbourne, on his side, had been generous—and ended by leaving them quite to themselves. Miss Miller's observations were not remarkable for logical consistency; for anything she wanted to say she was sure to find a pretext. She found a great many pretexts in the rugged embrasures of Chillon for asking Winterbourne sudden questions about himself—his family, his previous history, his tastes, his habits, his intentions—and for supplying information upon corresponding points in her own personality. Of her own tastes, habits and intentions Miss Miller was prepared to give the most definite, and indeed the most favourable, account.

"Well; I hope you know enough!" she said to her companion, after he had told her the history of the unhappy Bonivard. "I never saw a man that knew so much!" The history of Bonivard had evidently, as they say, gone into one ear and out of the other. But Daisy went on to say that she wished Winterbourne would travel with them and "go round" with them; they might know something, in that case. "Don't you want to come and teach Randolph?" she asked. Winterbourne said that nothing could possibly please him so much; but that he had unfortunately other occupations. "Other occupations? I don't believe it!" said Miss Daisy. "What do you mean? You are not in business." The young man admitted that he was not in business; but he had engagements which, even within a day or two would force him to go back to Geneva. "Oh, bother!" she said, "I don't believe it!" and she began to talk about something else. But a few moments later, when he was pointing out to her the pretty design of an antique fireplace, she broke out irrelevantly, "You don't mean to say you are going back to Geneva?"

"It is a melancholy fact that I shall have to return to Geneva to-morrow."

"Well, Mr. Winterbourne," said Daisy; "I think you're horrid!"

"Oh, don't say such dreadful things!" said Winterbourne— "just at the last."

"The last!" cried the young girl; "I call it the first. I have half a mind to leave you here and go straight back to the hotel alone." And for the next ten minutes she did nothing but call him horrid. Poor Winterbourne was fairly bewildered; no young lady had as yet done him the honour to be so agitated by the announcement of his movements. His companion, after this, ceased to pay any attention to the curiosities of Chillon or the beauties of the lake; she opened fire upon the mysterious charmer in Geneva, whom she appeared to have instantly taken it for granted that he was hurrying back to see. How did Miss Daisy Miller know that there was a charmer in Geneva? Winterbourne, who denied the existence of such a person, was quite unable to discover; and he was divided between amazement at the rapidity of her induction and amusement at the frankness of her *persiflage*. She seemed to him, in all this, an extraordinary mixture of innocence and crudity. "Does she never allow you more than three days at a time?" asked Daisy, ironically. "Doesn't she give you a vacation in summer? There's no one so hard worked but they can get leave to go off somewhere at this season. I suppose, if you stay another day, she'll come after you in the boat. Do wait over till Friday, and I will go down to the landing to see her arrive!" Winterbourne began to think he had been wrong to feel disappointed in the temper in which the young lady had embarked. If he had missed the personal accent, the personal accent was now making its appearance. It sounded very distinctly, at last, in her telling him she would stop "teasing" him if he would promise her solemnly to come down to Rome in the winter.

"That's not a difficult promise to make," said Winterbourne. "My aunt has taken an apartment in Rome for the winter, and has already asked me to come and see her."

"I don't want you to come for your aunt," said Daisy; "I want you to come for me." And this was the only allusion that the young man was ever to hear her make to his invidious kinswoman. He declared that, at any rate, he would certainly come. After this Daisy stopped teasing. Winterbourne took a carriage, and they drove back to Vevey in the dusk; the young girl was very quiet.

In the evening Winterbourne mentioned to Mrs. Costello that he had spent the afternoon at Chillon, with Miss Daisy Miller.

"The Americans—of the courier?" asked this lady.

"Ah, happily," said Winterbourne, "the courier stayed at home."

"She went with you all alone?"

"All alone."

Mrs. Costello sniffed a little at her smelling-bottle. "And that," she exclaimed, "is the young person you wanted me to know!"

III.

Winterbourne, who had returned to Geneva the day after his excursion to Chillon, went to Rome towards the end of January. His aunt had been established there for several weeks, and he had received a couple of letters from her. "Those people you were so devoted to last summer at Vevey have turned up here, courier and all," she wrote. "They seem to have made several acquaintances, but the courier continues to be the most *intime*. The young lady, however, is also very intimate with some third-rate Italians, with whom she rackets about in a way that makes much talk. Bring me that pretty novel of Cherbuliez's—'Paule Méré'—and don't come later than the 23rd."

In the natural course of events, Winterbourne, on arriving in Rome, would presently have ascertained Mrs. Miller's address at the American banker's and have gone to pay his compliments to Miss Daisy. "After what happened at Vevey I certainly think I may call upon them," he said to Mrs. Costello.

"If, after what happens—at Vevey and everywhere—you desire to keep up the acquaintance, you are very welcome. Of course a man may know every one. Men are welcome to the privilege!"

"Pray what is it that happens—here, for instance?" Winterbourne demanded.

"The girl goes about alone with her foreigners. As to what happens farther, you must apply elsewhere for information. She has picked up half-a-dozen of the regular Roman fortune-hunters, and she takes them about to people's houses. When she comes to a party she brings with her a gentleman with a good deal of manner and a wonderful moustache."

"And where is the mother?"

"I haven't the least idea. They are very dreadful people."

Winterbourne meditated a moment. "They are very ignorant—very innocent only. Depend upon it they are not bad."

"They are hopelessly vulgar," said Mrs. Costello. "Whether or no being hopelessly vulgar is being 'bad' is a question for the metaphysicians. They are bad enough to dislike, at any rate; and for this short life that is quite enough."

The news that Daisy Miller was surrounded by half-a-dozen wonderful moustaches checked Winterbourne's impulse to go straightway to see her. He had perhaps not definitely flattered himself that he had made an ineffaceable impression upon her heart, but he was annoyed at hearing of a state of affairs so little in harmony with an image that had lately flitted in and out of his own meditations; the image of a very pretty girl looking out of an old Roman window and asking herself urgently when Mr. Winterbourne would arrive. If, however, he determined to wait a little before reminding Miss Miller of his claims to her consideration, he went very soon to call upon two or three other friends. One of these friends was an American lady who had spent several winters at Geneva, where she had placed her children at school. She was a very accomplished woman and she lived in the Via Gregoriana. Winterbourne found her in a little crimson drawing-room, on a third floor; the room was filled with southern sunshine. He had not been there ten minutes when the servant came in, announcing "Madame Mila!" This announcement was presently followed by the entrance of little Randolph Miller, who stopped in the middle of the room and stood staring at Winterbourne. An instant later his pretty sister crossed the threshold; and then, after a considerable interval, Mrs. Miller slowly advanced.

"I know you!" said Randolph.

"I'm sure you know a great many things," exclaimed Winterbourne, taking him by the hand. "How is your education coming on?"

Daisy was exchanging greetings very prettily with her hostess; but when she heard Winterbourne's voice she quickly turned her head. "Well, I declare!" she said.

"I told you I should come, you know," Winterbourne rejoined, smiling.

"Well—I didn't believe it," said Miss Daisy.

"I am much obliged to you," laughed the young man.

"You might have come to see me!" said Daisy.

"I arrived only yesterday."

"I don't believe that!" the young girl declared.

Winterbourne turned with a protesting smile to her mother; but this lady evaded his glance, and seating herself, fixed her eyes upon her son. "We've got a bigger place than this," said Randolph. "It's all gold on the walls."

Mrs. Miller turned uneasily in her chair. "I told you if I were to bring you, you would say something!" she murmured.

"I told *you*!" Randolph exclaimed. "I tell *you*, sir!" he added jocosely, giving Winterbourne a thump on the knee. "It *is* bigger, too!"

Daisy had entered upon a lively conversation with her hostess; Winterbourne judged it becoming to address a few words to her mother. "I hope you have been well since we parted at Vevey," he said.

Mrs. Miller now certainly looked at him—at his chin. "Not very well, sir," she answered.

"She's got the dyspepsia," said Randolph. "I've got it too. Father's got it. I've got it worst!"

This announcement, instead of embarrassing Mrs. Miller, seemed to relieve her. "I suffer from the liver," she said. "I think it's this climate; it's less bracing than Schenectady, especially in the winter season. I don't know whether you know we reside at Schenectady. I was saying to Daisy that I certainly hadn't found any one like Dr. Davis, and I didn't believe I should. Oh, at Schenectady, he stands first; they think everything of him. He has so much to do, and yet there was nothing he wouldn't do for me. He said he never saw anything like my dyspepsia, but he was bound to cure it. I'm sure there was nothing he wouldn't try. He was just going to try something new when we came off. Mr. Miller wanted Daisy to see Europe for herself. But I wrote to Mr. Miller that it seems as if I couldn't get on without Dr. Davis. At Schenectady he stands at the very top; and there's a great deal of sickness there, too. It affects my sleep."

Winterbourne had a good deal of pathological gossip with Dr. Davis's patient, during which Daisy chattered unremittingly to her own companion. The young man asked Mrs. Miller how she was pleased with Rome. "Well, I must say I am disappointed," she answered. "We had heard so much about it; I suppose we had heard too much. But we couldn't help that. We had been led to expect something different."

"Ah, wait a little, and you will become very fond of it," said Winterbourne.

"I hate it worse and worse every day!" cried Randolph.

"You are like the infant Hannibal," said Winterbourne.

"No, I ain't!" Randolph declared, at a venture.

"You are not much like an infant," said his mother. "But we have seen places," she resumed, "that I should put a long way before Rome." And in reply to Winterbourne's interrogation, "There's Zurich," she observed; "I think Zurich is lovely; and we hadn't heard half so much about it."

"The best place we've seen is the City of Richmond!" said Randolph.

"He means the ship," his mother explained. "We crossed in that ship. Randolph had a good time on the City of Richmond."

"It's the best place I've seen," the child repeated. "Only it was turned the wrong way."

"Well, we've got to turn the right way some time," said Mrs. Miller, with a little laugh. Winterbourne expressed the hope that her daughter at least found some gratification in Rome, and she declared that Daisy was quite carried away. "It's on account of the society—the society's splendid. She goes round everywhere; she has made a great number of acquaintances. Of course she goes round more than I do. I must say they have been very sociable; they have taken her right in. And then she knows a great many gentlemen. Oh, she thinks there's nothing like Rome. Of course, it's a great deal pleasanter for a young lady if she knows plenty of gentlemen."

By this time Daisy had turned her attention again to Winterbourne. "I've been telling Mrs. Walker how mean you were!" the young girl announced.

"And what is the evidence you have offered?" asked Winterbourne, rather annoyed at Miss Miller's want of appreciation of the zeal of an admirer who on his way down to Rome had stopped neither at Bologna nor at Florence, simply because of a certain sentimental impatience. He remembered that a cynical compatriot had once told him that American women—the pretty ones, and this gave a largeness to the axiom—were at once the most exacting in the world and the least endowed with a sense of indebtedness.

"Why, you were awfully mean at Vevey," said Daisy. "You wouldn't do anything. You wouldn't stay there when I asked you."

"My dearest young lady," cried Winterbourne, with eloquence, "have I come all the way to Rome to encounter your reproaches?"

"Just hear him say that!" said Daisy to her hostess, giving a twist to a bow on this lady's dress. "Did you ever hear anything so quaint?"

"So quaint, my dear?" murmured Mrs. Walker, in the tone of a partisan of Winterbourne.

"Well, I don't know," said Daisy, fingering Mrs. Walker's ribbons. "Mrs. Walker, I want to tell you something."

"Motherr," interposed Randolph, with his rough ends to his words, "I tell you you've got to go. Eugenio'll raise something!"

"I'm not afraid of Eugenio," said Daisy, with a toss of her head. "Look here, Mrs. Walker," she went on, "you know I'm coming to your party."

"I am delighted to hear it."

"I've got a lovely dress."

"I am very sure of that."

"But I want to ask a favour—permission to bring a friend."

"I shall be happy to see any of your friends," said Mrs. Walker, turning with a smile to Mrs. Miller.

"Oh, they are not my friends," answered Daisy's mamma, smiling shyly, in her own fashion. "I never spoke to them!"

"It's an intimate friend of mine—Mr. Giovanelli," said Daisy, without a tremor in her clear little voice or a shadow on her brilliant little face.

Mrs. Walker was silent a moment, she gave a rapid glance at Winterbourne. "I shall be glad to see Mr. Giovanelli," she then said.

"He's an Italian," Daisy pursued, with the prettiest serenity. "He's a great friend of mine—he's the handsomest man in the world—except Mr. Winterbourne! He knows plenty of Italians, but he wants to know some Americans. He thinks ever so much of Americans. He's tremendously clever. He's perfectly lovely!"

It was settled that this brilliant personage should be brought to Mrs. Walker's party, and then Mrs. Miller prepared to take her leave. "I guess we'll go back to the hotel," she said.

"You may go back to the hotel, mother, but I'm going to take a walk," said Daisy.

"She's going to walk with Mr. Giovanelli," Randolph proclaimed.

"I am going to the Pincio," said Daisy, smiling.

"Alone, my dear—at this hour?" Mrs. Walker asked. The afternoon was drawing to a close—it was the hour for the throng of carriages and of contemplative pedestrians. "I don't think it's safe, my dear," said Mrs. Walker.

"Neither do I," subjoined Mrs. Miller. "You'll get the fever as sure as you live. Remember what Dr. Davis told you!"

"Give her some medicine before she goes," said Randolph.

The company had risen to its feet; Daisy, still showing her pretty teeth, bent over and kissed her hostess. "Mrs. Walker, you are too perfect," she said. "I'm not going alone; I am going to meet a friend."

"Your friend won't keep you from getting the fever," Mrs. Miller observed.

"Is it Mr. Giovanelli?" asked the hostess.

Winterbourne was watching the young girl; at this question his attention quickened. She stood there smiling and smoothing her bonnet-ribbons; she glanced at Winterbourne. Then, while she glanced and smiled, she answered without a shade of hesitation, "Mr. Giovanelli—the beautiful Giovanelli."

"My dear young friend," said Mrs. Walker, taking her hand, pleadingly, "don't walk off to the Pincio at this hour to meet a beautiful Italian."

"Well, he speaks English," said Mrs. Miller.

"Gracious me!" Daisy exclaimed, "I don't want to do anything improper. There's an easy way to settle it." She continued to glance at Winterbourne. "The Pincio is only a hundred yards distant, and if Mr. Winterbourne were as polite as he pretends he would offer to walk with me!"

Winterbourne's politeness hastened to affirm itself, and the young girl gave him gracious leave to accompany her. They passed down-stairs before her mother, and at the door Winterbourne perceived Mrs. Miller's carriage drawn up, with the ornamental courier whose acquaintance he had made at Vevey seated within. "Good-bye, Eugenio!" cried Daisy, "I'm going to take a walk." The distance from the Via Gregoriana to the beautiful garden at the other end of the Pincian Hill is, in fact, rapidly traversed. As the day was splendid, however, and the concourse of vehicles, walkers, and loungers numerous, the young Americans found their progress much delayed. This fact was highly agreeable to Winterbourne, in spite of his consciousness of his singular situation. The slow-moving, idly-gazing Roman crowd bestowed much attention upon the extremely pretty young foreign lady who was passing through it upon his arm; and he wondered what on earth had been in Daisy's mind when she proposed to expose herself, unattended, to its appreciation. His own mission, to her sense, apparently, was to consign her to the hands of Mr. Giovanelli; but Winterbourne, at once annoyed and gratified, resolved that he would do no such thing.

"Why haven't you been to see me?" asked Daisy. "You can't get out of that."

"I have had the honour of telling you that I have only just stepped out of the train."

"You must have stayed in the train a good while after it stopped!" cried the young girl, with her little laugh. "I suppose you were asleep. You have had time to go to see Mrs. Walker."

"I knew Mrs. Walker—" Winterbourne began to explain.

"I knew where you knew her. You knew her at Geneva. She told me so. Well, you knew me at Vevey. That's just as good. So you ought to have come." She asked him no other question than this; she began to prattle about her own affairs. "We've got splendid rooms at the hotel; Eugenio says they're the best rooms in Rome. We are going to stay all winter—if we don't die of the fever; and I guess we'll stay then. It's a great deal nicer than I thought; I thought it would be fearfully quiet; I was sure it would be awfully poky. I was sure we should be going round all the time with one of those dreadful old men that explain about the pictures and things. But we only had about a week of that, and now I'm enjoying myself. I know ever so many people, and they are all so charming. The society's extremely select. There are all kinds—English, and Germans, and Italians. I think I like the English best. I like their style of conversation. But there are some lovely Americans. I never saw anything so hospitable. There's something or other every day. There's not much dancing; but I must say I never thought dancing was everything. I was always fond of conversation. I guess I shall have plenty at Mrs. Walker's—her rooms are so small." When they had passed the gate of the Pincian Gardens, Miss Miller began to wonder where Mr. Giovanelli might be. "We had better go straight to that place in front," she said, "where you look at the view."

"I certainly shall not help you to find him," Winterbourne declared.

"Then I shall find him without you," said Miss Daisy.

"You certainly won't leave me!" cried Winterbourne.

She burst into her little laugh. "Are you afraid you'll get lost—or run over? But there's Giovanelli, leaning against that tree. He's staring at the women in the carriages: did you ever see anything so cool?"

Winterbourne perceived at some distance a little man standing with folded arms, nursing his cane. He had a handsome face, an artfully poised hat, a glass in one eye and a nosegay in his button-hole. Winterbourne looked at him a moment and then said, "Do you mean to speak to that man?"

"Do I mean to speak to him? Why, you don't suppose I mean to communicate by signs?"

"Pray understand, then," said Winterbourne, "that I intend to remain with you."

Daisy stopped and looked at him, without a sign of troubled consciousness in her face; with nothing but the presence of her charming eyes and her happy dimples. "Well, she's a cool one!" thought the young man.

"I don't like the way you say that," said Daisy. "It's too imperious."

"I beg your pardon if I say it wrong. The main point is to give you an idea of my meaning."

The young girl looked at him more gravely, but with eyes that were prettier than ever. "I have never allowed a gentleman to dictate to me, or to interfere with anything I do."

"I think you have made a mistake," said Winterbourne. "You should sometimes listen to a gentleman—the right one."

Daisy began to laugh again. "I do nothing but listen to gentlemen!" she exclaimed. "Tell me if Mr. Giovanelli is the right one?"

The gentleman with the nosegay in his bosom had now perceived our two friends, and was approaching the young girl with obsequious rapidity. He bowed to Winterbourne as well as to the latter's companion; he had a brilliant smile, an intelligent eye; Winterbourne thought him not a bad-looking fellow. But he nevertheless said to Daisy—"No, he's not the right one."

Daisy evidently had a natural talent for performing introductions; she mentioned the name of each of her companions to the other. She strolled along with one of them on each side

of her; Mr. Giovanelli, who spoke English very cleverly—
Winterbourne afterwards learned that he had practised the idiom upon a great many American heiresses—addressed her a
great deal of very polite nonsense; he was extremely urbane,
and the young American, who said nothing, reflected upon that
profundity of Italian cleverness which enables people to appear
more gracious in proportion as they are more acutely disappointed. Giovanelli, of course, had counted upon something
more intimate; he had not bargained for a party of three. But
he kept his temper in a manner which suggested far-stretching
intentions. Winterbourne flattered himself that he had taken
his measure. "He is not a gentleman," said the young American; "he is only a clever imitation of one. He is a music-master,
or a penny-a-liner, or a third-rate artist. Damn his good looks!"
Mr. Giovanelli had certainly a very pretty face; but Winterbourne felt a superior indignation at his own lovely fellow-
countrywoman's not knowing the difference between a spurious
gentleman and a real one. Giovanelli chattered and jested and
made himself wonderfully agreeable. It was true that if he was
an imitation the imitation was very skilful. "Nevertheless,"
Winterbourne said to himself, "a nice girl ought to know!"
And then he came back to the question whether this was in fact
a nice girl. Would a nice girl—even allowing for her being a little American flirt—make a rendezvous with a presumably low-
lived foreigner? The rendezvous in this case, indeed, had been
in broad daylight, and in the most crowded corner of Rome;
but was it not impossible to regard the choice of these circumstances as a proof of extreme cynicism? Singular though it may
seem, Winterbourne was vexed that the young girl, in joining
her *amoroso,* should not appear more impatient of his own
company, and he was vexed because of his inclination. It was
impossible to regard her as a perfectly well-conducted young
lady; she was wanting in a certain indispensable delicacy. It
would therefore simplify matters greatly to be able to treat her
as the object of one of those sentiments which are called by ro-
mancers "lawless passions." That she should seem to wish to
get rid of him would help him to think more lightly of her, and
to be able to think more lightly of her would make her much
less perplexing. But Daisy, on this occasion, continued to pre-

sent herself as an inscrutable combination of audacity and innocence.

She had been walking some quarter of an hour, attended by her two cavaliers, and responding in a tone of very childish gaiety, as it seemed to Winterbourne, to the pretty speeches of Mr. Giovanelli, when a carriage that had detached itself from the revolving train drew up beside the path. At the same moment Winterbourne perceived that his friend Mrs. Walker—the lady whose house he had lately left—was seated in the vehicle and was beckoning to him. Leaving Miss Miller's side, he hastened to obey her summons. Mrs. Walker was flushed; she wore an excited air. "It is really too dreadful," she said. "That girl must not do this sort of thing. She must not walk here with you two men. Fifty people have noticed her."

Winterbourne raised his eyebrows. "I think it's a pity to make too much fuss about it."

"It's a pity to let the girl ruin herself!"

"She is very innocent," said Winterbourne.

"She's very crazy!" cried Mrs. Walker. "Did you ever see anything so imbecile as her mother? After you had all left me, just now, I could not sit still for thinking of it. It seemed too pitiful, not even to attempt to save her. I ordered the carriage and put on my bonnet, and came here as quickly as possible. Thank heaven I have found you!"

"What do you propose to do with us?" asked Winterbourne, smiling.

"To ask her to get in, to drive her about here for half-an-hour, so that the world may see she is not running absolutely wild, and then to take her safely home."

"I don't think it's a very happy thought," said Winterbourne; "but you can try."

Mrs. Walker tried. The young man went in pursuit of Miss Miller, who had simply nodded and smiled at his interlocutrix in the carriage and had gone her way with her own companion. Daisy, on learning that Mrs. Walker wished to speak to her, retraced her steps with a perfect good grace and with Mr. Giovanelli at her side. She declared that she was delighted to have a chance to present this gentleman to Mrs. Walker. She immediately achieved the introduction, and declared that she had never in her life seen anything so lovely as Mrs. Walker's carriage-rug.

"I am glad you admire it," said this lady, smiling sweetly. "Will you get in and let me put it over you?"

"Oh, no, thank you," said Daisy. "I shall admire it much more as I see you driving round with it."

"Do get in and drive with me," said Mrs. Walker.

"That would be charming, but it's so enchanting just as I am!" and Daisy gave a brilliant glance at the gentlemen on either side of her.

"It may be enchanting, dear child, but it is not the custom here," urged Mrs. Walker, leaning forward in her victoria with her hands devoutly clasped.

"Well, it ought to be, then!" said Daisy. "If I didn't walk I should expire."

"You should walk with your mother, dear," cried the lady from Geneva, losing patience.

"With my mother dear!" exclaimed the young girl. Winterbourne saw that she scented interference. "My mother never walked ten steps in her life. And then, you know," she added with a laugh, "I am more than five years old."

"You are old enough to be more reasonable. You are old enough, dear Miss Miller, to be talked about."

Daisy looked at Mrs. Walker, smiling intensely. "Talked about? What do you mean?"

"Come into my carriage and I will tell you."

Daisy turned her quickened glance again from one of the gentlemen beside her to the other. Mr. Giovanelli was bowing to and fro, rubbing down his gloves and laughing very agreeably; Winterbourne thought it a most unpleasant scene. "I don't think I want to know what you mean," said Daisy presently. "I don't think I should like it."

Winterbourne wished that Mrs. Walker would tuck in her carriage-rug and drive away; but this lady did not enjoy being defied, as she afterwards told him. "Should you prefer being thought a very reckless girl?" she demanded.

"Gracious me!" exclaimed Daisy. She looked again at Mr. Giovanelli, then she turned to Winterbourne. There was a little pink flush in her cheek; she was tremendously pretty. "Does

Mr. Winterbourne think," she asked slowly, smiling, throwing back her head and glancing at him from head to foot, "that— to save my reputation—I ought to get into the carriage?"

Winterbourne coloured; for an instant he hesitated greatly. It seemed so strange to hear her speak that way of her "reputation." But he himself, in fact, must speak in accordance with gallantry. The finest gallantry, here, was simply to tell her the truth; and the truth, for Winterbourne, as the few indications I have been able to give have made him known to the reader, was that Daisy Miller should take Mrs. Walker's advice. He looked at her exquisite prettiness; and then he said very gently, "I think you should get into the carriage."

Daisy gave a violent laugh. "I never heard anything so stiff! If this is improper, Mrs. Walker," she pursued, "than I am all improper, and you must give me up. Good-bye; I hope you'll have a lovely ride!" and, with Mr. Giovanelli, who made a triumphantly obsequious salute, she turned away.

Mrs. Walker sat looking after her, and there were tears in Mrs. Walker's eyes. "Get in here, sir," she said to Winterbourne, indicating the place beside her. The young man answered that he felt bound to accompany Miss Miller; whereupon Mrs. Walker declared that if he refused her this favour she would never speak to him again. She was evidently in earnest. Winterbourne overtook Daisy and her companion and, offering the young girl his hand, told her that Mrs. Walker had made an imperious claim upon his society. He expected that in answer she would say something rather free, something to commit herself still farther to that "recklessness" from which Mrs. Walker had so charitably endeavoured to dissuade her. But she only shook his hand, hardly looking at him, while Mr. Giovanelli bade him farewell with a too emphatic flourish of the hat.

Winterbourne was not in the best possible humour as he took his seat in Mrs. Walker's victoria. "That was not clever of you," he said candidly, while the vehicle mingled again with the throng of carriages.

"In such a case," his companion answered, "I don't wish to be clever, I wish to be *earnest!*"

"Well, your earnestness has only offended her and put her off."

"It has happened very well," said Mrs. Walker. "If she is so perfectly determined to compromise herself, the sooner one knows it the better; one can act accordingly."

"I suspect she meant no harm," Winterbourne rejoined.

"So I thought a month ago. But she has been going too far."

"What has she been doing?"

"Everything that is not done here. Flirting with any man she could pick up; sitting in corners with mysterious Italians; dancing all the evening with the same partners; receiving visits at eleven o'clock at night. Her mother goes away when visitors come."

"But her brother," said Winterbourne, laughing, "sits up till midnight."

"He must be edified by what he sees. I'm told that at their hotel every one is talking about her, and that a smile goes round among the servants when a gentleman comes and asks for Miss Miller."

"The servants be hanged!" said Winterbourne angrily. "The poor girl's only fault," he presently added, "is that she is very uncultivated."

"She is naturally indelicate," Mrs. Walker declared. "Take that example this morning. How long had you known her at Vevey?"

"A couple of days."

"Fancy, then, her making it a personal matter that you should have left that place!"

Winterbourne was silent for some moments; then he said, "I suspect, Mrs. Walker, that you and I have lived too long at Geneva!" And he added a request that she should inform him with what particular design she had made him enter her carriage.

"I wished to beg you to cease your relations with Miss Miller—not to flirt with her—to give her no farther opportunity to expose herself—to let her alone, in short."

"I'm afraid I can't do that," said Winterbourne. "I like her extremely."

"All the more reason that you shouldn't help her to make a scandal."

"There shall be nothing scandalous in my attentions to her."

"There certainly will be in the way she takes them. But I have said what I had on my conscience," Mrs. Walker pursued. "If you wish to rejoin the young lady I will put you down. Here, by-the-way, you have chance."

The carriage was traversing that part of the Pincian Garden which overhangs the wall of Rome and overlooks the beautiful Villa Borghese. It is bordered by a large parapet, near which there are several seats. One of the seats, at a distance, was occupied by a gentleman and a lady, towards whom Mrs. Walker gave a toss of her head. At the same moment these persons rose and walked towards the parapet. Winterbourne had asked the coachman to stop; he now descended from the carriage. His companion looked at him a moment in silence; then, while he raised his hat, she drove majestically away. Winterbourne stood there; he had turned his eyes towards Daisy and her cavalier. They evidently saw no one; they were too deeply occupied with each other. When they reached the low garden-wall they stood a moment looking off at the great flat-topped pine-clusters of the Villa Borghese; then Giovanelli seated himself familiarly upon the broad ledge of the wall. The western sun in the opposite sky sent out a brilliant shaft through a couple of cloud-bars; whereupon Daisy's companion took her parasol out of her hands and opened it. She came a little nearer and he held the parasol over her; then, still holding it, he let it rest upon her shoulder, so that both of their heads were hidden from Winterbourne. This young man lingered a moment, then he began to walk. But he walked—not towards the couple with the parasol; towards the residence of his aunt, Mrs. Costello.

IV.

He flattered himself on the following day that there was no smiling among the servants when he, at least, asked for Mrs. Miller at her hotel. This lady and her daughter, however, were not at home; and on the next day after, repeating his visit, Winterbourne again had the misfortune not to find them. Mrs. Walker's party took place on the evening of the third day, and in spite of the frigidity of his last interview with the hostess

Winterbourne was among the guests. Mrs. Walker was one of those American ladies who, while residing abroad, make a point, in their own phrase, of studying European society; and she had on this occasion collected several specimens of her diversely-born fellow-mortals to serve, as it were, as text-books. When Winterbourne arrived Daisy Miller was not there; but in a few moments he saw her mother come in alone, very shyly and rue-fully. Mrs. Miller's hair, above her exposed-looking temples, was more frizzled than ever. As she approached Mrs. Walker, Winterbourne also drew near.

"You see I've come all alone," said poor Mrs. Miller. "I'm so frightened; I don't know what to do; it's the first time I've ever been to a party alone—especially in this country. I wanted to bring Randolph or Eugenio, or some one, but Daisy just pushed me off by myself. I ain't used to going round alone."

"And does not your daughter intend to favour us with her society?" demanded Mrs. Walker, impressively.

"Well, Daisy's all dressed," said Mrs. Miller, with that accent of the dispassionate, if not of the philosophic, historian with which she always recorded the current incidents of her daughter's career. "She got dressed on purpose before dinner. But she's got a friend of hers there; that gentleman—the Italian—that she wanted to bring. They've got going at the piano; it seems as if they couldn't leave off. Mr. Giovanelli sings splendidly. But I guess they'll come before very long," concluded Mrs. Miller hopefully.

"I'm sorry she should come—in that way," said Mrs. Walker.

"Well, I told her that there was no use in her getting dressed before dinner if she was going to wait three hours," responded Daisy's mamma. "I didn't see the use of her putting on such a dress as that to sit round with Mr. Giovanelli."

"This is most horrible!" said Mrs. Walker, turning away and addressing herself to Winterbourne. "*Elle s'affiche*. It's her re-venge for my having ventured to remonstrate with her. When she comes I shall not speak to her."

Daisy came after eleven o'clock, but she was not, on such an occasion, a young lady to wait to be spoken to. She rustled forward in radiant loveliness, smiling and chattering, carrying a large bouquet and attended by Mr. Giovanelli. Every one stopped talking, and turned and looked at her. She came straight to Mrs. Walker. "I'm afraid you thought I never was coming, so I sent mother off to tell you. I wanted to make Mr. Giovanelli practise some things before he came; you know he sings beautifully, and I want you to ask him to sing. This is Mr. Giovanelli; you know I introduced him to you; he's got the most lovely voice and he knows the most charming set of songs. I made him go over them this evening, on purpose; we had the greatest time at the hotel." Of all this Daisy delivered herself with the sweetest, brightest audibleness, looking now at her hostess and now round the room, while she gave a series of little pats, round her shoulders, to the edges of her dress. "Is there any one I know?" she asked.

"I think every one knows you!" said Mrs. Walker pregnantly, and she gave a very cursory greeting to Mr. Giovanelli. This gentleman bore himself gallantly. He smiled and bowed and showed his white teeth, he curled his moustaches and rolled his eyes, and performed all the proper functions of a handsome Italian at an evening party. He sang, very prettily, half-a-dozen songs, though Mrs. Walker afterwards declared that she had been quite unable to find out who asked him. It was apparently not Daisy who had given him his orders. Daisy sat a distance from the piano, and though she had publicly, as it were, professed a high admiration for his singing, talked, not inaudibly, while it was going on.

"It's a pity these rooms are so small; we can't dance," she said to Winterbourne, as if she had seen him five minutes before.

"I am not sorry we can't dance," Winterbourne answered; "I don't dance."

"Of course you don't dance; you're too stiff," said Miss Daisy. "I hope you enjoyed your drive with Mrs. Walker."

"No, I didn't enjoy it; I preferred walking with you."

"We paired off, that was much better," said Daisy. "But did you ever hear anything so cool as Mrs. Walker's wanting me to get into her carriage and drop poor Mr. Giovanelli; and under the pretext that it was proper? People have different ideas! It would have been most unkind; he had been talking about that walk for ten days."

"He should not have talked about it at all," said Winterbourne; "he would never have proposed to a young lady of this country to walk about the streets with him."

"About the streets?" cried Daisy, with her pretty stare. "Where then would he have proposed to her to walk? The Pincio is not the streets, either; and I, thank goodness, am not a young lady of this country. The young ladies of this country have a dreadfully poky time of it, so far as I can learn; I don't see why I should change my habits for *them*."

"I am afraid your habits are those of a flirt," said Winterbourne gravely.

"Of course they are," she cried, giving him her little smiling stare again. "I'm a fearful, frightful flirt! Did you ever hear of a nice girl that was not? But I suppose you will tell me now that I am not a very nice girl."

"You're a very nice girl, but I wish you would flirt with me, and me only," said Winterbourne.

"Ah! Thank you, thank you very much; you are the last man I should think of flirting with. As I have had the pleasure of informing you, you are too stiff."

"You say that too often," said Winterbourne.

Daisy gave a delighted laugh. "If I could have the sweet hope of making you angry, I would say it again."

"Don't do that, when I am angry I'm stiffer than ever. But if you won't flirt with me, do cease at least to flirt with your friend at the piano; they don't understand that sort of thing here."

"I thought they understood nothing else!" exclaimed Daisy.

"Not in young unmarried women."

"It seems to me much more proper in young unmarried women than in old married ones," Daisy declared.

"Well," said Winterbourne, "when you deal with natives you must go by the custom of the place. Flirting is a purely American custom; it doesn't exist here. So when you show yourself in public with Mr. Giovanelli and without your mother—"

"Gracious! poor mother!" interposed Daisy.

"Though you may be flirting, Mr. Giovanelli is not; he means something else."

"He isn't preaching, at any rate," said Daisy with vivacity.

"And if you want very much to know, we are neither of us flirting; we are too good friends for that; we are very intimate friends."

"Ah!" rejoined Winterbourne, "if you are in love with each other it is another affair."

She had allowed him up to this point to talk so frankly that he had no expectation of shocking her by this ejaculation; but she immediately got up, blushing visibly, and leaving him to exclaim mentally that little American flirts were the queerest creatures in the world. "Mr. Giovanelli, at least," she said, giving her interlocutor a single glance, "never says such very disagreeable things to me."

Winterbourne was bewildered; he stood staring. Mr. Giovanelli had finished singing; he left the piano and came over to Daisy. "Won't you come into the other room and have some tea?" he asked, bending before her with his decorative smile.

Daisy turned to Winterbourne, beginning to smile again. He was still more perplexed, for this inconsequent smile made nothing clear, though it seemed to prove, indeed, that she had a sweetness and softness that reverted instinctively to the pardon of offences. "It has never occurred to Mr. Winterbourne to offer me any tea," she said, with her little tormenting manner.

"I have offered you advice," Winterbourne rejoined.

"I prefer weak tea!" cried Daisy, and she went off with the brilliant Giovanelli. She sat with him in the adjoining room, in the embrasure of the window, for the rest of the evening. There was an interesting performance at the piano, but neither of these young people gave heed to it. When Daisy came to take leave of Mrs. Walker, this lady conscientiously repaired the weakness of which she had been guilty at the moment of the young girl's arrival. She turned her back straight upon Miss Miller and left her to depart with what grace she might. Winterbourne was standing near the door; he saw it all. Daisy turned very pale and looked at her mother, but Mrs. Miller was humbly unconscious of any violation of the usual social forms. She appeared, indeed, to have felt an incongruous impulse to draw attention to her own striking observance of them. "Good night, Mrs. Walker," she said; "we've had a beautiful evening. You see if I let Daisy come to parties without me, I don't want her to go away without me." Daisy turned away, looking with a pale, grave face at the circle near the door; Winterbourne saw that, for the first moment, she was too much shocked and puzzled even for indignation. He on his side was greatly touched.

"That was very cruel," he said to Mrs. Walker.

"She never enters my drawing-room again," replied his hostess.

Since Winterbourne was not to meet her in Mrs. Walker's drawing-room, he went as often as possible to Mrs. Miller's hotel. The ladies were rarely at home, but when he found them the devoted Giovanelli was always present. Very often the polished little Roman was in the drawing-room with Daisy alone, Mrs. Miller being apparently constantly of the opinion that discretion is the better part of surveillance. Winterbourne noted, at first with surprise, that Daisy on these occasions was never embarrassed or annoyed by his own entrance; but he very presently began to feel that she had no more surprises for him; the unexpected in her behavior was the only thing to expect. She showed no displeasure at her *tête-à-tête* with Giovanelli being interrupted; she could chatter as freshly and freely with two gentlemen as with one; there was always in her conversation, the same odd mixture of audacity and puerility. Winterbourne remarked to himself that if she was seriously interested in Giovanelli it was very singular that she should not take more trouble to preserve the sanctity of their interviews, and he liked her the more for her innocent-looking indifference and her apparently inexhaustible good humour. He could hardly have said why, but she seemed to him a girl who would never be jealous. At the risk of exciting a somewhat derisive smile on the reader's part, I may affirm that with regard to the women who had hitherto interested him it very often seemed to Winterbourne among the possibilities that, given certain contingencies, he should be afraid—literally afraid—of these ladies. He had a pleasant sense that he should never be afraid of Daisy Miller. It must be added that this sentiment was not altogether flattering to Daisy; it was part of his conviction, or rather of his apprehension, that she would prove a very light young person.

But she was evidently very much interested in Giovanelli. She looked at him whenever he spoke; she was perpetually telling him to do this and to do that; she was constantly "chaffing" and abusing him. She appeared completely to have forgotten that Winterbourne had said anything to displease her at Mrs. Walker's little party. One Sunday afternoon, having gone to St. Peter's with his aunt, Winterbourne perceived Daisy strolling about the great church in company with the inevitable Giovanelli. Presently he pointed out the young girl and her cavalier to Mrs. Costello. This lady looked at them a moment through her eyeglass, and then said:

"That's what makes you so pensive in these days, eh?"

"I had not the least idea I was pensive," said the young man.

"You are very much pre-occupied, you are thinking of something."

"And what is it," he asked, "that you accuse me of thinking of?"

"Of that young lady's—Miss Baker's, Miss Chandler's— what's her name?—Miss Miller's intrigue with that little barber's block."

"Do you call it an intrigue," Winterbourne asked—"an affair that goes on with such peculiar publicity?"

"That's their folly," said Mrs. Costello, "it's not their merit."

"No," rejoined Winterbourne, with something of that pensiveness to which his aunt had alluded. "I don't believe that there is anything to be called an intrigue."

"I have heard a dozen people speak of it; they say she is quite carried away by him."

"They are certainly very intimate," said Winterbourne.

Mrs. Costello inspected the young couple again with her optical instrument. "He is very handsome. One easily sees how it is. She thinks him the most elegant man in the world, the finest gentleman. She has never seen anything like him; he is better even than the courier. It was the courier probably who introduced him, and if he succeeds in marrying the young lady, the courier will come in for a magnificent commission."

"I don't believe she thinks of marrying him," said Winterbourne, "and I don't believe he hopes to marry her."

"You may be very sure she thinks of nothing. She goes on from day to day, from hour to hour, as they did in the Golden Age. I can imagine nothing more vulgar. And at the same time," added Mrs. Costello, "depend upon it that she may tell you any moment that she is 'engaged.' "

"I think that is more than Giovanelli expects," said Winterbourne.

"Who is Giovanelli?"

"The little Italian. I have asked questions about him and learned something. He is apparently a perfectly respectable little man. I believe he is in a small way a *cavaliere avvocato*. But he doesn't move in what are called the first circles. I think it is really not absolutely impossible that the courier introduced him. He is evidently immensely charmed with Miss Miller. If she thinks him the finest gentleman in the world, he, on his side, has never found himself in personal contact with such splendour, such opulence, such expensiveness, as this young lady's. And then she must seem to him wonderfully pretty and interesting. I rather doubt whether he dreams of marrying her. That must appear to him too impossible a piece of luck. He has nothing but his handsome face to offer, and there is a substantial Mr. Miller in that mysterious land of dollars. Giovanelli knows that he hasn't a title to offer. If he were only a count or a *marchese*! He must wonder at his luck at the way they have taken him up."

"He accounts for it by his handsome face, and thinks Miss Miller a young lady *qui se passe ses fantaisies*!" said Mrs. Costello.

"It is very true," Winterbourne pursued, "that Daisy and her mamma have not yet risen to that stage of—what shall I call it?—of culture, at which the idea of catching a count or a *marchese* begins. I believe that they are intellectually incapable of that conception."

"Ah! But the *cavaliere* can't believe it," said Mrs. Costello.

Of the observation excited by Daisy's "intrigue," Winterbourne gathered that day at St. Peter's sufficient evidence. A dozen of the American colonists in Rome came to talk with Mrs. Costello, who sat on a little portable stool at the base of one of the great pilasters. The vesper-service was going forward in splendid chants and organ-tones in the adjacent choir, and meanwhile, between Mrs. Costello and her friends, there was a great deal said about poor little Miss Miller's going really "too far." Winterbourne was not pleased with what he heard; but when, coming out upon the great steps of the church, he saw Daisy, who had emerged before him, get into an open cab with her accomplice and roll away through the cynical streets of Rome, he could not deny to himself that she was going very far indeed. He felt very sorry for her—not exactly that he believed that she had completely lost her head, but because it was painful to hear so much that was pretty and undefended and natural assigned to a vulgar place among the categories of disorder. He made an attempt after this to give a hint to Mrs. Miller. He met one day in the Corso a friend—a tourist like himself—who had just come out of the Doria Palace, where he had been walking through the beautiful gallery. His friend talked for a moment about the superb portrait of Innocent X. by Velasquez, which hangs in one of the cabinets of the palace, and then said, "And in the same cabinet, by-the-way, I had the pleasure of contemplating a picture of a different kind—that pretty American girl whom you pointed out to me last week." In answer to Winterbourne's inquiries, his friend narrated that the pretty American girl—prettier than ever—was seated with a companion in the secluded nook in which the great papal portrait is enshrined.

"Who was her companion?" asked Winterbourne.

"A little Italian with a bouquet in his button-hole. The girl is delightfully pretty, but I thought I understood from you the other day that she was a young lady *du meilleur monde.*"

"So she is!" answered Winterbourne; and having assured himself that his informant had seen Daisy and her companion but five minutes before, he jumped into a cab and went to call on Mrs. Miller. She was at home, but she apologised to him for receiving him in Daisy's absence.

"She's gone out somewhere with Mr. Giovanelli," said Mrs. Miller. "She's always going round with Mr. Giovanelli."

"I have noticed that they are very intimate," Winterbourne observed.

"Oh! It seems as if they couldn't live without each other!" said Mrs. Miller. "Well, he's a real gentleman, anyhow. I keep telling Daisy she's engaged!"

"And what does Daisy say?"

"Oh, she says she isn't engaged. But she might as well be!" this impartial parent resumed. "She goes on as if she was. But I've made Mr. Giovanelli promise to tell me, if *she* doesn't. I should want to write to Mr. Miller about it—shouldn't you?"

Winterbourne replied that he certainly should; and the state of mind of Daisy's mamma struck him as so unprecedented in the annals of parental vigilance that he gave up as utterly irrelevant the attempt to place her upon her guard.

After this Daisy was never at home, and Winterbourne ceased to meet her at the houses of their common acquaintance, because, as he perceived, these shrewd people had quite made up their minds that she was going too far. They ceased to invite her, and they intimated that they desired to express to observant Europeans the great truth that, though Miss Daisy Miller was a young American lady, her behaviour was not representative—was regarded by her compatriots as abnormal. Winterbourne wondered how she felt about all the cold shoulders that were turned towards her, and sometimes it annoyed him to suspect that she did not feel at all. He said to himself that she was too light and childish, too uncultivated and unreasoning, too provincial, to have reflected upon her ostracism or even to have perceived it. Then at other moments he believed that she carried about in her elegant and irresponsible little organism a defiant, passionate, perfectly observant consciousness of the impression she produced. He asked himself whether Daisy's defiance came from the consciousness of innocence or from her being, essentially, a young person of the reckless class. It must be admitted that holding oneself to a belief in Daisy's "innocence" came to seem to Winterbourne more and more a matter of fine-spun gallantry. As I have already had occasion to relate, he was angry at finding himself reduced to chopping logic about this young lady; he was vexed at his want of instinctive certitude as to how far her eccentricities were generic, national, and how far they were personal. From either view of them he had somehow missed her, and now it was too late. She was "carried away" by Mr. Giovanelli.

A few days after his brief interview with her mother, he encountered her in that beautiful abode of flowering desolation known as the Palace of the Cæsars. The early Roman spring had filled the air with bloom and perfume, and the rugged surface of the Palatine was muffled with tender verdure. Daisy was strolling along the top of one of those great mounds of ruin that are embanked with mossy marble and paved with monumental inscriptions. It seemed to him that Rome had never been so lovely as just then. He stood looking off at the enchanting harmony of line and colour that remotely encircles the city, inhaling the softly humid odours and feeling the freshness of the year and the antiquity of the place reaffirm themselves in mysterious interfusion. It seemed to him also that Daisy had never looked so pretty; but this had been an observation of his whenever he met her. Giovanelli was at her side, and Giovanelli, too, wore an aspect of even unwonted brilliancy.

"Well," said Daisy, "I should think you would be lonesome!"

"Lonesome?" asked Winterbourne.

"You are always going round by yourself. Can't you get any one to walk with you?"

"I am not so fortunate," said Winterbourne, "as your companion."

Giovanelli, from the first, had treated Winterbourne with distinguished politeness; he listened with a deferential air to his remarks; he laughed, punctiliously, at his pleasantries; he seemed disposed to testify to his belief that Winterbourne was a superior young man. He carried himself in no degree like a jealous wooer; he had obviously a great deal of tact; he had no objection to your expecting a little humility of him. It even seemed to Winterbourne at times that Giovanelli would find a certain mental relief in being able to have a private understanding with him—to say to him, as an intelligent man, that, bless you, *he* knew how extraordinary was this young lady, and didn't flatter himself with delusive—or at least *too* delusive—hopes of matrimony and dollars. On this occasion he strolled away from his companion to pluck a sprig of almond blossom, which he carefully arranged in his button-hole.

"I know why you say that," said Daisy, watching Giovanelli. "Because you think I go round too much with *him*!" And she nodded at her attendant.

"Every one thinks so—if you care to know," said Winterbourne.

"Of course I care to know!" Daisy exclaimed seriously. "But I don't believe it. They are only pretending to be shocked. They don't really care a straw what I do. Besides, I don't go round so much."

"I think you will find they do care. They will show it—disagreeably."

Daisy looked at him a moment. "How—disagreeably?"

"Haven't you noticed anything?" Winterbourne asked.

"I have noticed you. But I noticed you were as stiff as an umbrella the first time I saw you."

"You will find I am not so stiff as several others," said Winterbourne, smiling.

"How shall I find it?"

"By going to see the others."

"What will they do to me?"

"They will give you the cold shoulder. Do you know what that means?"

Daisy was looking at him intently; she began to colour. "Do you mean as Mrs. Walker did the other night?"

"Exactly!" said Winterbourne.

She looked away at Giovanelli, who was decorating himself with his almond-blossom. Then looking back at Winterbourne—"I shouldn't think you would let people be so unkind!" she said.

"How can I help it?" he asked.

"I should think you would say something."

"I do say something," and he paused a moment. "I say that your mother tells me that she believes you are engaged."

"Well, she does," said Daisy very simply.

Winterbourne began to laugh. "And does Randolph believe it?" he asked.

"I guess Randolph doesn't believe anything," said Daisy. Randolph's scepticism excited Winterbourne to farther hilarity, and he observed that Giovanelli was coming back to them. Daisy, observing it too, addressed herself again to her countryman. "Since you have mentioned it," she said, "I *am* engaged." . . . Winterbourne looked at her; he had stopped laughing. "You don't believe it!" she added.

He was silent a moment; and then, "Yes, I believe it!" he said.

"Oh, no, you don't," she answered. "Well, then—I am not!"

The young girl and her cicerone were on their way to the gate of the enclosure, so that Winterbourne, who had but lately entered, presently took leave of them. A week afterwards he went to dine at a beautiful villa on the Cælian Hill, and, on arriving, dismissed his hired vehicle. The evening was charming, and he promised himself the satisfaction of walking home beneath the Arch of Constantine and past the vaguely-lighted monuments of the Forum. There was a waning moon in the sky, and her radiance was not brilliant, but she was veiled in a thin cloud-curtain which seemed to diffuse and equalise it. When, on his return from the villa (it was eleven o'clock), Winterbourne approached the dusky circle of the Colosseum, it occurred to him, as a lover of the picturesque, that the interior, in the pale moonshine, would be well worth a glance. He turned aside and walked to one of the empty arches, near which, as he observed, an open carriage—one of the little Roman street-cabs—was stationed. Then he passed in among the cavernous shadows of the great structure, and emerged upon the clear and silent arena. The place had never seemed to him more impressive. One-half of the gigantic circus was in deep shade; the other was sleeping in the luminous dusk. As he stood there he began to murmur Byron's famous lines, out of "Manfred"; but before he had finished his quotation he remembered that if nocturnal meditations in the Colosseum are recommended by the poets, they are deprecated by the doctors. The historic atmosphere was there, certainly; but the historic atmosphere, scientifically considered, was no better than a villainous miasma. Winterbourne walked to the middle of the arena, to take a more general glance, intending thereafter to make a hasty retreat. The great cross in the centre was covered with shadow; it was only as he drew near it that he made it out distinctly. Then he saw that two persons were stationed upon the low steps which formed its base. One of these was a woman, seated; her companion was standing in front of her.

Presently the sound of the woman's voice came to him distinctly in the warm night-air. "Well, he looks at us as one of the old lions or tigers may have looked at the Christian martyrs!" These were the words he heard, in the familiar accent of Miss Daisy Miller.

"Let us hope he is not very hungry," responded the ingenious Giovanelli. "He will have to take me first; you will serve for dessert!"

Winterbourne stopped, with a sort of horror; and, it must be added, with a sort of relief. It was as if a sudden illumination had been flashed upon the ambiguity of Daisy's behaviour and the riddle had become easy to read. She was a young lady whom a gentleman need no longer be at pains to respect. He stood there looking at her—looking at her companion, and not reflecting that though he saw them vaguely, he himself must have been more brightly visible. He felt angry with himself that he had bothered so much about the right way of regarding Miss Daisy Miller. Then, as he was going to advance again, he checked himself; not from the fear that he was doing her injustice, but from a sense of the danger of appearing unbecomingly exhilarated by this sudden revulsion from cautious criticism. He turned away towards the entrance of the place; but as he did so he heard Daisy speak again.

"Why, it was Mr. Winterbourne! He saw me—and he cuts me!"

What a clever little reprobate she was, and how smartly she played an injured innocence! But he wouldn't cut her. Winterbourne came forward again, and went towards the great cross. Daisy had got up; Giovanelli lifted his hat. Winterbourne had now begun to think simply of the craziness, from a sanitary point of view, of a delicate young girl lounging away the evening in this nest of malaria. What if she *were* a clever little reprobate? that was no reason for her dying of the *perniciosa*. "How long have you been here?" he asked, almost brutally.

Daisy, lovely in the flattering moonlight, looked at him a moment. Then—"All the evening," she answered gently. . . . "I never saw anything so pretty."

"I am afraid," said Winterbourne, "that you will not think Roman fever very pretty. This is the way people catch it. I wonder," he added, turning to Giovanelli, "that you, a native Roman, should countenance such a terrible indiscretion."

"Ah," said the handsome native, "for myself, I am not afraid."

"Neither am I—for you! I am speaking for this young lady."

Giovanelli lifted his well-shaped eyebrows and showed his brilliant teeth. But he took Winterbourne's rebuke with docility. "I told the Signorina it was a grave indiscretion; but when was the Signorina ever prudent?"

"I never was sick, and I don't mean to be!" the Signorina declared. "I don't look like much, but I'm healthy! I was bound to see the Colosseum by moonlight; I shouldn't have wanted to go home without that; and we have had the most beautiful time, haven't we, Mr. Giovanelli? If there has been any danger, Eugenio can give me some pills. He has got some splendid pills."

"I should advise you," said Winterbourne, "to drive home as fast as possible and take one!"

"What you say is very wise," Giovanelli rejoined. "I will go and make sure the carriage is at hand." And he went forward rapidly.

Daisy followed with Winterbourne. He kept looking at her; she seemed not in the least embarrassed. Winterbourne said nothing; Daisy chattered about the beauty of the place. "Well, I *have* seen the Colosseum by moonlight!" she exclaimed. "That's one good thing." Then, noticing Winterbourne's silence, she asked him why he didn't speak. He made no answer; he only began to laugh. They passed under one of the dark archways; Giovanelli was in front with the carriage. Here Daisy stopped a moment, looking at the young American. "*Did* you believe I was engaged the other day?" she asked.

"It doesn't matter what I believed the other day," said Winterbourne, still laughing.

"Well, what do you believe now?"

"I believe that it makes very little difference whether you are engaged or not!"

He felt the young girl's pretty eyes fixed upon him through the thick gloom of the archway; she was apparently going to answer. But Giovanelli hurried her forward. "Quick, quick," he said; "if we get in by midnight we are quite safe."

Daisy took her seat in the carriage, and the fortunate Italian placed himself beside her. "Don't forget Eugenio's pills!" said Winterbourne, as he lifted his hat.

"I don't care," said Daisy, in a little strange tone, "whether I have Roman fever or not!" Upon this the cab-driver cracked his whip, and they rolled away over the desultory patches of the antique pavement.

Winterbourne—to do him justice, as it were—mentioned to no one that he had encountered Miss Miller, at midnight, in the Colosseum with a gentleman; but nevertheless, a couple of days later, the fact of her having been there under these circumstances was known to every member of the little American circle, and commented accordingly. Winterbourne reflected that they had of course known it at the hotel, and that, after Daisy's return, there had been an exchange of jokes between the porter and the cab-driver. But the young man was conscious at the same moment that it had ceased to be a matter of serious regret to him that the little American flirt should be "talked about" by low-minded menials. These people, a day or two later, had serious information to give: the little American flirt was alarmingly ill. Winterbourne, when the rumour came to him, immediately went to the hotel for more news. He found that two or three charitable friends had preceded him, and that they were being entertained in Mrs. Miller's salon by Randolph.

"It's going round at night," said Randolph—"that's what made her sick. She's always going round at night. I shouldn't think she'd want to—it's so plaguey dark. You can't see anything here at night, except when there's a moon. In America there's always a moon!" Mrs. Miller was invisible; she was now, at least, giving her daughter the advantage of her society. It was evident that Daisy was dangerously ill.

Winterbourne went often to ask for news of her, and once he saw Mrs. Miller, who, though deeply alarmed, was—rather to his surprise—perfectly composed, and, as it appeared, a most efficient and judicious nurse. She talked a good deal about Dr.

Davis, but Winterbourne paid her the compliment of saying to himself that she was not, after all, such a monstrous goose. "Daisy spoke of you the other day," she said to him. "Half the time she doesn't know what she's saying, but that time I think she did. She gave me a message; she told me to tell you. She told me to tell you that she never was engaged to that handsome Italian. I am sure I am very glad; Mr. Giovanelli hasn't been near us since she was taken ill. I thought he was so much of a gentleman; but I don't call that very polite! A lady told me that he was afraid I was angry with him for taking Daisy round at night. Well, so I am; but I suppose he knows I'm a lady. I would scorn to scold him. Any way, she says she's not engaged. I don't know why she wanted you to know; but she said to me three times—'Mind you tell Mr. Winterbourne.' And then she told me to ask if you remembered the time you went to that castle, in Switzerland. But I said I wouldn't give any such messages as that. Only, if she is not engaged, I'm sure I'm glad to know it."

But, as Winterbourne had said, it mattered very little. A week after this the poor girl died; it had been a terrible case of the fever. Daisy's grave was in the little Protestant cemetery, in an angle of the wall of imperial Rome, beneath the cypresses and the thick spring-flowers. Winterbourne stood there beside it, with a number of other mourners; a number larger than the scandal excited by the young lady's career would have led you to expect. Near him stood Giovanelli, who came nearer still before Winterbourne turned away. Giovanelli was very pale; on this occasion he had no flower in his button-hole; he seemed to wish to say something. At last he said, "She was the most beautiful young lady I ever saw, and the most amiable." And then he added in a moment, "And she was the most innocent."

Winterbourne looked at him, and presently repeated his words, "And the most innocent?"

"The most innocent!"

Winterbourne felt sore and angry. "Why the devil," he asked, "did you take her to that fatal place?"

Mr. Giovanelli's urbanity was apparently imperturbable. He looked on the ground a moment, and then he said, "For myself, I had no fear; and she wanted to go."

"That was no reason!" Winterbourne declared.

The subtle Roman again dropped his eyes. "If she had lived, I should have got nothing. She would never have married me, I am sure."

"She would never have married you?"

"For a moment I hoped so. But no. I am sure."

Winterbourne listened to him; he stood staring at the raw protuberance among the April daisies. When he turned away again Mr. Giovanelli, with his light slow step, had retired.

Winterbourne almost immediately left Rome; but the following summer he again met his aunt, Mrs. Costello, at Vevey. Mrs. Costello was fond of Vevey. In the interval Winterbourne had often thought of Daisy Miller and her mystifying manners. One day he spoke of her to his aunt—said it was on his conscience that he had done her injustice.

"I am sure I don't know," said Mrs. Costello. "How did your injustice affect her?"

"She sent me a message before her death which I didn't understand at the time. But I have understood it since. She would have appreciated one's esteem."

"Is that a modest way," asked Mrs. Costello, "of saying that she would have reciprocated one's affection?"

Winterbourne offered no answer to this question; but he presently said, "You were right in that remark that you made last summer. I was booked to make a mistake. I have lived too long in foreign parts."

Nevertheless, he went back to live at Geneva, whence there continue to come the most contradictory accounts of his motives of sojourn: a report that he is "studying" hard—an intimation that he is much interested in a very clever foreign lady.

Brooksmith

Harper's Weekly, *May 2, 1891. One of Ford Madox Hueffer's servants said, "It always gives me a turn to open the door for Mr. James. His eyes seem to look you through to the very backbone." "Brooksmith" considers a London butler who, according to James's New York Edition preface, had "caught a glimpse, all untimely, of 'la beauté parfaite'" of fine conversation in an ideal setting. Relating the "obscure tragedy" of a servant who loses his place at the fringes of such society, "Brooksmith" feels like a Jamesian version— supersaturated with acculturation though it may be—of Melville's "Bartleby."*

We are scattered now, the friends of the late Mr. Oliver Offord; but whenever we chance to meet I think we are conscious of a certain esoteric respect for each other. "Yes, you too have been in Arcadia," we seem not too grumpily to allow. When I pass the house in Mansfield Street I remember that Arcadia was there. I don't know who has it now, and I don't want to know; it's enough to be so sure that if I should ring the bell there would be no such luck for me as that Brooksmith should open the door. Mr. Offord, the most agreeable, the most lovable of bachelors, was a retired diplomatist, living on his pension, confined by his infirmities to his fireside and delighted to be found there any afternoon in the year by such visitors as Brooksmith allowed to come up. Brooksmith was his butler and his most intimate friend, to whom we all stood, or I should say sat, in the same relation in which the subject of the sovereign finds himself to the prime minister. By having been for years, in foreign lands, the most delightful Englishman any one had ever known, Mr. Offord had, in my opinion, rendered signal service to his country. But I suppose he had been too much liked—liked even by those who didn't like *it*—so that as people of that sort never get titles or dotations for the horrid things they have *not* done, his principal reward was simply that we went to see him.

Oh, we went perpetually, and it was not our fault if he was not overwhelmed with this particular honour. Any visitor who came once came again—to come merely once was a slight which nobody, I am sure, had ever put upon him. His circle, therefore, was essentially composed of *habitués,* who were *habitués* for each other as well as for him, as those of a happy *salon* should be. I remember vividly every element of the place, down to the intensely Londonish look of the grey opposite houses, in the gap of the white curtains of the high windows, and the exact spot where, on a particular afternoon, I put down my tea-cup for Brooksmith, lingering an instant, to gather it up as if he were plucking a flower. Mr. Offord's drawing-room was indeed Brooksmith's garden, his pruned and tended human *parterre,* and if we all flourished there and grew well in our places it was largely owing to his supervision.

Many persons have heard much, though most have doubtless seen little, of the famous institution of the *salon,* and many are born to the depression of knowing that this finest flower of social life refuses to bloom where the English tongue is spoken. The explanation is usually that our women have not the skill to cultivate it—the art to direct, between suggestive shores, the course of the stream of talk. My affectionate, my pious memory of Mr. Offord contradicts this induction only, I fear, more insidiously to confirm it. The very sallow and slightly smoked drawing-room in which he spent so large a portion of the last years of his life certainly deserved the distinguished name; but on the other hand it could not be said at all to owe its stamp to the soft pressure of the indispensable sex. The dear man had indeed been capable of one of those sacrifices to which women are deemed peculiarly apt; he had recognised (under the influence, in some degree, it is true, of physical infirmity), that if you wished people to find you at home you must manage not to be out. He had in short accepted the fact which many dabblers in the social art are slow to learn, that you must really, as they say, take a line and that the only way to be at home is to stay at home. Finally his own fireside had become a summary of his habits. Why should he ever have left it?—since this would have been leaving what was notoriously pleasantest in London, the compact charmed cluster (thinning away indeed into casual couples), round the fine old last century chimney-piece which, with the exception of the remarkable collection of miniatures, was the best thing the place contained. Mr. Offord was not rich; he had nothing but his pension and the use for life of the somewhat superannuated house.

When I am reminded by some uncomfortable contrast of to-day how perfectly we were all handled there I ask myself once more what had been the secret of such perfection. One had taken it for granted at the time, for anything that is supremely good produces more acceptance than surprise. I felt we were all happy, but I didn't consider how our happiness was managed. And yet there were questions to be asked, questions that strike me as singularly obvious now that there is nobody to answer them. Mr. Offord had solved the insoluble; he had, without feminine help (save in the sense that ladies were dying to come to him and he saved the lives of several), established a *salon;* but I might have guessed that there was a method in his madness—a law in his success. He had not hit it off by a mere fluke. There was an art in it all, and how was the art so hidden? Who, indeed, if it came to that, was the occult artist? Launching this inquiry the other day, I had already got hold of the tail of my reply. I was helped by the very wonder of some of the conditions that came back to me—those that used to seem as natural as sunshine in a fine climate.

How was it, for instance, that we never were a crowd, never either too many or too few, always the right people *with* the right people (there must really have been no wrong people at all), always coming and going, never sticking fast nor overstaying, yet never popping in or out with an indecorous familiarity? How was it that we all sat where we wanted and moved when we wanted and met whom we wanted and escaped whom we wanted; joining, according to the accident of inclination, the general circle or falling in with a single talker on a convenient sofa? Why were all the sofas so convenient, the accidents so happy, the talkers so ready, the listeners so willing, the subjects presented to you in a rotation as quickly fore-ordained as the courses at dinner? A dearth of topics would have been as unheard of as a lapse in the service. These speculations couldn't fail to lead me to the fundamental truth that Brooksmith had been somehow at the bottom of the mystery. If he had not established the *salon* at least he had carried it on. Brooksmith, in short, was the artist!

We felt this, covertly, at the time, without formulating it, and were conscious, as an ordered and prosperous community, of his evenhanded justice, untainted with flunkeyism. He had none of that vulgarity—his touch was infinitely fine. The delicacy of it was clear to me on the first occasion my eyes rested, as they were so often to rest again, on the domestic revealed, in the turbid light of the street, by the opening of the house-door. I saw on the spot that though he had plenty of school he carried it without arrogance—he had remained articulate and human. *L'Ecole Anglaise,* Mr. Offord used to call him, laughing, when, later, it happened more than once that we had some conversation about him. But I remember accusing Mr. Offord of not doing him quite ideal justice. That he was not one of the giants of the school, however, my old friend, who really understood him perfectly and was devoted to him, as I shall show, quite admitted; which doubtless poor Brooksmith had himself felt, to his cost, when his value in the market was originally determined. The utility of his class in general is estimated by the foot and the inch, and poor Brooksmith had only about five feet two to put into circulation. He acknowledged the inadequacy of this provision, and I am sure was penetrated with the everlasting fitness of the relation between service and stature. If *he* had been Mr. Offord he certainly would have found Brooksmith wanting, and indeed the laxity of his employer on this score was one of many things which he had had to condone and to which he had at last indulgently adapted himself.

I remember the old man's saying to me: "Oh, my servants, if they can live with me a fortnight they can live with me for ever.

But it's the first fortnight that tries 'em." It was in the first fortnight, for instance, that Brooksmith had had to learn that he
was exposed to being addressed as "my dear fellow" and "my
poor child." Strange and deep must such a probation have been
to him, and he doubtless emerged from it tempered and puri-
fied. This was written to a certain extent in his appearance; in
his spare, brisk little person, in his cloistered white face and extraordinarily polished hair, which told of responsibility, looked
as if it were kept up to the same high standard as the plate; in
his small, clear, anxious eyes, even in the permitted, though not
exactly encouraged tuft on his chin. "He thinks me rather mad,
but I've broken him in, and now he likes the place, he likes the
company," said the old man. I embraced this fully after I had
become aware that Brooksmith's main characteristic was a
deep and shy refinement, though I remember I was rather puzzled when, on another occasion, Mr. Offord remarked: "What
he likes is the talk—mingling in the conversation." I was conscious that I had never seen Brooksmith permit himself this
freedom, but I guessed in a moment that what Mr. Offord alluded to was a participation more intense than any speech
could have represented—that of being perpetually present on a
hundred legitimate pretexts, errands, necessities, and breathing
the very atmosphere of criticism, the famous criticism of life.
"Quite an education, sir, isn't it, sir?" he said to me one day at
the foot of the stairs, when he was letting me out; and I have always remembered the words and the tone as the first sign of the
quickening drama of poor Brooksmith's fate. It was indeed an
education, but to what was this sensitive young man of thirty-
five, of the servile class, being educated?

Practically and inevitably, for the time, to companionship, to
the perpetual, the even exaggerated reference and appeal of a
person brought to dependence by his time of life and his infirmities and always addicted moreover (this was the exaggera-
tion) to the art of giving you pleasure by letting you do things
for him. There were certain things Mr. Offord was capable of
pretending he liked you to do, even when he didn't, if he
thought *you* liked them. If it happened that you didn't either
(this was rare, but it might be), of course there were cross-

purposes; but Brooksmith was there to prevent their going very far. This was precisely the way he acted as moderator: he averted misunderstandings or cleared them up. He had been capable, strange as it may appear, of acquiring for this purpose an insight into the French tongue, which was often used at Mr. Offord's; for besides being habitual to most of the foreigners, and they were many, who haunted the place or arrived with letters (letters often requiring a little worried consideration, of which Brooksmith always had cognisance), it had really become the primary language of the master of the house. I don't know if all the *malentendus* were in French, but almost all the explanations were, and this didn't a bit prevent Brooksmith from following them. I know Mr. Offord used to read passages to him from Montaigne and Saint-Simon, for he read perpetually when he was alone—when they were alone, I should say— and Brooksmith was always about. Perhaps you'll say no wonder Mr. Offord's butler regarded him as "rather mad." However, if I'm not sure what he thought about Montaigne I'm convinced he admired Saint-Simon. A certain feeling for letters must have rubbed off on him from the mere handling of his master's books, which he was always carrying to and fro and putting back in their places.

I often noticed that if an anecdote or a quotation, much more a lively discussion, was going forward, he would, if busy with the fire or the curtains, the lamp or the tea, find a pretext for remaining in the room till the point should be reached. If his purpose was to catch it you were not discreet to call him off, and I shall never forget a look, a hard, stony stare (I caught it in its passage), which, one day when there were a good many people in the room, he fastened upon the footman who was helping him in the service and who, in an undertone, had asked him some irrelevant question. It was the only manifestation of harshness that I ever observed on Brooksmith's part, and at first I wondered what was the matter. Then I became conscious that Mr. Offord was relating a very curious anecdote, never before perhaps made so public, and imparted to the narrator by an eye-witness of the fact, bearing upon Lord Byron's life in Italy. Nothing would induce me to reproduce it here; but

Brooksmith had been in danger of losing it. If I ever should venture to reproduce it I shall feel how much I lose in not having my fellow-auditor to refer to.

The first day Mr. Offord's door was closed was therefore a dark date in contemporary history. It was raining hard and my umbrella was wet, but Brooksmith took it from me exactly as if this were a preliminary for going upstairs. I observed however that instead of putting it away he held it poised and trickling over the rug, and then I became aware that he was looking at me with deep, acknowledging eyes—his air of universal responsibility. I immediately understood; there was scarcely need of the question and the answer that passed between us. When I did understand that the old man had given up, for the first time, though only for the occasion, I exclaimed dolefully: "What a difference it will make—and to how many people!"

"I shall be one of them, sir!" said Brooksmith; and that was the beginning of the end.

Mr. Offord came down again, but the spell was broken, and the great sign of it was that the conversation was, for the first time, not directed. It wandered and stumbled, a little frightened, like a lost child—it had let go the nurse's hand. "The worst of it is that now we shall talk about my health—*c'est la fin de tout*," Mr. Offord said, when he reappeared; and then I recognised what a sign of change that would be—for he had never tolerated anything so provincial. The talk became ours, in a word—not his; and as ours, even when *he* talked, it could only be inferior. In this form it was a distress to Brooksmith, whose attention now wandered from it altogether: he had so much closer a vision of his master's intimate conditions than our superficialities represented. There were better hours, and he was more in and out of the room, but I could see that he was conscious that the great institution was falling to pieces. He seemed to wish to take counsel with me about it, to feel responsible for its going on in some form or other. When for the second period—the first had lasted several days—he had to tell me that our old friend didn't receive, I half expected to hear him say after a moment: "Do you think I ought to, sir, in his place?"—as he might have asked me, with the return of autumn, if I thought he had better light the drawing-room fire.

He had a resigned philosophic sense of what his guests—our guests, as I came to regard them in our colloquies—would expect. His feeling was that he wouldn't absolutely have approved of himself as a substitute for the host; but he was so saturated with the religion of habit that he would have made, for our friends, the necessary sacrifice to the divinity. He would take them on a little further, till they could look about them. I think I saw him also mentally confronted with the opportunity to deal—for once in his life—with some of his own dumb preferences, his limitations of sympathy, *weeding* a little, in prospect, and returning to a purer tradition. It was not unknown to me that he considered that toward the end of Mr. Offord's career a certain laxity of selection had crept in.

At last it came to be the case that we all found the closed door more often than the open one; but even when it was closed Brooksmith managed a crack for me to squeeze through; so that practically I never turned away without having paid a visit. The difference simply came to be that the visit was to Brooksmith. It took place in the hall, at the familiar foot of the stairs, and we didn't sit down—at least Brooksmith didn't; moreover it was devoted wholly to one topic and always had the air of being already over—beginning, as it were, at the end. But it was always interesting—it always gave me something to think about. It is true that the subject of my meditation was ever the same—ever "It's all very well, but what *will* become of Brooksmith?" Even my private answer to this question left me still unsatisfied. No doubt Mr. Offord would provide for him, but *what* would he provide? that was the great point. He couldn't provide society; and society had become a necessity of Brooksmith's nature. I must add that he never showed a symptom of what I may call sordid solitude—anxiety on his own account. He was rather livid and intensely grave, as befitted a man before whose eyes the "shade of that which once was great" was passing away. He had the solemnity of a person winding up, under depressing circumstances, a long established and celebrated business; he was a kind of social executor or liquidator. But his manner seemed to testify exclusively to the uncertainty of *our* future. I couldn't in those days have afforded it—I lived in two rooms in Jermyn Street and didn't "keep a man"; but even if my income had permitted I shouldn't have ventured to say to Brooksmith (emulating Mr. Offord), "My dear fellow, I'll take you on." The whole tone of our intercourse was so much more an implication that it was *I* who should now want a lift. Indeed there was a tacit assurance in Brooksmith's whole attitude that he would have me on his mind.

One of the most assiduous members of our circle had been Lady Kenyon, and I remember his telling me one day that her ladyship had, in spite of her own infirmities, lately much aggravated, been in person to inquire. In answer to this I remarked that she would feel it more than any one. Brooksmith was silent a moment; at the end of which he said, in a certain tone (there is no reproducing some of his tones), "I'll go and see her." I went to see her myself, and I learned that he had waited upon her; but when I said to her, in the form of a joke but with a core of earnest, that when all was over some of us ought to combine, to club together to set Brooksmith up on his own account, she replied a trifle disappointingly: "Do you mean in a public-house?" I looked at her in a way that I think Brooksmith himself would have approved, and then I answered: "Yes, the Offord Arms." What I had meant, of course, was that, for the love of art itself, we ought to look to it that such a peculiar faculty and so much acquired experience should not be wasted. I really think that if we had caused a few black-edged cards to be struck off and circulated—"Mr. Brooksmith will continue to receive on the old premises from four to seven; business carried on as usual during the alterations"—the majority of us would have rallied.

Several times he took me upstairs—always by his own proposal—and our dear old friend, in bed, in a curious flowered and brocaded *casaque* which made him, especially as his head was tied up in a handkerchief to match, look, to my imagination, like the dying Voltaire, held for ten minutes a sadly shrunken little *salon*. I felt indeed each time, as if I were attending the last *coucher* of some social sovereign. He was royally whimsical about his sufferings and not at all concerned—quite as if the Constitution provided for the case—about his successor. He glided over *our* sufferings charmingly, and none of his jokes—it was a gallant abstention, some of them would have been so easy—were at our expense. Now and again, I confess, there was one at Brooksmith's, but so pathetically sociable as to make the excellent man look at me in a way that seemed to say: "Do exchange a glance with me, or I sha'n't be able to stand it." What he was not able to stand was not what Mr. Offord said about him, but what he wasn't able to say in return. His notion of conversation, for himself, was giving you the convenience of speaking to him; and when he went to "see" Lady Kenyon, for instance, it was to carry her the tribute of his receptive silence. Where would the speech of his betters have been if proper service had been a manifestation of sound? In that case the fundamental difference would have had to be shown by *their* dumbness, and many of them, poor things, were dumb enough without that provision. Brooksmith took an unfailing interest in the preservation of the fundamental difference; it was the thing he had most on his conscience.

What had become of it, however, when Mr. Offord passed away like any inferior person—was relegated to eternal stillness like a butler upstairs? His aspect for several days after the expected event may be imagined, and the multiplication by funereal observance of the things he didn't say. When everything was over—it was late the same day—I knocked at the door of the house of mourning as I so often had done before. I could never call on Mr. Offord again, but I had come, literally, to call on Brooksmith. I wanted to ask him if there was anything I could do for him, tainted with vagueness as this inquiry could only be. My wild dream of taking him into my own service had died away: my service was not worth his being taken into. My offer to him could only be to help him to find another place, and yet there was an indelicacy, as it were, in taking for granted that his thoughts would immediately be fixed on another. I had a hope that he would be able to give his life a different form— though certainly not the form, the frequent result of such bereavements, of his setting up a little shop. That would have been dreadful; for I should have wished to further any enterprise that he might embark in, yet how could I have brought myself to go and pay him shillings and take back coppers over a counter? My visit then was simply an intended compliment.

He took it as such, gratefully and with all the tact in the world. He knew I really couldn't help him and that I knew he knew I couldn't; but we discussed the situation—with a good deal of elegant generality—at the foot of the stairs, in the hall already dismantled, where I had so often discussed other situations with him. The executors were in possession, as was still more apparent when he made me pass for a few minutes into the dining-room, where various objects were muffled up for removal.

Two definite facts, however, he had to communicate; one being that he was to leave the house for ever that night (servants, for some mysterious reason, seem always to depart by night), and the other—he mentioned it only at the last, with hesitation—that he had already been informed his late master had left him a legacy of eighty pounds. "I'm very glad," I said, and Brooksmith rejoined: "It was so like him to think of me." This was all that passed between us on the subject, and I know nothing of his judgment of Mr. Offord's memento. Eighty pounds are always eighty pounds, and no one has ever left *me* an equal sum; but, all the same, for Brooksmith, I was disappointed. I don't know what I had expected—in short I was disappointed. Eighty pounds might stock a little shop—a *very* little shop; but, I repeat, I couldn't bear to think of that. I asked my friend if he had been able to save a little, and he replied: "No, sir; I have had to do things." I didn't inquire what things he had had to do; they were his own affair, and I took his word for them as assentingly as if he had had the greatness of an ancient house to keep up; especially as there was something in his manner that seemed to convey a prospect of further sacrifice.

"I shall have to turn round a bit, sir—I shall have to look about me," he said; and then he added, indulgently, magnanimously: "If you should happen to hear of anything for me—"

I couldn't let him finish; this was, in its essence, too much in the really grand manner. It would be a help to my getting him off my mind to be able to pretend I *could* find the right place, and that help he wished to give me, for it was doubtless painful to him to see me in so false a position. I interposed with a few words to the effect that I was well aware that wherever he should go, whatever he should do, he would miss our old friend terribly—miss him even more than I should, having been with him so much more. This led him to make the speech that I have always remembered as the very text of the whole episode.

"Oh, sir, it's sad for *you*, very sad, indeed, and for a great many gentlemen and ladies; that it is, sir. But for me, sir, it is, if I may say so, still graver even than that: it's just the loss of something that was everything. For me, sir," he went on, with rising tears, "he was just *all*, if you know what I mean, sir. You have others, sir, I daresay—not that I would have you understand me to speak of them as in any way tantamount. But you have the pleasures of society, sir; if it's only in talking about him, sir, as I daresay you do freely—for all his blessed memory has to fear from it—with gentlemen and ladies who have had the same honour. That's not for me, sir, and I have to keep my associations to myself. Mr. Offord was *my* society, and now I have no more. You go back to conversation, sir, after all, and I go back to my place," Brooksmith stammered, without exaggerated irony or dramatic bitterness, but with a flat, unstudied veracity and his hand on the knob of the street-door. He turned it to let me out and then he added: "I just go downstairs, sir, again, and I stay there."

"My poor child," I replied, in my emotion, quite as Mr. Offord used to speak, "my dear fellow, leave it to me; we'll look after you, we'll all do something for you."

"Ah, if you could give me some one *like* him! But there ain't two in the world," said Brooksmith as we parted.

He had given me his address—the place where he would be to be heard of. For a long time I had no occasion to make use of the information; for he proved indeed, on trial, a very difficult case. In a word the people who knew him and had known Mr. Offord, didn't want to take him, and yet I couldn't bear to try to thrust him among people who didn't know him. I spoke to many of our old friends about him, and I found them all governed by the odd mixture of feelings of which I myself was conscious, and disposed, further, to entertain a suspicion that he was "spoiled," with which I then would have nothing to do. In plain terms a certain embarrassment, a sensible awkwardness, when they thought of it, attached to the idea of using him as a menial: they had met him so often in society. Many of them would have asked him, and did ask him, or rather did ask me to ask him, to come and see them; but a mere visiting-list was not what I wanted for him. He was too short for people who were very particular; nevertheless I heard of an opening in a diplomatic house-hold which led me to write him a note, though I was looking much less for something grand than for something human. Five days later I heard from him. The secretary's wife had decided, after keeping him waiting till then, that she couldn't take a servant out of a house in which there had not been a lady. The note had a P.S.: "It's a good job there wasn't, sir, such a lady as some."

A week later he came to see me and told me he was "suited"—committed to some highly respectable people (they were something very large in the City), who lived on the Bayswater side of the Park. "I daresay it will be rather poor, sir," he admitted; "but I've seen the fireworks, haven't I, sir?— it can't be fireworks *every* night. After Mansfield Street there ain't much choice." There was a certain amount, however, it seemed; for the following year, going one day to call on a country cousin, a lady of a certain age who was spending a fortnight in town with some friends of her own, a family unknown to me and resident in Chester Square, the door of the house was opened, to my surprise and gratification, by Brooksmith in person. When I came out I had some conversation with him, from which I gathered that he had found the large City people too dull for endurance, and I guessed, though he didn't say it, that he had found them vulgar as well. I don't know what judgment he would have passed on his actual patrons if my relative had not been their friend; but under the circumstances he abstained from comment.

None was necessary, however, for before the lady in question brought her visit to a close they honoured me with an invitation to dinner, which I accepted. There was a largeish party on the occasion, but I confess I thought of Brooksmith rather more than of the seated company. They required no depth of attention—they were all referable to usual, irredeemable, inevitable types. It was the world of cheerful common-place and conscious gentility and prosperous density, a full-fed, material, insular world, a world of hideous florid plate and ponderous order and thin conversation. There was not a word said about Byron. Nothing would have induced me to look at Brooksmith in the course of the repast, and I felt sure that not even my overturning the wine would have induced him to meet my eye. We were in intellectual sympathy—we felt, as regards each other, a kind of social responsibility. In short we had been in Arcadia together, and we had both come to *this!* No wonder we were ashamed to be confronted. When he helped on my overcoat, as I was going away, we parted, for the first time since the earliest days in Mansfield Street, in silence. I thought he looked lean and wasted, and I guessed that his new place was not more "human" than his previous one. There was plenty of beef and beer, but there was no reciprocity. The question for him to have asked before accepting the position would have been not "How many footmen are kept?" but "How much imagination?"

The next time I went to the house—I confess it was not very soon—I encountered his successor, a personage who evidently enjoyed the good fortune of never having quitted his natural level. Could any be higher? he seemed to ask—over the heads of three footmen and even of some visitors. He made me feel as if Brooksmith were dead; but I didn't dare to inquire—I couldn't have borne his "I haven't the least idea, sir." I despatched a note to the address Brooksmith had given me after Mr. Offord's death, but I received no answer. Six months later, however, I was favoured with a visit from an elderly, dreary, dingy person, who introduced herself to me as Mr. Brooksmith's aunt and from whom I learned that he was out of place and out of health and had allowed her to come and say to me that if I could spare half-an-hour to look in at him he would take it as a rare honour.

I went the next day—his messenger had given me a new address—and found my friend lodged in a short sordid street in Marylebone, one of those corners of London that wear the last expression of sickly meanness. The room into which I was shown was above the small establishment of a dyer and cleaner who had inflated kid gloves and discoloured shawls in his shop-front. There was a great deal of grimy infant life up and down the place, and there was a hot, moist smell within, as of the "boiling" of dirty linen. Brooksmith sat with a blanket over his legs at a clean little window, where, from behind stiff bluish-white curtains, he could look across at a huckster's and a tinsmith's and a small greasy public-house. He had passed through an illness and was convalescent, and his mother, as well as his aunt, was in attendance on him. I liked the mother, who was bland and intensely humble, but I didn't much fancy the aunt, whom I connected, perhaps unjustly, with the opposite public-house (she seemed somehow to be greasy with the same grease), and whose furtive eye followed every movement of my hand, as if to see if it were not going into my pocket. It didn't take this direction—I couldn't, unsolicited, put myself at that sort of ease with Brooksmith. Several times the door of the room opened, and mysterious old women peeped in and shuffled back again. I don't know who they were; poor Brooksmith seemed encompassed with vague, prying, beery females.

He was vague himself, and evidently weak, and much embarrassed, and not an allusion was made between us to Mansfield Street. The vision of the *salon* of which he had been an ornament hovered before me, however, by contrast, sufficiently. He assured me that he was really getting better, and his mother remarked that he would come round if he could only get his spirits up. The aunt echoed this opinion, and I became more sure that in her own case she knew where to go for such a purpose. I'm afraid I was rather weak with my old friend, for I neglected the opportunity, so exceptionally good, to rebuke the levity which had led him to throw up honourable positions—fine, stiff, steady berths, with morning prayers, as I knew, attached to one of them—in Bayswater and Belgravia. Very likely his reasons had been profane and sentimental; he didn't want morning prayers, he wanted to be somebody's dear fellow; but I couldn't be the person to rebuke him. He shuffled these episodes out of sight—I saw that he had no wish to discuss them. I perceived further, strangely enough, that it would probably be a questionable pleasure for him to see me again: he doubted now even of my power to condone his aberrations. He didn't wish to have to explain; and his behaviour, in future, was likely to need explanation. When I bade him farewell he looked at me a moment with eyes that said everything: "How can I talk about those exquisite years in this place, before these people, with the old women poking their heads in? It was very good of you to come to see me—it wasn't my idea; *she* brought you. We've said everything; it's over; you'll lose all patience with me, and I'd rather you shouldn't see the rest." I sent him some money, in a letter, the next day, but I saw the rest only in the light of a barren sequel.

A whole year after my visit to him I became aware once, in dining out, that Brooksmith was one of the several servants who hovered behind our chairs. He had not opened the door of the house to me, and I had not recognised him in the cluster of retainers in the hall. This time I tried to catch his eye, but he never gave me a chance, and when he handed me a dish I could only be careful to thank him audibly. Indeed I partook of two *entrées* of which I had my doubts, subsequently converted into certainties, in order not to snub him. He looked well enough in health, but much older, and wore, in an exceptionally marked degree, the glazed and expressionless mask of the British domestic *de race*. I saw with dismay that if I had not known him I should have taken him, on the showing of his countenance, for an extravagant illustration of irresponsive servile gloom. I said to myself that he had become a reactionary, gone over to the Philistines, thrown himself into religion, the religion of his "place," like a foreign lady *sur le retour*. I divined moreover that he was only engaged for the evening—he had become a mere waiter, had joined the band of the white-waistcoated who "go out." There was something pathetic in this fact, and it was a terrible vulgarisation of Brooksmith. It was the mercenary prose of butlerhood; he had given up the struggle for the poetry. If reciprocity was what he had missed, where was the reciprocity now? Only in the bottoms of the wine-glasses and the five shillings (or whatever they get), clapped into his hand by the permanent man. However, I supposed he had taken up a precarious branch of his profession because after all it sent him less downstairs. His relations with London society were more superficial, but they were of course more various. As I went away, on this occasion, I looked out for him eagerly among the four or five attendants whose perpendicular persons, fluting the walls of London passages, are supposed to lubricate the process of departure; but he was not on duty. I asked one of the others if he were not in the house, and received the prompt answer: "Just left, sir. Anything I can do for you, sir?" I wanted to say "Please give him my kind regards"; but I abstained; I didn't want to compromise him, and I never came across him again.

Often and often, in dining out, I looked for him, sometimes accepting invitations on purpose to multiply the chances of my meeting him. But always in vain; so that as I met many other members of the casual class over and over again, I at last adopted the theory that he always procured a list of expected guests beforehand and kept away from the banquets which he thus learned I was to grace. At last I gave up hope, and one day, at the end of three years, I received another visit from his aunt. She was drearier and dingier, almost squalid, and she was in great tribulation and want. Her sister, Mrs. Brooksmith, had been dead a year, and three months later her nephew had disappeared. He had always looked after her a bit—since her troubles; I never knew what her troubles had been—and now she hadn't so much as a petticoat to pawn. She had also a niece, to whom she had been everything, before her troubles, but the niece had treated her most shameful. These were details; the great and romantic fact was Brooksmith's final evasion of his fate. He had gone out to wait one evening, as usual, in a white waistcoat she had done up for him with her own hands, being due at a large party up Kensington way. But he had never come home again, and had never arrived at the large party, or at any party that any one could make out. No trace of him had come to light—no gleam of the white waistcoat had pierced the obscurity of his doom. This news was a sharp shock to me, for I had my ideas about his real destination. His aged relative had promptly, as she said, guessed the worst. Somehow and somewhere he had got out of the way altogether, and now I trust that, with characteristic deliberation, he is changing the plates of the immortal gods. As my depressing visitant also said, he never *had* got his spirits up. I was fortunately able to dismiss her with her own somewhat improved. But the dim ghost of poor Brooksmith is one of those that I see. He had indeed been spoiled.

The Real Thing

Black and White, April 16, 1892. James's 1891 note-book entry indicates that the donnée *of this tale was suggested by George du Maurier—the author of* Trilby—*when an "oldish, faded, ruined pair" asked him for help finding positions as models for an artist. Yet the idea of the "real" thing—"the idea—it can't be a 'story' in the vulgar sense of the word," as the notebook entry suggests—was James's own. For its form he sought "something as admirably compact and selected as Maupassant." Despite that compactness, the idea would find further complication in the later fiction, and, in each of the three novels of his major phase—*The Ambassadors, The Wings of the Dove, *and* The Golden Bowl—*the term "the real thing" is repeated frequently (it is also reiterated in the notebook entry, relating to "The Middle Years").*

I.

When the porter's wife (she used to answer the house-bell), announced "A gentleman—with a lady, sir," I had, as I often had in those days, for the wish was father to the thought, an immediate vision of sitters. Sitters my visitors in this case proved to be; but not in the sense I should have preferred. However, there was nothing at first to indicate that they might not have come for a portrait. The gentleman, a man of fifty, very high and very straight, with a moustache slightly grizzled and a dark grey walking-coat admirably fitted, both of which I noted professionally—I don't mean as a barber or yet as a tailor—would have struck me as a celebrity if celebrities often were striking. It was a truth of which I had for some time been conscious that a figure with a good deal of frontage was, as one might say, almost never a public institution. A glance at the lady helped to remind me of this paradoxical law: she also looked too distinguished to be a "personality." Moreover one would scarcely come across two variations together.

Neither of the pair spoke immediately—they only prolonged the preliminary gaze which suggested that each wished to give the other a chance. They were visibly shy; they stood there letting me take them in—which, as I afterwards perceived, was the most practical thing they could have done. In this way their embarrassment served their cause. I had seen people painfully reluctant to mention that they desired anything so gross as to be represented on canvas; but the scruples of my new friends appeared almost insurmountable. Yet the gentleman might have said "I should like a portrait of my wife," and the lady might have said "I should like a portrait of my husband." Perhaps they were not husband and wife—this naturally would make the matter more delicate. Perhaps they wished to be done together—in which case they ought to have brought a third person to break the news.

"We come from Mr. Rivet," the lady said at last, with a dim smile which had the effect of a moist sponge passed over a "sunk" piece of painting, as well as of a vague allusion to vanished beauty. She was as tall and straight, in her degree, as her companion, and with ten years less to carry. She looked as sad as a woman could look whose face was not charged with expression; that is her tinted oval mask showed friction as an exposed surface shows it. The hand of time had played over her freely, but only to simplify. She was slim and stiff, and so well-dressed, in dark blue cloth, with lappets and pockets and buttons, that it was clear she employed the same tailor as her husband. The couple had an indefinable air of prosperous thrift—they evidently got a good deal of luxury for their money. If I was to be one of their luxuries it would behove me to consider my terms.

"Ah, Claude Rivet recommended me?" I inquired; and I

added that it was very kind of him, though I could reflect that, as he only painted landscape, this was not a sacrifice.

The lady looked very hard at the gentleman, and the gentleman looked round the room. Then staring at the floor a moment and stroking his moustache, he rested his pleasant eyes on me with the remark: "He said you were the right one."

"I try to be, when people want to sit."

"Yes, we should like to," said the lady anxiously.

"Do you mean together?"

My visitors exchanged a glance. "If you could do anything with *me*, I suppose it would be double," the gentleman stammered.

"Oh yes, there's naturally a higher charge for two figures than for one."

"We should like to make it pay," the husband confessed.

"That's very good of you," I returned, appreciating so unwonted a sympathy—for I supposed he meant pay the artist.

A sense of strangeness seemed to dawn on the lady. "We mean for the illustrations—Mr. Rivet said you might put one in."

"Put one in—an illustration?" I was equally confused.

"Sketch her off, you know," said the gentleman, colouring.

It was only then that I understood the service Claude Rivet had rendered me; he had told them that I worked in black and white, for magazines, for story-books, for sketches of contemporary life, and consequently had frequent employment for models. These things were true, but it was not less true (I may confess it now—whether because the aspiration was to lead to everything or to nothing I leave the reader to guess), that I couldn't get the honours, to say nothing of the emoluments, of a great painter of portraits out of my head. My "illustrations" were my pot-boilers; I looked to a different branch of art (far and away the most interesting it had always seemed to me), to perpetuate my fame. There was no shame in looking to it also to make my fortune; but that fortune was by so much further from being made from the moment my visitors wished to be "done" for nothing. I was disappointed; for in the pictorial sense I had immediately *seen* them. I had seized their type—I had already settled what I would do with it. Something that wouldn't absolutely have pleased them, I afterwards reflected.

"Ah, you're—you're—a—?" I began, as soon as I had mastered my surprise. I couldn't bring out the dingy word "models"; it seemed to fit the case so little.

"We haven't had much practice," said the lady.

"We've got to *do* something, and we've thought that an artist in your line might perhaps make something of us," her husband threw off. He further mentioned that they didn't know many artists and that they had gone first, on the off-chance (he painted views of course, but sometimes put in figures—perhaps I remembered), to Mr. Rivet, whom they had met a few years before at a place in Norfolk where he was sketching.

"We used to sketch a little ourselves," the lady hinted.

"It's very awkward, but we absolutely *must* do something," her husband went on.

"Of course, we're not so *very* young," she admitted, with a wan smile.

With the remark that I might as well know something more about them, the husband had handed me a card extracted from a neat new pocket-book (their appurtenances were all of the freshest) and inscribed with the words "Major Monarch." Impressive as these words were they didn't carry my knowledge much further; but my visitor presently added: "I've left the army, and we've had the misfortune to lose our money. In fact our means are dreadfully small."

"It's an awful bore," said Mrs. Monarch.

They evidently wished to be discreet—to take care not to swagger because they were gentlefolks. I perceived they would have been willing to recognise this as something of a drawback, at the same time that I guessed at an underlying sense—their consolation in adversity—that they *had* their points. They certainly had; but these advantages struck me as preponderantly social; such for instance as would help to make a drawing-room look well. However, a drawing-room was always, or ought to be, a picture.

In consequence of his wife's allusion to their age Major Monarch observed: "Naturally, it's more for the figure that we thought of going in. We can still hold ourselves up." On the instant I saw that the figure was indeed their strong point. His "naturally" didn't sound vain, but it lighted up the question.

"*She* has got the best," he continued, nodding at his wife, with a pleasant after-dinner absence of circumlocution. I could only reply, as if we were in fact sitting over our wine, that this didn't prevent his own from being very good; which led him in turn to rejoin: "We thought that if you ever have to do people like us, we might be something like it. *She,* particularly—for a lady in a book, you know."

I was so amused by them that, to get more of it, I did my best to take their point of view; and though it was an embarrassment to find myself appraising physically, as if they were animals on hire or useful blacks, a pair whom I should have expected to meet only in one of the relations in which criticism is tacit, I looked at Mrs. Monarch judicially enough to be able to exclaim, after a moment, with conviction: "Oh yes, a lady in a book!" She was singularly like a bad illustration.

"We'll stand up, if you like," said the Major; and he raised himself before me with a really grand air.

I could take his measure at a glance—he was six feet two and a perfect gentleman. It would have paid any club in process of formation and in want of a stamp to engage him at a salary to stand in the principal window. What struck me immediately was that in coming to me they had rather missed their vocation; they could surely have been turned to better account for advertising purposes. I couldn't of course see the thing in detail, but I could see them make someone's fortune—I don't mean their own. There was something in them for a waistcoat-maker, an hotel-keeper or a soap-vendor. I could imagine "We always use it" pinned on their bosoms with the greatest effect; I had a vision of the promptitude with which they would launch a table d'hôte.

Mrs. Monarch sat still, not from pride but from shyness, and presently her husband said to her: "Get up my dear and show how smart you are." She obeyed, but she had no need to get up to show it. She walked to the end of the studio, and then she came back blushing, with her fluttered eyes on her husband. I was reminded of an incident I had accidentally had a glimpse of in Paris—being with a friend there, a dramatist about to produce a play—when an actress came to him to ask to be intrusted with a part. She went through her paces before him, walked up and down as Mrs. Monarch was doing. Mrs. Monarch did it quite as well, but I abstained from applauding. It was very odd to see such people apply for such poor pay. She looked as if she had ten thousand a year. Her husband had used the word that described her: she was, in the London current jargon, essentially and typically "smart." Her figure was, in the same order of ideas, conspicuously and irreproachably "good." For a woman of her age her waist was surprisingly small; her elbow moreover had the orthodox crook. She held her head at the conventional angle; but why did she come to *me?* She ought to have tried on jackets at a big shop. I feared my visitors were not only destitute, but "artistic"—which would be a great complication. When she sat down again I thanked her, observing that what a draughtsman most valued in his model was the faculty of keeping quiet.

"Oh, *she* can keep quiet," said Major Monarch. Then he added, jocosely: "I've always kept her quiet."

"I'm not a nasty fidget, am I?" Mrs. Monarch appealed to her husband.

He addressed his answer to me. "Perhaps it isn't out of place to mention—because we ought to be quite business-like, oughtn't we?—that when I married her she was known as the Beautiful Statue."

"Oh dear!" said Mrs. Monarch, ruefully.

"Of course I should want a certain amount of expression," I rejoined.

"Of *course!*" they both exclaimed.

"And then I suppose you know that you'll get awfully tired."

"Oh, we *never* get tired!" they eagerly cried.

"Have you had any kind of practice?"

They hesitated—they looked at each other. "We've been photographed, *immensely,*" said Mrs. Monarch.

"She means the fellows have asked us," added the Major.

"I see—because you're so good-looking."

"I don't know what they thought, but they were always after us."

"We always got our photographs for nothing," smiled Mrs. Monarch.

"We might have brought some, my dear," her husband remarked.

"I'm not sure we have any left. We've given quantities away," she explained to me.

"With our autographs and that sort of thing," said the Major.

"Are they to be got in the shops?" I inquired, as a harmless pleasantry.

"Oh, yes; *hers*—they used to be."

"Not now," said Mrs. Monarch, with her eyes on the floor.

II.

I could fancy the "sort of thing" they put on the presentation-copies of their photographs, and I was sure they wrote a beautiful hand. It was odd how quickly I was sure of everything that concerned them. If they were now so poor as to have to earn shillings and pence, they never had had much of a margin. Their good looks had been their capital, and they had good-humouredly made the most of the career that this resource marked out for them. It was in their faces, the blankness, the deep intellectual repose of the twenty years of country-house visiting which had given them pleasant intonations. I could see the sunny drawing-rooms, sprinkled with periodicals she didn't read, in which Mrs. Monarch had continuously sat; I could see the wet shrubberies in which she had walked, equipped to admiration for either exercise. I could see the rich covers the Major had helped to shoot and the wonderful garments in which, late at night, he repaired to the smoking-room to talk about them. I could imagine their leggings and waterproofs, their knowing tweeds and rugs, their rolls of sticks and cases of tackle and neat umbrellas; and I could evoke the exact appearance of their servants and the compact variety of their luggage on the platforms of country stations.

They gave small tips, but they were liked; they didn't do anything themselves, but they were welcome. They looked so well everywhere; they gratified the general relish for stature, complexion and "form." They knew it without fatuity or vulgarity, and they respected themselves in consequence. They were not superficial; they were thorough and kept themselves up—it had been their line. People with such a taste for activity had to have some line. I could feel how, even in a dull house, they could have been counted upon for cheerfulness. At present something had happened—it didn't matter what, their little income had grown less, it had grown least—and they had to do something for pocket-money. Their friends liked them, but didn't like to support them. There was something about them that represented credit—their clothes, their manners, their type; but if credit is a large empty pocket in which an occasional chink reverberates, the chink at least must be audible. What they wanted of me was to help to make it so. Fortunately they had no children—I soon divined that. They would also perhaps wish our relations to be kept secret: this was why it was "for the figure"—the reproduction of the face would betray them.

I liked them—they were so simple; and I had no objection to them if they would suit. But, somehow, with all their perfections I didn't easily believe in them. After all they were amateurs, and the ruling passion of my life was the detestation of the amateur. Combined with this was another perversity—an innate preference for the represented subject over the real one: the defect of the real one was so apt to be a lack of representation. I liked things that appeared; then one was sure. Whether they *were* or not was a subordinate and almost always a profitless question. There were other considerations, the first of which was that I already had two or three people in use, notably a young person with big feet, in alpaca, from Kilburn, who for a couple of years had come to me regularly for my illustrations and with whom I was still—perhaps ignobly—satisfied. I frankly explained to my visitors how the case stood; but they had taken more precautions than I supposed. They had reasoned out their opportunity, for Claude Rivet had told them of the projected *édition de luxe* of one of the writers of our day—the rarest of the novelists—who, long neglected by the multitudinous vulgar and dearly prized by the attentive (need I mention Philip Vincent?) had had the happy fortune of seeing, late in life, the dawn and then the full light of a higher criticism—an estimate in which, on the part of the public, there was something really of expiation. The edition in question, planned by a publisher of taste, was practically an act of high reparation; the wood-cuts with which it was to be enriched were the homage of English art to one of the most independent representatives of English letters. Major and Mrs. Monarch confessed to me that they had hoped I might be able to work *them* into my share of the enterprise. They knew I was to do the first of the books, "Rutland Ramsay," but I had to make clear to them that my participation in the rest of the affair— this first book was to be a test—was to depend on the satisfaction I should give. If this should be limited my employers would drop me without a scruple. It was therefore a crisis for me, and naturally I was making special preparations, looking about for new people, if they should be necessary, and securing the best types. I admitted however that I should like to settle down to two or three good models who would do for everything.

"Should we have often to—a—put on special clothes?" Mrs. Monarch timidly demanded.

"Dear, yes—that's half the business."

"And should we be expected to supply our own costumes?"

"Oh, no; I've got a lot of things. A painter's models put on— or put off—anything he likes."

"And do you mean—a—the same?"

"The same?"

Mrs. Monarch looked at her husband again.

"Oh, she was just wondering," he explained, "if the costumes are in *general* use." I had to confess that they were, and I mentioned further that some of them (I had a lot of genuine, greasy last-century things), had served their time, a hundred years ago, on living, world-stained men and women. "We'll put on anything that *fits*," said the Major.

"Oh, I arrange that—they fit in the pictures."

"I'm afraid I should do better for the modern books. I would come as you like," said Mrs. Monarch.

"She has got a lot of clothes at home: they might do for contemporary life," her husband continued.

"Oh, I can fancy scenes in which you'd be quite natural."

And indeed I could see the slipshod rearrangements of stale properties—the stories I tried to produce pictures for without the exasperation of reading them—whose sandy tracts the good lady might help to people. But I had to return to the fact that for this sort of work—the daily mechanical grind—I was already equipped; the people I was working with were fully adequate.

"We only thought we might be more like *some* characters," said Mrs. Monarch mildly, getting up.

Her husband also rose; he stood looking at me with a dim wistfulness that was touching in so fine a man. "Wouldn't it be rather a pull sometimes to have—a—to have—?" He hung fire; he wanted me to help him by phrasing what he meant. But I couldn't—I didn't know. So he brought it out, awkwardly: "The *real* thing; a gentleman, you know, or a lady." I was quite ready to give a general assent—I admitted that there was a great deal in that. This encouraged Major Monarch to say, following up his appeal with an unacted gulp: "It's awfully hard—we've tried everything." The gulp was communicative; it proved too much for his wife. Before I knew it Mrs. Monarch had dropped again upon a divan and burst into tears. Her husband sat down beside her, holding one of her hands; whereupon she quickly dried her eyes with the other, while I felt embarrassed as she looked up at me. "There isn't a confounded job I haven't applied for—waited for—prayed for. You can fancy we'd be pretty bad first. Secretaryships and that sort of thing? You might as well ask for a peerage. I'd be *anything*—I'm strong; a messenger or a coalheaver. I'd put on a gold-laced cap and open carriage-doors in front of the haberdasher's; I'd hang about a station, to carry portmanteaus; I'd be a postman. But they won't *look* at you; there are thousands, as good as yourself, already on the ground. *Gentlemen,* poor beggars, who have drunk their wine, who have kept their hunters!"

I was as reassuring as I knew how to be, and my visitors were presently on their feet again while, for the experiment, we agreed on an hour. We were discussing it when the door opened and Miss Churm came in with a wet umbrella. Miss Churm had to take the omnibus to Maida Vale and then walk half-a-mile. She looked a trifle blowsy and slightly splashed. I scarcely ever saw her come in without thinking afresh how odd it was that, being so little in herself, she should yet be so much in others. She was a meagre little Miss Churm, but she was an ample heroine of romance. She was only a freckled cockney, but she could represent everything, from a fine lady to a shepherdess; she had the faculty, as she might have had a fine voice or long hair. She couldn't spell, and she loved beer, but she had two or three "points," and practice, and a knack, and mother-wit, and a kind of whimsical sensibility, and a love of the theatre, and seven sisters, and not an ounce of respect, especially for the *h*. The first thing my visitors saw was that her umbrella was wet, and in their spotless perfection they visibly winced at it. The rain had come on since their arrival.

"I'm all in a soak; there *was* a mess of people in the 'bus. I wish you lived near a stytion," said Miss Churm. I requested her to get ready as quickly as possible, and she passed into the room in which she always changed her dress. But before going out she asked me what she was to get into this time.

"It's the Russian princess, don't you know?" I answered; "the one with the 'golden eyes,' in black velvet, for the long thing in the *Cheapside*."

"Golden eyes? I *say!*" cried Miss Churm, while my companions watched her with intensity as she withdrew. She always arranged herself, when she was late, before I could turn round, and I kept my visitors a little, on purpose, so that they might get an idea, from seeing her, what would be expected of themselves. I mentioned that she was quite my notion of an excellent model—she was really very clever.

"Do you think she looks like a Russian princess?" Major Monarch asked, with lurking alarm.

"When I make her, yes."

"Oh, if you have to *make* her—!" he reasoned, acutely.

"That's the most you can ask. There are so many that are not makeable."

"Well now, *here's* a lady"—and with a persuasive smile he passed his arm into his wife's—"who's already made!"

"Oh, I'm not a Russian princess," Mrs. Monarch protested, a little coldly. I could see that she had known some and didn't like them. There, immediately, was a complication of a kind that I never had to fear with Miss Churm.

This young lady came back in black velvet—the gown was rather rusty and very low on her lean shoulders—and with a Japanese fan in her red hands. I reminded her that in the scene I was doing she had to look over someone's head. "I forget whose it is; but it doesn't matter. Just look over a head."

"I'd rather look over a stove," said Miss Churm; and she took her station near the fire. She fell into position, settled herself into a tall attitude, gave a certain backward inclination to her head and a certain forward droop to her fan, and looked, at least to my prejudiced sense, distinguished and charming, foreign and dangerous. We left her looking so, while I went down-stairs with Major and Mrs. Monarch.

"I think I could come about as near it as that," said Mrs. Monarch.

"Oh, you think she's shabby, but you must allow for the alchemy of art."

However, they went off with an evident increase of comfort, founded on their demonstrable advantage in being the real thing. I could fancy them shuddering over Miss Churm. She was very droll about them when I went back, for I told her what they wanted.

"Well, if *she* can sit I'll tyke to bookkeeping," said my model.

"She's very lady-like," I replied, as an innocent form of aggravation.

"So much the worse for *you*. That means she can't turn round."

"She'll do for the fashionable novels."

"Oh yes, she'll *do* for them!" my model humorously declared. "Ain't they bad enough without her?" I had often sociably denounced them to Miss Churm.

III.

It was for the elucidation of a mystery in one of these works that I first tried Mrs. Monarch. Her husband came with her, to be useful if necessary—it was sufficiently clear that as a general thing he would prefer to come with her. At first I wondered if this were for "propriety's" sake—if he were going to be jealous and meddling. The idea was too tiresome, and if it had been confirmed it would speedily have brought our acquaintance to a close. But I soon saw there was nothing in it and that if he accompanied Mrs. Monarch it was (in addition to the chance of being wanted), simply because he had nothing else to do. When she was away from him his occupation was gone—she never *had* been away from him. I judged, rightly, that in their awkward situation their close union was their main comfort and that this union had no weak spot. It was a real marriage, an encouragement to the hesitating, a nut for pessimists to crack. Their address was humble (I remember afterwards thinking it had been the only thing about them that was really professional), and I could fancy the lamentable lodgings in which the Major would have been left alone. He could bear them with his wife—he couldn't bear them without her.

He had too much tact to try and make himself agreeable when he couldn't be useful; so he simply sat and waited, when I was too absorbed in my work to talk. But I liked to make him talk—it made my work, when it didn't interrupt it, less sordid, less special. To listen to him was to combine the excitement of going out with the economy of staying at home. There was only one hindrance: that I seemed not to know any of the people he and his wife had known. I think he wondered extremely, during the term of our intercourse, whom the deuce I *did* know. He hadn't a stray sixpence of an idea to fumble for; so we didn't spin it very fine—we confined ourselves to questions of leather and even of liquor (saddlers and breeches-makers and how to get good claret cheap), and matters like "good trains" and the habits of small game. His lore on these last subjects was astonishing, he managed to interweave the station-master with the ornithologist. When he couldn't talk about greater things he could talk cheerfully about smaller, and since I couldn't accompany him into reminiscences of the fashionable world he could lower the conversation without a visible effort to my level.

So earnest a desire to please was touching in a man who

could so easily have knocked one down. He looked after the
fire and had an opinion on the draught of the stove, without
my asking him, and I could see that he thought many of my
arrangements not half clever enough. I remember telling him
that if I were only rich I would offer him a salary to come and
teach me how to live. Sometimes he gave a random sigh, of
which the essence was: "Give me even such a bare old barrack
as *this,* and I'd do something with it!" When I wanted to use
him he came alone; which was an illustration of the superior
courage of women. His wife could bear her solitary second
floor, and she was in general more discreet; showing by various
small reserves that she was alive to the propriety of keeping our
relations markedly professional—not letting them slide into sociability. She wished it to remain clear that she and the Major
were employed, not cultivated, and if she approved of me as a
superior, who could be kept in his place, she never thought me
quite good enough for an equal.

She sat with great intensity, giving the whole of her mind to
it, and was capable of remaining for an hour almost as motionless as if she were before a photographer's lens. I could see
she had been photographed often, but somehow the very habit
that made her good for that purpose unfitted her for mine. At
first I was extremely pleased with her lady-like air, and it was a
satisfaction, on coming to follow her lines, to see how good
they were and how far they could lead the pencil. But after a
few times I began to find her too insurmountably stiff; do what
I would with it my drawing looked like a photograph or a copy
of a photograph. Her figure had no variety of expression—she
herself had no sense of variety. You may say that this was my
business, was only a question of placing her. I placed her in
every conceivable position, but she managed to obliterate their
differences. She was always a lady certainly, and into the bargain
was always the same lady. She was the real thing, but always the
same thing. There were moments when I was oppressed by the
serenity of her confidence that she *was* the real thing. All her
dealings with me and all her husband's were an implication
that this was lucky for *me.* Meanwhile I found myself trying to
invent types that approached her own, instead of making her
own transform itself—in the clever way that was not impossi-

ble, for instance, to poor Miss Churm. Arrange as I would and take the precautions I would, she always, in my pictures, came out too tall—landing me in the dilemma of having represented a fascinating woman as seven feet high, which, out of respect perhaps to my own very much scantier inches, was far from my idea of such a personage.

The case was worse with the Major—nothing I could do would keep *him* down, so that he became useful only for the representation of brawny giants. I adored variety and range, I cherished human accidents, the illustrative note; I wanted to characterise closely, and the thing in the world I most hated was the danger of being ridden by a type. I had quarrelled with some of my friends about it—I had parted company with them for maintaining that one *had* to be, and that if the type was beautiful (witness Raphael and Leonardo), the servitude was only a gain. I was neither Leonardo nor Raphael; I might only be a presumptuous young modern searcher, but I held that everything was to be sacrificed sooner than character. When they averred that the haunting type in question could easily *be* character, I retorted, perhaps superficially: "Whose?" It couldn't be everybody's—it might end in being nobody's.

After I had drawn Mrs. Monarch a dozen times I perceived more clearly than before that the value of such a model as Miss Churm resided precisely in the fact that she had no positive stamp, combined of course with the other fact that what she did have was a curious and inexplicable talent for imitation. Her usual appearance was like a curtain which she could draw up at request for a capital performance. This performance was simply suggestive; but it was a word to the wise—it was vivid and pretty. Sometimes, even, I thought it, though she was plain herself, too insipidly pretty; I made it a reproach to her that the figures drawn from her were monotonously (*bêtement*, as we used to say) graceful. Nothing made her more angry: it was so much her pride to feel that she could sit for characters that had nothing in common with each other. She would accuse me at such moments of taking away her "reputytion."

It suffered a certain shrinkage, this queer quantity, from the repeated visits of my new friends. Miss Churm was greatly in demand, never in want of employment, so I had no scruple in

putting her off occasionally, to try them more at my ease. It was
certainly amusing at first to do the real thing—it was amusing
to do Major Monarch's trousers. They *were* the real thing, even
if he did come out colossal. It was amusing to do his wife's back
hair (it was so mathematically neat,) and the particular "smart"
tension of her tight stays. She lent herself especially to positions
in which the face was somewhat averted or blurred; she
abounded in lady-like back views and *profils perdus*. When she
stood erect she took naturally one of the attitudes in which
court-painters represent queens and princesses; so that I found
myself wondering whether, to draw out this accomplishment, I
couldn't get the editor of the *Cheapside* to publish a really
royal romance, "A Tale of Buckingham Palace." Sometimes,
however, the real thing and the make-believe came into contact; by which I mean that Miss Churm, keeping an appointment or coming to make one on days when I had much work in
hand, encountered her invidious rivals. The encounter was not
on their part, for they noticed her no more than if she had been
the housemaid; not from intentional loftiness, but simply because, as yet, professionally, they didn't know how to fraternise, as I could guess that they would have liked—or at least
that the Major would. They couldn't talk about the omnibus—
they always walked; and they didn't know what else to try—
she wasn't interested in good trains or cheap claret. Besides,
they must have felt—in the air—that she was amused at them,
secretly derisive of their ever knowing how. She was not a person to conceal her scepticism if she had had a chance to show
it. On the other hand Mrs. Monarch didn't think her tidy; for
why else did she take pains to say to me (it was going out of the
way, for Mrs. Monarch), that she didn't like dirty women?

One day when my young lady happened to be present with
my other sitters (she even dropped in, when it was convenient,
for a chat), I asked her to be so good as to lend a hand in getting tea—a service with which she was familiar and which was
one of a class that, living as I did in a small way, with slender
domestic resources, I often appealed to my models to render.
They liked to lay hands on my property, to break the sitting,
and sometimes the china—I made them feel Bohemian. The
next time I saw Miss Churm after this incident she surprised

me greatly by making a scene about it—she accused me of having wished to humiliate her. She had not resented the outrage at the time, but had seemed obliging and amused, enjoying the comedy of asking Mrs. Monarch, who sat vague and silent, whether she would have cream and sugar, and putting an exaggerated simper into the question. She had tried intonations—as if she too wished to pass for the real thing; till I was afraid my other visitors would take offence.

Oh, *they* were determined not to do this; and their touching patience was the measure of their great need. They would sit by the hour, uncomplaining, till I was ready to use them; they would come back on the chance of being wanted and would walk away cheerfully if they were not. I used to go to the door with them to see in what magnificent order they retreated. I tried to find other employment for them—I introduced them to several artists. But they didn't "take," for reasons I could appreciate, and I became conscious, rather anxiously, that after such disappointments they fell back upon me with a heavier weight. They did me the honour to think that it was I who was most *their* form. They were not picturesque enough for the painters, and in those days there were not so many serious workers in black and white. Besides, they had an eye to the great job I had mentioned to them—they had secretly set their hearts on supplying the right essence for my pictorial vindica tion of our fine novelist. They knew that for this undertaking I should want no costume-effects, none of the frippery of past ages—that it was a case in which everything would be contemporary and satirical and, presumably, genteel. If I could work them into it their future would be assured, for the labour would of course be long and the occupation steady.

One day Mrs. Monarch came without her husband—she explained his absence by his having had to go to the City. While she sat there in her usual anxious stiffness there came, at the door, a knock which I immediately recognised as the subdued appeal of a model out of work. It was followed by the entrance of a young man whom I easily perceived to be a foreigner and who proved in fact an Italian acquainted with no English word but my name, which he uttered in a way that made it seem to include all others. I had not then visited his country, nor was I

proficient in his tongue; but as he was not so meanly constituted—what Italian is?—as to depend only on that member for
expression he conveyed to me, in familiar but graceful mimicry,
that he was in search of exactly the employment in which the
lady before me was engaged. I was not struck with him at first,
and while I continued to draw I emitted rough sounds of discouragement and dismissal. He stood his ground, however, not
importunately, but with a dumb, dog-like fidelity in his eyes
which amounted to innocent impudence—the manner of a devoted servant (he might have been in the house for years), unjustly suspected. Suddenly I saw that this very attitude and
expression made a picture, whereupon I told him to sit down
and wait till I should be free. There was another picture in the
way he obeyed me, and I observed as I worked that there were
others still in the way he looked wonderingly, with his head
thrown back, about the high studio. He might have been crossing himself in St. Peter's. Before I finished I said to myself: "The
fellow's a bankrupt orange-monger, but he's a treasure."

When Mrs. Monarch withdrew he passed across the room
like a flash to open the door for her, standing there with the
rapt, pure gaze of the young Dante spellbound by the young
Beatrice. As I never insisted, in such situations, on the blankness of the British domestic, I reflected that he had the making
of a servant (and I needed one, but couldn't pay him to be only
that), as well as of a model; in short I made up my mind to
adopt my bright adventurer if he would agree to officiate in the
double capacity. He jumped at my offer, and in the event my
rashness (for I had known nothing about him), was not
brought home to me. He proved a sympathetic though a desultory ministrant, and had in a wonderful degree the *sentiment
de la pose*. It was uncultivated, instinctive; a part of the happy
instinct which had guided him to my door and helped him to
spell out my name on the card nailed to it. He had had no other
introduction to me than a guess, from the shape of my high
north window, seen outside, that my place was a studio and
that as a studio it would contain an artist. He had wandered to
England in search of fortune, like other itinerants, and had embarked, with a partner and a small green handcart, on the sale
of penny ices. The ices had melted away and the partner had

dissolved in their train. My young man wore tight yellow trousers with reddish stripes and his name was Oronte. He was sallow but fair, and when I put him into some old clothes of my own he looked like an Englishman. He was as good as Miss Churm, who could look, when required, like an Italian.

IV.

I thought Mrs. Monarch's face slightly convulsed when, on her coming back with her husband, she found Oronte installed. It was strange to have to recognise in a scrap of a lazzarone a competitor to her magnificent Major. It was she who scented danger first, for the Major was anecdotically unconscious. But Oronte gave us tea, with a hundred eager confusions (he had never seen such a queer process), and I think she thought better of me for having at last an "establishment." They saw a couple of drawings that I had made of the establishment, and Mrs. Monarch hinted that it never would have struck her that he had sat for them. "Now the drawings you make from *us*, they look exactly like us," she reminded me, smiling in triumph; and I recognised that this was indeed just their defect. When I drew the Monarchs I couldn't, somehow, get away from them—get into the character I wanted to represent; and I had not the least desire my model should be discoverable in my picture. Miss Churm never was, and Mrs. Monarch thought I hid her, very properly, because she was vulgar; whereas if she was lost it was only as the dead who go to heaven are lost—in the gain of an angel the more.

By this time I had got a certain start with "Rutland Ramsay," the first novel in the great projected series; that is I had produced a dozen drawings, several with the help of the Major and his wife, and I had sent them in for approval. My understanding with the publishers, as I have already hinted, had been that I was to be left to do my work, in this particular case, as I liked, with the whole book committed to me; but my connection with the rest of the series was only contingent. There were moments when, frankly, it *was* a comfort to have the real thing under one's hand; for there were characters in "Rutland Ramsay"

that were very much like it. There were people presumably as
straight as the Major and women of as good a fashion as Mrs.
Monarch. There was a great deal of country-house life—
treated, it is true, in a fine, fanciful, ironical, generalised way—
and there was a considerable implication of knickerbockers
and kilts. There were certain things I had to settle at the outset;
such things for instance as the exact appearance of the hero,
the particular bloom of the heroine. The author of course gave
me a lead, but there was a margin for interpretation. I took the
Monarchs into my confidence, I told them frankly what I was
about, I mentioned my embarrassments and alternatives. "Oh,
take *him!*" Mrs. Monarch murmured sweetly, looking at her
husband; and "What could you want better than my wife?" the
Major inquired, with the comfortable candour that now prevailed between us.

I was not obliged to answer these remarks—I was only
obliged to place my sitters. I was not easy in mind, and I postponed, a little timidly perhaps, the solution of the question.
The book was a large canvas, the other figures were numerous,
and I worked off at first some of the episodes in which the hero
and the heroine were not concerned. When once I had set *them*
up I should have to stick to them—I couldn't make my young
man seven feet high in one place and five feet nine in another. I
inclined on the whole to the latter measurement, though the
Major more than once reminded me that *he* looked about as
young as anyone. It was indeed quite possible to arrange him,
for the figure, so that it would have been difficult to detect his
age. After the spontaneous Oronte had been with me a month,
and after I had given him to understand several different times
that his native exuberance would presently constitute an insurmountable barrier to our further intercourse, I waked to a
sense of his heroic capacity. He was only five feet seven, but the
remaining inches were latent. I tried him almost secretly at first,
for I was really rather afraid of the judgment my other models
would pass on such a choice. If they regarded Miss Churm as
little better than a snare, what would they think of the representation by a person so little the real thing as an Italian street-
vendor of a protagonist formed by a public school?

If I went a little in fear of them it was not because they bullied me, because they had got an oppressive foothold, but because in their really pathetic decorum and mysteriously permanent newness they counted on me so intensely. I was therefore very glad when Jack Hawley came home: he was always of such good counsel. He painted badly himself, but there was no one like him for putting his finger on the place. He had been absent from England for a year; he had been somewhere—I don't remember where—to get a fresh eye. I was in a good deal of dread of any such organ, but we were old friends; he had been away for months and a sense of emptiness was creeping into my life. I hadn't dodged a missile for a year.

He came back with a fresh eye, but with the same old black velvet blouse, and the first evening he spent in my studio we smoked cigarettes till the small hours. He had done no work himself, he had only got the eye; so the field was clear for the production of my little things. He wanted to see what I had done for the *Cheapside,* but he was disappointed in the exhibition. That at least seemed the meaning of two or three comprehensive groans which, as he lounged on my big divan, on a folded leg, looking at my latest drawings, issued from his lips with the smoke of the cigarette.

"What's the matter with you?" I asked.

"What's the matter with *you?*"

"Nothing save that I'm mystified."

"You are indeed. You're quite off the hinge. What's the meaning of this new fad?" And he tossed me, with visible irreverence, a drawing in which I happened to have depicted both my majestic models. I asked if he didn't think it good, and he replied that it struck him as execrable, given the sort of thing I had always represented myself to him as wishing to arrive at; but I let that pass, I was so anxious to see exactly what he meant. The two figures in the picture looked colossal, but I supposed this was *not* what he meant, inasmuch as, for aught he knew to the contrary, I might have been trying for that. I maintained that I was working exactly in the same way as when he last had done me the honour to commend me. "Well, there's a big hole somewhere," he answered; "wait a bit and I'll discover it." I depended upon him to do so: where else was the fresh eye? But he produced at last nothing more luminous than

"I don't know—I don't like your types." This was lame, for a
critic who had never consented to discuss with me anything but
the question of execution, the direction of strokes and the mystery of values.

"In the drawings you've been looking at I think my types are
very handsome."

"Oh, they won't do!"

"I've had a couple of new models."

"I see you have. *They* won't do."

"Are you very sure of that?"

"Absolutely—they're stupid."

"You mean *I* am—for I ought to get round that."

"You *can't*—with such people. Who are they?"

I told him, as far as was necessary, and he declared, heart-
lessly: "*Ce sont des gens qu'il faut mettre à la porte.*"

"You've never seen them; they're awfully good," I compas-
sionately objected.

"Not seen them? Why, all this recent work of yours drops to
pieces with them. It's all I want to see of them."

"No one else has said anything against it—the *Cheapside*
people are pleased."

"Everyone else is an ass, and the *Cheapside* people the
biggest asses of all. Come, don't pretend, at this time of day, to
have pretty illusions about the public, especially about publishers and editors. It's not for *such* animals you work—it's for
those who know, *coloro che sanno;* so keep straight for *me* if
you can't keep straight for yourself. There's a certain sort of
thing you tried for from the first—and a very good thing it is.
But this twaddle isn't *in* it." When I talked with Hawley later
about "Rutland Ramsay" and its possible successors he declared that I must get back into my boat again or I would go to
the bottom. His voice in short was the voice of warning.

I noted the warning, but I didn't turn my friends out of
doors. They bored me a good deal; but the very fact that they
bored me admonished me not to sacrifice them—if there was
anything to be done with them—simply to irritation. As I look
back at this phase they seem to me to have pervaded my life not
a little. I have a vision of them as most of the time in my studio,
seated, against the wall, on an old velvet bench to be out of the

way, and looking like a pair of patient courtiers in a royal ante-chamber. I am convinced that during the coldest weeks of the winter they held their ground because it saved them fire. Their newness was losing its gloss, and it was impossible not to feel that they were objects of charity. Whenever Miss Churm arrived they went away, and after I was fairly launched in "Rutland Ramsay" Miss Churm arrived pretty often. They managed to express to me tacitly that they supposed I wanted her for the low life of the book, and I let them suppose it, since they had attempted to study the work—it was lying about the studio—without discovering that it dealt only with the highest circles. They had dipped into the most brilliant of our novelists without deciphering many passages. I still took an hour from them, now and again, in spite of Jack Hawley's warning: it would be time enough to dismiss them, if dismissal should be necessary, when the rigour of the season was over. Hawley had made their acquaintance—he had met them at my fireside—and thought them a ridiculous pair. Learning that he was a painter they tried to approach him, to show him too that they were the real thing; but he looked at them, across the big room, as if they were miles away: they were a compendium of everything that he most objected to in the social system of his country. Such people as that, all convention and patent-leather, with ejaculations that stopped conversation, had no business in a studio. A studio was a place to learn to see, and how could you see through a pair of feather beds?

The main inconvenience I suffered at their hands was that, at first, I was shy of letting them discover how my artful little servant had begun to sit to me for "Rutland Ramsay." They knew that I had been odd enough (they were prepared by this time to allow oddity to artists,) to pick a foreign vagabond out of the streets, when I might have had a person with whiskers and credentials; but it was some time before they learned how high I rated his accomplishments. They found him in an attitude more than once, but they never doubted I was doing him as an organ-grinder. There were several things they never guessed, and one of them was that for a striking scene in the novel, in which a footman briefly figured, it occurred to me to make use of Major Monarch as the menial. I kept putting this off, I didn't

like to ask him to don the livery—besides the difficulty of finding a livery to fit him. At last, one day late in the winter, when
I was at work on the despised Oronte (he caught one's idea in
an instant), and was in the glow of feeling that I was going very
straight, they came in, the Major and his wife, with their society laugh about nothing (there was less and less to laugh at),
like country-callers—they always reminded me of that—who
have walked across the park after church and are presently per-
suaded to stay to luncheon. Luncheon was over, but they could
stay to tea—I knew they wanted it. The fit was on me, however,
and I couldn't let my ardour cool and my work wait, with the
fading daylight, while my model prepared it. So I asked Mrs.
Monarch if she would mind laying it out—a request which, for
an instant, brought all the blood to her face. Her eyes were on
her husband's for a second, and some mute telegraphy passed
between them. Their folly was over the next instant; his cheerful shrewdness put an end to it. So far from pitying their
wounded pride, I must add, I was moved to give it as complete
a lesson as I could. They bustled about together and got out the
cups and saucers and made the kettle boil. I know they felt as if
they were waiting on my servant, and when the tea was prepared I said: "He'll have a cup, please—he's tired." Mrs.
Monarch brought him one where he stood, and he took it from
her as if he had been a gentleman at a party, squeezing a crush-
hat with an elbow.

Then it came over me that she had made a great effort for
me—made it with a kind of nobleness—and that I owed her a
compensation. Each time I saw her after this I wondered what
the compensation could be. I couldn't go on doing the wrong
thing to oblige them. Oh, it *was* the wrong thing, the stamp of
the work for which they sat—Hawley was not the only person
to say it now. I sent in a large number of the drawings I had
made for "Rutland Ramsay," and I received a warning that
was more to the point than Hawley's. The artistic adviser of the
house for which I was working was of opinion that many of my
illustrations were not what had been looked for. Most of these
illustrations were the subjects in which the Monarchs had figured. Without going into the question of what *had* been looked
for, I saw at this rate I shouldn't get the other books to do. I

hurled myself in despair upon Miss Churm, I put her through all her paces. I not only adopted Oronte publicly as my hero, but one morning when the Major looked in to see if I didn't require him to finish a figure for the *Cheapside,* for which he had begun to sit the week before, I told him that I had changed my mind—I would do the drawing from my man. At this my visitor turned pale and stood looking at me. "Is *he* your idea of an English gentleman?" he asked.

I was disappointed, I was nervous, I wanted to get on with my work; so I replied with irritation: "Oh, my dear Major—I can't be ruined for *you!*"

He stood another moment; then, without a word, he quitted the studio. I drew a long breath when he was gone, for I said to myself that I shouldn't see him again. I had not told him definitely that I was in danger of having my work rejected, but I was vexed at his not having felt the catastrophe in the air, read with me the moral of our fruitless collaboration, the lesson that, in the deceptive atmosphere of art, even the highest respectability may fail of being plastic.

I didn't owe my friends money, but I did see them again. They re-appeared together, three days later, and under the circumstances there was something tragic in the fact. It was a proof to me that they could find nothing else in life to do. They had threshed the matter out in a dismal conference they had digested the bad news that they were not in for the series. If they were not useful to me even for the *Cheapside* their function seemed difficult to determine, and I could only judge at first that they had come, forgivingly, decorously, to take a last leave. This made me rejoice in secret that I had little leisure for a scene; for I had placed both my other models in position together and I was pegging away at a drawing from which I hoped to derive glory. It had been suggested by the passage in which Rutland Ramsay, drawing up a chair to Artemisia's pianostool, says extraordinary things to her while she ostensibly fingers out a difficult piece of music. I had done Miss Churm at the piano before—it was an attitude in which she knew how to take on an absolutely poetic grace. I wished the two figures to "compose" together, intensely, and my little Italian had entered perfectly into my conception. The pair were vividly before me, the piano had been pulled out; it was a charming picture of blended youth and murmured love, which I had only to catch and keep. My visitors stood and looked at it, and I was friendly to them over my shoulder.

They made no response, but I was used to silent company and went on with my work, only a little disconcerted (even though exhilarated by the sense that *this* was at least the ideal thing), at not having got rid of them after all. Presently I heard Mrs. Monarch's sweet voice beside, or rather above me: "I wish her hair was a little better done." I looked up and she was staring with a strange fixedness at Miss Churm, whose back was turned to her. "Do you mind my just touching it?" she went on—a question which made me spring up for an instant, as with the instinctive fear that she might do the young lady a harm. But she quieted me with a glance I shall never forget—I confess I should like to have been able to paint *that*—and went for a moment to my model. She spoke to her softly, laying a hand upon her shoulder and bending over her; and as the girl, understanding, gratefully assented, she disposed her rough curls, with a few quick passes, in such a way as to make Miss Churm's head twice as charming. It was one of the most heroic personal services I have ever seen tendered. Then Mrs. Monarch turned away with a low sigh and, looking about her as if for something to do, stooped to the floor with a noble humility and picked up a dirty rag that had dropped out of my paint-box.

The Major meanwhile had also been looking for something to do and, wandering to the other end of the studio, saw before him my breakfast things, neglected, unremoved. "I say, can't I be useful *here*?" he called out to me with an irrepressible quaver. I assented with a laugh that I fear was awkward and for the next ten minutes, while I worked, I heard the light clatter of china and the tinkle of spoons and glass. Mrs. Monarch assisted her husband—they washed up my crockery, they put it away. They wandered off into my little scullery, and I afterwards found that they had cleaned my knives and that my slender stock of plate had an unprecedented surface. When it came over me, the latent eloquence of what they were doing, I confess that my drawing was blurred for a moment—the picture swam. They had accepted their failure, but they couldn't accept their fate. They had bowed their heads in bewilderment to the perverse and cruel law in virtue of which the real thing could be so much less precious than the unreal; but they didn't want to starve. If my servants were my models, my models might be my servants. They would reverse the parts—the others would sit for the ladies and gentlemen, and *they* would do the work. They would still be in the studio—it was an intense dumb appeal to me not to turn them out. "Take us on," they wanted to say—"we'll do *anything*."

When all this hung before me the *afflatus* vanished—my pencil dropped from my hand. My sitting was spoiled and I got rid of my sitters, who were also evidently rather mystified and awestruck. Then, alone with the Major and his wife, I had a most uncomfortable moment. He put their prayer into a single sentence: "I say, you know—just let *us* do for you, can't you?" I couldn't—it was dreadful to see them emptying my slops; but I pretended I could, to oblige them, for about a week. Then I gave them a sum of money to go away; and I never saw them again. I obtained the remaining books, but my friend Hawley repeats that Major and Mrs. Monarch did me a permanent harm, got me into a second-rate trick. If it be true I am content to have paid the price—for the memory.

The Middle Years

Scribner's Magazine, *May 1893. In an 1892 note-book entry, the genesis of this tale concerns the "idea of the old artist, or man of letters, who, at the end, feels a kind of anguish of desire for a respite, a pro-longation—another period of life to do the real thing he has in him—the things for which all the others have been but a slow preparation." James's later pref-ace mainly addresses the tale's formal requirements— "not that of the nouvelle, but that of the concise anecdote"—and he notes the need "to squeeze my subject into the five or six thousand words" allowed him for the particular publication. He would use the title again; in 1913 he would begin work on the frag-mentary last volume—*The Middle Years—*of his three-volume autobiography.*

The April day was soft and bright, and poor Dencombe, happy in the conceit of reasserted strength, stood in the garden of the hotel, comparing, with a deliberation in which, however, there was still something of languor, the attractions of easy strolls. He liked the feeling of the south, so far as you could have it in the north, he liked the sandy cliffs and the clustered pines, he liked even the colourless sea. "Bournemouth as a health-resort" had sounded like a mere advertisement, but now he was reconciled to the prosaic. The sociable country postman, passing through the garden, had just given him a small parcel, which he took out with him, leaving the hotel to the right and creeping to a convenient bench that he knew of, a safe recess in the cliff. It looked to the south, to the tinted walls of the Island, and was protected behind by the sloping shoulder of the down. He was tired enough when he reached it, and for a moment he was disappointed; he was better, of course, but better, after all, than what? He should never again, as at one or two great moments of the past, be better than himself. The infinite of life had gone, and what was left of the dose was a small glass engraved like a thermometer by the apothecary. He sat and stared at the sea, which appeared all surface and twinkle, far shallower than the spirit of man. It was the abyss of human illusion that was the real, the tideless deep. He held his packet, which had come by book-post, unopened on his knee, liking, in the lapse of so many joys (his illness had made him feel his age), to know that it was there, but taking for granted there could be no complete renewal of the pleasure, dear to young experience, of seeing one's self "just out." Dencombe, who had a reputation, had come out too often and knew too well in advance how he should look.

His postponement associated itself vaguely, after a little, with a group of three persons, two ladies and a young man, whom, beneath him, straggling and seemingly silent, he could see move slowly together along the sands. The gentleman had his head bent over a book and was occasionally brought to a stop by the charm of this volume, which, as Dencombe could perceive even at a distance, had a cover alluringly red. Then his companions, going a little further, waited for him to come up, poking their parasols into the beach, looking around them at the sea and sky and clearly sensible of the beauty of the day. To these things the young man with the book was still more clearly indifferent; lingering, credulous, absorbed, he was an object of envy to an observer from whose connection with literature all such artlessness had faded. One of the ladies was large and mature; the other had the spareness of comparative youth and of a social situation possibly inferior. The large lady carried back Dencombe's imagination to the age of crinoline; she wore a hat of the shape of a mushroom, decorated with a blue veil, and had the air, in her aggressive amplitude, of clinging to a vanished fashion or even a lost cause. Presently her companion produced from under the folds of a mantle a limp, portable chair which she stiffened out and of which the large lady took possession. This act, and something in the movement of either party, instantly characterised the performers—they performed for Dencombe's recreation—as opulent matron and humble dependant. What, moreover, was the use of being an approved novelist if one couldn't establish a relation between such figures; the clever theory, for instance, that the young man was the son of the opulent matron, and that the humble dependant, the daughter of a clergyman or an officer, nourished a secret passion for him? Was that not visible from the way she stole behind her protectress to look back at him?—back to where he had let himself come to a full stop when his mother sat down to rest. His book was a novel; it had the catchpenny cover, and while the romance of life stood neglected at his side he lost himself in that of the circulating library. He moved mechanically to where the sand was softer, and ended by plumping down in it to finish his chapter at his ease. The humble dependant, discouraged by his remoteness, wandered, with a martyred droop of the head, in another direction, and the exorbitant lady, watching the waves, offered a confused resemblance to a flying-machine that had broken down.

When his drama began to fail Dencombe remembered that he had, after all, another pastime. Though such promptitude on the part of the publisher was rare, he was already able to draw from its wrapper his "latest," perhaps his last. The cover of "The Middle Years" was duly meretricious, the smell of the fresh pages the very odour of sanctity; but for the moment he went no further—he had become conscious of a strange alienation. He had forgotten what his book was about. Had the assault of his old ailment, which he had so fallaciously come to Bournemouth to ward off, interposed utter blankness as to what had preceded it? He had finished the revision of proof before quitting London, but his subsequent fortnight in bed had passed the sponge over colour. He couldn't have chanted to himself a single sentence, couldn't have turned with curiosity or confidence to any particular page. His subject had already gone from him, leaving scarcely a superstition behind. He uttered a low moan as he breathed the chill of this dark void, so desperately it seemed to represent the completion of a sinister process.

The tears filled his mild eyes; something precious had passed away. This was the pang that had been sharpest during the last few years—the sense of ebbing time, of shrinking opportunity; and now he felt not so much that his last chance was going as that it was gone indeed. He had done all that he should ever do, and yet he had not done what he wanted. This was the laceration—that practically his career was over: it was as violent as a rough hand at his throat. He rose from his seat nervously, like a creature hunted by a dread; then he fell back in his weakness and nervously opened his book. It was a single volume; he preferred single volumes and aimed at a rare compression. He began to read, and little by little, in this occupation, he was pacified and reassured. Everything came back to him, but came back with a wonder, came back, above all, with a high and magnificent beauty. He read his own prose, he turned his own leaves, and had, as he sat there with the spring sunshine on the page, an emotion peculiar and intense. His career was over, no doubt, but it was over, after all, with *that*.

He had forgotten during his illness the work of the previous year; but what he had chiefly forgotten was that it was extraordinarily good. He lived once more into his story and was drawn down, as by a siren's hand, to where, in the dim underworld of fiction, the great glazed tank of art, strange silent subjects float. He recognised his motive and surrendered to his talent. Never, probably, had that talent, such as it was, been so fine. His difficulties were still there, but what was also there, to his perception, though probably, alas! to nobody's else, was the art that in most cases had surmounted them. In his surprised enjoyment of this ability he had a glimpse of a possible reprieve. Surely its force was not spent—there was life and service in it yet. It had not come to him easily, it had been backward and roundabout. It was the child of time, the nursling of delay; he had struggled and suffered for it, making sacrifices not to be counted, and now that it was really mature was it to cease to yield, to confess itself brutally beaten? There was an infinite charm for Dencombe in feeling as he had never felt before that diligence *vincit omnia*. The result produced in his little book was somehow a result beyond his conscious intention: it was as if he had planted his genius, had trusted his method, and they

had grown up and flowered with this sweetness. If the achievement had been real, however, the process had been manful
enough. What he saw so intensely to-day, what he felt as a nail
driven in, was that only now, at the very last, had he come into
possession. His development had been abnormally slow, almost grotesquely gradual. He had been hindered and retarded
by experience, and for long periods had only groped his way. It
had taken too much of his life to produce too little of his art.
The art had come, but it had come after everything else. As
such a rate a first existence was too short—long enough only to
collect material; so that to fructify, to use the material, one
must have a second age, an extension. This extension was what
poor Dencombe sighed for. As he turned the last leaves of his
volume he murmured: "Ah for another go!—ah for a better
chance!"

The three persons he had observed on the sands had vanished and then reappeared; they had now wandered up a path,
an artificial and easy ascent, which led to the top of the cliff.
Dencombe's bench was half-way down, on a sheltered ledge,
and the large lady, a massive, heterogeneous person, with bold
black eyes and kind red cheeks, now took a few moments to
rest. She wore dirty gauntlets and immense diamond ear-rings;
at first she looked vulgar, but she contradicted this announcement in an agreeable off-hand tone. While her companions
stood waiting for her she spread her skirts on the end of Dencombe's seat. The young man had gold spectacles, through
which, with his finger still in his red-covered book, he glanced
at the volume, bound in the same shade of the same colour, lying on the lap of the original occupant of the bench. After an
instant Dencombe understood that he was struck with a resemblance, had recognised the gilt stamp on the crimson cloth,
was reading "The Middle Years," and now perceived that
somebody else had kept pace with him. The stranger was startled, possibly even a little ruffled, to find that he was not the
only person who had been favoured with an early copy. The
eyes of the two proprietors met for a moment, and Dencombe
borrowed amusement from the expression of those of his competitor, those, it might even be inferred, of his admirer. They
confessed to some resentment—they seemed to say: "Hang it,

has he got it *already?*—Of course he's a brute of a reviewer!" Dencombe shuffled his copy out of sight while the opulent matron, rising from her repose, broke out: "I feel already the good of this air!"

"I can't say I do," said the angular lady. "I find myself quite let down."

"I find myself horribly hungry. At what time did you order lunch?" her protectress pursued.

The young person put the question by. "Doctor Hugh always orders it."

"I ordered nothing to-day—I'm going to make you diet," said their comrade.

"Then I shall go home and sleep. *Qui dort dine!*"

"Can I trust you to Miss Vernham?" asked Doctor Hugh of his elder companion.

"Don't I trust *you?*" she archly inquired.

"Not too much!" Miss Vernham, with her eyes on the ground, permitted herself to declare. "You must come with us at least to the house," she went on, while the personage on whom they appeared to be in attendance began to mount higher. She had got a little out of ear-shot; nevertheless Miss Vernham became, so far as Dencombe was concerned, less distinctly audible to murmur to the young man: "I don't think you realise all you owe the Countess!"

Absently, a moment, Doctor Hugh caused his gold-rimmed spectacles to shine at her.

"Is that the way I strike you? I see—I see!"

"She's awfully good to us," continued Miss Vernham, compelled by her interlocutor's immovability to stand there in spite of his discussion of private matters. Of what use would it have been that Dencombe should be sensitive to shades had he not declared in that immovability a strange influence from the quiet old convalescent in the great tweed cape? Miss Vernham appeared suddenly to become aware of some such connection, for she added in a moment: "If you want to sun yourself here you can come back after you've seen us home."

Doctor Hugh, at this, hesitated, and Dencombe, in spite of a desire to pass for unconscious, risked a covert glance at him. What his eyes met this time, as it happened, was on the part of the young lady a queer stare, naturally vitreous, which made her aspect remind him of some figure (he couldn't name it) in a play or a novel, some sinister governess or tragic old maid. She seemed to scrutinise him, to challenge him, to say, from general spite: "What have you got to do with us?" At the same instant the rich humour of the Countess reached them from above: "Come, come, my little lambs, you should follow your old *bergère!*" Miss Vernham turned away at this, pursuing the ascent, and Doctor Hugh, after another mute appeal to Dencombe and a moment's evident demur, deposited his book on the bench, as if to keep his place or even as a sign that he would return, and bounded without difficulty up the rougher part of the cliff.

Equally innocent and infinite are the pleasures of observation and the resources engendered by the habit of analysing life. It amused poor Dencombe, as he dawdled in his tepid air-bath, to think that he was waiting for a revelation of something at the back of a fine young mind. He looked hard at the book on the end of the bench, but he wouldn't have touched it for the world. It served his purpose to have a theory which should not be exposed to refutation. He already felt better of his melancholy; he had, according to his old formula, put his head at the window. A passing Countess could draw off the fancy when, like the elder of the ladies who had just retreated, she was as obvious as the giantess of a caravan. It was indeed general views that were terrible; short ones, contrary to an opinion sometimes expressed, were the refuge, were the remedy. Doctor Hugh couldn't possibly be anything but a reviewer who had understandings for early copies with publishers or with newspapers. He reappeared in a quarter of an hour, with visible relief at finding Dencombe on the spot, and the gleam of white teeth in an embarrassed but generous smile. He was perceptibly disappointed at the eclipse of the other copy of the book; it was a pretext the less for speaking to the stranger. But he spoke notwithstanding; he held up his own copy and broke out pleadingly:

"*Do* say, if you have occasion to speak of it, that it's the best thing he has done yet!"

Dencombe responded with a laugh: "Done yet" was so amusing to him, made such a grand avenue of the future. Better still, the young man took *him* for a reviewer. He pulled out "The Middle Years" from under his cape, but instinctively concealed any tell-tale look of fatherhood. This was partly because a person was always a fool for calling attention to his work. "Is that what you're going to say yourself?" he inquired of his visitor.

"I'm not quite sure I shall write anything. I don't, as a regular thing—I enjoy in peace. But it's awfully fine."

Dencombe debated a moment. If his interlocutor had begun to abuse him he would have confessed on the spot to his identity, but there was no harm in drawing him on a little to praise. He drew him on with such success that in a few moments his new acquaintance, seated by his side, was confessing candidly that Dencombe's novels were the only ones he could read a second time. He had come the day before from London, where a friend of his, a journalist, had lent him his copy of the last—the copy sent to the office of the journal and already the subject of a "notice" which, as was pretended there (but one had to allow for "swagger") it had taken a full quarter of an hour to prepare. He intimated that he was ashamed for his friend, and in the case of a work demanding and repaying study, of such inferior manners; and, with his fresh appreciation and inexplicable wish to express it, he speedily became for poor Dencombe a remarkable, a delightful apparition. Chance had brought the weary man of letters face to face with the greatest admirer in the new generation whom it was supposable he possessed. The admirer, in truth, was mystifying, so rare a case was it to find a bristling young doctor—he looked like a German physiologist—enamoured of literary form. It was an accident, but happier than most accidents, so that Dencombe, exhilarated as well as confounded, spent half an hour in making his visitor talk while he kept himself quiet. He explained his premature possession of "The Middle Years" by an allusion to the friendship of the publisher, who, knowing he was at Bournemouth for his health, had paid him this graceful attention. He admitted that he had been ill, for Doctor Hugh would infallibly have guessed it; he even went so far as to wonder whether he mightn't look for some hygienic "tip" from a personage combining so bright an enthusiasm with a presumable knowledge of the remedies now in vogue. It would shake his faith a little perhaps to have to take a doctor seriously who could take *him* so seriously, but he enjoyed this gushing modern youth and he felt with an acute pang that there would still be work to do in a world in which such odd combinations were presented. It was not true, what he had tried for renunciation's sake to believe, that all the combinations were exhausted. They were not, they were not—they were infinite: the exhaustion was in the miserable artist.

Doctor Hugh was an ardent physiologist, saturated with the spirit of the age—in other words he had just taken his degree; but he was independent and various, he talked like a man who would have preferred to love literature best. He would fain have made fine phrases, but nature had denied him the trick. Some of the finest in "The Middle Years" had struck him inordinately, and he took the liberty of reading them to Dencombe in support of his plea. He grew vivid, in the balmy air, to his companion, for whose deep refreshment he seemed to have been sent; and was particularly ingenuous in describing how recently he had become acquainted, and how instantly infatuated, with the only man who had put flesh between the ribs of an art that was starving on superstitions. He had not yet written to him—he was deterred by a sentiment of respect. Dencombe at this moment felicitated himself more than ever on having never answered the photographers. His visitor's attitude promised him a luxury of intercourse, but he surmised that a certain security in it, for Doctor Hugh, would depend not a little on the Countess. He learned without delay with what variety of Countess they were concerned, as well as the nature of the tie that united the curious trio. The large lady, an Englishwoman by birth and the daughter of a celebrated baritone, whose taste, without his talent, she had inherited, was the widow of a French nobleman and mistress of all that remained of the handsome fortune, the fruit of her father's earnings, that had constituted her dower. Miss Vernham, an odd creature but an accomplished pianist, was attached to her person at a salary. The Countess was generous, independent, eccentric; she travelled with her minstrel and her medical man. Ignorant and passionate, she had nevertheless moments in which she was al-

most irresistible. Dencombe saw her sit for her portrait in Doctor Hugh's free sketch, and felt the picture of his young friend's
relation to her frame itself in his mind. This young friend, for a
representative of the new psychology, was himself easily hyp-
notised, and if he became abnormally communicative it was
only a sign of his real subjection. Dencombe did accordingly
what he wanted with him, even without being known as Dencombe.

Taken ill on a journey in Switzerland the Countess had
picked him up at an hotel, and the accident of his happening to
please her had made her offer him, with her imperious liberality, terms that couldn't fail to dazzle a practitioner without pa-
tients and whose resources had been drained dry by his studies.
It was not the way he would have elected to spend his time, but
it was time that would pass quickly, and meanwhile she was
wonderfully kind. She exacted perpetual attention, but it was
impossible not to like her. He gave details about his queer patient, a "type" if there ever was one, who had in connection
with her flushed obesity and in addition to the morbid strain of
a violent and aimless will a grave organic disorder; but he came
back to his loved novelist, whom he was so good as to pronounce more essentially a poet than many of those who went in
for verse, with a zeal excited, as all his indiscretion had been
excited, by the happy chance of Dencombe's sympathy and the
coincidence of their occupation. Dencombe had confessed to a
slight personal acquaintance with the author of "The Middle
Years," but had not felt himself as ready as he could have
wished when his companion, who had never yet encountered a
being so privileged, began to be eager for particulars. He even
thought that Doctor Hugh's eye at that moment emitted a glimmer of suspicion. But the young man was too inflamed to be
shrewd and repeatedly caught up the book to exclaim: "Did
you notice this?" or "Weren't you immensely struck with
that?" "There's a beautiful passage toward the end," he broke
out; and again he laid his hand upon the volume. As he turned
the pages he came upon something else, while Dencombe saw
him suddenly change colour. He had taken up, as it lay on the
bench, Dencombe's copy instead of his own, and his neighbour
immediately guessed the reason of his start. Doctor Hugh

looked grave an instant; then he said: "I see you've been altering the text!" Dencombe was a passionate corrector, a fingerer
of style; the last thing he ever arrived at was a form final for
himself. His ideal would have been to publish secretly, and
then, on the published text, treat himself to the terrified revise,
sacrificing always a first edition and beginning for posterity
and even for the collectors, poor dears, with a second. This
morning, in "The Middle Years," his pencil had pricked a dozen
lights. He was amused at the effect of the young man's reproach;
for an instant it made him change colour. He stammered, at any
rate, ambiguously; then, through a blur of ebbing consciousness, saw Doctor Hugh's mystified eyes. He only had time to feel
he was about to be ill again—that emotion, excitement, fatigue,
the heat of the sun, the solicitation of the air, had combined to
play him a trick, before, stretching out a hand to his visitor with
a plaintive cry, he lost his senses altogether.

Later he knew that he had fainted and that Doctor Hugh had
got him home in a bath-chair, the conductor of which, prowling within hail for custom, had happened to remember seeing
him in the garden of the hotel. He had recovered his perception
in the transit, and had, in bed, that afternoon, a vague recollection of Doctor Hugh's young face, as they went together,
bent over him in a comforting laugh and expressive of something more than a suspicion of his identity. That identity was
ineffaceable now, and all the more that he was disappointed,
disgusted. He had been rash, been stupid, had gone out too
soon, stayed out too long. He oughtn't to have exposed himself
to strangers, he ought to have taken his servant. He felt as if he
had fallen into a hole too deep to descry any little patch of
heaven. He was confused about the time that had elapsed—he
pieced the fragments together. He had seen his doctor, the real
one, the one who had treated him from the first and who had
again been very kind. His servant was in and out on tiptoe,
looking very wise after the fact. He said more than once something about the sharp young gentleman. The rest was vagueness, in so far as it wasn't despair. The vagueness, however,
justified itself by dreams, dozing anxieties from which he finally emerged to the consciousness of a dark room and a
shaded candle.

"You'll be all right again—I know all about you now," said a voice near him that he knew to be young. Then his meeting with Doctor Hugh came back. He was too discouraged to joke about it yet, but he was able to perceive, after a little, that the interest of it was intense for his visitor. "Of course I can't attend you professionally—you've got your own man, with whom I've talked and who's excellent," Doctor Hugh went on. "But you must let me come to see you as a good friend. I've just looked in before going to bed. You're doing beautifully, but it's a good job I was with you on the cliff. I shall come in early tomorrow. I want to do something for you. I want to do everything. You've done a tremendous lot for me." The young man held his hand, hanging over him, and poor Dencombe, weakly aware of this living pressure, simply lay there and accepted his devotion. He couldn't do anything less—he needed help too much.

The idea of the help he needed was very present to him that night, which he spent in a lucid stillness, an intensity of thought that constituted a reaction from his hours of stupor. He was lost, he was lost—he was lost if he couldn't be saved. He was not afraid of suffering, of death; he was not even in love with life; but he had had a deep demonstration of desire. It came over him in the long, quiet hours that only with "The Middle Years" had he taken his flight; only on that day, visited by soundless processions, had he recognised his kingdom. He had had a revelation of his range. What he dreaded was the idea that his reputation should stand on the unfinished. It was not with his past but with his future that it should properly be concerned. Illness and age rose before him like spectres with pitiless eyes: how was he to bribe such fates to give him the second chance? He had had the one chance that all men have—he had had the chance of life. He went to sleep again very late, and when he awoke Doctor Hugh was sitting by his head. There was already, by this time, something beautifully familiar in him.

"Don't think I've turned out your physician," he said; "I'm acting with his consent. He has been here and seen you. Somehow he seems to trust me. I told him how we happened to come together yesterday, and he recognises that I've a peculiar right."

Dencombe looked at him with a calculating earnestness. "How have you squared the Countess?"

The young man blushed a little, but he laughed. "Oh, never mind the Countess!"

"You told me she was very exacting."

Doctor Hugh was silent a moment. "So she is."

"And Miss Vernham's an *intrigante*."

"How do you know that?"

"I know everything. One *has* to, to write decently!"

"I think she's mad," said limpid Doctor Hugh.

"Well, don't quarrel with the Countess—she's a present help to you."

"I don't quarrel," Doctor Hugh replied. "But I don't get on with silly women." Presently he added: "You seem very much alone."

"That often happens at my age. I've outlived, I've lost by the way."

Doctor Hugh hesitated; then surmounting a soft scruple: "Whom have you lost?"

"Every one."

"Ah, no," the young man murmured, laying a hand on his arm.

"I once had a wife—I once had a son. My wife died when my child was born, and my boy, at school, was carried off by typhoid."

"I wish I'd been there!" said Doctor Hugh simply.

"Well—if you're here!" Dencombe answered, with a smile that, in spite of dimness, showed how much he liked to be sure of his companion's whereabouts.

"You talk strangely of your age. You're not old."

"Hypocrite—so early!"

"I speak physiologically."

"That's the way I've been speaking for the last five years, and it's exactly what I've been saying to myself. It isn't till we *are* old that we begin to tell ourselves we're not!"

"Yet I know I myself am young," Doctor Hugh declared.

"Not so well as I!" laughed his patient, whose visitor indeed would have established the truth in question by the honesty with which he changed the point of view, remarking that it

must be one of the charms of age—at any rate in the case of
high distinction—to feel that one has laboured and achieved.
Doctor Hugh employed the common phrase about earning
one's rest, and it made poor Dencombe, for an instant, almost
angry. He recovered himself, however, to explain, lucidly
enough, that if he, ungraciously, knew nothing of such a balm,
it was doubtless because he had wasted inestimable years. He
had followed literature from the first, but he had taken a lifetime to get alongside of her. Only to-day, at last, had he begun
to *see,* so that what he had hitherto done was a movement without a direction. He had ripened too late and was so clumsily
constituted that he had had to teach himself by mistakes.

"I prefer your flowers, then, to other people's fruit, and your
mistakes to other people's successes," said gallant Doctor
Hugh. "It's for your mistakes I admire you."

"You're happy—you don't know," Dencombe answered.

Looking at his watch the young man had got up; he named
the hour of the afternoon at which he would return. Dencombe
warned him against committing himself too deeply, and expressed again all his dread of making him neglect the Countess—perhaps incur her displeasure.

"I want to be like you—I want to learn by mistakes!" Doctor Hugh laughed.

"Take care you don't make too grave a one! But do come
back," Dencombe added, with the glimmer of a new idea.

"You should have had more vanity!" Doctor Hugh spoke as
if he knew the exact amount required to make a man of letters
normal.

"No, no—I only should have had more time. I want another
go."

"Another go?"

"I want an extension."

"An extension?" Again Doctor Hugh repeated Dencombe's
words, with which he seemed to have been struck.

"Don't you know?—I want to what they call 'live.'"

The young man, for good-bye, had taken his hand, which
closed with a certain force. They looked at each other hard a
moment. "You *will* live," said Doctor Hugh.

"Don't be superficial. It's too serious!"

"You *shall* live!" Dencombe's visitor declared, turning pale.

"Ah, that's better!" And as he retired the invalid, with a troubled laugh, sank gratefully back.

All that day and all the following night he wondered if it mightn't be arranged. His doctor came again, his servant was attentive, but it was to his confident young friend that he found himself mentally appealing. His collapse on the cliff was plausibly explained, and his liberation, on a better basis, promised for the morrow; meanwhile, however, the intensity of his meditations kept him tranquil and made him indifferent. The idea that occupied him was none the less absorbing because it was a morbid fancy. Here was a clever son of the age, ingenious and ardent, who happened to have set him up for connoisseurs to worship. This servant of his altar had all the new learning in science and all the old reverence in faith; wouldn't he therefore put his knowledge at the disposal of his sympathy, his craft at the disposal of his love? Couldn't he be trusted to invent a remedy for a poor artist to whose art he had paid a tribute? If he couldn't, the alternative was hard: Dencombe would have to surrender to silence, unvindicated and undivined. The rest of the day and all the next he toyed in secret with this sweet futility. Who would work the miracle for him but the young man who could combine such lucidity with such passion? He thought of the fairy-tales of science and charmed himself into forgetting that he looked for a magic that was not of this world. Doctor Hugh was an apparition, and that placed him above the law. He came and went while his patient, who sat up, followed him with supplicating eyes. The interest of knowing the great author had made the young man begin "The Middle Years" afresh, and would help him to find a deeper meaning in its pages. Dencombe had told him what he "tried for"; with all his intelligence, on a first perusal, Doctor Hugh had failed to guess it. The baffled celebrity wondered then who in the world *would* guess it: he was amused once more at the fine, full way with which an intention could be missed. Yet he wouldn't rail at the general mind to-day—consoling as that ever had been: the revelation of his own slowness had seemed to make all stupidity sacred.

Doctor Hugh, after a little, was visibly worried, confessing, on inquiry, to a source of embarrassment at home. "Stick to the Countess—don't mind me," Dencombe said, repeatedly; for his companion was frank enough about the large lady's attitude. She was so jealous that she had fallen ill—she resented such a breach of allegiance. She paid so much for his fidelity that she must have it all: she refused him the right to other sympathies, charged him with scheming to make her die alone, for it was needless to point out how little Miss Vernham was a resource in trouble. When Doctor Hugh mentioned that the Countess would already have left Bournemouth if he hadn't kept her in bed, poor Dencombe held his arm tighter and said with decision: "Take her straight away." They had gone out together, walking back to the sheltered nook in which, the other day, they had met. The young man, who had given his companion a personal support, declared with emphasis that his conscience was clear—he could ride two horses at once. Didn't he dream, for his future, of a time when he should have to ride five hundred? Longing equally for virtue, Dencombe replied that in that golden age no patient would pretend to have contracted with him for his whole attention. On the part of the Countess was not such an avidity lawful? Doctor Hugh denied it, said there was no contract but only a free understanding, and that a sordid servitude was impossible to a generous spirit; he liked moreover to talk about art, and that was the subject on which, this time, as they sat together on the sunny bench, he tried most to engage the author of "The Middle Years." Dencombe, soaring again a little on the weak wings of convalescence and still haunted by that happy notion of an organised rescue, found another strain of eloquence to plead the cause of a certain splendid "last manner," the very citadel, as it would prove, of his reputation, the stronghold into which his real treasure would be gathered. While his listener gave up the morning and the great still sea appeared to wait, he had a wonderful explanatory hour. Even for himself he was inspired as he told of what his treasure would consist—the precious metals he would dig from the mine, the jewels rare, strings of pearls, he would hang between the columns of his temple. He was wonderful for himself, so thick his convictions crowded; but he was still more wonderful for Doctor Hugh, who assured him, none the less,

that the very pages he had just published were already en-
crusted with gems. The young man, however, panted for the
combinations to come, and, before the face of the beautiful
day, renewed to Dencombe his guarantee that his profession
would hold itself responsible for such a life. Then he suddenly
clapped his hand upon his watch-pocket and asked leave to absent himself for half an hour. Dencombe waited there for his return, but was at last recalled to the actual by the fall of a
shadow across the ground. The shadow darkened into that of
Miss Vernham, the young lady in attendance on the Countess;
whom Dencombe, recognising her, perceived so clearly to have
come to speak to him that he rose from his bench to acknowledge the civility. Miss Vernham indeed proved not particularly
civil; she looked strangely agitated, and her type was now unmistakable.

"Excuse me if I inquire," she said, "whether it's too much to
hope that you may be induced to leave Doctor Hugh alone."
Then, before Dencombe, greatly disconcerted, could protest:
"You ought to be informed that you stand in his light; that you
may do him a terrible injury."

"Do you mean by causing the Countess to dispense with his
services?"

"By causing her to disinherit him." Dencombe started at this,
and Miss Vernham pursued, in the gratification of seeing she
could produce an impression: "It has depended on himself to
come into something very handsome. He has had a magnificent
prospect, but I think you've succeeded in spoiling it."

"Not intentionally, I assure you. Is there no hope the accident may be repaired?" Dencombe asked.

"She was ready to do anything for him. She takes great fancies, she lets herself go—it's her way. She has no relations, she's
free to dispose of her money, and she's very ill."

"I'm very sorry to hear it," Dencombe stammered.

"Wouldn't it be possible for you to leave Bournemouth?
That's what I've come to ask you."

Poor Dencombe sank down on his bench. "I'm very ill myself, but I'll try!"

Miss Vernham still stood there with her colourless eyes and
the brutality of her good conscience. "Before it's too late,

please!" she said; and with this she turned her back, in order, quickly, as if it had been a business to which she could spare but a precious moment, to pass out of his sight.

Oh, yes, after this Dencombe was certainly very ill. Miss Vernham had upset him with her rough, fierce news; it was the sharpest shock to him to discover what was at stake for a penniless young man of fine parts. He sat trembling on his bench, staring at the waste of waters, feeling sick with the directness of the blow. He was indeed too weak, too unsteady, too alarmed; but he would make the effort to get away, for he couldn't accept the guilt of interference, and his honour was really involved. He would hobble home, at any rate, and then he would think what was to be done. He made his way back to the hotel and, as he went, had a characteristic vision of Miss Vernham's great motive. The Countess hated women, of course; Dencombe was lucid about that; so the hungry pianist had no personal hopes and could only console herself with the bold conception of helping Doctor Hugh in order either to marry him after he should get his money or to induce him to recognise her title to compensation and buy her off. If she had befriended him at a fruitful crisis he would really, as a man of delicacy, and she knew what to think of that point, have to reckon with her.

At the hotel Dencombe's servant insisted on his going back to bed. The invalid had talked about catching a train and had begun with orders to pack; after which his humming nerves had yielded to a sense of sickness. He consented to see his physician, who immediately was sent for, but he wished it to be understood that his door was irrevocably closed to Doctor Hugh. He had his plan, which was so fine that he rejoiced in it after getting back to bed. Doctor Hugh, suddenly finding himself snubbed without mercy, would, in natural disgust and to the joy of Miss Vernham, renew his allegiance to the Countess. When his physician arrived Dencombe learned that he was feverish and that this was very wrong: he was to cultivate calmness and try, if possible, not to think. For the rest of the day he wooed stupidity; but there was an ache that kept him sentient, the probable sacrifice of his "extension," the limit of his course. His medical adviser was anything but pleased; his successive relapses were ominous. He charged this personage to put out a strong hand and take Doctor Hugh off his mind—it would contribute só much to his being quiet. The agitating name, in his room, was not mentioned again, but his security was a smothered fear, and it was not confirmed by the receipt, at ten o'clock that evening, of a telegram which his servant opened and read for him and to which, with an address in London, the signature of Miss Vernham was attached. "Beseech you to use all influence to make our friend join us here in the morning. Countess much the worse for dreadful journey, but everything may still be saved." The two ladies had gathered themselves up and had been capable in the afternoon of a spiteful revolution. They had started for the capital, and if the elder one, as Miss Vernham had announced, was very ill, she had wished to make it clear that she was proportionately reckless. Poor Dencombe, who was not reckless and who only desired that everything should indeed be "saved," sent this missive straight off to the young man's lodging and had on the morrow the pleasure of knowing that he had quitted Bournemouth by an early train.

Two days later he pressed in with a copy of a literary journal in his hand. He had returned because he was anxious and for the pleasure of flourishing the great review of "The Middle Years." Here at least was something adequate—it rose to the occasion; it was an acclamation, a reparation, a critical attempt to place the author in the niche he had fairly won. Dencombe accepted and submitted; he made neither objection nor inquiry, for old complications had returned and he had had two atrocious days. He was convinced not only that he should never again leave his bed, so that his young friend might pardonably remain, but that the demand he should make on the patience of beholders would be very moderate indeed. Doctor Hugh had been to town, and he tried to find in his eyes some confession that the Countess was pacified and his legacy clinched; but all he could see there was the light of his juvenile joy in two or three of the phrases of the newspaper. Dencombe couldn't read them, but when his visitor had insisted on repeating them more than once he was able to shake an unintoxicated head. "Ah, no; but they would have been true of what I *could* have done!"

"What people 'could have done' is mainly what they've in fact done," Doctor Hugh contended.

"Mainly, yes; but I've been an idiot!" said Dencombe.

Doctor Hugh did remain; the end was coming fast. Two days later Dencombe observed to him, by way of the feeblest of jokes, that there would now be no question whatever of a second chance. At this the young man stared; then he exclaimed: "Why, it has come to pass—it has come to pass! The second chance has been the public's—the chance to find the point of view, to pick up the pearl!"

"Oh, the pearl!" poor Dencombe uneasily sighed. A smile as cold as a winter sunset flickered on his drawn lips as he added: "The pearl is the unwritten—the pearl is the unalloyed, the *rest*, the lost!"

From that moment he was less and less present, heedless to all appearance of what went on around him. His disease was definitely mortal, of an action as relentless, after the short arrest that had enabled him to fall in with Doctor Hugh, as a leak in a great ship. Sinking steadily, though this visitor, a man of rare resources, now cordially approved by his physician, showed endless art in guarding him from pain, poor Dencombe kept no reckoning of favour or neglect, betrayed no symptom of regret or speculation. Yet toward the last he gave a sign of having noticed that for two days Doctor Hugh had not been in his room, a sign that consisted of his suddenly opening his eyes to ask of him if he had spent the interval with the Countess.

"The Countess is dead," said Doctor Hugh. "I knew that in a particular contingency she wouldn't resist. I went to her grave."

Dencombe's eyes opened wider. "She left you 'something handsome'?"

The young man gave a laugh almost too light for a chamber of woe. "Never a penny. She roundly cursed me."

"Cursed you?" Dencombe murmured.

"For giving her up. I gave her up for *you*. I had to choose," his companion explained.

"You chose to let a fortune go?"

"I chose to accept, whatever they might be, the consequences of my infatuation," smiled Doctor Hugh. Then, as a larger pleasantry: "A fortune be hanged! It's your own fault if I can't get your things out of my head."

The immediate tribute to his humour was a long, bewildered moan; after which, for many hours, many days, Dencombe lay motionless and absent. A response so absolute, such a glimpse of a definite result and such a sense of credit worked together in his mind and, producing a strange commotion, slowly altered and transfigured his despair. The sense of cold submersion left him—he seemed to float without an effort. The incident was extraordinary as evidence, and it shed an intenser light. At the last he signed to Doctor Hugh to listen, and, when he was down on his knees by the pillow, brought him very near.

"You've made me think it all a delusion."

"Not your glory, my friend," stammered the young man.

"Not my glory—what there is of it! It *is* glory—to have been tested, to have had our little quality and cast our little spell. The thing is to have made somebody care. You happen to be crazy, of course, but that doesn't affect the law."

"You're a great success!" said Doctor Hugh, putting into his young voice the ring of a marriage-bell.

Dencombe lay taking this in; then he gathered strength to speak once more. "A second chance—*that's* the delusion. There never was to be but one. We work in the dark—we do what we can—we give what we have. Our doubt is our passion and our passion is our task. The rest is the madness of art."

"If you've doubted, if you've despaired, you've always 'done' it," his visitor subtly argued.

"We've done something or other," Dencombe conceded.

"Something or other is everything. It's the feasible. It's *you!*"

"Comforter!" poor Dencombe ironically sighed.

"But it's true," insisted his friend.

"It's true. It's frustration that doesn't count."

"Frustration's only life," said Doctor Hugh.

"Yes, it's what passes." Poor Dencombe was barely audible, but he had marked with the words the virtual end of his first and only chance.

The Turn of the Screw

Collier's Weekly, *January 27–April 16, 1898. Oscar Wilde judged this work "a most wonderful, lurid, poisonous little tale, like an Elizabethan tragedy." Although it remains one of the most discussed works by Henry James, James himself soon dismissed it as "an inferior, a merely* pictorial, *subject and rather a shameless potboiler." But the 1908 New York Edition preface renewed interest when it called it "an amusette to catch those not easily caught (the 'fun' of the capture of the merely witless being ever but small), the jaded, the disillusioned, the fastidious." It took some years before, at least in print, anyone posited what its author might have meant. The suggestion finally came that perhaps the ghosts did not really exist, but were figments of a young woman's imagination. In 1924, when Edna Kenton published an article questioning the governess's perceptions, she noted "the irrepressible unconscious light she casts upon herself"* ("Henry James to the Ruminant Reader: The Turn of the Screw," The Arts, *November 1924, 245–255). In 1934 Edmund Wilson invoked the magic name Freud, as he recommended to the reader, "Observe, also, from the Freudian point of view, the significance of the governess' interest in the little girl's pieces of wood and of the fact that the male apparition first takes shape on a tower and the female apparition on a lake"* ("The Ambiguity of Henry James," Hound & Horn, *1934, 385–406). Criticism would thereafter become more alert to questions of sexual repression.*

The Turn of the Screw has been the subject of at least fifteen film or television adaptations (see Griffin, ed., Henry James Goes to the Movies), and in 1945 it was made into a distinguished opera by Benjamin Britten.

The story had held us, round the fire, sufficiently breathless, but except the obvious remark that it was gruesome, as, on Christmas eve in an old house, a strange tale should essentially be, I remember no comment uttered till somebody happened to say that it was the only case he had met in which such a visitation had fallen on a child. The case, I may mention, was that of an apparition in just such an old house as had gathered us for the occasion—an appearance, of a dreadful kind, to a little boy sleeping in the room with his mother and waking her up in the terror of it; waking her not to dissipate his dread and soothe him to sleep again, but to encounter also, herself, before she had succeeded in doing so, the same sight that had shaken him. It was this observation that drew from Douglas—not immediately, but later in the evening—a reply that had the interesting consequence to which I call attention. Someone else told a story not particularly effective, which I saw he was not following. This I took for a sign that he had himself something to produce and that we should only have to wait. We waited in fact till two nights later; but that same evening, before we scattered, he brought out what was in his mind.

"I quite agree—in regard to Griffin's ghost, or whatever it was—that its appearing first to the little boy, at so tender an age, adds a particular touch. But it's not the first occurrence of its charming kind that I know to have involved a child. If the child gives the effect another turn of the screw, what do you say to *two* children—?"

"We say, of course," somebody exclaimed, "that they give two turns! Also that we want to hear about them."

I can see Douglas there before the fire, to which he had got up to present his back, looking down at his interlocutor with his hands in his pockets. "Nobody but me, till now, has ever heard. It's quite too horrible." This, naturally, was declared by several voices to give the thing the utmost price, and our friend, with quiet art, prepared his triumph by turning his eyes over the rest of us and going on: "It's beyond everything. Nothing at all that I know touches it."

"For sheer terror?" I remember asking.

He seemed to say it was not so simple as that; to be really at a loss how to qualify it. He passed his hand over his eyes, made a little wincing grimace. "For dreadful—dreadfulness!"

"Oh, how delicious!" cried one of the women.

He took no notice of her; he looked at me, but as if, instead of me, he saw what he spoke of. "For general uncanny ugliness and horror and pain."

"Well then," I said, "just sit right down and begin."

He turned round to the fire, gave a kick to a log, watched it an instant. Then as he faced us again: "I can't begin. I shall have to send to town." There was a unanimous groan at this, and much reproach; after which, in his preoccupied way, he explained. "The story's written. It's in a locked drawer—it has not been out for years. I could write to my man and enclose the key; he could send down the packet as he finds it." It was to me in particular that he appeared to propound this—appeared almost to appeal for aid not to hesitate. He had broken a thickness of ice, the formation of many a winter: had had his reasons for a long silence. The others resented postponement, but it was just his scruples that charmed me. I adjured him to write by the first post and to agree with us for an early hearing; then I asked him if the experience in question had been his own. To this his answer was prompt. "Oh, thank God, no!"

"And is the record yours? You took the thing down?"

"Nothing but the impression. I took that *here*"—he tapped his heart. "I've never lost it."

"Then your manuscript—?"

"Is in old, faded ink, and in the most beautiful hand." He hung fire again. "A woman's. She has been dead these twenty years. She sent me the pages in question before she died." They were all listening now, and of course there was somebody to be arch, or at any rate to draw the inference. But if he put the inference by without a smile it was also without irritation. "She was a most charming person, but she was ten years older than I. She was my sister's governess," he quietly said. "She was the most agreeable woman I've ever known in her position; she would have been worthy of any whatever. It was long ago, and this episode was long before. I was at Trinity, and I found her at home on my coming down the second summer. I was much there that year—it was a beautiful one; and we had, in her off-hours, some strolls and talks in the garden—talks in which she struck me as awfully clever and nice. Oh yes; don't grin: I liked her extremely and am glad to this day to think she liked me too. If she hadn't she wouldn't have told me. She had never told anyone. It wasn't simply that she said so, but that I knew she hadn't. I was sure; I could see. You'll easily judge why when you hear."

"Because the thing had been such a scare?"

He continued to fix me. "You'll easily judge," he repeated: "*you* will."

I fixed him too. "I see. She was in love."

He laughed for the first time. "You *are* acute. Yes, she was in love. That is, she had been. That came out—she couldn't tell her story without its coming out. I saw it, and she saw I saw it; but neither of us spoke of it. I remember the time and the place—the corner of the lawn, the shade of the great beeches and the long, hot summer afternoon. It wasn't a scene for a shudder; but oh—!" He quitted the fire and dropped back into his chair.

"You'll receive the packet Thursday morning?" I inquired.

"Probably not till the second post."

"Well then; after dinner—"

"You'll all meet me here?" He looked us round again. "Isn't anybody going?" It was almost the tone of hope.

"Everybody will stay!"

"*I* will—and *I* will!" cried the ladies whose departure had been fixed. Mrs. Griffin, however, expressed the need for a little more light. "Who was it she was in love with?"

"The story will tell," I took upon myself to reply.

"Oh, I can't wait for the story!"

"The story *won't* tell," said Douglas; "not in any literal, vulgar way."

"More's the pity, then. That's the only way I ever understand."

"Won't *you* tell, Douglas?" somebody else inquired.

He sprang to his feet again. "Yes—to-morrow. Now I must go to bed. Good-night." And quickly catching up a candlestick, he left us slightly bewildered. From our end of the great brown hall we heard his step on the stair; whereupon Mrs. Griffin spoke. "Well, if I don't know who she was in love with, I know who *he* was."

"She was ten years older," said her husband.

"*Raison de plus*—at that age! But it's rather nice, his long reticence."

"Forty years!" Griffin put in.

"With this outbreak at last."

"The outbreak," I returned, "will make a tremendous occasion of Thursday night"; and everyone so agreed with me that, in the light of it, we lost all attention for everything else. The last story, however incomplete and like the mere opening of a serial, had been told; we handshook and "candlestuck," as somebody said, and went to bed.

I knew the next day that a letter containing the key had, by the first post, gone off to his London apartments; but in spite of—or perhaps just on account of—the eventual diffusion of this knowledge we quite let him alone till after dinner, till such an hour of the evening, in fact, as might best accord with the kind of emotion on which our hopes were fixed. Then he became as communicative as we could desire and indeed gave us his best reason for being so. We had it from him again before the fire in the hall, as we had had our mild wonders of the previous night. It appeared that the narrative he had promised to read us really required for a proper intelligence a few words of prologue. Let me say here distinctly, to have done with it, that this narrative, from an exact transcript of my own made much later, is what I shall presently give. Poor Douglas, before his death—when it was in sight—committed to me the manuscript that reached him on the third of these days and that, on the same spot, with immense effect, he began to read to our hushed little circle on the night of the fourth. The departing ladies who had said they would stay didn't, of course, thank heaven, stay: they departed, in consequence of arrangements made, in a rage of curiosity, as they professed, produced by the touches with which he had already worked us up. But that only made his little final auditory more compact and select, kept it, round the hearth, subject to a common thrill.

The first of these touches conveyed that the written statement took up the tale at a point after it had, in a manner, begun. The fact to be in possession of was therefore that his old friend, the youngest of several daughters of a poor country parson, had, at the age of twenty, on taking service for the first time in the schoolroom, come up to London, in trepidation, to answer in person an advertisement that had already placed her in brief correspondence with the advertiser. This person proved, on her presenting herself, for judgment, at a house in Harley Street, that impressed her as vast and imposing—this prospective patron proved a gentleman, a bachelor in the prime of life, such a figure as had never risen, save in a dream or an old novel, before a fluttered, anxious girl out of a Hampshire vicarage. One could easily fix his type; it never, happily, dies out. He was handsome and bold and pleasant, off-hand and gay and kind. He struck her, inevitably, as gallant and splendid, but what took her most of all and gave her the courage she afterwards showed was that he put the whole thing to her as a kind of favour, an obligation he should gratefully incur. She conceived him as rich, but as fearfully extravagant—saw him all in a glow of high fashion, of good looks, of expensive habits, of charming ways with women. He had for his own town residence a big house filled with the spoils of travel and the trophies of the chase; but it was to his country home, an old family place in Essex, that he wished her immediately to proceed.

He had been left, by the death of their parents in India, guardian to a small nephew and a small niece, children of a younger, a military brother, whom he had lost two years before. These children were, by the strangest of chances for a man in his position,—a lone man without the right sort of experience or a grain of patience,—very heavily on his hands. It had all been a great worry and, on his own part doubtless, a series of blunders, but he immensely pitied the poor chicks and had done all he could; had in particular sent them down to his other house, the proper place for them being of course the country, and kept them there, from the first, with the best people he could find to look after them, parting even with his own servants to wait on them and going down himself, whenever he might, to see how they were doing. The awkward thing was that they had practically no other relations and that his own affairs took up all his time. He had put them in possession of Bly, which was healthy and secure, and had placed at the head of their little establishment—but below stairs only—an excellent woman, Mrs. Grose, whom he was sure his visitor would like and who had formerly been maid to his mother. She was now housekeeper and was also acting for the time as superintendent to the little girl, of whom, without children of her own, she was, by good luck, extremely fond. There were plenty of people to help, but of course the young lady who should go down as governess would be in supreme authority. She would also have, in holidays, to look after the small boy, who had been for a term at school—young as he was to be sent, but what else could be done?—and who, as the holidays were about to begin, would be back from one day to the other. There had been for the two children at first a young lady whom they had had the misfortune to lose. She had done for them quite beautifully—she was a most respectable person—till her death, the great awkwardness of which had, precisely, left no alternative but the school for little Miles. Mrs. Grose, since then, in the way of manners and things, had done as she could for Flora; and there were, further, a cook, a housemaid, a dairywoman, an old pony, an old groom, and an old gardener, all likewise thoroughly respectable.

So far had Douglas presented his picture when someone put a question. "And what did the former governess die of?—of so much respectability?"

Our friend's answer was prompt. "That will come out. I don't anticipate."

"Excuse me—I thought that was just what you *are* doing."

"In her successor's place," I suggested, "I should have wished to learn if the office brought with it—"

"Necessary danger to life?" Douglas completed my thought. "She did wish to learn, and she did learn. You shall hear to-morrow what she learnt. Meanwhile, of course, the prospect struck her as slightly grim. She was young, untried, nervous: it was a vision of serious duties and little company, of really great loneliness. She hesitated—took a couple of days to consult and consider. But the salary offered much exceeded her modest measure, and on a second interview she faced the music, she engaged." And Douglas, with this, made a pause that, for the benefit of the company, moved me to throw in—

"The moral of which was of course the seduction exercised by the splendid young man. She succumbed to it."

He got up and, as he had done the night before, went to the fire, gave a stir to a log with his foot, then stood a moment with his back to us. "She saw him only twice."

"Yes, but that's just the beauty of her passion."

A little to my surprise, on this, Douglas turned round to me. "It *was* the beauty of it. There were others," he went on, "who hadn't succumbed. He told her frankly all his difficulty—that for several applicants the conditions had been prohibitive. They were, somehow, simply afraid. It sounded dull—it sounded strange; and all the more so because of his main condition."

"Which was—?"

"That she should never trouble him—but never, never: neither appeal nor complain nor write about anything; only meet all questions herself, receive all moneys from his solicitor, take the whole thing over and let him alone. She promised to do this, and she mentioned to me that when, for a moment, dis-burdened, delighted, he held her hand, thanking her for the sacrifice, she already felt rewarded."

"But was that all her reward?" one of the ladies asked.

"She never saw him again."

"Oh!" said the lady; which, as our friend immediately left us again, was the only other word of importance contributed to the subject till, the next night, by the corner of the hearth, in the best chair, he opened the faded red cover of a thin old-fashioned gilt-edged album. The whole thing took indeed more nights than one, but on the first occasion the same lady put an-other question. "What is your title?"

"I haven't one."

"Oh, *I* have!" I said. But Douglas, without heeding me, had begun to read with a fine clearness that was like a rendering to the ear of the beauty of his author's hand.

I.

I remember the whole beginning as a succession of flights and drops, a little see-saw of the right throbs and the wrong. After rising, in town, to meet his appeal, I had at all events a couple of very bad days—found myself doubtful again, felt indeed sure I had made a mistake. In this state of mind I spent the long hours of bumping, swinging coach that carried me to the stopping-place at which I was to be met by a vehicle from the house. This convenience, I was told, had been ordered, and I found, toward the close of the June afternoon, a commodious fly in waiting for me. Driving at that hour, on a lovely day, through a country to which the summer sweetness seemed to offer me a friendly welcome, my fortitude mounted afresh and, as we turned into the avenue, encountered a reprieve that was probably but a proof of the point to which it had sunk. I suppose I had expected, or had dreaded, something so melancholy that what greeted me was a good surprise. I remember as a most pleasant impression the broad, clear front, its open windows and fresh curtains and the pair of maids looking out; I remember the lawn and the bright flowers and the crunch of my wheels on the gravel and the clustered tree-tops over which the rooks circled and cawed in the golden sky. The scene had a greatness that made it a different affair from my own scant home, and there immediately appeared at the door, with a little girl in her hand, a civil person who dropped me as decent a curtsey as if I had been the mistress or a distinguished visitor. I had received in Harley Street a narrower notion of the place, and that, as I recalled it, made me think the proprietor still more of a gentleman, suggested that what I was to enjoy might be something beyond his promise.

I had no drop again till the next day, for I was carried triumphantly through the following hours by my introduction to

the younger of my pupils. The little girl who accompanied Mrs.
Grose appeared to me on the spot a creature so charming as to
make it a great fortune to have to do with her. She was the most
beautiful child I had ever seen, and I afterwards wondered that
my employer had not told me more of her. I slept little that
night—I was too much excited; and this astonished me too, I
recollect, remained with me, adding to my sense of the liberality with which I was treated. The large, impressive room, one
of the best in the house, the great state bed, as I almost felt it,
the full, figured draperies, the long glasses in which, for the first
time, I could see myself from head to foot, all struck me—like
the extraordinary charm of my small charge—as so many
things thrown in. It was thrown in as well, from the first moment, that I should get on with Mrs. Grose in a relation over
which, on my way, in the coach, I fear I had rather brooded.
The only thing indeed that in this early outlook might have
made me shrink again was the clear circumstance of her being
so glad to see me. I perceived within half an hour that she was
so glad—stout, simple, plain, clean, wholesome woman—as to
be positively on her guard against showing it too much. I wondered even then a little why she should wish not to show it, and
that, with reflection, with suspicion, might of course have
made me uneasy.

But it was a comfort that there could be no uneasiness in a
connection with anything so beatific as the radiant image of my
little girl, the vision of whose angelic beauty had probably
more than anything else to do with the restlessness that, before
morning, made me several times rise and wander about my
room to take in the whole picture and prospect; to watch, from
my open window, the faint summer dawn, to look at such portions of the rest of the house as I could catch, and to listen,
while, in the fading dusk, the first birds began to twitter, for the
possible recurrence of a sound or two, less natural and not
without, but within, that I had fancied I heard. There had been
a moment when I believed I recognised, faint and far, the cry of
a child; there had been another when I found myself just consciously starting as at the passage, before my door, of a light
footstep. But these fancies were not marked enough not to be

thrown off, and it is only in the light, or the gloom, I should rather say, of other and subsequent matters that they now come back to me. To watch, teach, "form" little Flora would too evidently be the making of a happy and useful life. It had been agreed between us downstairs that after this first occasion I should have her as a matter of course at night, her small white bed being already arranged, to that end, in my room. What I had undertaken was the whole care of her, and she had remained, just this last time, with Mrs. Grose only as an effect of our consideration for my inevitable strangeness and her natural timidity. In spite of this timidity—which the child herself, in the oddest way in the world, had been perfectly frank and brave about, allowing it, without a sign of uncomfortable consciousness, with the deep, sweet serenity indeed of one of Raphael's holy infants, to be discussed, to be imputed to her and to determine us—I felt quite sure she would presently like me. It was part of what I already liked Mrs. Grose herself for, the pleasure I could see her feel in my admiration and wonder as I sat at supper with four tall candles and with my pupil, in a high chair and a bib, brightly facing me, between them, over bread and milk. There were naturally things that in Flora's presence could pass between us only as prodigious and gratified looks, obscure and roundabout allusions.

"And the little boy—does he look like her? Is he too so very remarkable?"

One wouldn't flatter a child. "Oh, Miss, *most* remarkable. If you think well of this one!"—and she stood there with a plate in her hand, beaming at our companion, who looked from one of us to the other with placid heavenly eyes that contained nothing to check us.

"Yes; if I do—?"

"You *will* be carried away by the little gentleman!"

"Well, that, I think, is what I came for—to be carried away. I'm afraid, however," I remember feeling the impulse to add, "I'm rather easily carried away. I was carried away in London!"

I can still see Mrs. Grose's broad face as she took this in. "In Harley Street?"

"In Harley Street."

"Well, Miss, you're not the first—and you won't be the last."

"Oh, I've no pretension," I could laugh, "to being the only one. My other pupil, at any rate, as I understand, comes back tomorrow?"

"Not tomorrow—Friday, Miss. He arrives, as you did, by the coach, under care of the guard, and is to be met by the same carriage."

I forthwith expressed that the proper as well as the pleasant and friendly thing would be therefore that on the arrival of the public conveyance I should be in waiting for him with his little sister; an idea in which Mrs. Grose concurred so heartily that I somehow took her manner as a kind of comforting pledge—never falsified, thank heaven!—that we should on every question be quite at one. Oh, she was glad I was there!

What I felt the next day was, I suppose, nothing that could be fairly called a reaction from the cheer of my arrival; it was probably at the most only a slight oppression produced by a fuller measure of the scale, as I walked round them, gazed up at them, took them in, of my new circumstances. They had, as it were, an extent and mass for which I had not been prepared and in the presence of which I found myself, freshly, a little scared as well as a little proud. Lessons, in this agitation, certainly suffered some delay; I reflected that my first duty was, by the gentlest arts I could contrive, to win the child into the sense of knowing me. I spent the day with her out of doors; I arranged with her, to her great satisfaction, that it should be she, she only, who might show me the place. She showed it step by step and room by room and secret by secret, with droll, delightful, childish talk about it and with the result, in half an hour, of our becoming immense friends. Young as she was, I was struck, throughout our little tour, with her confidence and courage with the way, in empty chambers and dull corridors, on crooked staircases that made me pause and even on the summit of an old machicolated square tower that made me dizzy, her morning music, her disposition to tell me so many more things than she asked, rang out and led me on. I have not seen Bly since the day I left it, and I dare say that to my older and more informed eyes it would now appear sufficiently contracted. But as my little conductress, with her hair of gold and her frock of blue, danced before me round corners and pattered down passages, I had the view of a castle of romance inhabited by a rosy sprite, such a place as would somehow, for diversion of the young idea, take all colour out of storybooks and fairy-tales. Wasn't it just a storybook over which I had fallen a-doze and a-dream? No; it was a big, ugly, antique, but convenient house, embodying a few features of a building still older, half replaced and half utilised, in which I had the fancy of our being almost as lost as a handful of passengers in a great drifting ship. Well, I was, strangely, at the helm!

II.

This came home to me when, two days later, I drove over with Flora to meet, as Mrs. Grose said, the little gentleman; and all the more for an incident that, presenting itself the second evening, had deeply disconcerted me. The first day had been, on the whole, as I have expressed, reassuring; but I was to see it wind up in keen apprehension. The postbag, that evening,— it came late,—contained a letter for me, which, however, in the hand of my employer, I found to be composed but of a few words enclosing another, addressed to himself, with a seal still unbroken, "This, I recognise, is from the head-master, and the head-master's an awful bore. Read him, please; deal with him; but mind you don't report. Not a word. I'm off!" I broke the seal with a great effort—so great a one that I was a long time coming to it; took the unopened missive at last up to my room and only attacked it just before going to bed. I had better have let it wait till morning, for it gave me a second sleepless night. With no counsel to take, the next day, I was full of distress; and it finally got so the better of me that I determined to open myself at least to Mrs. Grose.

"What does it mean? The child's dismissed his school."

She gave me a look that I remarked at the moment; then, visibly, with a quick blankness, seemed to try to take it back. "But aren't they all—?"

"Sent home—yes. But only for the holidays. Miles may never go back at all."

Consciously, under my attention, she reddened. "They won't take him?"

"They absolutely decline."

At this she raised her eyes, which she had turned from me; I saw them fill with good tears. "What has he done?"

I hesitated; then I judged best simply to hand her my letter—which, however, had the effect of making her, without taking it, simply put her hands behind her. She shook her head sadly. "Such things are not for me, Miss."

My counsellor couldn't read! I winced at my mistake, which I attenuated as I could, and opened my letter again to repeat it to her; then, faltering in the act and folding it up once more, I put it back in my pocket. "Is he really *bad*?"

The tears were still in her eyes. "Do the gentlemen say so?"

"They go into no particulars. They simply express their regret that it should be impossible to keep him. That can have only one meaning." Mrs. Grose listened with dumb emotion; she forbore to ask me what this meaning might be; so that, presently, to put the thing with some coherence and with the mere aid of her presence to my own mind, I went on: "That he's an injury to the others."

At this, with one of the quick turns of simple folk, she suddenly flamed up. "Master Miles! *him* an injury?"

There was such a flood of good faith in it that, though I had not yet seen the child, my very fears made me jump to the absurdity of the idea. I found myself, to meet my friend the better, offering it, on the spot, sarcastically. "To his poor little innocent mates!"

"It's too dreadful," cried Mrs. Grose, "to say such cruel things! Why, he's scarce ten years old."

"Yes, yes; it would be incredible."

She was evidently grateful for such a profession. "See him, Miss, first. *Then* believe it!" I felt forthwith a new impatience to see him; it was the beginning of a curiosity that, for all the next hours, was to deepen almost to pain. Mrs. Grose was aware, I could judge, of what she had produced in me, and she followed it up with assurance. "You might as well believe it of the little lady. Bless her," she added the next moment—"*look* at her!"

I turned and saw that Flora, whom, ten minutes before, I had established in the schoolroom with a sheet of white paper, a pencil, and a copy of nice "round O's," now presented herself to view at the open door. She expressed in her little way an extraordinary detachment from disagreeable duties, looking to me, however, with a great childish light that seemed to offer it as a mere result of the affection she had conceived for my person, which had rendered necessary that she should follow me. I needed nothing more than this to feel the full force of Mrs. Grose's comparison, and, catching my pupil in my arms, covered her with kisses in which there was a sob of atonement.

None the less, the rest of the day, I watched for further occasion to approach my colleague, especially as, toward evening, I began to fancy she rather sought to avoid me. I overtook her, I remember, on the staircase; we went down together, and at the bottom I detained her, holding her there with a hand on her arm. "I take what you said to me at noon as a declaration that *you've* never known him to be bad."

She threw back her head; she had clearly, by this time, and very honestly, adopted an attitude. "Oh, never known him—I don't pretend *that!*"

I was upset again. "Then you *have* known him—?"

"Yes indeed, Miss, thank God!"

On reflection I accepted this. "You mean that a boy who never is—?"

"Is no boy for *me!*"

I held her tighter. "You like them with the spirit to be naughty?" Then, keeping pace with her answer, "So do I!" I eagerly brought out. "But not to the degree to contaminate—"

"To contaminate?"—my big word left her at a loss. I explained it. "To corrupt."

She stared, taking my meaning in; but it produced in her an odd laugh. "Are you afraid he'll corrupt *you?*" She put the question with such a fine bold humour that, with a laugh, a little silly doubtless, to match her own, I gave way for the time to the apprehension of ridicule.

But the next day, as the hour for my drive approached, I

cropped up in another place. "What was the lady who was here before?"

"The last governess? She was also young and pretty—almost as young and almost as pretty, Miss, even as you."

"Ah, then, I hope her youth and her beauty helped her!" I recollect throwing off. "He seems to like us young and pretty!"

"Oh, he *did*," Mrs. Grose assented: "it was the way he liked everyone!" She had no sooner spoken indeed than she caught herself up. "I mean that's *his* way—the master's."

I was struck. "But of whom did you speak first?"

She looked blank, but she coloured. "Why, of *him*."

"Of the master?"

"Of who else?"

There was so obviously no one else that the next moment I had lost my impression of her having accidentally said more than she meant; and I merely asked what I wanted to know. "Did *she* see anything in the boy—?"

"That wasn't right? She never told me."

I had a scruple, but I overcame it. "Was she careful—particular?"

Mrs. Grose appeared to try to be conscientious. "About some things—yes."

"But not about all?"

Again she considered. "Well, Miss—she's gone. I won't tell tales."

"I quite understand your feeling," I hastened to reply; but I thought it, after an instant, not opposed to this concession to pursue: "Did she die here?"

"No—she went off."

I don't know what there was in this brevity of Mrs. Grose's that struck me as ambiguous. "Went off to die?" Mrs. Grose looked straight out of the window, but I felt that, hypothetically, I had a right to know what young persons engaged for Bly were expected to do. "She was taken ill, you mean, and went home?"

"She was not taken ill, so far as appeared, in this house. She left it, at the end of the year, to go home, as she said, for a short holiday, to which the time she had put in had certainly given her a right. We had then a young woman—a nursemaid who had stayed on and who was a good girl and clever; and *she* took the children altogether for the interval. But our young lady never came back, and at the very moment I was expecting her I heard from the master that she was dead."

I turned this over. "But of what?"

"He never told me! But please, Miss," said Mrs. Grose, "I must get to my work."

III.

Her thus turning her back on me was fortunately not, for my just preoccupations, a snub that could check the growth of our mutual esteem. We met, after I had brought home little Miles, more intimately than ever on the ground of my stupefaction, my general emotion: so monstrous was I then ready to pronounce it that such a child as had now been revealed to me should be under an interdict. I was a little late on the scene, and I felt, as he stood wistfully looking out for me before the door of the inn at which the coach had put him down, that I had seen him, on the instant, without and within, in the great glow of freshness, the same positive fragrance of purity, in which I had, from the first moment, seen his little sister. He was incredibly beautiful, and Mrs. Grose had put her finger on it: everything but a sort of passion of tenderness for him was swept away by his presence. What I then and there took him to my heart for was something divine that I have never found to the same degree in any child—his indescribable little air of knowing nothing in the world but love. It would have been impossible to carry a bad name with a greater sweetness of innocence, and by the time I had got back to Bly with him I remained merely bewildered—so far, that is, as I was not outraged—by the sense of the horrible letter locked up in my room, in a drawer. As soon as I could compass a private word with Mrs. Grose I declared to her that it was grotesque.

She promptly understood me. "You mean the cruel charge—?"

"It doesn't live an instant. My dear woman, *look* at him!"

She smiled at my pretension to have discovered his charm. "I assure you, Miss, I do nothing else! What will you say, then?" she immediately added.

"In answer to the letter?" I had made up my mind. "Nothing."

"And to his uncle?"

I was incisive. "Nothing."

"And to the boy himself?"

I was wonderful. "Nothing."

She gave with her apron a great wipe to her mouth. "Then I'll stand by you. We'll see it out."

"We'll see it out!" I ardently echoed, giving her my hand to make it a vow.

She held me there a moment, then whisked up her apron again with her detached hand. "Would you mind, Miss, if I used the freedom—"

"To kiss me? No!" I took the good creature in my arms and, after we had embraced like sisters, felt still more fortified and indignant.

This, at all events, was for the time: a time so full that, as I recall the way it went, it reminds me of all the art I now need to make it a little distinct. What I look back at with amazement is the situation I accepted. I had undertaken, with my companion, to see it out, and I was under a charm, apparently, that could smooth away the extent and the far and difficult connections of such an effort. I was lifted aloft on a great wave of infatuation and pity. I found it simple, in my ignorance, my confusion, and perhaps my conceit, to assume that I could deal with a boy whose education for the world was all on the point of beginning. I am unable even to remember at this day what proposal I framed for the end of his holidays and the resumption of his studies. Lessons with me, indeed, that charming summer, we all had a theory that he was to have; but I now feel that, for weeks, the lessons must have been rather my own. I learnt something—at first certainly—that had not been one of the teachings of my small, smothered life; learnt to be amused, and even amusing, and not to think for the morrow. It was the first time, in a manner, that I had known space and air and freedom, all the music of summer and all the mystery of nature. And then there was consideration—and consideration was sweet. Oh, it was a trap—not designed, but deep—to my imagination, to my delicacy, perhaps to my vanity; to whatever, in me, was most excitable. The best way to picture it all is to say that I was off my guard. They gave me so little trouble—they were of a gentleness so extraordinary. I used to speculate—but even this with a dim disconnectedness—as to how the rough future (for all futures are rough!) would handle them and might bruise them. They had the bloom of health and happiness; and yet, as if I had been in charge of a pair of little grandees, of princes of the blood, for whom everything, to be right, would have to be enclosed and protected, the only form that, in my fancy, the after-years could take for them was that of a romantic, a really royal extension of the garden and the park. It may be, of course, above all, that what suddenly broke into this gives the previous time a charm of stillness—that hush in which something gathers or crouches. The change was actually like the spring of a beast.

In the first weeks the days were long; they often, at their finest, gave me what I used to call my own hour, the hour when, for my pupils, tea-time and bed-time having come and gone, I had, before my final retirement, a small interval alone. Much as I liked my companions, this hour was the thing in the day I liked most; and I liked it best of all when, as the light faded—or rather, I should say, the day lingered and the last calls of the last birds sounded, in a flushed sky, from the old trees—I could take a turn into the grounds and enjoy, almost with a sense of property that amused and flattered me, the beauty and dignity of the place. It was a pleasure at these moments to feel myself tranquil and justified; doubtless, perhaps, also to reflect that by my discretion, my quiet good sense and general high propriety, I was giving pleasure—if he ever thought of it!—to the person to whose pressure I had responded. What I was doing was what he had earnestly hoped and directly asked of me, and that I _could_, after all, do it proved even a greater joy than I had expected. I dare say I fancied myself, in short, a remarkable young woman and took comfort in the faith that this would more publicly appear. Well, I needed to be remarkable to offer a front to the remarkable things that presently gave their first sign.

It was plump, one afternoon, in the middle of my very hour: the children were tucked away and I had come out for my stroll. One of the thoughts that, as I don't in the least shrink now from noting, used to be with me in these wanderings was that it would be as charming as a charming story suddenly to meet someone. Someone would appear there at the turn of a path and would stand before me and smile and approve. I didn't ask more than that—I only asked that he should *know;* and the only way to be sure he knew would be to see it, and the kind light of it, in his handsome face. That was exactly present to me—by which I mean the face was—when, on the first of these occasions, at the end of a long June day, I stopped short on emerging from one of the plantations and coming into view of the house. What arrested me on the spot—and with a shock much greater than any vision had allowed for—was the sense that my imagination had, in a flash, turned real. He did stand there!—but high up, beyond the lawn and at the very top of the tower to which, on that first morning, little Flora had conducted me. This tower was one of a pair—square, incongruous, crenelated structures—that were distinguished, for some reason, though I could see little difference, as the new and the old. They flanked opposite ends of the house and were probably architectural absurdities, redeemed in a measure indeed by not being wholly disengaged nor of a height too pretentious, dating, in their gingerbread antiquity, from a romantic revival that was already a respectable past. I admired them, had fancies about them, for we could all profit in a degree, especially when they loomed through the dusk, by the grandeur of their actual battlements; yet it was not at such an elevation that the figure I had so often invoked seemed most in place.

It produced in me, this figure, in the clear twilight, I remember, two distinct gasps of emotion, which were, sharply, the shock of my first and that of my second surprise. My second was a violent perception of the mistake of my first: the man who met my eyes was not the person I had precipitately supposed. There came to me thus a bewilderment of vision of which, after these years, there is no living view that I can hope to give. An unknown man in a lonely place is a permitted object of fear to a young woman privately bred; and the figure that faced me was—a few more seconds assured me—as little anyone else I knew as it was the image that had been in my mind. I had not seen it in Harley Street—I had not seen it anywhere. The place, moreover, in the strangest way in the world, had, on the instant, and by the very fact of its appearance, become a solitude. To me at least, making my statement here with a deliberation with which I have never made it, the whole feeling of the moment returns. It was as if, while I took in—what I did take in—all the rest of the scene had been stricken with death. I can hear again, as I write, the intense hush in which the sounds of evening dropped. The rooks stopped cawing in the golden sky and the friendly hour lost, for the minute, all its voice. But there was no other change in nature, unless indeed it were a change that I saw with a stranger sharpness. The gold was still in the sky, the clearness in the air, and the man who looked at me over the battlements was as definite as a picture in a frame. That's how I thought, with extraordinary quickness, of each person that he might have been and that he was not. We were confronted across our distance quite long enough for me to ask myself with intensity who then he was and to feel, as an effect of my inability to say, a wonder that in a few instants more became intense.

The great question, or one of these, is, afterwards, I know, with regard to certain matters, the question of how long they have lasted. Well, this matter of mine, think what you will of it, lasted while I caught at a dozen possibilities, none of which made a difference for the better, that I could see, in there having been in the house—and for how long, above all?—a person of whom I was in ignorance. It lasted while I just bridled a little with the sense that my office demanded that there should be no such ignorance and no such person. It lasted while this visitant, at all events,—and there was a touch of the strange freedom, as I remember, in the sign of familiarity of his wearing no hat,—seemed to fix me, from his position, with just the question, just the scrutiny through the fading light, that his own presence provoked. We were too far apart to call to each other, but there was a moment at which, at shorter range, some challenge between us, breaking the hush, would have been the right result of our straight mutual stare. He was in one of the angles, the one away from the house, very erect, as it struck me, and with both hands on the ledge. So I saw him as I see the letters I

form on this page; then, exactly, after a minute, as if to add to
the spectacle, he slowly changed his place—passed, looking at
me hard all the while, to the opposite corner of the platform.
Yes, I had the sharpest sense that during this transit he never
took his eyes from me, and I can see at this moment the way his
hand, as he went, passed from one of the crenelations to the
next. He stopped at the other corner, but less long, and even as
he turned away still markedly fixed me. He turned away; that
was all I knew.

IV.

It was not that I didn't wait, on this occasion, for more, for I
was rooted as deeply as I was shaken. Was there a "secret" at
Bly—a mystery of Udolpho or an insane, an unmentionable relative kept in unsuspected confinement? I can't say how long I
turned it over, or how long, in a confusion of curiosity and
dread, I remained where I had had my collision; I only recall
that when I re-entered the house darkness had quite closed in.
Agitation, in the interval, certainly had held me and driven me,
for I must, in circling about the place, have walked three miles;
but I was to be, later on, so much more overwhelmed that this
mere dawn of alarm was a comparatively human chill. The
most singular part of it in fact—singular as the rest had been—
was the part I became, in the hall, aware of in meeting Mrs.
Grose. This picture comes back to me in the general train—the
impression, as I received it on my return, of the wide white
panelled space, bright in the lamplight and with its portraits
and red carpet, and of the good surprised look of my friend,
which immediately told me she had missed me. It came to me
straightway, under her contact, that, with plain heartiness,
mere relieved anxiety at my appearance, she knew nothing
whatever that could bear upon the incident I had there ready
for her. I had not suspected in advance that her comfortable
face would pull me up, and I somehow measured the importance of what I had seen by my thus finding myself hesitate to
mention it. Scarce anything in the whole history seems to me so
odd as this fact that my real beginning of fear was one, as I may

say, with the instinct of sparing my companion. On the spot, accordingly, in the pleasant hall and with her eyes on me, I, for a reason that I couldn't then have phrased, achieved an inward revolution—offered a vague pretext for my lateness and, with the plea of the beauty of the night and of the heavy dew and wet feet, went as soon as possible to my room.

Here it was another affair; here, for many days after, it was a queer affair enough. There were hours, from day to day,—or at least there were moments, snatched even from clear duties,—when I had to shut myself up to think. It was not so much yet that I was more nervous than I could bear to be as that I was remarkably afraid of becoming so; for the truth I had now to turn over was, simply and clearly, the truth that I could arrive at no account whatever of the visitor with whom I had been so inexplicably and yet, as it seemed to me, so intimately concerned. It took little time to see that I could sound without forms of inquiry and without exciting remark any domestic complication. The shock I had suffered must have sharpened all my senses; I felt sure, at the end of three days and as the result of mere closer attention, that I had not been practised upon by the servants nor made the object of any "game." Of whatever it was that I knew nothing was known around me. There was but one sane inference: someone had taken a liberty rather gross. That was what, repeatedly, I dipped into my room and locked the door to say to myself. We had been, collectively, subject to an intrusion; some unscrupulous traveller, curious in old houses, had made his way in unobserved, enjoyed the prospect from the best point of view, and then stolen out as he came. If he had given me such a bold hard stare, that was but a part of his indiscretion. The good thing, after all, was that we should surely see no more of him.

This was not so good a thing, I admit, as not to leave me to judge that what, essentially, made nothing else much signify was simply my charming work. My charming work was just my life with Miles and Flora, and through nothing could I so like it as through feeling that I could throw myself into it in trouble. The attraction of my small charges was a constant joy, leading me to wonder afresh at the vanity of my original fears, the distaste I had begun by entertaining for the probable grey prose of my office. There was to be no grey prose, it appeared, and no long grind; so how could work not be charming that presented itself as daily beauty? It was all the romance of the nursery and the poetry of the schoolroom. I don't mean by this, of course, that we studied only fiction and verse; I mean I can express no otherwise the sort of interest my companions inspired. How can I describe that except by saying that instead of growing used to them—and it's a marvel for a governess: I call the sisterhood to witness!—I made constant fresh discoveries. There was one direction, assuredly, in which these discoveries stopped: deep obscurity continued to cover the region of the boy's conduct at school. It had been promptly given me, I have noted, to face that mystery without a pang. Perhaps even it would be nearer the truth to say that—without a word—he himself had cleared it up. He had made the whole charge absurd. My conclusion bloomed there with the real rose-flush of his innocence: he was only too fine and fair for the little horrid, unclean school-world, and he had paid a price for it. I reflected acutely that the sense of such differences, such superiorities of quality, always, on the part of the majority—which could include even stupid, sordid headmasters—turns infallibly to the vindictive.

Both the children had a gentleness (it was their only fault, and it never made Miles a muff) that kept them—how shall I express it?—almost impersonal and certainly quite unpunishable. They were like the cherubs of the anecdote, who had—morally, at any rate—nothing to whack! I remember feeling with Miles in especial as if he had had, as it were, no history. We expect of a small child a scant one, but there was in this beautiful little boy something extraordinarily sensitive, yet extraordinarily happy, that, more than in any creature of his age I have seen, struck me as beginning anew each day. He had never for a second suffered. I took this as a direct disproof of his having really been chastised. If he had been wicked he would have "caught" it, and I should have caught it by the rebound—I should have found the trace. I found nothing at all, and he was therefore an angel. He never spoke of his school, never mentioned a comrade or a master; and I, for my part, was quite too much disgusted to allude to them. Of course I was under the spell, and the wonderful part is that, even at the time, I perfectly knew I was. But I gave myself up to it; it was an antidote to any pain, and I had more pains than one. I was in receipt in these days of disturbing letters from home, where things were not going well. But with my children, what things in the world mattered? That was the question I used to put to my scrappy retirements. I was dazzled by their loveliness.

There was a Sunday—to get on—when it rained with such force and for so many hours that there could be no procession to church; in consequence of which, as the day declined, I had arranged with Mrs. Grose that, should the evening show improvement, we would attend together the late service. The rain happily stopped, and I prepared for our walk, which, through the park and by the good road to the village, would be a matter of twenty minutes. Coming downstairs to meet my colleague in the hall, I remembered a pair of gloves that had required three stitches and that had received them—with a publicity perhaps not edifying—while I sat with the children at their tea, served on Sundays, by exception, in that cold, clean temple of mahogany and brass, the "grown-up" dining-room. The gloves had been dropped there, and I turned in to recover them. The day was grey enough, but the afternoon light still lingered, and it enabled me, on crossing the threshold, not only to recognise, on a chair near the wide window, then closed, the articles I wanted, but to become aware of a person on the other side of the window and looking straight in. One step into the room had sufficed; my vision was instantaneous; it was all there. The person looking straight in was the person who had already appeared to me. He appeared thus again with I won't say greater distinctness, for that was impossible, but with a nearness that represented a forward stride in our intercourse and made me, as I met him, catch my breath and turn cold. He was the same—he was the same, and seen, this time, as he had been seen before, from the waist up, the window, though the dining-room was on the ground-floor, not going down to the terrace on which he stood. His face was close to the glass, yet the effect of this better view was, strangely, only to show me how intense the former had been. He remained but a few seconds—long enough to convince me he also saw and recognised;

but it was as if I had been looking at him for years and had known him always. Something, however, happened this time that had not happened before; his stare into my face, through the glass and across the room, was as deep and hard as then, but it quitted me for a moment during which I could still watch it, see it fix successively several other things. On the spot there came to me the added shock of a certitude that it was not for me he had come there. He had come for someone else.

The flash of this knowledge—for it was knowledge in the midst of dread—produced in me the most extraordinary effect, started, as I stood there, a sudden vibration of duty and courage. I say courage because I was beyond all doubt already far gone. I bounded straight out of the door again, reached that of the house, got, in an instant, upon the drive, and, passing along the terrace as fast as I could rush, turned a corner and came full in sight. But it was in sight of nothing now—my visitor had vanished. I stopped, I almost dropped, with the real relief of this; but I took in the whole scene—I gave him time to reappear. I call it time, but how long was it? I can't speak to the purpose today of the duration of these things. That kind of measure must have left me: they couldn't have lasted as they actually appeared to me to last. The terrace and the whole place, the lawn and the garden beyond it, all I could see of the park, were empty with a great emptiness. There were shrubberies and big trees, but I remember the clear assurance I felt that none of them concealed him. He was there or was not there: not there if I didn't see him. I got hold of this; then, instinctively, instead of returning as I had come, went to the window. It was confusedly present to me that I ought to place myself where he had stood. I did so; I applied my face to the pane and looked, as he had looked, into the room. As if, at this moment, to show me exactly what his range had been, Mrs. Grose, as I had done for himself just before, came in from the hall. With this I had the full image of a repetition of what had already occurred. She saw me as I had seen my own visitant; she pulled up short as I had done; I gave her something of the shock that I had received. She turned white, and this made me ask myself if I had blanched as much. She stared, in short, and retreated on just *my* lines, and I knew she had then passed out and come round to me and that I should presently meet her. I remained where I was, and while I waited I thought of more things than one. But there's only one I take space to mention. I wondered why *she* should be scared.

V.

Oh, she let me know as soon as, round the corner of the house, she loomed again into view. "What in the name of goodness is the matter—?" She was now flushed and out of breath.

I said nothing till she came quite near. "With me?" I must have made a wonderful face. "Do I show it?"

"You're as white as a sheet. You look awful."

I considered; I could meet on this, without scruple, any innocence. My need to respect the bloom of Mrs. Grose's had dropped, without a rustle, from my shoulders, and if I wavered for the instant it was not with what I kept back. I put out my hand to her and she took it; I held her hard a little, liking to feel her close to me. There was a kind of support in the shy heave of her surprise. "You came for me for church, of course, but I can't go."

"Has anything happened?"

"Yes. You must know now. Did I look very queer?"

"Through this window? Dreadful!"

"Well," I said, "I've been frightened." Mrs. Grose's eyes expressed plainly that *she* had no wish to be, yet also that she knew too well her place not to be ready to share with me any marked inconvenience. Oh, it was quite settled that she *must* share! "Just what you saw from the dining-room a minute ago was the effect of that. What *I* saw—just before—was much worse."

Her hand tightened. "What was it?"

"An extraordinary man. Looking in."

"What extraordinary man?"

"I haven't the least idea."

Mrs. Grose gazed round us in vain. "Then where is he gone?"

"I know still less."

"Have you seen him before?"

"Yes—once. On the old tower."

She could only look at me harder. "Do you mean he's a stranger?"

"Oh, very much!"

"Yet you didn't tell me?"

"No—for reasons. But now that you've guessed—"

Mrs. Grose's round eyes encountered this charge. "Ah, I haven't guessed!" she said very simply. "How can I if *you* don't imagine?"

"I don't in the very least."

"You've seen him nowhere but on the tower?"

"And on this spot just now."

Mrs. Grose looked round again. "What was he doing on the tower?"

"Only standing there and looking down at me."

She thought a minute. "Was he a gentleman?"

I found I had no need to think. "No." She gazed in deeper wonder. "No."

"Then nobody about the place? Nobody from the village?"

"Nobody—nobody. I didn't tell you, but I made sure."

She breathed a vague relief: this was, oddly, so much to the good. It only went indeed a little way. "But if he isn't a gentleman—"

"What *is* he? He's a horror."

"A horror?"

"He's—God help me if I know *what* he is!"

Mrs. Grose looked round once more; she fixed her eyes on the duskier distance, then, pulling herself together, turned to me with abrupt inconsequence. "It's time we should be at church."

"Oh, I'm not fit for church!"

"Won't it do you good?"

"It won't do *them*—!" I nodded at the house.

"The children?"

"I can't leave them now."

"You're afraid—?"

I spoke boldly. "I'm afraid of *him*."

Mrs. Grose's large face showed me, at this, for the first time, the far-away faint glimmer of a consciousness more acute: I somehow made out in it the delayed dawn of an idea I myself had not given her and that was as yet quite obscure to me. It comes back to me that I thought instantly of this as something I could get from her; and I felt it to be connected with the desire she presently showed to know more. "When was it—on the tower?"

"About the middle of the month. At this same hour."

"Almost at dark," said Mrs. Grose.

"Oh no, not nearly. I saw him as I see you."

"Then how did he get in?"

"And how did he get out?" I laughed. "I had no opportunity to ask him! This evening, you see," I pursued, "he has not been able to get in."

"He only peeps?"

"I hope it will be confined to that!" She had now let go my hand; she turned away a little. I waited an instant; then I brought out: "Go to church. Good-bye. I must watch."

Slowly she faced me again. "Do you fear for them?"

We met in another long look. "Don't *you*?" Instead of answering she came nearer to the window and, for a minute, applied her face to the glass. "You see how he could see," I meanwhile went on.

She didn't move. "How long was he here?"

"Till I came out. I came to meet him."

Mrs. Grose at last turned round, and there was still more in her face. "*I* couldn't have come out."

"Neither could I!" I laughed again. "But I did come. I have my duty."

"So have I mine," she replied; after which she added: "What is he like?"

"I've been dying to tell you. But he's like nobody."

"Nobody?" she echoed.

"He has no hat." Then seeing in her face that she already, in this, with a deeper dismay, found a touch of picture, I quickly added stroke to stroke. "He has red hair, very red, close-curling, and a pale face, long in shape, with straight, good features and little, rather queer whiskers that are as red as his hair. His eyebrows are, somehow, darker; they look particularly arched and as if they might move a good deal. His eyes are sharp, strange—awfully; but I only know clearly that they're rather small and very fixed. His mouth's wide, and his lips are thin, and except for his little whiskers he's quite clean-shaven. He gives me a sort of sense of looking like an actor."

"An actor!" It was impossible to resemble one less, at least, than Mrs. Grose at that moment.

"I've never seen one, but so I suppose them. He's tall, active, erect," I continued, "but never—no, never!—a gentleman."

My companion's face had blanched as I went on; her round eyes started and her mild mouth gaped. "A gentleman?" she gasped, confounded, stupefied: "a gentleman *he?*"

"You know him then?"

She visibly tried to hold herself. "But he *is* handsome?"

I saw the way to help her. "Remarkably!"

"And dressed—?"

"In somebody's clothes. They're smart, but they're not his own."

She broke into a breathless affirmative groan. "They're the master's!"

I caught it up. "You *do* know him?"

She faltered but a second. "Quint!" she cried.

"Quint?"

"Peter Quint—his own man, his valet, when he was here!"

"When the master was?"

Gaping still, but meeting me, she pieced it all together. "He never wore his hat, but he did wear—well, there were waistcoats missed! They were both here—last year. Then the master went, and Quint was alone."

I followed, but halting a little. "Alone?"

"Alone with *us.*" Then, as from a deeper depth, "In charge," she added.

"And what became of him?"

She hung fire so long that I was still more mystified. "He went too," she brought out at last.

"Went where?"

Her expression, at this, became extraordinary. "God knows where! He died."

"Died?" I almost shrieked.

She seemed fairly to square herself, plant herself more firmly to utter the wonder of it. "Yes. Mr. Quint is dead."

VI.

It took of course more than that particular passage to place us together in presence of what we had now to live with as we could—my dreadful liability to impressions of the order so vividly exemplified, and my companion's knowledge, henceforth,—a knowledge half consternation and half compassion,—of that liability. There had been, this evening, after the revelation that left me, for an hour, so prostrate—there had been, for either of us, no attendance on any service but a little service of tears and vows, of prayers and promises, a climax to the series of mutual challenges and pledges that had straightway ensued on our retreating together to the schoolroom and shutting ourselves up there to have everything out. The result of our having everything out was simply to reduce our situation to the last rigour of its elements. She herself had seen nothing, not the shadow of a shadow, and nobody in the house but the governess was in the governess's plight; yet she accepted without directly impugning my sanity the truth as I gave it to her, and ended by showing me, on this ground, an awe-stricken tenderness, an expression of the sense of my more than questionable privilege, of which the very breath has remained with me as that of the sweetest of human charities.

What was settled between us, accordingly, that night, was that we thought we might bear things together; and I was not even sure that, in spite of her exemption, it was she who had the best of the burden. I knew at this hour, I think, as well as I knew later what I was capable of meeting to shelter my pupils; but it took me some time to be wholly sure of what my honest ally was prepared for to keep terms with so compromising a contract. I was queer company enough—quite as queer as the company I received; but as I trace over what we went through I see how much common ground we must have found in the one idea that, by good fortune, *could* steady us. It was the idea, the second movement, that led me straight out, as I may say, of the inner chamber

of my dread. I could take the air in the court, at least, and there
Mrs. Grose could join me. Perfectly can I recall now the particu-
lar way strength came to me before we separated for the night.
We had gone over and over every feature of what I had seen.

"He was looking for someone else, you say—someone who
was not you?"

"He was looking for little Miles." A portentous clearness
now possessed me. "*That's* whom he was looking for."

"But how do you know?"

"I know, I know, I know!" My exaltation grew. "And *you*
know, my dear!"

She didn't deny this, but I required, I felt, not even so much
telling as that. She resumed in a moment, at any rate: "What if
he should see him?"

"Little Miles? That's what he wants!"

She looked immensely scared again. "The child?"

"Heaven forbid! The man. He wants to appear to *them*."
That he might was an awful conception, and yet, somehow, I
could keep it at bay; which, moreover, as we lingered there,
was what I succeeded in practically proving. I had an absolute
certainty that I should see again what I had already seen, but
something within me said that by offering myself bravely as the
sole subject of such experience, by accepting, by inviting, by
surmounting it all, I should serve as an expiatory victim and
guard the tranquillity of my companions. The children, in especial, I should thus fence about and absolutely save. I recall
one of the last things I said that night to Mrs. Grose.

"It does strike me that my pupils have never mentioned—"

She looked at me hard as I musingly pulled up. "His having
been here and the time they were with him?"

"The time they were with him, and his name, his presence,
his history, in any way."

"Oh, the little lady doesn't remember. She never heard or
knew."

"The circumstances of his death?" I thought with some intensity. "Perhaps not. But Miles would remember—Miles
would know."

"Ah, don't try him!" broke from Mrs. Grose.

I returned her the look she had given me. "Don't be afraid." I continued to think. "It *is* rather odd."

"That he has never spoken of him?"

"Never by the least allusion. And you tell me they were 'great friends'?"

"Oh, it wasn't *him!*" Mrs. Grose with emphasis declared. "It was Quint's own fancy. To play with him, I mean—to spoil him." She paused a moment; then she added: "Quint was much too free."

This gave me, straight from my vision of his face—*such* a face!—a sudden sickness of disgust. "Too free with *my* boy?"

"Too free with everyone!"

I forbore, for the moment, to analyse this description further than by the reflection that a part of it applied to several of the members of the household, of the half-dozen maids and men who were still of our small colony. But there was everything, for our apprehension, in the lucky fact that no discomfortable legend, no perturbation of scullions, had ever, within anyone's memory, attached to the kind old place. It had neither bad name nor ill fame, and Mrs. Grose, most apparently, only desired to cling to me and to quake in silence. I even put her, the very last thing of all, to the test. It was when, at midnight, she had her hand on the schoolroom door to take leave. "I have it from you then—for it's of great importance—that he was definitely and admittedly bad?"

"Oh, not admittedly. *I* knew it—but the master didn't."

"And you never told him?"

"Well, he didn't like tale-bearing—he hated complaints. He was terribly short with anything of that kind, and if people were all right to *him*—"

"He wouldn't be bothered with more?" This squared well enough with my impression of him: he was not a trouble-loving gentleman, nor so very particular perhaps about some of the company *he* kept. All the same, I pressed my interlocutress. "I promise you *I* would have told!"

She felt my discrimination. "I dare say I was wrong. But, really, I was afraid."

"Afraid of what?"

"Of things that man could do. Quint was so clever—he was so deep."

I took this in still more than, probably, I showed. "You weren't afraid of anything else? Not of his effect—?"

"His effect?" she repeated with a face of anguish and waiting while I faltered.

"On innocent little precious lives. They were in your charge."

"No, they were not in mine!" she roundly and distressfully returned. "The master believed in him and placed him here because he was supposed not to be well and the country air so good for him. So he had everything to say. Yes"—she let me have it—"even about *them*."

"Them—that creature?" I had to smother a kind of howl. "And you could bear it!"

"No. I couldn't—and I can't now!" And the poor woman burst into tears.

A rigid control, from the next day, was, as I have said, to follow them; yet how often and how passionately, for a week, we came back together to the subject! Much as we had discussed it that Sunday night, I was, in the immediate later hours in especial—for it may be imagined whether I slept—still haunted with the shadow of something she had not told me. I myself had kept back nothing, but there was a word Mrs. Grose had kept back. I was sure, moreover, by morning, that this was not from a failure of frankness, but because on every side there were fears. It seems to me indeed, in retrospect, that by the time the morrow's sun was high I had restlessly read into the facts before us almost all the meaning they were to receive from subsequent and more cruel occurrences. What they gave me above all was just the sinister figure of the living man—the dead one would keep awhile!— and of the months he had continuously passed at Bly, which, added up, made a formidable stretch. The limit of this evil time had arrived only when, on the dawn of a winter's morning, Peter Quint was found, by a labourer going to early work, stone dead on the road from the village: a catastrophe explained—superficially at least—by a visible wound to his head; such a wound as might have been produced—and as, on the final evidence, *had* been—by a fatal slip, in the dark and after leaving the public house, on the steepish icy slope, a wrong path altogether, at the bottom of which he lay. The icy slope, the turn mistaken at night and in liquor, accounted for much—practically, in the end and after the inquest and boundless chatter, for everything; but there had been matters in his life—strange passages and perils, secret disorders, vices more than suspected—that would have accounted for a good deal more.

I scarce know how to put my story into words that shall be a credible picture of my state of mind; but I was in these days literally able to find a joy in the extraordinary flight of heroism the occasion demanded of me. I now saw that I had been asked for a service admirable and difficult; and there would be a greatness in letting it be seen—oh, in the right quarter!—that I could succeed where many another girl might have failed. It was an immense help to me—I confess I rather applaud myself as I look back!—that I saw my service so strongly and so simply. I was there to protect and defend the little creatures in the world the most bereaved and the most loveable, the appeal of whose helplessness had suddenly become only too explicit, a deep, constant ache of one's own committed heart. We were cut off, really, together; we were united in our danger. They had nothing but me, and I—well, I had *them*. It was in short a magnificent chance. This chance presented itself to me in an image richly material. I was a screen—I was to stand before them. The more I saw, the less they would. I began to watch them in a stifled suspense, a disguised excitement that might well, had it continued too long, have turned to something like madness. What saved me, as I now see, was that it turned to something else altogether. It didn't last as suspense—it was superseded by horrible proofs. Proofs, I say, yes—from the moment I really took hold.

This moment dated from an afternoon hour that I happened to spend in the grounds with the younger of my pupils alone. We had left Miles indoors, on the red cushion of a deep window-seat; he had wished to finish a book, and I had been glad to encourage a purpose so laudable in a young man whose only defect was an occasional excess of the restless. His sister, on the contrary, had been alert to come out, and I strolled with her half an hour, seeking the shade, for the sun was still high and the day exceptionally warm. I was aware afresh, with her, as we went, of how, like her brother, she contrived—it was the charming thing in both children—to let me alone without appearing to drop me and to accompany me without appearing to surround. They were never importunate and yet never listless. My attention to them all really went to seeing them amuse themselves immensely without me: this was a spectacle they seemed actively to prepare and that engaged me as an active admirer. I walked in a world of their invention—they had no occasion whatever to draw upon mine; so that my time was taken only with being, for them, some remarkable person or thing that the game of the moment required and that was merely, thanks to my superior, my exalted stamp, a happy and highly distinguished sinecure. I forget what I was on the present occasion; I only remember that I was something very important and very quiet and that Flora was playing very hard. We were on the edge of the lake, and, as we had lately begun geography, the lake was the Sea of Azof.

Suddenly, in these circumstances, I became aware that, on the other side of the Sea of Azof, we had an interested spectator. The way this knowledge gathered in me was the strangest thing in the world—the strangest, that is, except the very much stranger in which it quickly merged itself. I had sat down with a piece of work—for I was something or other that could sit—on the old stone bench which overlooked the pond; and in this position I began to take in with certitude, and yet without direct vision, the presence, at a distance, of a third person. The old trees, the thick shrubbery, made a great and pleasant shade, but it was all suffused with the brightness of the hot, still hour. There was no ambiguity in anything; none whatever, at least, in the conviction I from one moment to another found myself forming as to what I should see straight before me and across the lake as a consequence of raising my eyes. They were attached at this juncture to the stitching in which I was engaged, and I can feel once more the spasm of my effort not to move them till I should so have steadied myself as to be able to make up my mind what to do. There was an alien object in view—a figure whose right of presence I instantly, passionately questioned. I recollect counting over perfectly the possibilities, reminding myself that nothing was more natural, for instance, than the appearance of one of the men about the place, or even of a messenger, a postman or a tradesman's boy, from the village. That reminder had as little effect on my practical certitude as I was conscious—still even without looking—of its having upon the character and attitude of our visitor. Nothing was more natural than that these things should be the other things that they absolutely were not.

Of the positive identity of the apparition I would assure myself as soon as the small clock of my courage should have ticked out the right second; meanwhile, with an effort that was already sharp enough, I transferred my eyes straight to little Flora, who, at the moment, was about ten yards away. My heart had stood still for an instant with the wonder and terror of the question whether she too would see; and I held my breath while I waited for what a cry from her, what some sudden innocent sign either of interest or of alarm, would tell me. I waited, but nothing came; then, in the first place—and there is something more dire in this, I feel, than in anything I have to relate—I was determined by a sense that, within a minute, all sounds from her had previously dropped; and, in the second, by the circumstance that, also within the minute, she had, in her play, turned her back to the water. This was her attitude when I at last looked at her—looked with the confirmed conviction that we were still, together, under direct personal notice. She had picked up a small flat piece of wood, which happened to have in it a little hole that had evidently suggested to her the idea of sticking in another fragment that might figure as a mast and make the thing a boat. This second morsel, as I watched her, she was very markedly and intently attempting to tighten in its place. My apprehension of what she was doing sustained me so that after some seconds I felt I was ready for more. Then I again shifted my eyes—I faced what I had to face.

VII.

I got hold of Mrs. Grose as soon after this as I could; and I can give no intelligible account of how I fought out the interval. Yet I still hear myself cry as I fairly threw myself into her arms: "They *know*—it's too monstrous: they know, they know!"

"And what on earth—?" I felt her incredulity as she held me.

"Why, all that *we* know—and heaven knows what else be-sides!" Then, as she released me, I made it out to her, made it out perhaps only now with full coherency even to myself. "Two hours ago, in the garden"—I could scarce articulate—"Flora *saw!*"

Mrs. Grose took it as she might have taken a blow in the stomach. "She has told you?" she panted.

"Not a word—that's the horror. She kept it to herself! The child of eight, *that* child!" Unutterable still, for me, was the stupefaction of it.

Mrs. Grose, of course, could only gape the wider. "Then how do you know?"

"I was there—I saw with my eyes: saw that she was perfectly aware."

"Do you mean aware of *him?*"

"No—of *her.*" I was conscious as I spoke that I looked prodigious things, for I got the slow reflection of them in my companion's face. "Another person—this time; but a figure of quite as unmistakeable horror and evil: a woman in black, pale and dreadful—with such an air also, and such a face!—on the other side of the lake. I was there with the child—quiet for the hour; and in the midst of it she came."

"Came how—from where?"

"From where they come from! She just appeared and stood there—but not so near."

"And without coming nearer?"

"Oh, for the effect and the feeling, she might have been as close as you!"

My friend, with an odd impulse, fell back a step. "Was she someone you've never seen?"

"Yes. But someone the child has. Someone *you* have." Then, to show how I had thought it all out: "My predecessor—the one who died."

"Miss Jessel?"

"Miss Jessel. You don't believe me?" I pressed.

She turned right and left in her distress. "How can you be sure?"

This drew from me, in the state of my nerves, a flash of impatience. "Then ask Flora—*she's* sure!" But I had no sooner spoken than I caught myself up. "No, for God's sake, *don't!* She'll say she isn't—she'll lie!"

Mrs. Grose was not too bewildered instinctively to protest. "Ah, how *can* you?"

"Because I'm clear. Flora doesn't want me to know."

"It's only then to spare you."

"No, no—there are depths, depths! The more I go over it, the more I see in it, and the more I see in it the more I fear. I don't know what I *don't* see—what I *don't* fear!"

Mrs. Grose tried to keep up with me. "You mean you're afraid of seeing her again?"

"Oh, no; that's nothing—now!" Then I explained. "It's of *not* seeing her."

But my companion only looked wan. "I don't understand you."

"Why, it's that the child may keep it up—and that the child assuredly *will*—without my knowing it."

At the image of this possibility Mrs. Grose for a moment collapsed, yet presently to pull herself together again, as if from the positive force of the sense of what, should we yield an inch, there would really be to give way to. "Dear, dear—we must keep our heads! And after all, if she doesn't mind it—!" She even tried a grim joke. "Perhaps she likes it!"

"Likes *such* things—a scrap of an infant!"

"Isn't it just a proof of her blessed innocence?" my friend bravely inquired.

She brought me, for the instant, almost round. "Oh, we must clutch at *that*—we must cling to it! If it isn't a proof of what you say, it's a proof of—God knows what! For the woman's a horror of horrors."

Mrs. Grose, at this, fixed her eyes a minute on the ground; then at last raising them, "Tell me how you know," she said.

"Then you admit it's what she was?" I cried.

"Tell me how you know," my friend simply repeated.

"Know? By seeing her! By the way she looked."

"At you, do you mean—so wickedly?"

"Dear me, no—I could have borne that. She gave me never a glance. She only fixed the child."

Mrs. Grose tried to see it. "Fixed her?"

"Ah, with such awful eyes!"

She stared at mine as if they might really have resembled them. "Do you mean of dislike?"

"God help us, no. Of something much worse."

"Worse than dislike?"—this left her indeed at a loss.

"With a determination—indescribable. With a kind of fury of intention."

I made her turn pale. "Intention?"

"To get hold of her." Mrs. Grose—her eyes just lingering on mine—gave a shudder and walked to the window; and while she stood there looking out I completed my statement. "*That's* what Flora knows."

After a little she turned round. "The person was in black, you say?"

"In mourning—rather poor, almost shabby. But—yes—with extraordinary beauty." I now recognised to what I had at last, stroke by stroke, brought the victim of my confidence, for she quite visibly weighed this. "Oh, handsome—very, very," I insisted; "wonderfully handsome. But infamous."

She slowly came back to me. "Miss Jessel—*was* infamous." She once more took my hand in both her own, holding it as tight as if to fortify me against the increase of alarm I might draw from this disclosure. "They were both infamous," she finally said.

So, for a little, we faced it once more together; and I found absolutely a degree of help in seeing it now so straight. "I appreciate," I said, "the great decency of your not having hitherto spoken; but the time has certainly come to give me the whole thing." She appeared to assent to this, but still only in silence; seeing which I went on: "I must have it now. Of what did she die? Come, there was something between them."

"There was everything."

"In spite of the difference—?"

"Oh, of their rank, their condition"—she brought it woefully out. "*She* was a lady."

I turned it over; I again saw. "Yes—she was a lady."

"And he so dreadfully below," said Mrs. Grose.

I felt that I doubtless needn't press too hard, in such company, on the place of a servant in the scale; but there was nothing to prevent an acceptance of my companion's own measure of my predecessor's abasement. There was a way to deal with that, and I dealt; the more readily for my full vision—on the evidence—of our employer's late clever, good-looking "own" man; impudent, assured, spoiled, depraved. "The fellow was a hound."

Mrs. Grose considered as if it were perhaps a little a case for a sense of shades. "I've never seen one like him. He did what he wished."

"With *her*?"

"With them all."

It was as if now in my friend's own eyes Miss Jessel had again appeared. I seemed at any rate, for an instant, to see their evocation of her as distinctly as I had seen her by the pond; and I brought out with decision: "It must have been also what *she* wished!"

Mrs. Grose's face signified that it had been indeed, but she said at the same time: "Poor woman—she paid for it!"

"Then you do know what she died of?" I asked.

"No—I know nothing. I wanted not to know; I was glad enough I didn't; and I thanked heaven she was well out of this!"

"Yet you had, then, your idea—"

"Of her real reason for leaving? Oh, yes—as to that. She couldn't have stayed. Fancy it here—for a governess! And afterwards I imagined—and I still imagine. And what I imagine is dreadful."

"Not so dreadful as what *I* do," I replied; on which I must have shown her—as I was indeed but too conscious—a front of miserable defeat. It brought out again all her compassion for me, and at the renewed touch of her kindness my power to resist broke down. I burst, as I had, the other time, made her burst, into tears; she took me to her motherly breast, and my lamentation overflowed. "I don't do it!" I sobbed in despair; "I don't save or shield them! It's far worse than I dreamed—they're lost!"

VIII.

What I had said to Mrs. Grose was true enough: there were in the matter I had put before her depths and possibilities that I lacked resolution to sound; so that when we met once more in the wonder of it we were of a common mind about the duty of resistance to extravagant fancies. We were to keep our heads if we should keep nothing else—difficult indeed as that might be in the face of what, in our prodigious experience, was least to be questioned. Late that night, while the house slept, we had another talk in my room, when she went all the way with me as to its being beyond doubt that I had seen exactly what I had seen. To hold her perfectly in the pinch of that, I found I had only to ask her how, if I had "made it up," I came to be able to give, of each of the persons appearing to me, a picture disclosing, to the last detail, their special marks—a portrait on the exhibition of which she had instantly recognised and named them. She wished, of course,—small blame to her!—to sink the whole subject; and I was quick to assure her that my own interest in it had now violently taken the form of a search for the way to escape from it. I encountered her on the ground of a probability that with recurrence—for recurrence we took for granted—I should get used to my danger, distinctly professing that my personal exposure had suddenly become the least of my discomforts. It was my new suspicion that was intolerable; and yet even to this complication the later hours of the day had brought a little ease.

On leaving her, after my first outbreak, I had of course returned to my pupils, associating the right remedy for my dismay with that sense of their charm which I had already found to be a thing I could positively cultivate and which had never failed me yet. I had simply, in other words, plunged afresh into Flora's special society and there become aware—it was almost a luxury!—that she could put her little conscious hand straight upon the spot that ached. She had looked at me in sweet speculation and then had accused me to my face of having "cried." I had supposed I had brushed away the ugly signs: but I could literally—for the time, at all events—rejoice, under this fathomless charity, that they had not entirely disappeared. To gaze into the depths of blue of the child's eyes and pronounce their loveliness a trick of premature cunning was to be guilty of a cynicism in preference to which I naturally preferred to abjure my judgment and, so far as might be, my agitation. I couldn't abjure for merely wanting to, but I could repeat to Mrs. Grose—as I did there, over and over, in the small hours—that with their voices in the air, their pressure on one's heart and their fragrant faces against one's cheek, everything fell to the ground but their incapacity and their beauty. It was a pity that, somehow, to settle this once for all, I had equally to re-enumerate the signs of subtlety that, in the afternoon, by the lake, had made a miracle of my show of self-possession. It was a pity to be obliged to re-investigate the certitude of the moment itself and repeat how it had come to me as a revelation that the inconceivable communion I then surprised was a matter, for either party, of habit. It was a pity that I should have had to quaver out again the reasons for my not having, in my delusion, so much as questioned that the little girl saw our visitant even as I actually saw Mrs. Grose herself, and that she wanted, by just so much as she did thus see, to make me suppose she didn't, and at the same time, without showing anything, arrive at a guess as to whether I myself did! It was a pity that I needed once more to describe the portentous little activity by which she sought to divert my attention—the perceptible increase of movement, the greater intensity of play, the singing, the gabbling of nonsense, and the invitation to romp.

Yet if I had not indulged, to prove there was nothing in it, in this review, I should have missed the two or three dim elements of comfort that still remained to me. I should not for instance have been able to asseverate to my friend that I was certain— which was so much to the good—that *I* at least had not betrayed myself. I should not have been prompted, by stress of need, by desperation of mind,—I scarce know what to call it,— to invoke such further aid to intelligence as might spring from pushing my colleague fairly to the wall. She had told me, bit by bit, under pressure, a great deal; but a small shifty spot on the wrong side of it all still sometimes brushed my brow like the wing of a bat; and I remember how on this occasion—for the sleeping house and the concentration alike of our danger

and our watch seemed to help—I felt the importance of giving
the last jerk to the curtain. "I don't believe anything so horrible," I recollect saying; "no, let us put it definitely, my dear,
that I don't. But if I did, you know, there's a thing I should require now, just without sparing you the least bit more—oh, not
a scrap, come!—to get out of you. What was it you had in mind
when, in our distress, before Miles came back, over the letter
from his school, you said, under my insistence, that you didn't
pretend for him that he had not literally *ever* been 'bad'? He
has *not* literally 'ever,' in these weeks that I myself have lived
with him and so closely watched him; he has been an imperturbable little prodigy of delightful, loveable goodness. Therefore you might perfectly have made the claim for him if you
had not, as it happened, seen an exception to take. What was
your exception, and to what passage in your personal observation of him did you refer?"

It was a dreadfully austere inquiry, but levity was not our
note, and, at any rate, before the grey dawn admonished us to
separate I had got my answer. What my friend had had in mind
proved to be immensely to the purpose. It was neither more nor
less than the circumstance that for a period of several months
Quint and the boy had been perpetually together. It was in fact
the very appropriate truth that she had ventured to criticise the
propriety, to hint at the incongruity, of so close an alliance, and
even to go so far on the subject as a frank overture to Miss Jessel. Miss Jessel had, with a most strange manner, requested her
to mind her business, and the good woman had, on this, directly approached little Miles. What she had said to him, since
I pressed, was that *she* liked to see young gentlemen not forget
their station.

I pressed again, of course, at this. "You reminded him that
Quint was only a base menial?"

"As you might say! And it was his answer, for one thing, that
was bad."

"And for another thing?" I waited. "He repeated your words
to Quint?"

"No, not that. It's just what he *wouldn't!*" she could still impress upon me. "I was sure, at any rate," she added, "that he
didn't. But he denied certain occasions."

"What occasions?"

"When they had been about together quite as if Quint were his tutor—and a very grand one—and Miss Jessel only for the little lady. When he had gone off with the fellow, I mean, and spent hours with him."

"He then prevaricated about it—he said he hadn't?" Her assent was clear enough to cause me to add in a moment: "I see. He lied."

"Oh!" Mrs. Grose mumbled. This was a suggestion that it didn't matter; which indeed she backed up by a further remark. "You see, after all, Miss Jessel didn't mind. She didn't forbid him."

I considered. "Did he put that to you as a justification?"

At this she dropped again. "No, he never spoke of it."

"Never mentioned her in connection with Quint?"

She saw, visibly flushing, where I was coming out. "Well, he didn't show anything. He denied," she repeated; "he denied."

Lord, how I pressed her now! "So that you could see he knew what was between the two wretches?"

"I don't know—I don't know!" the poor woman groaned.

"You do know, you dear thing," I replied; "only you haven't my dreadful boldness of mind, and you keep back, out of timidity and modesty and delicacy, even the impression that, in the past, when you had, without my aid, to flounder about in silence, most of all made you miserable. But I shall get it out of you yet! There was something in the boy that suggested to you," I continued, "that he covered and concealed their relation."

"Oh, he couldn't prevent—"

"Your learning the truth? I dare say! But, heavens," I fell, with vehemence, a-thinking, "what it shows that they must, to that extent, have succeeded in making of him!"

"Ah, nothing that's not nice *now!*" Mrs. Grose lugubriously pleaded.

"I don't wonder you looked queer," I persisted, "when I mentioned to you the letter from his school!"

"I doubt if I looked as queer as you!" she retorted with homely force. "And if he was so bad then as that comes to, how is he such an angel now?"

"Yes, indeed—and if he was a fiend at school! How, how, how? Well," I said in my torment, "you must put it to me again, but I shall not be able to tell you for some days. Only, put it to me again!" I cried in a way that made my friend stare. "There are directions in which I must not for the present let myself go." Meanwhile I returned to her first example—the one to which she had just previously referred—of the boy's happy capacity for an occasional slip. "If Quint—on your remonstrance at the time you speak of—was a base menial, one of the things Miles said to you, I find myself guessing, was that you were another." Again her admission was so adequate that I continued: "And you forgave him that?"

"Wouldn't *you?*"

"Oh, yes!" And we exchanged there, in the stillness, a sound of the oddest amusement. Then I went on: "At all events, while he was with the man—"

"Miss Flora was with the woman. It suited them all!"

It suited me too, I felt, only too well; by which I mean that it suited exactly the particularly deadly view I was in the very act of forbidding myself to entertain. But I so far succeeded in checking the expression of this view that I will throw, just here, no further light on it than may be offered by the mention of my final observation to Mrs. Grose. "His having lied and been impudent are, I confess, less engaging specimens than I had hoped to have from you of the outbreak in him of the little natural man. Still," I mused, "they must do, for they make me feel more than ever that I must watch."

It made me blush, the next minute, to see in my friend's face how much more unreservedly she had forgiven him than her anecdote struck me as presenting to my own tenderness an occasion for doing. This came out when, at the schoolroom door, she quitted me. "Surely you don't accuse *him*—"

"Of carrying on an intercourse that he conceals from me? Ah, remember that, until further evidence, I now accuse nobody." Then, before shutting her out to go, by another passage, to her own place, "I must just wait," I wound up.

IX.

I waited and waited, and the days, as they elapsed, took something from my consternation. A very few of them, in fact, passing, in constant sight of my pupils, without a fresh incident, sufficed to give to grievous fancies and even to odious memories a kind of brush of the sponge. I have spoken of the surrender to their extraordinary childish grace as a thing I could actively cultivate, and it may be imagined if I neglected now to address myself to this source for whatever it would yield. Stranger than I can express, certainly, was the effort to struggle against my new lights; it would doubtless have been, however, a greater tension still had it not been so frequently successful. I used to wonder how my little charges could help guessing that I thought strange things about them; and the circumstance that these things only made them more interesting was not by itself a direct aid to keeping them in the dark. I trembled lest they should see that they *were* so immensely more interesting. Putting things at the worst, at all events, as in meditation I so often did, any clouding of their innocence could only be— blameless and foredoomed as they were—a reason the more for taking risks. There were moments when, by an irresistible impulse, I found myself catching them up and pressing them to my heart. As soon as I had done so I used to say to myself: "What will they think of that? Doesn't it betray too much?" It would have been easy to get into a sad, wild tangle about how much I might betray; but the real account, I feel, of the hours of peace that I could still enjoy was that the immediate charm of my companions was a beguilement still effective even under the shadow of the possibility that it was studied. For if it occurred to me that I might occasionally excite suspicion by the little outbreaks of my sharper passion for them, so too I remember wondering if I mightn't see a queerness in the traceable increase of their own demonstrations.

They were at this period extravagantly and preternaturally fond of me; which, after all, I could reflect, was no more than a graceful response in children perpetually bowed over and hugged. The homage of which they were so lavish succeeded, in truth, for my nerves, quite as well as if I never appeared to my-

self, as I may say, literally to catch them at a purpose in it. They
had never, I think, wanted to do so many things for their poor
protectress; I mean—though they got their lessons better and
better, which was naturally what would please her most—in
the way of diverting, entertaining, surprising her; reading her
passages, telling her stories, acting her charades, pouncing out
at her, in disguises, as animals and historical characters, and
above all astonishing her by the "pieces" they had secretly got
by heart and could interminably recite. I should never get to the
bottom—were I to let myself go even now—of the prodigious
private commentary, all under still more private correction,
with which, in these days, I over-scored their full hours. They
had shown me from the first a facility for everything, a general
faculty which, taking a fresh start, achieved remarkable flights.
They got their little tasks as if they loved them, and indulged,
from the mere exuberance of the gift, in the most unimposed
little miracles of memory. They not only popped out at me as
tigers and as Romans, but as Shakespeareans, astronomers,
and navigators. This was so singularly the case that it had presumably much to do with the fact as to which, at the present
day, I am at a loss for a different explanation: I allude to my unnatural composure on the subject of another school for Miles.
What I remember is that I was content not, for the time, to
open the question, and that contentment must have sprung
from the sense of his perpetually striking show of cleverness.
He was too clever for a bad governess, for a parson's daughter,
to spoil; and the strangest if not the brightest thread in the pensive embroidery I just spoke of was the impression I might have
got, if I had dared to work it out, that he was under some influence operating in his small intellectual life as a tremendous
incitement.

  If it was easy to reflect, however, that such a boy could post-
pone school, it was at least as marked that for such a boy to
have been "kicked out" by a school-master was a mystification
without end. Let me add that in their company now—and I
was careful almost never to be out of it—I could follow no
scent very far. We lived in a cloud of music and love and success
and private theatricals. The musical sense in each of the children was of the quickest, but the elder in especial had a mar-

vellous knack of catching and repeating. The school-room piano broke into all gruesome fancies; and when that failed there
were confabulations in corners, with a sequel of one of them
going out in the highest spirits in order to "come in" as something new. I had had brothers myself, and it was no revelation
to me that little girls could be slavish idolaters of little boys.
What surpassed everything was that there was a little boy in
the world who could have for the inferior age, sex, and intelligence so fine a consideration. They were extraordinarily at one,
and to say that they never either quarrelled or complained is to
make the note of praise coarse for their quality of sweetness.
Sometimes, indeed, when I dropped into coarseness, I perhaps
came across traces of little understandings between them by
which one of them should keep me occupied while the other
slipped away. There is a *naïf* side, I suppose, in all diplomacy;
but if my pupils practised upon me, it was surely with the minimum of grossness. It was all in the other quarter that, after a
lull, the grossness broke out.

I find that I really hang back; but I must take my plunge. In
going on with the record of what was hideous at Bly, I not only
challenge the most liberal faith—for which I little care; but—
and this is another matter—I renew what I myself suffered, I
again push my way through it to the end. There came suddenly
an hour after which, as I look back, the affair seems to me to
have been all pure suffering; but I have at least reached the
heart of it, and the straightest road out is doubtless to advance.
One evening—with nothing to lead up or to prepare it—I felt
the cold touch of the impression that had breathed on me the
night of my arrival and which, much lighter then, as I have
mentioned, I should probably have made little of in memory
had my subsequent sojourn been less agitated. I had not gone
to bed; I sat reading by a couple of candles. There was a room-
ful of old books at Bly—last-century fiction, some of it, which,
to the extent of a distinctly deprecated renown, but never to so
much as that of a stray specimen, had reached the sequestered
home and appealed to the unavowed curiosity of my youth. I
remember that the book I had in my hand was Fielding's
Amelia; also that I was wholly awake. I recall further both a
general conviction that it was horribly late and a particular ob-

jection to looking at my watch. I figure, finally, that the white curtain draping, in the fashion of those days, the head of Flora's little bed, shrouded, as I had assured myself long before, the perfection of childish rest. I recollect in short that, though I was deeply interested in my author, I found myself, at the turn of a page and with his spell all scattered, looking straight up from him and hard at the door of my room. There was a moment during which I listened, reminded of the faint sense I had had, the first night, of there being something undefineably astir in the house, and noted the soft breath of the open casement just move the half-drawn blind. Then, with all the marks of a deliberation that must have seemed magnificent had there been anyone to admire it, I laid down my book, rose to my feet, and, taking a candle, went straight out of the room and, from the passage, on which my light made little impression, noiselessly closed and locked the door.

I can say now neither what determined nor what guided me, but I went straight along the lobby, holding my candle high, till I came within sight of the tall window that presided over the great turn of the staircase. At this point I precipitately found myself aware of three things. They were practically simultaneous, yet they had flashes of succession. My candle, under a bold flourish, went out, and I perceived, by the uncovered window, that the yielding dusk of earliest morning rendered it unnecessary. Without it, the next instant, I saw that there was someone on the stair. I speak of sequences, but I required no lapse of seconds to stiffen myself for a third encounter with Quint. The apparition had reached the landing half-way up and was therefore on the spot nearest the window, where at sight of me, it stopped short and fixed me exactly as it had fixed me from the tower and from the garden. He knew me as well as I knew him; and so, in the cold, faint twilight, with a glimmer in the high glass and another on the polish of the oak stair below, we faced each other in our common intensity. He was absolutely, on this occasion, a living, detestable, dangerous presence. But that was not the wonder of wonders; I reserve this distinction for quite another circumstance: the circumstance that dread had unmistakeably quitted me and that there was nothing in me there that didn't meet and measure him.

I had plenty of anguish after that extraordinary moment, but I had, thank God, no terror. And he knew I had not—I found myself at the end of an instant magnificently aware of this. I felt, in a fierce rigour of confidence, that if I stood my ground a minute I should cease—for the time, at least—to have him to reckon with; and during the minute, accordingly, the thing was as human and hideous as a real interview: hideous just because it *was* human, as human as to have met alone, in the small hours, in a sleeping house, some enemy, some adventurer, some criminal. It was the dead silence of our long gaze at such close quarters that gave the whole horror, huge as it was, its only note of the unnatural. If I had met a murderer in such a place and at such an hour, we still at least would have spoken. Something would have passed, in life, between us; if nothing had passed one of us would have moved. The moment was so prolonged that it would have taken but little more to make me doubt if even *I* were in life. I can't express what followed it save by saying that the silence itself—which was indeed in a manner an attestation of my strength—became the element into which I saw the figure disappear; in which I definitely saw it turn as I might have seen the low wretch to which it had once belonged turn on receipt of an order, and pass, with my eyes on the villainous back that no hunch could have more disfigured, straight down the staircase and into the darkness in which the next bend was lost.

X.

I remained awhile at the top of the stair, but with the effect presently of understanding that when my visitor had gone, he had gone: then I returned to my room. The foremost thing I saw there by the light of the candle I had left burning was that Flora's little bed was empty; and on this I caught my breath with all the terror that, five minutes before, I had been able to resist. I dashed at the place in which I had left her lying and over which (for the small silk counterpane and the sheets were disarranged) the white curtains had been deceivingly pulled forward; then my step, to my unutterable relief, produced an answering sound: I perceived an agitation of the window-blind, and the child, ducking down, emerged rosily from the other side of it. She stood there in so much of her candour and so little of her nightgown, with her pink bare feet and the golden glow of her curls. She looked intensely grave, and I had never had such a sense of losing an advantage acquired (the thrill of which had just been so prodigious) as on my consciousness that she addressed me with a reproach. "You naughty: where *have* you been?"—instead of challenging her own irregularity I found myself arraigned and explaining. She herself explained, for that matter, with the loveliest, eagerest simplicity. She had known suddenly, as she lay there, that I was out of the room, and had jumped up to see what had become of me. I had dropped, with the joy of her reappearance, back into my chair—feeling then, and then only, a little faint; and she had pattered straight over to me, thrown herself upon my knee, given herself to be held with the flame of the candle full in the wonderful little face that was still flushed with sleep. I remember closing my eyes an instant, yieldingly, consciously, as before the excess of something beautiful that shone out of the blue of her own. "You were looking for me out of the window?" I said. "You thought I might be walking in the grounds?"

"Well, you know, I thought someone was"—she never blanched as she smiled out that at me.

Oh, how I looked at her now! "And did you see anyone?"

"Ah, *no!*" she returned, almost with the full privilege of childish inconsequence, resentfully, though with a long sweetness in her little drawl of the negative.

At that moment, in the state of my nerves, I absolutely believed she lied; and if I once more closed my eyes it was before the dazzle of the three or four possible ways in which I might take this up. One of these, for a moment, tempted me with such singular intensity that, to withstand it, I must have gripped my little girl with a spasm that, wonderfully, she submitted to without a cry or a sign of fright. Why not break out at her on the spot and have it all over?—give it to her straight in her lovely little lighted face? "You see, you see, you *know* that you do and that you already quite suspect I believe it; therefore why not frankly confess it to me, so that we may at least live with it together and learn perhaps, in the strangeness of our fate, where we are and what it means?" This solicitation dropped, alas, as it came: if I could immediately have succumbed to it I might have spared myself—well you'll see what. Instead of succumbing I sprang again to my feet, looked at her bed, and took a helpless middle way. "Why did you pull the curtain over the place to make me think you were still there?"

Flora luminously considered; after which, with her little divine smile: "Because I don't like to frighten you!"

"But if I had, by your idea, gone out—?"

She absolutely declined to be puzzled; she turned her eyes to the flame of the candle as if the question were as irrelevant, or at any rate as impersonal, as Mrs. Marcet or nine-times-nine. "Oh, but you know," she quite adequately answered, "that you might come back, you dear, and that you *have!*" And after a little, when she had got into bed, I had, for a long time, by almost sitting on her to hold her hand, to prove that I recognised the pertinence of my return.

You may imagine the general complexion, from that moment, of my nights. I repeatedly sat up till I didn't know when; I selected moments when my room-mate unmistakeably slept, and, stealing out, took noiseless turns in the passage and even pushed as far as to where I had last met Quint. But I never met him there again; and I may as well say at once that I on no other occasion saw him in the house. I just missed, on the staircase, on the other hand, a different adventure. Looking down it from the top I once recognised the presence of a woman seated on one of the lower steps with her back presented to me, her body half bowed and her head, in an attitude of woe, in her hands. I had been there but an instant, however, when she vanished without looking round at me. I knew, none the less, exactly what dreadful face she had to show; and I wondered whether, if instead of being above I had been below, I should have had, for going up, the same nerve I had lately shown Quint. Well, there continued to be plenty of chance for nerve. On the eleventh night after my latest encounter with that gentleman—they were all numbered now—I had an alarm that perilously skirted it and that indeed, from the particular quality of its unexpectedness, proved quite my sharpest shock. It was precisely the first night during this series that, weary with watching, I had felt that I might again without laxity lay myself down at my old hour. I slept immediately and, as I afterwards knew, till about one o'clock; but when I woke it was to sit straight up, as completely roused as if a hand had shook me. I had left a light burning, but it was now out, and I felt an instant certainty that Flora had extinguished it. This brought me to my feet and straight, in the darkness, to her bed, which I found she had left. A glance at the window enlightened me further, and the striking of a match completed the picture.

The child had again got up—this time blowing out the taper, and had again, for some purpose of observation or response, squeezed in behind the blind and was peering out into the night. That she now saw—as she had not, I had satisfied myself, the previous time—was proved to me by the fact that she was disturbed neither by my re-illumination nor by the haste I made to get into slippers and into a wrap. Hidden, protected, absorbed, she evidently rested on the sill—the casement opened forward—and gave herself up. There was a great still moon to help her, and this fact had counted in my quick decision. She was face to face with the apparition we had met at the lake, and could now communicate with it as she had not then been able to do. What I, on my side, had to care for was, without disturbing her, to reach, from the corridor, some other window in the same quarter. I got to the door without her hearing me; I got out of it, closed it and listened, from the other side, for some sound from her. While I stood in the passage I had my eyes on her brother's door, which was but ten steps off and which, indescribably, produced in me a renewal of the strange impulse that I lately spoke of as my temptation. What if I should go straight in and march to *his* window?—what if, by risking to his boyish bewilderment a revelation of my motive, I should throw across the rest of the mystery the long halter of my boldness?

This thought held me sufficiently to make me cross to his threshold and pause again. I preternaturally listened; I figured to myself what might portentously be; I wondered if his bed were also empty and he too were secretly at watch. It was a deep, soundless minute, at the end of which my impulse failed. He was quiet; he might be innocent; the risk was hideous; I turned away. There was a figure in the grounds—a figure prowling for a sight, the visitor with whom Flora was engaged; but it was not the visitor most concerned with my boy. I hesitated afresh, but on other grounds and only a few seconds; then I had made my choice. There were empty rooms at Bly, and it was only a question of choosing the right one. The right one suddenly presented itself to me as the lower one—though high above the gardens— in the solid corner of the house that I have spoken of as the old tower. This was a large, square chamber, arranged with some state as a bedroom, the extravagant size of which made it so inconvenient that it had not for years, though kept by Mrs. Grose in exemplary order, been occupied. I had often admired it and I knew my way about in it; I had only, after just faltering at the first chill gloom of its disuse, to pass across it and unbolt as quietly as I could one of the shutters. Achieving this transit, I uncovered the glass without a sound and, applying my face to the pane, was able, the darkness without being much less than within, to see that I commanded the right direction. Then I saw something more. The moon made the night extraordinarily penetrable and showed me on the lawn a person, diminished by distance, who stood there motionless and as if fascinated, looking up to where I had appeared—looking, that is, not so much straight at me as at something that was apparently above me. There was clearly another person above me—there was a person on the tower; but the presence on the lawn was not in the least what I had conceived and had confidently hurried to meet. The presence on the lawn—I felt sick as I made it out—was poor little Miles himself.

XI.

It was not till late next day that I spoke to Mrs. Grose; the rigour with which I kept my pupils in sight making it often difficult to meet her privately, and the more as we each felt the importance of not provoking—on the part of the servants quite as much as on that of the children—any suspicion of a secret flurry or of a discussion of mysteries. I drew a great security in this particular from her mere smooth aspect. There was noth-

ing in her fresh face to pass on to others my horrible confi-
dences. She believed me, I was sure, absolutely: if she hadn't I
don't know what would have become of me, for I couldn't have
borne the business alone. But she was a magnificent monument
to the blessing of a want of imagination, and if she could see in
our little charges nothing but their beauty and amiability, their
happiness and cleverness, she had no direct communication
with the sources of my trouble. If they had been at all visibly
blighted or battered, she would doubtless have grown, on tracing it back, haggard enough to match them; as matters stood,
however, I could feel her, when she surveyed them, with her
large white arms folded and the habit of serenity in all her look,
thank the Lord's mercy that if they were ruined the pieces
would still serve. Flights of fancy gave place, in her mind, to a
steady fireside glow, and I had already begun to perceive how,
with the development of the conviction that—as time went on
without a public accident—our young things could, after all,
look out for themselves, she addressed her greatest solicitude to
the sad case presented by their instructress. That, for myself,
was a sound simplification: I could engage that, to the world,
my face should tell no tales, but it would have been, in the conditions, an immense added strain to find myself anxious about
hers.

At the hour I now speak of she had joined me, under pressure, on the terrace, where, with the lapse of the season, the afternoon sun was now agreeable; and we sat there together
while, before us, at a distance, but within call if we wished, the
children strolled to and fro in one of their most manageable
moods. They moved slowly, in unison, below us, over the lawn,
the boy, as they went, reading aloud from a storybook and
passing his arm round his sister to keep her quite in touch. Mrs.
Grose watched them with positive placidity; then I caught the
suppressed intellectual creak with which she conscientiously
turned to take from me a view of the back of the tapestry. I had
made her a receptacle of lurid things, but there was an odd
recognition of my superiority—my accomplishments and my
function—in her patience under my pain. She offered her mind
to my disclosures as, had I wished to mix a witch's broth and
proposed it with assurance, she would have held out a large

clean saucepan. This had become thoroughly her attitude by
the time that, in my recital of the events of the night, I reached
the point of what Miles had said to me when, after seeing him,
at such a monstrous hour, almost on the very spot where he
happened now to be, I had gone down to bring him in; choosing then, at the window, with a concentrated need of not
alarming the house, rather that method than a signal more res-
onant. I had left her meanwhile in little doubt of my small hope
of representing with success even to her actual sympathy my
sense of the real splendour of the little inspiration with which,
after I had got him into the house, the boy met my final articulate challenge. As soon as I appeared in the moonlight on the
terrace, he had come to me as straight as possible; on which I
had taken his hand without a word and led him, through the
dark spaces, up the staircase where Quint had so hungrily hovered for him, along the lobby where I had listened and trembled, and so to his forsaken room.

Not a sound, on the way, had passed between us, and I had
wondered—oh, *how* I had wondered!—if he were groping
about in his little mind for something plausible and not too
grotesque. It would tax his invention, certainly, and I felt, this
time, over his real embarrassment, a curious thrill of triumph.
It was a sharp trap for the inscrutable! He couldn't play any
longer at innocence; so how the deuce would he get out of it?
There beat in me indeed, with the passionate throb of this question, an equal dumb appeal as to how the deuce *I* should. I was
confronted at last, as never yet, with all the risk attached even
now to sounding my own horrid note. I remember in fact that
as we pushed into his little chamber, where the bed had not
been slept in at all and the window, uncovered to the moonlight, made the place so clear that there was no need of striking
a match—I remember how I suddenly dropped, sank upon the
edge of the bed from the force of the idea that he must know
how he really, as they say, "had" me. He could do what he
liked, with all his cleverness to help him, so long as I should
continue to defer to the old tradition of the criminality of those
caretakers of the young who minister to superstitions and
fears. He "had" me indeed, and in a cleft stick; for who would
ever absolve me, who would consent that I should go unhung,

if, by the faintest tremor of an overture, I were the first to introduce into our perfect intercourse an element so dire? No, no: it was useless to attempt to convey to Mrs. Grose, just as it is scarcely less so to attempt to suggest here, how, in our short, stiff brush in the dark, he fairly shook me with admiration. I was of course thoroughly kind and merciful; never, never yet had I placed on his little shoulders hands of such tenderness as those with which, while I rested against the bed, I held him there well under fire. I had no alternative but, in form at least, to put it to him.

"You must tell me now—and all the truth. What did you go out for? What were you doing there?"

I can still see his wonderful smile, the whites of his beautiful eyes, and the uncovering of his little teeth shine to me in the dusk. "If I tell you why, will you understand?" My heart, at this, leaped into my mouth. *Would* he tell me why? I found no sound on my lips to press it, and I was aware of replying only with a vague, repeated, grimacing nod. He was gentleness itself, and while I wagged my head at him he stood there more than ever a little fairy prince. It was his brightness indeed that gave me a respite. Would it be so great if he were really going to tell me? "Well," he said at last, "just exactly in order that you should do this."

"Do what?"

"Think me—for a change—*bad!*" I shall never forget the sweetness and gaiety with which he brought out the word, nor how, on top of it, he bent forward and kissed me. It was practically the end of everything. I met his kiss and I had to make, while I folded him for a minute in my arms, the most stupendous effort not to cry. He had given exactly the account of himself that permitted least of my going behind it, and it was only with the effect of confirming my acceptance of it that, as I presently glanced about the room, I could say—

"Then you didn't undress at all?"

He fairly glittered in the gloom. "Not at all. I sat up and read."

"And when did you go down?"

"At midnight. When I'm bad I *am* bad!"

"I see, I see—it's charming. But how could you be sure I would know it?"

"Oh, I arranged that with Flora." His answers rang out with a readiness! "She was to get up and look out."

"Which is what she did do." It was I who fell into the trap!

"So she disturbed you, and, to see what she was looking at, you also looked—you saw."

"While you," I concurred, "caught your death in the night air!"

He literally bloomed so from this exploit that he could afford radiantly to assent. "How otherwise should I have been bad enough?" he asked. Then, after another embrace, the incident and our interview closed on my recognition of all the reserves of goodness that, for his joke, he had been able to draw upon.

XII.

The particular impression I had received proved in the morning light, I repeat, not quite successfully presentable to Mrs. Grose, though I reinforced it with the mention of still another remark that he had made before we separated. "It all lies in half-a-dozen words," I said to her, "words that really settle the matter. 'Think, you know, what I *might* do!' He threw that off to show me how good he is. He knows down to the ground what he 'might' do. That's what he gave them a taste of at school."

"Lord, you do change!" cried my friend.

"I don't change—I simply make it out. The four, depend upon it, perpetually meet. If on either of these last nights you had been with either child, you would clearly have understood. The more I've watched and waited the more I've felt that if there were nothing else to make it sure it would be made so by the systematic silence of each. *Never,* by a slip of the tongue, have they so much as alluded to either of their old friends, any more than Miles has alluded to his expulsion. Oh yes, we may sit here and look at them, and they may show off to us there to their fill; but even while they pretend to be lost in their fairy-tale they're steeped in their vision of the dead restored. He's not reading to her," I declared; "they're talking of *them*—they're talking horrors! I go on, I know, as if I were crazy; and it's a wonder I'm not. What I've seen would have made *you* so; but it has only made me more lucid, made me get hold of still other things."

My lucidity must have seemed awful, but the charming creatures who were victims of it, passing and repassing in their interlocked sweetness, gave my colleague something to hold on by; and I felt how tight she held as, without stirring in the breath of my passion, she covered them still with her eyes. "Of what other things have you got hold?"

"Why, of the very things that have delighted, fascinated, and yet, at bottom, as I now so strangely see, mystified and troubled me. Their more than earthly beauty, their absolutely unnatural goodness. It's a game," I went on; "it's a policy and a fraud!"

"On the part of little darlings—?"

"As yet mere lovely babies? Yes, mad as that seems!" The very act of bringing it out really helped me to trace it—follow it all up and piece it all together. "They haven't been good—they've only been absent. It has been easy to live with them, because they're simply leading a life of their own. They're not mine—they're not ours. They're his and they're hers!"

"Quint's and that woman's?"

"Quint's and that woman's. They want to get to them."

Oh, how, at this, poor Mrs. Grose appeared to study them! "But for what?"

"For the love of all the evil that, in those dreadful days, the pair put into them. And to ply them with that evil still, to keep up the work of demons, is what brings the others back."

"Laws!" said my friend under her breath. The exclamation was homely, but it revealed a real acceptance of my further proof of what, in the bad time—for there had been a worse even than this!—must have occurred. There could have been no such justification for me as the plain assent of her experience to whatever depth of depravity I found credible in our brace of scoundrels. It was in obvious submission of memory that she brought out after a moment: "They *were* rascals! But what can they now do?" she pursued.

"Do?" I echoed so loud that Miles and Flora, as they passed at their distance, paused an instant in their walk and looked at us. "Don't they do enough?" I demanded in a lower tone, while the children, having smiled and nodded and kissed hands to us, resumed their exhibition. We were held by it a minute; then I answered: "They can destroy them!" At this my companion did turn, but the inquiry she launched was a silent one, the effect of which was to make me more explicit. "They don't know, as yet, quite how—but they're trying hard. They're seen only across, as it were, and beyond—in strange places and on high places, the top of towers, the roof of houses, the outside of windows, the further edge of pools; but there's a deep design, on either side, to shorten the distance and overcome the obstacle; and the success of the tempters is only a question of time. They've only to keep to their suggestions of danger."

"For the children to come?"

"And perish in the attempt!" Mrs. Grose slowly got up, and I scrupulously added: "Unless, of course, we can prevent!"

Standing there before me while I kept my seat, she visibly turned things over. "Their uncle must do the preventing. He must take them away."

"And who's to make him?"

She had been scanning the distance, but she now dropped on me a foolish face. "You, Miss."

"By writing to him that his house is poisoned and his little nephew and niece mad?"

"But if they *are,* Miss?"

"And if I am myself, you mean? That's charming news to be sent him by a governess whose prime undertaking was to give him no worry."

Mrs. Grose considered, following the children again. "Yes, he do hate worry. That was the great reason—"

"Why those fiends took him in so long? No doubt, though his indifference must have been awful. As I'm not a fiend, at any rate, I shouldn't take him in."

My companion, after an instant and for all answer, sat down

again and grasped my arm. "Make him at any rate come to you."

I stared. "To *me?*" I had a sudden fear of what she might do. " 'Him'?"

"He ought to *be* here—he ought to help."

I quickly rose, and I think I must have shown her a queerer face than ever yet. "You see me asking him for a visit?" No, with her eyes on my face she evidently couldn't. Instead of it even—as a woman reads another—she could see what I myself saw: his derision, his amusement, his contempt for the breakdown of my resignation at being left alone and for the fine machinery I had set in motion to attract his attention to my slighted charms. She didn't know—no one knew—how proud I had been to serve him and to stick to our terms; yet she none the less took the measure, I think, of the warning I now gave her. "If you should so lose your head as to appeal to him for me—"

She was really frightened. "Yes, Miss?"

"I would leave, on the spot, both him and you."

XIII.

It was all very well to join them, but speaking to them proved quite as much as ever an effort beyond my strength—offered, in close quarters, difficulties as insurmountable as before. This situation continued a month, and with new aggravations and particular notes, the note above all, sharper and sharper, of the small ironic consciousness on the part of my pupils. It was not, I am as sure today as I was sure then, my mere infernal imagination: it was absolutely traceable that they were aware of my predicament and that this strange relation made, in a manner, for a long time, the air in which we moved. I don't mean that they had their tongues in their cheeks or did anything vulgar, for that was not one of their dangers: I do mean, on the other hand, that the element of the unnamed and untouched became, between us, greater than any other, and that so much avoidance could not have been so successfully effected without a great deal of tacit arrangement. It was as if, at moments, we

were perpetually coming into sight of subjects before which we
must stop short, turning suddenly out of alleys that we perceived to be blind, closing with a little bang that made us look
at each other—for, like all bangs, it was something louder than
we had intended—the doors we had indiscreetly opened. All
roads lead to Rome, and there were times when it might have
struck us that almost every branch of study or subject of conversation skirted forbidden ground. Forbidden ground was the
question of the return of the dead in general and of whatever,
in especial, might survive, in memory, of the friends little children had lost. There were days when I could have sworn that
one of them had, with a small invisible nudge, said to the other:
"She thinks she'll do it this time—but she *won't!*" To "do it"
would have been to indulge for instance—and for once in a
way—in some direct reference to the lady who had prepared
them for my discipline. They had a delightful endless appetite
for passages in my own history, to which I had again and again
treated them; they were in possession of everything that had
ever happened to me, had had, with every circumstance the
story of my smallest adventures and of those of my brothers
and sisters and of the cat and the dog at home, as well as many
particulars of the eccentric nature of my father, of the furniture
and arrangement of our house, and of the conversation of the
old women of our village. There were things enough, taking
one with another, to chatter about, if one went very fast and
knew by instinct when to go round. They pulled with an art of
their own the strings of my invention and my memory; and
nothing else perhaps, when I thought of such occasions afterwards, gave me so the suspicion of being watched from under
cover. It was in any case over *my* life, *my* past, and *my* friends
alone that we could take anything like our ease—a state of affairs that led them sometimes without the least pertinence to
break out into sociable reminders. I was invited—with no visible connection—to repeat afresh Goody Gosling's celebrated
mot or to confirm the details already supplied as to the cleverness of the vicarage pony.

It was partly at such junctures as these and partly at quite
different ones that, with the turn my matters had now taken,
my predicament, as I have called it, grew most sensible. The

fact that the days passed for me without another encounter ought, it would have appeared, to have done something toward soothing my nerves. Since the light brush, that second night on the upper landing, of the presence of a woman at the foot of the stair, I had seen nothing, whether in or out of the house, that one had better not have seen. There was many a corner round which I expected to come upon Quint, and many a situation that, in a merely sinister way, would have favoured the appearance of Miss Jessel. The summer had turned, the summer had gone; the autumn had dropped upon Bly and had blown out half our lights. The place, with its grey sky and withered garlands, its bared spaces and scattered dead leaves, was like a theatre after the performance—all strewn with crumpled playbills. There were exactly states of the air, conditions of sound and of stillness, unspeakable impressions of the *kind* of ministering moment, that brought back to me, long enough to catch it, the feeling of the medium in which, that June evening out-of-doors, I had had my first sight of Quint, and in which, too, at those other instants, I had, after seeing him through the window, looked for him in vain in the circle of shrubbery. I recognised the signs, the portents—I recognised the moment, the spot. But they remained unaccompanied and empty, and I continued unmolested; if unmolested one could call a young woman whose sensibility had, in the most extraordinary fashion, not declined but deepened. I had said in my talk with Mrs. Grose on that horrid scene of Flora's by the lake—and had perplexed her by so saying—that it would from that moment distress me much more to lose my power than to keep it. I had then expressed what was vividly in my mind: the truth that, whether the children really saw or not—since, that is, it was not yet definitely proved—I greatly preferred, as a safeguard, the fulness of my own exposure. I was ready to know the very worst that was to be known. What I had then had an ugly glimpse of was that my eyes might be sealed just while theirs were most opened. Well, my eyes *were* sealed, it appeared, at present—a consummation for which it seemed blasphemous not to thank God. There was, alas, a difficulty about that: I would have thanked him with all my soul had I not had in a proportionate measure this conviction of the secret of my pupils.

How can I retrace today the strange steps of my obsession? There were times of our being together when I would have been ready to swear that, literally, in my presence, but with my direct sense of it closed, they had visitors who were known and were welcome. Then it was that, had I not been deterred by the very chance that such an injury might prove greater than the injury to be averted, my exultation would have broken out. "They're here, they're here, you little wretches," I would have cried, "and you can't deny it now!" The little wretches denied it with all the added volume of their sociability and their tenderness, in just the crystal depths of which—like the flash of a fish in a stream—the mockery of their advantage peeped up. The shock, in truth, had sunk into me still deeper than I knew on the night when, looking out to see either Quint or Miss Jessel under the stars, I had beheld the boy over whose rest I watched and who had immediately brought in with him—had straightway, there, turned it on me—the lovely upward look with which, from the battlements above me, the hideous apparition of Quint had played. If it was a question of a scare, my discovery on this occasion had scared me more than any other, and it was in the condition of nerves produced by it that I made my actual inductions. They harassed me so that sometimes, at odd moments, I shut myself up audibly to rehearse—it was at once a fantastic relief and a renewed despair—the manner in which I might come to the point. I approached it from one side and the other while, in my room, I flung myself about, but I always broke down in the monstrous utterance of names. As they died away on my lips, I said to myself that I should indeed help them to represent something infamous if, by pronouncing them, I should violate as rare a little case of instinctive delicacy as any schoolroom, probably, had ever known. When I said to myself: "*They* have the manners to be silent, and you, trusted as you are, the baseness to speak!" I felt myself crimson and I covered my face with my hands. After these secret scenes I chattered more than ever, going on volubly enough till one of our prodigious, palpable hushes occurred—I can call them nothing else—the strange, dizzy lift or swim (I try for terms!) into a stillness, a pause of all life, that had nothing to do with the more or less noise that at the moment we might be engaged

in making and that I could hear through any deepened exhilaration or quickened recitation or louder strum of the piano.
Then it was that the others, the outsiders, were there. Though
they were not angels, they "passed," as the French say, causing
me, while they stayed, to tremble with the fear of their addressing to their younger victims some yet more infernal message or more vivid image than they had thought good enough
for myself.

What it was most impossible to get rid of was the cruel idea
that, whatever I had seen, Miles and Flora saw *more*—things
terrible and unguessable and that sprang from dreadful passages of intercourse in the past. Such things naturally left on
the surface, for the time, a chill which we vociferously denied
that we felt; and we had, all three, with repetition, got into
such splendid training that we went, each time, almost automatically, to mark the close of the incident, through the very
same movements. It was striking of the children, at all events,
to kiss me inveterately with a kind of wild irrelevance and
never to fail—one or the other—of the precious question that
had helped us through many a peril. "When do you think he
will come? Don't you think we *ought* to write?"—there was
nothing like that inquiry, we found by experience, for carrying
off an awkwardness. "He" of course was their uncle in Harley
Street; and we lived in much profusion of theory that he might
at any moment arrive to mingle in our circle. It was impossible
to have given less encouragement than he had done to such a
doctrine, but if we had not had the doctrine to fall back upon
we should have deprived each other of some of our finest exhibitions. He never wrote to them—that may have been selfish,
but it was a part of the flattery of his trust of me; for the way in
which a man pays his highest tribute to a woman is apt to be
but by the more festal celebration of one of the sacred laws of
his comfort; and I held that I carried out the spirit of the pledge
given not to appeal to him when I let my charges understand
that their own letters were but charming literary exercises. They
were too beautiful to be posted; I kept them myself; I have
them all to this hour. This was a rule indeed which only added
to the satiric effect of my being plied with the supposition that
he might at any moment be among us. It was exactly as if my

charges knew how almost more awkward than anything else that might be for me. There appears to me, moreover, as I look back, no note in all this more extraordinary than the mere fact that, in spite of my tension and of their triumph, I never lost patience with them. Adorable they must in truth have been, I now reflect, that I didn't in these days hate them! Would exasperation, however, if relief had longer been postponed, finally have betrayed me? It little matters, for relief arrived. I call it relief, though it was only the relief that a snap brings to a strain or the burst of a thunderstorm to a day of suffocation. It was at least change, and it came with a rush.

XIV.

Walking to church a certain Sunday morning, I had little Miles at my side and his sister, in advance of us and at Mrs. Grose's, well in sight. It was a crisp, clear day, the first of its order for some time; the night had brought a touch of frost, and the autumn air, bright and sharp, made the church-bells almost gay. It was an odd accident of thought that I should have happened at such a moment to be particularly and very gratefully struck with the obedience of my little charges. Why did they never resent my inexorable, my perpetual society? Something or other had brought nearer home to me that I had all but pinned the boy to my shawl and that, in the way our companions were marshalled before me, I might have appeared to provide against some danger of rebellion. I was like a gaoler with an eye to possible surprises and escapes. But all this belonged—I mean their magnificent little surrender—just to the special array of the facts that were most abysmal. Turned out for Sunday by his uncle's tailor, who had had a free hand and a notion of pretty waistcoats and of his grand little air, Miles's whole title to independence, the rights of his sex and situation, were so stamped upon him that if he had suddenly struck for freedom I should have had nothing to say. I was by the strangest of chances wondering how I should meet him when the revolution unmistakably occurred. I call it a revolution because I now see how, with the word he spoke, the curtain rose on the last act of my dreadful drama and the catastrophe was precipitated. "Look here, my dear, you know," he charmingly said, "when in the world, please, am I going back to school?"

Transcribed here the speech sounds harmless enough, particularly as uttered in the sweet, high, casual pipe with which, at all interlocutors, but above all at his eternal governess, he threw off intonations as if he were tossing roses. There was something in them that always made one "catch," and I caught, at any rate, now so effectually that I stopped as short as if one of the trees of the park had fallen across the road. There was something new, on the spot, between us, and he was perfectly aware that I recognised it, though, to enable me to do so, he had no need to look a whit less candid and charming than usual. I could feel in him how he already, from my at first finding nothing to reply, perceived the advantage he had gained. I was so slow to find anything that he had plenty of time, after a minute, to continue with his suggestive but inconclusive smile: "You know, my dear, that for a fellow to be with a lady *always*—!" His "my dear" was constantly on his lips for me, and nothing could have expressed more the exact shade of the sentiment with which I desired to inspire my pupils than its fond familiarity. It was so respectfully easy.

But, oh, how I felt that at present I must pick my own phrases! I remember that, to gain time, I tried to laugh, and I seemed to see in the beautiful face with which he watched me how ugly and queer I looked. "And always with the same lady?" I returned.

He neither blenched nor winked. The whole thing was virtually out between us. "Ah, of course, she's a jolly, 'perfect' lady; but, after all, I'm a fellow, don't you see? that's—well, getting on."

I lingered there with him an instant ever so kindly. "Yes, you're getting on." Oh, but I felt helpless!

I have kept to this day the heartbreaking little idea of how he seemed to know that and to play with it. "And you can't say I've not been awfully good, can you?"

I laid my hand on his shoulder, for, though I felt how much better it would have been to walk on, I was not yet quite able. "No, I can't say that, Miles."

"Except just that one night, you know—!"

"That one night?" I couldn't look as straight as he.

"Why, when I went down—went out of the house."

"Oh, yes. But I forget what you did it for."

"You forget?"—he spoke with the sweet extravagance of childish reproach. "Why, it was to show you I could!"

"Oh, yes, you could."

"And I can again."

I felt that I might, perhaps, after all, succeed in keeping my wits about me. "Certainly. But you won't."

"No, not *that* again. It was nothing."

"It was nothing," I said. "But we must go on."

He resumed our walk with me, passing his hand into my arm. "Then when *am* I going back?"

I wore, in turning it over, my most responsible air. "Were you very happy at school?"

He just considered. "Oh, I'm happy enough anywhere!"

"Well, then," I quavered, "if you're just as happy here—!"

"Ah, but that isn't everything! Of course *you* know a lot—"

"But you hint that you know almost as much?" I risked as he paused.

"Not half I want to!" Miles honestly professed. "But it isn't so much that."

"What is it, then?"

"Well—I want to see more life."

"I see; I see." We had arrived within sight of the church and of various persons, including several of the household of Bly, on their way to it and clustered about the door to see us go in. I quickened our step; I wanted to get there before the question between us opened up much further; I reflected hungrily that, for more than an hour, he would have to be silent; and I thought with envy of the comparative dusk of the pew and of the almost spiritual help of the hassock on which I might bend my knees. I seemed literally to be running a race with some confusion to which he was about to reduce me, but I felt that he had got in first when, before we had even entered the churchyard, he threw out—

"I want my own sort!"

It literally made me bound forward. "There are not many of

your own sort, Miles!" I laughed. "Unless perhaps dear little Flora!"

"You really compare me to a baby girl?"

This found me singularly weak. "Don't you, then, *love* our sweet Flora?"

"If I didn't—and you too; if I didn't—!" he repeated as if retreating for a jump, yet leaving his thought so unfinished that, after we had come into the gate, another stop, which he imposed on me by the pressure of his arm, had become inevitable. Mrs. Grose and Flora had passed into the church, the other worshippers had followed, and we were, for the minute, alone among the old, thick graves. We had paused, on the path from the gate, by a low oblong, table-like tomb.

"Yes, if you didn't—?"

He looked, while I waited, about at the graves. "Well, you know what!" But he didn't move, and he presently produced something that made me drop straight down on the stone slab, as if suddenly to rest. "Does my uncle think what *you* think?"

I markedly rested. "How do you know what I think?"

"Ah, well, of course I don't; for it strikes me you never tell me. But I mean does *he* know?"

"Know what, Miles?"

"Why, the way I'm going on."

I perceived quickly enough that I could make, to this inquiry, no answer that would not involve something of a sacrifice of my employer. Yet it appeared to me that we were all, at Bly, sufficiently sacrificed to make that venial. "I don't think your uncle much cares."

Miles, on this, stood looking at me. "Then don't you think he can be made to?"

"In what way?"

"Why, by his coming down."

"But who'll get him to come down?"

"*I* will!" the boy said with extraordinary brightness and emphasis. He gave me another look charged with that expression and then marched off alone into church.

XV.

The business was practically settled from the moment I never followed him. It was a pitiful surrender to agitation, but my being aware of this had somehow no power to restore me. I only sat there on my tomb and read into what my little friend had said to me the fulness of its meaning; by the time I had grasped the whole of which I had also embraced, for absence, the pretext that I was ashamed to offer my pupils and the rest of the congregation such an example of delay. What I said to myself above all was that Miles had got something out of me and that the proof of it, for him, would be just this awkward collapse. He had got out of me that there was something I was much afraid of and that he should probably be able to make use of my fear to gain, for his own purpose, more freedom. My fear was of having to deal with the intolerable question of the grounds of his dismissal from school, for that was really but the question of the horrors gathered behind. That his uncle should arrive to treat with me of these things was a solution that, strictly speaking, I ought now to have desired to bring on; but I could so little face the ugliness and the pain of it that I simply procrastinated and lived from hand to mouth. The boy, to my deep discomposure, was immensely in the right, was in a position to say to me: "Either you clear up with my guardian the mystery of this interruption of my studies, or you cease to expect me to lead with you a life that's so unnatural for a boy." What was so unnatural for the particular boy I was concerned with was this sudden revelation of a consciousness and a plan.

That was what really overcame me, what prevented my going in. I walked round the church, hesitating, hovering; I reflected that I had already, with him, hurt myself beyond repair. Therefore I could patch up nothing, and it was too extreme an effort to squeeze beside him into the pew: he would be so much more sure than ever to pass his arm into mine and make me sit there for an hour in close, silent contact with his commentary on our talk. For the first minute since his arrival I wanted to get away from him. As I paused beneath the high east window and listened to the sounds of worship, I was taken with an impulse that might master me, I felt, completely should I give it the least encouragement. I might easily put an end to my predicament by getting away altogether. Here was my chance; there was no one to stop me; I could give the whole thing up—turn my back and retreat. It was only a question of hurrying again, for a few preparations, to the house which the attendance at church of so many of the servants would practically have left unoccupied. No one, in short, could blame me if I should just drive desperately off. What was it to get away if I got away only till dinner? That would be in a couple of hours, at the end of which—I had the acute prevision—my little pupils would play at innocent wonder about my non-appearance in their train.

"What *did* you do, you naughty, bad thing? Why in the world, to worry us so—and take our thoughts off too, don't you know?—did you desert us at the very door?" I couldn't meet such questions nor, as they asked them, their false little lovely eyes; yet it was all so exactly what I should have to meet that, as the prospect grew sharp to me, I at last let myself go.

I got, so far as the immediate moment was concerned, away; I came straight out of the churchyard and, thinking hard, retracted my steps through the park. It seemed to me that by the time I reached the house I had made up my mind I would fly. The Sunday stillness both of the approaches and of the interior, in which I met no one, fairly excited me with a sense of opportunity. Were I to get off quickly, this way, I should get off without a scene, without a word. My quickness would have to be remarkable, however, and the question of a conveyance was the great one to settle. Tormented, in the hall, with difficulties and obstacles, I remember sinking down at the foot of the staircase—suddenly collapsing there on the lowest step and then, with a revulsion, recalling that it was exactly where more than a month before, in the darkness of night and just so bowed with evil things, I had seen the spectre of the most horrible of women. At this I was able to straighten myself; I went the rest of the way up; I made, in my bewilderment, for the schoolroom, where there were objects belonging to me that I should have to take. But I opened the door to find again, in a flash, my eyes unsealed. In the presence of what I saw I reeled straight back upon my resistance.

Seated at my own table in clear noonday light I saw a person whom, without my previous experience, I should have taken at the first blush for some housemaid who might have stayed at home to look after the place and who, availing herself of rare relief from observation and of the schoolroom table and my pens, ink, and paper, had applied herself to the considerable effort of a letter to her sweetheart. There was an effort in the way that, while her arms rested on the table, her hands with evident weariness supported her head; but at the moment I took this in I had already become aware that, in spite of my entrance, her attitude strangely persisted. Then it was—with the very act of its announcing itself—that her identity flared up in a change of posture. She rose, not as if she had heard me, but with an indescribable grand melancholy of indifference and detachment, and, within a dozen feet of me, stood there as my vile predecessor. Dishonoured and tragic, she was all before me; but even as I fixed and, for memory, secured it, the awful image passed away. Dark as midnight in her black dress, her haggard beauty and her unutterable woe, she had looked at me long enough to appear to say that her right to sit at my table was as good as mine to sit at hers. While these instants lasted indeed I had the extraordinary chill of a feeling that it was I who was the intruder. It was as a wild protest against it that, actually addressing her—"You terrible, miserable woman!"—I heard myself break into a sound that, by the open door, rang through the long passage and the empty house. She looked at me as if she heard me, but I had recovered myself and cleared the air. There was nothing in the room the next minute but the sunshine and a sense that I must stay.

XVI.

I had so perfectly expected that the return of my pupils would be marked by a demonstration that I was freshly upset at having to take into account that they were dumb about my absence. Instead of gaily denouncing and caressing me, they made no allusion to my having failed them, and I was left, for the time, on perceiving that she too said nothing, to study Mrs. Grose's odd face. I did this to such purpose that I made sure they had in some way bribed her to silence; a silence that, however, I would engage to break down on the first private opportunity. This opportunity came before tea: I secured five minutes with her in the housekeeper's room, where, in the twilight, amid a smell of lately-baked bread, but with the place all swept and garnished, I found her sitting in pained placidity before the fire. So I see her still, so I see her best: facing the flame from her straight chair in the dusky, shining room, a large clean image of the "put away"—of drawers closed and locked and rest without a remedy.

"Oh, yes, they asked me to say nothing; and to please them—so long as they were there—of course I promised. But what had happened to you?"

"I only went with you for the walk," I said. "I had then to come back to meet a friend."

She showed her surprise. "A friend—*you*?"

"Oh, yes, I have a couple!" I laughed. "But did the children give you a reason?"

"For not alluding to your leaving us? Yes; they said you would like it better. Do you like it better?"

My face had made her rueful. "No, I like it worse!" But after an instant I added: "Did they say why I should like it better?"

"No; Master Miles only said, 'We must do nothing but what she likes!'"

"I wish indeed he would! And what did Flora say?"

"Miss Flora was too sweet. She said, 'Oh, of course, of course!'—and I said the same."

I thought a moment. "You were too sweet too—I can hear you all. But none the less, between Miles and me, it's now all out."

"All out?" My companion stared. "But what, Miss?"

"Everything. It doesn't matter. I've made up my mind. I came home, my dear," I went on, "for a talk with Miss Jessel."

I had by this time formed the habit of having Mrs. Grose literally well in hand in advance of my sounding that note; so that even now, as she bravely blinked under the signal of my word, I could keep her comparatively firm. "A talk! Do you mean she spoke?"

"It came to that. I found her, on my return, in the school-room."

"And what did she say?" I can hear the good woman still, and the candour of her stupefaction.

"That she suffers the torments—!"

It was this, of a truth, that made her, as she filled out my picture, gape. "Do you mean," she faltered, "—of the lost?"

"Of the lost. Of the damned. And that's why, to share them—" I faltered myself with the horror of it.

But my companion, with less imagination, kept me up. "To share them—?"

"She wants Flora." Mrs. Grose might, as I gave it to her, fairly have fallen away from me had I not been prepared. I still held her there, to show I was. "As I've told you, however, it doesn't matter."

"Because you've made up your mind? But to what?"

"To everything."

"And what do you call 'everything'?"

"Why, sending for their uncle."

"Oh, Miss, in pity do," my friend broke out.

"Ah, but I will, I *will!* I see it's the only way. What's 'out,' as I told you, with Miles is that if he thinks I'm afraid to—and has ideas of what he gains by that—he shall see he's mistaken. Yes, yes; his uncle shall have it here from me on the spot (and before the boy himself if necessary) that if I'm to be reproached with having done nothing again about more school—"

"Yes, Miss—" my companion pressed me.

"Well, there's that awful reason."

There were now clearly so many of these for my poor colleague that she was excusable for being vague. "But—a—which?"

"Why, the letter from his old place."

"You'll show it to the master?"

"I ought to have done so on the instant."

"Oh, no!" said Mrs. Grose with decision.

"I'll put it before him," I went on inexorably, "that I can't undertake to work the question on behalf of a child who has been expelled—"

"For we've never in the least known what!" Mrs. Grose declared.

"For wickedness. For what else—when he's so clever and beautiful and perfect? Is he stupid? Is he untidy? Is he infirm? Is he ill-natured? He's exquisite—so it can be only *that;* and that would open up the whole thing. After all," I said, "it's their uncle's fault. If he left here such people—!"

"He didn't really in the least know them. The fault's mine." She had turned quite pale.

"Well, you shan't suffer," I answered.

"The children shan't!" she emphatically returned.

I was silent awhile; we looked at each other. "Then what am I to tell him?"

"You needn't tell him anything. *I'll* tell him."

I measured this. "Do you mean you'll write—?" Remembering she couldn't, I caught myself up. "How do you communicate?"

"I tell the bailiff. *He* writes."

"And should you like him to write our story?"

My question had a sarcastic force that I had not fully intended, and it made her, after a moment, inconsequently break down. The tears were again in her eyes. "Ah, Miss, *you* write!"

"Well—tonight," I at last answered; and on this we separated.

XVII.

I went so far, in the evening, as to make a beginning. The weather had changed back, a great wind was abroad, and beneath the lamp, in my room, with Flora at peace beside me, I sat for a long time before a blank sheet of paper and listened to the lash of the rain and the batter of the gusts. Finally I went out, taking a candle; I crossed the passage and listened a minute at Miles's door. What, under my endless obsession, I had been impelled to listen for was some betrayal of his not being at rest, and I presently caught one, but not in the form I had expected. His voice tinkled out. "I say, you there—come in." It was a gaiety in the gloom!

I went in with my light and found him, in bed, very wide awake, but very much at his ease. "Well, what are *you* up to?" he asked with a grace of sociability in which it occurred to me that Mrs. Grose, had she been present, might have looked in vain for proof that anything was "out."

I stood over him with my candle. "How did you know I was there?"

"Why, of course I heard you. Did you fancy you made no noise? You're like a troop of cavalry!" he beautifully laughed.

"Then you weren't asleep?"

"Not much! I lie awake and think."

I had put my candle, designedly, a short way off, and then, as he held out his friendly old hand to me, had sat down on the edge of his bed. "What is it," I asked, "that you think of?"

"What in the world, my dear, but *you?*"

"Ah, the pride I take in your appreciation doesn't insist on that! I had so far rather you slept."

"Well, I think also, you know, of this queer business of ours."

I marked the coolness of his firm little hand. "Of what queer business, Miles?"

"Why, the way you bring me up. And all the rest!"

I fairly held my breath a minute, and even from my glimmering taper there was light enough to show how he smiled up at me from his pillow. "What do you mean by all the rest?"

"Oh, you know, you know!"

I could say nothing for a minute, though I felt, as I held his hand and our eyes continued to meet, that my silence had all the air of admitting his charge and that nothing in the whole world of reality was perhaps at that moment so fabulous as our actual relation. "Certainly you shall go back to school," I said, "if it be that that troubles you. But not to the old place—we must find another, a better. How could I know it did trouble you, this question, when you never told me so, never spoke of it at all?" His clear, listening face, framed in its smooth whiteness, made him for the minute as appealing as some wistful patient in a children's hospital; and I would have given, as the resemblance came to me, all I possessed on earth really to be the nurse or the sister of charity who might have helped to cure him. Well, even as it was, I perhaps might help! "Do you know you've never said a word to me about your school—I mean the old one; never mentioned it in any way?"

He seemed to wonder; he smiled with the same loveliness. But he clearly gained time; he waited, he called for guidance. "Haven't I?" It wasn't for *me* to help him—it was for the thing I had met!

Something in his tone and the expression of his face, as I got this from him, set my heart aching with such a pang as it had never yet known; so unutterably touching was it to see his little brain puzzled and his little resources taxed to play, under the spell laid on him, a part of innocence and consistency. "No, never—from the hour you came back. You've never mentioned to me one of your masters, one of your comrades, nor the least little thing that ever happened to you at school. Never, little Miles—no, never—have you given me an inkling of anything that *may* have happened there. Therefore you can fancy how much I'm in the dark. Until you came out, that way, this morning, you had, since the first hour I saw you, scarce even made a reference to anything in your previous life. You seemed so perfectly to accept the present." It was extraordinary how my absolute conviction of his secret precocity (or whatever I might call the poison of an influence that I dared but half to phrase) made him, in spite of the faint breath of his inward trouble, appear as accessible as an older person—imposed him almost as an intellectual equal. "I thought you wanted to go on as you are."

It struck me that at this he just faintly coloured. He gave, at any rate, like a convalescent slightly fatigued, a languid shake of his head. "I don't—I don't. I want to get away."

"You're tired of Bly?"

"Oh, no, I like Bly."

"Well, then—?"

"Oh, *you* know what a boy wants!"

I felt that I didn't know so well as Miles, and I took temporary refuge. "You want to go to your uncle?"

Again, at this, with his sweet ironic face, he made a movement on the pillow. "Ah, you can't get off with that!"

I was silent a little, and it was I, now, I think, who changed colour. "My dear, I don't want to get off!"

"You can't, even if you do. You can't, you can't!"—he lay beautifully staring. "My uncle must come down, and you must completely settle things."

"If we do," I returned with some spirit, "you may be sure it will be to take you quite away."

"Well, don't you understand that that's exactly what I'm working for? You'll have to tell him—about the way you've let it all drop; you'll have to tell him a tremendous lot!"

The exultation with which he uttered this helped me somehow, for the instant, to meet him rather more. "And how much will *you*, Miles, have to tell him? There are things he'll ask you!"

He turned it over. "Very likely. But what things?"

"The things you've never told me. To make up his mind what to do with you. He can't send you back—"

"Oh, I don't want to go back!" he broke in. "I want a new field."

He said it with admirable serenity, with positive unimpeachable gaiety; and doubtless it was that very note that most evoked for me the poignancy, the unnatural childish tragedy, of his probable reappearance at the end of three months with all this bravado and still more dishonour. It overwhelmed me now that I should never be able to bear that, and it made me let myself go. I threw myself upon him and in the tenderness of my pity I embraced him. "Dear little Miles, dear little Miles—!"

My face was close to his, and he let me kiss him, simply taking it with indulgent good-humour. "Well, old lady?"

"Is there nothing—nothing at all that you want to tell me?"

He turned off a little, facing round toward the wall and holding up his hand to look at as one had seen sick children look. "I've told you—I told you this morning."

Oh, I was sorry for him! "That you just want me not to worry you?"

He looked round at me now, as if in recognition of my understanding him; then ever so gently, "To let me alone," he replied.

There was even a singular little dignity in it, something that made me release him, yet, when I had slowly risen, linger beside him. God knows I never wished to harass him, but I felt that merely, at this, to turn my back on him was to abandon or, to put it more truly, to lose him. "I've just begun a letter to your uncle," I said.

"Well, then, finish it!"

I waited a minute. "What happened before?"

He gazed up at me again. "Before what?"

"Before you came back. And before you went away."

For some time he was silent, but he continued to meet my eyes. "What happened?"

It made me, the sound of the words, in which it seemed to me that I caught for the very first time a small faint quaver of consenting consciousness—it made me drop on my knees beside the bed and seize once more the chance of possessing him. "Dear little Miles, dear little Miles, if you *knew* how I want to help you! It's only that, it's nothing but that, and I'd rather die than give you a pain or do you a wrong—I'd rather die than hurt a hair of you. Dear little Miles"—oh, I brought it out now even if I *should* go too far—"I just want you to help me to save you!" But I knew in a moment after this that I had gone too far. The answer to my appeal was instantaneous, but it came in the form of an extraordinary blast and chill, a gust of frozen air and a shake of the room as great as if, in the wild wind, the casement had crashed in. The boy gave a loud, high shriek, which, lost in the rest of the shock of sound, might have seemed, indistinctly, though I was so close to him, a note either of jubilation or of terror. I jumped to my feet again and was conscious of darkness. So for a moment we remained, while I stared about me and saw that the drawn curtains were unstirred and the window tight. "Why, the candle's out!" I then cried.

"It was I who blew it, dear!" said Miles.

XVIII.

The next day, after lessons, Mrs. Grose found a moment to say to me quietly: "Have you written, Miss?"

"Yes—I've written." But I didn't add—for the hour—that my letter, sealed and directed, was still in my pocket. There would be time enough to send it before the messenger should go to the village. Meanwhile there had been, on the part of my pupils, no more brilliant, more exemplary morning. It was exactly as if they had both had at heart to gloss over any recent little friction. They performed the dizziest feats of arithmetic, soaring quite out of *my* feeble range, and perpetrated, in higher spirits than ever, geographical and historical jokes. It was conspicuous of course in Miles in particular that he appeared to wish to show how easily he could let me down. This child, to my memory, really lives in a setting of beauty and misery that no words can translate; there was a distinction all his own in every impulse he revealed; never was a small natural creature, to the uninitiated eye all frankness and freedom, a more ingenious, a more extraordinary little gentleman. I had perpetually to guard against the wonder of contemplation into which my initiated view betrayed me; to check the irrelevant gaze and discouraged sigh in which I constantly both attacked and renounced the enigma of what such a little gentleman could have done that deserved a penalty. Say that, by the dark prodigy I knew, the imagination of all evil *had* been opened up to him: all the justice within me ached for the proof that it could ever have flowered into an act.

He had never, at any rate, been such a little gentleman as when, after our early dinner on this dreadful day, he came round to me and asked if I shouldn't like him, for half an hour, to play to me. David playing to Saul could never have shown a finer sense of the occasion. It was literally a charming exhibition of tact, of magnanimity, and quite tantamount to his saying outright: "The true knights we love to read about never push an advantage too far. I know what you mean now: you mean that—to be let alone yourself and not followed up—you'll cease to worry and spy upon me, won't keep me so close to you, will let me go and come. Well, I 'come,' you see—but I don't go! There'll be plenty of time for that. I do really delight in your society, and I only want to show you that I contended for a principle." It may be imagined whether I resisted this appeal or failed to accompany him again, hand in hand, to the schoolroom. He sat down at the old piano and played as he had never played, and if there are those who think he had better have been kicking a football I can only say that I wholly agree with them. For at the end of a time that under his influence I had quite ceased to measure I started up with a strange sense of having literally slept at my post. It was after luncheon, and by the schoolroom fire, and yet I hadn't really, in the least, slept: I had only done something much worse—I had forgotten. Where, all this time, was Flora? When I put the question to Miles he played on a minute before answering, and then could only say: "Why, my dear, how do *I* know?"—breaking moreover into a happy laugh which, immediately after, as if it were a vocal accompaniment, he prolonged into incoherent, extravagant song.

I went straight to my room, but his sister was not there; then, before going downstairs, I looked into several others. As she was nowhere about she would surely be with Mrs. Grose, whom, in the comfort of that theory, I accordingly proceeded in quest of. I found her where I had found her the evening before, but she met my quick challenge with blank, scared ignorance. She had only supposed that, after the repast, I had carried off both the children; as to which she was quite in her right, for it was the very first time I had allowed the little girl out of my sight without some special provision. Of course now indeed she might be with the maids, so that the immediate thing was to look for her without an air of alarm. This we promptly arranged between us; but when, ten minutes later and in pursuance of our arrangement, we met in the hall, it was only to report on either side that after guarded inquiries we had altogether failed to trace her. For a minute there, apart from observation, we exchanged mute alarms, and I could feel with what high interest my friend returned me all those I had from the first given her.

"She'll be above," she presently said—"in one of the rooms you haven't searched."

"No; she's at a distance." I had made up my mind. "She has gone out."

Mrs. Grose stared. "Without a hat?"

I naturally also looked volumes. "Isn't that woman always without one?"

"She's with *her?*"

"She's with *her!*" I declared. "We must find them."

My hand was on my friend's arm, but she failed for the moment, confronted with such an account of the matter, to respond to my pressure. She communed, on the contrary, on the spot, with her uneasiness. "And where's Master Miles?"

"Oh, *he's* with Quint. They're in the schoolroom."

"Lord, Miss!" My view, I was myself aware—and therefore I suppose my tone—had never yet reached so calm an assurance.

"The trick's played," I went on; "they've successfully worked their plan. He found the most divine little way to keep me quiet while she went off."

" 'Divine'?" Mrs. Grose bewilderedly echoed.

"Infernal, then!" I almost cheerfully rejoined. "He has provided for himself as well. But come!"

She had helplessly gloomed at the upper regions. "You leave him—?"

"So long with Quint? Yes—I don't mind that now."

She always ended, at these moments, by getting possession of my hand, and in this manner she could at present still stay me. But after gasping an instant at my sudden resignation, "Because of your letter?" she eagerly brought out.

I quickly, by way of answer, felt for my letter, drew it forth, held it up, and then, freeing myself, went and laid it on the great hall-table. "Luke will take it," I said as I came back. I reached the house-door and opened it; I was already on the steps.

My companion still demurred: the storm of the night and the early morning had dropped, but the afternoon was damp and grey. I came down to the drive while she stood in the doorway. "You go with nothing on?"

"What do I care when the child has nothing? I can't wait to dress," I cried, "and if you must do so, I leave you. Try meanwhile, yourself, upstairs."

"With *them*?" Oh, on this, the poor woman promptly joined me!

XIX.

We went straight to the lake, as it was called at Bly, and I dare say rightly called, though I reflect that it may in fact have been a sheet of water less remarkable than it appeared to my untravelled eyes. My acquaintance with sheets of water was small, and the pool of Bly, at all events on the few occasions of my consenting, under the protection of my pupils, to affront its surface in the old flat-bottomed boat moored there for our use, had impressed me both with its extent and its agitation. The usual place of embarkation was half a mile from the house, but I had an intimate conviction that, wherever Flora might be, she was not near home. She had not given me the slip for any small adventure, and, since the day of the very great one that I had shared with her by the pond, I had been aware, in our walks, of the quarter to which she most inclined. This was why I had now given to Mrs. Grose's steps so marked a direction—a direction that made her, when she perceived it, oppose a resistance that showed me she was freshly mystified. "You're going to the water, Miss?—you think she's *in*—?"

"She may be, though the depth is, I believe, nowhere very great. But what I judge most likely is that she's on the spot from which, the other day, we saw together what I told you."

"When she pretended not to see—?"

"With that astounding self-possession! I've always been sure she wanted to go back alone. And now her brother has managed it for her."

Mrs. Grose still stood where she had stopped. "You suppose they really *talk* of them?"

I could meet this with a confidence! "They say things that, if we heard them, would simply appall us."

"And if she *is* there—?"

"Yes?"

"Then Miss Jessel is?"

"Beyond a doubt. You shall see."

"Oh, thank you!" my friend cried, planted so firm that, taking it in, I went straight on without her. By the time I reached the pool, however, she was close behind me, and I knew that, whatever, to her apprehension, might befall me, the exposure of my society struck her as her least danger. She exhaled a moan of relief as we at last came in sight of the greater part of the water without a sight of the child. There was no trace of Flora on that nearer side of the bank where my observation of her had been most startling, and none on the opposite edge, where, save for a margin of some twenty yards, a thick copse came down to the water. The pond, oblong in shape, had a width so scant compared to its length that, with its ends out of view, it might have been taken for a scant river. We looked at the empty expanse, and then I felt the suggestion of my friend's eyes. I knew what she meant and I replied with a negative head-shake.

"No, no; wait! She has taken the boat."

My companion stared at the vacant mooring-place and then again across the lake. "Then where is it?"

"Our not seeing it is the strongest of proofs. She has used it to go over, and then has managed to hide it."

"All alone—that child?"

"She's not alone, and at such times she's not a child: she's an old, old woman." I scanned all the visible shore while Mrs. Grose took again, into the queer element I offered her, one of her plunges of submission; then I pointed out that the boat might perfectly be in a small refuge formed by one of the re-cesses of the pool, an indentation masked, for the hither side, by a projection of the bank and by a clump of trees growing close to the water.

"But if the boat's there, where on earth's *she?*" my colleague anxiously asked.

"That's exactly what we must learn." And I started to walk further.

"By going all the way round?"

"Certainly, far as it is. It will take us but ten minutes, but it's far enough to have made the child prefer not to walk. She went straight over."

"Laws!" cried my friend again; the chain of my logic was ever too much for her. It dragged her at my heels even now, and when we had got half-way round—a devious, tiresome process, on ground much broken and by a path choked with over-growth—I paused to give her breath. I sustained her with a grateful arm, assuring her that she might hugely help me; and this started us afresh, so that in the course of but few minutes more we reached a point from which we found the boat to be where I had supposed it. It had been intentionally left as much as possible out of sight and was tied to one of the stakes of a fence that came, just there, down to the brink and that had been an assistance to disembarking. I recognised, as I looked at the pair of short, thick oars, quite safely drawn up, the prodigious character of the feat for a little girl; but I had lived, by this time, too long among wonders and had panted to too many livelier measures. There was a gate in the fence, through which we passed, and that brought us, after a trifling interval, more into the open. Then, "There she is!" we both exclaimed at once.

Flora, a short way off, stood before us on the grass and smiled as if her performance was now complete. The next thing she did, however, was to stoop straight down and pluck—quite as if it were all she was there for—a big, ugly spray of withered fern. I instantly became sure she had just come out of the copse. She waited for us, not herself taking a step, and I was conscious of the rare solemnity with which we presently approached her. She smiled and smiled, and we met; but it was all done in a silence by this time flagrantly ominous. Mrs. Grose was the first to break the spell: she threw herself on her knees and, drawing the child to her breast, clasped in a long embrace the little tender, yielding body. While this dumb convulsion lasted I could only watch it—which I did the more intently when I saw Flora's face peep at me over our companion's shoulder. It was serious now—the flicker had left it; but it strengthened the pang with which I at that moment envied Mrs. Grose the simplicity of *her* relation. Still, all this while, nothing more passed between us save that Flora had let her foolish fern again drop to the ground. What she and I had virtually said to each other was that pretexts were useless now. When Mrs. Grose finally got up she kept the child's hand, so that the two were still before me; and the singular reticence of our communion was even more marked in the frank look she launched me. "I'll be hanged," it said, "if *I'll* speak!"

It was Flora who, gazing all over me in candid wonder, was

the first. She was struck with our bareheaded aspect. "Why, where are your things?"

"Where yours are, my dear!" I promptly returned.

She had already got back her gaiety, and appeared to take this as an answer quite sufficient. "And where's Miles?" she went on.

There was something in the small valour of it that quite finished me: these three words from her were, in a flash like the glitter of a drawn blade, the jostle of the cup that my hand, for weeks and weeks, had held high and full to the brim and that now, even before speaking, I felt overflow in a deluge. "I'll tell you if you'll tell *me*—" I heard myself say, then heard the tremor in which it broke.

"Well, what?"

Mrs. Grose's suspense blazed at me, but it was too late now, and I brought the thing out handsomely. "Where, my pet, is Miss Jessel?"

XX.

Just as in the churchyard with Miles, the whole thing was upon us. Much as I had made of the fact that this name had never once, between us, been sounded, the quick, smitten glare with which the child's face now received it fairly likened my breach of the silence to the smash of a pane of glass. It added to the interposing cry, as if to stay the blow, that Mrs. Grose, at the same instant, uttered over my violence—the shriek of a creature scared, or rather wounded, which, in turn, within a few seconds, was completed by a gasp of my own. I seized my colleague's arm. "She's there, she's there!"

Miss Jessel stood before us on the opposite bank exactly as she had stood the other time, and I remember, strangely, as the first feeling now produced in me, my thrill of joy at having brought on a proof. She was there, and I was justified; she was there, and I was neither cruel nor mad. She was there for poor scared Mrs. Grose, but she was there most for Flora; and no moment of my monstrous time was perhaps so extraordinary as that in which I consciously threw out to her—with the sense that, pale and ravenous demon as she was, she would catch and understand it—an inarticulate message of gratitude. She rose erect on the spot my friend and I had lately quitted, and there was not, in all the long reach of her desire, an inch of her evil that fell short. This first vividness of vision and emotion were things of a few seconds, during which Mrs. Grose's dazed blink across to where I pointed struck me as a sovereign sign that she too at last saw, just as it carried my own eyes precipitately to the child. The revelation then of the manner in which Flora was affected startled me, in truth, far more than it would have done to find her also merely agitated, for direct dismay was of course not what I had expected. Prepared and on her guard as our pursuit had actually made her, she would repress every betrayal; and I was therefore shaken, on the spot, by my first glimpse of the particular one for which I had not allowed. To see her, without a convulsion of her small pink face, not even feign to glance in the direction of the prodigy I announced, but only, instead of that, turn at *me* an expression of hard, still gravity, an expression absolutely new and unprecedented and that appeared to read and accuse and judge me—this was a stroke that somehow converted the little girl herself into the very presence that could make me quail. I quailed even though my certitude that she thoroughly saw was never greater than at that instant, and in the immediate need to defend myself I called it passionately to witness. "She's there, you little unhappy thing—there, there, *there,* and you see her as well as you see me!" I had said shortly before to Mrs. Grose that she was not at these times a child, but an old, old woman, and that description of her could not have been more strikingly confirmed than in the way in which, for all answer to this, she simply showed me, without a concession, an admission, of her eyes, a countenance of deeper and deeper, of indeed suddenly quite fixed, reprobation. I was by this time—if I can put the whole thing at all together—more appalled at what I may properly call her manner than at anything else, though it was simultaneously with this that I became aware of having Mrs. Grose also, and very formidably, to reckon with. My elder companion, the next moment, at any rate, blotted out everything but her own flushed face and her loud, shocked protest, a burst of high disapproval. "What a dreadful turn, to be sure, Miss! Where on earth do you see anything?"

I could only grasp her more quickly yet, for even while she spoke the hideous plain presence stood undimmed and undaunted. It had already lasted a minute, and it lasted while I continued, seizing my colleague, quite thrusting her at it and presenting her to it, to insist with my pointing hand. "You don't see her exactly as *we* see?—you mean to say you don't now—*now?* She's as big as a blazing fire! Only look, dearest woman, *look*—!" She looked, even as I did, and gave me, with her deep groan of negation, repulsion, compassion—the mixture with her pity of her relief at her exemption—a sense, touching to me even then, that she would have backed me up if she could. I might well have needed that, for with this hard blow of the proof that her eyes were hopelessly sealed I felt my own situation horribly crumble, I felt—I saw—my livid predecessor press, from her position, on my defeat, and I was conscious, more than all, of what I should have from this instant to deal with in the astounding little attitude of Flora. Into this attitude Mrs. Grose immediately and violently entered, breaking, even while there pierced through my sense of ruin a prodigious private triumph, into breathless reassurance.

"She isn't there, little lady, and nobody's there—and you never see nothing, my sweet! How can poor Miss Jessel—when poor Miss Jessel's dead and buried? *We* know, don't we, love?"—and she appealed, blundering in, to the child. "It's all a mere mistake and a worry and a joke—and we'll go home as fast as we can!"

Our companion, on this, had responded with a strange, quick primness of propriety, and they were again, with Mrs. Grose on her feet, united, as it were, in pained opposition to me. Flora continued to fix me with her small mask of reprobation, and even at that minute I prayed God to forgive me for seeming to see that, as she stood there holding tight to our friend's dress, her incomparable childish beauty had suddenly failed, had quite vanished. I've said it already—she was literally, she was hideously, hard; she had turned common and almost ugly. "I don't know what you mean. I see nobody. I see nothing. I never *have*. I think you're cruel. I don't like you!"

Then, after this deliverance, which might have been that of a vulgarly pert little girl in the street, she hugged Mrs. Grose more closely and buried in her skirts the dreadful little face. In this position she produced an almost furious wail. "Take me away, take me away—oh, take me away from *her!*"

"From *me?*" I panted.

"From you—from you!" she cried.

Even Mrs. Grose looked across at me dismayed, while I had nothing to do but communicate again with the figure that, on the opposite bank, without a movement, as rigidly still as if catching, beyond the interval, our voices, was as vividly there for my disaster as it was not there for my service. The wretched child had spoken exactly as if she had got from some outside source each of her stabbing little words, and I could therefore, in the full despair of all I had to accept, but sadly shake my head at her. "If I had ever doubted, all my doubt would at present have gone. I've been living with the miserable truth, and now it has only too much closed round me. Of course I've lost you: I've interfered, and you've seen—under *her* dictation"— with which I faced, over the pool again, our infernal witness— "the easy and perfect way to meet it. I've done my best, but I've lost you. Good-bye." For Mrs. Grose I had an imperative, an almost frantic "Go, go!" before which, in infinite distress, but mutely possessed of the little girl and clearly convinced, in spite of her blindness, that something awful had occurred and some collapse engulfed us, she retreated, by the way we had come, as fast as she could move.

Of what first happened when I was left alone I had no subsequent memory. I only knew that at the end of, I suppose, a quarter of an hour, an odorous dampness and roughness, chilling and piercing my trouble, had made me understand that I must have thrown myself, on my face, on the ground and given way to a wildness of grief. I must have lain there long and cried and sobbed, for when I raised my head the day was almost done. I got up and looked a moment, through the twilight, at the grey pool and its blank, haunted edge, and then I took, back to the house, my dreary and difficult course. When I reached the gate in the fence the boat, to my surprise, was gone, so that I had a fresh reflection to make on Flora's extraordinary command of the situation. She passed that night, by the most tacit, and I should add, were not the word so grotesque a false note, the happiest of arrangements, with Mrs. Grose. I saw neither of them on my return, but, on the other hand, as by an ambiguous compensation, I saw a great deal of Miles. I saw—I can use no other phrase—so much of him that it was as if it were more than it had ever been. No evening I had passed at Bly had the portentous quality of this one; in spite of which—and in spite also of the deeper depths of consternation that had opened beneath my feet—there was literally, in the ebbing actual, an extraordinarily sweet sadness. On reaching the house I had never so much as looked for the boy; I had simply gone straight to my room to change what I was wearing and to take in, at a glance, much material testimony to Flora's rupture. Her little belongings had all been removed. When later, by the schoolroom fire, I was served with tea by the usual maid, I indulged, on the article of my other pupil, in no inquiry whatever. He had his freedom now—he might have it to the end! Well, he did have it; and it consisted—in part at least—of his coming in at about eight o'clock and sitting down with me in silence. On the removal of the tea-things I had blown out the candles and drawn my chair closer: I was conscious of a mortal coldness and felt as if I should never again be warm. So, when he appeared, I was sitting in the glow with my thoughts. He paused a moment by the door as if to look at me; then—as if to share them—came to the other side of the hearth and sank into a chair. We sat there in absolute stillness; yet he wanted, I felt, to be with me.

XXI.

Before a new day, in my room, had fully broken, my eyes opened to Mrs. Grose, who had come to my bedside with worse news. Flora was so markedly feverish that an illness was perhaps at hand; she had passed a night of extreme unrest, a night agitated above all by fears that had for their subject not in the least her former, but wholly her present, governess. It was not against the possible re-entrance of Miss Jessel on the scene that she protested—it was conspicuously and passionately against mine. I was promptly on my feet of course, and with an immense deal to ask; the more that my friend had discernibly now girded her loins to meet me once more. This I felt as soon as I had put to her the question of her sense of the child's sincerity as against my own. "She persists in denying to you that she saw, or has ever seen, anything?"

My visitor's trouble, truly, was great. "Ah, Miss, it isn't a matter on which I can push her! Yet it isn't either, I must say, as if I much needed to. It has made her, every inch of her, quite old."

"Oh, I see her perfectly from here. She resents, for all the world like some high little personage, the imputation on her truthfulness and, as it were, her respectability. 'Miss Jessel indeed—*she!*' Ah, she's 'respectable,' the chit! The impression she gave me there yesterday was, I assure you, the very strangest of all; it was quite beyond any of the others. I *did* put my foot in it! She'll never speak to me again."

Hideous and obscure as it all was, it held Mrs. Grose briefly silent; then she granted my point with a frankness which, I made sure, had more behind it. "I think indeed, Miss, she never will. She do have a grand manner about it!"

"And that manner"—I summed it up—"is practically what's the matter with her now!"

Oh, that manner, I could see in my visitor's face, and not a little else besides! "She asks me every three minutes if I think you're coming in."

"I see—I see." I too, on my side, had so much more than worked it out. "Has she said to you since yesterday—except to repudiate her familiarity with anything so dreadful—a single other word about Miss Jessel?"

"Not one, Miss. And of course you know," my friend added, "I took it from her, by the lake, that, just then and there at least, there *was* nobody."

"Rather! And, naturally, you take it from her still."

"I don't contradict her. What else can I do?"

"Nothing in the world! You've the cleverest little person to deal with. They've made them—their two friends, I mean—still cleverer even than nature did; for it was wondrous material to play on! Flora has now her grievance, and she'll work it to the end."

"Yes, Miss; but to *what* end?"

"Why, that of dealing with me to her uncle. She'll make me out to him the lowest creature—!"

I winced at the fair show of the scene in Mrs. Grose's face; she looked for a minute is if she sharply saw them together. "And him who thinks so well of you!"

"He has an odd way—it comes over me now," I laughed, "—of proving it! But that doesn't matter. What Flora wants, of course, is to get rid of me."

My companion bravely concurred. "Never again to so much as look at you."

"So that what you've come to me now for," I asked, "is to speed me on my way?" Before she had time to reply, however, I had her in check. "I've a better idea—the result of my reflections. My going *would* seem the right thing, and on Sunday I was terribly near it. Yet that won't do. It's *you* who must go. You must take Flora."

My visitor, at this, did speculate. "But where in the world—?"

"Away from here. Away from *them*. Away, even most of all, now, from me. Straight to her uncle."

"Only to tell on you—?"

"No, not 'only'! To leave me, in addition, with my remedy."

She was still vague. "And what *is* your remedy?"

"Your loyalty, to begin with. And then Miles's."

She looked at me hard. "Do you think he—?"

"Won't, if he has the chance, turn on me? Yes, I venture still to think it. At all events, I want to try. Get off with his sister as soon as possible and leave me with him alone." I was amazed, myself, at the spirit I had still in reserve, and therefore perhaps a trifle the more disconcerted at the way in which, in spite of this fine example of it, she hesitated. "There's one thing, of course," I went on: "they mustn't, before she goes, see each other for three seconds." Then it came over me that, in spite of Flora's presumable sequestration from the instant of her return from the pool, it might already be too late. "Do you mean," I anxiously asked, "that they *have* met?"

At this she quite flushed. "Ah, Miss, I'm not such a fool as that! If I've been obliged to leave her three or four times, it has been each time with one of the maids, and at present, though she's alone, she's locked in safe. And yet—and yet!" There were too many things.

"And yet what?"

"Well, are you so sure of the little gentleman?"

"I'm not sure of anything but *you*. But I have, since last evening, a new hope. I think he wants to give me an opening. I do believe that—poor little exquisite wretch!—he wants to speak. Last evening, in the firelight and the silence, he sat with me for two hours as if it were just coming."

Mrs. Grose looked hard, through the window, at the grey, gathering day. "And did it come?"

"No, though I waited and waited, I confess it didn't, and it was without a breach of the silence or so much as a faint allusion to his sister's condition and absence that we at last kissed for good-night. All the same," I continued, "I can't, if her uncle sees her, consent to his seeing her brother without my having given the boy—and most of all because things have got so bad—a little more time."

My friend appeared on this ground more reluctant than I could quite understand. "What do you mean by more time?"

"Well, a day or two—really to bring it out. He'll then be on *my* side—of which you see the importance. If nothing comes, I shall only fail, and you will, at the worst, have helped me by doing, on your arrival in town, whatever you may have found possible." So I put it before her, but she continued for a little so inscrutably embarrassed that I came again to her aid. "Unless, indeed," I wound up, "you really want *not* to go."

I could see it, in her face, at last clear itself; she put out her hand to me as a pledge. "I'll go—I'll go. I'll go this morning."

I wanted to be very just. "If you *should* wish still to wait, I would engage she shouldn't see me."

"No, no: it's the place itself. She must leave it." She held me a moment with heavy eyes, then brought out the rest. "Your idea's the right one. I myself, Miss—"

"Well?"

"I can't stay."

The look she gave me with it made me jump at possibilities. "You mean that, since yesterday, you *have* seen—?"

She shook her head with dignity. "I've *heard*—!"

"Heard?"

"From that child—horrors! There!" she sighed with tragic relief. "On my honour, Miss, she says things—!" But at this evocation she broke down; she dropped, with a sudden sob, upon my sofa and, as I had seen her do before, gave way to all the grief of it.

It was quite in another manner that I, for my part, let myself go. "Oh, thank God!"

She sprang up again at this, drying her eyes with a groan. "'Thank God'?"

"It so justifies me!"

"It does that, Miss!"

I couldn't have desired more emphasis, but I just hesitated. "She's so horrible?"

I saw my colleague scarce knew how to put it. "Really shocking."

"And about me?"

"About you, Miss—since you must have it. It's beyond everything, for a young lady; and I can't think wherever she must have picked up—"

"The appalling language she applied to me? I can, then!" I broke in with a laugh that was doubtless significant enough.

It only, in truth, left my friend still more grave. "Well, perhaps I ought to also—since I've heard some of it before! Yet I can't bear it," the poor woman went on while, with the same movement, she glanced, on my dressing-table, at the face of my watch. "But I must go back."

I kept her, however. "Ah, if you can't bear it—!"

"How can I stop with her, you mean? Why, just *for* that: to get her away. Far from this," she pursued, "far from *them*—"

"She may be different? she may be free?" I seized her almost with joy. "Then, in spite of yesterday, you *believe*—"

"In such doings?" Her simple description of them required, in the light of her expression, to be carried no further, and she gave me the whole thing as she had never done. "I believe."

Yes, it was a joy, and we were still shoulder to shoulder: if I might continue sure of that I should care but little what else happened. My support in the presence of disaster would be the same as it had been in my early need of confidence, and if my friend would answer for my honesty, I would answer for all the rest. On the point of taking leave of her, none the less, I was to some extent embarrassed. "There's one thing of course—it occurs to me—to remember. My letter, giving the alarm, will have reached town before you."

I now perceived still more how she had been beating about the bush and how weary at last it had made her. "Your letter won't have got there. Your letter never went."

"What then became of it?"

"Goodness knows! Master Miles—"

"Do you mean *he* took it?" I gasped.

She hung fire, but she overcame her reluctance. "I mean that I saw yesterday, when I came back with Miss Flora, that it wasn't where you had put it. Later in the evening I had the chance to question Luke, and he declared that he had neither noticed nor touched it." We could only exchange, on this, one of our deeper mutual soundings, and it was Mrs. Grose who first brought up the plumb with an almost elate "You see!"

"Yes, I see that if Miles took it instead he probably will have read it and destroyed it."

"And don't you see anything else?"

I faced her a moment with a sad smile. "It strikes me that by this time your eyes are open even wider than mine."

They proved to be so indeed, but she could still blush, almost, to show it. "I make out now what he must have done at school." And she gave, in her simple sharpness, an almost droll disillusioned nod. "He stole!"

I turned it over—I tried to be more judicial. "Well—perhaps."

She looked as if she found me unexpectedly calm. "He stole *letters!*"

She couldn't know my reasons for a calmness after all pretty shallow; so I showed them off as I might. "I hope then it was to more purpose than in this case! The note, at any rate, that I put on the table yesterday," I pursued, "will have given him so scant an advantage—for it contained only the bare demand for an interview—that he is already much ashamed of having gone so far for so little, and that what he had on his mind last evening was precisely the need of confession." I seemed to myself, for the instant, to have mastered it, to see it all. "Leave us, leave us"—I was already, at the door, hurrying her off. "I'll get it out of him. He'll meet me—he'll confess. If he confesses, he's saved. And if he's saved—"

"Then *you* are?" The dear woman kissed me on this, and I took her farewell. "I'll save you without him!" she cried as she went.

XXII.

Yet it was when she had got off—and I missed her on the spot—that the great pinch really came. If I had counted on what it would give me to find myself alone with Miles, I speedily perceived, at least, that it would give me a measure. No hour of my stay in fact was so assailed with apprehensions as that of my coming down to learn that the carriage containing Mrs. Grose and my younger pupil had already rolled out of the gates. Now I *was*, I said to myself, face to face with the elements, and for much of the rest of the day, while I fought my weakness, I could consider that I had been supremely rash. It was a tighter place still than I had yet turned round in; all the more that, for the first time, I could see in the aspect of others a confused reflection of the crisis. What had happened naturally caused them all to stare; there was too little of the explained, throw out whatever we might, in the suddenness of my colleague's act. The maids and the men looked blank; the effect of which on my nerves was an aggravation until I saw the necessity of making it a positive aid. It was precisely, in short, by just clutching the helm that I avoided total wreck; and I dare say that, to bear up at all, I became, that morning, very grand and very dry. I welcomed the consciousness that I was charged with much to do, and I caused it to be known as well that, left thus to myself, I was quite remarkably firm. I wandered with that manner, for the next hour or two, all over the place and

looked, I have no doubt, as if I were ready for any onset. So, for
the benefit of whom it might concern, I paraded with a sick
heart.

The person it appeared least to concern proved to be, till dinner, little Miles himself. My perambulations had given me,
meanwhile, no glimpse of him, but they had tended to make
more public the change taking place in our relation as a consequence of his having at the piano, the day before, kept me, in
Flora's interest, so beguiled and befooled. The stamp of publicity had of course been fully given by her confinement and departure, and the change itself was now ushered in by our
non-observance of the regular custom of the schoolroom. He
had already disappeared when, on my way down, I pushed
open his door, and I learned below that he had breakfasted—in
the presence of a couple of the maids—with Mrs. Grose and his
sister. He had then gone out, as he said, for a stroll; than which
nothing, I reflected, could better have expressed his frank view
of the abrupt transformation of my office. What he would now
permit this office to consist of was yet to be settled: there was a
queer relief, at all events—I mean for myself in especial—in the
renouncement of one pretension. If so much had sprung to the
surface, I scarce put it too strongly in saying that what had perhaps sprung highest was the absurdity of our prolonging the
fiction that I had anything more to teach him. It sufficiently
stuck out that, by tacit little tricks in which even more than
myself he carried out the care for my dignity, I had had to appeal to him to let me off straining to meet him on the ground of
his true capacity. He had at any rate his freedom now; I was
never to touch it again; as I had amply shown, moreover, when,
on his joining me in the schoolroom the previous night, I had
uttered, on the subject of the interval just concluded, neither
challenge nor hint. I had too much, from this moment, my other
ideas. Yet when he at last arrived the difficulty of applying them,
the accumulations of my problem, were brought straight home
to me by the beautiful little presence on which what had occurred had as yet, for the eye, dropped neither stain nor shadow.

To mark, for the house, the high state I cultivated I decreed
that my meals with the boy should be served, as we called it,
downstairs; so that I had been awaiting him in the ponderous

pomp of the room outside of the window of which I had had from Mrs. Grose, that first scared Sunday, my flash of something it would scarce have done to call light. Here at present I felt afresh—for I had felt it again and again—how my equilibrium depended on the success of my rigid will, the will to shut my eyes as tight as possible to the truth that what I had to deal with was, revoltingly, against nature. I could only get on at all by taking "nature" into my confidence and my account, by treating my monstrous ordeal as a push in a direction unusual, of course, and unpleasant, but demanding, after all, for a fair front, only another turn of the screw of ordinary human virtue. No attempt, none the less, could well require more tact than just this attempt to supply, one's self, *all* the nature. How could I put even a little of that article into a suppression of reference to what had occurred? How, on the other hand, could I make a reference without a new plunge into the hideous obscure? Well, a sort of answer, after a time, had come to me, and it was so far confirmed as that I was met, incontestably, by the quickened vision of what was rare in my little companion. It was indeed as if he had found even now—as he had so often found at lessons—still some other delicate way to ease me off. Wasn't there light in the fact which, as we shared our solitude, broke out with a specious glitter it had never yet quite worn?—the fact that (opportunity aiding, precious opportunity which had now come) it would be preposterous, with a child so endowed, to forgo the help one might wrest from absolute intelligence? What had his intelligence been given him for but to save him? Mightn't one, to reach his mind, risk the stretch of an angular arm over his character? It was as if, when we were face to face in the dining-room, he had literally shown me the way. The roast mutton was on the table, and I had dispensed with attendance. Miles, before he sat down, stood a moment with his hands in his pockets and looked at the joint, on which he seemed on the point of passing some humorous judgment. But what he presently produced was: "I say, my dear, is she really very awfully ill?"

"Little Flora? Not so bad but that she'll presently be better. London will set her up. Bly had ceased to agree with her. Come here and take your mutton."

He alertly obeyed me, carried the plate carefully to his seat, and, when he was established, went on. "Did Bly disagree with her so terribly suddenly?"

"Not so suddenly as you might think. One had seen it coming on."

"Then why didn't you get her off before?"

"Before what?"

"Before she became too ill to travel."

I found myself prompt. "She's *not* too ill to travel: she only might have become so if she had stayed. This was just the moment to seize. The journey will dissipate the influence"—oh, I was grand!—"and carry it off."

"I see, I see"—Miles, for that matter, was grand too. He settled to his repast with the charming little "table manner" that, from the day of his arrival, had relieved me of all grossness of admonition. Whatever he had been driven from school for, it was not for ugly feeding. He was irreproachable, as always, today; but he was unmistakeably more conscious. He was discernibly trying to take for granted more things than he found, without assistance, quite easy; and he dropped into peaceful silence while he felt his situation. Our meal was of the briefest—mine a vain pretence, and I had the things immediately removed. While this was done Miles stood again with his hands in his little pockets and his back to me—stood and looked out of the wide window through which, that other day, I had seen what pulled me up. We continued silent while the maid was with us—as silent, it whimsically occurred to me, as some young couple who, on their wedding-journey, at the inn, feel shy in the presence of the waiter. He turned round only when the waiter had left us. "Well—so we're alone!"

XXIII.

"Oh, more or less." I fancy my smile was pale. "Not absolutely. We shouldn't like that!" I went on.

"No—I suppose we shouldn't. Of course we have the others."

"We have the others—we have indeed the others," I concurred.

"Yet even though we have them," he returned, still with his hands in his pockets and planted there in front of me, "they don't much count, do they?"

I made the best of it, but I felt wan. "It depends on what you call 'much'!"

"Yes"—with all accommodation—"everything depends!" On this, however, he faced to the window again and presently reached it with his vague, restless, cogitating step. He remained there awhile, with his forehead against the glass, in contemplation of the stupid shrubs I knew and the dull things of November. I had always my hypocrisy of "work," behind which, now, I gained the sofa. Steadying myself with it there as I had repeatedly done at those moments of torment that I have described as the moments of my knowing the children to be given to something from which I was barred, I sufficiently obeyed my habit of being prepared for the worst. But an extraordinary impression dropped on me as I extracted a meaning from the boy's embarrassed back—none other than the impression that I was not barred now. This inference grew in a few minutes to sharp intensity and seemed bound up with the direct perception that it was positively *he* who was. The frames and squares of the great window were a kind of image, for him, of a kind of failure. I felt that I saw him, at any rate, shut in or shut out. He was admirable, but not comfortable: I took it in with a throb of hope. Wasn't he looking, through the haunted pane, for something he couldn't see?—and wasn't it the first time in the whole business that he had known such a lapse? The first, the very first: I found it a splendid portent. It made him anxious, though he watched himself; he had been anxious all day and, even while in his usual sweet little manner he sat at table, had needed all his small strange genius to give it a gloss. When he at last turned round to meet me, it was almost as if this genius had succumbed. "Well, I think I'm glad Bly agrees with *me!*"

"You would certainly seem to have seen, these twenty-four hours, a good deal more of it than for some time before. I hope," I went on bravely, "that you've been enjoying yourself."

"Oh, yes, I've been ever so far; all round about—miles and miles away. I've never been so free."

He had really a manner of his own, and I could only try to keep up with him. "Well, do you like it?"

He stood there smiling; then at last he put into two words— "Do *you?*"—more discrimination than I had ever heard two words contain. Before I had time to deal with that, however, he continued as if with the sense that this was an impertinence to be softened. "Nothing could be more charming than the way you take it, for of course if we're alone together now it's you that are alone most. But I hope," he threw in, "you don't particularly mind!"

"Having to do with you?" I asked. "My dear child, how can I help minding? Though I've renounced all claim to your company,—you're so beyond me,—I at least greatly enjoy it. What else should I stay on for?"

He looked at me more directly, and the expression of his face, graver now, struck me as the most beautiful I had ever found in it. "You stay on just for *that?*"

"Certainly. I stay on as your friend and from the tremendous interest I take in you till something can be done for you that may be more worth your while. That needn't surprise you." My voice trembled so that I felt it impossible to suppress the shake. "Don't you remember how I told you, when I came and sat on your bed the night of the storm, that there was nothing in the world I wouldn't do for you?"

"Yes, yes!" He, on his side, more and more visibly nervous, had a tone to master; but he was so much more successful than I that, laughing out through his gravity, he could pretend we were pleasantly jesting. "Only that, I think, was to get me to do something for *you!*"

"It was partly to get you to do something," I conceded. "But, you know, you didn't do it."

"Oh, yes," he said with the brightest superficial eagerness, "you wanted me to tell you something."

"That's it. Out, straight out. What you have on your mind, you know."

"Ah, then, is *that* what you've stayed over for?"

He spoke with a gaiety through which I could still catch the finest little quiver of resentful passion; but I can't begin to express the effect upon me of an implication of surrender even so faint. It was as if what I had yearned for had come at last only to astonish me. "Well, yes—I may as well make a clean breast of it. It was precisely for that."

He waited so long that I supposed it for the purpose of repudiating the assumption on which my action had been founded; but what he finally said was: "Do you mean now—here?"

"There couldn't be a better place or time." He looked round him uneasily, and I had the rare—oh, the queer!—impression of the very first symptom I had seen in him of the approach of immediate fear. It was as if he were suddenly afraid of me— which struck me indeed as perhaps the best thing to make him. Yet in the very pang of the effort I felt it vain to try sternness, and I heard myself the next instant so gentle as to be almost grotesque. "You want so to go out again?"

"Awfully!" He smiled at me heroically, and the touching little bravery of it was enhanced by his actually flushing with pain. He had picked up his hat, which he had brought in, and stood twirling it in a way that gave me, even as I was just nearly reaching port, a perverse horror of what I was doing. To do it in *any* way was an act of violence, for what did it consist of but the obtrusion of the idea of grossness and guilt on a small helpless creature who had been for me a revelation of the possibilities of beautiful intercourse? Wasn't it base to create for a being so exquisite a mere alien awkwardness? I suppose I now read into our situation a clearness it couldn't have had at the time, for I seem to see our poor eyes already lighted with some spark of a prevision of the anguish that was to come. So we circled about, with terrors and scruples, like fighters not daring to close. But it was for each other we feared! That kept us a little longer suspended and unbruised. "I'll tell you everything," Miles said—"I mean I'll tell you anything you like. You'll stay on with me, and we shall both be all right and I *will* tell you— I *will*. But not now."

"Why not now?"

My insistence turned him from me and kept him once more at his window in a silence during which, between us, you might have heard a pin drop. Then he was before me again with the air of a person for whom, outside, someone who had frankly to be reckoned with was waiting. "I have to see Luke."

I had not yet reduced him to quite so vulgar a lie, and I felt proportionately ashamed. But, horrible as it was, his lies made up my truth. I achieved thoughtfully a few loops of my knitting. "Well, then, go to Luke, and I'll wait for what you promise. Only, in return for that, satisfy, before you leave me, one very much smaller request."

He looked as if he felt he had succeeded enough to be able still a little to bargain. "Very much smaller—?"

"Yes, a mere fraction of the whole. Tell me"—oh, my work preoccupied me, and I was off-hand!—"if, yesterday afternoon, from the table in the hall, you took, you know, my letter."

XXIV.

My sense of how he received this suffered for a minute from something that I can describe only as a fierce split of my attention—a stroke that at first, as I sprang straight up, reduced me to the mere blind movement of getting hold of him, drawing him close, and, while I just fell for support against the nearest piece of furniture, instinctively keeping him with his back to the window. The appearance was full upon us that I had already had to deal with here: Peter Quint had come into view like a sentinel before a prison. The next thing I saw was that, from outside, he had reached the window, and then I knew that, close to the glass and glaring in through it, he offered once more to the room his white face of damnation. It represents but grossly what took place within me at the sight to say that on the second my decision was made; yet I believe that no woman so overwhelmed ever in so short a time recovered her grasp of the *act*. It came to me in the very horror of the immediate presence that the act would be, seeing and facing what I saw and faced, to keep the boy himself unaware. The inspiration—I can call it by no other name—was that I felt how voluntarily, how transcendently, I *might*. It was like fighting with a demon for a human soul, and when I had fairly so appraised it I saw how the human soul—held out, in the tremor of my hands, at arm's length—had a perfect dew of sweat on a lovely childish forehead. The face that was close to mine was as white as the face against the glass, and out of it presently came a sound, not low nor weak, but as if from much further away, that I drank like a waft of fragrance.

"Yes—I took it."

At this, with a moan of joy, I enfolded, I drew him close; and while I held him to my breast, where I could feel in the sudden fever of his little body the tremendous pulse of his little heart, I kept my eyes on the thing at the window and saw it move and shift its posture. I have likened it to a sentinel, but its slow wheel, for a moment, was rather the prowl of a baffled beast. My present quickened courage, however, was such that, not too much to let it through, I had to shade, as it were, my flame. Meanwhile the glare of the face was again at the window, the scoundrel fixed as if to watch and wait. It was the very confidence that I might now defy him, as well as the positive certitude, by this time, of the child's unconsciousness, that made me go on. "What did you take it for?"

"To see what you said about me."

"You opened the letter?"

"I opened it."

My eyes were now, as I held him off a little again, on Miles's own face, in which the collapse of mockery showed me how complete was the ravage of uneasiness. What was prodigious was that at last, by my success, his sense was scaled and his communication stopped: he knew that he was in presence, but knew not of what, and knew still less that I also was and that I did know. And what did this strain of trouble matter when my eyes went back to the window only to see that the air was clear again and—by my personal triumph—the influence quenched? There was nothing there. I felt that the cause was mine and that I should surely get *all*. "And you found nothing!"—I let my elation out.

He gave the most mournful, thoughtful little headshake. "Nothing."

"Nothing, nothing!" I almost shouted in my joy.

"Nothing, nothing," he sadly repeated.

I kissed his forehead; it was drenched. "So what have you done with it?"

"I've burnt it."

"Burnt it?" It was now or never. "Is that what you did at school?"

Oh, what this brought up! "At school?"

"Did you take letters?—or other things?"

"Other things?" He appeared now to be thinking of something far off and that reached him only through the pressure of his anxiety. Yet it did reach him. "Did I *steal*?"

I felt myself redden to the roots of my hair as well as wonder if it were more strange to put to a gentleman such a question or to see him take it with allowances that gave the very distance of his fall in the world. "Was it for that you mightn't go back?"

The only thing he felt was rather a dreary little surprise. "Did you know I mightn't go back?"

"I know everything."

He gave me at this the longest and strangest look. "Everything?"

"Everything. Therefore *did* you—?" But I couldn't say it again.

Miles could, very simply. "No. I didn't steal."

My face must have shown him I believed him utterly; yet my hands—but it was for pure tenderness—shook him as if to ask him why, if it was all for nothing, he had condemned me to months of torment. "What then did you do?"

He looked in vague pain all round the top of the room and drew his breath, two or three times over, as if with difficulty. He might have been standing at the bottom of the sea and raising his eyes to some faint green twilight. "Well—I said things."

"Only that?"

"They thought it was enough!"

"To turn you out for?"

Never, truly, had a person "turned out" shown so little to explain it as this little person! He appeared to weigh my question, but in a manner quite detached and almost helpless. "Well, I suppose I oughtn't."

"But to whom did you say them?"

He evidently tried to remember, but it dropped—he had lost it. "I don't know!"

He almost smiled at me in the desolation of his surrender,

which was indeed practically, by this time, so complete that I ought to have left it there. But I was infatuated—I was blind with victory, though even then the very effect that was to have brought him so much nearer was already that of added separation. "Was it to everyone?" I asked.

"No; it was only to—" But he gave a sick little headshake. "I don't remember their names."

"Were they then so many?"

"No—only a few. Those I liked."

Those he liked? I seemed to float not into clearness, but into a darker obscure, and within a minute there had come to me out of my very pity the appalling alarm of his being perhaps innocent. It was for the instant confounding and bottomless, for if he *were* innocent, what then on earth was *I*? Paralysed, while it lasted, by the mere brush of the question, I let him go a little, so that, with a deep-drawn sigh, he turned away from me again; which, as he faced toward the clear window, I suffered, feeling that I had nothing now there to keep him from. "And did they repeat what you said?" I went on after a moment.

He was soon at some distance from me, still breathing hard and again with the air, though now without anger for it, of being confined against his will. Once more, as he had done before, he looked up at the dim day as if, of what had hitherto sustained him, nothing was left but an unspeakable anxiety. "Oh, yes," he nevertheless replied—"they must have repeated them. To those *they* liked," he added.

There was, somehow, less of it than I had expected; but I turned it over. "And these things came round—?"

"To the masters? Oh, yes!" he answered very simply. "But I didn't know they'd tell."

"The masters? They didn't—they've never told. That's why I ask you."

He turned to me again his little beautiful fevered face. "Yes, it was too bad."

"Too bad?"

"What I suppose I sometimes said. To write home."

I can't name the exquisite pathos of the contradiction given to such a speech by such a speaker; I only know that the next instant I heard myself throw off with homely force: "Stuff and nonsense!" But the next after that I must have sounded stern enough. "What *were* these things?"

My sternness was all for his judge, his executioner; yet it made him avert himself again, and that movement made *me*, with a single bound and an irrepressible cry, spring straight upon him. For there again, against the glass, as if to blight his confession and stay his answer, was the hideous author of our woe—the white face of damnation. I felt a sick swim at the drop of my victory and all the return of my battle, so that the wildness of my veritable leap only served as a great betrayal. I saw him, from the midst of my act, meet it with a divination, and on the perception that even now he only guessed, and that the window was still to his own eyes free, I let the impulse flame up to convert the climax of his dismay into the very proof of his liberation. "No more, no more, no more!" I shrieked, as I tried to press him against me, to my visitant.

"Is she *here*?" Miles panted as he caught with his sealed eyes the direction of my words. Then as his strange "she" staggered me and, with a gasp, I echoed it, "Miss Jessel, Miss Jessel!" he with a sudden fury gave me back.

I seized, stupefied, his supposition—some sequel to what we had done to Flora, but this made me only want to show him that it was better still than that. "It's not Miss Jessel! But it's at the window—straight before us. It's *there*—the coward horror, there for the last time!"

At this, after a second in which his head made the movement of a baffled dog's on a scent and then gave a frantic little shake for air and light, he was at me in a white rage, bewildered, glaring vainly over the place and missing wholly, though it now, to my sense, filled the room like the taste of poison, the wide, overwhelming presence. "It's *he*?"

I was so determined to have all my proof that I flashed into ice to challenge him. "Whom do you mean by 'he'?"

"Peter Quint—you devil!" His face gave again, round the room, its convulsed supplication. "*Where*?"

They are in my ears still, his supreme surrender of the name and his tribute to my devotion. "What does he matter now, my own?—what will he *ever* matter? *I* have you," I launched at the beast, "but he has lost you for ever!" Then, for the demonstration of my work, "There, *there!*" I said to Miles.

But he had already jerked straight round, stared, glared again, and seen but the quiet day. With the stroke of the loss I was so proud of he uttered the cry of a creature hurled over an abyss, and the grasp with which I recovered him might have been that of catching him in his fall. I caught him, yes, I held him—it may be imagined with what a passion; but at the end of a minute I began to feel what it truly was that I held. We were alone with the quiet day, and his little heart, dispossessed, had stopped.

The Beast in the Jungle

In The Better Sort, *1903. Discussing "The Beast in the Jungle" in his 1909 New York Edition preface, James admits that "my attested predilection for poor sensitive gentlemen almost embarrasses me as I march." Perhaps that admission has been responsible for the fact that so much biographical criticism has been heaped upon this great tale—even if the earlier 1901 notebook entry suggests no hint of self-reflection. Early criticism felt comfortable discovering a link between the halfhearted attachment of John Marcher and May Bartram, and whatever went on between Henry James and Constance Fenimore Woolson—a friend who had died, an apparent suicide, a decade before the tale was written. More recently the tale has been central to the discussion of James's sexuality and the related potential for homosexual coding in his fiction (see Eve Kosofsky Sedgwick, "The Beast in the Closet," in* Epistemology of the Closet, *Berkeley: University of California Press, 1990)—although not all critics accept the centrality or validity of the homosexual reading.*

I.

What determined the speech that startled him in the course of their encounter scarcely matters, being probably but some words spoken by himself quite without intention—spoken as they lingered and slowly moved together after their renewal of acquaintance. He had been conveyed by friends, an hour or two before, to the house at which she was staying; the party of visitors at the other house, of whom he was one, and thanks to whom it was his theory, as always, that he was lost in the crowd, had been invited over to luncheon. There had been after luncheon much dispersal, all in the interest of the original motive, a view of Weatherend itself and the fine things, intrinsic features, pictures, heirlooms, treasures of all the arts, that made the place almost famous; and the great rooms were so numerous that guests could wander at their will, hang back from the principal group, and, in cases where they took such matters with the last seriousness, give themselves up to mysterious appreciations and measurements. There were persons to be observed, singly or in couples, bending toward objects in out-of-the-way corners with their hands on their knees and their heads nodding quite as with the emphasis of an excited sense of smell. When they were two they either mingled their sounds of ecstasy or melted into silences of even deeper import, so that there were aspects of the occasion that gave it for Marcher much the air of the "look round," previous to a sale highly advertised, that excites or quenches, as may be, the dream of acquisition. The dream of acquisition at Weatherend would have had to be wild indeed, and John Marcher found himself, among such suggestions, disconcerted almost equally by the presence of those who knew too much and by that of those who knew nothing. The great rooms caused so much poetry and history to press upon him that he needed to wander apart to feel in a proper relation with them, though his doing so was not, as happened, like the gloating of some of his companions, to be compared to the movements of a dog sniffing a cupboard. It had an issue promptly enough in a direction that was not to have been calculated.

It led, in short, in the course of the October afternoon, to his closer meeting with May Bartram, whose face, a reminder, yet not quite a remembrance, as they sat, much separated, at a very long table, had begun merely by troubling him rather pleasantly. It affected him as the sequel of something of which he had lost the beginning. He knew it, and for the time quite welcomed it, as a continuation, but didn't know what it continued, which was an interest, or an amusement, the greater as he was also somehow aware—yet without a direct sign from her—that the young woman herself had not lost the thread. She had not lost it, but she wouldn't give it back to him, he saw, without some putting forth of his hand for it; and he not only saw that, but saw several things more, things odd enough in the light of the fact that at the moment some accident of grouping brought them face to face he was still merely fumbling with the idea that any contact between them in the past would have had no importance. If it had had no importance he scarcely knew why his actual impression of her should so seem to have so much; the answer to which, however, was that in such a life as they all appeared to be leading for the moment one could but take things as they came. He was satisfied, without in the least being able to say why, that this young lady might roughly have ranked in the house as a poor relation; satisfied also that she was not there on a brief visit, but was more or less a part of the establishment—almost a working, a remunerated part. Didn't she enjoy at periods a protection that she paid for by helping, among other services, to show the place and explain it, deal with the tiresome people, answer questions about the dates of the buildings, the styles of the furniture, the authorship of the pictures, the favourite haunts of the ghost? It wasn't that she looked as if you could have given her shillings—it was impossible to look less so. Yet when she finally drifted toward him, distinctly handsome, though ever so much older—older than when he had seen her before—it might have been as an effect of her guessing that he had, within the couple of hours, devoted more imagination to her than to all the others put together, and had thereby penetrated to a kind of truth that the others were too stupid for. She *was* there on harder terms than anyone; she was there as a consequence of things suffered, in one way and another, in the interval of years; and she remembered him very much as she was remembered—only a good deal better.

By the time they at last thus came to speech they were alone in one of the rooms—remarkable for a fine portrait over the chimney-place—out of which their friends had passed, and the charm of it was that even before they had spoken they had practically arranged with each other to stay behind for talk.

The charm, happily, was in other things too; it was partly in there being scarce a spot at Weatherend without something to stay behind for. It was in the way the autumn day looked into the high windows as it waned; in the way the red light, breaking at the close from under a low, sombre sky, reached out in a long shaft and played over old wainscots, old tapestry, old gold, old colour. It was most of all perhaps in the way she came to him as if, since she had been turned on to deal with the simpler sort, he might, should he choose to keep the whole thing down, just take her mild attention for a part of her general business. As soon as he heard her voice, however, the gap was filled up and the missing link supplied; the slight irony he divined in her attitude lost its advantage. He almost jumped at it to get there before her. "I met you years and years ago in Rome. I remember all about it." She confessed to disappointment— she had been so sure he didn't; and to prove how well he did he began to pour forth the particular recollections that popped up as he called for them. Her face and her voice, all at his service now, worked the miracle—the impression operating like the torch of a lamplighter who touches into flame, one by one, a long row of gas jets. Marcher flattered himself that the illumination was brilliant, yet he was really still more pleased on her showing him, with amusement, that in his haste to make everything right he had got most things rather wrong. It hadn't been at Rome—it had been at Naples; and it hadn't been seven years before—it had been more nearly ten. She hadn't been either with her uncle and aunt, but with her mother and her brother; in addition to which it was not with the Pembles that *he* had been, but with the Boyers, coming down in their company from Rome—a point on which she insisted, a little to his confusion, and as to which she had her evidence in hand. The Boyers she had known, but she didn't know the Pembles, though she had heard of them, and it was the people he was with who had made them acquainted. The incident of the thunderstorm that had raged round them with such violence as to drive them for refuge into an excavation—this incident had not occurred at the Palace of the Cæsars, but at Pompeii, on an occasion when they had been present there at an important find.

He accepted her amendments, he enjoyed her corrections,

though the moral of them was, she pointed out, that he *really* didn't remember the least thing about her; and he only felt it as a drawback that when all was made conformable to the truth there didn't appear much of anything left. They lingered together still, she neglecting her office—for from the moment he was so clever she had no proper right to him—and both neglecting the house, just waiting as to see if a memory or two more wouldn't again breathe upon them. It had not taken them many minutes, after all, to put down on the table, like the cards of a pack, those that constituted their respective hands; only what came out was that the pack was unfortunately not perfect—that the past, invoked, invited, encouraged, could give them, naturally, no more than it had. It had made them meet—her at twenty, him at twenty-five; but nothing was so strange, they seemed to say to each other, as that, while so occupied, it hadn't done a little more for them. They looked at each other as with the feeling of an occasion missed; the present one would have been so much better if the other, in the far distance, in the foreign land, hadn't been so stupidly meagre. There weren't, apparently, all counted, more than a dozen little old things that had succeeded in coming to pass between them; trivialities of youth, simplicities of freshness, stupidities of ignorance, small possible germs, but too deeply buried—too deeply (didn't it seem?) to sprout after so many years. Marcher said to himself that he ought to have rendered her some service—saved her from a capsized boat in the Bay, or at least recovered her dressing-bag, filched from her cab, in the streets of Naples, by a lazzarone with a stiletto. Or it would have been nice if he could have been taken with fever, alone, at his hotel, and she could have come to look after him, to write to his people, to drive him out in convalescence. *Then* they would be in possession of the something or other that their actual show seemed to lack. It yet somehow presented itself, this show, as too good to be spoiled; so that they were reduced for a few minutes more to wondering a little helplessly why—since they seemed to know a certain number of the same people—their reunion had been so long averted. They didn't use that name for it, but their delay from minute to minute to join the others was a kind of confession that they didn't quite want it to be a failure. Their attempted supposition of reasons for their not having met but showed how little they knew of each other. There came in fact a moment when Marcher felt a positive pang. It was vain to pretend she was an old friend, for all the communities were wanting, in spite of which it was as an old friend that he saw she would have suited him. He had new ones enough—was surrounded with them, for instance, at that hour at the other house; as a new one he probably wouldn't have so much as noticed her. He would have liked to invent something, get her to make-believe with him that some passage of a romantic or critical kind *had* originally occurred. He was really almost reaching out in imagination—as against time—for something that would do, and saying to himself that if it didn't come this new incident would simply and rather awkwardly close. They would separate, and now for no second or for no third chance. They would have tried and not succeeded. Then it was, just at the turn, as he afterwards made it out to himself, that, everything else failing, she herself decided to take up the case and, as it were, save the situation. He felt as soon as she spoke that she had been consciously keeping back what she said and hoping to get on without it; a scruple in her that immensely touched him when, by the end of three or four minutes more, he was able to measure it. What she brought out, at any rate, quite cleared the air and supplied the link—the link it was such a mystery he should frivolously have managed to lose.

"You know you told me something that I've never forgotten and that again and again has made me think of you since; it was that tremendously hot day when we went to Sorrento, across the bay, for the breeze. What I allude to was what you said to me, on the way back, as we sat, under the awning of the boat, enjoying the cool. Have you forgotten?"

He had forgotten, and he was even more surprised than ashamed. But the great thing was that he saw it was no vulgar reminder of any "sweet" speech. The vanity of women had long memories, but she was making no claim on him of a compliment or a mistake. With another woman, a totally different one, he might have feared the recall possibly even some imbecile "offer." So, in having to say that he had indeed forgotten, he was conscious rather of a loss than of a gain; he already saw an interest in the matter of her reference. "I try to think—but I give it up. Yet I remember the Sorrento day."

"I'm not very sure you do," May Bartram after a moment said; "and I'm not very sure I ought to want you to. It's dreadful to bring a person back, at any time, to what he was ten years before. If you've lived away from it," she smiled, "so much the better."

"Ah, if *you* haven't why should I?" he asked.

"Lived away, you mean, from what I myself was?"

"From what *I* was. I was of course an ass," Marcher went on; "but I would rather know from you just the sort of ass I was than—from the moment you have something in your mind—not know anything."

Still, however, she hesitated. "But if you've completely ceased to be that sort—?"

"Why, I can then just so all the more bear to know. Besides, perhaps I haven't."

"Perhaps. Yet if you haven't," she added, "I should suppose you would remember. Not indeed that *I* in the least connect with my impression the invidious name you use. If I had only thought you foolish," she explained, "the thing I speak of wouldn't so have remained with me. It was about yourself." She waited, as if it might come to him; but as, only meeting her eyes in wonder, he gave no sign, she burnt her ships. "Has it ever happened?"

Then it was that, while he continued to stare, a light broke for him and the blood slowly came to his face, which began to burn with recognition. "Do you mean I told you—?"

But he faltered, lest what came to him shouldn't be right, lest he should only give himself away.

"It was something about yourself that it was natural one shouldn't forget—that is if one remembered you at all. That's why I ask you," she smiled, "if the thing you then spoke of has ever come to pass?"

Oh, then he saw, but he was lost in wonder and found himself embarrassed. This, he also saw, made her sorry for him, as if her allusion had been a mistake. It took him but a moment, however, to feel that it had not been, much as it had been a surprise. After the first little shock of it her knowledge on the contrary began, even if rather strangely, to taste sweet to him. She was the only other person in the world then who would have it, and she had had it all these years, while the fact of his having so breathed his secret had unaccountably faded from him. No wonder they couldn't have met as if nothing had happened. "I judge," he finally said, "that I know what you mean. Only I had strangely enough lost the consciousness of having taken you so far into my confidence."

"Is it because you've taken so many others as well?"

"I've taken nobody. Not a creature since then."

"So that I'm the only person who knows?"

"The only person in the world."

"Well," she quickly replied, "I myself have never spoken. I've never, never repeated of you what you told me." She looked at him so that he perfectly believed her. Their eyes met over it in such a way that he was without a doubt. "And I never will."

She spoke with an earnestness that, as if almost excessive, put him at ease about her possible derision. Somehow the whole question was a new luxury to him—that is, from the moment she was in possession. If she didn't take the ironic view she clearly took the sympathetic, and that was what he had had, in all the long time, from no one whomsoever. What he felt was that he couldn't at present have begun to tell her and yet could profit perhaps exquisitely by the accident of having done so of old. "Please don't then. We're just right as it is."

"Oh, I am," she laughed, "if you are!" To which she added: "Then you do still feel in the same way?"

It was impossible to him not to take to himself that she was really interested, and it all kept coming as a sort of revelation. He had thought of himself so long as abominably alone, and, lo, he wasn't alone a bit. He hadn't been, it appeared, for an hour—since those moments on the Sorrento boat. It was *she* who had been, he seemed to see as he looked at her—she who had been made so by the graceless fact of his lapse of fidelity. To tell her what he had told her—what had it been but to ask something of her? something that she had given, in her charity, without his having, by a remembrance, by a return of the spirit, failing another encounter, so much as thanked her. What he had asked of her had been simply at first not to laugh at him. She had beautifully not done so for ten years, and she was not doing so now. So he had endless gratitude to make up. Only for that he must see just how he had figured to her. "What, exactly, was the account I gave—?"

"Of the way you did feel? Well, it was very simple. You said you had had from your earliest time, as the deepest thing within you, the sense of being kept for something rare and strange, possibly prodigious and terrible, that was sooner or later to happen to you, that you had in your bones the foreboding and the conviction of, and that would perhaps overwhelm you."

"Do you call that very simple?" John Marcher asked.

She thought a moment. "It was perhaps because I seemed, as you spoke, to understand it."

"You do understand it?" he eagerly asked.

Again she kept her kind eyes on him. "You still have the belief?"

"Oh!" he exclaimed helplessly. There was too much to say.

"Whatever it is to be," she clearly made out, "it hasn't yet come."

He shook his head in complete surrender now. "It hasn't yet come. Only, you know, it isn't anything I'm to *do*, to achieve in the world, to be distinguished or admired for. I'm not such an ass as *that*. It would be much better, no doubt, if I were."

"It's to be something you're merely to suffer?"

"Well, say to wait for—to have to meet, to face, to see suddenly break out in my life; possibly destroying all further consciousness, possibly annihilating me; possibly, on the other hand, only altering everything, striking at the root of all my world and leaving me to the consequences, however they shape themselves."

She took this in, but the light in her eyes continued for him not to be that of mockery. "Isn't what you describe perhaps but the expectation—or, at any rate, the sense of danger, familiar to so many people—of falling in love?"

John Marcher thought. "Did you ask me that before?"

"No—I wasn't so free-and-easy then. But it's what strikes me now."

"Of course," he said after a moment, "it strikes you. Of course it strikes *me*. Of course what's in store for me may be no more than that. The only thing is," he went on, "that I think that if it had been that, I should by this time know."

"Do you mean because you've *been* in love?" And then as he but looked at her in silence: "You've been in love, and it hasn't meant such a cataclysm, hasn't proved the great affair?"

"Here I am, you see. It hasn't been overwhelming."

"Then it hasn't been love," said May Bartram.

"Well, I at least thought it was. I took it for that—I've taken it till now. It was agreeable, it was delightful, it was miserable," he explained. "But it wasn't strange. It wasn't what *my* affair's to be."

"You want something all to yourself—something that nobody else knows or *has* known?"

"It isn't a question of what I 'want'—God knows I don't want anything. It's only a question of the apprehension that haunts me—that I live with day by day."

He said this so lucidly and consistently that, visibly, it further imposed itself. If she had not been interested before she would have been interested now. "Is it a sense of coming violence?"

Evidently now too, again, he liked to talk of it. "I don't think of it as—when it does come—necessarily violent. I only think of it as natural and as of course, above all, unmistakeable. I think of it simply as *the* thing. *The* thing will of itself appear natural."

"Then how will it appear strange?"

Marcher bethought himself. "It won't—to *me*."

"To whom then?"

"Well," he replied, smiling at last, "say to you."

"Oh then, I'm to be present?"

"Why, you *are* present—since you know."

"I see." She turned it over. "But I mean at the catastrophe."

At this, for a minute, their lightness gave way to their gravity; it was as if the long look they exchanged held them together. "It will only depend on yourself—if you'll watch with me."

"Are you afraid?" she asked.

"Don't leave me *now*," he went on.

"Are you afraid?" she repeated.

"Do you think me simply out of my mind?" he pursued instead of answering. "Do I merely strike you as a harmless lunatic?"

"No," said May Bartram. "I understand you. I believe you."

"You mean you feel how my obsession—poor old thing!—may correspond to some possible reality?"

"To some possible reality."

"Then you *will* watch with me?"

She hesitated, then for the third time put her question. "Are you afraid?"

"Did I tell you I was—at Naples?"

"No, you said nothing about it."

"Then I don't know. And I should *like* to know," said John Marcher. "You'll tell me yourself whether you think so. If you'll watch with me you'll see."

"Very good then." They had been moving by this time across the room, and at the door, before passing out, they paused as if for the full wind-up of their understanding. "I'll watch with you," said May Bartram.

II.

The fact that she "knew"—knew and yet neither chaffed him nor betrayed him—had in a short time begun to constitute between them a sensible bond, which became more marked when, within the year that followed their afternoon at Weatherend, the opportunities for meeting multiplied. The event that thus promoted these occasions was the death of the ancient lady, her great-aunt, under whose wing, since losing her mother, she had to such an extent found shelter, and who, though but the widowed mother of the new successor to the property, had succeeded—thanks to a high tone and a high temper—in not forfeiting the supreme position at the great house. The deposition of this personage arrived but with her death, which, followed by many changes, made in particular a difference for the young woman in whom Marcher's expert attention had recognised from the first a dependent with a pride that might ache though it didn't bristle. Nothing for a long time had made him easier than the thought that the aching must have been much soothed by Miss Bartram's now finding herself able to set up a small home in London. She had acquired property, to an amount that made that luxury just possible, under her aunt's extremely complicated will, and when the whole matter began to be straightened out, which indeed took time, she let him know that the happy issue was at last in view. He had seen her again before that day, both because she had more than once accompanied the ancient lady to town and because he had paid another visit to the friends who so conveniently made of Weatherend one of the charms of their own hospitality. These friends had taken him back there; he had achieved there again with Miss Bartram some quiet detachment; and he had in London succeeded in persuading her to more than one brief absence from her aunt. They went together, on these latter occasions, to the National Gallery and the South Kensington Museum, where, among vivid reminders, they talked of Italy at large—not now attempting to recover, as at first, the taste of their youth and their ignorance. That recovery, the first day at Weatherend, had served its purpose well, had given them quite enough; so that they were, to Marcher's sense, no longer hovering about the head-waters of their stream, but had felt their boat pushed sharply off and down the current.

They were literally afloat together; for our gentleman this was marked, quite as marked as that the fortunate cause of it was just the buried treasure of her knowledge. He had with his own hands dug up this little hoard, brought to light—that is to within reach of the dim day constituted by their discretions and privacies—the object of value the hiding-place of which he had, after putting it into the ground himself, so strangely, so long forgotten. The exquisite luck of having again just stumbled on the spot made him indifferent to any other question; he would doubtless have devoted more time to the odd accident of his lapse of memory if he had not been moved to devote so much to the sweetness, the comfort, as he felt, for the future, that this accident itself had helped to keep fresh. It had never entered into his plan that anyone should "know," and mainly for the reason that it was not in him to tell anyone. That would have been impossible, since nothing but the amusement of a cold world would have waited on it. Since, however, a mysterious fate had opened his mouth in youth, in spite of him, he would count that a compensation and profit by it to the utmost. That the right person *should* know tempered the asperity of his secret more even than his shyness had permitted him to imagine; and May Bartram was clearly right, because—well, because there she was. Her knowledge simply settled it; he would have been sure enough by this time had she been wrong. There was that in his situation, no doubt, that disposed him too much to see her as a mere confidant, taking all her light for him from the fact—the fact only—of her interest in his predicament, from her mercy, sympathy, seriousness, her consent not to regard him as the funniest of the funny. Aware, in fine, that her price for him was just in her giving him this constant sense of his being admirably spared, he was careful to remember that she had, after all, also a life of her own, with things that might happen to *her*, things that in friendship one should likewise take account of. Something fairly remarkable came to pass with him, for that matter, in this connection—something represented by a certain passage of his consciousness, in the suddenest way, from one extreme to the other.

He had thought himself, so long as nobody knew, the most disinterested person in the world, carrying his concentrated burden, his perpetual suspense, ever so quietly, holding his tongue about it, giving others no glimpse of it nor of its effect upon his life, asking of them no allowance and only making on his side all those that were asked. He had disturbed nobody with the queerness of having to know a haunted man, though he had had moments of rather special temptation on hearing people say that they were "unsettled." If they were as unsettled as he was—he who had never been settled for an hour in his life—they would know what it meant. Yet it wasn't, all the same, for him to make them, and he listened to them civilly enough. This was why he had such good—though possibly such rather colourless—manners; this was why, above all, he could regard himself, in a greedy world, as decently—as, in fact, perhaps even a little sublimely—unselfish. Our point is accordingly that he valued this character quite sufficiently to measure his present danger of letting it lapse, against which he promised himself to be much on his guard. He was quite ready, none the less, to be selfish just a little, since, surely, no more charming occasion for it had come to him. "Just a little," in a word, was just as much as Miss Bartram, taking one day with another, would let him. He never would be in the least coercive, and he would keep well before him the lines on which consideration for her—the very highest—ought to proceed. He would thoroughly establish the heads under which her affairs, her requirements, her peculiarities—he went so far as to give them the latitude of that name—would come into their intercourse. All this naturally was a sign of how much he took the intercourse itself for granted. There was nothing more to be done about *that*. It simply existed; had sprung into being with her first penetrating question to him in the autumn light there at Weatherend. The real form it should have taken on the basis that stood out large was the form of their marrying. But the devil in this was that the very basis itself put marrying out of the question. His conviction, his apprehension, his obsession, in short, was not a condition he could invite a woman to share; and that consequence of it was precisely what was the matter with him. Something or other lay in wait for him, amid the twists and the turns of the months and the years, like a crouching beast in the jungle. It signified little whether the crouching beast were destined to slay him or to be slain. The definite point was the inevitable spring of the creature; and the definite lesson from that was that a man of feeling didn't cause himself to be accompanied by a lady on a tiger-hunt. Such was the image under which he had ended by figuring his life.

They had at first, none the less, in the scattered hours spent together, made no allusion to that view of it; which was a sign he was handsomely ready to give that he didn't expect, that he in fact didn't care always to be talking about it. Such a feature in one's outlook was really like a hump on one's back. The difference it made every minute of the day existed quite independently of discussion. One discussed, of course, *like* a hunchback, for there was always, if nothing else, the hunchback face. That remained, and she was watching him; but people watched best, as a general thing, in silence, so that such would be predominantly the manner of their vigil. Yet he didn't want, at the same time, to be solemn; solemn was what he imagined he too much tended to be with other people. The thing to be, with the one person who knew, was easy and natural—to make the reference rather than be seeming to avoid it, to avoid it rather than be seeming to make it, and to keep it, in any case, familiar, facetious even, rather than pedantic and portentous. Some such consideration as the latter was doubtless in his mind, for instance, when he wrote pleasantly to Miss Bartram that perhaps the great thing he had so long felt as in the lap of the gods was no more than this circumstance, which touched him so nearly, of her acquiring a house in London. It was the first allusion they had yet again made, needing any other hitherto so little; but when she replied, after having given him the news, that she was by no means satisfied with such a trifle, as the climax to so special a suspense, she almost set him wondering if she hadn't even a larger conception of singularity for him than he had for himself. He was at all events destined to become aware little by little, as time went by, that she was all the while looking at his life, judging it, measuring it, in the light of the thing she knew, which grew to be at last, with the consecration of the years, never mentioned between them save as "the real truth" about him. That had always been his own form of reference to it, but she adopted the form so quietly that, looking back at the end of a period, he knew there was no moment at which it was traceable that she had, as he might say, got inside his condition, or exchanged the attitude of beautifully indulging for that of still more beautifully believing him.

It was always open to him to accuse her of seeing him but as the most harmless of maniacs, and this, in the long run—since it covered so much ground—was his easiest description of their friendship. He had a screw loose for her, but she liked him in spite of it, and was practically, against the rest of the world, his kind, wise keeper, unremunerated, but fairly amused and, in the absence of other near ties, not disreputably occupied. The rest of the world of course thought him queer, but she, she only, knew how, and above all why, queer; which was precisely what enabled her to dispose the concealing veil in the right folds. She took his gaiety from him—since it had to pass with them for gaiety—as she took everything else; but she certainly so far justified by her unerring touch his finer sense of the degree to which he had ended by convincing her. *She* at least never spoke of the secret of his life except as "the real truth about you," and she had in fact a wonderful way of making it seem, as such, the secret of her own life too. That was in fine how he so constantly felt her as allowing for him; he couldn't on the whole call it anything else. He allowed for himself, but she, exactly, allowed still more; partly because, better placed for a sight of the matter, she traced his unhappy perversion through portions of its course into which he could scarce follow it. He knew how he felt, but, besides knowing that, she knew how he *looked* as well; he knew each of the things of importance he was insidiously kept from doing, but she could add up the amount they made, understand how much, with a lighter weight on his spirit, he might have done, and thereby establish how, clever as he was, he fell short. Above all she was in the secret of the difference between the forms he went through—those of his little office under Government, those of caring for his modest patrimony, for his library, for his garden in the country, for the people in London whose invitations he accepted and repaid—and the detachment that reigned beneath them and that made of all behaviour, all that could in the least be called behaviour, a long act of dissimulation. What it had come to was that he wore a mask painted with the social simper, out of the eyeholes of which there looked eyes of an expression not in the least matching the other features. This the stupid world, even after years, had never more than half discovered. It was only May Bartram who had, and she achieved, by an art indescribable, the feat of at once—or perhaps it was only alternately—meeting the eyes from in front and mingling her own vision, as from over his shoulder, with their peep through the apertures.

So, while they grew older together, she did watch with him, and so she let this association give shape and colour to her own existence. Beneath *her* forms as well detachment had learned to sit, and behaviour had become for her, in the social sense, a false account of herself. There was but one account of her that would have been true all the while, and that she could give, directly, to nobody, least of all to John Marcher. Her whole attitude was a virtual statement, but the perception of that only

seemed destined to take its place for him as one of the many
things necessarily crowded out of his consciousness. If she had,
moreover, like himself, to make sacrifices to their real truth, it
was to be granted that her compensation might have affected
her as more prompt and more natural. They had long periods,
in this London time, during which, when they were together, a
stranger might have listened to them without in the least prick-
ing up his ears; on the other hand, the real truth was equally liable at any moment to rise to the surface, and the auditor
would then have wondered indeed what they were talking
about. They had from an early time made up their mind that
society was, luckily, unintelligent, and the margin that this gave
them had fairly become one of their commonplaces. Yet there
were still moments when the situation turned almost fresh—
usually under the effect of some expression drawn from herself.
Her expressions doubtless repeated themselves, but her intervals were generous. "What saves us, you know, is that we answer so completely to so usual an appearance: that of the man
and woman whose friendship has become such a daily habit, or
almost, as to be at last indispensable." That, for instance, was
a remark she had frequently enough had occasion to make,
though she had given it at different times different developments. What we are especially concerned with is the turn it
happened to take from her one afternoon when he had come to
see her in honour of her birthday. This anniversary had fallen
on a Sunday, at a season of thick fog and general outward
gloom; but he had brought her his customary offering, having
known her now long enough to have established a hundred little customs. It was one of his proofs to himself, the present he
made her on her birthday, that he had not sunk into real selfishness. It was mostly nothing more than a small trinket, but it
was always fine of its kind, and he was regularly careful to pay
for it more than he thought he could afford. "Our habit saves
you, at least, don't you see? because it makes you, after all, for
the vulgar, indistinguishable from other men. What's the most
inveterate mark of men in general? Why, the capacity to spend
endless time with dull women—to spend it, I won't say without
being bored, but without minding that they are, without being
driven off at a tangent by it; which comes to the same thing.

I'm your dull woman, a part of the daily bread for which you pray at church. That covers your tracks more than anything."

"And what covers yours?" asked Marcher, whom his dull woman could mostly to this extent amuse. "I see of course what you mean by your saving me, in one way and another, so far as other people are concerned—I've seen it all along. Only, what is it that saves *you*? I often think, you know, of that."

She looked as if she sometimes thought of that too, but in rather a different way. "Where other people, you mean, are concerned?"

"Well, you're really so in with me, you know—as a sort of result of my being so in with yourself. I mean of my having such an immense regard for you, being so tremendously grateful for all you've done for me. I sometimes ask myself if it's quite fair. Fair I mean to have so involved and—since one may say it—interested you. I almost feel as if you hadn't really had time to do anything else."

"Anything else but be interested?" she asked. "Ah, what else does one ever want to be? If I've been 'watching' with you, as we long ago agreed that I was to do, watching is always in itself an absorption."

"Oh, certainly," John Marcher said, "if you hadn't had your curiosity—! Only, doesn't it sometimes come to you, as time goes on, that your curiosity is not being particularly repaid?"

May Bartram had a pause. "Do you ask that, by any chance, because you feel at all that yours isn't? I mean because you have to wait so long."

Oh, he understood what she meant. "For the thing to happen that never does happen? For the beast to jump out? No, I'm just where I was about it. It isn't a matter as to which I can *choose*, I can decide for a change. It isn't one as to which there *can* be a change. It's in the lap of the gods. One's in the hands of one's law—there one is. As to the form the law will take, the way it will operate, that's its own affair."

"Yes," Miss Bartram replied; "of course one's fate is coming, of course it *has* come, in its own form and its own way, all the while. Only, you know, the form and the way in your case were to have been—well, something so exceptional and, as one may say, so particularly *your* own."

Something in this made him look at her with suspicion. "You say 'were to *have* been,' as if in your heart you had begun to doubt."

"Oh!" she vaguely protested.

"As if you believed," he went on, "that nothing will now take place."

She shook her head slowly, but rather inscrutably. "You're far from my thought."

He continued to look at her. "What then is the matter with you?"

"Well," she said after another wait, "the matter with me is simply that I'm more sure than ever my curiosity, as you call it, will be but too well repaid."

They were frankly grave now; he had got up from his seat, had turned once more about the little drawing-room to which, year after year, he brought his inevitable topic; in which he had, as he might have said, tasted their intimate community with every sauce, where every object was as familiar to him as the things of his own house and the very carpets were worn with his fitful walk very much as the desks in old counting-houses are worn by the elbows of generations of clerks. The generations of his nervous moods had been at work there, and the place was the written history of his whole middle life. Under the impression of what his friend had just said he knew himself, for some reason, more aware of these things, which made him, after a moment, stop again before her. "Is it, possibly, that you've grown afraid?"

"Afraid?" He thought, as she repeated the word, that his question had made her, a little, change colour; so that, lest he should have touched on a truth, he explained very kindly, "You remember that that was what you asked *me* long ago—that first day at Weatherend."

"Oh yes, and you told me you didn't know—that I was to see for myself. We've said little about it since, even in so long a time."

"Precisely," Marcher interposed—"quite as if it were too delicate a matter for us to make free with. Quite as if we might find, on pressure, that I *am* afraid. For then," he said, "we shouldn't, should we? quite know what to do."

She had for the time no answer to this question. "There have been days when I thought you were. Only, of course," she added, "there have been days when we have thought almost anything."

"Everything. Oh!" Marcher softly groaned as with a gasp, half spent, at the face, more uncovered just then than it had been for a long while, of the imagination always with them. It had always had its incalculable moments of glaring out, quite as with the very eyes of the very Beast, and, used as he was to them, they could still draw from him the tribute of a sigh that rose from the depths of his being. All that they had thought, first and last, rolled over him; the past seemed to have been reduced to mere barren speculation. This in fact was what the place had just struck him as so full of—the simplification of everything but the state of suspense. That remained only by seeming to hang in the void surrounding it. Even his original fear, if fear it had been, had lost itself in the desert. "I judge, however," he continued, "that you see I'm not afraid now."

"What I see is, as I make it out, that you've achieved something almost unprecedented in the way of getting used to danger. Living with it so long and so closely, you've lost your sense of it; you know it's there, but you're indifferent, and you cease even, as of old, to have to whistle in the dark. Considering what the danger is," May Bartram wound up, "I'm bound to say that I don't think your attitude could well be surpassed."

John Marcher faintly smiled. "It's heroic?"

"Certainly—call it that."

He considered. "I *am*, then, a man of courage?"

"That's what you were to show me."

He still, however, wondered. "But doesn't the man of courage know what he's afraid of—or *not* afraid of? I don't know *that*, you see. I don't focus it. I can't name it. I only know I'm exposed."

"Yes, but exposed—how shall I say?—so directly. So intimately. That's surely enough."

"Enough to make you feel, then—as what we may call the end of our watch—that I'm not afraid?"

"You're not afraid. But it isn't," she said, "the end of our

watch. That is it isn't the end of yours. You've everything still
to see."

"Then why haven't *you?*" he asked. He had had, all along,
to-day, the sense of her keeping something back, and he still
had it. As this was his first impression of that, it made a kind of
date. The case was the more marked as she didn't at first answer; which in turn made him go on. "You know something I
don't." Then his voice, for that of a man of courage, trembled
a little. "You know what's to happen." Her silence, with the
face she showed, was almost a confession—it made him sure.
"You know, and you're afraid to tell me. It's so bad that you're
afraid I'll find out."

All this might be true, for she did look as if, unexpectedly to
her, he had crossed some mystic line that she had secretly
drawn round her. Yet she might, after all, not have worried;
and the real upshot was that he himself, at all events, needn't.
"You'll never find out."

III.

It was all to have made, none the less, as I have said, a date; as
came out in the fact that again and again, even after long intervals, other things that passed between them wore, in relation to
this hour, but the character of recalls and results. Its immediate
effect had been indeed rather to lighten insistence—almost to
provoke a reaction; as if their topic had dropped by its own
weight and as if moreover, for that matter, Marcher had been
visited by one of his occasional warnings against egotism. He
had kept up, he felt, and very decently on the whole, his consciousness of the importance of not being selfish, and it was
true that he had never sinned in that direction without
promptly enough trying to press the scales the other way. He
often repaired his fault, the season permitting, by inviting his
friend to accompany him to the opera; and it not infrequently
thus happened that, to show he didn't wish her to have but one
sort of food for her mind, he was the cause of her appearing
there with him a dozen nights in the month. It even happened
that, seeing her home at such times, he occasionally went in

with her to finish, as he called it, the evening, and, the better to make his point, sat down to the frugal but always careful little supper that awaited his pleasure. His point was made, he thought, by his not eternally insisting with her on himself; made for instance, at such hours, when it befell that, her piano at hand and each of them familiar with it, they went over passages of the opera together. It chanced to be on one of these occasions, however, that he reminded her of her not having answered a certain question he had put to her during the talk that had taken place between them on her last birthday. "What is it that saves *you?*"—saved her, he meant, from that appearance of variation from the usual human type. If he had practically escaped remark, as she pretended, by doing, in the most important particular, what most men do—find the answer to life in patching up an alliance of a sort with a woman no better than himself—how had she escaped it, and how could the alliance, such as it was, since they must suppose it had been more or less noticed, have failed to make her rather positively talked about?

"I never said," May Bartram replied, "that it hadn't made me talked about."

"Ah well then, you're not 'saved.' "

"It has not been a question for me. If you've had your woman, I've had," she said, "my man."

"And you mean that makes you all right?"

She hesitated. "I don't know why it shouldn't make me—humanly, which is what we're speaking of—as right as it makes you."

"I see," Marcher returned. " 'Humanly,' no doubt, as showing that you're living for something. Not, that is, just for me and my secret."

May Bartram smiled. "I don't pretend it exactly shows that I'm not living for you. It's my intimacy with you that's in question."

He laughed as he saw what she meant. "Yes, but since, as you say, I'm only, so far as people make out, ordinary, you're—aren't you?—no more than ordinary either. You help me to pass for a man like another. So if I *am*, as I understand you, you're not compromised. Is that it?"

She had another hesitation, but she spoke clearly enough. "That's it. It's all that concerns me—to help you to pass for a man like another."

He was careful to acknowledge the remark handsomely. "How kind, how beautiful, you are to me! How shall I ever repay you?"

She had her last grave pause, as if there might be a choice of ways. But she chose. "By going on as you are."

It was into this going on as he was that they relapsed, and really for so long a time that the day inevitably came for a further sounding of their depths. It was as if these depths, constantly bridged over by a structure that was firm enough in spite of its lightness and of its occasional oscillation in the somewhat vertiginous air, invited on occasion, in the interest of their nerves, a dropping of the plummet and a measurement of the abyss. A difference had been made moreover, once for all, by the fact that she had, all the while, not appeared to feel the need of rebutting his charge of an idea within her that she didn't dare to express, uttered just before one of the fullest of their later discussions ended. It had come up for him then that she "knew" something and that what she knew was bad—too bad to tell him. When he had spoken of it as visibly so bad that she was afraid he might find it out, her reply had left the matter too equivocal to be let alone and yet, for Marcher's special sensibility, almost too formidable again to touch. He circled about it at a distance that alternately narrowed and widened and that yet was not much affected by the consciousness in him that there was nothing she could "know," after all, any better than he did. She had no source of knowledge that he hadn't equally—except of course that she might have finer nerves. That was what women had where they were interested; they made out things, where people were concerned, that the people often couldn't have made out for themselves. Their nerves, their sensibility, their imagination, were conductors and revealers, and the beauty of May Bartram was in particular that she had given herself so to his case. He felt in these days what, oddly enough, he had never felt before, the growth of a dread of losing her by some catastrophe—some catastrophe that yet wouldn't at all be *the* catastrophe: partly because she had, almost of a sudden, begun to strike him as useful to him as never yet, and partly by reason of an appearance of uncertainty in her health, coincident and equally new. It was characteristic of the inner detachment he had hitherto so successfully cultivated and to which our whole account of him is a reference, it was characteristic that his complications, such as they were, had never yet seemed so as at this crisis to thicken about him, even to the point of making him ask himself if he were, by any chance, of a truth, within sight or sound, within touch or reach, within the immediate jurisdiction of the thing that waited.

When the day came, as come it had to, that his friend confessed to him her fear of a deep disorder in her blood, he felt somehow the shadow of a change and the chill of a shock. He immediately began to imagine aggravations and disasters, and above all to think of her peril as the direct menace for himself of personal privation. This indeed gave him one of those partial recoveries of equanimity that were agreeable to him—it showed him that what was still first in his mind was the loss she herself might suffer. "What if she should have to die before knowing, before seeing—?" It would have been brutal, in the early stages of her trouble, to put that question to her; but it had immediately sounded for him to his own concern, and the possibility was what most made him sorry for her. If she did "know," moreover, in the sense of her having had some—what should he think?—mystical, irresistible light, this would make the matter not better, but worse, inasmuch as her original adoption of his own curiosity had quite become the basis of her life. She had been living to see what would *be* to be seen, and it would be cruel to her to have to give up before the accomplishment of the vision. These reflections, as I say, refreshed his generosity; yet, make them as he might, he saw himself, with the lapse of the period, more and more disconcerted. It lapsed for him with a strange, steady sweep, and the oddest oddity was that it gave him, independently of the threat of much inconvenience, almost the only positive surprise his career, if career it could be called, had yet offered him. She kept the house as she had never done; he had to go to her to see her—she could meet him nowhere now, though there was scarce a corner of their loved old London in which she had not in the past, at one time or another, done so; and he found her always seated by her fire in the deep, old-fashioned chair she was less and less able to leave. He had been struck one day, after an absence exceeding his usual measure, with her suddenly looking much older to him than he had ever thought of her being; then he recognised that the suddenness was all on his side—he had just been suddenly struck. She looked older because inevitably, after so many years, she *was* old, or almost; which was of course true in still greater measure of her companion. If she was old, or almost, John Marcher assuredly was, and yet it was her showing of the lesson, not his own, that brought the truth home to him. His surprises began here; when once they had begun they multiplied; they came rather with a rush: it was as if, in the oddest way in the world, they had all been kept back, sown in a thick cluster, for the late afternoon of life, the time at which, for people in general, the unexpected has died out.

One of them was that he should have caught himself—for he *had* so done—*really* wondering if the great accident would take form now as nothing more than his being condemned to see this charming woman, this admirable friend, pass away from him. He had never so unreservedly qualified her as while confronted in thought with such a possibility; in spite of which there was small doubt for him that as an answer to his long riddle the mere effacement of even so fine a feature of his situation would be an abject anticlimax. It would represent, as connected with his past attitude, a drop of dignity under the shadow of which his existence could only become the most grotesque of failures. He had been far from holding it a failure—long as he had waited for the appearance that was to make it a success. He had waited for a quite other thing, not for such a one as that. The breath of his good faith came short, however, as he recognised how long he had waited, or how long, at least, his companion had. That she, at all events, might be recorded as having waited in vain—this affected him sharply, and all the more because of his at first having done little more than amuse himself with the idea. It grew more grave as the gravity of her condition grew, and the state of mind it produced in him, which he ended by watching, himself, as if it had been some definite disfigurement of his outer person, may pass for another of his surprises. This conjoined itself still with another, the really stupefying consciousness of a question that he would have allowed to shape itself had he dared. What did everything mean—what, that is, did *she* mean, she and her vain waiting and her probable death and the soundless admonition of it all—unless that, at this time of day, it was simply, it was overwhelmingly too late? He had never, at any stage of his queer consciousness, admitted the whisper of such a correction; he had never, till within these last few months, been so false to his conviction as not to hold that what was to come to him had time, whether *he* struck himself as having it or not. That at last, at last, he certainly hadn't it, to speak of, or had it but in the scantiest measure—such, soon enough, as things went with him, became the inference with which his old obsession had to reckon: and this it was not helped to do by the more and more confirmed appearance that the great vagueness casting the long shadow in which he had lived had, to attest itself, almost no margin left. Since it was in Time that he was to have met his fate, so it was in Time that his fate was to have acted; and as he waked up to the sense of no longer being young, which was exactly the sense of being stale, just as that, in turn, was the sense of being weak, he waked up to another matter beside. It all hung together; they were subject, he and the great vagueness, to an equal and indivisible law. When the possibilities themselves had, accordingly, turned stale, when the secret of the gods had grown faint, had perhaps even quite evaporated, that, and that only, was failure. It wouldn't have been failure to be bankrupt, dishonoured, pilloried, hanged; it was failure not to be anything. And so, in the dark valley into which his path had taken its unlooked-for twist, he wondered not a little as he groped. He didn't care what awful crash might overtake him, with what ignominy or what monstrosity he might yet be associated—since he wasn't, after all, too utterly old to suffer—if it would only be decently proportionate to the posture he had kept, all his life, in the promised presence of it. He had but one desire left—that he shouldn't have been "sold."

IV.

Then it was that one afternoon, while the spring of the year was young and new, she met, all in her own way, his frankest betrayal of these alarms. He had gone in late to see her, but evening had not settled, and she was presented to him in that long, fresh light of waning April days which affects us often with a sadness sharper than the greyest hours of autumn. The week had been warm, the spring was supposed to have begun early, and May Bartram sat, for the first time in the year, without a fire, a fact that, to Marcher's sense, gave the scene of which she formed part a smooth and ultimate look, an air of knowing, in its immaculate order and its cold, meaningless cheer, that it would never see a fire again. Her own aspect—he could scarce have said why—intensified this note. Almost as white as wax, with the marks and signs in her face as numerous and as fine as if they had been etched by a needle, with soft white draperies relieved by a faded green scarf, the delicate tone of which had been consecrated by the years, she was the picture of a serene, exquisite, but impenetrable sphinx, whose head, or indeed all whose person, might have been powdered with silver. She was a sphinx, yet with her white petals and green fronds she might have been a lily too—only an artificial lily, wonderfully imitated and constantly kept, without dust or stain, though not exempt from a slight droop and a complexity of faint creases, under some clear glass bell. The perfection of household care, of high polish and finish, always reigned in her rooms, but they especially looked to Marcher at present as if everything had been wound up, tucked in, put away, so that she might sit with folded hands and with nothing more to do. She was "out of it," to his vision; her work was over; she communicated with him as across some gulf, or from some island of rest that she had already reached, and it made him feel strangely abandoned. Was it—or, rather, wasn't it—that if for so long she had been watching with him the answer to their question had swum into her ken and taken on its name, so that her occupation was verily gone? He had as much as charged her with this in saying to her, many months before, that she even then knew something she was keeping from him. It was a

point he had never since ventured to press, vaguely fearing, as
he did, that it might become a difference, perhaps a disagreement, between them. He had in short, in this later time, turned
nervous, which was what, in all the other years, he had never
been; and the oddity was that his nervousness should have
waited till he had begun to doubt, should have held off so long
as he was sure. There was something, it seemed to him, that the
wrong word would bring down on his head, something that
would so at least put an end to his suspense. But he wanted not
to speak the wrong word; that would make everything ugly. He
wanted the knowledge he lacked to drop on him, if drop it
could, by its own august weight. If she was to forsake him it
was surely for her to take leave. This was why he didn't ask her
again, directly, what she knew; but it was also why, approaching the matter from another side, he said to her in the course of
his visit: "What do you regard as the very worst that, at this
time of day, *can* happen to me?"

He had asked her that in the past often enough; they had, with
the odd, irregular rhythm of their intensities and avoidances, exchanged ideas about it and then had seen the ideas washed away
by cool intervals, washed like figures traced in sea-sand. It had
ever been the mark of their talk that the oldest allusions in it required but a little dismissal and reaction to come out again,
sounding for the hour as new. She could thus at present meet his
inquiry quite freshly and patiently. "Oh yes, I've repeatedly
thought, only it always seemed to me of old that I couldn't quite
make up my mind. I thought of dreadful things, between which
it was difficult to choose; and so must you have done."

"Rather! I feel now as if I had scarce done anything else. I
appear to myself to have spent my life in thinking of nothing
but dreadful things. A great many of them I've at different
times named to you, but there were others I couldn't name."

"They were too, too dreadful?"

"Too, too dreadful—some of them."

She looked at him a minute, and there came to him as he met
it an inconsequent sense that her eyes, when one got their full
clearness, were still as beautiful as they had been in youth, only
beautiful with a strange, cold light—a light that somehow was
a part of the effect, if it wasn't rather a part of the cause, of the

pale, hard sweetness of the season and the hour. "And yet," she said at last, "there are horrors we have mentioned."

It deepened the strangeness to see her, as such a figure in such a picture, talk of "horrors," but she was to do, in a few minutes, something stranger yet—though even of this he was to take the full measure but afterwards—and the note of it was already in the air. It was, for the matter of that, one of the signs that her eyes were having again such a high flicker of their prime. He had to admit, however, what she said. "Oh yes, there were times when we did go far." He caught himself in the act of speaking as if it all were over. Well, he wished it were; and the consummation depended, for him, clearly, more and more on his companion.

But she had now a soft smile. "Oh, far—!"

It was oddly ironic. "Do you mean you're prepared to go further?"

She was frail and ancient and charming as she continued to look at him, yet it was rather as if she had lost the thread. "Do you consider that we went so far?"

"Why, I thought it the point you were just making—that we *had* looked most things in the face."

"Including each other?" She still smiled. "But you're quite right. We've had together great imaginations, often great fears; but some of them have been unspoken."

"Then the worst—we haven't faced that. I *could* face it, I believe, if I knew what you think it. I feel," he explained, "as if I had lost my power to conceive such things." And he wondered if he looked as blank as he sounded. "It's spent."

"Then why do you assume," she asked, "that mine isn't?"

"Because you've given me signs to the contrary. It isn't a question for you of conceiving, imagining, comparing. It isn't a question now of choosing." At last he came out with it. "You know something that I don't. You've shown me that before."

These last words affected her, he could see in a moment, remarkably, and she spoke with firmness, "I've shown you, my dear, nothing."

He shook his head. "You can't hide it."

"Oh, oh!" May Bartram murmured over what she couldn't hide. It was almost a smothered groan.

"You admitted it months ago, when I spoke of it to you as of something you were afraid I would find out. Your answer was that I couldn't, that I wouldn't, and I don't pretend I have. But you had something therefore in mind, and I see now that it must have been, that it still is, the possibility that, of all possibilities, has settled itself for you as the worst. This," he went on, "is why I appeal to you. I'm only afraid of ignorance now—I'm not afraid of knowledge." And then as for a while she said nothing: "What makes me sure is that I see in your face and feel here, in this air and amid these appearances, that you're out of it. You've done. You've had your experience. You leave me to my fate."

Well, she listened, motionless and white in her chair, as if she had in fact a decision to make, so that her whole manner was a virtual confession, though still with a small, fine, inner stiffness, an imperfect surrender. "It *would* be the worst," she finally let herself say. "I mean the thing that I've never said."

It hushed him a moment. "More monstrous than all the monstrosities we've named?"

"More monstrous. Isn't that what you sufficiently express," she asked, "in calling it the worst?"

Marcher thought. "Assuredly—if you mean, as I do, something that includes all the loss and all the shame that are thinkable."

"It would if it *should* happen," said May Bartram. "What we're speaking of, remember, is only my idea."

"It's your belief," Marcher returned. "That's enough for me. I feel your beliefs are right. Therefore if, having this one, you give me no more light on it, you abandon me."

"No, no!" she repeated. "I'm with you—don't you see?—still." And as if to make it more vivid to him she rose from her chair—a movement she seldom made in these days—and showed herself, all draped and all soft, in her fairness and slimness. "I haven't forsaken you."

It was really, in its effort against weakness, a generous assurance, and had the success of the impulse not, happily, been great, it would have touched him to pain more than to pleasure. But the cold charm in her eyes had spread, as she hovered before him, to all the rest of her person, so that it was, for the minute, almost like a recovery of youth. He couldn't pity her for that; he could only take her as she showed—as capable still of helping him. It was as if, at the same time, her light might at any instant go out; wherefore he must make the most of it. There passed before him with intensity the three or four things he wanted most to know; but the question that came of itself to his lips really covered the others. "Then tell me if I shall consciously suffer."

She promptly shook her head. "Never!"

It confirmed the authority he imputed to her, and it produced on him an extraordinary effect. "Well, what's better than that? Do you call that the worst?"

"You think nothing is better?" she asked.

She seemed to mean something so special that he again sharply wondered, though still with the dawn of a prospect of relief. "Why not, if one doesn't *know?*" After which, as their eyes, over his question, met in a silence, the dawn deepened and something to his purpose came, prodigiously, out of her very face. His own, as he took it in, suddenly flushed to the forehead, and he gasped with the force of a perception to which, on the instant, everything fitted. The sound of his gasp filled the air; then he became articulate. "I see—if I don't suffer!"

In her own look, however, was doubt. "You see what?"

"Why, what you mean—what you've always meant."

She again shook her head. "What I mean isn't what I've always meant. It's different."

"It's something new?"

She hesitated. "Something new. It's not what you think. I see what you think."

His divination drew breath then; only her correction might be wrong. "It isn't that I *am* a donkey?" he asked between faintness and grimness. "It isn't that it's all a mistake?"

"A mistake?" she pityingly echoed. *That* possibility, for her, he saw, would be monstrous; and if she guaranteed him the immunity from pain it would accordingly not be what she had in mind. "Oh, no," she declared; "it's nothing of that sort. You've been right."

Yet he couldn't help asking himself if she weren't, thus pressed, speaking but to save him. It seemed to him he should be most lost if his history should prove all a platitude. "Are you telling me the truth, so that I sha'n't have been a bigger idiot than I can bear to know? I *haven't* lived with a vain imagination, in the most besotted illusion? I haven't waited but to see the door shut in my face?"

She shook her head again. "However the case stands *that* isn't the truth. Whatever the reality, it *is* a reality. The door isn't shut. The door's open," said May Bartram.

"Then something's to come?"

She waited once again, always with her cold, sweet eyes on him. "It's never too late." She had, with her gliding step, diminished the distance between them, and she stood nearer to him, close to him, a minute, as if still full of the unspoken. Her movement might have been for some finer emphasis of what she was at once hesitating and deciding to say. He had been standing by the chimney-piece, fireless and sparely adorned, a small, perfect old French clock and two morsels of rosy Dresden constituting all its furniture; and her hand grasped the shelf while she kept him waiting, grasped it a little as for support and encouragement. She only kept him waiting, however; that is he only waited. It had become suddenly, from her movement and attitude, beautiful and vivid to him that she had something more to give him; her wasted face delicately shone with it, and it glittered, almost as with the white lustre of silver, in her expression. She was right, incontestably, for what he saw in her face was the truth, and strangely, without consequence, while their talk of it as dreadful was still in the air, she appeared to present it as inordinately soft. This, prompting bewilderment, made him but gape the more gratefully for her revelation, so that they continued for some minutes silent, her face shining at him, her contact imponderably pressing, and his stare all kind, but all expectant. The end, none the less, was that what he had expected failed to sound. Something else took place instead, which seemed to consist at first in the mere closing of her eyes. She gave way at the same instant to a slow, fine shudder, and though be remained staring—though he stared, in fact, but the harder—she turned off and regained her chair. It was the end of what she had been intending, but it left him thinking only of that.

"Well, you don't say——?"

She had touched in her passage a bell near the chimney and had sunk back, strangely pale. "I'm afraid I'm too ill."

"Too ill to tell me?" It sprang up sharp to him, and almost to his lips, the fear that she would die without giving him light. He checked himself in time from so expressing his question, but she answered as if she had heard the words.

"Don't you know——now?"

" 'Now'——?" She had spoken as if something that had made a difference had come up within the moment. But her maid, quickly obedient to her bell, was already with them. "I know nothing." And he was afterwards to say to himself that he must have spoken with odious impatience, such an impatience as to show that, supremely disconcerted, he washed his hands of the whole question.

"Oh!" said May Bartram.

"Are you in pain?" he asked, as the woman went to her.

"No," said May Bartram.

Her maid, who had put an arm round her as if to take her to her room, fixed on him eyes that appealingly contradicted her; in spite of which, however, he showed once more his mystification. "What then has happened?"

She was once more, with her companion's help, on her feet, and, feeling withdrawal imposed on him, he had found, blankly, his hat and gloves and had reached the door. Yet he waited for her answer. "What *was* to," she said.

V.

He came back the next day, but she was then unable to see him, and as it was literally the first time this had occurred in the long stretch of their acquaintance he turned away, defeated and sore, almost angry—or feeling at least that such a break in their custom was really the beginning of the end—and wandered alone with his thoughts, especially with one of them that he was unable to keep down. She was dying, and he would lose her; she was dying, and his life would end. He stopped in the park, into which he had passed, and stared before him at his recurrent doubt. Away from her the doubt pressed again; in her presence he had believed her, but as he felt his forlornness he threw himself into the explanation that, nearest at hand, had most of a miserable warmth for him and least of a cold torment. She had deceived him to save him—to put him off with something in which he should be able to rest. What could the thing that was to happen to him be, after all, but just this thing that had begun to happen? Her dying, her death, his consequent solitude—*that* was what he had figured as the beast in the jungle, that was what had been in the lap of the gods. He had had her word for it as he left her; for what else, on earth, could she have meant? It wasn't a thing of a monstrous order; not a fate rare and distinguished; not a stroke of fortune that overwhelmed and immortalised; it had only the stamp of the common doom. But poor Marcher, at this hour, judged the common doom sufficient. It would serve his turn, and even as the consummation of infinite waiting he would bend his pride to accept it. He sat down on a bench in the twilight. He hadn't been a fool. Something had *been*, as she had said, to come. Before he rose indeed it had quite struck him that the final fact really matched with the long avenue through which he had had to reach it. As sharing his suspense, and as giving herself all, giving her life, to bring it to an end, she had come with him every step of the way. He had lived by her aid, and to leave her behind would be cruelly, damnably to miss her. What could be more overwhelming than that?

Well, he was to know within the week, for though she kept him a while at bay, left him restless and wretched during a series of days on each of which he asked about her only again to have to turn away, she ended his trial by receiving him where she had always received him. Yet she had been brought out at some hazard into the presence of so many of the things that were, consciously, vainly, half their past, and there was scant service left in the gentleness of her mere desire, all too visible, to check his obsession and wind up his long trouble. That was clearly what she wanted; the one thing more, for her own peace, while she could still put out her hand. He was so af-

fected by her state that, once seated by her chair, he was moved
to let everything go; it was she herself therefore who brought
him back, took up again, before she dismissed him, her last
word of the other time. She showed how she wished to leave
their affair in order. "I'm not sure you understood. You've
nothing to wait for more. It *has* come."

Oh, how he looked at her! "Really?"

"Really."

"The thing that, as you said, *was* to?"

"The thing that we began in our youth to watch for."

Face to face with her once more he believed her; it was a claim
to which he had so abjectly little to oppose. "You mean that it has
come as a positive, definite occurrence, with a name and a date?"

"Positive. Definite. I don't know about the 'name,' but, oh,
with a date!"

He found himself again too helplessly at sea. "But come in
the night—come and passed me by?"

May Bartram had her strange, faint smile. "Oh no, it hasn't
passed you by!"

"But if I haven't been aware of it, and it hasn't touched
me—?"

"Ah, your not being aware of it," and she seemed to hesitate
an instant to deal with this—"your not being aware of it is the
strangeness *in* the strangeness. It's the wonder *of* the wonder."
She spoke as with the softness almost of a sick child, yet now at
last, at the end of all, with the perfect straightness of a sibyl.
She visibly knew that she knew, and the effect on him was of
something co-ordinate, in its high character, with the law that
had ruled him. It was the true voice of the law; so on her lips
would the law itself have sounded. "It *has* touched you," she
went on. "It has done its office. It has made you all its own."

"So utterly without my knowing it?"

"So utterly without your knowing it." His hand, as he leaned
to her, was on the arm of her chair, and, dimly smiling always
now, she placed her own on it. "It's enough if *I* know it."

"Oh!" he confusedly sounded, as she herself of late so often
had done.

"What I long ago said is true. You'll never know now, and I

think you ought to be content. You've *had* it," said May Bartram.

"But had what?"

"Why, what was to have marked you out. The proof of your law. It has acted. I'm too glad," she then bravely added, "to have been able to see what it's *not*."

He continued to attach his eyes to her, and with the sense that it was all beyond him, and that *she* was too, he would still have sharply challenged her, had he not felt it an abuse of her weakness to do more than take devoutly what she gave him, take it as hushed as to a revelation. If he did speak, it was out of the foreknowledge of his loneliness to come. "If you're glad of what it's 'not,' it might then have been worse?"

She turned her eyes away, she looked straight before her with which, after a moment: "Well, you know our fears."

He wondered. "It's something then we never feared?"

On this, slowly, she turned to him. "Did we ever dream, with all our dreams, that we should sit and talk of it thus?"

He tried for a little to make out if they had; but it was as if their dreams, numberless enough, were in solution in some thick, cold mist, in which thought lost itself. "It might have been that we couldn't talk?"

"Well"—she did her best for him—"not from this side. This, you see," she said, "is the *other* side."

"I think," poor Marcher returned, "that all sides are the same to me." Then, however, as she softly shook her head in correction: "We mightn't, as it were, have got across—?"

"To where we are—no. We're *here*"—she made her weak emphasis.

"And much good does it do us!" was her friend's frank comment.

"It does us the good it can. It does us the good that *it* isn't here. It's past. It's behind," said May Bartram. "Before—" but her voice dropped.

He had got up, not to tire her, but it was hard to combat his yearning. She after all told him nothing but that his light had failed—which he knew well enough without her. "Before—?" he blankly echoed.

"Before, you see, it was always to *come*. That kept it present."

"Oh, I don't care what comes now! Besides," Marcher added, "it seems to me I liked it better present, as you say, than I can like it absent with *your* absence."

"Oh, mine!"—and her pale hands made light of it.

"With the absence of everything." He had a dreadful sense of standing there before her for—so far as anything but this proved, this bottomless drop was concerned—the last time of their life. It rested on him with a weight he felt he could scarce bear, and this weight it apparently was that still pressed out what remained in him of speakable protest. "I believe you; but I can't begin to pretend I understand. *Nothing*, for me, is past; nothing *will* pass until I pass myself, which I pray my stars may be as soon as possible. Say, however," he added, "that I've eaten my cake, as you contend, to the last crumb—how can the thing I've never felt at all be the thing I was marked out to feel?"

She met him, perhaps, less directly, but she met him unperturbed. "You take your 'feelings' for granted. You were to suffer your fate. That was not necessarily to know it."

"How in the world—when what is such knowledge but suffering?"

She looked up at him a while, in silence. "No—you don't understand."

"I suffer," said John Marcher.

"Don't, don't!"

"How can I help at least *that*?"

"*Don't!*" May Bartram repeated.

She spoke it in a tone so special, in spite of her weakness, that he stared an instant—stared as if some light, hitherto hidden, had shimmered across his vision. Darkness again closed over it, but the gleam had already become for him an idea. "Because I haven't the right—?"

"Don't *know*—when you needn't," she mercifully urged. "You needn't—for we shouldn't."

"Shouldn't?" If he could but know what she meant!

"No—it's too much."

"Too much?" he still asked—but with a mystification that

was the next moment, of a sudden, to give way. Her words, if they meant something, affected him in this light—the light also of her wasted face—as meaning *all,* and the sense of what knowledge had been for herself came over him with a rush which broke through into a question. "Is it of that, then, you're dying?"

She but watched him, gravely at first, as if to see, with this, where he was, and she might have seen something, or feared something, that moved her sympathy. "I would live for you still—if I could." Her eyes closed for a little, as if, withdrawn into herself, she were, for a last time, trying. "But I can't!" she said as she raised them again to take leave of him.

She couldn't indeed, as but too promptly and sharply appeared, and he had no vision of her after this that was anything but darkness and doom. They had parted forever in that strange talk; access to her chamber of pain, rigidly guarded, was almost wholly forbidden him; he was feeling now moreover, in the face of doctors, nurses, the two or three relatives attracted doubtless by the presumption of what she had to "leave," how few were the rights, as they were called in such cases, that he had to put forward, and how odd it might even seem that their intimacy shouldn't have given him more of them. The stupidest fourth cousin had more, even though she had been nothing in such a person's life. She had been a feature of features in *his,* for what else was it to have been so indispensable? Strange beyond saying were the ways of existence, baffling for him the anomaly of his lack, as he felt it to be, of producible claim. A woman might have been, as it were, everything to him, and it might yet present him in no connection that anyone appeared obliged to recognise. If this was the case in these closing weeks it was the case more sharply on the occasion of the last offices rendered, in the great grey London cemetery, to what had been mortal, to what had been precious, in his friend. The concourse at her grave was not numerous, but he saw himself treated as scarce more nearly concerned with it than if there had been a thousand others. He was in short from this moment face to face with the fact that he was to profit extraordinarily little by the interest May Bartram had taken in him. He couldn't quite have said what he expected, but he had somehow not expected this approach to a double privation. Not only had her interest failed him, but he seemed to feel himself unattended—and for a reason he couldn't sound—by the distinction, the dignity, the propriety, if nothing else, of the man markedly bereaved. It was as if, in the view of society, he had not *been* markedly bereaved, as if there still failed some sign or proof of it, and as if, none the less, his character could never be affirmed, nor the deficiency ever made up. There were moments, as the weeks went by, when he would have liked, by some almost aggressive act, to take his stand on the intimacy of his loss, in order that it *might* be questioned and his retort, to the relief of his spirit, so recorded; but the moments of an irritation more helpless followed fast on these, the moments during which, turning things over with a good conscience but with a bare horizon, he found himself wondering if he oughtn't to have begun, so to speak, further back.

He found himself wondering indeed at many things, and this last speculation had others to keep it company. What could he have done, after all, in her lifetime, without giving them both, as it were, away? He couldn't have made it known she was watching him, for that would have published the superstition of the Beast. This was what closed his mouth now—now that the Jungle had been threshed to vacancy and that the Beast had stolen away. It sounded too foolish and too flat; the difference for him in this particular, the extinction in his life of the element of suspense, was such in fact as to surprise him. He could scarce have said what the effect resembled; the abrupt cessation, the positive prohibition, of music perhaps, more than anything else, in some place all adjusted and all accustomed to sonority and to attention. If he could at any rate have conceived lifting the veil from his image at some moment of the past (what had he done, after all, if not lift it to *her?*), so to do this to-day, to talk to people at large of the jungle cleared and confide to them that he now felt it as safe, would have been not only to see them listen as to a goodwife's tale, but really to hear himself tell one. What it presently came to in truth was that poor Marcher waded through his beaten grass, where no life stirred, where no breath sounded, where no evil eye seemed to gleam from a possible lair, very much as if vaguely looking for the Beast, and still more as if missing it. He walked about in an existence that had grown strangely more spacious, and, stopping fitfully in places where the undergrowth of life struck him as closer, asked himself yearningly, wondered secretly and sorely, if it would have lurked here or there. It would have at all events *sprung;* what was at least complete was his belief in the truth itself of the assurance given him. The change from his old sense to his new was absolute and final: what was to happen *had* so absolutely and finally happened that he was as little able to know a fear for his future as to know a hope; so absent in short was any question of anything still to come. He was to live entirely with the other question, that of his unidentified past, that of his having to see his fortune impenetrably muffled and masked.

The torment of this vision became then his occupation; he couldn't perhaps have consented to live but for the possibility of guessing. She had told him, his friend, not to guess; she had forbidden him, so far as he might, to know, and she had even in a sort denied the power in him to learn: which were so many things, precisely, to deprive him of rest. It wasn't that he wanted, he argued for fairness, that anything that had happened to him should happen over again; it was only that he shouldn't, as an anticlimax, have been taken sleeping so sound as not to be able to win back by an effort of thought the lost stuff of consciousness. He declared to himself at moments that he would either win it back or have done with consciousness for ever; he made this idea his one motive, in fine, made it so much his passion that none other, to compare with it, seemed ever to have touched him. The lost stuff of consciousness became thus for him as a strayed or stolen child to an unappeasable father; he hunted it up and down very much as if he were knocking at doors and inquiring of the police. This was the spirit in which, inevitably, he set himself to travel; he started on a journey that was to be as long as he could make it; it danced before him that, as the other side of the globe couldn't possibly have less to say to him, it might, by a possibility of suggestion, have more. Before he quitted London, however, he made a pilgrimage to May Bartram's grave, took his way to it through the endless avenues of the grim suburban necropolis,

sought it out in the wilderness of tombs, and, though he had
come but for the renewal of the act of farewell, found himself,
when he had at last stood by it, beguiled into long intensities.
He stood for an hour, powerless to turn away and yet powerless to penetrate the darkness of death; fixing with his eyes her
inscribed name and date, beating his forehead against the fact
of the secret they kept, drawing his breath, while he waited as
if, in pity of him, some sense would rise from the stones. He
kneeled on the stones, however, in vain; they kept what they
concealed; and if the face of the tomb did become a face for
him it was because her two names were like a pair of eyes that
didn't know him. He gave them a last long look, but no palest
light broke.

VI.

He stayed away, after this, for a year; he visited the depths of
Asia, spending himself on scenes of romantic interest, of superlative sanctity; but what was present to him everywhere was
that for a man who had known what *he* had known the world
was vulgar and vain. The state of mind in which he had lived
for so many years shone out to him, in reflection, as a light that
coloured and refined, a light beside which the glow of the East
was garish, cheap and thin. The terrible truth was that he had
lost—with everything else—a distinction as well; the things
he saw couldn't help being common when he had become
common to look at them. He was simply now one of them
himself—he was in the dust, without a peg for the sense of
difference; and there were hours when, before the temples of
gods and the sepulchres of kings, his spirit turned, for nobleness of association, to the barely discriminated slab in the London suburb. That had become for him, and more intensely with
time and distance, his one witness of a past glory. It was all that
was left to him for proof or pride, yet the past glories of
Pharaohs were nothing to him as he thought of it. Small wonder then that he came back to it on the morrow of his return.
He was drawn there this time as irresistibly as the other, yet
with a confidence, almost, that was doubtless the effect of the

many months that had elapsed. He had lived, in spite of himself, into his change of feeling, and in wandering over the earth had wandered, as might be said, from the circumference to the centre of his desert. He had settled to his safety and accepted perforce his extinction; figuring to himself, with some colour, in the likeness of certain little old men he remembered to have seen, of whom, all meagre and wizened as they might look, it was related that they had in their time fought twenty duels or been loved by ten princesses. They indeed had been wondrous for others, while he was but wondrous for himself; which, however, was exactly the cause of his haste to renew the wonder by getting back, as he might put it, into his own presence. That had quickened his steps and checked his delay. If his visit was prompt it was because he had been separated so long from the part of himself that alone he now valued.

It is accordingly not false to say that he reached his goal with a certain elation and stood there again with a certain assurance. The creature beneath the sod *knew* of his rare experience, so that, strangely now, the place had lost for him its mere blankness of expression. It met him in mildness—not, as before, in mockery; it wore for him the air of conscious greeting that we find, after absence, in things that have closely belonged to us and which seem to confess of themselves to the connection. The plot of ground, the graven tablet, the tended flowers affected him so as belonging to him that he quite felt for the hour like a contented landlord reviewing a piece of property. Whatever had happened—well, had happened. He had not come back this time with the vanity of that question, his former worrying, "What, *what?*" now practically so spent. Yet he would, none the less, never again so cut himself off from the spot; he would come back to it every month, for if he did nothing else by its aid he at least held up his head. It thus grew for him, in the oddest way, a positive resource; he carried out his idea of periodical returns, which took their place at last among the most inveterate of his habits. What it all amounted to, oddly enough, was that, in his now so simplified world, this garden of death gave him the few square feet of earth on which he could still most live. It was as if, being nothing anywhere else for anyone, nothing even for himself, he were just everything here, and if not for a crowd of witnesses, or indeed for any witness but John Marcher, then by clear right of the register that he could scan like an open page. The open page was the tomb of his friend, and *there* were the facts of the past, there the truth of his life, there the backward reaches in which he could lose himself. He did this, from time to time, with such effect that he seemed to wander through the old years with his hand in the arm of a companion who was, in the most extraordinary manner, his other, his younger self; and to wander, which was more extraordinary yet, round and round a third presence—not wandering she, but stationary, still, whose eyes, turning with his revolution, never ceased to follow him, and whose seat was his point, so to speak, of orientation. Thus in short he settled to live—feeding only on the sense that he once *had* lived, and dependent on it not only for a support but for an identity.

It sufficed him, in its way, for months, and the year elapsed; it would doubtless even have carried him further but for an accident, superficially slight, which moved him, in a quite other direction, with a force beyond any of his impressions of Egypt or of India. It was a thing of the merest chance—the turn, as he afterwards felt, of a hair, though he was indeed to live to believe that if light hadn't come to him in this particular fashion it would still have come in another. He was to live to believe this, I say, though he was not to live, I may not less definitely mention, to do much else. We allow him at any rate the benefit of the conviction, struggling up for him at the end, that, whatever might have happened or not happened, he would have come round of himself to the light. The incident of an autumn day had put the match to the train laid from of old by his misery. With the light before him he knew that even of late his ache had only been smothered. It was strangely drugged, but it throbbed; at the touch it began to bleed. And the touch, in the event, was the face of a fellow-mortal. This face, one grey afternoon when the leaves were thick in the alleys, looked into Marcher's own, at the cemetery, with an expression like the cut of a blade. He felt it, that is, so deep down that he winced at the steady thrust. The person who so mutely assaulted him was a figure he had noticed, on reaching his own goal, absorbed by a grave a short distance away, a grave apparently fresh, so that the emotion of the visitor would probably match it for frankness. This fact alone forbade further attention, though during the time he stayed he remained vaguely conscious of his neighbour, a middle-aged man apparently, in mourning, whose bowed back, among the clustered monuments and mortuary yews, was constantly presented. Marcher's theory that these were elements in contact with which he himself revived, had suffered, on this occasion, it may be granted, a sensible though inscrutable check. The autumn day was dire for him as none had recently been, and he rested with a heaviness he had not yet known on the low stone table that bore May Bartram's name. He rested without power to move, as if some spring in him, some spell vouchsafed, had suddenly been broken forever. If he could have done that moment as he wanted he would simply have stretched himself on the slab that was ready to take him, treating it as a place prepared to receive his last sleep. What in all the wide world had he now to keep awake for? He stared before him with the question, and it was then that, as one of the cemetery walks passed near him, he caught the shock of the face.

His neighbour at the other grave had withdrawn, as he himself, with force in him to move, would have done by now, and was advancing along the path on his way to one of the gates. This brought him near, and his pace was slow, so that—and all the more as there was a kind of hunger in his look—the two men were for a minute directly confronted. Marcher felt him on the spot as one of the deeply stricken—a perception so sharp that nothing else in the picture lived for it, neither his dress, his age, nor his presumable character and class; nothing lived but the deep ravage of the features that he showed. He *showed* them—that was the point; he was moved, as he passed, by some impulse that was either a signal for sympathy or, more possibly, a challenge to another sorrow. He might already have been aware of our friend, might, at some previous hour, have noticed in him the smooth habit of the scene, with which the state of his own senses so scantly consorted, and might thereby have been stirred as by a kind of overt discord. What Marcher was at all events conscious of was, in the first place, that the

image of scarred passion presented to him was conscious too—
of something that profaned the air; and, in the second, that,
roused, startled, shocked, he was yet the next moment looking
after it, as it went, with envy. The most extraordinary thing
that had happened to him—though he had given that name to
other matters as well—took place, after his immediate vague
stare, as a consequence of this impression. The stranger passed,
but the raw glare of his grief remained, making our friend wonder in pity what wrong, what wound it expressed, what injury
not to be healed. What had the man *had* to make him, by the
loss of it, so bleed and yet live?

Something—and this reached him with a pang—that *he*,
John Marcher, hadn't; the proof of which was precisely John
Marcher's arid end. No passion had ever touched him, for this
was what passion meant; he had survived and maundered and
pined, but where had been *his* deep ravage? The extraordinary
thing we speak of was the sudden rush of the result of this
question. The sight that had just met his eyes named to him, as
in letters of quick flame, something he had utterly, insanely
missed, and what he had missed made these things a train of
fire, made them mark themselves in an anguish of inward
throbs. He had seen *outside* of his life, not learned it within, the
way a woman was mourned when she had been loved for herself; such was the force of his conviction of the meaning of the
stranger's face, which still flared for him like a smoky torch. It
had not come to him, the knowledge, on the wings of experience; it had brushed him, jostled him, upset him, with the dis-
respect of chance, the insolence of an accident. Now that the
illumination had begun, however, it blazed to the zenith, and
what he presently stood there gazing at was the sounded void
of his life. He gazed, he drew breath, in pain; he turned in his
dismay, and, turning, he had before him in sharper incision
than ever the open page of his story. The name on the table
smote him as the passage of his neighbour had done, and what
it said to him, full in the face, was that *she* was what he had
missed. This was the awful thought, the answer to all the past,
the vision at the dread clearness of which he turned as cold as
the stone beneath him. Everything fell together, confessed, ex-

plained, overwhelmed; leaving him most of all stupefied at the blindness he had cherished. The fate he had been marked for he had met with a vengeance—he had emptied the cup to the lees; he had been the man of his time, *the* man, to whom nothing on earth was to have happened. That was the rare stroke—that was his visitation. So he saw it, as we say, in pale horror, while the pieces fitted and fitted. So *she* had seen it, while he didn't, and so she served at this hour to drive the truth home. It was the truth, vivid and monstrous, that all the while he had waited the wait was itself his portion. This the companion of his vigil had at a given moment perceived, and she had then offered him the chance to baffle his doom. One's doom, however, was never baffled, and on the day she had told him that his own had come down she had seen him but stupidly stare at the escape she offered him.

The escape would have been to love her; then, *then* he would have lived. *She* had lived—who could say now with what passion?—since she had loved him for himself; whereas he had never thought of her (ah, how it hugely glared at him!) but in the chill of his egotism and the light of her use. Her spoken words came back to him, and the chain stretched and stretched. The beast had lurked indeed, and the beast, at its hour, had sprung; it had sprung in that twilight of the cold April when, pale, ill, wasted, but all beautiful, and perhaps even then recoverable, she had risen from her chair to stand before him and let him imaginably guess. It had sprung as he didn't guess; it had sprung as she hopelessly turned from him, and the mark, by the time he left her, had fallen where it *was* to fall. He had justified his fear and achieved his fate; he had failed, with the last exactitude, of all he was to fail of; and a moan now rose to his lips as he remembered she had prayed he mightn't know. This horror of waking—*this* was knowledge, knowledge under the breath of which the very tears in his eyes seemed to freeze. Through them, none the less, he tried to fix it and hold it; he kept it there before him so that he might feel the pain. That at least, belated and bitter, had something of the taste of life. But the bitterness suddenly sickened him, and it was as if, horribly, he saw, in the truth, in the cruelty of his image, what had been appointed and done. He saw the Jungle of his life and saw the lurking Beast; then, while he looked, perceived it, as by a stir of the air, rise, huge and hideous, for the leap that was to settle him. His eyes darkened—it was close; and, instinctively turning, in his hallucination, to avoid it, he flung himself, on his face, on the tomb.

The Jolly Corner

The English Review, December 1908. Returning to England after his 1904–1905 American tour—his first time back in the United States in over twenty years—James was soon engaged in several projects. Among them were the travel essays he would publish in The American Scene; *but in the summer of 1906 he took time apart to begin work on an "American" tale that would become "The Jolly Corner." In it, a fifty-six-year-old expatriate (James was sixty-one when he made his American tour) returns to his old home, or, more precisely, to his old house in New York, for the first time in thirty years; there he wonders—obsessively—what might have become of him had he never left. Although this late tale's architectural framing is by no means unique—for even in his criticism James had developed metaphors of the "chamber of consciousness" and "the house of fiction"—the architectural complexity of "The Jolly Corner" is prodigious. As Leon Edel observed, it is "as if the house on 'the jolly corner' were a mind, a brain, and Spencer Brydon were walking through its passages finding certain doors of resistance closed to truths hidden from himself."*

I.

"Every one asks me what I 'think' of everything," said Spencer Brydon; "and I make answer as I can—begging or dodging the question, putting them off with any nonsense. It wouldn't matter to any of them really," he went on, "for, even were it possible to meet in that stand-and-deliver way so silly a demand on so big a subject, my 'thoughts' would still be almost altogether about something that concerns only myself." He was talking to Miss Staverton, with whom for a couple of months now he had availed himself of every possible occasion to talk; this disposition and this resource, this comfort and support, as the situation in fact presented itself, having promptly enough taken the first place in the considerable array of rather unattenuated surprises attending his so strangely belated return to America. Everything was somehow a surprise; and that might be natural when one had so long and so consistently neglected everything, taken pains to give surprises so much margin for play. He had given them more than thirty years—thirty-three, to be exact; and they now seemed to him to have organised their performance quite on the scale of that licence. He had been twenty-three on leaving New York—he was fifty-six to-day: unless indeed he were to reckon as he had sometimes, since his repatriation, found himself feeling; in which case he would have lived longer than is often allotted to man. It would have taken a century, he repeatedly said to himself, and said also to Alice Staverton, it would have taken a longer absence and a more averted mind than those even of which he had been guilty, to pile up the differences, the newnesses, the queernesses, above all the bignesses, for the better or the worse, that at present assaulted his vision wherever he looked.

The great fact all the while however had been the incalculability; since he *had* supposed himself, from decade to decade, to be allowing, and in the most liberal and intelligent manner, for brilliancy of change. He actually saw that he had allowed for nothing; he missed what he would have been sure of finding, he found what he would never have imagined. Proportions and values were upside-down; the ugly things he had expected, the ugly things of his far-away youth, when he had too promptly waked up to a sense of the ugly—these uncanny phenomena placed him rather, as it happened, under the charm; whereas the "swagger" things, the modern, the monstrous, the famous things, those he had more particularly, like thousands of ingenuous enquirers every year, come over to see, were exactly his sources of dismay. They were as so many set traps for displeasure, above all for reaction, of which his restless tread was constantly pressing the spring. It was interesting, doubtless, the whole show, but it would have been too disconcerting hadn't a certain finer truth saved the situation. He had distinctly not, in this steadier light, come over *all* for the monstrosities; he had come, not only in the last analysis but quite on the face of the act, under an impulse with which they had nothing to do. He had come—putting the thing pompously—to look at his "property," which he had thus for a third of a century not been within four thousand miles of; or, expressing it less sordidly, he had yielded to the humour of seeing again his house on the jolly corner, as he usually, and quite fondly, described it—the one in which he had first seen the light, in which various members of his family had lived and had died, in which the holidays of his overschooled boyhood had been passed and the few social flowers of his chilled adolescence gathered, and which, alienated then for so long a period, had, through the successive deaths of his two brothers and the termination of old arrangements, come wholly into his hands. He was the owner of another, not quite so "good"—the jolly corner having been, from far back, superlatively extended and consecrated; and the value of the pair represented his main capital, with an income consisting, in these later years, of their respective rents which (thanks precisely to their original excellent type) had never been depressingly low. He could live in "Europe," as he had been in the habit of living, on the product of these flourishing New York leases, and all the better since, that of the second structure, the mere number in its long row, having within a twelvemonth fallen in, renovation at a high advance had proved beautifully possible.

These were items of property indeed, but he had found himself since his arrival distinguishing more than ever between them. The house within the street, two bristling blocks westward, was already in course of reconstruction as a tall mass of flats; he had acceded, some time before, to overtures for this conversion—in which, now that it was going forward, it had been not the least of his astonishments to find himself able, on the spot, and though without a previous ounce of such experience, to participate with a certain intelligence, almost with a certain authority. He had lived his life with his back so turned to such concerns and his face addressed to those of so different an order that he scarce knew what to make of this lively stir, in a compartment of his mind never yet penetrated, of a capacity for business and a sense for construction. These virtues, so common all round him now, had been dormant in his own organism—where it might be said of them perhaps that they had slept the sleep of the just. At present, in the splendid autumn weather—the autumn at least was a pure boon in the terrible place—he loafed about his "work" undeterred, secretly agitated; not in the least "minding" that the whole proposition, as they said, was vulgar and sordid, and ready to climb ladders, to walk the plank, to handle materials and look wise about them, to ask questions, in fine, and challenge explanations and really "go into" figures.

It amused, it verily quite charmed him; and, by the same stroke, it amused, and even more, Alice Staverton, though perhaps charming her perceptibly less. She wasn't however going to be better-off for it, as *he* was—and so astonishingly much: nothing was now likely, he knew, ever to make her better-off than she found herself, in the afternoon of life, as the delicately frugal possessor and tenant of the small house in Irving Place to which she had subtly managed to cling through her almost unbroken New York career. If he knew the way to it now better than to any other address among the dreadful multiplied numberings which seemed to him to reduce the whole place to some vast ledger-page, overgrown, fantastic, of ruled and crisscrossed lines and figures—if he had formed, for his consolation, that habit, it was really not a little because of the charm of his having encountered and recognised, in the vast wilderness of the wholesale, breaking through the mere gross generalisation of wealth and force and success, a small still scene where items and shades, all delicate things, kept the sharpness of the notes of a high voice perfectly trained, and where economy hung about like the scent of a garden. His old friend lived with one maid and herself dusted her relics and trimmed her lamps and polished her silver; she stood off, in the awful modern crush, when she could, but she sallied forth and did battle

when the challenge was really to "spirit," the spirit she after all
confessed to, proudly and a little shyly, as to that of the better
time, that of *their* common, their quite far-away and antediluvian social period and order. She made use of the street-cars
when need be, the terrible things that people scrambled for as
the panic-stricken at sea scramble for the boats; she affronted,
inscrutably, under stress, all the public concussions and or-
deals; and yet, with that slim mystifying grace of her appearance, which defied you to say if she were a fair young woman
who looked older through trouble, or a fine smooth older one
who looked young through successful indifference; with her
precious reference, above all, to memories and histories into
which he could enter, she was as exquisite for him as some pale
pressed flower (a rarity to begin with), and, failing other sweet-
nesses, she was a sufficient reward of his effort. They had communities of knowledge, "their" knowledge (this discriminating
possessive was always on her lips) of presences of the other age,
presences all overlaid, in his case, by the experience of a man
and the freedom of a wanderer, overlaid by pleasure, by infi-
delity, by passages of life that were strange and dim to her, just
by "Europe" in short, but still unobscured, still exposed and
cherished, under that pious visitation of the spirit from which
she had never been diverted.

She had come with him one day to see how his "apartment-
house" was rising; he had helped her over gaps and explained
to her plans, and while they were there had happened to have,
before her, a brief but lively discussion with the man in charge,
the representative of the building-firm that had undertaken his
work. He had found himself quite "standing-up" to this personage over a failure on the latter's part to observe some detail
of one of their noted conditions, and had so lucidly argued his
case that, besides ever so prettily flushing, at the time, for sympathy in his triumph, she had afterwards said to him (though to
a slightly greater effect of irony) that he had clearly for too
many years neglected a real gift. If he had but stayed at home
he would have anticipated the inventor of the sky-scraper. If he
had but stayed at home he would have discovered his genius in
time really to start some new variety of awful architectural
hare and run it till it burrowed in a gold-mine. He was to re-

member these words, while the weeks elapsed, for the small silver ring they had sounded over the queerest and deepest of his
own lately most disguised and most muffled vibrations.

It had begun to be present to him after the first fortnight, it
had broken out with the oddest abruptness, this particular
wanton wonderment: it met him there—and this was the image
under which he himself judged the matter, or at least, not a little, thrilled and flushed with it—very much as he might have
been met by some strange figure, some unexpected occupant, at
a turn of one of the dim passages of an empty house. The
quaint analogy quite hauntingly remained with him, when he
didn't indeed rather improve it by a still intenser form: that of
his opening a door behind which he would have made sure of
finding nothing, a door into a room shuttered and void, and yet
so coming, with a great suppressed start, on some quite erect
confronting presence, something planted in the middle of the
place and facing him through the dusk. After that visit to the
house in construction he walked with his companion to see
the other and always so much the better one, which in the east-
ward direction formed one of the corners, the "jolly" one precisely, of the street now so generally dishonoured and disfigured
in its westward reaches, and of the comparatively conservative
Avenue. The Avenue still had pretensions, as Miss Staverton
said, to decency; the old people had mostly gone, the old names
were unknown, and here and there an old association seemed
to stray, all vaguely, like some very aged person, out too late,
whom you might meet and feel the impulse to watch or follow,
in kindness, for safe restoration to shelter.

They went in together, our friends; he admitted himself with
his key, as he kept no one there, he explained, preferring, for
his reasons, to leave the place empty, under a simple arrangement with a good woman living in the neighbourhood and who
came for a daily hour to open windows and dust and sweep.
Spencer Brydon had his reasons and was growingly aware of
them; they seemed to him better each time he was there, though
he didn't name them all to his companion, any more than he
told her as yet how often, how quite absurdly often, he himself
came. He only let her see for the present, while they walked
through the great blank rooms, that absolute vacancy reigned

and that, from top to bottom, there was nothing but Mrs. Muldoon's broomstick, in a corner, to tempt the burglar. Mrs. Muldoon was then on the premises, and she loquaciously attended the visitors, preceding them from room to room and pushing back shutters and throwing up sashes—all to show them, as she remarked, how little there was to see. There was little indeed to see in the great gaunt shell where the main dispositions and the general apportionment of space, the style of an age of ampler allowances, had nevertheless for its master their honest pleading message, affecting him as some good old servant's, some lifelong retainer's appeal for a character, or even for a retiring-pension; yet it was also a remark of Mrs. Muldoon's that, glad as she was to oblige him by her noonday round, there was a request she greatly hoped he would never make of her. If he should wish her for any reason to come in after dark she would just tell him, if he "plased," that he must ask it of somebody else.

The fact that there was nothing to see didn't militate for the worthy woman against what one *might* see, and she put it frankly to Miss Staverton that no lady could be expected to like, could she? "craping up to thim top storeys in the ayvil hours." The gas and the electric light were off the house, and she fairly evoked a gruesome vision of her march through the great grey rooms—so many of them as there were too!—with her glimmering taper. Miss Staverton met her honest glare with a smile and the profession that she herself certainly would recoil from such an adventure. Spencer Brydon meanwhile held his peace—for the moment; the question of the "evil" hours in his old home had already become too grave for him. He had begun some time since to "crape," and he knew just why a packet of candles addressed to that pursuit had been stowed by his own hand, three weeks before, at the back of a drawer of the fine old sideboard that occupied, as a "fixture," the deep recess in the dining-room. Just now he laughed at his companions—quickly however changing the subject; for the reason that, in the first place, his laugh struck him even at that moment as starting the odd echo, the conscious human resonance (he scarce knew how to qualify it) that sounds made while he was there alone sent back to his ear or his fancy; and that, in the second, he imagined Alice Staverton for the instant on the point of asking him, with a divination, if he ever so prowled. There were divinations he was unprepared for, and he had at all events averted enquiry by the time Mrs. Muldoon had left them, passing on to other parts.

There was happily enough to say, on so consecrated a spot, that could be said freely and fairly; so that a whole train of declarations was precipitated by his friend's having herself broken out, after a yearning look round: "But I hope you don't mean they want you to pull *this* to pieces!" His answer came, promptly, with his re-awakened wrath: it was of course exactly what they wanted, and what they were "at" him for, daily, with the iteration of people who couldn't for their life understand a man's liability to decent feelings. He had found the place, just as it stood and beyond what he could express, an interest and a joy. There were values other than the beastly rent-values, and in short, in short—! But it was thus Miss Staverton took him up. "In short you're to make so good a thing of your skyscraper that, living in luxury on *those* ill-gotten gains, you can afford for a while to be sentimental here!" Her smile had for him, with the words, the particular mild irony with which he found half her talk suffused; an irony without bitterness and that came, exactly, from her having so much imagination—not, like the cheap sarcasms with which one heard most people, about the world of "society," bid for the reputation of cleverness, from nobody's really having any. It was agreeable to him at this very moment to be sure that when he had answered, after a brief demur, "Well yes: so, precisely, you may put it!" her imagination would still do him justice. He explained that even if never a dollar were to come to him from the other house he would nevertheless cherish this one; and he dwelt, further, while they lingered and wandered, on the fact of the stupefaction he was already exciting, the positive mystification he felt himself create.

He spoke of the value of all he read into it, into the mere sight of the walls, mere shapes of the rooms, mere sound of the floors, mere feel, in his hand, of the old silver-plated knobs of the several mahogany doors, which suggested the pressure of the palms of the dead; the seventy years of the past in fine that these things represented, the annals of nearly three generations, counting his grandfather's, the one that had ended there, and the impalpable ashes of his long-extinct youth, afloat in the very air like microscopic motes. She listened to everything; she was a woman who answered intimately but who utterly didn't chatter. She scattered abroad therefore no cloud of words; she could assent, she could agree, above all she could encourage, without doing that. Only at the last she went a little further than he had done himself. "And then how do you know? You may still, after all, want to live here." It rather indeed pulled him up, for it wasn't what he had been thinking, at least in her sense of the words. "You mean I may decide to stay on for the sake of it?"

"Well, *with* such a home—!" But, quite beautifully, she had too much tact to dot so monstrous an *i*, and it was precisely an illustration of the way she didn't rattle. How could any one— of any wit—insist on any one else's "wanting" to live in New York?

"Oh," he said, "I *might* have lived here (since I had my opportunity early in life); I might have put in here all these years. Then everything would have been different enough—and, I dare say, 'funny' enough. But that's another matter. And then the beauty of it—I mean of my perversity, of my refusal to agree to a 'deal'—is just in the total absence of a reason. Don't you see that if I had a reason about the matter at all it would *have* to be the other way, and would then be inevitably a reason of dollars? There are no reasons here *but* of dollars. Let us therefore have none whatever—not the ghost of one."

They were back in the hall then for departure, but from where they stood the vista was large, through an open door, into the great square main saloon, with its almost antique felicity of brave spaces between windows. Her eyes came back from that reach and met his own a moment. "Are you very sure the 'ghost' of one doesn't, much rather, serve—?"

He had a positive sense of turning pale. But it was as near as they were then to come. For he made answer, he believed, between a glare and a grin: "Oh ghosts—of course the place must swarm with them! I should be ashamed of it if it didn't. Poor Mrs. Muldoon's right, and it's why I haven't asked her to do more than look in."

Miss Staverton's gaze again lost itself, and things she didn't utter, it was clear, came and went in her mind. She might even for the minute, off there in the fine room, have imagined some element dimly gathering. Simplified like the death-mask of a handsome face, it perhaps produced for her just then an effect akin to the stir of an expression in the "set" commemorative plaster. Yet whatever her impression may have been she produced instead a vague platitude. "Well, if it were only furnished and lived in—!"

She appeared to imply that in case of its being still furnished he might have been a little less opposed to the idea of a return. But she passed straight into the vestibule, as if to leave her words behind her, and the next moment he had opened the house-door and was standing with her on the steps. He closed the door and, while he re-pocketed his key, looking up and down, they took in the comparatively harsh actuality of the Avenue, which reminded him of the assault of the outer light of the Desert on the traveller emerging from an Egyptian tomb. But he risked before they stepped into the street his gathered answer to her speech. "For me it *is* lived in. For me it *is* furnished." At which it was easy for her to sigh "Ah yes—!" all vaguely and discreetly; since his parents and his favourite sister, to say nothing of other kin, in numbers, had run their course and met their end there. That represented, within the walls, ineffaceable life.

It was a few days after this that, during an hour passed with her again, he had expressed his impatience of the too flattering curiosity—among the people he met—about his appreciation of New York. He had arrived at none at all that was socially producible, and as for that matter of his "thinking" (thinking the better or the worse of anything there) he was wholly taken up with one subject of thought. It was mere vain egoism, and it was moreover, if she liked, a morbid obsession. He found all things come back to the question of what he personally might have been, how he might have led his life and "turned out," if he had not so, at the outset, given it up. And confessing for the

first time to the intensity within him of this absurd speculation—which but proved also, no doubt, the habit of too self-
ishly thinking—he affirmed the impotence there of any other
source of interest, any other native appeal. "What would it
have made of me, what would it have made of me? I keep for
ever wondering, all idiotically; as if I could possibly know! I see
what it has made of dozens of others, those I meet, and it positively aches within me, to the point of exasperation, that it
would have made something of me as well. Only I can't make
out *what,* and the worry of it, the small rage of curiosity never
to be satisfied, brings back what I remember to have felt, once
or twice, after judging best, for reasons, to burn some impor-.
tant letter unopened. I've been sorry, I've hated it—I've never
known what was in the letter. You may of course say it's a
trifle—!"

"I don't say it's a trifle," Miss Staverton gravely interrupted.
She was seated by her fire, and before her, on his feet and
restless, he turned to and fro between this intensity of his idea
and a fitful and unseeing inspection, through his single eye-
glass, of the dear little old objects on her chimney-piece. Her
interruption made him for an instant look at her harder. "I
shouldn't care if you did!" he laughed, however; "and it's only
a figure, at any rate, for the way I now feel. *Not* to have followed my perverse young course—and almost in the teeth of
my father's curse, as I may say; not to have kept it up, so, 'over
there,' from that day to this, without a doubt or a pang; not,
above all, to have liked it, to have loved it, so much, loved it,
no doubt, with such an abysmal conceit of my own preference:
some variation from *that,* I say, must have produced some different effect for my life and for my 'form.' I should have stuck
here—if it had been possible; and I was too young, at twenty-
three, to judge, *pour deux sous,* whether it *were* possible. If I
had waited I might have seen it was, and then I might have
been, by staying here, something nearer to one of these types
who have been hammered so hard and made so keen by their
conditions. It isn't that I admire them so much—the question of
any charm in them, or of any charm, beyond that of the rank
money-passion, exerted by their conditions *for* them, has nothing to do with the matter: it's only a question of what fantastic,

yet perfectly possible, development of my own nature I mayn't have missed. It comes over me that I had then a strange *alter ego* deep down somewhere within me, as the full-blown flower is in the small tight bud, and that I just took the course, I just transferred him to the climate, that blighted him for once and for ever."

"And you wonder about the flower," Miss Staverton said. "So do I, if you want to know; and so I've been wondering these several weeks. I believe in the flower," she continued, "I feel it would have been quite splendid, quite huge and monstrous."

"Monstrous above all!" her visitor echoed; "and I imagine, by the same stroke, quite hideous and offensive."

"You don't believe that," she returned; "if you did you wouldn't wonder. You'd know, and that would be enough for you. What you feel—and what I feel *for* you—is that you'd have had power."

"You'd have liked me that way?" he asked.

She barely hung fire. "How should I not have liked you?"

"I see. You'd have liked me, have preferred me, a billionaire!"

"How should I not have liked you?" she simply again asked.

He stood before her still—her question kept him motionless. He took it in, so much there was of it; and indeed his not otherwise meeting it testified to that. "I know at least what I am," he simply went on; "the other side of the medal's clear enough. I've not been edifying—I believe I'm thought in a hundred quarters to have been barely decent. I've followed strange paths and worshipped strange gods; it must have come to you again and again—in fact you've admitted to me as much—that I was leading, at any time these thirty years, a selfish frivolous scandalous life. And you see what it has made of me."

She just waited, smiling at him. "You see what it has made of *me*."

"Oh you're a person whom nothing can have altered. You were born to be what you are, anywhere, anyway: you've the perfection nothing else could have blighted. And don't you see how, without my exile, I shouldn't have been waiting till now—?" But he pulled up for the strange pang.

"The great thing to see," she presently said, "seems to me to be that it has spoiled nothing. It hasn't spoiled your being here at last. It hasn't spoiled this. It hasn't spoiled your speaking—" She also however faltered.

He wondered at everything her controlled emotion might mean. "Do you believe then—too dreadfully!—that I *am* as good as I might ever have been?"

"Oh no! Far from it!" With which she got up from her chair and was nearer to him. "But I don't care," she smiled.

"You mean I'm good enough?"

She considered a little. "Will you believe it if I say so? I mean will you let that settle your question for you?" And then as if making out in his face that he drew back from this, that he had some idea which, however absurd, he couldn't yet bargain away: "Oh you don't care either—but very differently: you don't care for anything but yourself."

Spencer Brydon recognised it—it was in fact what he had absolutely professed. Yet he importantly qualified. "*He* isn't myself. He's the just so totally other person. But I do want to see him," he added. "And I can. And I shall."

Their eyes met for a minute while he guessed from something in hers that she divined his strange sense. But neither of them otherwise expressed it, and her apparent understanding, with no protesting shock, no easy derision, touched him more deeply than anything yet, constituting for his stifled perversity, on the spot, an element that was like breatheable air. What she said however was unexpected. "Well, *I've* seen him."

"You—?"

"I've seen him in a dream."

"Oh a 'dream'—!" It let him down.

"But twice over," she continued. "I saw him as I see you now."

"You've dreamed the same dream—?"

"Twice over," she repeated. "The very same."

This did somehow a little speak to him, as it also gratified him. "You dream about me at that rate?"

"Ah about *him!*" she smiled.

His eyes again sounded her. "Then you know all about him." And as she said nothing more: "What's the wretch like?"

She hesitated, and it was as if he were pressing her so hard that, resisting for reasons of her own, she had to turn away. "I'll tell you some other time!"

II.

It was after this that there was most of a virtue for him, most of a cultivated charm, most of a preposterous secret thrill, in the particular form of surrender to his obsession and of address to what he more and more believed to be his privilege. It was what in these weeks he was living for—since he really felt life to begin but after Mrs. Muldoon had retired from the scene and, visiting the ample house from attic to cellar, making sure he was alone, he knew himself in safe possession and, as he tacitly expressed it, let himself go. He sometimes came twice in the twenty-four hours; the moments he liked best were those of gathering dusk, of the short autumn twilight; this was the time of which, again and again, he found himself hoping most. Then he could, as seemed to him, most intimately wander and wait, linger and listen, feel his fine attention, never in his life before so fine, on the pulse of the great vague place: he preferred the lampless hour and only wished he might have prolonged each day the deep crepuscular spell. Later—rarely much before midnight, but then for a considerable vigil—he watched with his glimmering light; moving slowly, holding it high, playing it far, rejoicing above all, as much as he might, in open vistas, reaches of communication between rooms and by passages; the long straight chance or show, as he would have called it, for the revelation he pretended to invite. It was a practice he found he could perfectly "work" without exciting remark; no one was in the least the wiser for it; even Alice Staverton, who was moreover a well of discretion, didn't quite fully imagine.

He let himself in and let himself out with the assurance of calm proprietorship; and accident so far favoured him that, if a fat Avenue "officer" had happened on occasion to see him entering at eleven-thirty, he had never yet, to the best of his belief, been noticed as emerging at two. He walked there on the crisp November nights, arrived regularly at the evening's end; it was as easy to do this after dining out as to take his way to a club or to his hotel. When he left his club, if he hadn't been dining out, it was ostensibly to go to his hotel; and when he left his hotel, if he had spent a part of the evening there, it was ostensibly to go to his club. Everything was easy in fine; everything conspired and promoted: there was truly even in the strain of his experience something that glossed over, something that salved and simplified, all the rest of consciousness. He circulated, talked, renewed, loosely and pleasantly, old relations—met indeed, so far as he could, new expectations and seemed to make out on the whole that in spite of the career, of such different contacts, which he had spoken of to Miss Staverton as ministering so little, for those who might have watched it, to edification, he was positively rather liked than not. He was a dim secondary social success—and all with people who had truly not an idea of him. It was all mere surface sound, this murmur of their welcome, this popping of their corks—just as his gestures of response were the extravagant shadows, emphatic in proportion as they meant little, of some game of *ombres chinoises*. He projected himself all day, in thought, straight over the bristling line of hard unconscious heads and into the other, the real, the waiting life; the life that, as soon as he had heard behind him the click of his great house-door, began for him, on the jolly corner, as beguilingly as the slow opening bars of some rich music follows the tap of the conductor's wand.

He always caught the first effect of the steel point of his stick on the old marble of the hall pavement, large black-and-white squares that he remembered as the admiration of his childhood and that had then made in him, as he now saw, for the growth of an early conception of style. This effect was the dim reverberating tinkle as of some far-off bell hung who should say where?—in the depths of the house, of the past, of that mystical other world that might have flourished for him had he not, for weal or woe, abandoned it. On this impression he did ever the same thing; he put his stick noiselessly away in a corner— feeling the place once more in the likeness of some great glass bowl, all precious concave crystal, set delicately humming by the play of a moist finger round its edge. The concave crystal held, as it were, this mystical other world, and the indescrib-

ably fine murmur of its rim was the sigh there, the scarce audible pathetic wail to his strained ear, of all the old baffled for-
sworn possibilities. What he did therefore by this appeal of his
hushed presence was to wake them into such measure of
ghostly life as they might still enjoy. They were shy, all but un-
appeasably shy, but they weren't really sinister; at least they
weren't as he had hitherto felt them—before they had taken the
Form he so yearned to make them take, the Form he at moments saw himself in the light of fairly hunting on tiptoe, the
points of his evening-shoes, from room to room and from
storey to storey.

That was the essence of his vision—which was all rank folly,
if one would, while he was out of the house and otherwise occupied, but which took on the last verisimilitude as soon as he
was placed and posted. He knew what he meant and what he
wanted; it was as clear as the figure on a cheque presented in
demand for cash. His *alter ego* "walked"—that was the note of
his image of him, while his image of his motive for his own odd
pastime was the desire to waylay him and meet him. He
roamed, slowly, warily, but all restlessly, he himself did—Mrs.
Muldoon had been right, absolutely, with her figure of their
"craping"; and the presence he watched for would roam restlessly too. But it would be as cautious and as shifty; the conviction of its probable, in fact its already quite sensible, quite
audible evasion of pursuit grew for him from night to night,
laying on him finally a rigour to which nothing in his life had
been comparable. It had been the theory of many superficially-
judging persons, he knew, that he was wasting that life in a surrender to sensations, but he had tasted of no pleasure so fine as
his actual tension, had been introduced to no sport that demanded at once the patience and the nerve of this stalking of a
creature more subtle, yet at bay perhaps more formidable, than
any beast of the forest. The terms, the comparisons, the very
practices of the chase positively came again into play; there
were even moments when passages of his occasional experience
as a sportsman, stirred memories, from his younger time, of
moor and mountain and desert, revived for him—and to the increase of his keenness—by the tremendous force of analogy. He
found himself at moments—once he had placed his single light

on some mantel-shelf or in some recess—stepping back into shelter or shade, effacing himself behind a door or in an embrasure, as he had sought of old the vantage of rock and tree; he found himself holding his breath and living in the joy of the instant, the supreme suspense created by big game alone.

He wasn't afraid (though putting himself the question as he believed gentlemen on Bengal tiger-shoots or in close quarters with the great bear of the Rockies had been known to confess to having put it); and this indeed—since here at least he might be frank!—because of the impression, so intimate and so strange, that he himself produced as yet a dread, produced certainly a strain, beyond the liveliest he was likely to feel. They fell for him into categories, they fairly became familiar, the signs, for his own perception, of the alarm his presence and his vigilance created; though leaving him always to remark, portentously, on his probably having formed a relation, his probably enjoying a consciousness, unique in the experience of man. People enough, first and last, had been in terror of apparitions, but who had ever before so turned the tables and become himself, in the apparitional world, an incalculable terror? He might have found this sublime had he quite dared to think of it; but he didn't too much insist, truly, on that side of his privilege. With habit and repetition he gained to an extraordinary degree the power to penetrate the dusk of distances and the darkness of corners, to resolve back into their innocence the treacheries of uncertain light, the evil-looking forms taken in the gloom by mere shadows, by accidents of the air, by shifting effects of perspective; putting down his dim luminary he could still wander on without it, pass into other rooms and, only knowing it was there behind him in case of need, see his way about, visually project for his purpose a comparative clearness. It made him feel, this acquired faculty, like some monstrous stealthy cat; he wondered if he would have glared at these moments with large shining yellow eyes, and what it mightn't verily be, for the poor hard-pressed *alter ego,* to be confronted with such a type.

He liked however the open shutters; he opened everywhere those Mrs. Muldoon had closed, closing them as carefully afterwards, so that she shouldn't notice: he liked—oh this he did like, and above all in the upper rooms!—the sense of the hard silver of the autumn stars through the window-panes, and scarcely less the flare of the street-lamps below, the white electric lustre which it would have taken curtains to keep out. This was human actual social; this was of the world he had lived in, and he was more at his ease certainly for the countenance, coldly general and impersonal, that all the while and in spite of his detachment it seemed to give him. He had support of course mostly in the rooms at the wide front and the prolonged side; it failed him considerably in the central shades and the parts at the back. But if he sometimes, on his rounds, was glad of his optical reach, so none the less often the rear of the house affected him as the very jungle of his prey. The place was there more subdivided; a large "extension" in particular, where small rooms for servants had been multiplied, abounded in nooks and corners, in closets and passages, in the ramifications especially of an ample back staircase over which he leaned, many a time, to look far down—not deterred from his gravity even while aware that he might, for a spectator, have figured some solemn simpleton playing at hide-and-seek. Outside in fact he might himself make that ironic *rapprochement*; but within the walls, and in spite of the clear windows, his consistency was proof against the cynical light of New York.

It had belonged to that idea of the exasperated consciousness of his victim to become a real test for him; since he had quite put it to himself from the first that, oh distinctly! he could "cultivate" his whole perception. He had felt it as above all open to cultivation—which indeed was but another name for his manner of spending his time. He was bringing it on, bringing it to perfection, by practice; in consequence of which it had grown so fine that he was now aware of impressions, attestations of his general postulate, that couldn't have broken upon him at once. This was the case more specifically with a phenomenon at last quite frequent for him in the upper rooms, the recognition—absolutely unmistakeable, and by a turn dating from a particular hour, his resumption of his campaign after a diplomatic drop, a calculated absence of three nights—of his being definitely followed, tracked at a distance carefully taken and to the express end that he should the less confidently, less arrogantly, appear to himself merely to pursue. It worried, it finally quite broke him up, for it proved, of all the conceivable impressions, the one least suited to his book. He was kept in sight while remaining himself—as regards the essence of his position—sightless, and his only recourse then was in abrupt turns, rapid recoveries of ground. He wheeled about, retracing his steps, as if he might so catch in his face at least the stirred air of some other quick revolution. It was indeed true that his fully dislocalised thought of these manoeuvres recalled to him Pantaloon, at the Christmas farce, buffeted and tricked from behind by ubiquitous Harlequin; but it left intact the influence of the conditions themselves each time he was re-exposed to them, so that in fact this association, had he suffered it to become constant, would on a certain side have but ministered to his intenser gravity. He had made, as I have said, to create on the premises the baseless sense of a reprieve, his three absences; and the result of the third was to confirm the after-effect of the second.

On his return, that night—the night succeeding his last intermission—he stood in the hall and looked up the staircase with a certainty more intimate than any he had yet known. "He's *there,* at the top, and waiting—not, as in general, falling back for disappearance. He's holding his ground, and it's the first time—which is a proof, isn't it? that something has happened for him." So Brydon argued with his hand on the banister and his foot on the lowest stair; in which position he felt as never before the air chilled by his logic. He himself turned cold in it, for he seemed of a sudden to know what now was involved. "Harder pressed?—yes, he takes it in, with its thus making clear to him that I've come, as they say, 'to stay.' He finally doesn't like and can't bear it, in the sense, I mean, that his wrath, his menaced interest, now balances with his dread. I've hunted him till he has 'turned': that, up there, is what has happened—he's the fanged or the antlered animal brought at last to bay." There came to him, as I say—but determined by an influence beyond my notation!—the acuteness of this certainty; under which however the next moment he had broken into a sweat that he would as little have consented to attribute to fear as he would have dared immediately to act upon it for enterprise. It marked none the less a prodigious thrill, a thrill that represented sudden dismay, no doubt, but also represented, and with the selfsame throb, the strangest, the most joyous, possibly the next minute almost the proudest, duplication of consciousness.

"He has been dodging, retreating, hiding, but now, worked up to anger, he'll fight!"—this intense impression made a single mouthful, as it were, of terror and applause. But what was wondrous was that the applause, for the felt fact, was so eager, since, if it was his other self he was running to earth, this ineffable identity was thus in the last resort not unworthy of him. It bristled there—somewhere near at hand, however unseen still—as the hunted thing, even as the trodden worm of the adage *must* at last bristle; and Brydon at this instant tasted probably of a sensation more complex than had ever before found itself consistent with sanity. It was as if it would have shamed him that a character so associated with his own should triumphantly succeed in just skulking, should to the end not risk the open; so that the drop of this danger was, on the spot, a great lift of the whole situation. Yet with another rare shift of the same subtlety he was already trying to measure by how much more he himself might now be in peril of fear; so rejoicing that he could, in another form, actively inspire that fear, and simultaneously quaking for the form in which he might passively know it.

The apprehension of knowing it must after a little have grown in him, and the strangest moment of his adventure perhaps, the most memorable or really most interesting, afterwards, of his crisis, was the lapse of certain instants of concentrated conscious *combat,* the sense of a need to hold on to something, even after the manner of a man slipping and slipping on some awful incline; the vivid impulse, above all, to move, to act, to charge, somehow and upon something—to show himself, in a word, that he wasn't afraid. The state of "holding-on" was thus the state to which he was momentarily reduced; if there had been anything, in the great vacancy, to seize, he would presently have been aware of having clutched it as he might under a shock at home have clutched the nearest chair-back. He had been surprised at any rate—of this he *was* aware—into something unprecedented since his original appropriation of the place; he had closed his eyes, held them tight, for a long minute, as with that instinct of dismay and that terror of vision. When he opened them the room, the other contiguous rooms, extraordinarily, seemed lighter—so light, almost, that at first he took the change for day. He stood firm, however that might be, just where he had paused; his resistance had helped him—it was as if there were something he had tided over. He knew after a little what this was—it had been in the imminent danger of flight. He had stiffened his will against going; without this he would have made for the stairs, and it seemed to him that, still with his eyes closed, he would have descended them, would have known how, straight and swiftly, to the bottom.

Well, as he had held out, here he was—still at the top, among the more intricate upper rooms and with the gauntlet of the others, of all the rest of the house, still to run when it should be his time to go. He would go at his time—only at his time: didn't he go every night very much at the same hour? He took out his watch—there was light for that: it was scarcely a quarter past one, and he had never withdrawn so soon. He reached his lodgings for the most part at two—with his walk of a quarter of an hour. He would wait for the last quarter—he wouldn't stir till then; and he kept his watch there with his eyes on it, reflecting while he held it that this deliberate wait, a wait with an effort, which he recognised, would serve perfectly for the attestation he desired to make. It would prove his courage—unless indeed the latter might most be proved by his budging at last from his place. What he mainly felt now was that, since he hadn't originally scuttled, he had his dignities—which had never in his life seemed so many—all to preserve and to carry aloft. This was before him in truth as a physical image, an image almost worthy of an age of greater romance. That remark indeed glimmered for him only to glow the next instant with a finer light; since what age of romance, after all, could have matched either the state of his mind or, "objectively," as they said, the wonder of his situation? The only difference would have been that, brandishing his dignities over his head as in a parchment scroll, he might then—that is in the heroic time—have proceeded downstairs with a drawn sword in his other grasp.

At present, really, the light he had set down on the mantel of the next room would have to figure his sword; which utensil, in the course of a minute, he had taken the requisite number of steps to possess himself of. The door between the rooms was open, and from the second another door opened to a third. These rooms, as he remembered, gave all three upon a common corridor as well, but there was a fourth, beyond them, without issue save through the preceding. To have moved, to have heard his step again, was appreciably a help; though even in recognising this he lingered once more a little by the chimney-piece on which his light had rested. When he next moved, just hesitating where to turn, he found himself considering a circumstance that, after his first and comparatively vague apprehension of it, produced in him the start that often attends some pang of recollection, the violent shock of having ceased happily to forget. He had come into sight of the door in which the brief chain of communication ended and which he now surveyed from the nearer threshold, the one not directly facing it. Placed at some distance to the left of this point, it would have admitted him to the last room of the four, the room without other approach or egress, had it not, to his intimate conviction, been closed *since* his former visitation, the matter probably of a quarter of an hour before. He stared with all his eyes at the wonder of the fact, arrested again where he stood and again holding his breath while he sounded its sense. Surely it had been *subsequently* closed—that is it had been on his previous passage indubitably open!

He took it full in the face that something had happened between—that he couldn't not have noticed before (by which he meant on his original tour of all the rooms that evening) that such a barrier had exceptionally presented itself. He had indeed since that moment undergone an agitation so extraordinary that it might have muddled for him any earlier view; and he tried to convince himself that he might perhaps then have gone into the room and, inadvertently, automatically, on coming out, have drawn the door after him. The difficulty was that this exactly was what he never did; it was against his whole policy, as he might have said, the essence of which was to keep vistas clear. He had them from the first, as he was well aware, quite on the brain: the strange apparition, at the far end of one of them, of his baffled "prey" (which had become by so sharp an irony so little the term now to apply!) was the form of success his imagination had most cherished, projecting into it always a refinement of beauty. He had known fifty times the start of perception that had afterwards dropped; had fifty times gasped to himself "There!" under some fond brief hallucination. The house, as the case stood, admirably lent itself; he might wonder at the taste, the native architecture of the particular time, which could rejoice so in the multiplication of doors—the opposite extreme to the modern, the actual almost complete proscription of them; but it had fairly contributed to provoke this obsession of the presence encountered telescopically, as he might say, focussed and studied in diminishing perspective and as by a rest for the elbow.

It was with these considerations that his present attention was charged—they perfectly availed to make what he saw portentous. He *couldn't*, by any lapse, have blocked that aperture; and if he hadn't, if it was unthinkable, why what else was clear but that there had been another agent? Another agent?—he had been catching, as he felt, a moment back, the very breath of him; but when had he been so close as in this simple, this logical, this completely personal act? It was so logical, that is, that one might have *taken* it for personal; yet for what did Brydon take it, he asked himself, while, softly panting, he felt his eyes almost leave their sockets. Ah this time at last they *were*, the two, the opposed projections of him, in presence; and this time, as much as one would, the question of danger loomed. With it rose, as not before, the question of courage—for what he knew the blank face of the door to say to him was "Show us how much you have!" It stared, it glared back at him with that challenge; it put to him the two alternatives: should he just push it open or not? Oh to have this consciousness was to *think*—and to think, Brydon knew, as he stood there, was, with the lapsing moments, not to have acted! Not to have acted—that was the misery and the pang—was even still not to act; was in fact *all* to feel the thing in another, in a new and terrible way. How long did he pause and how long did he debate? There was presently nothing to measure it; for his vibration had already changed—as just by the effect of its intensity. Shut up there, at bay, defiant, and with the prodigy of the thing palpably proveably *done,* thus giving notice like some stark signboard—under that accession of accent the situation itself had turned; and Brydon at last remarkably made up his mind on what it had turned to.

It had turned altogether to a different admonition; to a supreme hint, for him, of the value of Discretion! This slowly dawned, no doubt—for it could take its time; so perfectly, on his threshold, had he been stayed, so little as yet had he either advanced or retreated. It was the strangest of all things that now when, by his taking ten steps and applying his hand to a latch, or even his shoulder and his knee, if necessary, to a panel, all the hunger of his prime need might have been met, his high curiosity crowned, his unrest assuaged—it was amazing, but it was also exquisite and rare, that insistence should have, at a touch, quite dropped from him. Discretion—he jumped at that; and yet not, verily, at such a pitch, because it saved his nerves or his skin, but because, much more valuably, it saved the situation. When I say he "jumped" at it I feel the consonance of this term with the fact that—at the end indeed of I know not how long—he did move again, he crossed straight to the door. He wouldn't touch it—it seemed now that he might *if* he would: he would only just wait there a little, to show, to prove, that he wouldn't. He had thus another station, close to the thin partition by which revelation was denied him; but with his eyes bent and his hands held off in a mere intensity of stillness. He listened as if there had been something to hear, but this attitude, while it lasted, was his own communication. "If you won't then—good: I spare you and I give up. You affect me as by the appeal positively for pity: you convince me that for reasons rigid and sublime—what do I know?—we both of us should have suffered. I respect them then, and, though moved and privileged as, I believe, it has never been given to man, I retire, I renounce—never, on my honour, to try again. So rest for ever—and let *me!*"

That, for Brydon was the deep sense of this last demonstration—solemn, measured, directed, as he felt it to be. He brought it to a close, he turned away; and now verily he knew

how deeply he had been stirred. He retraced his steps, taking
up his candle, burnt, he observed, well-nigh to the socket, and
marking again, lighten it as he would, the distinctness of his
footfall; after which, in a moment, he knew himself at the other
side of the house. He did here what he had not yet done at these
hours—he opened half a casement, one of those in the front,
and let in the air of the night; a thing he would have taken at
any time previous for a sharp rupture of his spell. His spell was
broken now, and it didn't matter—broken by his concession
and his surrender, which made it idle henceforth that he should
ever come back. The empty street—its other life so marked
even by the great lamplit vacancy—was within call, within
touch; he stayed there as to be in it again, high above it though
he was still perched; he watched as for some comforting common fact, some vulgar human note, the passage of a scavenger
or a thief, some night-bird however base. He would have
blessed that sign of life; he would have welcomed positively the
slow approach of his friend the policeman, whom he had hitherto only sought to avoid, and was not sure that if the patrol
had come into sight he mightn't have felt the impulse to get into
relation with it, to hail it, on some pretext, from his fourth
floor.

The pretext that wouldn't have been too silly or too compromising, the explanation that would have saved his dignity
and kept his name, in such a case, out of the papers, was not
definite to him: he was so occupied with the thought of recording his Discretion—as an effect of the vow he had just uttered
to his intimate adversary—that the importance of this loomed
large and something had overtaken all ironically his sense of
proportion. If there had been a ladder applied to the front of
the house, even one of the vertiginous perpendiculars employed
by painters and roofers and sometimes left standing overnight,
he would have managed somehow, astride of the window-sill,
to compass by outstretched leg and arm that mode of descent.
If there had been some such uncanny thing as he had found in
his room at hotels, a workable fire-escape in the form of
notched cable or a canvas shoot, he would have availed himself
of it as a proof—well, of his present delicacy. He nursed that
sentiment, as the question stood, a little in vain, and even—at

the end of he scarce knew, once more, how long—found it, as by the action on his mind of the failure of response of the outer world, sinking back to vague anguish. It seemed to him he had waited an age for some stir of the great grim hush; the life of the town was itself under a spell—so unnaturally, up and down the whole prospect of known and rather ugly objects, the blankness and the silence lasted. Had they ever, he asked himself, the hard-faced houses, which had begun to look livid in the dim dawn, had they ever spoken so little to any need of his spirit? Great builded voids, great crowded stillnesses put on, often, in the heart of cities, for the small hours, a sort of sinister mask, and it was of this large collective negation that Brydon presently became conscious—all the more that the break of day was, almost incredibly, now at hand, proving to him what a night he had made of it.

He looked again at his watch, saw what had become of his time-values (he had taken hours for minutes—not, as in other tense situations, minutes for hours) and the strange air of the streets was but the weak, the sullen flush of a dawn in which everything was still locked up. His choked appeal from his own open window had been the sole note of life, and he could but break off at last as for a worse despair. Yet while so deeply demoralised he was capable again of an impulse denoting—at least by his present measure—extraordinary resolution; of retracing his steps to the spot where he had turned cold with the extinction of his last pulse of doubt as to there being in the place another presence than his own. This required an effort strong enough to sicken him; but he had his reason, which overmastered for the moment everything else. There was the whole of the rest of the house to traverse, and how should he screw himself to that if the door he had seen closed were at present open? He could hold to the idea that the closing had practically been for him an act of mercy, a chance offered him to descend, depart, get off the ground and never again profane it. This conception held together, it worked; but what it meant for him depended now clearly on the amount of forbearance his recent action, or rather his recent inaction, had engendered. The image of the "presence," whatever it was, waiting there for him to go—this image had not yet been so concrete for his nerves as when he stopped short of the point at which certainty would have come to him. For, with all his resolution, or more exactly with all his dread, he did stop short—he hung back from really seeing. The risk was too great and his fear too definite: it took at this moment an awful specific form.

He knew—yes, as he had never known anything—that, *should* he see the door open, it would all too abjectly be the end of him. It would mean that the agent of his shame—for his shame was the deep abjection—was once more at large and in general possession; and what glared him thus in the face was the act that this would determine for him. It would send him straight about to the window he had left open, and by that window, be long ladder and dangling rope as absent as they would, he saw himself uncontrollably insanely fatally take his way to the street. The hideous chance of this he at least could avert; but he could only avert it by recoiling in time from assurance. He had the whole house to deal with, this fact was still there; only he now knew that uncertainty alone could start him. He stole back from where he had checked himself—merely to do so was suddenly like safety—and, making blindly for the greater staircase, left gaping rooms and sounding passages behind. Here was the top of the stairs, with a fine large dim descent and three spacious landings to mark off. His instinct was all for mildness, but his feet were harsh on the floors, and, strangely, when he had in a couple of minutes become aware of this, it counted somehow for help. He couldn't have spoken, the tone of his voice would have scared him, and the common conceit or resource of "whistling in the dark" (whether literally or figuratively) have appeared basely vulgar; yet he liked none the less to hear himself go, and when he had reached his first landing—taking it all with no rush, but quite steadily—that stage of success drew from him a gasp of relief.

The house, withal, seemed immense, the scale of space again inordinate; the open rooms, to no one of which his eyes deflected, gloomed in their shuttered state like mouths of caverns; only the high skylight that formed the crown of the deep well created for him a medium in which he could advance, but which might have been, for queerness of colour, some watery under-world. He tried to think of something noble, as that his

property was really grand, a splendid possession; but this nobleness took the form too of the clear delight with which he
was finally to sacrifice it. They might come in now, the builders,
the destroyers—they might come as soon as they would. At
the end of two flights he had dropped to another zone, and
from the middle of the third, with only one more left, he recognised the influence of the lower windows, of half-drawn blinds,
of the occasional gleam of streetlamps, of the glazed spaces of
the vestibule. This was the bottom of the sea, which showed an
illumination of its own and which he even saw paved—when at
a given moment he drew up to sink a long look over the banis-
ters—with the marble squares of his childhood. By that time indubitably he felt, as he might have said in a commoner cause,
better; it had allowed him to stop and draw breath, and the
ease increased with the sight of the old black-and-white slabs.
But what he most felt was that now surely, with the element of
impunity pulling him as by hard firm hands, the case was settled for what he might have seen above had he dared that last
look. The closed door, blessedly remote now, was still closed—
and he had only in short to reach that of the house.

He came down further, he crossed the passage forming the
access to the last flight; and if here again he stopped an instant
it was almost for the sharpness of the thrill of assured escape.
It made him shut his eyes—which opened again to the straight
slope of the remainder of the stairs. Here was impunity still,
but impunity almost excessive; inasmuch as the sidelights and
the high fan-tracery of the entrance were glimmering straight
into the hall; an appearance produced, he the next instant saw,
by the fact that the vestibule gaped wide, that the hinged halves
of the inner door had been thrown far back. Out of that again
the *question* sprang at him, making his eyes, as he felt, half-
start from his head, as they had done, at the top of the house,
before the sign of the other door. If he had left that one open,
hadn't he left this one closed, and wasn't he now in *most* immediate presence of some inconceivable occult activity? It was
as sharp, the question, as a knife in his side, but the answer
hung fire still and seemed to lose itself in the vague darkness to
which the thin admitted dawn, glimmering archwise over the
whole outer door, made a semicircular margin, a cold silvery

nimbus that seemed to play a little as he looked—to shift and expand and contract.

It was as if there had been something within it, protected by indistinctness and corresponding in extent with the opaque surface behind, the painted panels of the last barrier to his escape, of which the key was in his pocket. The indistinctness mocked him even while he stared, affected him as somehow shrouding or challenging certitude, so that after faltering an instant on his step he let himself go with the sense that here *was* at last something to meet, to touch, to take, to know—something all unnatural and dreadful, but to advance upon which was the condition for him either of liberation or of supreme defeat. The penumbra, dense and dark, was the virtual screen of a figure which stood in it as still as some image erect in a niche or as some black-vizored sentinel guarding a treasure. Brydon was to know afterwards, was to recall and make out, the particular thing he had believed during the rest of his descent. He saw, in its great grey glimmering margin, the central vagueness diminish, and he felt it to be taking the very form toward which, for so many days, the passion of his curiosity had yearned. It gloomed, it loomed, it was something, it was somebody, the prodigy of a personal presence.

Rigid and conscious, spectral yet human, a man of his own substance and stature waited there to measure himself with his power to dismay. This only could it be—this only till he recognised, with his advance, that what made the face dim was the pair of raised hands that covered it and in which, so far from being offered in defiance, it was buried as for dark deprecation. So Brydon, before him, took him in; with every fact of him now, in the higher light, hard and acute—his planted stillness, his vivid truth, his grizzled bent head and white masking hands, his queer actuality of evening-dress, of dangling double eye-glass, of gleaming silk lappet and white linen, of pearl button and gold watch-guard and polished shoe. No portrait by a great modern master could have presented him with more intensity, thrust him out of his frame with more art, as if there had been "treatment," of the consummate sort, in his every shade and salience. The revulsion, for our friend, had become, before he knew it, immense—this drop, in the act of apprehension, to the sense of his adversary's inscrutable manœuvre. That meaning at least, while he gaped, it offered him; for he could but gape at his other self in this other anguish, gape as a proof that *he,* standing there for the achieved, the enjoyed, the triumphant life, couldn't be faced in his triumph. Wasn't the proof in the splendid covering hands, strong and completely spread?—so spread and so intentional that, in spite of a special verity that surpassed every other, the fact that one of these hands had lost two fingers, which were reduced to stumps, as if accidentally shot away, the face was effectually guarded and saved.

"Saved," though, *would* it be?—Brydon breathed his wonder till the very impunity of his attitude and the very insistence of his eyes produced, as he felt, a sudden stir which showed the next instant as a deeper portent, while the head raised itself, the betrayal of a braver purpose. The hands, as he looked, began to move, to open; then, as if deciding in a flash, dropped from the face and left it uncovered and presented. Horror, with the sight, had leaped into Brydon's throat, gasping there in a sound he couldn't utter; for the bared identity was too hideous as *his,* and his glare was the passion of his protest. The face, *that* face, Spencer Brydon's?—he searched it still, but looking away from it in dismay and denial, falling straight from his height of sublimity. It was unknown, inconceivable, awful, disconnected from any possibility—! He had been "sold," he inwardly moaned, stalking such game as this: the presence before him was a presence, the horror within him a horror, but the waste of his nights had been only grotesque and the success of his adventure an irony. Such an identity fitted his at *no* point, made its alternative monstrous. A thousand times yes, as it came upon him nearer now—the face was the face of a stranger. It came upon him nearer now, quite as one of those expanding fantastic images projected by the magic lantern of childhood; for the stranger, whoever he might be, evil, odious, blatant, vulgar, had advanced as for aggression, and he knew himself give ground. Then harder pressed still, sick with the force of his shock, and falling back as under the hot breath and the roused passion of a life larger than his own, a rage of personality before which his own collapsed, he felt the whole vision turn to darkness and his very feet give way. His head went round; he was going; he had gone.

III.

What had next brought him back, clearly—though after how long?—was Mrs. Muldoon's voice, coming to him from quite near, from so near that he seemed presently to see her as kneeling on the ground before him while he lay looking up at her; himself not wholly on the ground, but half-raised and upheld—conscious, yes, of tenderness of support and, more particularly, of a head pillowed in extraordinary softness and faintly refreshing fragrance. He considered, he wondered, his wit but half at his service; then another face intervened, bending more directly over him, and he finally knew that Alice Staverton had made her lap an ample and perfect cushion to him, and that she had to this end seated herself on the lowest degree of the staircase, the rest of his long person remaining stretched on his old black-and-white slabs. They were cold, these marble squares of his youth; but *he* somehow was not, in this rich return of consciousness—the most wonderful hour, little by little, that he had ever known, leaving him, as it did, so gratefully, so abysmally passive, and yet as with a treasure of intelligence waiting all round him for quiet appropriation; dissolved, he might call it, in the air of the place and producing the golden glow of a late autumn afternoon. He had come back, yes—come back from further away than any man but himself had ever travelled; but it was strange how with this sense what he had come back *to* seemed really the great thing, and as if his prodigious journey had been all for the sake of it. Slowly but surely his consciousness grew, his vision of his state thus completing itself: he had been miraculously *carried* back—lifted and carefully borne as from where he had been picked up, the uttermost end of an interminable grey passage. Even with this he was suffered to rest, and what had now brought him to knowledge was the break in the long mild motion.

It had brought him to knowledge, to knowledge—yes, this was the beauty of his state; which came to resemble more and more that of a man who has gone to sleep on some news of a great inheritance, and then, after dreaming it away, after profaning it with matters strange to it, has waked up again to serenity of certitude and has only to lie and watch it grow. This was the drift of his patience—that he had only to let it shine on him. He must moreover, with intermissions, still have been lifted and borne; since why and how else should he have known himself, later on, with the afternoon glow intenser, no longer at the foot of his stairs—situated as these now seemed at that dark other end of his tunnel—but on a deep window-bench of his high saloon, over which had been spread, couch-fashion, a mantle of soft stuff lined with grey fur that was familiar to his eyes and that one of his hands kept fondly feeling as for its pledge of truth. Mrs. Muldoon's face had gone, but the other, the second he had recognised, hung over him in a way that showed how he was still propped and pillowed. He took it all in, and the more he took it the more it seemed to suffice: he was as much at peace as if he had had food and drink. It was the two women who had found him, on Mrs. Muldoon's having plied, at her usual hour, her latch-key—and on her having above all arrived while Miss Staverton still lingered near the house. She had been turning away, all anxiety, from worrying the vain bell-handle—her calculation having been of the hour of the good woman's visit; but the latter, blessedly, had come up while she was still there, and they had entered together. He had then lain, beyond the vestibule, very much as he was lying now—quite, that is, as he appeared to have fallen, but all so wondrously without bruise or gash; only in a depth of stupor. What he most took in, however, at present, with the steadier clearance, was that Alice Staverton had for a long unspeakable moment not doubted he was dead.

"It must have been that I *was*." He made it out as she held him. "Yes—I can only have died. You brought me literally to life. Only," he wondered, his eyes rising to her, "only, in the name of all the benedictions, how?"

It took her but an instant to bend her face and kiss him, and something in the manner of it, and in the way her hands clasped and locked his head while he felt the cool charity and virtue of her lips, something in all this beatitude somehow answered everything. "And now I keep you," she said.

"Oh keep me, keep me!" he pleaded while her face still hung over him: in response to which it dropped again and stayed close, clingingly close. It was the seal of their situation—of which he tasted the impress for a long blissful moment in silence. But he came back. "Yet how did you know—?"

"I was uneasy. You were to have come, you remember—and you had sent no word."

"Yes, I remember—I was to have gone to you at one to-day." It caught on to their "old" life and relation—which were so near and so far. "I was still out there in my strange darkness—where was it, what was it? I must have stayed there so long." He could but wonder at the depth and the duration of his swoon.

"Since last night?" she asked with a shade of fear for her possible indiscretion.

"Since this morning—it must have been: the cold dim dawn of to-day. Where have I been," he vaguely wailed, "where have I been?" He felt her hold him close, and it was as if this helped him now to make in all security his mild moan. "What a long dark day!"

All in her tenderness she had waited a moment. "In the cold dim dawn?" she quavered.

But he had already gone on piecing together the parts of the whole prodigy. "As I didn't turn up you came straight—?"

She barely cast about. "I went first to your hotel—where they told me of your absence. You had dined out last evening and hadn't been back since. But they appeared to know you had been at your club."

"So you had the idea of *this*—?"

"Of what?" she asked in a moment.

"Well—of what has happened."

"I believed at least you'd have been here. I've known, all along," she said, "that you've been coming."

" 'Known' it—?"

"Well, I've believed it. I said nothing to you after that talk we had a month ago—but I felt sure. I knew you *would*," she declared.

"That I'd persist, you mean?"

"That you'd see him."

"Ah but I didn't!" cried Brydon with his long wail. "There's somebody—an awful beast; whom I brought, too horribly, to bay. But it's not me."

At this she bent over him again, and her eyes were in his eyes. "No—it's not you." And it was as if, while her face hovered, he might have made out in it, hadn't it been so near, some particular meaning blurred by a smile. "No, thank heaven," she repeated—"it's not you! Of course it wasn't to have been."

"Ah but it *was*," he gently insisted. And he stared before him now as he had been staring for so many weeks. "I was to have known myself."

"You couldn't!" she returned consolingly. And then reverting, and as if to account further for what she had herself done, "But it wasn't only *that*, that you hadn't been at home," she went on. "I waited till the hour at which we had found Mrs. Muldoon that day of my going with you; and she arrived, as I've told you, while, failing to bring any one to the door, I lingered in my despair on the steps. After a little, if she hadn't come, by such a mercy, I should have found means to hunt her up. But it wasn't," said Alice Staverton, as if once more with her fine intention—"it wasn't only that."

His eyes, as he lay, turned back to her. "What more then?"

She met it, the wonder she had stirred. "In the cold dim dawn, you say? Well, in the cold dim dawn of this morning I too saw you."

"Saw *me*—?"

"Saw *him*," said Alice Staverton. "It must have been at the same moment."

He lay an instant taking it in—as if he wished to be quite reasonable. "At the same moment?"

"Yes—in my dream again, the same one I've named to you. He came back to me. Then I knew it for a sign. He had come to you."

At this Brydon raised himself; he had to see her better. She helped him when she understood his movement, and he sat up, steadying himself beside her there on the window-bench and with his right hand grasping her left. "*He* didn't come to me."

"You came to yourself," she beautifully smiled.

"Ah I've come to myself now—thanks to you, dearest. But this brute, with his awful face—this brute's a black stranger. He's none of *me*, even as I *might* have been," Brydon sturdily declared.

But she kept the clearness that was like the breath of infallibility. "Isn't the whole point that you'd have been different?"

He almost scowled for it. "As different as *that*—?"

Her look again was more beautiful to him than the things of this world. "Haven't you exactly wanted to know *how* different? So this morning," she said, "you appeared to me."

"Like *him?*"

"A black stranger!"

"Then how did you know it was I?"

"Because, as I told you weeks ago, my mind, my imagination, had worked so over what you might, what you mightn't have been—to show you, you see, how I've thought of you. In the midst of that you came to me—that my wonder might be answered. So I knew," she went on; "and believed that, since the question held you too so fast, as you told me that day, you too would see for yourself. And when this morning I again saw I knew it would be because you had—and also then, from the first moment, because you somehow wanted me. *He* seemed to tell me of that. So why," she strangely smiled, "shouldn't I like him?"

It brought Spencer Brydon to his feet. "You 'like' that horror—?"

"I *could* have liked him. And to me," she said, "he was no horror. I had accepted him."

"'Accepted'—?" Brydon oddly sounded.

"Before, for the interest of his difference—yes. And as *I* didn't disown him, as *I* knew him—which you at last, confronted with him in his difference, so cruelly didn't, my dear—well, he must have been, you see, less dreadful to me. And it may have pleased him that I pitied him."

She was beside him on her feet, but still holding his hand—

still with her arm supporting him. But though it all brought for him thus a dim light, "You 'pitied' him?" he grudgingly, resentfully asked.

"He has been unhappy, he has been ravaged," she said.

"And haven't I been unhappy? Am not I—you've only to look at me!—ravaged?"

"Ah I don't say I like him *better,*" she granted after a thought. "But he's grim, he's worn—and things have happened to him. He doesn't make shift, for sight, with your charming monocle."

"No"—it struck Brydon: "I couldn't have sported mine 'downtown.' They'd have guyed me there."

"His great convex pince-nez—I saw it, I recognised the kind—is for his poor ruined sight. And his poor right hand—!"

"Ah!" Brydon winced—whether for his proved identity or for his lost fingers. Then, "He has a million a year," he lucidly added. "But he hasn't you."

"And he isn't—no, he isn't—*you!*" she murmured as he drew her to his breast.

II

REVISIONS

James's final *New York Edition* preface speaks of his passion for revision, that process whereby "The 'old' matter is there, re-accepted, re-tasted, exquisitely re-assimilated, and re-enjoyed—believed in, to be brief with the same 'old' grateful faith. . . ." Generally his works were published in book form only after first appearance in magazines, and for the secondary publication he always made changes. Then for subsequent editions he made more changes. But the final revisions for the *New York Edition* of 1907–1909 could be dramatic, especially when he reconsidered a work written in relative youth.

There remains disagreement as to which texts should be recommended to the general reader. Although the late revised texts tend to be more "difficult," highly wrought, and often exquisite in vocabulary, they frequently offer fresh power and deepened insight. And as indicated by the final *Portrait of a Lady* collations that are provided here, in his maturity James was more ready to explore expressions of human passion and sexuality.

But there were indications that James eventually regretted the wholesale task of revision, and the revenues from the *New York Edition* were sufficiently disappointing to explain some bitterness concerning that effort. In a 1943 reminiscence, Compton Mackenzie recalled that James was appalled when he learned that the young writer was planning to "rewrite" his own successful 1912 novel, *Carnival*. According to Mackenzie, the Master responded as follows: " 'I wasted months of labour upon the thankless, the sterile, the preposterous, the monstrous task of revision. There is not an hour of such labour that I have not regretted since. You have been granted the most precious gift that can be granted a young writer—the ability to toss up a ball against the wall of life and catch it securely at the first rebound . . . I on the contrary, am compelled to toss the ball so that it travels from wall to wall . . .' here with a gesture he seemed to indicate that he was standing in a titanic fives-court, following with anxious eyes the ball he had just tossed against the wall of life . . . 'from wall to wall until at last, losing momentum with every new angle from which it rebounds, the ball returns to earth and dribbles slowly at my feet, when I arduously bend over, all my bones creaking, and with infinite difficulty manage to reach it and pick it up.'" In *Henry James: A Life in Letters,* Philip Horne cites a letter from that same year, where, in reference to a Uniform Edition of some of his tales, James states, "I shall not ask to see the proofs—I hate so reading over my old things!" (545).

The following collation provides a very small sampling of extensive revisions made for the *New York Edition.*

Daisy Miller

Daisy Miller: A Study, *in* Cornhill Magazine, *1878;*
Daisy Miller, *New York: Harper and Brothers, 1879;*
Daisy Miller: A Study, An International Episode, Four
Meetings, *London: Macmillan, 1879. This collation
provides texts from the first English book edition of
1879 and from the* New York Edition *(volume XVIII)
of 1909.*

1879 "Oh, blazes, it's har-r-d!" he exclaimed, pronouncing the
adjective in a peculiar manner.

NYE "Oh blazes; it's har-r-d!" he exclaimed, divesting vowel
and consonants, pertinently enough, of any taint of softness.

1879 He had a great relish for feminine beauty; he was addicted to observing and analysing it. . . .

NYE He took a great interest generally in that range of effects
and was addicted to noting and, as it were, recording them. . . .

1879 Certainly she was very charming; but how deucedly sociable!

NYE Certainly she was very charming, but how extraordinarily communicative and how tremendously easy.

1879 Winterbourne stood looking after her; and as she moved
away, drawing her muslin furbelows over the gravel, said to
himself that she had the *tournure* of a princess.

NYE Winterbourne stood watching her, and as she moved away, drawing her muslin furbelows over the walk, he spoke to himself of her natural elegance.

1879 "They are very common," Mrs. Costello declared. "They are the sort of Americans that one does one's duty by not—not accepting."

NYE "They are horribly common"—it was perfectly simple. "They're the sort of Americans that one does one's duty by just ignoring."

1879 "Of course she's pretty. But she is very common."

NYE "Of course she's very pretty. But she's of the last crudity."

1879 "Well, if Daisy feels up to it—," said Mrs. Miller, in a tone impregnated with a sense of the magnitude of the enterprise.

NYE "Well, if Daisy feels up to it—," said Mrs. Miller in a tone that seemed to break under the burden of such conceptions.

1879 "Yes, it would be lovely!" said Daisy. But she made no movement to accompany him; she only stood there laughing.

NYE "Yes, it would be lovely!" But she made no movement to accompany him; she only remained an elegant image of free light irony.

1879 But he saw that she cared little for feudal antiquities, and that the dusky traditions of Chillon made but a slight impression on her.

NYE But he saw she cared little for mediaeval history and that the grim ghosts of Chillon loomed but faintly before her.

1879 This announcement, instead of embarrassing Mrs. Miller, seemed to relieve her.

NYE This proclamation, instead of embarrassing Mrs. Miller, seemed to soothe her by reconstituting the environment to which she was most accustomed.

1879 "My dearest young lady," cried Winterbourne, with eloquence, "have I come all the way to Rome to encounter your reproaches?"

NYE "Dearest young lady," cried Winterbourne, with generous passion, "have I come all the way to Rome only to be riddled by your silver shafts?"

1879 "She's very crazy!" cried Walker. . . .

NYE "She's very reckless," cried Walker. . . .

1879 "Who is Giovanelli?" "The little Italian."

NYE "And who is Giovanelli?" "The shiny—but, to do him justice, not greasy—little Roman."

1879 . . . the riddle had become easy to read. She was a young lady whom a gentleman need no longer be at pains to respect.

NYE . . . the whole riddle of her contradictions had grown easy to read. She was a lady about the *shades* of whose perversity a foolish puzzled gentleman need no longer trouble his head or his heart. That once questionable quantity *had* no shades—it was a mere black little blot.

1879 Mr. Giovanelli's urbanity was apparently imperturbable. He looked on the ground a moment, and then he said, "For myself, I had no fear, and she wanted to go." "That was no reason!" Winterbourne declared.

NYE Giovanelli raised his neat shoulders and eyebrows to within a suspicion of a shrug. "For myself I had no fear; and *she*—she did what she liked." Winterbourne's eyes attached themselves to the ground. "She did what she liked!"

The Portrait of a Lady

The Portrait of a Lady, *published in* Macmillan's Magazine, *October 1880–November 1881. This collation provides texts from the first English book edition (London: Macmillan, 1881) and from the* New York Edition *(volumes III and IV) of 1908.*

1881 Deprived of this advantage, however, Isabel's visitors retained that of an extreme sweetness and shyness of demeanor, and having, as she thought, the kindest eyes in the world.

NYE Deprived of this advantage, however, Isabel's visitors retained that of an extreme sweetness and shyness of demeanor, and having, as she thought, eyes liked balanced basins, the circles of "ornamental water," set, in parterres, among the geraniums.

———————

1881 Miss Stackpole directed her gaze to the Constable again, and Ralph bespoke her attention for a small Watteau hanging near it. . . .

NYE Miss Stackpole directed her gaze to the Constable again, and Ralph bespoke her attention for a small Lancret hanging near it. . . .

———————

1881 . . . something told her that she should not be satisfied, . . .

NYE . . . something assured her there was a fallacy somewhere in the glowing logic of the proposition—as *he* saw it—

even though she mightn't put her very finest finger-point on it; . . .

1881 There was something too forcible, something oppressive and restrictive, in the manner in which he presented himself.

NYE There was a disagreeable strong push, a kind of hardness of presence, in his way of rising before her.

1881 Caspar Goodwood raised his eyes to her own again; they wore an expression of ardent remonstrance.

NYE Caspar Goodwood raised his eyes to her again; they seemed to shine through a vizard of a helmet.

1881 She was an excitable creature, and now she was much excited.

NYE Vibration was easy to her, was in fact too constant with her, and she found herself now humming like a smitten harp. She only asked, however, to put on the cover, to case herself again in brown holland.

1881 "I'm afraid there are moments in life when even Beethoven has nothing to say to us. We must admit, however, that they are our worst moments."

NYE "I'm afraid there are moments in life when even Schubert has nothing to say to us. We must admit, however, that they are our worst."

1881 Madame Merle had thick, fair hair, which was arranged with picturesque simplicity.

NYE Madame Merle had thick, fair hair, arranged somehow "classically" and as if she were a Bust, Isabel judged—a Juno or a Niobe.

1881 Isabel heard the Countess say something extravagant.

NYE Isabel heard the Countess, at something said by her companion, plunge into the latter's lucidity as a poodle splashes after a thrown stick.

1881 To like her was impossible; but the intenser sentiment might be managed. Madame Merle managed it beautifully.

NYE She mightn't be inhaled as a rose, but she might be grasped as a nettle. Madame Merle genially squeezed her into insignificance.

1881 Into this freshness of Madame Merle she obtained a considerable insight; she saw that it was, after all, a tolerably artificial bloom.

NYE Into this freshness of Madame Merle she obtained a considerable insight; she seemed to see it as professional, as slightly mechanical, carried about in its case like the fiddle of the virtuoso, or blanketed and bridled like the "favorite" of a jockey.

1881 His face wore its pleasant and perpetual smile, which perhaps suggested wit rather than achieved it; . . .

NYE Blighted and battered, but still responsive and still ironic, his face was like a lighted lantern patched with paper and unsteadily held; . . .

1881 "Touchett and I have kept up a sort of parliamentary debate all the way from London. I tell him he's the last of the Tories, and he calls me the head of the Communists."

NYE "Touchett and I have kept up a sort of parliamentary debate all the way from London. I tell him he's the last of the Tories, and he calls me the King of the Goths—says I have, down to the details of my personal appearance, every sign of the brute."

1881 The finest individual she had ever known was hers; the simple knowledge was a sort of act of devotion.

NYE The finest—in the sense of being the subtlest—manly organism she had ever known had become her property, and the recognition of her having but to put out her hands and take it had been originally a sort of act of devotion.

1881 Her eye had lost none of its serenity, her toilet none of its crispness, her opinions none of their national flavour.

NYE Her remarkably open eyes, lighted like great glared railway-stations, had put up no shutters; her attire had lost none of its crispness, her opinions none of their national reference.

1881 She sat in her corner, so motionless, so passive, simply with the sense of being carried, so detached from hope and regret, that if her spirit was haunted with sudden pictures, it might have been the spirit disembarrassed of the flesh.

NYE She sat in her corner, so motionless, so passive, simply with the sense of being carried, so detached from hope and regret, that she recalled to herself one of those Etruscan figures couched upon the receptacle of their ashes.

1881 "To get away from you!" she answered. But this expressed only a little of what she felt. The rest was that she had never been loved before. It lifted her off her feet.

NYE "To get away from *you*!" she answered. But this expressed only a little of what she felt. The rest was that she had never been loved before. She had believed it, but this was different; this was the hot wind of the desert, at the approach of which the others dropped dead, like mere sweet airs of the garden. It wrapped her about; it lifted her off her feet, while the very taste of it, as of something potent, acrid, and strange, forced open her set teeth.

1881 His kiss was like a flash of lightning; when it was dark again she was free.

NYE His kiss was like white lightning, a flash that spread, and spread again, and stayed; and it was extraordinarily as if, while she took it, she felt each thing in his hard manhood that had least pleased her, each aggressive fact of his face, his figure, his presence, justified of its intense identity and made one with this act of possession. So had she heard of those wrecked and under water following a train of images before they sink. But when darkness returned she was free.

III

TRAVEL

James once wrote to his publisher and friend Frederick Macmillan that, "Like the German woman of letters mentioned by Heine, who always wrote with one eye fixed on her MS. & the other on some man—I too pass my life in a sort of divergent squint. One of my orbs of vision rests (complacently enough) on the scenes that surround me here; the other constantly wanders away to the shores of Old England." Having made his first trip to Europe—in the company of his parents and older brother William—before his first birthday, James remained a traveler all his life. He took the genre of travel writing seriously and produced a fine book of essays on each of the four countries that provided the settings of his fiction.

From
English Hours

English Hours, *1905, a collection of sixteen travel essays written mostly in the 1870s (the earliest dated
1872), with only one essay composed after 1890 (in
1901). They are generally less probing than James's
Italian essays, perhaps because they consider his
adopted home rather than the far-off ideal that Italy—
in its various states and at various stages—remained
for him until the end of his life. In his brief introductory "Note" to* English Hours, *James acknowledges
that the essays offer "a good many wonderments and
judgments and emotions, whether felicities or mistakes, the fine freshness of which the author has—to
his misfortune, no doubt—outlived."*

LONDON AT MIDSUMMER
(1877)

I believe it is supposed to require a good deal of courage to confess that one has spent the month of so-called social August in
London; and I will therefore, taking the bull by the horns,
plead guilty at the very outset to this poorness of spirit. I might
attempt some ingenious extenuation of it; I might say that my
remaining in town had been the most unexpected necessity
or the merest inadvertence; I might pretend I liked it—that I
had done it in fact for the perverse love of the thing; I might
claim that you don't really know the charms of London until
on one of the dog-days you have imprinted your boot-sole in the

slumbering dust of Belgravia, or, gazing along the empty vista of the Drive, in Hyde Park, have beheld, for almost the first time in England, a landscape without figures. But little would remain of these specious apologies save the bald circumstance that I had distinctly failed to pack and be off—either on the first of August with the ladies and children, or on the thirteenth with the members of Parliament, or on the twelfth when the grouse-shooting began. (I am not sure that I have got my dates right to a day, but these were about the proper opportunities.) I have, in fact, survived the departure of everything genteel, and the three millions of persons who remained behind with me have been witnesses of my shame.

I cannot pretend, on the other hand, that, having lingered in town, I have found it a very odious or painful experience. Being a stranger, I have not felt it necessary to incarcerate myself during the day and steal abroad only under cover of the darkness—a line of conduct imposed by public opinion, if I am to trust the social criticism of the weekly papers (which I am far from doing), upon the native residents who allow themselves to be overtaken by the unfashionable season. I have indeed always held that few things are pleasanter, during very hot weather, than to have a great city, and a large house within it, quite to one's self. Yet these majestic conditions have not embellished my own metropolitan sojourn, and I have received an impression that in London it would be rather difficult for a visitor not having the command of a good deal of powerful machinery to find them united. English summer weather is rarely hot enough to make it necessary to darken one's house and denude one's person. The present year has indeed in this respect been "exceptional," as any year is, for that matter, that one spends anywhere. But the manners of the people are, to alien eyes, a sufficient indication that at the best (or the worst) even the highest flights of the thermometer in the united Kingdom betray a broken wing. People live with closed windows in August very much as they do in January, and there is to the eye no appreciable difference in the character—that is in the thickness and stiffness—of their coats and boots. A "bath" in England, for the most part, all the year round, means a little portable tin tub and a sponge. Peaches and pears, grapes and melons, are not a more obvious ornament of the market at midsummer than at Christmas. This matter of peaches and melons, by the way, offers one of the best examples of that fact to which a commentator on English manners from afar finds himself constantly recurring, and to which he grows at last almost ashamed of alluding—the fact that the beauty and luxury of the country, that elaborate system known and revered all over the world as "English comfort," is a limited and restricted, an essentially private, affair. I am not one of those irreverent strangers who talk of English fruit as a rather audacious *plaisanterie,* though I could see very well what was meant a short time since by an anecdote related to me in a tone of contemptuous generalisation by a couple of my fellow countrywomen. They had arrived in London in the dog-days, and, lunching at their hotel, had asked to be served with some fruit. The hotel was of the stateliest pattern, and they were waited upon by a functionary whose grandeur was proportionate. This personage bowed and retired, and, after a long delay, reappearing, placed before them with an inimitable gesture a dish of gooseberries and currants. It appeared upon investigation that these acrid vegetables were the only things of succulence that the establishment could undertake to supply; and it seemed to increase the irony of the situation that the establishment was as near as possible to Buckingham Palace. I say that the heroines of my anecdote seemed disposed to generalise: this was sufficiently the case, I mean, to give me a pretext for assuring them that on a thousand fine properties the most beautiful peaches and melons were at that moment ripening either under glass or in warm old walled gardens. My auditors tossed their heads of course at the fine properties, the glass, and the walled gardens; and indeed at their place of privation close to Buckingham Palace such a piece of knowledge was but scantily consoling.

It is to a more public fund of entertainment that the desultory stranger in any country chiefly appeals, especially in summer weather; and as I have implied that there is little encouragement in England to such an appeal it may appear remarkable that I should not have felt London, at this season, void of all beguilement. But one's liking for London—a stranger's liking at least— has at the best a kind of perversity and infirmity often rather difficult to reduce to a statement. I am far from meaning by this that there are not in this mighty metropolis a thousand sources of interest, entertainment, and delight: what I mean is that, for one reason and another, with all its social resources, the place lies heavy on the imported consciousness. It seems grim and lurid, fierce and unmerciful. And yet the imported consciousness accepts it at last with an active satisfaction and finds something warm and comfortable, something that if removed would be greatly missed, in its portentous pressure. It must be admitted, however, that, granting that every one is out of town, your choice of pastimes is not embarrassing. If you have happened to spend a certain amount of time in places where public manners have more frankness London will seem to you scantly provided with innocent diversions. This indeed brings us back simply to that question of the absence of a "public fund" of amusement to which reference was just now made. You must give up the idea of going to sit somewhere in the open air, to eat an ice and listen to a band of music. You will find neither the seat, the ice, nor the band; but on the other hand, faithful at once to your interest and your detachment, you may supply the place of these delights by a little private meditation on the deep-lying causes of the English indifference to them. In such reflections nothing is idle—every grain of testimony counts; and one need therefore not be accused of jumping too suddenly from small things to great if one traces a connection between the absence of ices and music and the essentially hierarchical plan of English society. This hierarchical plan of English society is the great and ever-present fact to the mind of a stranger: there is hardly a detail of life that does not in some degree betray it. It is really only in a country in which a good deal of democratic feeling prevails that people of "refinement," as we say in America, will be willing to sit at little round tables, on a pavement or a gravel-walk, at the door of a café. The better sort are too "genteel" and the inferior sort too base. One must hasten to add too, in justice, that the better sort are, as a general thing, quite too well furnished with entertainments of their own; they have those special resources to which I alluded a moment since. They are persons for whom the private machinery of ease has been made to work with extraordinary smoothness.

If you can sit on a terrace overlooking gardens and have your *café noir* handed you in old Worcester cups by servants who are models of consideration, you have hardly a decent pretext for going to a public house. In France and Italy, in Germany and Spain, the count and countess will sally forth and encamp for the evening, under a row of coloured lamps, upon the paving-stones, but it is ten to one that the count and countess live on a single floor and up several pair of stairs. They are, however, I think, not appreciably affected by considerations which operate potently in England. An Englishman who should propose to sit down, in his own country, at a café-door, would find himself remembering that he is pretending to participations, contacts, fellowships the absolute impracticability of which is expressed in all the rest of his doings.

The study of these reasons, however, would lead us very far from the potential little tables for ices in—where shall I say?— in Oxford Street. But, after all, there is no reason why our imagination should hover about any such articles of furniture. I am afraid they would not strike us as at the best happily situated. In such matters everything hangs together, and I am certain that the customs of the Boulevard des Italiens and the Piazza Colonna would not harmonise with the scenery of the great London thoroughfare. A gin-palace right and left and a detachment of the London rabble in an admiring semicircle— these strike one as some of the more obvious features of the affair. Yet at the season of which I write one's social studies must at the least be studies of low life, for wherever one may go for a stroll or to spend the summer afternoon the comparatively sordid side of things is uppermost. There is no one in the parks save the rough characters who are lying on their faces in the sheep-polluted grass. These people are always tolerably numerous in the Green Park, through which I frequently pass, and are always an occasion for deep wonder. But your wonder will go far if it begins to bestir itself on behalf of the recumbent British tramp. You perceive among them some rich possibilities. Their velveteen legs and their colossal high-lows, their purple necks and ear-tips, their knotted sticks and little greasy hats, make them look like stage-villains of realistic melodrama. I may do them injustice, but consistent character in them mostly requires that they shall have had a taste of penal servitude—that they shall have paid the penalty of stamping on some weaker human head with those huge square heels that are turned up to the summer sky. Actually, however, they are innocent enough, for they are sleeping as peacefully as the most accomplished philanthropist, and it is their look of having walked over half England, and of being pennilessly hungry and thirsty, that constitutes their romantic attractiveness. These six square feet of brown grass are their present sufficiency; but how long will they sleep, whither will they go next, and whence did they come last? You permit yourself to wish that they might sleep for ever and go nowhere else at all.

The month of August is so uncountenanced in London that, going a few days since to Greenwich, that famous resort, I found it possible to get but half a dinner. The celebrated hotel had put out its stoves and locked up its pantry. But for this discovery I should have mentioned the little expedition to Greenwich as a charming relief to the monotony of a London August. Greenwich and Richmond are, classically, the two suburban dining-places. I know not how it may be at this time with Richmond, but the Greenwich incident brings me back (I hope not once too often) to the element of what has lately been called "particularism" in English pleasures. It was in obedience to a perfectly logical argument that the Greenwich hotel had, as I say, locked up its pantry. All well-bred people leave London after the first week in August, *ergo* those who remain behind are not well-bred, and cannot therefore rise to the conception of a "fish dinner." Why then should we have anything ready? I had other impressions, fortunately, of this interesting suburb, and I hasten to declare that during the period of good-breeding the dinner at Greenwich is the most amusing of all dinners. It begins with fish and it continues with fish: what it ends with—except songs and speeches and affectionate partings—I hesitate to affirm. It is a kind of mermaid reversed; for I do know, in a vague way, that the tail of the creature is elaborately and interminably fleshy. If it were not grossly indiscreet I should risk an allusion to the particular banquet which was the occasion of my becoming acquainted with the Greenwich *cuisine*. I would try to express how pleasant it may be to sit in a company of clever and distinguished men before the large windows that look out upon the broad brown Thames. The ships swim by confidently, as if they were part of the entertainment and put down in the bill; the light of the afternoon fades ever so slowly. We eat all the fish of the sea, and wash them down with liquids that bear no resemblance to salt water. We partake of any number of those sauces with which, according to the French adage, one could swallow one's grandmother with a good conscience. To touch on the identity of my companions would indeed be indiscreet, but there is nothing indelicate in marking a high appreciation of the frankness and robustness of English conviviality. The stranger—the American at least—who finds himself in the company of a number of Englishmen assembled for a convivial purpose becomes conscious of an indefinable and delectable something which, for want of a better name, he is moved to call their superior richness of temperament. He takes note of the liberal share of the individual in the magnificent temperament of the people. This seems to him one of the finest things in the world, and his satisfaction will take a keener edge from such an incident as the single one I may permit myself to mention. It was one of those little incidents which can occur only in an old society—a society in which every one that a newly-arrived observer meets strikes him as having in some degree or other a sort of historic identity, being connected with some one or something that he has heard of, that he has wondered about. If they are not the rose they have lived more or less near it. There is an old English song-writer whom we all know and admire—whose songs are sung wherever the language is spoken. Of course, according to the law I just hinted at, one of the gentlemen sitting opposite must needs be his great-grandson. After dinner there are songs, and the gentleman trolls out one of his ancestral ditties with the most charming voice and the most finished art.

I have still other memories of Greenwich, where there is a charming old park, on a summit of one of whose grassy undulations the famous observatory is perched. To do the thing completely you must take passage upon one of the little grimy sixpenny steamers that ply upon the Thames, perform the journey by water, and then, disembarking, take a stroll in the park

to get up an appetite for dinner. I find an irresistible charm in
any sort of river-navigation, but I scarce know how to speak of
the little voyage from Westminster Bridge to Greenwich. It is in
truth the most prosaic possible form of being afloat, and to be
recommended rather to the enquiring than to the fastidious
mind. It initiates you into the duskiness, the blackness, the
crowdedness, the intensely commercial character of London.
Few European cities have a finer river than the Thames, but
none certainly has expended more ingenuity in producing a
sordid river-front. For miles and miles you see nothing but the
sooty backs of warehouses, or perhaps they are the sooty faces:
in buildings so utterly expressionless it is impossible to distinguish. They stand massed together on the banks of the wide
turbid stream, which is fortunately of too opaque a quality to
reflect the dismal image. A damp-looking, dirty blackness is the
universal tone. The river is almost black, and is covered with
black barges; above the black housetops, from among the far-
stretching docks and basins, rises a dusky wilderness of masts.
The little puffing steamer is dingy and gritty—it belches a sable
cloud that keeps you company as you go. In this carboniferous
shower your companions, who belong chiefly indeed to the
classes bereft of lustre, assume an harmonious greyness; and
the whole picture, glazed over with the glutinous London mist,
becomes a masterly composition. But it is very impressive in
spite of its want of lightness and brightness, and though it is
ugly it is anything but trivial. Like so many of the aspects of
English civilisation that are untouched by elegance or grace, it
has the merit of expressing something very serious. Viewed in
this intellectual light the polluted river, the sprawling barges,
the dead-faced warehouses, the frowsy people, the atmospheric
impurities become richly suggestive. It sounds rather absurd,
but all this smudgy detail may remind you of nothing less than
the wealth and power of the British empire at large; so that a
kind of metaphysical magnificence hovers over the scene, and
supplies what may be literally wanting. I don't exactly understand the association, but I know that when I look off to the
left at the East India Docks, or pass under the dark hugely-
piled bridges, where the railway trains and the human processions are for ever moving, I feel a kind of imaginative thrill.

The tremendous piers of the bridges, in especial, seem the very pillars of the empire aforesaid.

It is doubtless owing to this habit of obtrusive and unprofitable reverie that the sentimental tourist thinks it very fine to see the Greenwich observatory lifting its two modest little brick towers. The sight of this useful edifice gave me a pleasure which may at first seem extravagant. The reason was simply that I used to see it as a child, in woodcuts, in school geographies, and in the corners of large maps which had a glazed, sallow surface, and which were suspended in unexpected places, in dark halls and behind doors. The maps were hung so high that my eyes could reach only to the lower corners, and these corners usually contained a print of a strange-looking house perched among trees upon a grassy bank that swept down before it with the most engaging steepness. I used always to think of the joy it must be to roll at one's length down this curved incline. Close at hand was usually something printed about something being at such and such a number of degrees "east of Greenwich." Why east of Greenwich? The vague wonder that the childish mind felt on this point gave the place a mysterious importance and seemed to put it into relation with the difficult and fascinating parts of geography—the countries of unintentional outline and the lonely-looking pages of the atlas. Yet there it stood the other day, the precise point from which the great globe is measured; there was the plain little façade with the old-fashioned cupolas; there was the bank on which it would be so delightful not to be able to stop running. It made me feel terribly old to find that I was not even tempted to begin. There are indeed a great many steep banks in Greenwich Park, which tumbles up and down in the most adventurous fashion. It is a charming place, rather shabby and footworn, as befits a strictly popular resort, but with a character all its own. It is filled with magnificent foreign-looking trees, of which I know nothing but that they have a vain appearance of being chestnuts, planted in long, convergent avenues, with trunks of extraordinary girth and limbs that fling a dusky shadow far over the grass; there are plenty of benches, and there are deer as tame as sleepy children; and from the tops of the bosky hillocks there are views of the widening Thames and the moving ships and the two classic inns by the waterside and the great pompous buildings, designed by Inigo Jones, of the old Hospital, which have been despoiled of their ancient pensioners and converted into a naval academy.

Taking note of all this, I arrived at a far-away angle in the wall of the park, where a little postern door stood ajar. I pushed the door open and found myself, by a thrilling transition, upon Blackheath Common. One had often heard, in vague, irrecoverable, anecdotic connections, of Blackheath: well, here it was—a great green, breezy place where lads in corduroys were playing cricket. I am, as a rule, moved to disproportionate ecstasy by an English common; it may be curtailed and cockneyfied, as this one was—which had lamp-posts stuck about on its turf and a fresh-painted banister all around—but it generally abounds in the note of English breeziness, and you always seem to have seen it water-coloured or engraved. Even if the turf be too much trodden there is to foreign eyes an intimate insular reference in it and in the way the high-piled, weather-bearing clouds hang over it and drizzle down their grey light. Still further to identify this spot, here was the British soldier emerging from two or three of the roads, with his cap upon his ear, his white gloves in one hand and his foppish little cane in the other. He wore the uniform of the artillery, and I asked him where he had come from. I learned that he had walked over from Woolwich and that this feat might be accomplished in half an hour. Inspired again by vague associations I proceeded to accomplish its equivalent. I bent my steps to Woolwich, a place which I knew, in a general way, to be a nursery of British valour. At the end of my half hour I emerged upon another common, where the water-colour bravery had even a higher pitch. The scene was like a chapter of some forgotten record. The open grassy expanse was immense, and, the evening being beautiful, it was dotted with strolling soldiers and townsfolk. There were half a dozen cricket-matches, both civil and military. At one end of this peaceful *campus martius,* which stretches over a hilltop, rises an interminable façade—one of the fronts of the Royal Artillery barracks. It has a very honourable air, and more windows and doors, I imagine, than any building in Britain. There is a great clean parade before it, and there are many sentinels pacing in front of neatly-kept places of ingress to officers' quarters. Everything it looks out upon is in the smartest military trim—the distinguished college (where the poor young man whom it would perhaps be premature to call the last of the Bonapartes lately studied the art of war) on one side; a sort of model camp, a collection of the tidiest plank huts, on the other; a hospital, on a well-ventilated site, at the remoter end. And then in the town below there are a great many more military matters: barracks on an immense scale; a dockyard that presents an interminable dead wall to the street; an arsenal which the gatekeeper (who refused to admit me) declared to be "five miles" in circumference; and, lastly, grogshops enough to inflame the most craven spirit. These latter institutions I glanced at on my way to the railway-station at the bottom of the hill; but before departing I had spent half an hour in strolling about the common in vague consciousness of certain emotions that are called into play (I speak but for myself) by almost any glimpse of the imperial machinery of this great country. The glimpse may be of the slightest; it stirs a peculiar sentiment. I know not what to call this sentiment unless it be simply an admiration for the greatness of England. The greatness of England; that is a very off-hand phrase, and of course I don't pretend to use it analytically. I use it romantically, as it sounds in the ears of any American who remounts the stream of time to the head waters of his own loyalties. I think of the great part that England has played in human affairs, the great space she has occupied, her tremendous might, her far-stretching rule. That these clumsily-general ideas should be suggested by the sight of some infinitesimal fraction of the English administrative system may seem to indicate a cast of fancy too hysterical; but if so I must plead guilty to the weakness. Why should a sentry-box more or less set one thinking of the glory of this little island, which has found in her mere genius the means of such a sway? This is more than I can tell; and all I shall attempt to say is that in the difficult days that are now elapsing a sympathising stranger finds his meditations singularly quickened. It is the imperial element in English history that he has chiefly cared for, and he finds himself wondering whether the imperial epoch is completely closed. It is a moment when all the nations of Europe seem to be doing something, and he waits to see what England, who has done so much, will do. He has been meeting of late a good many of his country-people—Americans who live on the Continent and pretend to speak with assurance of continental ways of feeling. These people have been passing through London, and many of them are in that irritated condition of mind which appears to be the portion of the American sojourner in the British metropolis when he is not given up to the delights of the historic sentiment. They have declared with assurance that the continental nations have ceased to care a straw for what England thinks, that her traditional prestige is completely extinct and that the affairs of Europe will be settled quite independently of her action and still more of her inaction. England will do nothing, will risk nothing; there is no cause bad enough for her not to find a selfish interest in it—there is no cause good enough for her to fight about it. Poor old England is defunct; it is about time she should seek the most decent burial possible. To all this the sympathetic stranger replies that in the first place he doesn't believe a word of it, and in the second doesn't care a fig for it—care, that is, what the continental nations think. If the greatness of England were really waning it would be to him as a personal grief; and as he strolls about the breezy common of Woolwich, with all those mementoes of British dominion around him, he vibrates quite too richly to be distracted by such vapours.

He wishes nevertheless, as I said before, that England would *do* something—something striking and powerful, which should be at once characteristic and unexpected. He asks himself what she can do, and he remembers that this greatness of England which he so much admires was formerly much exemplified in her "taking" something. Can't she "take" something now? There is the "Spectator," who wants her to occupy Egypt: can't she occupy Egypt? The "Spectator" considers this her moral duty—enquires even whether she has a right *not* to bestow the blessings of her beneficent rule upon the down-trodden Fellaheen. I found myself in company with an acute young Frenchman a day or two after this eloquent plea for a partial annexation of the Nile had appeared in the supersubtle sheet. Some allusion was made to it, and my companion of course pronounced it the most finished example conceivable of insular hypocrisy. I don't know how powerful a defence I made of it, but while I read it I had found the hypocrisy contagious. I recalled it while I pursued my contemplations, but I recalled at the same time that sadly prosaic speech of Mr. Gladstone's to which it had been a reply. Mr. Gladstone had said that England had much more urgent duties than the occupation of Egypt: she had to attend to the great questions of—What were the great questions? Those of local taxation and the liquor-laws! Local taxation and the liquor-laws! The phrase, to my ears, just then, sounded almost squalid. These were not the things I had been thinking of; it was not as she should bend anxiously over these doubtless interesting subjects that the sympathising stranger would seem to see England in his favourite posture—that, as Macaulay says, of hurling defiance at her foes. Mr. Gladstone may perhaps have been right, but Mr. Gladstone was far from being a sympathising stranger.

From
Italian Hours

Italian Hours, 1909, a collection (with several new essays and several added sections in old essays) of twenty-two travel essays written from 1872 to 1909. "Two Old Houses," Independent, *September 1899. "The Saint's Afternoon," parts I–V first published in* The May Book, *compiled by Eliza Aria, 1901; parts VI and VII published for the first time in* Italian Hours. *This work is of particular interest in providing the range of James's voice at various stages of his development, from the expression of youth to that of full maturity. The volume is also notable in its arrangement—the essays are often printed out of chronology—beginning with youthful consideration of the aesthetic experience of Venice, and then, somewhat surprisingly for Henry James, finally asserting "the last word" of Italy as the vigor of Naples. The distance traveled in terms of sensibility is enormous.*

TWO OLD HOUSES AND THREE YOUNG WOMEN
(1899, VENICE, FLORENCE)

There are times and places that come back yet again, but that, when the brooding tourist puts out his hand to them, meet it a little slowly, or even seem to recede a step, as if in slight fear of some liberty he may take. Surely they should know by this time that he is capable of taking none. He has his own way—he makes it all right. It now becomes just a part of the charming solicitation that it presents precisely a problem—that of *giving* the particular thing as much as possible without at the same time giving it, as we say, away. There are considerations, proprieties, a necessary indirectness—he must use, in short, a little art. No necessity, however, more than this, makes him warm to his work, and thus it is that, after all, he hangs his three pictures.

I.

The evening that was to give me the first of them was by no means the first occasion of my asking myself if that inveterate "style" of which we talk so much be absolutely conditioned—in dear old Venice and elsewhere—on decrepitude. Is it the style that has brought about the decrepitude, or the decrepitude that has, as it were, intensified and consecrated the style? There is an ambiguity about it all that constantly haunts and beguiles. Dear old Venice has lost her complexion, her figure, her reputation, her self-respect; and yet, with it all, has so puzzlingly not lost a shred of her distinction. Perhaps indeed the case is simpler than it seems, for the poetry of misfortune is familiar to us all, whereas, in spite of a stroke here and there of some happy justice that charms, we scarce find ourselves anywhere arrested by the poetry of a run of luck. The misfortune of Venice being, accordingly, at every point, what we most touch, feel and see, we end by assuming it to be of the essence of her dignity; a consequence, we become aware, by the way, sufficiently discouraging to the general application or pretension of style, and all the more that, to make the final felicity deep, the original greatness must have been something tremendous. If it be the ruins that are noble we have known plenty that were not, and moreover there are degrees and varieties: certain monuments, solid survivals, hold up their heads and decline to ask for a grain of your pity. Well, one knows of course when to keep one's pity to oneself; yet one clings, even in the face of the colder stare, to one's prized Venetian privilege of making the sense of doom and decay a part of every impression. Cheerful work, it may be said of course; and it is doubtless only in Venice that you gain more by such a trick than you lose. What was most beautiful is gone; what was next most beautiful is, thank goodness, going—that, I think, is the monstrous description of the better part of your thought. Is it really your fault if the place makes you want so desperately to read history into everything?

You do that wherever you turn and wherever you look, and you do it, I should say, most of all at night. It comes to you there with longer knowledge, and with all deference to what flushes and shimmers, that the night is the real time. It perhaps even wouldn't take much to make you award the palm to the nights of winter. This is certainly true for the form of progression that is most characteristic, for every question of departure and arrival by gondola. The little closed cabin of this perfect vehicle, the movement, the darkness and the plash, the indistinguishable swerves and twists, all the things you don't see and all the things you do feel—each dim recognition and obscure arrest is a possible throb of your sense of being floated to your doom, even when the truth is simply and sociably that you are going out to tea. Nowhere else is anything as innocent so mysterious, nor anything as mysterious so pleasantly deterrent to protest. These are the moments when you are most daringly Venetian, most content to leave cheap trippers and other aliens the high light of the mid-lagoon and the pursuit of pink and gold. The splendid day is good enough for *them;* what is best for you is to stop at last, as you are now stopping, among clustered *pali* and softly-shifting poops and prows, at a great flight of water-steps that play their admirable part in the general effect of a great entrance. The high doors stand open from them to the paved chamber of a basement tremendously tall and not vulgarly lighted, from which, in turn, mounts the slow stone staircase that draws you further on. The great point is, that if you are worthy of this impression at all, there isn't a single item of it of which the association isn't noble. Hold to it fast that there is no other such dignity of arrival as arrival by water. Hold to it that to float and slacken and gently bump, to creep out of the low, dark *felze* and make the few guided movements and find the strong crooked and offered arm, and then, beneath lighted palace-windows, pass up the few damp steps on the precautionary carpet—hold to it that these things constitute a preparation of which the only defect is that it may sometimes perhaps really prepare too much. It's so stately that what can come after?—it's so good in itself that what, upstairs, as we comparative vulgarians say, can be better? Hold to it, at any rate, that if a lady, in especial, scrambles out of a carriage, tumbles out of a cab, flops out of a tram-car, and hurtles, projectile-like, out of a "lightning-elevator," she alights from the Venetian conveyance as Cleopatra may have stepped from her barge. Upstairs—whatever may be yet in store for her—her entrance shall still advantageously enjoy the support most opposed to the "momentum" acquired. The beauty of the matter has been in the absence of all momentum—elsewhere so scientifically applied to us, from behind, by the terrible life of our day—and in the fact that, as the elements of slowness, the felicities of deliberation, doubtless thus all hang together, the last of calculable dangers is to enter a great Venetian room with a rush.

Not the least happy note, therefore, of the picture I am trying to frame is that there was absolutely no rushing; not only in the sense of a scramble over marble floors, but, by reason of something dissuasive and distributive in the very air of the place, a suggestion, under the fine old ceilings and among types of face and figure abounding in the unexpected, that here were many things to consider. Perhaps the simplest rendering of a scene into the depths of which there are good grounds of discretion for not sinking would be just this emphasis on the value of the unexpected for such occasions—with due qualification, naturally, of its degree. Unexpectedness pure and simple, it is needless to say, may easily endanger any social gathering, and I hasten to add moreover that the figures and faces I speak of were probably not in the least unexpected to each other. The stage they occupied was a stage of variety—Venice has ever been a garden of strange social flowers. It is only as reflected in the consciousness of the visitor from afar—brooding tourist even call him, or sharp-eyed bird on the branch—that I attempt to give you the little drama; beginning with the felicity that most appealed to him, the visible, unmistakable fact that he was the only representative of his class. The whole of the rest of the business was but what he saw and felt and fancied— what he was to remember and what he was to forget. Through

it all, I may say distinctly, he clung to his great Venetian clue—
the explanation of everything by the historic idea. It was a high
historic house, with such a quantity of recorded past twinkling
in the multitudinous candles that one grasped at the idea of
something waning and displaced, and might even fondly and
secretly nurse the conceit that what one was having was just
the very last. Wasn't it certainly, for instance, no mere illusion
that there is no appreciable future left for such manners—an
urbanity so comprehensive, a form so transmitted, as those of
such a hostess and such a host? The future is for a different
conception of the graceful altogether—so far as it's for a conception of the graceful at all. Into that computation I shall not
attempt to enter; but these representative products of an antique culture, at least, and one of which the secret seems more
likely than not to be lost, were not common, nor indeed was
any one else—in the circle to which the picture most insisted on
restricting itself.

Neither, on the other hand, was any one either very beautiful
or very fresh: which was again, exactly, a precious "value" on
an occasion that was to shine most, to the imagination, by the
complexity of its references. Such old, old women with such
old, old jewels; such ugly, ugly ones with such handsome, becoming names; such battered, fatigued gentlemen with such inscrutable decorations; such an absence of youth, for the most
part, in either sex—of the pink and white, the "bud" of new
worlds; such a general personal air, in fine, of being the worse
for a good deal of wear in various old ones. It was not a society—that was clear—in which little girls and boys set the tune;
and there was that about it all that might well have cast a
shadow on the path of even the most successful little girl. Yet
also—let me not be rudely inexact—it was in honour of youth
and freshness that we had all been convened. The *fiançailles* of
the last—unless it were the last but one—unmarried daughter
of the house had just been brought to a proper climax; the contract had been signed, the betrothal rounded off—I'm not sure
that the civil marriage hadn't, that day, taken place. The occasion then had in fact the most charming of heroines and the
most ingenuous of heroes, a young man, the latter, all happily
suffused with a fair Austrian blush. The young lady had had,

besides other more or less shining recent ancestors, a very famous paternal grandmother, who had played a great part in the political history of her time and whose portrait, in the taste and dress of 1830, was conspicuous in one of the rooms. The granddaughter of this celebrity, of royal race, was strikingly like her and, by a fortunate stroke, had been habited, combed, curled in a manner exactly to reproduce the portrait. These things were charming and amusing, as indeed were several other things besides. The great Venetian beauty of our period was there, and nature had equipped the great Venetian beauty for her part with the properest sense of the suitable, or in any case with a splendid generosity—since on the ideally suitable *character* of so brave a human symbol who shall have the last word? This responsible agent was at all events the beauty in the world about whom probably, most, the absence of question (an absence never wholly propitious) would a little smugly and monotonously flourish: the one thing wanting to the interest she inspired was thus the possibility of ever discussing it. There were plenty of suggestive subjects round about, on the other hand, as to which the exchange of ideas would by no means necessarily have dropped. You profit to the full at such times by all the old voices, echoes, images—by that element of the history of Venice which represents all Europe as having at one time and another revelled or rested, asked for pleasure or for patience there; which gives you the place supremely as the refuge of endless strange secrets, broken fortunes and wounded hearts.

II.

There had been, on lines of further or different speculation, a young Englishman to luncheon, and the young Englishman had proved "sympathetic"; so that when it was a question afterwards of some of the more hidden treasures, the browner depths of the old churches, the case became one for mutual guidance and gratitude—for a small afternoon tour and the wait of a pair of friends in the warm little *campi,* at locked doors for which the nearest urchin had scurried off to fetch the

keeper of the key. There are few brown depths to-day into which
the light of the hotels doesn't shine, and few hidden treasures
about which pages enough, doubtless, haven't already been
printed: my business, accordingly, let me hasten to say, is not
now with the fond renewal of any discovery—at least in the
order of impressions most usual. Your discovery may be, for
that matter, renewed every week; the only essential is the good
luck—which a fair amount of practice has taught you to count
upon—of not finding, for the particular occasion, other discov-
erers in the field. Then, in the quiet corner, with the closed
door—then in the presence of the picture and of your companion's sensible emotion—not only the original happy moment,
but everything else, is renewed. Yet once again it can all come
back. The old custode, shuffling about in the dimness, jerks
away, to make sure of his tip, the old curtain that isn't much
more modern than the wonderful work itself. He does his best
to create light where light can never be; but you have your
practised groping gaze, and in guiding the young eyes of your
less confident associate, moreover, you feel you possess the
treasure. These are the most refined pleasures that Venice has
still to give, these odd happy passages of communication and
response.

But the point of my reminiscence is that there were other
communications that day, as there were certainly other re-
sponses. I have forgotten exactly what it was we were looking
for—without much success—when we met the three Sisters.
Nothing requires more care, as a long knowledge of Venice
works in, than not to lose the useful faculty of getting lost. I
had so successfully done my best to preserve it that I could at
that moment conscientiously profess an absence of any suspicion of where we might be. It proved enough that, wherever we
were, we were where the three sisters found us. This was on a
little bridge near a big campo, and a part of the charm of the
matter was the theory that it was very much out of the way.
They took us promptly in hand—they were only walking over
to San Marco to match some coloured wool for the manufacture of such belated cushions as still bloom with purple and
green in the long leisures of old palaces; and that mild errand
could easily open a parenthesis. The obscure church we had

feebly imagined we were looking for proved, if I am not mistaken, that of the sisters' parish; as to which I have but a confused recollection of a large grey void and of admiring for the first time a fine work of art of which I have now quite lost the identity. This was the effect of the charming beneficence of the three sisters, who presently were to give our adventure a turn in the emotion of which everything that had preceded seemed as nothing. It actually strikes me even as a little dim to have been told by them, as we all fared together, that a certain low, wide house, in a small square as to which I found myself without particular association, had been in the far-off time the residence of George Sand. And yet this was a fact that, though I could then only feel it must be for another day, would in a different connection have set me richly reconstructing.

Madame Sand's famous Venetian year has been of late immensely in the air—a tub of soiled linen which the muse of history, rolling her sleeves well up, has not even yet quite ceased energetically and publicly to wash. The house in question must have been the house to which the wonderful lady betook herself when, in 1834, after the dramatic exit of Alfred de Musset, she enjoyed that remarkable period of rest and refreshment with the so long silent, the but recently rediscovered, reported, extinguished, Doctor Pagello. As an old Sandist—not exactly indeed of the *première heure,* but of the fine high noon and golden afternoon of the great career—I had been, though I confess too inactively, curious as to a few points in the topography of the eminent adventure to which I here allude; but had never got beyond the little public fact, in itself always a bit of a thrill to the Sandist, that the present Hotel Danieli had been the scene of its first remarkable stages. I am not sure indeed that the curiosity I speak of has not at last, in my breast, yielded to another form of wonderment—truly to the rather rueful question of why we have so continued to concern ourselves, and why the fond observer of the footprints of genius is likely so to continue attentive to an altercation neither in itself and in its day, nor in its preserved and attested records, at all positively edifying. The answer to such an inquiry would doubtless reward patience, but I fear we can now glance at its possibilities only long enough to say that interesting persons—so they be of a sufficiently approved and established interest—render in some degree interesting whatever happens to them, and give it an importance even when very little else (as in the case I refer to) may have operated to give it a dignity. Which is where I leave the issue of further identifications.

For the three sisters, in the kindest way in the world, had asked us if we already knew their sequestered home and whether, in case we didn't, we should be at all amused to see it. My own acquaintance with them, though not of recent origin, had hitherto lacked this enhancement, at which we both now grasped with the full instinct, indescribable enough, of what it was likely to give. But how, for that matter, either, can I find the right expression of what was to remain with us of this episode? It is the fault of the sad-eyed old witch of Venice that she so easily puts more into things that can pass under the common names that do for them elsewhere. Too much for a rough sketch was to be seen and felt in the home of the three sisters, and in the delightful and slightly pathetic deviation of their doing us so simply and freely the honours of it. What was most immediately marked was their resigned cosmopolite state, the effacement of old conventional lines by foreign contact and example; by the action, too, of causes full of a special interest, but not to be emphasised perhaps—granted indeed they be named at all—without a certain sadness of sympathy. If "style," in Venice, sits among ruins, let us always lighten our tread when we pay her a visit.

Our steps were in fact, I am happy to think, almost soft enough for a death-chamber as we stood in the big, vague *sala* of the three sisters, spectators of their simplified state and their beautiful blighted rooms, the memories, the portraits, the shrunken relics of nine Doges. If I wanted a first chapter it was here made to my hand; the painter of life and manners, as he glanced about, could only sigh—as he so frequently has to—over the vision of so much more truth than he can use. What on earth is the need to "invent," in the midst of tragedy and comedy that never cease? Why, with the subject itself, all round, so inimitable, condemn the picture to the silliness of trying not to be aware of it? The charming lonely girls, carrying so simply their great name and fallen fortunes, the despoiled *decaduta* house, the unfailing Italian grace, the space so out of scale with actual needs, the absence of books, the presence of ennui, the sense of the length of the hours and the shortness of everything else—all this was a matter not only for a second chapter and a third, but for a whole volume, a *dénoûment* and a sequel.

This time, unmistakably, it *was* the last—Wordsworth's stately "shade of that which once was great"; and it was almost as if our distinguished young friends had consented to pass away slowly in order to treat us to the vision. Ends are only ends in truth, for the painter of pictures, when they are more or less conscious and prolonged. One of the sisters had been to London, whence she had brought back the impression of having seen at the British Museum a room exclusively filled with books and documents devoted to the commemoration of her family. She must also then have encountered at the National Gallery the exquisite specimen of an early Venetian master in which one of her ancestors, then head of the State, kneels with so sweet a dignity before the Virgin and Child. She was perhaps old enough, none the less, to have seen this precious work taken down from the wall of the room in which we sat and—on terms so far too easy—carried away for ever; and not too young, at all events, to have been present, now and then, when her candid elders, enlightened too late as to what their sacrifice might really have done for them, looked at each other with the pale hush of the irreparable. We let ourselves note that these were matters to put a great deal of old, old history into sweet young Venetian faces.

III.

In Italy, if we come to that, this particular appearance is far from being only in the streets, where we are apt most to observe it—in countenances caught as we pass and in the objects marked by the guide-books with their respective stellar allowances. It is behind the walls of the houses that old, old history is thick and that the multiplied stars of Baedeker might often best find their application. The feast of St. John the Baptist is the feast of the year in Florence, and it seemed to me on that night that I could have scattered about me a handful of these signs. I had the pleasure of spending a couple of hours on a signal high terrace that overlooks the Arno, as well as in the galleries that open out to it, where I met more than ever the pleasant curious question of the disparity between the old conditions and the new manners. Make our manners, we moderns, as good as we can, there is still no getting over it that they are not good enough for many of the great places. This was one of those scenes, and its greatness came out to the full into the hot Florentine evening, in which the pink and golden fires of the pyrotechnics arranged on Ponte Carraja—the occasion of our assembly—lighted up the large issue. The "good people" beneath were a huge, hot, gentle, happy family; the fireworks on the bridge, kindling river as well as sky, were delicate and charming; the terrace connected the two wings that give bravery to the front of the palace, and the close-hung pictures in the rooms, open in a long series, offered to a lover of quiet perambulation an alternative hard to resist.

Wherever he stood—on the broad loggia, in the cluster of company, among bland ejaculations and liquefied ices, or in the presence of the mixed masters that led him from wall to wall—such a seeker for the spirit of each occasion could only turn it over that in the first place this was an intenser, finer little Florence than ever, and that in the second the testimony was again wonderful to former fashions and ideas. What did they do, in the other time, the time of so much smaller a society, smaller and fewer fortunes, more taste perhaps as to some particulars, but fewer tastes, at any rate, and fewer habits and wants—what did they do with chambers so multitudinous and so vast? Put their "state" at its highest—and we know of many ways in which it must have broken down—how did they live in them without the aid of variety? How did they, in minor communities in which every one knew every one, and every one's impression and effect had been long, as we say, discounted, find representation and emulation sufficiently amusing? Much of the charm of thinking of it, however, is doubtless that we are not able to say. This leaves us with the conviction that does them most honour: the old generations built and arranged greatly for the simple reason that they liked it, and they could bore themselves—to say nothing of each other, when it came to that—better in noble conditions than in mean ones.

It was not, I must add, of the far-away Florentine age that I most thought, but of periods more recent and of which the sound and beautiful house more directly spoke. If one had always been homesick for the Arno-side of the seventeenth and eighteenth centuries, here was a chance, and a better one than ever, to taste again of the cup. Many of the pictures—there was a charming quarter of an hour when I had them to myself— were bad enough to have passed for good in those delightful years. Shades of Grand-Dukes encompassed me—Dukes of the pleasant later sort who weren't really grand. There was still the sense of having come too late—yet not too late, after all, for this glimpse and this dream. My business was to people the place—its own business had never been to save us the trouble of understanding it. And then the deepest spell of all was perhaps that just here I was supremely out of the way of the so terribly actual Florentine question. This, as all the world knows, is a battle-ground, to-day, in many journals, with all Italy practically pulling on one side and all England, America and Germany pulling on the other: I speak of course of the more or less articulate opinion. The "improvement," the rectification of Florence is in the air, and the problem of the particular ways in which, given such desperately delicate cases, these matters should be understood. The little treasure-city is, if there ever was one, a delicate case—more delicate perhaps than any other in the world save that of our taking on ourselves to persuade the Italians that they mayn't do as they like with their own. They so absolutely may that I profess I see no happy issue from the fight. It will take more tact than our combined tactful genius may at all probably muster to convince them that their own is, by an ingenious logic, much rather *ours*. It will take more subtlety still to muster for them that truly dazzling show of examples from which they may learn that what in general is "ours" shall appear to them as a rule a sacrifice to beauty and a triumph of taste. The situation, to the truly analytic mind, offers in short, to perfection, all the elements of despair; and I am afraid that if I hung back, at the Corsini palace, to woo illusions and invoke the irrelevant, it was because I could think, in the conditions, of no better way to meet the acute responsibility of the critic than just to shirk it.

THE SAINT'S AFTERNOON AND OTHERS
(1901, 1909, THE BAY OF NAPLES)

Before and above all was the sense that, with the narrow limits of past adventure, I had never yet had such an impression of what the summer could be in the south or the south in the summer; but I promptly found it, for the occasion, a good fortune that my terms of comparison were restricted. It was really something, at a time when the stride of the traveller had become as long as it was easy, when the seven-league boots positively hung, for frequent use, in the closet of the most sedentary, to have kept one's self so innocent of strange horizons that the Bay of Naples in June might still seem quite final. That picture struck me—a particular corner of it at least, and for many reasons—as the last word; and it is this last word that comes back to me, after a short interval, in a green, grey northern nook, and offers me again its warm, bright golden meaning before it also inevitably catches the chill. Too precious, surely, for us not to suffer it to help us as it may is the faculty of putting together again in an order the sharp minutes and hours that the wave of time has been as ready to pass over as the salt sea to wipe out the letters and words your stick has traced in the sand. Let me, at any rate, recover a sufficient number of such signs to make a sort of sense.

I.

Far aloft on the great rock was pitched, as the first note, and indeed the highest, of the wondrous concert, the amazing creation of the friend who had offered me hospitality, and whom, more almost than I had ever envied any one anything, I envied the privilege of being able to reward a heated, artless pilgrim with a revelation of effects so incalculable. There was none but the loosest prefigurement as the creaking and puffing little boat, which had conveyed me only from Sorrento, drew closer beneath the prodigious island—beautiful, horrible and haunted— that does most, of all the happy elements and accidents, towards making the Bay of Naples, for the study of composition, a lesson in the grand style. There was only, above and below, through the blue of the air and sea, a great confused shining of hot cliffs and crags and buttresses, a loss, from nearness, of the splendid couchant outline and the more comprehensive mass, and an opportunity—oh, not lost, I assure you—to sit and meditate, even moralise, on the empty deck, while a happy brotherhood of American and German tourists, including, of course, many sisters, scrambled down into little waiting, rocking tubs and, after a few strokes, popped systematically into the small orifice of the Blue Grotto. There was an appreciable moment when they were all lost to view in that receptacle, the daily "psychological" moment during which it must so often befall the recalcitrant observer on the deserted deck to find himself aware of how delightful it might be if none of them should come out again. The charm, the fascination of the idea is not a little—though also not wholly—in the fact that, as the wave rises over the aperture, there is the most encouraging appearance that they perfectly may not. There it is. There is no more of them. It is a case to which nature has, by the neatest stroke and with the best taste in the world, just quietly attended.

Beautiful, horrible, haunted: that is the essence of what, about itself, Capri says to you—dip again into your Tacitus and see why; and yet, while you roast a little under the awning and in the vaster shadow, it is not because the trail of Tiberius is ineffaceable that you are most uneasy. The trail of Germanicus in Italy to-day ramifies further and bites perhaps even deeper; a proof of which is, precisely, that his eclipse in the Blue Grotto is inexorably brief, that here he is popping out again, bobbing enthusiastically back and scrambling triumphantly back. The spirit, in truth, of his effective appropriation of Capri has a broad-faced candour against which there is no standing up, supremely expressive as it is of the well-known "love that kills," of Germanicus's fatal susceptibility. If I were to let my-

self, however, incline to *that* aspect of the serious case of Capri
I should embark on strange depths. The straightness and simplicity, the classic, synthetic directness of the German passion
for Italy, make this passion probably the sentiment in the world
that is in the act of supplying enjoyment in the largest, sweetest
mouthfuls; and there is something unsurpassably marked in the
way that on this irresistible shore it has seated itself to rumi-
nate and digest. It keeps the record in its own loud accents; it
breaks out in the folds of the hills and on the crests of the crags
into every manner of symptom and warning. Huge advertise-
ments and portents stare across the bay; the acclivities bristle
with breweries and "restorations" and with great ugly Gothic
names. I hasten, of course, to add that some such general consciousness as this may well oppress, under any sky, at the century's end, the brooding tourist who makes himself a prey by
staying anywhere, when the gong sounds, "behind." It is behind, in the track and the reaction, that he least makes out the
end of it all, perceives that to visit any one's country for any
one's sake is more and more to find some one quite other in
possession. No one, least of all the brooder himself, is in his
own.

II.

I certainly, at any rate, felt the force of this truth when, on
scaling the general rock with the eye of apprehension, I made
out at a point much nearer its summit than its base the gleam
of a dizzily-perched white sea-gazing front which I knew for
my particular landmark and which promised so much that it
would have been welcome to keep even no more than half. Let
me instantly say that it kept still more than it promised, and by
no means least in the way of leaving far below it the worst of
the outbreak of restorations and breweries. There is a road at
present to the upper village, with which till recently communication was all by rude steps cut in the rock and diminutive
donkeys scrambling on the flints; one of those fine flights of
construction which the great road-making "Latin races" take,
wherever they prevail, without advertisement or bombast; and

even while I followed along the face of the cliff its climbing consolidated ledge, I asked myself how I could think so well of it without consistently thinking better still of the temples of beer so obviously destined to enrich its terminus. The perfect answer to that was of course that the brooding tourist is never bound to be consistent. What happier law for him than this very one, precisely, when on at last alighting, high up in the blue air, to stare and gasp and almost disbelieve, he embraced little by little the beautiful truth particularly, on this occasion, reserved for himself, and took in the stupendous picture? For here above all had the thought and the hand come from far away—even from *ultima Thule,* and yet were in possession triumphant and acclaimed. Well, all one could say was that the way they had felt their opportunity, the divine conditions of the place, spoke of the advantage of some such intellectual perspective as a remote original standpoint alone perhaps can give. If what had finally, with infinite patience, passion, labour, taste, got itself done there, was like some supreme reward of an old dream of Italy, something perfect after long delays, was it not verily in *ultima Thule* that the vow would have been piously enough made and the germ tenderly enough nursed? For a certain art of asking of Italy all she can give, you must doubtless either be a rare *raffiné* or a rare genius, a sophisticated Norseman or just a Gabriele d'Annunzio.

All she can give appeared to me, assuredly, for that day and the following, gathered up and enrolled there: in the wondrous cluster and dispersal of chambers, corners, courts, galleries, arbours, arcades, long white ambulatories and vertiginous points of view. The greatest charm of all perhaps was that, thanks to the particular conditions, she seemed to abound, to overflow, in directions in which I had never yet enjoyed the chance to find her so free. The indispensable thing was therefore, in observation, in reflection, to press the opportunity hard, to recognise that as the abundance was splendid, so, by the same stroke, it was immensely suggestive. It dropped into one's lap, naturally, at the end of an hour or two, the little white flower of its formula: the brooding tourist, in other words, could only continue to brood till he had made out in a measure, as I may say, what was so wonderfully the matter with him. He was simply then in the presence, more than ever yet, of the possible poetry of the personal and social life of the south, and the fun would depend much—as occasions are fleeting—on his arriving in time, in the interest of that imagination which is his only field of sport, at adequate new notations of it. The sense of all this, his obscure and special fun in the general bravery, mixed, on the morrow, with the long, human hum of the bright, hot day and filled up the golden cup with questions and answers. The feast of St. Antony, the patron of the upper town, was the one thing in the air, and of the private beauty of the place, there on the narrow shelf, in the shining, shaded loggias and above the blue gulfs, all comers were to be made free.

III.

The church-feast of its saint is of course for Anacapri, as for any self-respecting Italian town, the great day of the year, and the smaller the small "country," in native parlance, as well as the simpler, accordingly, the life, the less the chance for leakage, on other pretexts, of the stored wine of loyalty. This pure fluid, it was easy to feel overnight, had not sensibly lowered its level; so that nothing indeed, when the hour came, could well exceed the outpouring. All up and down the Sorrentine promontory the early summer happens to be the time of the saints, and I had just been witness there of a week on every day of which one might have travelled, through kicked-up clouds and other demonstrations, to a different hot holiday. There had been no bland evening that, somewhere or other, in the hills or by the sea, the white dust and the red glow didn't rise to the dim stars. Dust, perspiration, illumination, conversation—these were the regular elements. "They're very civilised," a friend who knows them as well as they can be known had said to me of the people in general; "plenty of fireworks and plenty of talk—that's all they ever want." That they were "civilised"—on the side on which they were most to show—was therefore to be the word of the whole business, and nothing could have, in fact, had more interest than the meaning that for the thirty-six hours I read into it.

Seen from below and diminished by distance, Anacapri makes scarce a sign, and the road that leads to it is not traceable over the rock; but it sits at its ease on its high, wide table, of which it covers—and with picturesque southern culture as well—as much as it finds convenient. As much of it as possible was squeezed all the morning, for St. Antony, into the piazzetta before the church, and as much more into that edifice as the robust odour mainly prevailing there allowed room for. It was the odour that was in prime occupation, and one could only wonder how so many men, women and children could cram themselves into so much smell. It was surely the smell, thick and resisting, that was least successfully to be elbowed. Meanwhile the good saint, before he could move into the air, had, among the tapers and the tinsel, the opera-music and the pulpit poundings, bravely to snuff it up. The shade outside was hot, and the sun was hot; but we waited as densely for him to come out, or rather to come "on," as the pit at the opera waits for the great tenor. There were people from below and people from the mainland and people from Pomerania and a brass band from Naples. There were other figures at the end of longer strings—strings that, some of them indeed, had pretty well given way and were now but little snippets trailing in the dust. Oh, the queer sense of the good old Capri of artistic legend, of which the name itself was, in the more benighted years—years of the contadina and the pifferaro—a bright evocation! Oh, the echo, on the spot, of each romantic tale. Oh, the loafing painters, so bad and so happy, the conscious models, the vague personalities! The "beautiful Capri girl" was of course not missed, though not perhaps so beautiful as in her ancient glamour, which none the less didn't at all exclude the probable presence—with *his* legendary light quite undimmed—of the English lord in disguise who will at no distant date marry her. The whole thing was there; one held it in one's hand.

The saint comes out at last, borne aloft in long procession and under a high canopy: a rejoicing, staring, smiling saint, openly delighted with the one happy hour in the year on which he may take his own walk. Frocked and tonsured, but not at all macerated, he holds in his hand a small wax puppet of an infant Jesus and shows him to all their friends, to whom he nods and bows: to whom, in the dazzle of the sun he literally seems to grin and wink, while his litter sways and his banners flap and every one gaily greets him. The ribbons and draperies flutter, and the white veils of the marching maidens, the music blares and the guns go off and the chants resound, and it is all as holy and merry and noisy as possible. The procession—down to the delightful little tinselled and bare-bodied babies, miniature St. Antonys irrespective of sex, led or carried by proud papas or brown grandsires—includes so much of the population that you marvel there is such a muster to look on—like the charades given in a family in which every one wants to act. But it is all indeed in a manner one house, the little high-niched island community, and nobody therefore, even in the presence of the head of it, puts on an air of solemnity. Singular and suggestive before everything else is the absence of any approach to our notion of the posture of respect, and this among people whose manners in general struck one as so good and, in particular, as so cultivated. The office of the saint—of which the festa is but the annual reaffirmation—involves not the faintest attribute of remoteness or mystery.

While, with my friend, I waited for him, we went for coolness into the second church of the place, a considerable and bedizened structure, with the rare curiosity of a wondrous pictured pavement of majolica, the garden of Eden done in large coloured tiles or squares, with every beast, bird and river, and a brave *diminuendo*, in especial, from portal to altar, of perspective, so that the animals and objects of the foreground are big and those of the successive distances differ with much propriety. Here in the sacred shade the old women were knitting, gossiping, yawning, shuffling about; here the children were romping and "larking"; here, in a manner, were the open parlour, the nursery, the kindergarten and the conversazione of the poor. This is everywhere the case by the southern sea. I remember near Sorrento a wayside chapel that seemed the scene of every function of domestic life, including cookery and others. The odd thing is that it all appears to interfere so little with that special civilised note—the note of manners—which is so constantly touched. It is barbarous to expectorate in the temple of your faith, but that doubtless is an extreme case. Is civilisation really measured by the number of things people do respect? There would seem to be much evidence against it. The oldest societies, the societies with most traditions, are naturally not the least ironic, the least *blasées,* and the African tribes who take so many things into account that they fear to quit their huts at night are not the fine flower.

IV.

Where, on the other hand, it was impossible not to feel to the full all the charming *riguardi*—to use their own good word—in which our friends *could* abound, was, that afternoon, in the extraordinary temple of art and hospitality that had been benignantly opened to me. Hither, from three o'clock to seven, all the world, from the small in particular to the smaller and the smallest, might freely flock, and here, from the first hour to the last, the huge straw-bellied flasks of purple wine were tilted for all the thirsty. They were many, the thirsty, they were three hundred, they were unending; but the draughts they drank were neither countable nor counted. This boon was dispensed in a long, pillared portico, where everything was white and light save the blue of the great bay as it played up from far below or as you took it in, between shining columns, with your elbows on the parapet. Sorrento and Vesuvius were over against you; Naples furthest off, melted, in the middle of the picture, into shimmering vagueness and innocence; and the long arm of Posilippo and the presence of the other islands, Procida, the stricken Ischia, made themselves felt to the left. The grand air of it all was in one's very nostrils and seemed to come from sources too numerous and too complex to name. It was antiquity in solution, with every brown, mild figure, every note of the old speech, every tilt of the great flask, every shadow cast by every classic fragment, adding its touch to the impression. What was the secret of the surprising amenity?—to the essence of which one got no nearer than simply by feeling afresh the old story of the deep interfusion of the present with the past. You had felt that often before, and all that could, at the most, help you now was that, more than ever yet, the present appeared to become again really classic, to sigh with strange elusive sounds of Virgil and Theocritus. Heaven only knows how little they would in truth have had to say to it, but we yield to these visions as we must, and when the imagination fairly turns in its pain almost any soft name is good enough to soothe it.

It threw such difficulties but a step back to say that the secret of the amenity was "style"; for what in the world was the secret of style, which you might have followed up and down the abysmal old Italy for so many a year only to be still vainly calling for it? Everything, at any rate, that happy afternoon, in that place of poetry, was bathed and blessed with it. The castle of Barbarossa had been on the height behind; the villa of black Tiberius had overhung the immensity from the right; the white arcades and the cool chambers offered to every step some sweet old "piece" of the past, some rounded porphyry pillar supporting a bust, some shaft of pale alabaster upholding a trellis, some mutilated marble image, some bronze that had roughly resisted. Our host, if we came to that, had the secret; but he could only express it in grand practical ways. One of them was precisely this wonderful "afternoon tea," in which tea only— *that*, good as it is, has never the note of style—was not to be found. The beauty and the poetry, at all events, were clear enough, and the extraordinary uplifted distinction; but where, in all this, it may be asked was the element of "horror" that I have spoken of as sensible?—what obsession that was not charming could find a place in that splendid light, out of which the long summer squeezes every secret and shadow? I'm afraid I'm driven to plead that these evils were exactly in one's imagination, a predestined victim always of the cruel, the fatal historic sense. To make so much distinction, how much history had been needed!—so that the whole air still throbbed and ached with it, as with an accumulation of ghosts to whom the very climate was pitiless, condemning them to blanch for ever in the general glare and grandeur, offering them no dusky northern nook, no place at the friendly fireside, no shelter of legend or song.

V.

My friend had, among many original relics, in one of his white galleries—and how he understood the effect and the "value" of whiteness!—two or three reproductions of the finest bronzes of the Naples museum, the work of a small band of brothers whom he had found himself justified in trusting to deal with their problem honourably and to bring forth something as different as possible from the usual compromise of commerce. They had brought forth, in especial, for him, a copy of the young resting, slightly-panting Mercury which it was a pure delight to live with, and they had come over from Naples on St. Antony's eve, as they had done the year before, to report themselves to their patron, to keep up good relations, to drink Capri wine and to join in the tarantella. They arrived late, while we were at supper; they received their welcome and their billet, and I am not sure it was not the conversation and the beautiful manners of these obscure young men that most fixed in my mind for the time the sense of the side of life that, all around, was to come out strongest. It would be artless, no doubt, to represent them as high types of innocence or even of energy— at the same time that, weighing them against *some* ruder folk of our own race, we might perhaps have made bold to place their share even of these qualities in the scale. It was an impression indeed never infrequent in Italy, of which I might, in these days, first have felt the force during a stay, just earlier, with a friend at Sorento—a friend who had good-naturedly "had in," on his wondrous terrace, after dinner, for the pleasure of the gaping alien, the usual local quartette, violins, guitar and flute, the musical barber, the musical tailor, sadler, joiner, humblest sons of the people and exponents of Neapolitan song. Neapolitan song, as we know, has been blown well about the world, and it is late in the day to arrive with a ravished ear for it. That, however, was scarcely at all, for me, the question: the question, on the Sorrento terrace, so high up in the cool Capri night, was of the present outlook, in the world, for the races with whom it has been a tradition, in intercourse, positively to please.

The personal civilisation, for intercourse, of the musical barber and tailor, of the pleasant young craftsmen of my other friend's company, was something that could be trusted to make the brooding tourist brood afresh—to say more to him in fact, all the rest of the second occasion, than everything else put together. The happy address, the charming expression, the indistinctive discretion, the complete eclipse, in short, of vulgarity and brutality—these things easily became among these people the supremely suggestive note, begetting a hundred hopes and fears as to the place that, with the present general turn of affairs about the globe, is being kept for them. They are perhaps what the races politically feeble have still most to contribute—but what appears to be the happy prospect for the races politically feeble? And so the afternoon waned, among the mellow marbles and the pleasant folk—the purple wine flowed, the golden light faded, song and dance grew free and circulation slightly embarrassed. But the great impression remained and finally was exquisite. It was all purple wine, all art and song, and nobody a grain the worse. It was fireworks and conversation—the former, in the piazzetta, were to come later; it was civilisation and amenity. I took in the greater picture, but I lost nothing else; and I talked with the contadini about antique sculpture. No, nobody was a grain the worse; and I had plenty to think of. So it was I was quickened to remember that we others, we of my own country, as a race politically *not* weak, had—by what I had somewhere just heard—opened "three hundred 'saloons'" at Manilla.

VI.

The "other" afternoons I here pass on to—and I may include in them, for that matter, various mornings scarce less charmingly sacred to memory—were occasions of another and a later year; a brief but all felicitous impression of Naples itself, and of the approach to it from Rome, as well as of the return to Rome by a different wonderful way, which I feel I shall be wise never to attempt to "improve on." Let me muster assurance to confess that this comparatively recent and superlatively rich reminiscence gives me for its first train of ineffable images those of a motor-run that, beginning betimes of a splendid June day, and seeing me, with my genial companions, blissfully out of Porta San Paolo, hung over us thus its benediction till the splendour had faded in the lamplit rest of the Chiaja. "We'll go by the mountains," my friend, of the winged chariot, had said, "and we'll come back, after three days, by the sea"; which handsome promise flowered into such flawless performance that I could but feel it to have closed and rounded for me, beyond any further rehandling, the long-drawn rather indeed than thick-studded chaplet of my visitations of Naples—from the first, seasoned with the highest sensibility of youth, forty years ago, to this last the other day. I find myself noting with interest—and just to be able to emphasise it is what inspires me with these remarks—that, in spite of the milder and smoother and perhaps, pictorially speaking, considerably emptier, Neapolitan face of things, things in general, of our later time, I recognised in my final impression a grateful, a beguiling serenity. The place is at the best wild and weird and sinister, and yet seemed on this occasion to be seated more at her ease in her immense natural dignity. My disposition to feel that, I hasten to add, was doubtless my own secret; my three beautiful days, at any rate, filled themselves with the splendid harmony, several of the minor notes of which ask for a place, such as it may be, just here.

Wondrously, it was a clean and cool and, as who should say, quiet and amply interspaced Naples—in tune with itself, no harsh jangle of *forestieri* vulgarising the concert. I seemed in fact, under the blaze of summer, the only stranger—though the blaze of summer itself was, for that matter, everywhere but a higher pitch of light and colour and tradition, and a lower pitch of everything else; even, it struck me, of sound and fury. The appeal in short was genial, and, faring out to Pompeii of a Sunday afternoon, I enjoyed there, for the only time I can recall, the sweet chance of a late hour or two, the hour of the lengthening shadows, absolutely alone. The impression remains ineffaceable—it was to supersede half-a-dozen other mixed memories, the sense that had remained with me, from far back, of a pilgrimage always here beset with traps and shocks and vulgar importunities, achieved under fatal discouragements. Even Pompeii, in fine, haunt of *all* the cockneys of

creation, burned itself, in the warm still eventide, as clear as
glass, or as the glow of a pale topaz, and the particular cockney
who roamed without a plan and at his ease, but with his feet on
Roman slabs, his hands on Roman stones, his eyes on the Roman void, his consciousness really at last of some good to him,
could open himself as never before to the fond luxurious fallacy of a close communion, a direct revelation. With which
there were other moments for him not less the fruit of the slow
unfolding of time; the clearest of these again being those enjoyed on the terrace of a small island-villa—the island a rock
and the villa a wondrous little rock-garden, unless a better term
would be perhaps rock-salon, just off the extreme point of
Posilippo and where, thanks to a friendliest hospitality, he was
to hang ecstatic, through another sublime afternoon, on the
wave of a magical wand. Here, as happened, were charming
wise, original people even down to delightful amphibious American children, enamelled by the sun of the Bay as for figures of
miniature Tritons and Nereids on a Renaissance plaque; and
above all, on the part of the general prospect, a demonstration
of the grand style of composition and effect that one was never
to wish to see bettered. The way in which the Italian scene on
such occasions as this seems to purify itself to the transcendent
and perfect *idea* alone—idea of beauty, of dignity, of comprehensive grace, with all accidents merged, all defects disowned,
all experience outlived, and to gather itself up into the mere
mute eloquence of what has just incalculably *been,* remains
forever the secret and the lesson of the subtlest daughter of History. All one could do, at the heart of the overarching crystal,
and in presence of the relegated City, the far-trailing Mount,
the grand Sorrentine headland, the islands incomparably stationed and related, was to wonder what may well become of
the so many other elements of any poor human and social com-
plexus, what might become of any successfully-working or
only struggling and floundering civilisation at all, when high
Natural Elegance proceeds to take such exclusive charge and
recklessly assume, as it were, *all* the responsibilities.

VII.

This indeed had been quite the thing I was asking myself all the wondrous way down from Rome, and was to ask myself afresh, on the return, largely within sight of the sea, as our earlier course had kept to the ineffably romantic inland valleys, the great decorated blue vistas in which the breasts of the mountains shine vaguely with strange high-lying city and castle and church and convent, even as shoulders of no diviner line might be hung about with dim old jewels. It was odd, at the end of time, long after those initiations, of comparative youth, that had then struck one as extending the very field itself of felt charm, as exhausting the possibilities of fond surrender, it was odd to have positively a new basis of enjoyment, a new gate of triumphant passage, thrust into one's consciousness and opening to one's use; just as I confess I have to brace myself a little to call by such fine names our latest, our ugliest and most monstrous aid to motion. It is true of the monster, as we have known him up to now, that one can neither quite praise him nor quite blame him without a blush—he reflects so the nature of the company he's condemned to keep. His splendid easy power addressed to noble aims make him assuredly on occasion a purely beneficent creature. I parenthesise at any rate that I know him in no other light—counting out of course the acquaintance that consists of a dismayed arrest in the road, with back flattened against wall or hedge, for the dusty, smoky, stenchy shock of his passage. To no end is his easy power more blest than to that of ministering to the ramifications, as it were, of curiosity, or to that, in other words, of achieving for us, among the kingdoms of the earth, the grander and more genial, the comprehensive and *complete* introduction. Much as was ever to be said for our old forms of pilgrimage—and I am convinced that they are far from wholly superseded—they left, they had to leave, dreadful gaps in our yearning, dreadful lapses in our knowledge, dreadful failures in our energy; there were always things off and beyond, goals of delight and dreams of desire, that dropped as a matter of course into the unattainable, and over to which our wonder-working agent now flings the firm straight bridge. Curiosity has lost, under this amazing extension, its salutary renouncements perhaps; contemplation has become one with action and satisfaction one with desire—speaking always in the spirit of the inordinate lover of an enlightened use of our eyes. That may represent, for all I know, an insolence of advantage on which there will be eventual heavy charges, as yet obscure and incalculable, to pay, and I glance at the possibility only to avoid all thought of the lesson of the long run, and to insist that I utter this dithyramb but in the immediate flush and fever of the short. For such a beat of time as our fine courteous and contemplative advance upon Naples, and for such another as our retreat northward under the same fine law of observation and homage, the bribed consciousness could only decline to question its security. The sword of Damocles suspended over that presumption, the skeleton at the banquet of extravagant ease, would have been that even at our actual inordinate rate—leaving quite apart "improvements" to come—such savings of trouble begin to use up the world; some hard grain of difficulty being always a necessary part of the composition of pleasure. The hard grain in our old comparatively pedestrian mixture, before this business of our learning not so much even to fly (which might indeed involve trouble) as to be mechanically and prodigiously flown, quite another matter, was the element of uncertainty, effort and patience; the handful of silver nails which, I admit, drove many an impression home. The seated motorist misses the silver nails, I fully acknowledge, save in so far as his æsthetic (let alone his moral) conscience may supply him with some artful subjective substitute; in which case the thing becomes a precious secret of his own.

However, I wander wild—by which I mean I look too far ahead; my intention having been only to let my sense of the merciless June beauty of Naples Bay at the sunset hour and on the island terrace associate itself with the whole inexpressible taste of our two motor-days' feast of scenery. That queer question of the exquisite grand manner as the most emphasised *all* of things—of what it may, seated so predominant in nature, insidiously, through the centuries, let generations and populations "in for," hadn't in the least waited for the special emphasis I speak of to hang about me. I must have found myself more or less consciously entertaining it by the way—since how couldn't it be of the very essence of the truth, constantly and intensely before us, that Italy is really so much the most beautiful country in the world, taking all things together, that others must stand off and be hushed while she speaks? Seen thus in great comprehensive iridescent stretches, it is the incomparable wrought *fusion,* fusion of human history and mortal passion with the elements of earth and air, of colour, composition and form, that constitute her appeal and give it the supreme heroic grace. The chariot of fire favours fusion rather than promotes analysis, and leaves much of that first June picture for me, doubtless, a great accepted blur of violet and silver. The various hours and successive aspects, the different strong passages of our reverse process, on the other hand, still figure for me even as some series of sublime landscape-frescoes—if the great Claude, say, had ever used that medium—in the immense gallery of a palace; the homeward run by Capua, Terracina, Gaeta and its storied headland fortress, across the deep, strong, indescribable Pontine Marshes, white-cattled, strangely pastoral, sleeping in the afternoon glow, yet stirred by the near sea-breath. Thick somehow to the imagination as some full-bodied sweetness of syrup is thick to the palate the atmosphere of that region— thick with the sense of history and the very taste of time; as if the haunt and home (which indeed it is) of some great fair bovine aristocracy attended and guarded by halberdiers in the form of the mounted and long-lanced herdsmen, admirably congruous with the whole picture at every point, and never more so than in their manner of gaily taking up, as with bell-voices of golden bronze, the offered wayside greeting.

There had been this morning among the impressions of our first hour an unforgettable specimen of that general type—the image of one of those human figures on which our perception of the romantic so often pounces in Italy as on the genius of the scene personified; with this advantage, that as the scene there has, at its best, an unsurpassable distinction, so the physiognomic representative, standing for it all, and with an animation, a complexion, an expression, a fineness and fulness of humanity that appear to have gathered it in and to sum it up, becomes beautiful by the same simple process, very much, that makes the heir to a great capitalist rich. Our early start, our roundabout descent from Posilippo by shining Baiae for avoidance of the city, had been an hour of enchantment beyond any notation I can here recover; all lustre and azure, yet all composition and classicism, the prospect developed and spread, till after extraordinary upper reaches of radiance and horizons of pearl we came at the turn of a descent upon a stalwart young gamekeeper, or perhaps substantial young farmer, who, well-appointed and blooming, had unslung his gun and, resting on it beside a hedge, just lived for us, in the rare felicity of his whole look, during that moment and while, in recognition, or almost, as we felt, in homage, we instinctively checked our speed. He pointed, as it were, the lesson, giving the supreme right accent or final exquisite turn to the immense magnificent phrase; which from those moments on, and on and on, resembled doubtless nothing so much as a page written, by a consummate verbal economist and master of style, in the noblest of all tongues. Our splendid human plant by the wayside had flowered thus into style—and there wasn't to be, all day, a lapse of eloquence, a wasted word or a cadence missed.

These things are personal memories, however, with the logic of certain insistences of that sort often difficult to seize. Why should I have kept so sacredly uneffaced, for instance, our small afternoon wait at tea-time or, as we made it, coffee-time, in the little brown piazzetta of Velletri, just short of the final push on through the flushed Castelli Romani and the drop and home-stretch across the darkening Campagna? We had been dropped into the very lap of the ancient civic family, after the inveterate fashion of one's sense of such stations in small Italian towns. There was a narrow raised terrace, with steps, in front of the best of the two or three local cafés, and in the soft enclosed, the warm waning light of June various benign contemplative worthies sat at disburdened tables and, while they smoked long black weeds, enjoyed us under those probable workings of subtlety with which we invest so many quite unimaginably blank (I dare say) Italian simplicities. The charm was, as always in Italy, in the tone and the air and the happy hazard of things, which made any positive pretension or claimed importance a comparatively trifling question. We slid, in the steep little place, more or less down hill; we wished, stomachically, we had rather addressed ourselves to a tea-basket; we suffered importunity from unchidden infants who swarmed about our chairs and romped about our feet; we stayed no long time, and "went to see" nothing; yet we communicated to intensity, we lay at our ease in the bosom of the past, we practised intimacy, in short, an intimacy so much greater than the mere accidental and ostensible: the difficulty for the right and grateful expression of which makes the old, the familiar tax on the luxury of loving Italy.

From
The American Scene

The American Scene, 1907. This work collects and adds to the essays published during James's American tour of 1904–1905. It is unique among the travel books in providing views written entirely in James's maturity. Although many contemporary travel books described the wonders of New York City, few—and none of the practical guidebooks—paid attention to the Bowery or the immigrant quarters of the city. James's focus is therefore surprising, and it has raised controversy, with assertions—and refutations—of anti-Semitism. The American Scene provides varied impressions of the regions and cities of the east coast of the United States, from New England to Florida. Although James also traveled to California, his ambition to write a separate volume on that part of his trip went unfulfilled.

THE BOWERY AND THEREABOUTS
(1907, NEW YORK)

I.

I scarce know, once more, if such a matter be a sign of the city itself, or only another perversity on the part of a visitor apt to press a little too hard, everywhere, on the spring of the show; but wherever I turned, I confess, wherever any aspect seemed to put forth a freshness, there I found myself saying that this aspect was one's strongest impression. It is impossible, as I now recollect, not to be amused at the great immediate differences of scene and occasion that could produce such a judgment, and this remark directly applies, no doubt, to the accident of a visit, one afternoon of the dire midwinter, to a theatre in the Bowery at which a young actor in whom I was interested had found for the moment a fine melodramatic opportunity. This small adventure—if the adventures of rash observation be ever small—was to remain embalmed for me in all its odd, sharp notes, and perhaps in none more than in its element of contrast with an image antediluvian, the memory of the conditions of a Bowery theatre, *the* Bowery Theatre in fact, contemporary with my more or less gaping youth. Was that vast dingy edifice, with its illustrious past, still standing?—a point on which I was to remain vague while I electrically travelled through a strange, a sinister over-roofed clangorous darkness, a wide thoroughfare beset, for all its width, with sound and fury, and bristling, amid the traffic, with posts and piles that were as the supporting columns of a vast cold, yet also uncannily-animated, sepulchre. It was like moving the length of an interminable cage, beyond the remoter of whose bars lighted shops, struggling dimly under other penthouse effects, offered their Hebrew faces and Hebrew names to a human movement that affected one even then as a breaking of waves that had rolled, for their welter on this very strand, from the other side of the globe. I was on my way to enjoy, no doubt, some peculiarly "American" form of the theatric mystery, but my way led me, apparently, through depths of the Orient, and I should clearly take my place with an Oriental public.

I took it in fact in such a curtained corner of a private box as might have appeared to commit me to the most intimate interest possible—might have done so, that is, if all old signs had not seemed visibly to fail and new questions, mockingly insoluble, to rise. The old signs would have been those of some "historic" community, so to speak, between the play and the public, between those opposed reciprocal quantities: such a consciousness of the same general terms of intercourse for instance, as I seemed to have seen prevail, long years ago, under the great dim, bleak, sonorous dome of the old Bowery. Nothing so much imposed itself at first as this suggestive contrast—

the vision of the other big bare ranting stupid stage, the grey
void, smelling of dust and tobacco-juice, of a scene on which
realism was yet to dawn, but which addressed itself, on the
other hand, to an audience at one with it. Audience and "production" had been then of the same stripe and the same "tradition"; the pitch, that is, had been of our own domestic and
romantic tradition (to apply large words to a loose matter, a
matter rich in our very own aesthetic idiosyncrasy). I should
say, in short, if it didn't savour of pedantry, that if this ancient
"poetic" had been purely a home-grown thing, nursed in the
English intellectual cradle, and in the American of a time when
the American resembled the English closely enough, so the instincts from which it sprang were instincts familiar to the
whole body of spectators, whose dim sense of art (to use again
the big word) was only not thoroughly English because it must
have been always so abundantly Irish. The foreign note, in that
thinner air, was, at the most, the Irish, and I think of the elements of the "Jack Sheppard" and "Claude Duval" Bowery, including the peanuts and the orange-peel, as quite harmoniously
Irish. From the corner of the box of my so improved playhouse
further down, the very name of which moreover had the cosmopolite lack of point, I made out, in the audience, the usual
mere monotony of the richer exoticism. No single face, beginning with those close beside me (for my box was a shared luxury), but referred itself, by my interpretation, to some such
strange outland form as we had not dreamed of in my day. There
they all sat, the representatives of the races we have nothing "in
common" with, as naturally, as comfortably, as munchingly, as if
the theatre were their constant practice—and, as regards the
munching, I may add, I was struck with the appearance of quality and cost in the various confections pressed from moment to
moment upon our notice by the little playhouse peddlers.

It comes over me under this branch of my reminiscence, that
these almost "high-class" luxuries, circulating in such a company, were a sort of supreme symbol of the *promoted* state of
the aspirant to American conditions. He, or more particularly
she, had been promoted, and, more or less at a bound, to the
habitual use of chocolate-creams, and indeed of other dainties,
refined and ingenious, compared with which these are quite

vieux jeu. This last remark might in fact open up for us, had I space, a view, interesting to hold a moment, or to follow as far as it might take us, of the wondrous consumption by the "people," over the land, of the most elaborate solid and liquid sweets, such products as form in other countries an expensive and select dietary. The whole phenomenon of this omnipresent and essentially "popular" appeal of the confectioner and pastry-cook, I can take time but to note, is more significant of the eco-nomic, and even of the social situation of the masses than many a circumstance honoured with more attention. I found myself again and again—in presence, for example, of the great glitter-ing temples, the bristling pagodas, erected to the worship in question wherever men and women, perhaps particularly women, most congregate, and above all under the high domes of the great modern railway stations—I found myself wonder-ing, I say, what such facts represented, what light they might throw upon manners and wages. Wages, in the country at large, *are* largely manners—the only manners, I think it fair to say, one mostly encounters; the market and the home therefore look alike dazzling, at first, in this reflected, many-coloured lustre. It speaks somehow, beyond anything else, of the diffused sense of material ease—since the solicitation of sugar couldn't be so hugely and artfully organized if the response were not clearly proportionate. But how is the response itself organized, and what are the other items of that general budget of labour, what in especial are the attenuations of that general state of fa-tigue, in which so much purchasing-power can flow to the sup-posedly superfluous? The wage-earners, the toilers of old, notably in other climes, were known by the wealth of their songs; and has it, on these lines, been given to the American people to be known by the number of their "candies"?

I must not let the question, however, carry me too far—quite away from the point I was about to make of my sense of the queer chasm over which, on the Saturday afternoon at the Windsor Theatre, I seemed to see the so domestic drama reach out to the so exotic audience and the so exotic audience reach out to the so domestic drama. The play (a masterpiece of its type, if I may so far strain a point, in such a case, and in the in-terest of my young friend's excellent performance, as to predi-

cate "type") was American, to intensity, in its blank conformity to convention, the particular implanted convention of the
place. This convention, simply expressed, was that there should
never be anything different in a play (the most conservative of
human institutions) from what there had always been before;
that *that place,* in a word, should always know the very same
theatric thing, any deviation from which might be phrenology,
or freemasonry, or iron-mongery, or anything else in the world,
but would never be drama, especially drama addressed to the
heart of the people. The tricks and the traps, the *trucs,* the
whole stage-carpentry, might freely renew themselves, to create
for artless minds the illusion of a difference; but the sense of the
business would still have to reside in our ineradicable Anglo-
Saxon policy, or our seemingly deep-seated necessity, of keeping, where "representation" is concerned, so far away from the
truth and the facts of life as really to betray a fear in us of possibly doing something like them should we be caught nearer.
"Foreigners," in general, unmistakably, in any attempt to render life, obey the instinct of keeping closer, positively recognize
the presence and the solicitation of the deep waters; yet here
was my houseful of foreigners, physiognomically branded as
such, confronted with our pale poetic—fairly caught for
schooling in our art of making the best of it. Nothing (in the
texture of the occasion) could have had a sharper interest than
this demonstration that, since what we most pretend to do with
them is thoroughly to school them, the schooling, by our system, cannot begin too soon nor pervade their experience too
much. Were they going to rise to it, or rather to fall to it—to
our instinct, as distinguished from their own, for picturing life?
Were they to take our lesson, submissively, in order to get with
it our smarter traps and tricks, our superior Yankee machinery
(illustrated in the case before them, for instance, by a wonderful folding bed in which the villain of the piece, pursuing the
virtuous heroine round and round the room and trying to leap
over it after her, is, at the young lady's touch of a hidden spring,
engulfed as in the jaws of a crocodile)? Or would it be their dim
intellectual resistance, a vague stir in them of some unwitting
heritage—of the finer irony, that I should make out, on the contrary, as withstanding the effort to corrupt them, and thus per-

haps really promising to react, over the head of our offered me-
chanic bribes, on our ingrained intellectual platitude?

One had only to formulate that question to seem to see the
issue hang there, for the excitement of the matter, quite as if the
determination were to be taken on the spot. For the opposition
over the chasm of the footlights, as I have called it, grew intense truly, as I took in on one side the hue of the Galician
cheek, the light of the Moldavian eye, the whole pervasive facial mystery, swaying, at the best, for the moment, over the
gulf, on the vertiginous bridge of American confectionery—
and took in on the other the perfect "Yankee" quality of the
challenge which stared back at them as in the white light of its
hereditary thinness. I needn't say that when I departed—perhaps from excess of suspense—it was without seeing the balance drop to either quarter, and I am afraid I think of the odd
scene as still enacted in many places and many ways, the inevitable rough union in discord of the two groups of instincts,
the fusion of the two camps by a queer, clumsy, wasteful social
chemistry. Such at all events are the round-about processes of
peaceful history, the very history that succeeds, for our edification, in *not* consisting of battles and blood and tears.

II.

I was happily to find, at all events, that I had not, on that occasion, done with the Bowery, or with its neighbourhood—as
how could one not rejoice to return to an air in which such infinite suggestion might flower? The season had advanced,
though the summer night was no more than genial, and the
question, for this second visit, was of a "look-in," with two or
three friends, at three or four of the most "characteristic"
evening resorts (for reflection and conversation) of the dwellers
on the East side. It was definitely not, the question, of any gaping view of the policed underworld—unanimously pronounced
an imposture, in general, at the best, and essentially less interesting than the exhibition of public manners. I found on the
spot, in harmony with this preference, that nothing better
could have been desired, in the way of pure presentable picture,

subject always to the swinging lantern-light of the individual imagination, than the first (as I think it was, for the roaming hour) of our penetrated "haunts"—a large semi-subterranean establishment, a beer-cellar rich in the sporting note, adorned with images of strong men and lovely women, prize-fighters and *ballerine,* and finding space in its deep bosom for a billiard-room and a bowling-alley, all sociably squeezed together; finding space, above all, for a collection of extraordinarily equivocal types of consumers: an intensity of equivocation indeed planted, just as if to await direct and convenient study, in the most typical face of the collection, a face which happened, by good fortune, to be that of the most officious presence. When the element of the equivocal in personal character and history takes on, in New York, an addition from all the rest of the swarming ambiguity and fugacity of race and tongue, the result becomes, for the picture-seeker, indescribably, luridly strong. There always comes up, at view of the "low" physiognomy shown in conditions that denote a measure of impunity and ease, the question—than which few, I think, are more interesting to the psychologist—of the forms of ability *consistent* with lowness; the question of the quality of intellect, the subtlety of character, the mastery of the art of life, with which the extremity of baseness may yet be associated. That question held me, I confess, so under its spell during those almost first steps of our ingenuous *enquête,* that I would gladly have prolonged, just there, my opportunity to sound it.

The fascination was of course in the perfection of the baseness, and the puzzle in the fact that it could be subject, without fatally muddling, without tearing and rending them, to those arts of life, those quantities of conformity, the numerous involved accommodations and patiences, that are *not* in the repertory of the wolf and the snake. Extraordinary, we say to ourselves on such occasions, the amount of formal tribute that civilization is after all able to gouge out of apparently hopeless stuff; extraordinary that it can make a presentable sheath for such fangs and such claws. The mystery is in the *how* of the process, in the wonderful little wavering borderland between nature and art, the place of the crooked seam where, if psychology had the adequate lens, the white stitches would show. All this played through one's thought, to the infinite extension of the sufficiently close and thoroughly *banal* beer-cellar. There happened to be reasons, not to be shaded over, why one of my companions should cause a particular chord of recognition to vibrate, and the very convergence of hushed looks, in the so "loud" general medium, seemed to lay bare, from table to table, the secret of the common countenance (common to that place) put off its guard by curiosity, almost by amiability. The secret was doubtless in many cases but the poor familiar human secret of the vulgar mind, of the soul unfurnished, so to speak, in respect to delicacy, probity, pity, with a social decoration of the mere bleak walls of instinct; but it was the unforgettable little personality that I have referred to as the presiding spirit, it was the spokesman of our welcome, the master of the scene himself, who struck me as presenting my question in its finest terms. To conduct a successful establishment, to *be* a spokesman, an administrator, an employer of labour and converser on subjects, let alone a citizen and a tax-payer, was to have an existence abounding in relations and to be subject to the law that a relation, however imperfectly human or social, is at the worst a matter that can only be described as delicate. Well, in presence of the abysmal obliquity of such a face, of the abysmal absence of traceability or coherency in such antecedents, where did the different delicacies involved come in at all?—how did intercourse emerge at all, and, much more, emerge so brilliantly, as it were, from its dangers? The answer had to be, for the moment, no doubt, that if there be such a state as that of misrepresenting your value and use, there is also the rare condition of being so sunk beneath the level of appearance as not to be able to represent them at all. Appearance, in you, has thus not only no notes, no language, no authority, but is literally condemned to operate *as* the treacherous sum of your poverties.

The jump was straight, after this, to a medium so different that I seem to see, as the one drawback to evoking it again, however briefly, the circumstance that it started the speculative hare for even a longer and straighter run. This irrepressible animal covered here, however, a much goodlier country, covered it in the interest of a happy generalization—the bold truth that even when apparently done to death by that property of the American air which reduces so many aspects to a common denominator, certain finer shades of saliency and consistency do often, by means known to themselves, recover their rights. They are like swimmers who have had to plunge, to come round and under water, but who pop out a panting head and shine for a moment in the sun. My image is perhaps extravagant, for the question is only of the kept recollection of a café pure and simple, particularly pure and particularly simple in fact, inasmuch as it dispensed none but "soft" drinks and presented itself thus in the light, the quiet, tempered, intensely individual light, of a beerhouse innocent of beer. I have indeed no other excuse for calling it a beerhouse than the fact that it offered to every sense such a deep Germanic peace as abides, for the most part (though not always even then), where the deep-lidded tankard balances with the scarce shallower bowl of the meditative pipe. This modest asylum had its tone, which I found myself, after a few minutes, ready to take for exquisite, if on no other ground than its almost touching suggestion of discriminations made and preserved in the face of no small difficulty. That is what I meant just now by my tribute to the occasional patience of unquenched individualism—the practical subtlety of the spirit unashamed of its preference for the minor key, clinging, through thick and thin, to its conception of decency and dignity, and finding means to make it good even to the exact true shade. These are the real triumphs of art—the discriminations in favour of taste produced not by the gilded and guarded "private room," but by making publicity itself delicate, making your barrier against vulgarity consist but in a few tables and chairs, a few coffee-cups and boxes of dominoes. Money in quantities enough can always create tone, but it had been created here by mere unbuyable instinct. The charm of the place in short was that its note of the exclusive had been arrived at with such a beautifully fine economy. I try, in memory, and for the value of the lesson, to analyze, as it were, the elements, and seem to recall as the most obvious the contemplative stillness in which the faint click of the moved domino could be heard, and into which the placid attention of the quiet, honest men who were thus testifying for the exquisite could be read. The exquisite, yes, *was* the triumph of their tiny temple, with all the loud surrounding triumphs, those of the coarse and the common, making it but stick the faster, like a well-inserted wedge. And fully to catch this was to catch by the same stroke the main ground of the effect, to see that it came most of all from felicity of suppression and omission. There was so visibly too much everywhere else of everything vulgar, that there reigned here, for the difference, the learnt lesson that there could scarce be in such an air of infection little enough, in quantity and mass, of anything. The felicity had its climax in the type, or rather in the individual character, of our host, who, officiating alone, had apparently suppressed all aids to service and succeeded, as by an inspiration of genius, in omitting, for all his years, to learn the current American. He spoke but a dozen words of it, and that was doubtless how he best kept the key of the old Germanic peace—of the friendly stillness in which, while the East side roared, a new metaphysic might have been thought out or the scheme of a new war intellectualized.

III.

After this there were other places, mostly higher in the scale, and but a couple of which my memory recovers. There was also, as I recall, a snatched interlude—an associated dash into a small crammed convivial theatre, an oblong hall, bristling with pipe and glass, at the end of which glowed for a moment, a little dingily, some broad passage of a Yiddish comedy of manners. It hovered there, briefly, as if seen through a spy-glass reaching, across the world, to some far-off dowdy Jewry; then our sense of it became too mixed a matter—it was a scent, literally, not further to be followed. There remained with me none the less the patch of alien comedy, with all it implied of esoteric vision on the part of the public. Something of that admonition had indeed, earlier in the season, been sharp—so much had one heard of a brilliant Yiddish actress who was drawing the town to the East side by the promise of a new note. This lady, however, had disconcerted my own purpose by suddenly appearing, in the orthodox quarter, in a language only definable as not in *intention* Yiddish—not otherwise definable; and I also missed, through a like alarm, the opportunity of hearing an admired actor of the same school. He was Yiddish on the East side, but he cropped up, with a wild growth, in Broadway as well, and his auditors seemed to know as little as care to what idiom they supposed themselves to be listening. Marked in New York, by many indications, this vagueness of ear as to differences, as to identities, of idiom.

I must not, however, under that interference, lose the echo of a couple of other of the impressions of my crowded summer night—and all the less that they kept working it, as I seem to remember, up to a higher and higher pitch. It had been intimated to me that one of these scenes of our climax had entered the sophisticated phase, that of sacrificing to a self-consciousness that was to be regretted—that of making eyes, so to speak, at the larger, the up-town public; that pestilent favour of "society" which is fatal to everything it touches and which so quickly leaves the places of its passage unfit for its own use and uninteresting for any other. This establishment had learned to lay on local colour with malice prepense—the local colour of its "Slav" origin—and was the haunt, on certain evenings of the week, of yearning groups from Fifth Avenue sated with familiar horizons. Yet there were no yearning groups—none, that is, save our own—at the time of our visit; there was only, very amply and pleasantly presented, another aspect of the perpetual process of the New York intermarriage. As the Venetian Republic, in the person of the Doge, used to go forth, on occasion, to espouse the Adriatic, so it is quite as if the American, incarnate in its greatest port, were for ever throwing the nuptial ring to the still more richly-dowered Atlantic. I speak again less of the nuptial rites themselves than of those immediate fruits that struck me everywhere as so characteristic—so equally characteristic, I mean, of each party to the union. The flourishing establishment of my present reference offered distinctly its outland picture, but showed it in an American frame, and the features of frame and picture arranged themselves shrewdly together. Quiet couples, elderly bourgeois husbands and wives, sat there over belated sausage and cheese, potato-salad and Hungarian wine, the wife with her knitting produced while the husband finished his cigar; and the indication, for the moment, might have been of some evening note of Dantzig or of Buda-Pesth.

But the conditioning foreign, and the visibility of their quite so happily conjugal give-and-take, in New York, is my reason for this image of the repeated espousals. Why were the quiet easy couples, with their homely café habit (kept in the best relation to the growth, under the clicking needles, of the marital stocking), such remote and indirect results of our local anecdotic past, our famous escape, at our psychological moment, from King George and his works, with all sorts of inevitable lapses and hitches in any grateful consciousness they might ever have of that prime cause of their new birth? Yet why, on the other hand, could they affect one, even with the Fatherland planked under them in the manner of the praying-carpet spread beneath the good Mahometan, as still more disconnected from the historic consciousness implied in their own type, and with the mere moral identity of German or Slav, or whatever it might be, too extinct in them for any possibility of renewal? The exotic boss here did speak, I remember, fluent East-side New Yorkese, and it was in this wonderful tongue that he expressed to us his superior policy, his refined philosophy, announced his plans for the future and presented himself, to my vision, as a possibly far-reaching master-spirit. What remains with me is this expression, and the colour and the quality of it, and the free familiarity and the "damned foreign impudence," with so much taken for granted, and all the hitches and lapses, all the solutions of continuity, in *his* inward assimilation of our heritage and point of view, matched, as these were, on our own side, by such signs of large and comparatively witless concession. What, oh, what again, were he and his going to make of us?

Well, there was the impression, and that was a question on which, for a certain intensity in it, our adventure might have closed; but it was so far from closing that, late though the hour, it presently opened out into a vast and complicated picture which I find myself thinking of, after an interval, as the splendid crown of the evening. Here were we still on the East side, but we had moved up, by stages artfully inspired, into the higher walks, into a pavilion of light and sound and savoury science that struck one as vaguely vast, as possibly gardened about, and that, blazing into the stillness of the small hours, dazzled one with the show of its copious and various activity.

The whole vision was less intimate than elsewhere, but it was a world of custom quite away from any mere Delmonico tradition of one's earlier time, and rich, as one might reckon it, in its own queer marks, marks probably never yet reduced—inspiring thought!—to literary notation; with which it would seem better to form a point of departure for fresh exploration than serve as tail-piece to the end of a chapter. Who were all the people, and whence and whither and why, in the good New York small hours? Where *was* the place after all, and what might it, or might it not, truly, represent to slightly-fatigued feasters who, in a recess like a privileged opera-box at a *bal masqué*, and still communing with polyglot waiters, looked down from their gallery at a multitudinous supper, a booming orchestra, an elegance of disposed plants and flowers, a perfect organization and an abyss of mystery? Was it "on" Third Avenue, on Second, on fabulous unattempted First? Nothing would induce me to cut down the romance of it, in remembrance, to a mere address, least of all to an awful New York one; New York addresses falling so below the grace of a city where the very restaurants may on occasion, under restless analysis, flash back the likeness of Venetian palaces flaring with the old carnival. The ambiguity is the element in which the whole thing swims for me—so nocturnal, so bacchanal, so hugely hatted and feathered and flounced, yet apparently so innocent, almost so patriarchal again, and matching, in its mixture, with nothing one had elsewhere known. It breathed its simple "New York! New York!" at every impulse of inquiry; so that I can only echo contentedly, with analysis for once quite agreeably baffled, "Remarkable, unspeakable New York!"

from BOSTON
(1907)

It sometimes uncomfortably happens for a writer, consulting his remembrance, that he remembers too much and finds himself knowing his subject too well; which is but the case of the bottle too full for the wine to start. There has to be room for the air to circulate between one's impressions, between the parts of one's knowledge, since it is the air, or call it the intervals on the sea of one's ignorance, of one's indifference, that sets these floating fragments into motion. This is more or less what I feel in presence of the invitation—even the invitation written on the very face of the place itself, of its actual aspects and appearances—to register my "impression" of Boston. Can one *have*, in the conditions, an impression of Boston, any that has not been for long years as inappreciable as a "sunk" picture?—that dead state of surface which requires a fresh application of varnish. The situation I speak of is the consciousness of "old" knowledge, knowledge so compacted by the years as to be unable, like the bottled wine, to flow. The answer to such questions as these, no doubt, however, is the practical one of trying a shake of the bottle or a brushful of the varnish. My "sunk" sense of Boston found itself vigorously varnished by mere renewal of vision at the end of long years; though I confess that under this favouring influence I ask myself why I should have had, after all, the notion of overlaid deposits of experience. The experience had anciently been small—so far as smallness may be imputed to any of our prime initiations; yet it had left consequences out of proportion to its limited seeming self. Early contacts had been brief and few, and the slight bridge had long ago collapsed, wherefore the impressed condition that acquired again, on the spot, an intensity, struck me as but half explained by the inordinate power of assimilation of the imaginative young. I should have had none the less to content myself with this evidence of the magic of past sensibilities had not the question suddenly been lighted for me as by a sudden flicker of the torch—and for my special benefit—carried in the hand of history. This light, waving for an instant over the scene, gave me the measure of my relation to it, both as to immense little extent and to quite subjective character.

I.

It was in strictness only a matter of noting the harshness of change—since I scarce know what else to call it—on the part of the approaches to a particular spot I had wished to revisit. I made out, after a little, the entrance to Ashburton Place; but I missed on that spacious summit of Beacon Hill more than I can say the pleasant little complexity of the other time, marked with its share of the famous old-world "crookedness" of Boston, that element of the mildly tortuous which did duty, for the story-seeker, as an ancient and romantic note, and was half envied, half derided by the merely rectangular criticism. Didn't one re-member the day when New Yorkers, when Philadelphians, when pilgrims from the West, sated with their eternal equidis-tances, with the quadrilateral scheme of life, "raved" about Cornhill and appeared to find in the rear of the State House a recall of one of the topographical, the architectural jumbles of Europe or Asia? And did not indeed the small happy accidents of the disappearing Boston exhale in a comparatively sensible manner the warm breath of history, the history of something as against the history of nothing?—so that, being gone, or gener-ally going, they enabled one at last to feel and almost to talk about them as one had found one's self feeling and talking about the sacrificed relics of old Paris and old London. In this immediate neigbourhood of the enlarged State House, where a great raw clearance has been made, memory met that pang of loss, knew itself sufficiently bereft to see the vanished objects, a scant but adequate cluster of "nooks," of such odds and ends as parochial schemes of improvement sweep away, positively overgrown, within one's own spirit, by a wealth of legend. There was at least the gain, at any rate, that one was now go-ing to be free to picture them, to embroider them, at one's ease—to tangle them up in retrospect, and make the real ro-mantic claim for them. This accordingly is what I am doing, but I am doing it in particular for the sacrificed end of Ashbur-ton Place, the Ashburton Place that I anciently knew. This em-inently respectable by-way, on my return to question it, opened its short vista for me honestly enough, though looking rather exposed and undermined, since the mouth of the passage to the west, formerly measured and narrow, had begun to yawn into space, a space peopled in fact, for the eye of appreciation, with the horrific glazed perpendiculars of the future. But the pair of ancient houses I was in quest of kept their tryst; a pleasant individual pair, mated with nothing else in the street, yet looking at that hour as if their old still faces had lengthened, their shuttered, lidded eyes had closed, their brick complexions had paled, above the good granite basements, to a fainter red—all as with the cold consciousness of a possible doom.

That possibility, on the spot, was not present to me, occupied as I was with reading into one of them a short page of history that I had my own reasons for finding of supreme interest, the history of two years of far-away youth spent there at a period—the closing-time of the War—full both of public and of intimate vibrations. The two years had been those of a young man's, a very young man's earliest fond confidence in a "literary career," and the effort of actual attention was to recover on the spot some echo of ghostly footsteps—the sound as of taps on the window-pane heard in the dim dawn. The place itself was meanwhile, at all events, a conscious memento, with old secrets to keep and old stories to witness for, a saturation of life as closed together and preserved in it as the scent lingering in a folded pocket-handkerchief. But when, a month later, I returned again (a justly-rebuked mistake) to see if another whiff of the fragrance were not to be caught, I found but a gaping void, the brutal effacement, at a stroke, of every related object, of the whole precious past. Both the houses had been levelled and the space to the corner cleared; hammer and pickaxe had evidently begun to swing on the very morrow of my previous visit—which had moreover been precisely the imminent doom announced, without my understanding it, in the poor scared faces. I had been present, by the oddest hazard, at the very last moments of the victim in whom I was most interested; the act of obliteration had been breathlessly swift, and if I had often seen how fast history could be made I had doubtless never so felt that it could be unmade still faster. It was as if the bottom had fallen out of one's own biography, and one plunged backward into space without meeting anything. That, however, seemed just to give me, as I have hinted, the whole figure of my connection with everything about, a connection that had been sharp, in spite of brevity, and then had broken short off. Thus it was the sense of the rupture, more than of anything else, that I was, and for a still much briefer time, to carry with me. It seemed to leave me with my early impression of the place on my hands, inapt, as might be, for use; so that I could only try, rather vainly, to fit it to present conditions, among which it tended to shrink and stray.

It was on two or three such loitering occasions, wondering and invoking pauses that had, a little vaguely and helplessly perhaps, the changed crest of Beacon Hill for their field—it was at certain of these moments of charged, yet rather chilled, contemplation that I felt my small cluster of early associations shrivel to a scarce discernible point. I recall a Sunday afternoon in particular when I hung about on the now vaster platform of the State House for a near view of the military monuments erected there, the statues of Generals Hooker and Devens, and for the charm at once and the pang of feeling the whole backward vista, with all its features, fall from that eminence into grey perspective. The top of Beacon Hill quite rakes, with a but slightly shifting range, the old more definite Boston; for there seemed no item, nor any number, of that remarkable sum that it would not anciently have helped one to distinguish or divine. There all these things essentially were at the moment I speak of, but only again as something ghostly and dim, something overlaid and smothered by the mere modern thickness. I lingered half-an-hour, much of the new disposition of the elements here involved being duly impressive, and the old uplifted front of the State House, surely, in its spare and austere, its ruled and pencilled kind, a thing of beauty, more delightful and harmonious even than I had remembered it; one of the inestimable values again, in the eye of the town, for taste and temperance, as the perfectly felicitous "Park Street" Church hard by, was another. The irresistible spell, however, I think, was something sharper yet—the coercion, positively, of feeling one's case, the case of one's deeper discomfiture, completely made out. The day itself, toward the winter's end, was all benignant, like the immense majority of the days of the American year, and there went forward across the top of the hill a continuous passage of men and women, in couples and talkative companies, who struck me as labouring wage-earners, of the simpler sort, arrayed, very comfortably, in their Sunday best and decently enjoying their leisure. They came up as from over the Common, they passed or they paused, exchanging remarks on the beauty of the scene, but rapidly presenting themselves to me as of more interest, for the moment, than anything it contained.

For no sound of English, in a single instance, escaped their lips; the greater number spoke a rude form of Italian, the others some outland dialect unknown to me—though I waited and waited to catch an echo of antique refrains. No note of any shade of American speech struck my ear, save in so far as the sounds in question represent today so much of the substance of that idiom. The types and faces bore them out; the people before me were gross aliens to a man, and they were in serene and triumphant possession. Nothing, as I say, could have been more effective for figuring the hitherward bars of a grating through which I might make out, far-off in space, "my" small homogeneous Boston of the more interesting time. It was not of course that our gross little aliens were immediate "social" figures in the narrower sense of the term, or that any personal commerce of which there might be question could colour itself, to its detriment, from their presence; but simply that they expressed, as everywhere and always, the great cost at which every place on my list had become braver and louder, and that they gave the measure of the distance by which the general movement was *away*—away, always and everywhere, from the old presumptions and conceivabilities. Boston, the bigger, braver, louder Boston, was "away," and it was quite, at that hour, as if each figure in my procession were there on purpose to leave me no doubt of it. Therefore had I the vision, as filling the sky, no longer of the great Puritan "whip," the whip for the conscience and the nerves, of the local legend, but that of a huge applied sponge, a sponge saturated with the foreign mixture and passed over almost everything I remembered and might still have recovered. The detail of this obliteration would take me too far, but I had even then (on a previous day as well as only half-an-hour before) caught at something that might stand for a vivid symbol of the general effect of it. To come up from School Street into Beacon was to approach the Athenaeum— exquisite institution, to fond memory, joy of the aspiring prime; yet to approach the Athenaeum only to find all disposition to enter it drop as dead as if from quick poison, what did *that* de-

note but the dreadful chill of change, and of the change in especial that was most completely dreadful? For had not this honoured haunt of all the most civilized—library, gallery, temple
of culture, the place that was to Boston at large as Boston at
large was to the rest of New England—had it not with peculiar
intensity had a "value," the most charming of its kind, no
doubt, in all the huge country, and had not this value now, evidently, been brought so low that one shrank, in delicacy, from
putting it to the test?

It was a case of the detestable "tall building" again, and of
its instant destruction of quality in everything it overtowers.
Put completely out of countenance by the mere masses of brute
ugliness beside it, the temple of culture looked only rueful and
snubbed, hopelessly down in the world; so that, far from being
moved to hover or to penetrate, one's instinct was to pass by on
the other side, averting one's head from an humiliation one
could do nothing to make less. And this indeed though one
would have liked to do something; the brute masses, above the
comparatively small refined façade (one saw how happy one
had always thought it) having for the inner ear the voice of a
pair of school-bullies who hustle and pummel some studious
little boy. "'Exquisite' was what they called you, eh? We'll teach
you, then, little sneak, to be exquisite! We allow none of that
rot round here." It was heart-breaking, this presentation of a
Boston practically void of an Athenaeum; though perhaps not
without interest as showing how much one's own sense of the
small city of the earlier time had been dependent on that institution. I found it of no use, at any rate, to think, for a compen-
satory sign of the new order, of the present Public Library; the
present Public Library, however remarkable in its pomp and
circumstance, and of which I had at that hour received my severe impression, being neither exquisite nor on the way to become so—a difficult, an impassable way, no doubt, for Public
Libraries. Nor did I cast about, in fact, very earnestly, for consolation—so much more was I held by the vision of the closed
order which shaped itself, continually, in the light of the differing present; an order gaining an interest for this backward view
precisely as one felt that all the parts and tokens of it, while it
lasted, had hung intimately together. Missing those parts and

tokens, or as many of them as one could, became thus a constant slightly painful joy: it made them fall so into their place as items of the old character, or proofs, positively, as one might say, of the old distinction. It was impossible not to see Park Street itself, for instance—while I kept looking at the matter from my more "swagger" hilltop as violently vulgarized; and it was incontestable that, whatever might be said, there had anciently not been, on the whole continent, taking everything together, an equal animated space more exempt from vulgarity. There had probably been comparable spaces—impressions, in New York, in Philadelphia, in Baltimore, almost as good; but only almost, by reason of their lacking (which was just the point) the indefinable perfection of Park Street.

It seems odd to have to borrow from the French the right word in this association—or would seem so, rather, had it been less often indicated that that people have better names than ours even for the qualities we are apt to suppose ourselves more in possession of than they. Park Street, in any case, had been magnificently *honnête*—the very type and model, for a pleasant street-view, of the character. The aspects that might elsewhere have competed were *honnêtes* and weak, whereas Park Street was *honnête* and strong—strong as founded on all the moral, material, social solidities, instead of on some of them only, which made again all the difference. Personal names, as notes of that large emanation, need scarcely be invoked—they might even have a weakening effect; the force of the statement was in its collective, cumulative look, as if each member of the row, from the church at the Tremont Street angle to the amplest, squarest, most purple presence at the Beacon Street corner (where it always had a little the air of a sturdy proprietor with back to the fire, legs apart and thumbs in the armholes of an expanse of high-coloured plush waistcoat), was but a syllable in the word Respectable several times repeated. One had somehow never heard it uttered with so convincing an emphasis. But the shops, up and down, are making all this as if it had never been, pleasant "premises" as they have themselves acquired; and it was to strike me from city to city, I fear, that the American shop in general pleads but meagrely—whether on its outer face or by any more intimate art—for indulgence to its tendency to swarm, to bristle, to vociferate. The shop-front, observed at random, produced on me from the first, and almost everywhere alike, a singular, a sinister impression, which left me uneasy till I had found a name for it: the sense of an economic law of which one had not for years known the unholy rigour, the vision of "protected" production and of commodities requiring certainly, in many cases, every advantage Protection could give them. They looked to me always, these exhibitions, consciously and defiantly protected—insolently safe, able to be with impunity anything they would; and when once that lurid light had settled on them I could see them, I confess, in none other; so that the objects composing them fell, throughout, into a vicious and villainous category—quite as if audibly saying: "Oh come; don't look among us for what you won't, for what you shan't find, the best quality attainable; but only for that quite other matter, the best value we allow you. You must take us or go without, and if you feel your nose thus held to the grindstone by the hard fiscal hand, it's no more than you deserve for harbouring treasonable thoughts."

So it was, therefore, that while the imagination and the memory strayed—strayed away to other fiscal climates, where the fruits of competition so engagingly ripen and flush—the streets affected one at moments as a prolonged show-case for every arrayed vessel of humiliation. The fact that several classes of the protected products appeared to consist of articles that one might really anywhere have preferred did little, oddly enough, to diminish the sense of severe discipline awaiting the restored absentee on contact with these occasions of traffic. The discipline indeed is general, proceeding as it does from so many sources, but it earns its name, in particular, from the predicament of the ingenuous inquirer who asks himself if he can "really bear" the combination of such general manners and such general prices, of such general prices and such general manners. He has a helpless bewildered moment during which he wonders if he mightn't bear the prices a little better if he were a little better addressed, or bear the usual form of address a little better if the prices were in themselves, given the commodity offered, a little less humiliating to the purchaser. Neither of these elements of his dilemma strikes him as likely to abate—the general cost of the things to drop, or the general grimness of the person he deals with over the counter to soften; so that he reaches out again for balm to where he has had to seek it under other wounds, falls back on the cultivation of patience and regret, on large international comparison. He is confronted too often, to his sense, with the question of what may be "borne"; but what does he see about him if not a vast social order in which the parties to certain relations are all the while marvellously, inscrutably, desperately "bearing" each other? He may wonder, at his hours, how, under the strain, social cohesion does not altogether give way; but that is another question, which belongs to a different plane of speculation. For he asks himself quite as much as anything else how the shopman or the shoplady can bear to be barked at in the manner he constantly hears used to them by customers—he recognizes that no agreeable form of intercourse *could* survive a day in such air: so that what is the only relation finding ground there but a necessary vicious circle of gross mutual endurance?

* * * * *

Oh, for business, for a commercial, an organizing energy of the first order, the indications would seem to abound; the air being full of them as of one loud voice, and nowhere so full perhaps as at that Park Street corner, precisely, where it was to be suggested to me that their meaning was capable on occasion of turning to the sinister. The commercial energy at least was educated, up to the eyes—Harvard was still caring for that more than for anything else—but the wonderments, or perhaps rather the positive impressions I have glanced at, bore me constant company, keeping the last word, all emphasis of answer, back as if for the creation of a dramatic suspense. I liked the suspense, none the less, for what it had in common with "intellectual curiosity," and it gave me a light, moreover, which was highly convenient, helping me to look at everything in some related state to this proposition of the value of the Puritan residuum—the question of whether value *is* expressed, for instance, by the little tales, mostly by ladies, and about and for children romping through the ruins of the Language, in the monthly magazines. Some of my perceptions of relation might seem forced, for other minds, but it sufficed me that they were straight and clear for myself—straight and clear again, for example, when (always on my hilltop and raking the prospect over for memories) I quite assented to the tacit intimation that a long aesthetic period had closed with the disappearance of the old Museum Theatre. This had been the theatre of the "great" period—so far as such a description may fit an establishment that never produced during that term a play either by a Bostonian or by any other American; or it had at least, with however unequal steps, kept the great period company, made the Boston of those years quite complacently participate in its genial continuity. This character of its *being* an institution, its really being a theatre, with a repertory and a family of congruous players, not one of them the baleful actor-manager, head and front of all the so rank and so acclaimed vulgarities of our own day— this nature in it of not being the mere empty shelf, the indifferent cave of the winds, that yields a few nights' lodging, under stress, to the passing caravan, gave it a dignity of which I seemed to see the ancient city gratefully conscious, fond and jealous, and the thought of which invites me to fling over it now perhaps too free a fold of the mantle of romance. And yet why too free? is what I ask myself as I remember that the Museum had for long years a repertory—the repertory of its age— a company and a cohesion, theatrical trifles of the cultivation of which no present temple of the drama from end to end of the country appears to show a symptom. Therefore I spare a sigh to its memory, and, though I doubtless scarce think of it as the haunt of Emerson, of Hawthorne or of Mr. Ticknor, the common conscience of the mid-century in the New England capital insists on showing, at this distance of time, as the richer for it.

France

"France," in The Book of France in Aid of the French Parliamentary Committee's Fund for the Relief of the Invaded Departments, *1915. In 1884 James's* A Little Tour in France *had delivered "a few informal notes"—actually forty short essays—on a six-week journey mostly outside Paris, but this final retrospective consideration—as much a wartime address as a travel essay—offers a more general appreciation of the spirit of the place.*

I think that if there is a general ground in the world, on which an appeal might be made, in a civilised circle, with a sense of its being uttered only to meet at once and beyond the need of in-sistence a certain supreme recognition and response, the idea of what France and the French mean to the educated spirit of man would be the nameable thing. It would be the cause uniting us most quickly in an act of glad intelligence, uniting us with the least need of any wondering why. We should understand and answer together just by the magic of the mention, the touch of the two or three words, and this in proportion to our feeling ourselves social and communicating creatures—to the point in fact of a sort of shame at any imputation of our not liberally understanding, of our waiting in any degree to be nudged or hustled. The case of France, as one may hold it, where the per-ceptive social mind is concerned and set in motion, is thus only to be called exquisite—so far as we don't seem so to qualify things *down*. We certainly all feel, in the beautiful connection, in two general ways; one of these being that the spring pressed with such happy effect lifts the sense by its mere vibration into the lightest and brightest air in which, taking our world all round, it is given to our finer interest about things to breathe and move; and the other being that just having our intelligence, our experience at its freest and bravest, taken for granted, is a compliment to us, as not purely instinctive persons, which we should miss, if it were not paid, rather to the degree of finding the omission an insult.

Such, I say, is our easy relation to the sound of a voice raised, even however allusively and casually, on behalf of that great national and social presence which has always most appositely, most sensibly, most obsessively, as I surely may put it, and above all most dazzlingly, neighboured and admonished us here: after such a fashion as really to have made the felt breath of its life, across an interval constantly narrowing, a part of our education as distinguished from our luck. Our luck in all our past has been enormous, the greatest luck on the whole, assuredly, that any race has ever had; but it has never been a conscious reaction or a gathered fruition, as one may say; it has just been a singular felicity of position and of temperament, and this felicity has made us observe and perceive and reflect much less than it has made us directly act and profit and enjoy: enjoy of course by attending tremendously to all the business involved in our position. So far as we have had reactions, therefore, they have not sprung, when they have been at all intensified, from the extraordinary good fortune of our state. Unless indeed I may put it that what they *have* very considerably sprung from has been exactly a part of our general prodigy— the good fortune itself of our being neighboured by a native genius so different from our own, so suggestive of wondrous and attaching comparisons, as to keep us chronically aware of the difference and the contrast and yet all the while help us to see into them and through them.

We were not, to all appearance, appointed by fate for the most perceptive and penetrative offices conceivable; so that to have over against us and within range a proposition, as we nowadays say, that could only grow more and more vivid, more and more engaging and inspiring, in the measure of our growth of criticism and curiosity, or, in other words, of the capacity just to pay attention, pay attention otherwise than by either sticking very fast at home or inquiring of the Antipodes, the Antipodes almost exclusively—what has that practically been for us but one of the very choicest phases of our luck aforesaid, one of the most appraisable of our felicities? the very one, doubtless, that our dissimilarity of temperament and taste would have most contradictiously and most correctively prescribed from the moment we were not to be left simply to stew in our juice! If the advantage I so characterise was to be in its own way thoroughly affirmative, there was yet nothing about it to do real or injurious violence to that abysmal good nature which sometimes strikes me as our most effective contribution to human history. The vision of France, at any rate, so close and so clear at propitious hours, was to grow happily illustrational for us as nothing else in any like relation to us could possibly have become. Other families have a way, on good opportunity, of interesting us more than our own, and here was this immense acquaintance extraordinarily mattering for us and at the same time not irritating us by a single claim of cousinship or a single liberty taken on any such score. Any liberties taken were much rather liberties, I think, of ours—always abounding as we did in quite free, and perhaps slightly rough, and on the whole rather superficial, movement beyond our island circle and toward whatever lay in our path. France lay very much in our path, our path to almost everything that could beckon us forth from our base—and there were very few things in the world or places on the globe that didn't so beckon us; according to which she helped us along on our expansive course a good deal more, doubtless, than either she or we always knew.

All of which, you see, is but a manner of making my point that her name means more than anything in the world to us but just our own. Only at present it means ever so much more, almost unspeakably more, than it has ever done in the past, and I can't help inviting you to feel with me, for a very few moments, what the real force of this association to which we now throb consists of, and why it so moves us. We enjoy generous emotions *because* they are generous, because generosity is a noble passion and a glow, because we spring with it for the time above our common pedestrian pace—and this just in proportion as all questions and doubts about it drop to the ground. But great reasons never spoil a great sympathy, and to see an inspiring object in a strong light never made any such a shade less inspiring. So, therefore, in these days when our great neighbour and Ally is before us in a beauty that is tragic, tragic because menaced and overdarkened, the closest possible appreciation of what it is that is thereby in peril for ourselves and for the world makes the image shine with its highest brightness at the same time that the cloud upon it is made more black. When I sound the depth of my own affection so fondly excited, I take the like measure for all of us and feel the glad recognition I meet in thus putting it to you, for our full illumination, that what happens to France happens to all that part of ourselves which we are most proud, and most finely advised, to enlarge and cultivate and consecrate.

Our heroic friend sums up for us, in other words, and has always summed up, the life of the mind and the life of the senses alike, taken together, in the most irrepressible freedom of either—and, after that fashion, positively lives *for* us, carries on experience for us; does it under our tacit and our at present utterly ungrudging view of her being formed and endowed and constantly prompted, toward such doing, on all sorts of sides that are simply so many reasons for our standing off, standing off in a sort of awed intellectual hush or social suspense, and watching and admiring and thanking her. She is sole and single in this, that she takes charge of those of the interests of man which most dispose him to fraternise with himself, to pervade all his possibilities and to taste all his faculties, and in consequence to find and to make the earth a friendlier, an easier, and especially a more various sojourn; and the great thing is the amiability and the authority, intimately combined, with which she has induced us all to trust her on this ground. There are matters as to which every set of people has of course most to trust itself, most to feel its own genius and its own stoutness— as we are here and all round about us knowing and abiding by that now as we have never done. But I verily think there has never been anything in the world—since the most golden aspect of antiquity at least—like the way in which France has been trusted to gather the rarest and fairest and sweetest fruits

of our so tremendously and so mercilessly turned-up garden of
life. She has gardened where the soil of humanity has been
most grateful and the aspect, so to call it, most toward the sun,
and there, at the high and yet mild and fortunate centre, she has
grown the precious, intimate, the nourishing, finishing things
that she has inexhaustibly scattered abroad. And if we have all
so taken them from her, so expected them from her as our
right, to the point that she would have seemed positively to fail
of a passed pledge to help us to happiness if she had disappointed us, this has been because of her treating us to the impression of genius as no nation since the Greeks has treated the
watching world, and because of our feeling that genius at that
intensity is infallible.

What it has all amounted to, as I say, is that we have never
known otherwise an agent so beautifully organised, organised
from within, for a mission, and that such an organisation at
free play has made us really want never to lift a finger to break
the charm. We catch at every turn of our present long-drawn
crisis indeed that portentous name: it's displayed to us on a
measureless scale that our Enemy is organised, organised possibly to the effect of binding us with a spell if anything *could*
keep us passive. The term has been in a manner, by that association, compromised and vulgarised: I say vulgarised because
any history of organisation from without and for intended aggression and self-imposition, however elaborate the thing may
be, shows for merely mechanical and bristling compared with
the condition of being naturally and functionally endowed and
appointed. This last is the only fair account of the complete
and perfect case that France has shown us and that civilisation
has depended on for half its assurances. Well, now, we have before us this boundless extension of the case, that, as we have always known what it was to see the wonderful character I speak
of range through its variety and keep shining with another and
still another light, so in these days we assist at what we may
verily call the supreme evidence of its incomparable gift for
vivid exhibition. It takes our great Ally, and her only, to be as
vivid for concentration, for reflection, for intelligent, inspired
contraction of life toward an end all but smothered in sacrifice,
as she has ever been for the most splendidly wasteful diffusion

and communication; and to give us a view of her nature and her mind in which, laying down almost every advantage, every art and every appeal that we have generally known her by, she takes on energies, forms of collective sincerity, silent eloquence and selected example that are fresh revelations—and so, bleeding at every pore, while at no time in all her history so completely erect, makes us feel her perhaps as never before our incalculable, immortal France.

IV

CRITICISM

Five months after seeing his first story in print, Henry James published his first critical essay. The 1864 tale "A Tragedy of Error" is surprisingly lurid: a woman hires a boatman to kill her lame husband, but in what seems a nightmare out of *Rigoletto,* the boatman mistakenly drowns her lover, and at the end the husband comes limping toward her from out of the night. Yet the review of Nassau W. Senior's *Essays on Fiction* still holds interest, and not just because its twenty-one-year-old author already speaks with such confidence ("Individually respectable enough in their time and place, they yet make a very worthless book," "half a dozen empty articles," "singularly pointless," "hardly worth the trouble of reading"). It is also notable that Henry James submitted his first review essay on a book that was itself a book of criticism, and it was a book of criticism on achievement in the novel. But—as early as 1864—the young James would already "be embittered by disappointment" in a hope of finding "some attempt to codify the vague and desultory canons, which cannot, indeed, be said to govern, but which in some measure define, this department of literature."

After decades of writing on the French, English, American, German, Russian, and Italian novel—as well as on various poets, essayists, dramatists, actors, and painters—James's greatest critical achievement came more than forty years after his Nassau Senior essay. In the eighteen prefaces to the *New York Edition* of 1907–09, he would return to considering the principles of fiction as he reveals the "steps taken and obstacles mastered" in the evolution of his own tales and novels. No one before James had attempted such a pragmatic demystification of the novel's "rich, ambiguous aesthetic air." Perhaps no one since has had such a profound influence on how fiction is evaluated.

On Whitman

"brute sublimity"

"Walt Whitman, Drum-Taps," The Nation, November 16, 1865. Although James notes the "melancholy task" of reviewing Whitman's volume of war poetry, Edith Wharton's 1934 A Backward Glance *speaks of his later enthusiasm for the poet. She recalls how one day "someone spoke of Whitman, and it was a joy to me to discover that James thought him, as I did, the greatest of American poets. 'Leaves of Grass' was put into his hands, and all evening we sat rapt while he wandered from 'The Song of Myself' to 'When lilacs last in the door-yard bloomed' (when he read 'Lovely and soothing Death' his voice filled the hushed room like an organ adagio). . . ."*

It has been a melancholy task to read this book; and it is a still more melancholy one to write about it. Perhaps since the day of Mr. Tupper's "Philosophy" there has been no more difficult reading of the poetic sort. It exhibits the effort of an essentially prosaic mind to lift itself, by a prolonged muscular strain, into poetry. Like hundreds of other good patriots, during the last four years, Mr. Walt Whitman has imagined that a certain amount of violent sympathy with the great deeds and sufferings of our soldiers, and of admiration for our national energy, together with a ready command of picturesque language, are sufficient inspiration for a poet. If this were the case, we had been a nation of poets. The constant developments of the war moved us continually to strong feeling and to strong expression of it. But in those cases in which these expressions were written out and printed with all due regard to prosody, they failed to make poetry, as any one may see by consulting now in cold blood the back volumes of the "Rebellion Record." *Of course* the city of Manhattan, as Mr. Whitman delights to call it, when regiments poured through it in the first months of the war, and its own sole god, to borrow the words of a real poet, ceased for a while to be the millionaire, was a noble spectacle, and a poetical statement to this effect is possible. *Of course* the tumult of a battle is grand, the results of a battle tragic, and the untimely deaths of young men a theme for elegies. But he is not a poet who merely reiterates these plain facts *ore rotundo*. He only sings them worthily who views them from a height. Every tragic event collects about it a number of persons who delight to dwell upon its superficial points—of minds which are bullied by the *accidents* of the affair. The temper of such minds seems to us to be the reverse of the poetic temper; for the poet, although he incidentally masters, grasps, and uses the superficial traits of his theme, is really a poet only in so far as he extracts its latent meaning and holds it up to common eyes. And yet from such minds most of our war-verses have come, and Mr. Whitman's utterances, much as the assertion may surprise his friends, are in this respect no exception to general fashion. They are an exception, however, in that they openly pretend to be something better; and this it is that makes them melancholy reading. Mr. Whitman is very fond of blowing his own trumpet, and he has made very explicit claims for his book. "Shut not your doors," he exclaims at the outset—

Shut not your doors to me, proud libraries,
For that which was lacking among you all, yet needed most, I bring;
A book I have made for your dear sake, O soldiers,
And for you, O soul of man, and you, love of comrades;
The words of my book nothing, the life of it everything;
A book separate, not link'd with the rest, nor felt by the intellect;
But you will feel every word, O Libertad! arm'd Libertad!
It shall pass by the intellect to swim the sea, the air,
With joy with you, O soul of man.

These are great pretensions, but it seems to us that the following are even greater:

> From Paumanok starting, I fly like a bird,
> Around and around to soar, to sing the idea of all;
> To the north betaking myself, to sing there arctic songs,
> To Kanada, 'till I absorb Kanada in myself—to Michigan then,
> To Wisconsin, Iowa, Minnesota, to sing their songs (they are
>   inimitable);
> Then to Ohio and Indiana, to sing theirs—to Missouri and
>   Kansas and Arkansas to sing theirs,
> To Tennessee and Kentucky—to the Carolinas and Georgia, to
>   sing theirs,
> To Texas, and so along up toward California, to roam accepted
>   everywhere;
> To sing first (to the tap of the war-drum, if need be)
> The idea of all—of the western world, one and inseparable,
> And then the song of each member of these States.

Mr. Whitman's primary purpose is to celebrate the greatness of our armies; his secondary purpose is to celebrate the greatness of the city of New York. He pursues these objects through a hundred pages of matter which remind us irresistibly of the story of the college professor who, on a venturesome youth's bringing him a theme done in blank verse, reminded him that it was not customary in writing prose to begin each line with a capital. The frequent capitals are the only marks of verse in Mr. Whitman's writing. There is, fortunately, but one attempt at rhyme. We say fortunately, for if the inequality of Mr. Whitman's lines were self-registering, as it would be in the case of an anticipated syllable at their close, the effect would be painful in the extreme. As the case stands, each line starts off by itself, in resolute independence of its companions, without a visible goal. But if Mr. Whitman does not write verse, he does not write ordinary prose. The reader has seen that liberty is "libertad." In like manner, comrade is "camerado"; Americans are "Americanos"; a pavement is a "trottoir," and Mr. Whitman himself is a "chansonnier." If there is one thing that Mr. Whitman is not, it is this, for Béranger was a *chansonnier*. To appreciate the force of our conjunction, the reader should compare his military lyrics with Mr. Whitman's declamations. Our author's novelty, however, is not in his words, but in the form of his writing. As we have said, it begins for all the world like verse and turns out to be arrant prose. It is more like Mr. Tupper's proverbs than anything we have met. But what if, in form, it *is* prose? it may be asked. Very good poetry has come out of prose before this. To this we would reply that it must first have gone into it. Prose, in order to be good poetry, must first be good prose. As a general principle, we know of no circumstance more likely to impugn a writer's earnestness than the adoption of an anomalous style. He must have something very original to say if none of the old vehicles will carry his thoughts. Of course he *may* be surprisingly original. Still, presumption is against him. If on examination the matter of his discourse proves very valuable, it justifies, or at any rate excuses, his literary innovation.

But if, on the other hand, it is of a common quality, with nothing new about it but its manners, the public will judge the writer harshly. The most that can be said of Mr. Whitman's vaticinations is, that, cast in a fluent and familiar manner, the average substance of them might escape unchallenged. But we have seen that Mr. Whitman prides himself especially on the substance—the life—of his poetry. It may be rough, it may be grim, it may be clumsy—such we take to be the author's argument—but it is sincere, it is sublime, it appeals to the soul of man, it is the voice of a people. He tells us, in the lines quoted, that the words of his book are nothing. To our perception they are everything, and very little at that. A great deal of verse that is nothing but words has, during the war, been sympathetically sighed over and cut out of newspaper corners, because it has possessed a certain simple melody. But Mr. Whitman's verse, we are confident, would have failed even of this triumph, for the simple reason that no triumph, however small, is won but through the exercise of art, and that this volume is an offense against art. It is not enough to be grim and rough and careless; common sense is also necessary, for it is by common sense that we are judged. There exists in even the commonest minds, in literary matters, a certain precise instinct of conservatism, which is very shrewd in detecting wanton eccentricities. To this instinct Mr. Whitman's attitude seems monstrous. It is monstrous because it pretends to persuade the soul while it slights the intellect; because it pretends to gratify the feelings while it outrages the taste. The point is that it does this *on theory,* wilfully, consciously, arrogantly. It is the little nursery game of "open your mouth and shut your eyes." Our hearts are often touched through a compromise with the artistic sense, but never in direct violation of it. Mr. Whitman sits down at the outset and counts out the intelligence. This were indeed a wise precaution on his part if the intelligence were only submissive! But when she is deliberately insulted, she takes her revenge by simply standing erect and open-eyed. This is assuredly the best she can do. And if she could find a voice she would probably address Mr. Whitman as follows: "You came to woo my sister, the human soul. Instead of giving me a kick as you approach, you should either greet me courteously, or, at least, steal in unobserved. But now you have me on your hands. Your chances are poor. What the human heart desires above all is sincerity, and you do not appear to me sincere. For a lover you talk entirely too much about yourself. In one place you threaten to absorb Kanada. In another you call upon the city of New York to incarnate you, as you have incarnated it. In another you inform us that neither youth pertains to you nor 'delicatesse,' that you are awkward in the parlor, that you do not dance, and that you have neither bearing, beauty, knowledge, nor fortune. In another place, by an allusion to your 'little songs,' you seem to identify yourself with the third person of the Trinity. For a poet who claims to sing 'the idea of all,' this is tolerably egotistical. We look in vain, however, through your book for a single idea. We find nothing but flashy imitations of ideas. We find a medley of extravagances and commonplaces. We find art, measure, grace, sense sneered at on every page, and nothing positive given us in their stead. To be positive one must have something to say; to be positive requires reason, labor, and art; and art requires, above all things, a suppression of one's self, a subordination of one's self to an idea. This will never do for you, whose plan is to adapt the scheme of the universe to your own limitations. You cannot entertain and exhibit ideas; but, as we have seen, you are prepared to incarnate them. It is for this reason, doubtless, that when once you have planted yourself squarely before the public, and in view of the great service you have done to the ideal, have become, as you say, 'accepted everywhere,' you can afford to deal exclusively in words. What would be bald nonsense and dreary platitudes in any one else becomes sublimity in you. But all this is a mistake. To become adopted as a national poet, it is not enough to discard everything in particular and to accept everything in general, to amass crudity upon crudity, to discharge the undigested contents of your blotting-book into the lap of the public. You must respect the public which you address; for it has taste, if you have not. It delights in the grand, the heroic, and the masculine; but it delights to see these conceptions cast into worthy form. It is indifferent to brute sublimity. It will never do for you to thrust your hands into your pockets and cry out that, as the research of form is an intolerable bore, the shortest and most economical way for the public to embrace its idols—for the nation to realize its genius—is in your own person. This democratic, liberty-loving, American populace, this stern and war-tried people, is a great civilizer. It is devoted to refinement. If it has sustained a monstrous war, and practised human nature's best in so many ways for the last five years, it is not to put up with spurious poetry afterwards. To sing aright our battles and our glories it is not enough to have served in a hospital (however praiseworthy the task in itself), to be aggressively careless, inelegant, and ignorant, and to be constantly preoccupied with yourself. It is not enough to be rude, lugubrious, and grim. You must also be serious. You must forget yourself in your ideas. Your personal qualities—the vigor of your temperament, the manly independence of your nature, the tenderness of your heart—these facts are impertinent. You must be *possessed*, and you must strive to possess your possession. If in your striving you break into divine eloquence, then you are a poet. If the idea which possesses you is the idea of your country's greatness, then you are a national poet; and not otherwise."

On Baudelaire

"This is not Evil . . . it is simply the nasty!"

From "Charles Baudelaire," Nation, April 27, 1876. At the outset of his discussion of Baudelaire's 1857 Les fleurs du mal, James makes clear that he is not shocked by any of it. He voices impatience with Baudelaire's enthusiasm for Edgar Allan Poe—"vastly the greater charlatan of the two, as well as the greater genius"—finding that enthusiasm to be the mark of a "decidedly primitive stage of reflection." In his 1879 Hawthorne volume he would label Poe's critical judgments as "pretentious, spiteful, and vulgar." Finally the thirty-three-year-old critic dismisses Baudelaire with a withering assessment: "What the poet wishes, doubtless, was to seem to be always in the poetic attitude, what the reader sees is a gentleman in a painful-looking posture, staring very hard at a mass of things from which, more intelligently, we avert our heads."

As a brief discussion was lately carried on touching the merits of the writer whose name we have prefixed to these lines, it may not be amiss to introduce him to some of those readers who must have observed the contest with little more than a vague sense of the strangeness of its subject. Charles Baudelaire is not a novelty in literature; his principal work dates from 1857, and his career terminated a few years later. But his admirers have made a classic of him and elevated him to the rank of one of those subjects which are always in order. Even if we differ with them on this point, such attention as Baudelaire demands will not lead us very much astray. He is not, in quantity (whatever he may have been in quality), a formidable writer; having died young, he was not prolific, and the most noticeable of his original productions are contained in two small volumes.

His celebrity began with the publication of "Les Fleurs du Mal," a collection of verses of which some had already appeared in periodicals. The "Revue des Deux Mondes" had taken the responsibility of introducing a few of them to the world—or rather, though it held them at the baptismal font of public opinion, it had declined to stand godfather. An accompanying note in the "Revue" disclaimed all editorial approval of their morality. This of course procured them a good many readers; and when, on its appearance, the volume we have mentioned was overhauled by the police a still greater number of persons desired to possess it. Yet in spite of the service rendered him by the censorship, Baudelaire has never become in any degree popular; the lapse of twenty years has seen but five editions of "Les Fleurs du Mal." The foremost feeling of the reader of the present day will be one of surprise, and even amusement, at Baudelaire's audacities having provoked this degree of scandal. The world has travelled fast since then, and the French censorship must have been, in the year 1857, in a very prudish mood. There is little in "Les Fleurs du Mal" to make the reader of either French or English prose and verse of the present day even open his eyes. We have passed through the fiery furnace and profited by experience. We are happier than Racine's heroine, who had not

   Su se faire un front qui ne rougit jamais.

Baudelaire's verses do not strike us as being dictated by a spirit of bravado—though we have heard that, in talk, it was his habit, to an even tiresome degree, to cultivate the quietly outrageous—to pile up monstrosities and blasphemies without winking and with the air of uttering proper commonplaces.

"Les Fleurs du Mal" is evidently a sincere book—so far as anything for a man of Baudelaire's temper and culture could be sincere. Sincerity seems to us to belong to a range of qualities with which Baudelaire and his friends were but scantily concerned. His great quality was an inordinate cultivation of the sense of the picturesque, and his care was for how things looked, and whether some kind of imaginative amusement was not to be got out of them, much more than for what they meant and whither they led and what was their use in human life at large. The later editions of "Les Fleurs du Mal" (with some of the interdicted pieces still omitted and others, we believe, restored) contain a long preface by Théophile Gautier, which throws a curious side-light upon what the Spiritualist newspapers would call Baudelaire's "mentality." Of course Baudelaire is not to be held accountable for what Gautier says of him, but we cannot help judging a man in some degree by the company he keeps. To admire Gautier is certainly excellent taste, but to be admired by Gautier we cannot but regard as rather compromising. He gives a magnificently picturesque account of the author of "Les Fleurs du Mal," in which, indeed, the question of pure exactitude is evidently so very subordinate that it seems grossly ill-natured for us to appeal to such a standard. While we are reading him, however, we find ourselves wishing that Baudelaire's analogy with the author himself were either greater or less. Gautier was perfectly sincere, because he dealt only with the picturesque and pretended to care only for appearances. But Baudelaire (who, to our mind, was an altogether inferior genius to Gautier) applied the same process of interpretation to things as regards which it was altogether inadequate; so that one is constantly tempted to suppose he cares more for his process—for making grotesquely-pictorial verse—than for the things themselves. On the whole, as we have said, this inference would be unfair. Baudelaire had a certain groping sense of the moral complexities of life, and if the best that he succeeds in doing is to drag them down into the very turbid element in which he himself plashes and flounders, and there present them to us much besmirched and bespattered, this was not a want of goodwill in him, but rather a dulness and permanent immaturity of vision. For American readers, furthermore, Baudelaire is compromised by his having made himself the apostle of our own Edgar Poe. He translated, very carefully and exactly, all of Poe's prose writings, and, we believe, some of his very valueless verses. With all due respect to the very original genius of the author of the "Tales of Mystery," it seems to us that to take him with more than a certain degree of seriousness is to lack seriousness one's self. An enthusiasm for Poe is the mark of a decidedly primitive stage of reflection. Baudelaire thought him a profound philosopher, the neglect of whose golden utterances stamped his native land with infamy. Nevertheless, Poe was vastly the greater charlatan of the two, as well as the greater genius.

"Les Fleurs du Mal" was a very happy title for Baudelaire's verses, but it is not altogether a just one. Scattered flowers incontestably do bloom in the quaking swamps of evil, and the poet who does not mind encountering bad odours in his pursuit of sweet ones is quite at liberty to go in search of them. But Baudelaire has, as a general thing, not plucked the flowers—he has plucked the evil-smelling weeds (we take it that he did not use the word flowers in a purely ironical sense) and he has often taken up mere cupfuls of mud and bog-water. He had said to himself that it was a great shame that the realm of evil and unclean things should be fenced off from the domain of poetry; that it was full of subjects, of chances and effects; that it had its light and shade, its logic and its mystery; and that there was the making of some capital verses in it. So he leaped the barrier and was soon immersed in it up to his neck. Baudelaire's imagination was of a melancholy and sinister kind, and, to a considerable extent, this plunging into darkness and dirt was doubtless very spontaneous and disinterested. But he strikes us on the whole as passionless, and this, in view of the unquestionable pluck and acuteness of his fancy, is a great pity. He knew evil not by experience, not as something within himself, but by contemplation and curiosity, as something outside of himself, by which his own intellectual agility was not in the least discomposed, rather, indeed (as we say his fancy was of a dusky cast) agreeably flattered and stimulated. In the former case, Baudelaire, with his other gifts, might have been a great poet. But, as it is, evil for him begins outside and not inside, and consists primarily of a great deal of lurid landscape and unclean furniture. This is an almost ludicrously puerile view of the matter. Evil is represented as an affair of blood and carrion and physical sickness—there must be stinking corpses and starving prostitutes and empty laudanum bottles in order that the poet shall be effectively inspired.

A good way to embrace Baudelaire at a glance is to say that he was, in his treatment of evil, exactly what Hawthorne was not—Hawthorne, who felt the thing at its source, deep in the human consciousness. Baudelaire's infinitely slighter volume of genius apart, he was a sort of Hawthorne reversed. It is the absence of this metaphysical quality in his treatment of his favourite subjects (Poe was his metaphysician, and his devotion sustained him through a translation of "Eureka!") that exposes him to that class of accusations of which M. Edmond Schérer's accusation of feeding upon *pourriture* is an example; and, in fact, in his pages we never know with what we are dealing. We encounter an inextricable confusion of sad emotions and vile things, and we are at a loss to know whether the subject pretends to appeal to our conscience or—we were going to say—to our olfactories. "Le Mal?" we exclaim; "you do yourself too much honour. This is not Evil; it is not the wrong; it is simply the nasty!" Our impatience is of the same order as that which we should feel if a poet, pretending to pluck "the flowers of good," should come and present us, as specimens, a rhapsody on plumcake and *eau du Cologne*. Independently of the question of his subjects, the charm of Baudelaire's verse is often of a very high order. He belongs to the class of geniuses in whom we ourselves find but a limited pleasure—the laborious, deliberate, economical writers, those who fumble a long time in their pockets before they bring out their hand with a coin in the palm. But the coin, when Baudelaire at last produced it, was often of a high value. He had an extraordinary verbal instinct and an exquisite felicity of epithet. . . .

From
Hawthorne

"No sovereign, no court, no personal loyalty,
no aristocracy, no church"

From Hawthorne, *1879, a seven-chapter critical biography published in London by Macmillan, for "The English Men of Letters Series." James begins by noting that "Out of the soil of New England he sprang—in the crevice of that immitigable granite he sprouted and bloomed." From the perspective of a literary realist, James discusses Hawthorne's romances with occasional disdain but generally with praise, as when he judges that* The Scarlet Letter *was "the finest piece of imaginative writing yet put forth in the country." The following passage catalogues the deficiencies which made Hawthorne's task as a novelist difficult in America; at the time he writes, James himself had already decided to remain in England as an expatriate.*

He was poor, he was solitary, and he undertook to devote himself to literature in a community in which the interest in literature was as yet of the smallest. It is not too much to say that even to the present day it is a considerable discomfort in the United States not to be "in business." The young man who attempts to launch himself in a career that does not belong to the so-called practical order; the young man who has not, in a word, an office in the business-quarter of the town, with his name painted on the door, has but a limited place in the social system, finds no particular bough to perch upon. He is not looked at askance, he is not regarded as an idler; literature and the arts have always been held in extreme honour in the American world, and those who practise them are received on easier terms than in other countries. If the tone of the American world is in some respects provincial, it is in none more so than in this matter of the exaggerated homage rendered to authorship. The gentleman or the lady who has written a book is in many circles the object of an admiration too indiscriminating to operate as an encouragement to good writing. There is no reason to suppose that this was less the case fifty years ago; but fifty years ago, greatly more than now, the literary man must have lacked the comfort and inspiration of belonging to a class. The best things come, as a general thing, from the talents that are members of a group; every man works better when he has companions working in the same line, and yielding the stimulus of suggestion, comparison, emulation. Great things of course have been done by solitary workers; but they have usually been done with double the pains they would have cost if they had been produced in more genial circumstances. The solitary worker loses the profit of example and discussion; he is apt to make awkward experiments; he is in the nature of the case more or less of an empiric. The empiric may, as I say, be treated by the world as an expert; but the drawbacks and discomforts of empiricism remain to him, and are in fact increased by the suspicion that is mingled with his gratitude, of a want in the public taste of a sense of the proportions of things. Poor Hawthorne, beginning to write subtle short tales at Salem, was empirical enough; he was one of, at most, some dozen Americans who had taken up literature as a profession. The profession in the United States is still very young, and of diminutive stature; but in the year 1830 its head could hardly have been seen above ground. It strikes the observer of to-day that Hawthorne showed great courage in entering a field in which the honours and emoluments were so scanty as the profits of authorship must have been at that time. I have said that in the United States at present authorship is a pedestal, and literature is the fashion; but Hawthorne's history is a proof that it was possible, fifty years ago, to write a great many little masterpieces without becoming known. He begins the preface to the *Twice-Told Tales* by remarking that he was "for many years the obscurest man of letters in America." When once this work obtained recognition, the recognition left little to be desired.

Hawthorne never, I believe, made large sums of money by his
writings, and the early profits of these charming sketches could
not have been considerable; for many of them, indeed, as they
appeared in journals and magazines, he had never been paid at
all; but the honour, when once it dawned—and it dawned tolerably early in the author's career—was never thereafter wanting. Hawthorne's countrymen are solidly proud of him, and the
tone of Mr. Lathrop's *Study* is in itself sufficient evidence of the
manner in which an American story-teller may in some cases
look to have his eulogy pronounced.

*   *   *   *   *

I know not at what age he began to keep a diary; the first entries in the American volumes are of the summer of 1835.
There is a phrase in the preface to his novel of *Transformation,*
which must have lingered in the minds of many Americans who
have tried to write novels and to lay the scene of them in the
western world. "No author, without a trial, can conceive of the
difficulty of writing a romance about a country where there is no
shadow, no antiquity, no mystery, no picturesque and gloomy
wrong, nor anything but a commonplace prosperity, in broad
and simple daylight, as is happily the case with my dear native
land." The perusal of Hawthorne's American Note-Books operates as a practical commentary upon this somewhat ominous
text. It does so at least to my own mind; it would be too much
perhaps to say that the effect would be the same for the usual
English reader. An American reads between the lines—he com-
pletes the suggestions—he constructs a picture. I think I am not
guilty of any gross injustice in saying that the picture he constructs from Hawthorne's American diaries, though by no
means without charms of its own, is not, on the whole, an interesting one. It is characterised by an extraordinary blankness—a curious paleness of colour and paucity of detail.
Hawthorne, as I have said, has a large and healthy appetite for
detail, and one is therefore the more struck with the lightness
of the diet to which his observation was condemned. For myself, as I turn the pages of his journals, I seem to see the image
of the crude and simple society in which he lived. I use these ep-
ithets, of course, not invidiously, but descriptively; if one desire

to enter as closely as possible into Hawthorne's situation, one must endeavour to reproduce his circumstances. We are struck with the large number of elements that were absent from them, and the coldness, the thinness, the blankness, to repeat my epithet, present themselves so vividly that our foremost feeling is that of compassion for a romancer looking for subjects in such a field. It takes so many things, as Hawthorne must have felt later in life, when he made the acquaintance of the denser, richer, warmer European spectacle—it takes such an accumulation of history and custom, such a complexity of manners and types, to form a fund of suggestion for a novelist. If Hawthorne had been a young Englishman, or a young Frenchman of the same degree of genius, the same cast of mind, the same habits, his consciousness of the world around him would have been a very different affair; however obscure, however reserved, his own personal life, his sense of the life of his fellow-mortals would have been almost infinitely more various. The negative side of the spectacle on which Hawthorne looked out, in his contemplative saunterings and reveries, might, indeed, with a little ingenuity, be made almost ludicrous; one might enumerate the items of high civilization, as it exists in other countries, which are absent from the texture of American life, until it should become a wonder to know what was left. No State, in the European sense of the word, and indeed barely a specific national name. No sovereign, no court, no personal loyalty, no aristocracy, no church, no clergy, no army, no diplomatic service, no country gentlemen, no palaces, no castles, nor manors, nor old country-houses, nor parsonages, nor thatched cottages nor ivied ruins; no cathedrals, nor abbeys, nor little Norman churches; no great Universities nor public schools—no Oxford, nor Eton, nor Harrow; no literature, no novels, no museums, no pictures, no political society, no sporting class—no Epsom nor Ascot! Some such list as that might be drawn up of the absent things in American life—especially in the American life of forty years ago, the effect of which, upon an English or a French imagination, would probably as a general thing be appalling. The natural remark, in the almost lurid light of such an indictment, would be that if these things are left out, everything is left out. The American knows that a good deal remains; what it is that remains—that is his secret, his joke, as one may say. It would be cruel, in this terrible denudation, to deny him the consolation of his national gift, that "American humour" of which of late years we have heard so much.

*   *   *   *   *

The writer of these lines, who was a child at the time, remembers dimly the sensation the book produced, and the little shudder with which people alluded to it, as if a peculiar horror were mixed with its attractions. He was too young to read it himself, but its title, upon which he fixed his eyes as the book lay upon the table, had a mysterious charm. He had a vague belief indeed that the "letter" in question was one of the documents that come by the post, and it was a source of perpetual wonderment to him that it should be of such an unaccustomed hue. Of course it was difficult to explain to a child the significance of poor Hester Prynne's blood-coloured A. But the mystery was at last partly dispelled by his being taken to see a collection of pictures (the annual exhibition of the National Academy), where he encountered a representation of a pale, handsome woman, in a quaint black dress and a white coif, holding between her knees an elfish-looking little girl, fantastically dressed and crowned with flowers. Embroidered on the woman's breast was a great crimson A, over which the child's fingers, as she glanced strangely out of the picture, were maliciously playing. I was told that this was Hester Prynne and little Pearl, and that when I grew older I might read their interesting history. But the picture remained vividly imprinted on my mind; I had been vaguely frightened and made uneasy by it; and when, years afterwards, I first read the novel, I seemed to myself to have read it before, and to be familiar with its two strange heroines. I mention this incident simply as an indication of the degree to which the success of The Scarlet Letter had made the book what is called an actuality. Hawthorne himself was very modest about it; he wrote to his publisher, when there was a question of his undertaking another novel, that what had given the history of Hester Prynne its "vogue" was simply the introductory chapter. In fact, the publication of The Scarlet Letter was in the United States a literary event of the first importance. The book was the finest piece of imaginative writing yet put forth in the country. There was a consciousness of this in the welcome that was given it—a satisfaction in the idea of America having produced a novel that belonged to literature, and to the forefront of it. Something might at last be sent to Europe as exquisite in quality as anything that had been received, and the best of it was that the thing was absolutely American; it belonged to the soil, to the air; it came out of the very heart of New England.

It is beautiful, admirable, extraordinary; it has in the highest degree that merit which I have spoken of as the mark of Hawthorne's best things—an indefinable purity and lightness of conception, a quality which in a work of art affects one in the same way as the absence of grossness does in a human being. His fancy, as I just now said, had evidently brooded over the subject for a long time; the situation to be represented had disclosed itself to him in all its phases. When I say in all its phases, the sentence demands modification; for it is to be remembered that if Hawthorne laid his hand upon the well-worn theme, upon the familiar combination of the wife, the lover, and the husband, it was after all but to one period of the history of these three persons that he attached himself. The situation is the situation after the woman's fault has been committed, and the current of expiation and repentance has set in. In spite of the relation between Hester Prynne and Arthur Dimmesdale, no story of love was surely ever less of a "love story." To Hawthorne's imagination the fact that these two persons had loved each other too well was of an interest comparatively vulgar; what appealed to him was the idea of their moral situation in the long years that were to follow. The story indeed is in a secondary degree that of Hester Prynne; she becomes, really, after the first scene, an accessory figure; it is not upon her the *dénoûment* depends. It is upon her guilty lover that the author projects most frequently the cold, thin rays of his fitfully-moving lantern, which makes here and there a little luminous circle, on the edge of which hovers the livid and sinister figure of the injured and retributive husband. The story goes on for the most part between the lover and the husband—the tormented young Puritan minister, who carries the secret of his own lapse from pastoral purity locked up beneath an exterior that commends

itself to the reverence of his flock, while he sees the softer partner of his guilt standing in the full glare of exposure and hum-
bling herself to the misery of atonement—between this more
wretched and pitiable culprit, to whom dishonour would come
as a comfort and the pillory as a relief, and the older, keener,
wiser man, who, to obtain satisfaction for the wrong he has
suffered, devises the infernally ingenious plan of conjoining
himself with his wronger, living with him, living upon him, and
while he pretends to minister to his hidden ailment and to sym-
pathise with his pain, revels in his unsuspected knowledge of
these things and stimulates them by malignant arts. The attitude of Roger Chillingworth, and the means he takes to com-
pensate himself—these are the highly original elements in the
situation that Hawthorne so ingeniously treats. None of his
works are so impregnated with that after-sense of the old Puritan consciousness of life to which allusion has so often been
made. If, as M. Montégut says, the qualities of his ancestors *fil-
tered* down through generations into his composition, *The
Scarlet Letter* was, as it were, the vessel that gathered up the
last of the precious drops. And I say this not because the story
happens to be of so-called historical cast, to be told of the early
days of Massachusetts and of people in steeple-crowned hats
and sad coloured garments. The historical colouring is rather
weak than otherwise; there is little elaboration of detail, of the
modern realism of research; and the author has made no great
point of causing his figures to speak the English of their period.
Nevertheless, the book is full of the moral presence of the race
that invented Hester's penance—diluted and complicated with
other things, but still perfectly recognisable. Puritanism, in a
word, is there, not only objectively, as Hawthorne tried to
place it there, but subjectively as well. Not, I mean, in his judgment of his characters, in any harshness of prejudice, or in the
obtrusion of a moral lesson; but in the very quality of his own
vision, in the tone of the picture, in a certain coldness and ex-
clusiveness of treatment.

*   *   *   *   *

He was a beautiful, natural, original genius, and his life had
been singularly exempt from worldly preoccupations and vul-

gar efforts. It had been as pure, as simple, as unsophisticated, as his work. He had lived primarily in his domestic affections, which were of the tenderest kind; and then—without eagerness, without pretension, but with a great deal of quiet devotion—in his charming art. His work will remain; it is too original and exquisite to pass away; among the men of imagination he will always have his niche. No one has had just that vision of life, and no one has had a literary form that more successfully expressed his vision. He was not a moralist, and he was not simply a poet. The moralists are weightier, denser, richer, in a sense; the poets are more purely inconclusive and irresponsible. He combined in a singular degree the spontaneity of the imagination with a haunting care for moral problems. Man's conscience was his theme, but he saw it in the light of a creative fancy which added, out of its own substance, an interest, and, I may almost say, an importance.

On Emerson

"salt is wanting"

From "Review of Carlyle and Emerson," Century Magazine, 1883. Thomas Carlyle and particularly Ralph Waldo Emerson—who had died in 1881 and 1882—had been friends of Henry James's father, and Henry James himself had visited Emerson in Concord and later had guided him through the Louvre. As is the case with his opinion of Hawthorne, James judges the insufficiencies of New England culture as partly responsible for the fact that a remarkable writer failed to live up to his potential.

Emerson speaks the word in that passage; he was an optimist, and this in spite of the fact that he was the inspiration of the considerable body of persons who at that time, in New England, were seeking a better way. Carlyle, on the other hand, was a pessimist—a pessimist of pessimists—and this great difference between them includes many of the others. The American public has little more to learn in regard to the extreme amenity of Emerson, his eminently gentle spirit, his almost touching tolerance, his deference toward every sort of human manifestation; but many of his letters remind us afresh of his singular modesty of attitude and of his extreme consideration for that blundering human family whom he believed to be in want of light. His optimism makes us wonder at times where he discovered the errors that it would seem well to set right, and what there was in his view of the world on which the spirit of criticism could feed. He had a high and noble conception of good, without having, as it would appear, a definite conception of evil. The few words I have just quoted in regard to the America of 1841, "intelligent, sensual, and avaricious," have as sharp an ironical ring in them as any that I remember to have noticed in his part of the Correspondence. He has not a grain of current contempt; one feels, at times, that he has not enough. This salt is wanting in his taste of things.

The Art of Fiction

"the chamber of consciousness"
"Try to be one . . . on whom nothing is lost!"

Longman's Magazine, September 1884. This piece was written in response to Walter Besant's overly prescriptive 1884 essay, "Fiction as one of the Arts." Among other pronouncements, Besant insists that one should not attempt to write on any "experience" that is remote from one's own social experience. Here James redefines experience as a process of analysis in "the chamber of consciousness" and considerably complicates any definition of fictive realism.

I should not have affixed so comprehensive a title to these few remarks, necessarily wanting in any completeness upon a subject the full consideration of which would carry us far, did I not seem to discover a pretext for my temerity in the interesting pamphlet lately published under this name by Mr. Walter Besant. Mr. Besant's lecture at the Royal Institution—the original form of his pamphlet—appears to indicate that many persons are interested in the art of fiction, and are not indifferent to such remarks, as those who practise it may attempt to make about it. I am therefore anxious not to lose the benefit of this favourable association, and to edge in a few words under cover of the attention which Mr. Besant is sure to have excited. There is something very encouraging in his having put into form certain of his ideas on the mystery of story-telling.

It is a proof of life and curiosity—curiosity on the part of the brotherhood of novelists as well as on the part of their readers. Only a short time ago it might have been supposed that the English novel was not what the French call *discutable*. It had no air of having a theory, a conviction, a consciousness of itself behind it—of being the expression of an artistic faith, the result of choice and comparison. I do not say it was necessarily the worse for that: it would take much more courage than I possess to intimate that the form of the novel as Dickens and Thackeray (for instance) saw it had any taint of incompleteness. It was, however, *naïf* (if I may help myself out with another French word); and evidently if it be destined to suffer in any way for having lost its *naïveté* it has now an idea of making sure of the corresponding advantages. During the period I have alluded to there was a comfortable, good-humoured feeling abroad that a novel is a novel, as a pudding is a pudding, and that our only business with it could be to swallow it. But within a year or two, for some reason or other, there have been signs of returning animation—the era of discussion would appear to have been to a certain extent opened. Art lives upon discussion, upon experiment, upon curiosity, upon variety of attempt, upon the exchange of views and the comparison of standpoints; and there is a presumption that those times when no one has anything particular to say about it, and has no reason to give for practice or preference, though they may be times of honour, are not times of development—are times, possibly even, a little of dulness. The successful application of any art is a delightful spectacle, but the theory too is interesting; and though there is a great deal of the latter without the former I suspect there has never been a genuine success that has not had a latent core of conviction. Discussion, suggestion, formulation, these things are fertilizing when they are frank and sincere. Mr. Besant has set an excellent example in saying what he thinks, for his part, about the way in which fiction should be written, as well as about the way in which it should be published; for his view of the "art," carried on into an appendix, covers that too. Other labourers in the same field will doubtless take up the argument, they will give it the light of their experience, and the effect will surely be to make our interest in the novel a little more what it had for some time threatened to fail to be—a serious, active, inquiring interest, under protection of which this delightful study may, in moments of confidence, venture to say a little more what it thinks of itself.

It must take itself seriously for the public to take it so. The old superstition about fiction being "wicked" has doubtless died out in England; but the spirit of it lingers in a certain oblique regard directed toward any story which does not more or less admit that it is only a joke. Even the most jocular novel feels in some degree the weight of the proscription that was formerly directed against literary levity; the jocularity does not always succeed in passing for orthodoxy. It is still expected, though perhaps people are ashamed to say it, that a production which is after all only a "make-believe" (for what else is a "story"?) shall be in some degree apologetic—shall renounce the pretension of attempting really to represent life. This, of course, any sensible, wide-awake story declines to do, for it quickly perceives that the tolerance granted to it on such a condition is only an attempt to stifle it disguised in the form of generosity. The old evangelical hostility to the novel, which was as explicit as it was narrow, and which regarded it as little less favourable to our immortal part than a stage-play, was in reality far less insulting. The only reason for the existence of a novel is that it does attempt to represent life. When it relinquishes this attempt, the same attempt that we see on the canvas of the painter, it will have arrived at a very strange pass. It is not expected of the picture that it will make itself humble in order to be forgiven; and the analogy between the art of the painter and the art of the novelist is, so far as I am able to see, complete. Their inspiration is the same, their process (allowing for the different quality of the vehicle), is the same, their success is the same. They may learn from each other, they may explain and sustain each other. Their cause is the same, and the honour of one is the honour of another. The Mahometans think a picture an unholy thing, but it is a long time since any Christian did, and it is therefore the more odd that in the Christian mind the traces (dissimulated though they may be) of a suspicion of the sister art should linger to this day. The only effectual way to lay it to rest is to emphasize the analogy to which I just alluded— to insist on the fact that as the picture is reality, so the novel is history. That is the only general description (which does it justice) that we may give of the novel. But history also is allowed to represent life; it is not, any more than painting, expected to apologize. The subject-matter of fiction is stored up likewise in documents and records, and if it will not give itself away, as they say in California, it must speak with assurance, with the tone of the historian. Certain accomplished novelists have a habit of giving themselves away which must often bring tears to the eyes of people who take their fiction seriously. I was lately struck, in reading over many pages of Anthony Trollope, with his want of discretion in this particular. In a digression, a parenthesis or an aside, he concedes to the reader that he and this trusting friend are only "making believe." He admits that the events he narrates have not really happened, and that he can give his narrative any turn the reader may like best. Such a betrayal of a sacred office seems to me, I confess, a terrible crime; it is what I mean by the attitude of apology, and it shocks me every whit as much in Trollope as it would have shocked me in Gibbon or Macaulay. It implies that the novelist is less occupied in looking for the truth (the truth, of course I mean, that he assumes, the premises that we must grant him, whatever they may be), than the historian, and in doing so it deprives him at a stroke of all his standing-room. To represent and illustrate the past, the actions of men, is the task of either writer, and the only difference that I can see is, in proportion as he succeeds, to the honour of the novelist, consisting as it does in his having more difficulty in collecting his evidence, which is so far from being purely literary. It seems to me to give him a great character, the fact that he has at once so much in common with the philosopher and the painter; this double analogy is a magnificent heritage.

It is of all this evidently that Mr. Besant is full when he insists upon the fact that fiction is one of the *fine* arts, deserving in its turn of all the honours and emoluments that have hitherto been reserved for the successful profession of music, poetry, painting, architecture. It is impossible to insist too much on so important a truth, and the place that Mr. Besant demands for the work of the novelist may be represented, a trifle less abstractly, by saying that he demands not only that it shall be reputed artistic, but that it shall be reputed very artistic indeed. It is excellent that he should have struck this note, for his doing so indicates that there was need of it, that his proposition may be to many people a novelty. One rubs one's eyes at the thought; but the rest of Mr. Besant's essay confirms the revelation. I suspect in truth that it would be possible to confirm it still further, and that one would not be far wrong in saying that in addition to the people to whom it has never occurred that a novel ought to be artistic, there are a great many others who, if this principle were urged upon them, would be filled with an indefinable mistrust. They would find it difficult to explain their repugnance, but it would operate strongly to put them on their guard. "Art," in our Protestant communities, where so many things have got so strangely twisted about, is supposed in certain circles to have some vaguely injurious effect upon those who make it an important consideration, who let it weigh in the balance. It is assumed to be opposed in some mysterious manner to morality, to amusement, to instruction. When it is embodied in the work of the painter (the sculptor is another affair!) you know what it is: it stands there before you, in the honesty of pink and green and a gilt frame; you can see the worst of it at a glance, and you can be on your guard. But when it is introduced into literature it becomes more insidious—there is danger of its hurting you before you know it. Literature should be either instructive or amusing, and there is in many minds an impression that these artistic preoccupations, the search for form, contribute to neither end, interfere indeed with both. They are too frivolous to be edifying, and too serious to be diverting; and they are moreover priggish and paradoxical and superfluous. That, I think, represents the manner in which the latent thought of many people who read novels as an exercise in skipping would explain itself if it were to become articulate. They would argue, of course, that a novel ought to be "good," but they would interpret this term in a fashion of their own, which indeed would vary considerably from one critic to another. One would say that being good means representing virtuous and aspiring characters, placed in prominent positions; another would say that it depends on a "happy ending," on a distribution at the last of prizes, pensions, husbands, wives, babies, millions, appended paragraphs, and cheerful remarks. Another still would say that it means being full of incident and movement, so that we shall wish to jump ahead, to see who was the mysterious stranger, and if the stolen will was ever found, and shall not be distracted from this pleasure by any tiresome analysis or "description." But they would all agree that the "artistic" idea would spoil some of their fun. One would hold it accountable for all the description, another would see it revealed in the absence of sympathy. Its hostility to a happy ending would be evident, and it might even in some cases render any ending at all impossible. The "ending" of a novel is, for many persons, like that of a good dinner, a course of dessert and ices, and the artist in fiction is regarded as a sort of meddlesome doctor who forbids agreeable aftertastes. It is therefore true that this conception of Mr. Besant's of the novel as a superior form encounters not only a negative but a positive indifference. It matters little that as a work of art it should really be as little or as much of its essence to supply happy endings, sympathetic characters, and an objective tone, as if it were a work of mechanics: the association of ideas, however incongruous, might easily be too much for it if an eloquent voice were not sometimes raised to call attention to the fact that it is at once as free and as serious a branch of literature as any other.

Certainly this might sometimes be doubted in presence of the enormous number of works of fiction that appeal to the credulity of our generation, for it might easily seem that there could be no great character in a commodity so quickly and easily produced. It must be admitted that good novels are much compromised by bad ones, and that the field at large suffers discredit from overcrowding. I think, however, that this injury is only superficial, and that the superabundance of written fiction proves nothing against the principle itself. It has been vulgarized, like all other kinds of literature, like everything else to-day, and it has proved more than some kinds accessible to vulgarization. But there is as much difference as there ever was between a good novel and a bad one: the bad is swept with all the daubed canvases and spoiled marble into some unvisited limbo, or infinite rubbish-yard beneath the back-windows of the world, and the good subsists and emits its light and stimulates our desire for perfection. As I shall take the liberty of making but a single criticism of Mr. Besant, whose tone is so full of the love of his art, I may as well have done with it at once. He seems to me to mistake in attempting to say so definitely beforehand what sort of an affair the good novel will be. To indicate the danger of such an error as that has been the purpose of these few pages; to suggest that certain traditions on the subject, applied *a priori*, have already had much to answer for, and that the good health of an art which undertakes so immediately to reproduce life must demand that it be perfectly free. It lives upon exercise, and the very meaning of exercise is freedom. The only obligation to which in advance we may hold a novel, without incurring the accusation of being arbitrary, is that it be interesting. That general responsibility rests upon it, but it is the only one I can think of. The ways in which it is at liberty to accomplish this result (of interesting us) strike me as innumerable, and such as can only suffer from being marked out or fenced in by prescription. They are as various as the temperament of man, and they are successful in proportion as they reveal a particular mind, different from others. A novel is in its broadest definition a personal, a direct impression of life: that, to begin with, constitutes its value, which is greater or less according to the intensity of the impression. But there will be no intensity at all, and therefore no value, unless there is freedom to feel and say. The tracing of a line to be followed, of a tone to be taken, of a form to be filled out, is a limitation of that freedom and a suppression of the very thing that we are most curious about. The form, it seems to me, is to be appreciated after the fact: then the author's choice has been made, his standard has been indicated; then we can follow lines and directions and compare tones and resemblances. Then in a word we can enjoy one of the most charming of pleasures, we can estimate quality, we can apply the test of execution. The execution belongs to the author alone; it is what is most personal to him, and we measure him by that. The advantage, the luxury, as well as the torment and responsibility of the novelist, is that there is no limit to what he may attempt as an executant—no limit to his possible experiments, efforts, discoveries, successes. Here it is especially that he works, step by step, like his brother of the brush, of whom we may always say that he has painted his picture in a manner best known to himself. His manner is his secret, not necessarily a jealous one. He cannot disclose it as a general thing if he would; he would be at a loss to teach it to others. I say this with a due recollection of having insisted on the community of method of the artist who paints a picture and the artist who writes a novel. The painter *is* able to teach the rudiments of his practice, and it is possible, from the study of good work (granted the aptitude), both to learn how to paint and to learn how to write. Yet it remains true, without injury to the *rapprochement,* that the literary artist would be obliged to say to his pupil much more than the other, "Ah, well, you must do it as you can!" It is a question of degree, a matter of delicacy. If there are exact sciences, there are also exact arts, and the grammar of painting is so much more definite that it makes the difference.

I ought to add, however, that if Mr. Besant says at the beginning of his essay that the "laws of fiction may be laid down and taught with as much precision and exactness as the laws of harmony, perspective, and proportion," he mitigates what might appear to be an extravagance by applying his remark to "general" laws, and by expressing most of these rules in a manner with which it would certainly be unaccommodating to disagree. That the novelist must write from his experience, that his "characters must be real and such as might be met with in actual life"; that "a young lady brought up in a quiet country village should avoid descriptions of garrison life," and "a writer whose friends and personal experiences belong to the lower middle-class should carefully avoid introducing his characters into society"; that one should enter one's notes in a commonplace book; that one's figures should be clear in outline; that making them clear by some trick of speech or of carriage is a bad method, and "describing them at length" is a worse one; that English Fiction should have a "conscious moral purpose"; that "it is almost impossible to estimate too highly the value of careful workmanship—that is, of style"; that "the most important point of all is the story," that "the story is everything": these are principles with most of which it is surely impossible not to sympathize. That remark about the lower middle-class writer and his knowing his place is perhaps rather chilling; but for the rest I should find it difficult to dissent from any one of

these recommendations. At the same time, I should find it difficult positively to assent to them, with the exception, perhaps,
of the injunction as to entering one's notes in a common-place
book. They scarcely seem to me to have the quality that Mr. Besant attributes to the rules of the novelist—the "precision and
exactness" of "the laws of harmony, perspective, and proportion." They are suggestive, they are even inspiring, but they are
not exact, though they are doubtless as much so as the case admits of: which is a proof of that liberty of interpretation for
which I just contended. For the value of these different injunc-
tions—so beautiful and so vague—is wholly in the meaning
one attaches to them. The characters, the situation, which
strike one as real will be those that touch and interest one most,
but the measure of reality is very difficult to fix. The reality of
Don Quixote or of Mr. Micawber is a very delicate shade; it is
a reality so coloured by the author's vision that, vivid as it may
be, one would hesitate to propose it as a model: one would expose one's self to some very embarrassing questions on the part
of a pupil. It goes without saying that you will not write a good
novel unless you possess the sense of reality; but it will be difficult to give you a recipe for calling that sense into being. Humanity is immense, and reality has a myriad forms; the most
one can affirm is that some of the flowers of fiction have the
odour of it, and others have not; as for telling you in advance
how your nosegay should be composed, that is another affair.
It is equally excellent and inconclusive to say that one must
write from experience; to our supposititious aspirant such a
declaration might savour of mockery. What kind of experience
is intended, and where does it begin and end? Experience is
never limited, and it is never complete; it is an immense sensibility, a kind of huge spider-web of the finest silken threads
suspended in the chamber of consciousness, and catching every
air-borne particle in its tissue. It is the very atmosphere of the
mind; and when the mind is imaginative—much more when it
happens to be that of a man of genius—it takes to itself the
faintest hints of life, it converts the very pulses of the air into
revelations. The young lady living in a village has only to be a
damsel upon whom nothing is lost to make it quite unfair (as it
seems to me) to declare to her that she shall have nothing to say

about the military. Greater miracles have been seen than that, imagination assisting, she should speak the truth about some of these gentlemen. I remember an English novelist, a woman of genius, telling me that she was much commended for the impression she had managed to give in one of her tales of the nature and way of life of the French Protestant youth. She had been asked where she learned so much about this recondite being, she had been congratulated on her peculiar opportunities. These opportunities consisted in her having once, in Paris, as she ascended a staircase, passed an open door where, in the household of a *pasteur*, some of the young Protestants were seated at table round a finished meal. The glimpse made a picture; it lasted only a moment, but that moment was experience. She had got her direct personal impression, and she turned out her type. She knew what youth was, and what Protestantism; she also had the advantage of having seen what it was to be French, so that she converted these ideas into a concrete image and produced a reality. Above all, however, she was blessed with the faculty which when you give it an inch takes an ell, and which for the artist is a much greater source of strength than any accident of residence or of place in the social scale. The power to guess the unseen from the seen, to trace the implication of things, to judge the whole piece by the pattern, the condition of feeling life in general so completely that you are well on your way to knowing any particular corner of it—this cluster of gifts may almost be said to constitute experience, and they occur in country and in town, and in the most differing stages of education. If experience consists of impressions, it may be said that impressions *are* experience, just as (have we not seen it?) they are the very air we breathe. Therefore, if I should certainly say to a novice, "Write from experience and experience only," I should feel that this was rather a tantalizing monition if I were not careful immediately to add, "Try to be one of the people on whom nothing is lost!"

I am far from intending by this to minimize the importance of exactness—of truth of detail. One can speak best from one's own taste, and I may therefore venture to say that the air of reality (solidity of specification) seems to me to be the supreme virtue of a novel—the merit on which all its other merits (including that conscious moral purpose of which Mr. Besant speaks) helplessly and submissively depend. If it be not there they are all as nothing, and if these be there, they owe their effect to the success with which the author has produced the illusion of life. The cultivation of this success, the study of this exquisite process, form, to my taste, the beginning and the end of the art of the novelist. They are his inspiration, his despair, his reward, his torment, his delight. It is here in very truth that he competes with life; it is here that he competes with his brother the painter in *his* attempt to render the look of things, the look that conveys their meaning, to catch the colour, the relief, the expression, the surface, the substance of the human spectacle. It is in regard to this that Mr. Besant is well inspired when he bids him take notes. He cannot possibly take too many, he cannot possibly take enough. All life solicits him, and to "render" the simplest surface, to produce the most momentary illusion, is a very complicated business. His case would be easier, and the rule would be more exact, if Mr. Besant had been able to tell him what notes to take. But this, I fear, he can never learn in any manual; it is the business of his life. He has to take a great many in order to select a few, he has to work them up as he can, and even the guides and philosophers who might have most to say to him must leave him alone when it comes to the application of precepts, as we leave the painter in communion with his palette. That his characters "must be clear in outline," as Mr. Besant says—he feels that down to his boots; but how he shall make them so is a secret between his good angel and himself. It would be absurdly simple if he could be taught that a great deal of "description" would make them so, or that on the contrary the absence of description and the cultivation of dialogue, or the absence of dialogue and the multiplication of "incident," would rescue him from his difficulties. Nothing, for instance, is more possible than that he be of a turn of mind for which this odd, literal opposition of description and dialogue, incident and description, has little meaning and light. People often talk of these things as if they had a kind of internecine distinctness, instead of melting into each other at every breath, and being intimately associated parts of one general effort to expression. I cannot imagine composition existing in a series of blocks, nor conceive, in any novel worth discussing at all, of a passage of description that is not in its intention narrative, a passage of dialogue that is not in its intention descriptive, a touch of truth of any sort that does not partake of the nature of incident, or an incident that derives its interest from any other source than the general and only source of the success of a work of art—that of being illustrative. A novel is a living thing, all one and continuous, like any other organism, and in proportion as it lives will it be found, I think, that in each of the parts there is something of each of the other parts. The critic who over the close texture of a finished work shall pretend to trace a geography of items will mark some frontiers as artificial, I fear, as any that have been known to history. There is an old-fashioned distinction between the novel of character and the novel of incident which must have cost many a smile to the intending fabulist who was keen about his work. It appears to me as little to the point as the equally celebrated distinction between the novel and the romance—to answer as little to any reality. There are bad novels and good novels, as there are bad pictures and good pictures; but that is the only distinction in which I see any meaning, and I can as little imagine speaking of a novel of character as I can imagine speaking of a picture of character. When one says picture one says of character, when one says novel one says of incident, and the terms may be transposed at will. What is character but the determination of incident? What is incident but the illustration of character? What is either a picture or a novel that is *not* of character? What else do we seek in it and find in it? It is an incident for a woman to stand up with her hand resting on a table and look out at you in a certain way; or if it be not an incident I think it will be hard to say what it is. At the same time it is an expression of character. If you say you don't see it (character in *that—allons donc!*), this is exactly what the artist who has reasons of his own for thinking he *does* see it undertakes to show you. When a young man makes up his mind that he has not faith enough after all to enter the church as he intended, that is an incident, though you may not hurry to the end of the chapter to see whether perhaps he doesn't change once more. I do not say that these are extraordinary or startling incidents. I do not pretend to estimate the degree of interest proceeding from them, for this will depend upon the skill of the painter. It sounds almost puerile to say that some incidents are intrinsically much more important than others, and I need not take this precaution after having professed my sympathy for the major ones in remarking that the only classification of the novel that I can understand is into that which has life and that which has it not.

The novel and the romance, the novel of incident and that of character—these clumsy separations appear to me to have been made by critics and readers for their own convenience, and to help them out of some of their occasional queer predicaments, but to have little reality or interest for the producer, from whose point of view it is of course that we are attempting to consider the art of fiction. The case is the same with another shadowy category which Mr. Besant apparently is disposed to set up—that of the "modern English novel"; unless indeed it be that in this matter he has fallen into an accidental confusion of standpoints. It is not quite clear whether he intends the remarks in which he alludes to it to be didactic or historical. It is as difficult to suppose a person intending to write a modern English as to suppose him writing an ancient English novel: that is a label which begs the question. One writes the novel, one paints the picture, of one's language and of one's time, and calling it modern English will not, alas! make the difficult task any easier. No more, unfortunately, will calling this or that work of one's fellow-artist a romance—unless it be, of course, simply for the pleasantness of the thing, as for instance when Hawthorne gave this heading to his story of *Blithedale*. The French, who have brought the theory of fiction to remarkable completeness, have but one name for the novel, and have not attempted smaller things in it, that I can see, for that. I can think of no obligation to which the "romancer" would not be held equally with the novelist; the standard of execution is equally high for each. Of course it is of execution that we are talking—that being the only point of a novel that is open to contention. This is perhaps too often lost sight of, only to produce interminable confusions and cross-purposes. We must grant the artist his subject, his idea, his *donnée:* our criticism is applied only to what

THE ART OF FICTION

he makes of it. Naturally I do not mean that we are bound to like it or find it interesting: in case we do not our course is perfectly simple—to let it alone. We may believe that of a certain idea even the most sincere novelist can make nothing at all, and the event may perfectly justify our belief; but the failure will have been a failure to execute, and it is in the execution that the fatal weakness is recorded. If we pretend to respect the artist at all, we must allow him his freedom of choice, in the face, in particular cases, of innumerable presumptions that the choice will not fructify. Art derives a considerable part of its beneficial exercise from flying in the face of presumptions, and some of the most interesting experiments of which it is capable are hidden in the bosom of common things. Gustave Flaubert has written a story about the devotion of a servant-girl to a parrot, and the production, highly finished as it is, cannot on the whole be called a success. We are perfectly free to find it flat, but I think it might have been interesting; and I, for my part, am extremely glad he should have written it; it is a contribution to our knowledge of what can be done—or what cannot. Ivan Turgenieff has written a tale about a deaf and dumb serf and a lap-dog, and the thing is touching, loving, a little masterpiece. He struck the note of life where Gustave Flaubert missed it—he flew in the face of a presumption and achieved a victory.

Nothing, of course, will ever take the place of the good old fashion of "liking" a work of art or not liking it: the most improved criticism will not abolish that primitive, that ultimate test. I mention this to guard myself from the accusation of intimating that the idea, the subject, of a novel or a picture, does not matter. It matters, to my sense, in the highest degree, and if I might put up a prayer it would be that artists should select none but the richest. Some, as I have already hastened to admit, are much more remunerative than others, and it would be a world happily arranged in which persons intending to treat them should be exempt from confusions and mistakes. This fortunate condition will arrive only, I fear, on the same day that critics become purged from error. Meanwhile, I repeat, we do not judge the artist with fairness unless we say to him, "Oh, I grant you your starting-point, because if I did not I should seem to prescribe to you, and heaven forbid I should take that responsibility. If I pretend to tell you what you must not take, you will call upon me to tell you then what you must take; in which case I shall be prettily caught. Moreover, it isn't till I have accepted your data that I can begin to measure you. I have the standard, the pitch; I have no right to tamper with your flute and then criticize your music. Of course I may not care for your idea at all; I may think it silly, or stale, or unclean; in which case I wash my hands of you altogether. I may content myself with believing that you will not have succeeded in being interesting, but I shall, of course, not attempt to demonstrate it, and you will be as indifferent to me as I am to you. I needn't remind you that there are all sorts of tastes: who can know it better? Some people, for excellent reasons, don't like to read about carpenters; others, for reasons even better, don't like to read about courtesans. Many object to Americans. Others (I believe they are mainly editors and publishers) won't look at Italians. Some readers don't like quiet subjects; others don't like bustling ones. Some enjoy a complete illusion, others the consciousness of large concessions. They choose their novels accordingly, and if they don't care about your idea they won't, *a fortiori*, care about your treatment."

So that it comes back very quickly, as I have said, to the liking: in spite of M. Zola, who reasons less powerfully than he represents, and who will not reconcile himself to this absoluteness of taste, thinking that there are certain things that people ought to like, and that they can be made to like. I am quite at a loss to imagine anything (at any rate in this matter of fiction) that people *ought* to like or to dislike. Selection will be sure to take care of itself, for it has a constant motive behind it. That motive is simply experience. As people feel life, so they will feel the art that is most closely related to it. This closeness of relation is what we should never forget in talking of the effort of the novel. Many people speak of it as a factitious, artificial form, a product of ingenuity, the business of which is to alter and arrange the things that surround us, to translate them into conventional, traditional moulds. This, however, is a view of the matter which carries us but a very short way, condemns the art to an eternal repetition of a few familiar *clichés*, cuts short its development, and leads us straight up to a dead wall. Catching the very note and trick, the strange irregular rhythm of life, that is the attempt whose strenuous force keeps Fiction upon her feet. In proportion as in what she offers us we see life *without* rearrangement do we feel that we are touching the truth; in proportion as we see it *with* rearrangement do we feel that we are being put off with a substitute, a compromise and convention. It is not uncommon to hear an extraordinary assurance of remark in regard to this matter of rearranging, which is often spoken of as if it were the last word of art. Mr. Besant seems to me in danger of falling into the great error with his rather unguarded talk about "selection." Art is essentially selection, but it is a selection whose main care is to be typical, to be inclusive. For many people art means rose-coloured window-panes, and selection means picking a bouquet for Mrs. Grundy. They will tell you glibly that artistic considerations have nothing to do with the disagreeable, with the ugly; they will rattle off shallow commonplaces about the province of art and the limits of art till you are moved to some wonder in return as to the province and the limits of ignorance. It appears to me that no one can ever have made a seriously artistic attempt without becoming conscious of an immense increase—a kind of revelation—of freedom. One perceives in that case—by the light of a heavenly ray—that the province of art is all life, all feeling, all observation, all vision. As Mr. Besant so justly intimates, it is all experience. That is a sufficient answer to those who maintain that it must not touch the sad things of life, who stick into its divine unconscious bosom little prohibitory inscriptions on the end of sticks, such as we see in public gardens—"It is forbidden to walk on the grass; it is forbidden to touch the flowers; it is not allowed to introduce dogs or to remain after dark; it is requested to keep to the right." The young aspirant in the line of fiction whom we continue to imagine will do nothing without taste, for in that case his freedom would be of little use to him; but the first advantage of his taste will be to reveal to him the absurdity of the little sticks and tickets. If he have taste, I must add, of course he will have ingenuity, and my disrespectful reference to that quality just now was not meant to imply that it is useless in fiction. But it is only a secondary aid; the first is a capacity for receiving straight impressions.

Mr. Besant has some remarks on the question of "the story" which I shall not attempt to criticize, though they seem to me to contain a singular ambiguity, because I do not think I understand them. I cannot see what is meant by talking as if there were a part of a novel which is the story and part of it which for mystical reasons is not—unless indeed the distinction be made in a sense in which it is difficult to suppose that any one should attempt to convey anything. "The story," if it represents anything, represents the subject, the idea, the *donnée* of the novel; and there is surely no "school"—Mr. Besant speaks of a school—which urges that a novel should be all treatment and no subject. There must assuredly be something to treat; every school is intimately conscious of that. This sense of the story being the idea, the starting-point, of the novel, is the only one that I see in which it can be spoken of as something different from its organic whole; and since in proportion as the work is successful the idea permeates and penetrates it, informs and animates it, so that every word and every punctuation-point contribute directly to the expression, in that proportion do we lose our sense of the story being a blade which may be drawn more or less out of its sheath. The story and the novel, the idea and the form, are the needle and thread, and I never heard of a guild of tailors who recommended the use of the thread without the needle, or the needle without the thread. Mr. Besant is not the only critic who may be observed to have spoken as if there were certain things in life which constitute stories, and certain others which do not. I find the same odd implication in an entertaining article in the *Pall Mall Gazette*, devoted, as it happens, to Mr. Besant's lecture. "The story is the thing!" says this graceful writer, as if with a tone of opposition to some other idea. I should think it was, as every painter who, as the time for "sending in" his picture looms in the distance, finds himself still in quest of a subject—as every belated artist not fixed about his theme will heartily agree. There are some subjects which speak to us and others which do not, but he would be a clever man who should undertake to give a rule—an index expurgatorius—by which the story and the no-story should be known apart. It is impossible (to me at least) to imagine any such rule which shall not be altogether arbitrary. The writer in the *Pall Mall* opposes the delightful (as I suppose) novel of *Margot la Balafrée* to certain tales in which "Bostonian nymphs" appear to have "rejected English dukes for psychological reasons." I am not acquainted with the romance just designated, and can scarcely forgive the *Pall Mall* critic for not mentioning the name of the author, but the title appears to refer to a lady who may have received a scar in some heroic adventure. I am inconsolable at not being acquainted with this episode, but am utterly at a loss to see why it is a story when the rejection (or acceptance) of a duke is not, and why a reason, psychological or other, is not a subject when a cicatrix is. They are all particles of the multitudinous life with which the novel deals, and surely no dogma which pretends to make it lawful to touch the one and unlawful to touch the other will stand for a moment on its feet. It is the special picture that must stand or fall, according as it seem to possess truth or to lack it. Mr. Besant does not, to my sense, light up the subject by intimating that a story must, under penalty of not being a story, consist of "adventures." Why of adventures more than of green spectacles? He mentions a category of impossible things, and among them he places "fiction without adventure." Why without adventure, more than without matrimony, or celibacy, or parturition, or cholera, or hydropathy, or Jansenism? This seems to me to bring the novel back to the hapless little *rôle* of being an artificial, ingenious thing—bring it down from its large, free character of an immense and exquisite correspondence with life. And what *is* adventure, when it comes to that, and by what sign is the listening pupil to recognize it? It is an adventure—an immense one—for me to write this little article; and for a Bostonian nymph to reject an English duke is an adventure only less stirring, I should say, than for an English duke to be rejected by a Bostonian nymph. I see dramas within dramas in that, and innumerable points of view. A psychological reason is, to my imagination, an object adorably pictorial; to catch the tint of its complexion—I feel as if that idea might inspire one to Titianesque efforts. There are few things more exciting to me, in short, than a psychological reason, and yet, I protest, the novel seems to me the most magnificent form of art. I have just been reading, at the same time, the delightful story of *Treasure*

Island, by Mr. Robert Louis Stevenson and, in a manner less consecutive, the last tale from M. Edmond de Goncourt, which is entitled *Chérie.* One of these works treats of murders, mysteries, islands of dreadful renown, hairbreadth escapes, miraculous coincidences and buried doubloons. The other treats of a little French girl who lived in a fine house in Paris, and died of wounded sensibility because no one would marry her. I call *Treasure Island* delightful, because it appears to me to have succeeded wonderfully in what it attempts; and I venture to bestow no epithet upon *Chérie,* which strikes me as having failed deplorably in what it attempts—that is in tracing the development of the moral consciousness of a child. But one of these productions strikes me as exactly as much of a novel as the other, and as having a "story" quite as much. The moral consciousness of a child is as much a part of life as the islands of the Spanish Main, and the one sort of geography seems to me to have those "surprises" of which Mr. Besant speaks quite as much as the other. For myself (since it comes back in the last resort, as I say, to the preference of the individual), the picture of the child's experience has the advantage that I can at successive steps (an immense luxury, near to the "sensual pleasure" of which Mr. Besant's critic in the *Pall Mall* speaks) say Yes or No, as it may be, to what the artist puts before me. I have been a child in fact, but I have been on a quest for a buried treasure only in supposition, and it is a simple accident that with M. de Goncourt I should have for the most part to say No. With George Eliot, when she painted that country with a far other intelligence, I always said Yes.

The most interesting part of Mr. Besant's lecture is unfortunately the briefest passage—his very cursory allusion to the "conscious moral purpose" of the novel. Here again it is not very clear whether he be recording a fact or laying down a principle; it is a great pity that in the latter case he should not have developed his idea. This branch of the subject is of immense importance, and Mr. Besant's few words point to considerations of the widest reach, not to be lightly disposed of. He will have treated the art of fiction but superficially who is not prepared to go every inch of the way that these considerations will carry him. It is for this reason that at the beginning of these re-

marks I was careful to notify the reader that my reflections on
so large a theme have no pretension to be exhaustive. Like Mr.
Besant, I have left the question of the morality of the novel till
the last, and at the last I find I have used up my space. It is a
question surrounded with difficulties, as witness the very first
that meets us, in the form of a definite question, on the threshold. Vagueness, in such a discussion, is fatal, and what is the
meaning of your morality and your conscious moral purpose?
Will you not define your terms and explain how (a novel being
a picture) a picture can be either moral or immoral? You wish
to paint a moral picture or carve a moral statue: will you not
tell us how you would set about it? We are discussing the Art
of Fiction; questions of art are questions (in the widest sense) of
execution; questions of morality are quite another affair, and
will you not let us see how it is that you find it so easy to mix
them up? These things are so clear to Mr. Besant that he has de-
duced from them a law which he sees embodied in English Fiction, and which is "a truly admirable thing and a great cause
for congratulation." It is a great cause for congratulation indeed when such thorny problems become as smooth as silk. I
may add that in so far as Mr. Besant perceives that in point of
fact English Fiction has addressed itself preponderantly to
these delicate questions he will appear to many people to have
made a vain discovery. They will have been positively struck,
on the contrary, with the moral timidity of the usual English
novelist; with his (or with her) aversion to face the difficulties
with which on every side the treatment of reality bristles. He is
apt to be extremely shy (whereas the picture that Mr. Besant
draws is a picture of boldness), and the sign of his work, for the
most part, is a cautious silence on certain subjects. In the English novel (by which of course I mean the American as well),
more than in any other, there is a traditional difference between
that which people know and that which they agree to admit
that they know, that which they see and that which they speak
of, that which they feel to be a part of life and that which they
allow to enter into literature. There is the great difference, in
short, between what they talk of in conversation and what they
talk of in print. The essence of moral energy is to survey the
whole field, and I should directly reverse Mr. Besant's remark

and say not that the English novel has a purpose, but that it has a diffidence. To what degree a purpose in a work of art is a source of corruption I shall not attempt to inquire; the one that seems to me least dangerous is the purpose of making a perfect work. As for our novel, I may say lastly on this score that as we find it in England today it strikes me as addressed in a large degree to "young people," and that this in itself constitutes a presumption that it will be rather shy. There are certain things which it is generally agreed not to discuss, not even to mention, before young people. That is very well, but the absence of discussion is not a symptom of the moral passion. The purpose of the English novel—"a truly admirable thing, and a great cause for congratulation"—strikes me therefore as rather negative.

There is one point at which the moral sense and the artistic sense lie very near together; that is in the light of the very obvious truth that the deepest quality of a work of art will always be the quality of the mind of the producer. In proportion as that intelligence is fine will the novel, the picture, the statue partake of the substance of beauty and truth. To be constituted of such elements is, to my vision, to have purpose enough. No good novel will ever proceed from a superficial mind; that seems to me an axiom which, for the artist in fiction, will cover all needful moral ground: if the youthful aspirant take it to heart it will illuminate for him many of the mysteries of "purpose." There are many other useful things that might be said to him, but I have come to the end of my article, and can only touch them as I pass. The critic in the *Pall Mall Gazette,* whom I have already quoted, draws attention to the danger, in speaking of the art of fiction, of generalizing. The danger that he has in mind is rather, I imagine, that of particularizing, for there are some comprehensive remarks which, in addition to those embodied in Mr. Besant's suggestive lecture, might without fear of misleading him be addressed to the ingenuous student. I should remind him first of the magnificence of the form that is open to him, which offers to sight so few restrictions and such innumerable opportunities. The other arts, in comparison, appear confined and hampered; the various conditions under which they are exercised are so rigid and definite. But the only condition that I can think of attaching to the composition of the novel is, as I have already said, that it be sincere. This freedom is a splendid privilege, and the first lesson of the young novelist is to learn to be worthy of it. "Enjoy it as it deserves," I should say to him; "take possession of it, explore it to its utmost extent, publish it, rejoice in it. All life belongs to you, and do not listen either to those who would shut you up into corners of it and tell you that it is only here and there that art inhabits, or to those who would persuade you that this heavenly messenger wings her way outside of life altogether, breathing a superfine air, and turning away her head from the truth of things. There is no impression of life, no manner of seeing it and feeling it, to which the plan of the novelist may not offer a place; you have only to remember that talents so dissimilar as those of Alexandre Dumas and Jane Austen, Charles Dickens and Gustave Flaubert have worked in this field with equal glory. Do not think too much about optimism and pessimism; try and catch the colour of life itself. In France to-day we see a prodigious effort (that of Emile Zola, to whose solid and serious work no explorer of the capacity of the novel can allude without respect), we see an extraordinary effort vitiated by a spirit of pessimism on a narrow basis. M. Zola is magnificent, but he strikes an English reader as ignorant; he has an air of working in the dark; if he had as much light as energy, his results would be of the highest value. As for the aberrations of a shallow optimism, the ground (of English fiction especially) is strewn with their brittle particles as with broken glass. If you must indulge in conclusions, let them have the taste of a wide knowledge. Remember that your first duty is to be as complete as possible—to make as perfect a work. Be generous and delicate and pursue the prize."

From
The Question of Our Speech

"Our national use of vocal sound, in men
and women alike, *is* slovenly."

Appleton's Booklover's Magazine, *August 1905. "The
Question of Our Speech" was delivered in 1905 as
the Bryn Mawr College commencement address during the American tour of 1904–1905. In this quietly
hammering lecture, James aims to correct the careless
speech patterns and unappealing "tonal quality" of
the young American woman. As Leon Edel notes in
Henry James: The Master, the lecture raised controversy. Letters to the editor objected to James's own
overly complex language, and Woodrow Wilson, then
president of Princeton University, declared a preference for the direct prose of the American newspaper
over the novelist's "laborious" style.*

These truths, you see, are incontestable; yet though you are
daughters, fortunate in many respects, of great common-
wealths that have been able to render you many attentions, to
surround you with most of the advantages of peace and plenty,
it is none the less definite that there will have been felt to reign
among you, in general, no positive mark whatever, public or
private, of an effective consciousness of any of them; the consciousness, namely—a sign of societies truly possessed of light—
that no civilized body of men and women has ever left so vital
an interest to run wild, to shift, as we say, all for itself, to stumble and flounder, through mere adventure and accident, in the
common dust of life, to pick up a living, in fine, by the wayside
and the ditch. Of the degree in which a society is civilized the
vocal form, the vocal tone, the personal, social accent and

sound of its intercourse, have always been held to give a direct reflection. That sound, that vocal form, the touchstone of manners, is the note, the representative note—representative of its having (in our poor, imperfect human degree) achieved civilization. Judged in this light, it must frankly be said, our civilization remains strikingly *un*achieved: the last of American idiosyncrasies, the last by which we can be conceived as "represented" in the international concert of culture, would be the pretension to a tone-standard, to our wooing comparison with that of other nations. The French, the Germans, the Italians, the English perhaps in particular, and many other people, Occidental and Oriental, I surmise, not excluding the Turks and the Chinese, have for the symbol of education, of civility, a tone-standard; we alone flourish in undisturbed and—as in the sense of so many other of our connections—in something like sublime unconsciousness of any such possibility.

It is impossible, in very fact, to have a tone-standard without the definite preliminary of a *care* for tone, and against a care for tone, it would very much appear, the elements of life in this country, as at present conditioned, violently and increasingly militate. At one or two reasons for this strange but consummate conspiracy I shall in a moment ask you to glance with me, but in the meanwhile I should go any length in agreeing with you about any such perversity, on the part of parents and guardians, pastors and masters, as their expecting the generations, whether of young women or young men, to arrive at a position of such comparative superiority alone—unsupported and unguided. There is no warrant for the placing on these inevitably rather light heads and hearts, on any company of you, assaulted, in our vast vague order, by many pressing wonderments, the *whole* of the burden of a care for tone. A care for tone is part of a care for many other things besides; for the fact, for the value, of good breeding, above all, as to which tone unites with various other personal, social signs to bear testimony. The idea of good breeding—without which intercourse fails to flower into fineness, without which human relations bear but crude and tasteless fruit—is one of the most precious conquests of civilization, the very core of our social heritage; but in the transmission of which it becomes us much more to be active and interested than merely passive and irresponsible participants. It is an idea, the idea of good breeding (in other words, simply the idea of *secure* good manners), for which, always, in every generation, there is yet more, and yet more, to be done; and no danger would be more lamentable than that of the real extinction, in our hands, of so sacred a flame. Flames, however, even the most sacred, do not go on burning of themselves; they require to be kept up; handed on the torch needs to be from one group of patient and competent watchers to another. The possibility, the preferability, of people's speaking as people speak when their speech has had for them a signal importance, is a matter to be kept sharply present; from that comes support, comes example, comes authority—from that comes the inspiration of those comparative beginners of life, the hurrying children of time, who are but too exposed to be worked upon, by a hundred circumstances, in a different and inferior sense. You don't speak soundly and agreeably, you don't speak neatly and consistently, unless you *know* how you speak, how you may, how you should, how you shall speak, unless you have discriminated, unless you have noticed differences and suffered from violations and vulgarities; and you have not this positive consciousness, you are incapable of any reaction of taste or sensibility worth mentioning, unless a great deal of thought of the matter has been taken *for* you.

Taking thought, in this connection, is what I mean by obtaining a tone-standard—a clear criterion of the best usage and example: which is but to recognize, once for all, that avoiding vulgarity, arriving at lucidity, pleasantness, charm, and contributing by the mode and the degree of utterance a colloquial, a genial value even to an inevitably limited quantity of intention, of thought, is an art to be acquired and cultivated, just as much as any of the other, subtler, arts of life. There are plenty of influences round about us that make for an imperfect disengagement of the human side of vocal sound, that make for the confused, the ugly, the flat, the thin, the mean, the helpless, that reduce articulation to an easy and ignoble minimum, and so keep it as little distinct as possible from the grunting, the squealing, the barking or the roaring of animals. I do not mean to say that civility of utterance may not become an all but unconscious beautiful habit—I mean to say, thank goodness, that this is exactly what it *may* become. But so to succeed it must be a collective and associated habit; for the greater the number of persons speaking well, in given conditions, the more that number will tend to increase, and the smaller the number the more that number will tend to shrink and lose itself in the desert of the common. Contact and communication, a beneficent contagion, bring about the happy state—the state of sensibility to tone, the state of recognizing, and responding to, certain vocal sounds *as* tone, and recognizing and reacting from certain others as negations of tone: negations the more offensive in proportion as they have most enjoyed impunity. You will have, indeed, in any at all aspiring cultivation of tone, a vast mass of assured impunity, of immunity on the wrong side of the line, to reckon with. There are in every quarter, in our social order, impunities of aggression and corruption in plenty; but there are none, I think, showing so unperturbed a face—wearing, I should slangily say, if slang were permitted me here, so impudent a "mug"—as the forces assembled to make you believe that no form of speech is provably better than another, and that just this matter of "care" is an affront to the majesty of sovereign ignorance. Oh, I don't mean to say that you will find in the least a clear field and nothing but favor! The difficulty of your case is exactly the ground of my venturing thus to appeal to you. That there is difficulty, that there is a great blatant, blowing dragon to slay, can only constitute, as it appears to me, a call of honor for generous young minds, something of a trumpet-sound for tempers of high courage.

*   *   *   *   *

Our national use of vocal sound, in men and women alike, *is* slovenly—an absolutely inexpert daub of unapplied tone. It leaves us at the mercy of a medium that, as I say, is incomplete; which sufficiently accounts, as regards our whole vocal manifestation, for the effect of a want of finish. Noted sounds have their extent and their limits, their mass, however concentrated, and their edges; and what is the speech of a given society but a series, a more or less rich complexity, of noted sounds? Nothing is commoner than to see throughout our country, young persons of either sex—for the phenomenon is most marked, I think, for reasons I will touch on, in the newer generations— whose utterance can only be indicated by pronouncing it destitute of any approach to an emission of the consonant. It becomes thus a mere helpless slobber of disconnected vowel noises—the weakest and cheapest attempt at human expression that we shall easily encounter, I imagine, in any community pretending to the general instructed state. Observe, too, that the vowel sounds in themselves, at this rate, quite fail of any purity, for the reason that our consonants contribute to the drawing and modeling of our vowels—just as our vowels contribute to the coloring, to the painting, as we may call it, of our consonants, and that any frequent repetition of a vowel depending for all rounding and shaping on another vowel alone lays upon us an effort of the thorax under which we inevitably break down. Hence the undefined noises that I refer to when consonantal sound drops out; drops as it drops, for example, among those vast populations to whose lips, to whose ear, it is so rarely given to form the terminal letter of our "Yes," or to hear it formed. The abject "Yeh-eh" (the ugliness of the drawl is not easy to represent) which usurps the place of that interesting vocable makes its nearest approach to deviating into the decency of a final consonant when it becomes a still more questionable "Yeh-ep."

Vast numbers of people, indeed, even among those who speak very badly, appear to grope instinctively for some restoration of the missing value even at the cost of inserting it between words that begin and end with vowels. You will perfectly hear persons supposedly "cultivated," the very instructors of youth sometimes themselves, talk of vanilla-r-ice-cream, of California-r-oranges, of Cuba-r-and Porto Rico, of Atalanta-r- in Calydon, and (very resentfully) of "the idea-r-of" any intimation that their performance and example in these respects may not be immaculate. You will perfectly hear the sons and daughters of the most respectable families disfigure in this interest, and for this purpose, the pleasant old names of Papa and Mamma. "Is Popper-up stairs?" and "is Mommer-in the parlor?" pass for excellent household speech in millions of honest homes. If the English say throughout, and not only sometimes, Papa and

Mama, and the French say Papa and Maman, they say them consistently—and Popper, with an "r," but illustrates our loss, much to be regretted, alas, of the power to emulate the clearness of the vowel-cutting, an art as delicate in its way as gemcutting, in the French word. You will, again, perfectly hear a gentle hostess, solicitous for your comfort, tell you that if you wish to lie down there is a sofa-r-in your room. No one is "thought any the worse of" for saying these things; even though it be distinct that there are circles, in other communities, the societies still keeping the touchstone of manners, as I have called our question, in its place, where they would be punctually noted. It is not always a question of an *r*, however—though the letter, I grant, gets terribly little rest among those great masses of our population who strike us, in the boundless West perhaps especially, as, under some strange impulse received toward consonantal recovery of balance, making it present even in words from which it is absent, bringing it in everywhere as with the small vulgar effect of a sort of morose grinding of the back teeth. There are, you see, sounds of a mysterious intrinsic meanness, and there are sounds of a mysterious intrinsic frankness and sweetness; and I think the recurrent note I have indicated—fatherr and motherr and otherr, waterr and matterr and scatterr, harrd and barrd, parrt, starrt, and (dreadful to say) arrt (the repetition it is that drives home the ugliness), are signal specimens of what becomes of a custom of utterance out of which the principle of taste has dropped.

From
The Lesson of Balzac

"plated and burnished and bright"

Atlantic Monthly, August 1905. "The Lesson of Balzac" was first delivered in Philadelphia during the American lecture tour of 1905 ("five or six hundred people in a hall stuffed to suffocation, tho' very large and with perfect audibility, and making for a 'literary address' an inevitably rather false and 'fashionable' milieu"). The first of James's five essays on Balzac had appeared in 1875, the last was to be published in 1913, with his final opus on Balzac filling 120 tightly printed pages in a collected edition. With its aim of presenting the social structure of France at every level, Balzac's La comédie humaine—*over ninety novels in all—is grouped into Studies of Marriage, Studies of Manners, and Studies of Philosophy; it had great influence on James's development.*

He at all events robustly loved the sense of another explored, assumed, assimilated identity—enjoyed it as the hand enjoys the glove when the glove ideally fits. My image indeed is loose; for what he liked was absolutely to get into the constituted consciousness, into all the clothes, gloves and whatever else, into the very skin and bones, of the habited, featured, colored, articulated form of life that he desired to present. How do we know given persons, for any purpose of demonstration, unless we know their situation for themselves, unless we see it from their point of vision, that is from their point of pressing consciousness or sensation?—without our allowing for which there is no appreciation. Balzac loved his Valérie then as Thackeray

did not love his Becky, or his Blanche Amory in "Pendennis."
But his prompting was not to expose her; it could only be, on
the contrary—intensely aware as he was of all the lengths she
might go, and paternally, maternally alarmed about them—to
cover her up and protect her, in the interest of her special genius and freedom. All his impulse was to *la faire valoir*, to give
her all her value, just as Thackeray's attitude was the opposite
one, a desire positively to expose and desecrate poor Becky—to
follow her up, catch her in the act and bring her to shame:
though with a mitigation, an admiration, an inconsequence,
now and then wrested from him by an instinct finer, in his
mind, than the so-called "moral" eagerness. The English writer
wants to make sure, first of all, of your moral judgment; the
French is willing, while it waits a little, to risk, for the sake of
his subject and its interest, your spiritual salvation. Madame
Marneffe, detrimental, fatal as she is, is "exposed," so far as
anything in life, or in art, may be, by the working-out of the situation and the subject themselves; so that when they have done
what they would, what they logically had to, with her, we are
ready to take it from them. We do not feel, very irritatedly, very
lecturedly, in other words with superfluous edification, that she
has been sacrificed. Who can say, on the contrary, that Blanche
Amory, in "Pendennis," with the author's lash about her little
bare white back from the first—who can feel that she has *not*
been sacrificed, or that her little bareness and whiteness, and all
the rest of her, have been, by such a process, presented as they
had a right to demand?

It all comes back, in fine, to that respect for the liberty of the
subject which I should be willing to name as *the* great sign of
the painter of the first order. Such a witness to the human comedy fairly holds his breath for fear of arresting or diverting that
natural license; the witness who begins to breathe so uneasily
in presence of it that his respiration not only warns off the little prowling or playing creature he is supposed to be studying,
but drowns, for our ears, the ingenuous sounds of the animal,
as well as the general, truthful hum of the human scene at
large—this demonstrator has no sufficient warrant for his task.
And if such an induction as this is largely the moral of our renewed glance at Balzac, there is a lesson, of a more essential

sort, I think, folded still deeper within—the lesson that there is no convincing art that is not ruinously expensive. I am unwilling to say, in the presence of such of his successors as George Eliot and Tolstoi and Zola (to name, for convenience, only three of them), that he was the last of the novelists to do the thing handsomely; but I will say that we get the impression at least of his having had more to spend. Many of those who have followed him affect us as doing it, in the vulgar phrase, "on the cheap"; by reason mainly, no doubt, of their having been, all helplessly, foredoomed to cheapness. Nothing counts, of course, in art, but the excellent; nothing exists, however briefly, for estimation, for appreciation, but the superlative—always in its kind; and who shall declare that the severe economy of the vast majority of those apparently emulous of the attempt to "render" the human subject and the human scene proceeds from anything worse than the consciousness of a limited capital? This flourishing frugality operates happily, no doubt—given all the circumstances—for the novelist; but it has had terrible results for the novel, so far as the novel is a form with which criticism may be moved to concern itself. Its misfortune, its discredit, what I have called its bankrupt state among us, is the not unnatural consequence of its having ceased, for the most part, to be artistically interesting. It has become an object of easy manufacture, showing on every side the stamp of the machine; it has become the article of commerce, produced in quantity, and as we so see it we inevitably turn from it, under the rare visitations of the critical impulse, to compare it with those more precious products of the same general nature that we used to think of as belonging to the class of the handmade.

The lesson of Balzac, under this comparison, is extremely various, and I should prepare myself much too large a task were I to attempt a list of the separate truths he brings home. I have to choose among them, and I choose the most important; the three or four that more or less include the others. In reading him over, in opening him almost anywhere to-day, what immediately strikes us is the part assigned by him, in any picture, to the *conditions* of the creatures with whom he is concerned. Contrasted with him other prose painters of life scarce seem to see the conditions at all. He clearly held pretended por-

trayal as nothing, as less than nothing, as a most vain thing, unless it should be, in spirit and intention, the art of complete representation. "Complete" is of course a great word, and there is
no art at all, we are often reminded, that is not on too many
sides an abject compromise. The element of compromise is always there; it is of the essence; we live with it, and it may serve
to keep us humble. The formula of the whole matter is sufficiently expressed perhaps in a reply I found myself once making to an inspired but discouraged friend, a fellow-craftsman
who had declared in his despair that there was no use trying,
that it was a form, the novel, absolutely too difficult. "Too difficult indeed; yet there is one way to master it—which is to pretend consistently that it isn't." We are all of us, all the while,
pretending—as consistently as we can—that it isn't, and
Balzac's great glory is that he pretended hardest. He never had
to pretend so hard as when he addressed himself to that evocation of the medium, that distillation of the natural and social
air, of which I speak, the things that most require on the part of
the painter preliminary possession—so definitely require it
that, terrified at the requisition when conscious of it, many a
painter prefers to beg the whole question. He has thus, this ingenious person, to invent some *other* way of making his characters interesting—some other way, that is, than the arduous
way, demanding so much consideration, of presenting them to
us. They are interesting, in fact, as subjects of fate, the figures
round whom a situation closes, in proportion as, sharing their
existence, we feel where fate comes in and just how it gets at
them. In the void they are not interesting—and Balzac, like Nature herself, abhorred a vacuum. Their situation takes hold of
us because it is theirs, not because it is somebody's, any one's,
that of creatures unidentified. Therefore it is not superfluous
that their identity shall first be established for us, and their adventures, in that measure, have a relation to it, and therewith
an appreciability. There is no such thing in the world as an adventure pure and simple; there is only mine and yours, and his
and hers—it being the greatest adventure of all, I verily think,
just to *be* you or I, just to be he or she. To Balzac's imagination
that was indeed in itself an immense adventure—and nothing
appealed to him more than to show *how* we all are, and how

we are placed and built-in for being so. What befalls us is but
another name for the way our circumstances press upon us—so
that an account of what befalls us is an account of our circumstances.

Add to this, then, that the fusion of all the elements of the
picture, under his hand, is complete—of what people are with
what they do, of what they do with what they are, of the action
with the agents, of the medium with the action, of all the parts
of the drama with each other. Such a production as "Le Père
Goriot" for example, or as "Eugénie Grandet," or as "Le Curé
de Village," has, in respect to this fusion, a kind of inscrutable
perfection. The situation sits shrouded in its circumstances,
and then, by its inner expansive force, emerges from them, the
action marches, to the rich rustle of this great tragic and ironic
train, the embroidered heroic mantle, with an art of keeping together that makes of "Le Père Goriot" in especial a supreme
case of composition, a model of that high virtue that we know
as economy of effect, economy of line and touch. An inveterate
sense of proportion was not, in general, Balzac's distinguishing
mark; but with great talents one has great surprises, and the effect of this large handling of the conditions was more often
than not to make the work, whatever it might be, appear admirably composed. Of all the costly charms of a "story" this
interest derived from composition is the costliest—and there is
perhaps no better proof of our present penury than the fact
that, in general, when one makes a plea for it, the plea might
seemingly (for all it is understood!) be for trigonometry or osteol-
ogy. "Composition?—what may that happen to *be,* and, whatever it is, what has it to do with the matter?" I shall take for
granted here that every one perfectly knows, for without that
assumption I shall not be able to wind up, as I must immediately do. The presence of the conditions, when really presented,
when made vivid, provides for the action—which is, from step
to step, constantly implied in them; whereas the process of suspending the action in the void and dressing it there with the
tinkling bells of what is called dialogue only makes no provision at all for the other interest. There are two elements of the
art of the novelist which, as they present, I think, the greatest
difficulty, tend thereby most to fascinate us: in the first place

that mystery of the foreshortened procession of facts and figures, of appearances of whatever sort, which is in some lights
but another name for the picture governed by the principle of
composition, and which has at any rate as little as possible in
common with the method now usual among us, the juxtaposition of items emulating the column of numbers of a schoolboy's
sum in addition. It is the art of the brush, I know, as opposed
to the art of the slate-pencil; but to the art of the brush the novel
must return, I hold, to recover whatever may be still recoverable
of its sacrificed honor.

The second difficulty that I commend for its fascination, at
all events, the most attaching when met and the most rewarding when triumphantly met—though I hasten to add that it also
strikes me as not only the least "met," in general, but the least
suspected—this second difficulty is that of representing, to put
it simply, the lapse of time, the duration of the subject: representing it, that is, more subtly than by a blank space, or a row
of stars, on the historic page. With the blank space and the row
of stars Balzac's genius had no affinity, and he is therefore as
unlike as possible those narrators—so numerous, all round us,
it would appear, to-day in especial—the succession of whose
steps and stages, the development of whose action, in the given
case, affects us as occupying but a week or two. No one begins,
to my sense, to handle the time-element and produce the time-
effect with the authority of Balzac in his amplest sweeps—by
which I am far from meaning in his longest passages. That
study of the foreshortened image, of the neglect of which I suggest the ill consequence, is precisely the enemy of the tiresome
procession of would-be narrative items, seen all in profile, like
the rail-heads of a fence; a substitute for the baser device of ac-
counting for the time-quantity by mere quantity of statement.
Quality and manner of statement account for it in a finer
way—always assuming, as I say, that unless it is accounted for
nothing else really is. The fashion of our day is to account for
it almost exclusively by an inordinate abuse of the colloquial
resource, of the report, from page to page, from chapter to
chapter, from beginning to end, of the talk, between the persons involved, in which situation and action may be conceived
as registered. Talk between persons is perhaps, of all the parts

of the novelist's plan, the part that Balzac most scrupulously weighed and measured and kept in its place; judging it, I think—though he perhaps even had an undue suspicion of its possible cheapness, as feeling it the thing that can least afford to be cheap—a precious and supreme resource, the very flower of illustration of the subject and thereby not to be inconsiderately discounted. It was his view, discernibly, that the flower must keep its bloom, or in other words not to be too much handled, in order to have a fragrance when nothing but its fragrance will serve.

It was his view indeed positively that there is a *law* in these things, and that, admirable for illustration, functional for illustration, dialogue has its function perverted, and therewith its life destroyed, when forced, all clumsily, into the constructive office. It is in the drama, of course, that it is constructive; but the drama lives by a law so different, verily, that everything that is right for it seems wrong for the prose picture, and everything that is right for the prose picture addressed directly, in turn, to the betrayal of the "play." These are questions, however, that bore deep—if I have successfully braved the danger that they absolutely do bore; so that I must content myself, as a glance at this point, with the claim for the author of "Le Père Goriot" that colloquial illustration, in his work, suffers less, on the whole, than in any other I know, from its attendant, its besetting and haunting penalty of springing, unless watched, a leak in its effect. It is as if the master of the ship were keeping his eye on the pump; the pump, I mean, of relief and alternation, the pump that keeps the vessel free of too much water. We must always remember that, save in the cases where "dialogue" is organic, is the very law of the game—in which case, as I say, the game is another business altogether—it is essentially the fluid element: as, for instance (to cite, conveniently, Balzac's most eminent prose contemporary), was strikingly its character in the elder Dumas; just as its character in the younger, the dramatist, illustrates supremely what I call the other game. The current, in old Dumas, the large, loose, facile flood of talked movement, talked interest, as much as you will, is, in virtue of this fluidity, a current indeed, with so little of wrought texture that we float and splash in it; feeling it thus resemble much more some capacious tepid tank than the figured tapestry, all over-scored with objects in fine perspective, which symbolizes to me (if one may have a symbol) the last word of the achieved fable. Such a tapestry, with its wealth of expression of its subject, with its myriad ordered stitches, its harmonies of tone and felicities of taste, is a work, above all, of closeness—and therefore the more pertinent image here as it is in the name of closeness that I am inviting you to let Balzac once more appeal to you.

It will strike you perhaps that I speak as if we all, as if you all, without exception were novelists, haunting the back shop, the laboratory, or, more nobly expressed, the inner shrine of the temple; but such assumptions, in this age of print—if I may not say this age of poetry—are perhaps never too wide of the mark, and I have at any rate taken your interest sufficiently for granted to ask you to close up with me for an hour at the feet of the master of us all. Many of us may stray, but he always remains—he is fixed by virtue of his weight. Do not look too knowing at that—as a hint that you were already conscious he is heavy, and that if this is what I have mainly to suggest my lesson might have been spared. He is, I grant, too heavy to be moved; many of us may stray and straggle, as I say—since we have not his inaptitude largely to circulate. There is none the less such an odd condition as circulating without motion, and I am not so sure that even in our own way we do move. We do not, at any rate, get away from him; he is behind us, at the worst, when he is not before, and I feel that any course about the country we explore is ever best held by keeping him, through the trees of the forest, in sight. So far as we do move, we move round him; every road comes back to him; he sits there, in spite of us, so massively, for orientation. "Heavy" therefore if we like, but heavy because weighted with his fortune; the extraordinary fortune that has survived all the extravagance of his career, his twenty years of royal intellectual spending, and that has done so by reason of the rare value of the original property—the high, prime genius so tied-up from him that that was safe. And "that," through all that has come and gone, has steadily, has enormously appreciated. Let us then also, if we see him, in the sacred grove, as our towering idol, see him as gilded thick, with so much gold—plated and burnished and bright, in the manner of towering idols. It is for the lighter and looser and poorer among us to be gilded thin!

On Shakespeare

the "absolute value of Style"

From "Introduction to The Tempest," *in* The Complete Works of William Shakespeare, *ed. Sidney Lee, 1907. Before the publication of this essay James had never provided more than a passing commentary on Shakespeare, and yet the curiosity of this "introduction" is that it scarcely mentions the play itself or the figures of Prospero, Miranda, Ariel, or Caliban. The focus is on two potentially self-referential issues, the richness of Shakespeare's style and "the abrupt stoppage of his pulse after* The Tempest"—*the mysterious fact that after that play Shakespeare lived another five years and yet apparently wrote no more. When James wrote this essay, his last completed novel,* The Golden Bowl, *was three years behind him; in his case, however, he continued to produce important work in nonfiction genres.*

The man himself, in the Plays, we directly touch, to my consciousness, positively nowhere: we are dealing too perpetually with the artist, the monster and magician of a thousand masks, not one of which we feel him drop long enough to gratify with the breath of the interval that strained attention in us which would be yet, so quickened, ready to become deeper still. Here at last the artist is, comparatively speaking, so generalised, so consummate and typical, so frankly amused with himself, that is with his art, with his power, with his theme, that it is as if he came to meet us more than his usual half-way, and as if, thereby, in meeting *him,* and touching him, we were nearer to meeting and touching the man. The man everywhere, in Shake-speare's work, is so effectually locked up and imprisoned in the artist that we but hover at the base of thick walls for a sense of him; while, in addition, the artist is so steeped in the abysmal objectivity of his characters and situations that the great billows of the medium itself play with him, to our vision, very much as, over a ship's side, in certain waters, we catch, through transparent tides, the flash of strange sea-creatures. What we are present at in this fashion is a series of incalculable plunges—the series of those that have taken effect, I mean, after the great primary plunge, made once for all, of the man into the artist: the successive plunges of the artist himself into Romeo and into Juliet, into Shylock, Hamlet, Macbeth, Coriolanus, Cleopatra, Antony, Lear, Othello, Falstaff, Hotspur; immersions during which, though he always ultimately finds his feet, the very violence of the movements involved troubles and distracts our sight. In The Tempest, by the supreme felicity I speak of, is no violence; he sinks as deep as we like, but what he sinks into, beyond all else, is the lucid stillness of his style.

One can speak, in these matters, but from the impression determined by one's own inevitable standpoint; again and again, at any rate, such a masterpiece puts before me the very act of the momentous conjunction taking place for the poet, at a given hour, between his charged inspiration and his clarified experience: or, as I should perhaps better express it, between his human curiosity and his aesthetic passion. Then, if he happens to have been, all his career, with his equipment for it, more or less the victim and the slave of the former, he yields, by way of a change, to the impulse of allowing the latter, for a magnificent moment, the upper hand. The human curiosity, as I call it, is always there—with no more need of making provision for it than use in taking precautions against it; the surrender to the luxury of expertness may therefore go forward on its own conditions. I can offer no better description of The Tempest as fresh re-perusal lights it for me than as such a surrender, sublimely enjoyed; and I may frankly say that, under this impression of it, there is no refinement of the artistic consciousness that I do not see my way—or feel it, better, perhaps, since we but grope, at the best, in our darkness—to attribute to the author. It is a way that one follows to the end, because it is a road, I repeat, on which one least misses some glimpse of him face to face. If it be true that the thing was concocted to meet a particular demand, that of the master of the King's revels, with his prescription of date, form, tone and length, this, so far from interfering with the Poet's perception of a charming opportunity to taste for *himself,* for himself above all, and as he had almost never so tasted, not even in A Midsummer Night's Dream, of the quality of his mind and the virtue of his skill, would have exceedingly favoured the happy case. Innumerable one may always suppose these delicate debates and intimate understandings of an artist with himself. "How much *taste,* in the world, may I conceive that I have?—and what a charming idea to snatch a moment for finding out! What moment could be better than this—a bridal evening before the Court, with extra candles and the handsomest company—if I can but put my hand on the right 'scenario'?" We can catch, across the ages, the searching sigh and the look about; we receive the stirred breath of the ripe, amused genius; and, stretching, as I admit I do at least, for a still closer conception of the beautiful crisis, I find it pictured for me in some such presentment as that of a divine musician who, alone in his room, preludes or improvises at close of day. He sits at the harpsichord, by the open window, in the summer dusk; his hands wander over the keys. They stray far, for his motive, but at last he finds and holds it; then he lets himself go, embroidering and refining: it is the thing for the hour and his mood. The neighbours may gather in the garden, the nightingale be hushed on the bough; it is none the less a private occasion, a concert of one, both performer and auditor, who plays for his own ear, his own hand, his own innermost sense, and for the bliss and capacity of his instrument. Such are the only hours at which the artist *may,* by any measure of his own (too many things, at others, make heavily against it); and their challenge to him is irresistible if he has known, all along, too much compromise and too much sacrifice.

The face that beyond any other, however, I seem to see The Tempest turn to us is the side on which it so superlatively speaks of that endowment for Expression, expression as a primary force, a consuming, an independent passion, which was the greatest ever laid upon man. It is for Shakespeare's power of constitutive speech quite as if he had swum into our ken with it from another planet, gathering it up there, in its wealth, as something antecedent to the occasion and the need, and if possible quite in excess of them; something that was to make of our poor world a great flat table for receiving the glitter and clink of outpoured treasure. The idea and the motive are more often than not so smothered in it that they scarce know themselves, and the resources of such a style, the provision of images, emblems, energies of every sort, laid up in advance, affects us as the storehouse of a king before a famine or a siege—which not only, by its scale, braves depletion or exhaustion, but bursts, through mere excess of quantity or presence, out of all doors and windows. It renders the poverties and obscurities of our world, as I say, in the dazzling terms of a richer and better. It constitutes, by a miracle, more than half the author's material; so much more usually does it happen, for the painter or the poet, that life itself, in its appealing, overwhelming crudity, offers itself as the paste to be kneaded. Such a personage works in general in the very elements of experience; whereas we see Shakespeare working predominantly in the terms of expression, *all* in the terms of the artist's specific vision and genius; with a thicker cloud of images to attest his approach, at any point, than the comparatively meagre given case ever has to attest its own identity. He points for us as no one else the relation of style to meaning and of manner to motive; a matter on which, right and left, we hear such rank ineptitudes uttered. Unless it be true that these things, on either hand, are inseparable; unless it be true that the phrase, the cluster and order of terms, *is* the object and the sense, in as close a compression as that of body and soul, so that any consideration of them as distinct, from the moment style is an active, applied force, becomes a gross stupidity: unless we recognise this reality the author of The Tempest has no lesson for us. It is by his expression of it exactly as the expression stands that the particular thing is created, created as interesting, as beautiful, as strange, droll or terrible—as related, in short, to our understanding or our sensibility; in consequence of which we reduce it to naught when we begin to talk of either of its presented parts as matters by themselves.

All of which considerations indeed take us too far; what it is important to note being simply our Poet's high testimony to this independent, absolute value of Style, and to its need thoroughly to project and seat itself. It had been, as so seating itself, the very home of his mind, for his all too few twenty years; it had been the supreme source to him of the joy of life. It had been in fine his material, his plastic clay; since the more subtly he applied it the more secrets it had to give him, and the more these secrets might appear to him, at every point, one with the lights and shades of the human picture, one with the myriad pulses of the spirit of man. Thus it was that, as he passed from one application of it to another, tone became, for all its suggestions, more and more sovereign to him, and the subtlety of its secrets an exquisite interest. If I see him, at the last, over The Tempest, as the composer, at the harpsichord or the violin, extemporising in the summer twilight, it is exactly that he is feeling there for tone and by the same token, finding it—finding it as The Tempest, beyond any register of ours, immortally gives it. This surrender to the highest sincerity of virtuosity, as we nowadays call it, is to my perception *all* The Tempest; with no possible depth or delicacy in it that such an imputed character does not cover and provide for. The subject to be treated was the simple fact (if one may call anything in the matter simple) that refinement, selection, economy, the economy not of poverty, but of wealth a little weary of congestion—the very air of the lone island and the very law of the Court celebration—were here implied and imperative things. Anything was a subject, always, that offered to sight an aperture of size enough for expression and its train to pass in and deploy themselves. If they filled up all the space, none the worse; they occupied it as nothing else could do. The subjects of the Comedies are, without exception, old wives' tales—which we are not too insufferably aware of only because the iridescent veil so perverts their proportions. The subjects of the Histories are no subjects at all; each is but a row of pegs for the hanging of the cloth of gold that is to muffle them. Such a thing as The Merchant of Venice declines, for very shame, to be reduced to its elements of witless "story"; such things as the two Parts of Henry the Fourth form no more than a straight convenient channel for the procession of evoked images that is to pour through it like a torrent. Each of these productions is none the less of incomparable splendour; by which splendour we are bewildered till we see how it comes. Then we see that every inch of it is personal tone, or in other words brooding expression raised to the highest energy. Push such energy far enough—far enough if you can!—and, being what it is, it then inevitably provides for Character. Thus we see character, in every form of which the "story" gives the thinnest hint, marching through the pieces I have named in its habit as it lives, and so filling out the scene that nothing is missed. The "story" in The Tempest is a thing of naught, for any story will provide a remote island, a shipwreck and a coincidence. Prospero and Miranda, awaiting their relatives, are, in the present case, for the relatives, the coincidence—just as the relatives are the coincidence for them. Ariel and Caliban, and the island-airs and island-scents, and all the rest of the charm and magic and the ineffable delicacy (a delicacy positively at its highest in the conception and execution of Caliban) are the style handed over to its last disciplined passion of curiosity; a curiosity which flowers, at this pitch, into the freshness of each of the characters.

From
the Preface to Roderick Hudson

"Really, universally, relations stop nowhere"

The Preface to Roderick Hudson, *volume I,* The Novels and Tales of Henry James, *New York: Scribners, 1907. As the first of the eighteen prefaces to the popularly termed* New York Edition *addresses the "exquisite problem of the artist," James notes he will be making many changes in the texts—"reading over, for revision, correction and republication, the volumes here in hand."*

"Roderick Hudson" was begun in Florence in the spring of 1874, designed from the first for serial publication in "The Atlantic Monthly," where it opened in January 1875 and persisted through the year. I yield to the pleasure of placing these circumstances on record, as I shall place others, and as I have yielded to the need of renewing acquaintance with the book after a quarter of a century. This revival of an all but extinct relation with an early work may often produce for an artist, I think, more kinds of interest and emotion than he shall find it easy to express, and yet will light not a little, to his eyes, that veiled face of his Muse which he is condemned for ever and all anxiously to study. The art of representation bristles with questions the very terms of which are difficult to apply and to appreciate; but whatever makes it arduous makes it, for our refreshment, infinite, causes the practice of it, with experience, to spread around us in a widening, not in a narrowing circle. Therefore it is that experience has to organise, for convenience and cheer, some system of observation—for fear, in the admirable immensity, of losing its way. We see it as pausing from time to time to consult its notes, to measure, for guidance, as many aspects and distances as possible, as many steps taken and obstacles mastered and fruits gathered and beauties enjoyed. Everything counts, nothing is superfluous in such a survey; the explorer's note-book strikes me here as endlessly receptive. This accordingly is what I mean by the contributive value—or put it simply as, to one's own sense, the beguiling charm—of the *accessory* facts in a given artistic case. This is why, as one looks back, the private history of any sincere work, however modest its pretensions, looms with its own completeness in the rich, ambiguous aesthetic air, and seems at once to borrow a dignity and to mark, so to say, a station. This is why, reading over, for revision, correction and republication, the volumes here in hand, I find myself, all attentively, in presence of some such recording scroll or engraved commemorative table—from which the "private" character, moreover, quite insists on dropping out. These notes represent, over a considerable course, the continuity of an artist's endeavour, the growth of his whole operative consciousness and, best of all, perhaps, their own tendency to multiply, with the implication, thereby, of a memory much enriched. Addicted to "stories" and inclined to retrospect, he fondly takes, under this backward view, his whole unfolding, his process of production, for a thrilling tale, almost for a wondrous adventure, only asking himself at what stage of remembrance the mark of the relevant will begin to fail. He frankly proposes to take this mark everywhere for granted.

"Roderick Hudson" was my first attempt at a novel, a long fiction with a "complicated" subject, and I recall again the quite uplifted sense with which my idea, such as it was, permitted me at last to put quite out to sea. I had but hugged the shore on sundry previous small occasions; bumping about, to acquire skill, in the shallow waters and sandy coves of the "short story" and master as yet of no vessel constructed to carry a sail. The subject of "Roderick" figured to me vividly this employment of canvas, and I have not forgotten, even after long years, how the blue southern sea seemed to spread immediately before me and the breath of the spice-islands to be already in the breeze. Yet it must even then have begun for me too, the ache of fear, that was to become so familiar, of being unduly tempted and led on by "developments"; which is but the desperate discipline of the question involved in them. They are of the very essence of the novelist's process, and it is by their aid, fundamentally, that his idea takes form and lives; but they impose on him, through the principle of continuity that rides them, a proportionate anxiety. They are the very condition of interest, which languishes and drops without them; the painter's subject consisting ever, obviously, of the related state, to each other, of certain figures and things. To exhibit these relations, once they have all been recognised, is to "treat" his idea, which involves neglecting none of those that directly minister to interest; the degree of that directness remaining meanwhile a matter of highly difficult appreciation, and one on which felicity of form and composition, as a part of the total effect, mercilessly rests. Up to what point is such and such a development *indispensable* to the interest? What is the point beyond which it ceases to be rigorously so? Where, for the complete expression of one's subject, does a particular relation stop—giving way to some other not concerned in that expression?

Really, universally, relations stop nowhere, and the exquisite problem of the artist is eternally but to draw, by a geometry of his own, the circle within which they shall happily *appear* to do so. He is in the perpetual predicament that the continuity of things is the whole matter, for him, of comedy and tragedy; that this continuity is never, by the space of an instant or an inch, broken, and that, to do anything at all, he has at once intensely to consult and intensely to ignore it. All of which will perhaps pass but for a supersubtle way of pointing the plain moral that a young embroiderer of the canvas of life soon began to work in terror, fairly, of the vast expanse of that surface, of the boundless number of its distinct perforations for the needle, and of the tendency inherent in his many-coloured flowers and figures to cover and consume as many as possible of the little holes. The development of the flower, of the figure, involved thus an immense counting of holes and a careful selection among them. That would have been, it seemed to him, a brave enough process, were it not the very nature of the holes so to invite, to solicit, to persuade, to practise positively a thousand lures and deceits. The prime effect of so sustained a system, so prepared a surface, is to lead on and on; while the fascination of following resides, by the same token, in the presumability *somewhere* of a convenient, of a visibly-appointed stopping-place. Art would be easy indeed if, by a fond power disposed to "patronise" it, such conveniences, such simplifications, had been provided. We have, as the case stands, to invent and establish them, to arrive at them by a difficult, dire process of selection and comparison, of surrender and sacrifice. The very meaning of expertness is acquired courage to brace one's self for the cruel crisis from the moment one sees it grimly loom.

From
the Preface to The Portrait of a Lady

"The house of fiction has in short
not one window, but a million"

The Preface to The Portrait of a Lady, *volume III,*
The Novels and Tales of Henry James, New York:
Scribners, 1908. In an undated notebook entry, prob-
ably of late 1880 or early 1881, James had recognized
that the "obvious criticism of course will be that I
have not seen the heroine to the end of her situation—
that I have left her en l'air.*—This is both true and*
false. The whole of anything is never told; you can
only take what groups together." Almost thirty years
later he asserts "all the varieties of outlook on life,"
as he continues to resist demands for a rigidly pre-
scribed fictional structure.

The house of fiction has in short not one window, but a million—a number of possible windows not to be reckoned,
rather; every one of which has been pierced, or is still pierce-
able, in its vast front, by the need of the individual vision and
by the pressure of the individual will. These apertures, of dissimilar shape and size, hang so, all together, over the human
scene that we might have expected of them a greater sameness
of report than we find. They are but windows at the best, mere
holes in a dead wall, disconnected, perched aloft; they are not
hinged doors opening straight upon life. But they have this
mark of their own that at each of them stands a figure with a
pair of eyes, or at least with a field-glass, which forms, again
and again, for observation, a unique instrument, insuring to
the person making use of it an impression distinct from every
other. He and his neighbours are watching the same show, but

one seeing more where the other sees less, one seeing black where the other sees white, one seeing big where the other sees small, one seeing coarse where the other sees fine. And so on, and so on; there is fortunately no saying on what, for the particular pair of eyes, the window may *not* open; "fortunately" by reason, precisely, of this incalculability of range. The spreading field, the human scene, is the "choice of subject"; the pierced aperture, either broad or balconied or slit-like and low-browed, is the "literary form"; but they are, singly or together, as nothing without the posted presence of the watcher—without, in other words, the consciousness of the artist. Tell me what the artist is, and I will tell you of what he has *been* conscious. Thereby I shall express to you at once his boundless freedom and his "moral" reference.

All this is a long way round, however, for my word about my dim first move toward "The Portrait," which was exactly my grasp of a single character—an acquisition I had made, moreover, after a fashion not here to be retraced. Enough that I was, as seemed to me, in complete possession of it, that I had been so for a long time, that this had made it familiar and yet had not blurred its charm, and that, all urgently, all tormentingly, I saw it in motion and, so to speak, in transit. This amounts to saying that I saw it as bent upon its fate—some fate or other; *which,* among the possibilities, being precisely the question. Thus I had my vivid individual—vivid, so strangely, in spite of being still at large, not confined by the conditions, not engaged in the tangle, to which we look for much of the impress that constitutes an identity. If the apparition was still all to be placed how came it to be vivid?—since we puzzle such quantities out, mostly, just by the business of placing them. One could answer such a question beautifully, doubtless, if one could do so subtle, if not so monstrous, a thing as to write the history of the growth of one's imagination. One would describe then what, at a given time, had extraordinarily happened to it, and one would so, for instance, be in a position to tell, with an approach to clearness, how, under favour of occasion, it had been able to take over (take over straight from life) such and such a constituted, animated figure or form. The figure has to that extent, as you see, *been* placed—placed in the imagination that detains it, preserves, protects, enjoys it, conscious of its presence in the dusky, crowded, heterogeneous back-shop of the mind very much as a wary dealer in precious odds and ends, competent to make an "advance" on rare objects confided to him, is conscious of the rare little "piece" left in deposit by the reduced, mysterious lady of title or the speculative amateur, and which is already there to disclose its merit afresh as soon as a key shall have clicked in a cupboard-door.

From
the Preface to The Tragic Muse

"large loose baggy monsters"

The Preface to The Tragic Muse, *volume VII,* The Novels and Tales of Henry James, *New York: Scribners, 1908. In a preface particularly concerned with matters of form, and the need for artistic structure, James notes the plaguing defects of immense novels by Thackeray, Dumas, and Tolstoy.*

The more I turn my pieces over, at any rate, the more I now see I must have found in them, and I remember how, once well in presence of my three typical examples, my fear of too ample a canvas quite dropped. The only question was that if I had marked my political case, from so far back, for "a story by itself," and then marked my theatrical case for another, the joining together of these interests, originally seen as separate, might, all disgracefully, betray the seam, show for mechanical and superficial. A story was a story, a picture a picture, and I had a mortal horror of two stories, two pictures, in one. The reason of this was the clearest—my subject was immediately, under that disadvantage, so cheated of its indispensable centre as to become of no more use for expressing a main intention than a wheel without a hub is of use for moving a cart. It was a fact, apparently, that one *had* on occasion seen two pictures in one; were there not for instance certain sublime Tintorettos at Venice, a measureless Crucifixion in especial, which showed without loss of authority half a dozen actions separately taking place? Yes, that might be, but there had surely been nevertheless a mighty pictorial fusion, so that the virtue of composition had somehow thereby come all mysteriously to its own. Of course the affair would be simple enough if composition could be kept out of the question; yet by what art or process, what bars and bolts, what unmuzzled dogs and pointed guns, perform that feat? I had to know myself utterly inapt for any such valour and recognise that, to make it possible, sundry things should have begun for me much further back than I had felt them even in their dawn. A picture without composition slights its most precious chance for beauty, and is moreover not composed at all unless the painter knows *how* that principle of health and safety, working as an absolutely premeditated art, has prevailed. There may in its absence be life, incontestably, as "The Newcomes" has life, as "Les Trois Mousquetaires," as Tolstoi's "Peace and War," have it; but what do such large loose baggy monsters, with their queer elements of the accidental and the arbitrary, artistically *mean?* We have heard it maintained, we well remember, that such things are "superior to art"; but we understand least of all what *that* may mean, and we look in vain for the artist, the divine explanatory genius, who will come to our aid and tell us. There is life and life, and as waste is only life sacrificed and thereby prevented from "counting," I delight in a deep-breathing economy and an organic form. My business was accordingly to "go in" for complete pictorial fusion, some such common interest between my two first notions as would, in spite of their birth under quite different stars, do them no violence at all.

AUTOBIOGRAPHY

Forty years after James's death, *A Small Boy and Others* (1913), *Notes of a Son and Brother* (1914), and the fragmentary *The Middle Years* (1917) were republished as a one-volume *Autobiography*, a title James himself had never used. The title stuck, although James might not have been happy with its assumptions. In 1911 he had complained to H. G. Wells of the "accurst autobiographical form which puts a premium on the loose, the improvised, the cheap & the easy." The habits of the novelist did not die easily, and his "autobiography" has a particularly shrewd and complex structure. Furthermore, the first volume is somewhat ambiguous as to whether the "small boy" of the title is in fact Henry or William James.

Henry James's concern for his privacy, and for his family's privacy, may have further disposed him against work in the genre. When copies of his sister Alice's diary were privately published in 1894, he became "scared and disconcerted—I mean alarmed—by the sight of so many private allusions and names in print." He burned his copy, one of only four published. In 1909 he burned most of the letters he had received over the years, and then in 1915 he destroyed many other personal papers.

Yet if James resisted the form and even the impulse of autobiography, the memoir of his childhood with his sister and brothers, in that wild intellectual house, remains distinguished and often joyous. In her 1924 *Henry James at Work,* his secretary Theodora Bosanquet recalled "the flood of remembrance" when he began a volume on William's early letters—"But an entire volume of memories was finished before bringing William to an age for writing letters, and *A Small Boy* came to a rather abrupt end as a result of the writer's sudden decision that a break must be made at once if the flood of remembrance was not to drown his pious intention." "It was," Bosanquet said, "extraordinarily easy for him to recover the past." Also in 1913, but a few months after *A Small Boy and Others* was published in New York, the first volume of Proust's *À la recherche du temps perdu* was published in Paris.

The peaches d'antan

From A Small Boy and Others, *1913. In* The Portrait
of a Lady *Isabel Archer recalls "a long garden, sloping down to the stable and containing peach-trees of
barely credible familiarity. Isabel had stayed with her
grandmother at various seasons, but somehow all her
visits had a flavour of peaches." Here James recalls
the impression that New York in summer made on
him as a twelve-year-old.*

I should wrong the whole impression if I didn't figure it first
and foremost as that of some vast succulent cornucopia. What
did the stacked boxes and baskets of our youth represent but
the boundless fruitage of that more bucolic age of the American world, and what was after all of so strong an assault as the
rankness of such a harvest? Where is that fruitage now, where
in particular are the peaches *d'antan?* where the mounds of Is-
abella grapes and Seckel pears in the sticky sweetness of which
our childhood seems to have been steeped? It was surely, save
perhaps for oranges, a more informally and familiarly fruit-
eating time, and bushels of peaches in particular, peaches big
and peaches small, peaches white and peaches yellow, played a
part in life from which they have somehow been deposed; every
garden, almost every bush and the very boys' pockets grew
them; they were "cut up" and eaten with cream at every meal;
domestically "brandied" they figured, the rest of the year,
scarce less freely—if they were rather a "party dish" it was because they made the party whenever they appeared, and when
ice-cream was added, or they were added *to* it, they formed the

highest revel we knew. Above all the public heaps of them, the high-piled receptacles at every turn, touched the street as with a sort of southern plenty; the note of the rejected and scattered fragments, the memory of the slippery skins and rinds and kernels with which the old dislocated flags were bestrown, is itself endeared to me and contributes a further pictorial grace. We ate everything in those days by the bushel and the barrel, as from stores that were infinite; we handled watermelons as freely as cocoanuts, and the amount of stomach-ache involved was negligible in the general Eden-like consciousness.

The dancing teacher Madame Dubreil

From A Small Boy and Others, *1913. When they traveled abroad, the James children received a polyglot education, but even in New York their instructors often spoke foreign languages. In the section from which this passage is taken, James describes the New York musical soirées that involved Madame Dubreil and other teachers, as he reports that "Europe, by the stroke, had come to us in such force that we had but to enjoy it on the spot."*

Intenser than these vague shades meanwhile is my vision of the halls of Ferrero—where the orgy of the senses and even the riot of the mind, of which I have just spoken, must quite literally have led me more of a dance than anywhere. Let this sketch of a lost order note withal that under so scant a general provision for infant exercise, as distinguished from infant ease, our hopping and sliding in tune had to be deemed urgent. It was the sense for this form of relief that clearly was general, superseding as the ampler Ferrero scene did previous limited exhibitions; even those, for that matter, coming back to me in the ancient person of M. Charriau—I guess at the writing of his name—whom I work in but confusedly as a professional visitor, a subject gaped at across a gulf of fear, in one of our huddled schools; all the more that I perfectly evoke him as resembling, with a difference or two, the portraits of the aged Voltaire, and that he had, fiddle in hand and *jarret tendu,* incited the young agility of our mother and aunt. Edward Ferrero was another matter; in the prime of life, good-looking, romantic and moustachio'd, he was suddenly to figure, on the outbreak of the Civil War, as a General of volunteers—very much as if he had been one of Bonaparte's improvised young marshals; in anticipation of which, however, he wasn't at all fierce or superior, to my remembrance, but most kind to sprawling youth, in a charming man of the world fashion and as if *we* wanted but a touch to become also men of the world. Remarkably good-looking, as I say, by the measure of that period, and extraordinarily agile—he could so gracefully leap and bound that his bounding into the military saddle, such occasion offering, had all the felicity, and only wanted the pink fleshings, of the circus—he was still more admired by the mothers, with whom he had to my eyes a most elegant relation, than by the pupils; among all of whom, at the frequent and delightful soirées, he caused trays laden with lucent syrups repeatedly to circulate. The scale of these entertainments, as I figured it, and the florid frescoes, just damp though they were with newness, and the free lemonade, and the freedom of remark, equally great, with the mothers, were the lavish note in him—just as the fact that he never himself fiddled, but was followed, over the shining parquet, by attendant fiddlers, represented doubtless a shadow the less on his later dignity, so far as that dignity was compassed. Dignity marked in full measure even at the time the presence of his sister Madame Dubreuil, a handsome authoritative person who instructed us equally, in fact preponderantly, and who, though comparatively not sympathetic, so engaged, physiognomically, my wondering interest, that I hear to this hour her shrill Franco-American accent: "Don't look at *me*, little boy—look at my feet." I see them now, these somewhat fat members, beneath the uplifted skirt, encased in "bronzed" slippers, without heels but attached, by graceful cross-bands over her white stockings, to her solid ankles—an emphatic sign of the time; not less than I recover my surprised sense of their supporting her without loss of balance, substantial as she was, in the "first position"; her command of which, her ankles clapped close together and her body very erect, was so perfect that even with her toes, right and left, fairly turning the corner backward, she never fell prone on her face.

It consorted somehow with this wealth of resource in her

that she appeared at the soirées, or at least at the great fancy-dress soirée in which the historic truth of my experience, free lemonade and all, is doubtless really shut up, as the "genius of California," a dazzling vision of white satin and golden flounces—her brother meanwhile maintaining that more distinctively European colour which I feel to have been for my young presumption the convincing essence of the scene in the character of a mousquetaire de Louis Quinze, highly consonant with his type. There hovered in the background a flushed, full-chested and tawnily short-bearded M. Dubreuil, who, as a singer of the heavy order, at the Opera, carried us off into larger things still—the Opera having at last about then, after dwelling for years, down town, in shifty tents and tabernacles, set up its own spacious pavilion and reared its head as the Academy of Music: all at the end, or what served for the end, of our very street, where, though it wasn't exactly near and Union Square bristled between, I could yet occasionally gape at the great bills beside the portal, in which M. Dubreuil always so serviceably came in at the bottom of the cast. A subordinate artist, a "grand utility" at the best, I believe, and presently to become, on that scene, slightly ragged I fear even in its freshness, permanent stage-manager or, as we say nowadays, producer, he had yet eminently, to my imagination, the richer, the "European" value; especially for instance when our air thrilled, in the sense that our attentive parents re-echoed, with the visit of the great Grisi and the great Mario, and I seemed, though the art of advertisement was then comparatively so young and so chaste, to see our personal acquaintance, as he could almost be called, thickly sandwiched between them. Such was one's strange sense for the connections of things that they drew out the halls of Ferrero till these too seemed fairly to resound with Norma and Lucrezia Borgia, as if opening straight upon the stage, and Europe, by the stroke, had come to us in such force that we had but to enjoy it on the spot. That could never have been more the case than on the occasion of my assuming, for the famous fancy-ball—not at the operatic Academy, but at the dancing-school, which came so nearly to the same thing—the dress of a débardeur, whatever that might be, which carried in its puckered folds of dark green relieved with scarlet and silver such an exotic fragrance and appealed to me by such a legend. The legend had come round to us, it was true, by way of Albany, whence we learned at the moment of our need, that one of the adventures, one of the least lamentable, of our cousin Johnny had been his figuring as a *débardeur* at some Parisian revel; the elegant evidence of which, neatly packed, though with but vague instructions for use, was helpfully sent on to us. The instructions for use were in fact so vague that I was afterward to become a bit ruefully conscious of having sadly dishonoured, or at least abbreviated, my model. I fell, that is I stood, short of my proper form by no less than half a leg; the essence of the *débardeur* being, it appeared, that he emerged at the knees, in white silk stockings and with neat calves, from the beribboned breeches which I artlessly suffered to flap at my ankles. The discovery, after the fact, was disconcerting—yet had been best made withal, too late; for it would have seemed, I conceive, a less monstrous act to attempt to lengthen my legs than to shorten Johnny's *culotte*. The trouble had been that we hadn't really known what a *débardeur* *was*, and I am not sure indeed that I know to this day. It had been more fatal still that even fond Albany couldn't tell us.

A *daguerreotype taken by Mathew Brady*

From A Small Boy and Others, *1913. In 1844, only a few years after Louis-Jacques-Mandé Daguerre developed his revolutionary daguerreotype process, the pioneer American photographer Mathew Brady opened his first studio in New York. Brady would go on to become famous for his photographic record of the Civil War, as well as for sensitive portraits of President Abraham Lincoln.*

I shall have strained the last drop of romance from this vision of our towny summers with the quite sharp reminiscence of my first sitting for my daguerreotype. I repaired with my father on an August day to the great Broadway establishment of Mr. Brady, supreme in that then beautiful art, and it is my impression—the only point vague with me—that though we had come up by the Staten Island boat for the purpose we were to keep the affair secret till the charming consequence should break, at home, upon my mother. Strong is my conviction that our mystery, in the event, yielded almost at once to our elation, for no tradition had a brighter household life with us than that of our father's headlong impatience. He moved in a cloud, if not rather in a high radiance, of precipitation and divulgation, a chartered rebel against cold reserves. The good news in his hand refused under any persuasion to grow stale, the sense of communicable pleasure in his breast was positively explosive; so that we saw those "surprises" in which he had conspired with our mother for our benefit converted by him in every case, under our shamelessly encouraged guesses, into common conspiracies against her—against her knowing, that is, how thoroughly we were all compromised. He had a special and delightful sophistry at the service of his overflow, and never so fine a fancy as in defending it on "human" grounds. He was something very different withal from a parent of weak mercies; weakness was never so positive and plausible, nor could the attitude of sparing you be more handsomely or on occasion even more comically aggressive.

My small point is simply, however, that the secresy of our conjoined portrait was probably very soon, by his act, to begin a public and shining life and to enjoy it till we received the picture; as to which moreover still another remembrance steals on me, a proof of the fact that our adventure was improvised. Sharp again is my sense of not being so adequately dressed as I should have taken thought for had I foreseen my exposure; though the resources of my wardrobe as then constituted could surely have left me but few alternatives. The main resource of a small New York boy in this line at that time was the little sheath-like jacket, tight to the body, closed at the neck and adorned in front with a single row of brass buttons—a garment of scant grace assuredly and compromised to my consciousness, above all, by a strange ironic light from an unforgotten source. It was but a short time before those days that the great Mr. Thackeray had come to America to lecture on The English Humourists, and still present to me is the voice proceeding from my father's library, in which some glimpse of me hovering, at an opening of the door, in passage or on staircase, prompted him to the formidable words: "Come here, little boy, and show me your extraordinary jacket!" My sense of my jacket became from that hour a heavy one—further enriched as my vision is by my shyness of posture before the seated, the celebrated visitor, who struck me, in the sunny light of the animated room, as enormously big and who, though he laid on my shoulder the hand of benevolence, bent on my native costume the spectacles of wonder. I was to know later on why he had been so amused and why, after asking me if this were the common uniform of my age and class, he remarked that in England, were I to go there, I should be addressed as "Buttons." It had been revealed to me thus in a flash that we were somehow *queer*, and though never exactly crushed by it I became aware that I at least felt so as I stood with my head in Mr. Brady's vise. Beautiful most decidedly the lost art of the daguerreotype; I remember the "exposure" as on this occasion interminably long, yet with the result of a facial anguish far less harshly reproduced than my suffered snapshots of a later age. Too few, I may here interject, were to remain my gathered impressions of the great humourist, but one of them, indeed almost the only other, bears again on the play of his humour over our perversities of dress. It belongs to a later moment, an occasion on which I see him familiarly seated with us, in Paris, during the spring of 1857, at some repast at which the younger of us too, by that time, habitually flocked, in our affluence of five. Our youngest was beside him, a small sister, then not quite in her eighth year, and arrayed apparently after the fashion of the period and place; and the tradition lingered long of his having suddenly laid his hand on her little flounced person and exclaimed with ludicrous horror: "Crinoline?—I was suspecting it! So young and so depraved!"

The Galerie d'Apollon

From A Small Boy and Others, *1913. The Louvre's*
Galerie d'Apollon provided both the youthful and the
mature Henry James with a turbulent image of artis-
tic promise. Here the seventy-year-old novelist records
how as a thirteen-year-old he was overcome by the
"vast deafening chorus" of the museum's treasures;
and then he recounts that many years later he had the
"most admirable nightmare of my life"—a "dream-
adventure" in which he fled from someone or some-
thing across the splendid hall's "far-gleaming floor."

We were not yet aware of style, though on the way to become
so, but were aware of mystery, which indeed was one of its
forms—while we saw all the others, without exception, exhib-
ited at the Louvre, where at first they simply overwhelmed and
bewildered me.

It was as if they had gathered there into a vast deafening chorus; I shall never forget how—speaking, that is, for my own
sense—they filled those vast halls with the influence rather of
some complicated sound, diffused and reverberant, than of
such visibilities as one could directly deal with. To distinguish
among these, in the charged and coloured and confounding air,
was difficult—it discouraged and defied; which was doubtless
why my impression originally best entertained was that of
those magnificent parts of the great gallery simply not inviting
us to distinguish. They only arched over us in the wonder of
their endless golden riot and relief, figured and flourished in
perpetual revolution, breaking into great high-hung circles and

symmetries of squandered picture, opening into deep outward embrasures that threw off the rest of monumental Paris somehow as a told story, a sort of wrought effect or bold ambiguity for a vista, and yet held it there, at every point, as a vast bright gage, even at moments a felt adventure of experience. This comes to saying that in those beginnings I felt myself most happily cross that bridge over to Style constituted by the wondrous Galerie d'Apollon, drawn out for me as a long but assured initiation and seeming to form with its supreme coved ceiling and inordinately shining parquet a prodigious tube or tunnel through which I inhaled little by little, that is again and again, a general sense of *glory*. The glory meant ever so many things at once, not only beauty and art and supreme design, but history and fame and power, the world in fine raised to the richest and noblest expression. The world there was at the same time, by an odd extension or intensification, the local present fact, to my small imagination, of the Second Empire, which was (for my notified consciousness) new and queer and perhaps even wrong, but on the spot so amply radiant and elegant that it took to itself, took under its protection with a splendour of insolence, the state and ancientry of the whole scene, profiting thus, to one's dim historic vision, confusedly though it might be, by the unparalleled luxury and variety of its heritage. But who shall count the sources at which an intense young fancy (when a young fancy *is* intense) capriciously, absurdly drinks?—so that the effect is, in twenty connections, that of a love-philtre or fear-philtre which fixes for the senses their supreme symbol of the fair or the strange. The Galerie d'Apollon became for years what I can only term a splendid scene of things, even of the quite irrelevant or, as might be, almost unworthy; and I recall to this hour, with the last vividness, what a precious part it played for me, and exactly by that continuity of honour, on my awaking, in a summer dawn many years later, to the fortunate, the instantaneous recovery and capture of the most appalling yet most admirable nightmare of my life. The climax of this extraordinary experience—which stands alone for me as a dream-adventure founded in the deepest, quickest, clearest act of cogitation and comparison, act indeed of life-saving energy, as well as in unutterable fear—was the sudden pursuit, through an open door, along a huge high saloon, of a just dimly-described figure that retreated in terror before my rush and dash (a glare of inspired reaction from irresistible but shameful dread,) out of the room I had a moment before been desperately, and all the more abjectly, defending by the push of my shoulder against hard pressure on lock and bar from the other side. The lucidity, not to say the sublimity, of the crisis had consisted of the great thought that I, in my appalled state, was probably still more appalling than the awful agent, creature or presence, whatever he was, whom I had guessed, in the suddenest wild start from sleep, the sleep within my sleep, to be making for my place of rest. The triumph of my impulse, perceived in a flash as I acted on it by myself at a bound, forcing the door outward, was the grand thing, but the great point of the whole was the wonder of my final recognition. Routed, dismayed, the tables turned upon him by my so surpassing him for straight aggression and dire intention, my visitant was already but a diminished spot in the long perspective, the tremendous, glorious hall, as I say, over the far-gleaming floor of which, cleared for the occasion of its great line of priceless vitrines down the middle, he sped for *his* life, while a great storm of thunder and lightning played through the deep embrasures of high windows at the right. The lightning that revealed the retreat revealed also the wondrous place and, by the same amazing play, my young imaginative life in it of long before, the sense of which, deep within me, had kept it whole, preserved it to this thrilling use; for what in the world were the deep embrasures and the so polished floor but those of the Galerie d'Apollon of my childhood? The "scene of something" I had vaguely then felt it? Well I might, since it was to be the scene of that immense hallucination.

Of what, at the same time, in those years, were the great rooms of the Louvre almost equally, above and below, not the scene, from the moment they so wrought, stage by stage, upon our perceptions?—literally on almost all of these, in one way and another; quite in such a manner, I more and more see, as to have been educative, formative, fertilising, in a degree which no other "intellectual experience" our youth was to know could pretend, as a comprehensive, conducive thing, to rival.

The sharp and strange, the quite heart-shaking little prevision
had come to me, for myself, I make out, on the occasion of our
very first visit of all, my brother's and mine, under conduct of
the good Jean Nadali, before-mentioned, trustfully deputed by
our parents, in the Rue de la Paix, on the morrow of our first
arrival in Paris (July 1855) and while they were otherwise concerned. I hang again, appalled but uplifted, on brave Nadali's
arm—his professional acquaintance with the splendours about
us added for me on the spot to the charm of his "European"
character: I cling to him while I gape at Géricault's Radeau de
la Méduse, *the* sensation, for splendour and terror of interest,
of that juncture to me, and ever afterwards to be associated,
along with two or three other more or less contemporary products, Guérin's Burial of Atala, Prudhon's Cupid and Psyche,
David's helmetted Romanisms, Madame Vigée-Lebrun's "rav-
ishing" portrait of herself and her little girl, with how can I say
what foretaste (as determined by that instant as if the hour had
struck from a clock) of all the fun, confusedly speaking, that
one was going to have, and the kind of life, always of the queer
so-called inward sort, tremendously "sporting" in its way—
though that description didn't then wait upon it, that one was
going to lead. It came of itself, this almost awful apprehension
in all the presences, under our courier's protection and in my
brother's company—it came just there and so; there was alarm
in it somehow as well as bliss. The bliss in fact I think scarce
disengaged itself at all, but only the sense of a freedom of contact and appreciation really too big for one, and leaving such a
mark on the very place, the pictures, the frames themselves, the
figures within them, the particular parts and features of each,
the look of the rich light, the smell of the massively enclosed
air, that I have never since renewed the old exposure without
renewing again the old emotion and taking up the small scared
consciousness. *That,* with so many of the conditions repeated,
is the charm—to feel afresh the beginning of so much that was
to be. The beginning in short was with Géricault and David,
but it went on and on and slowly spread; so that one's
stretched, one's even strained, perceptions, one's discoveries
and extensions piece by piece, come back, on the great premises, almost as so many explorations of the house of life, so

many circlings and hoverings round the image of the world. I
have dim reminiscences of permitted independent visits, uncor-
rectedly juvenile though I might still be, during which the
house of life and the palace of art became so mixed and inter-
changeable—the Louvre being, under a general description, the
most peopled of all scenes not less than the most hushed of all
temples—that an excursion to look at pictures would have but
half expressed my afternoon. I had looked at pictures, looked
and looked again, at the vast Veronese, at Murillo's moon-borne
Madonna, at Leonardo's almost unholy dame with the folded
hands, treasures of the Salon Carré as that display was then
composed; but I had also looked at France and looked at Europe, looked even at America as Europe itself might be conceived so to look, looked at history, as a still-felt past and a
complacently personal future, at society, manners, type, characters, possibilities and prodigies and mysteries of fifty sorts;
and all in the light of being splendidly "on my own," as I supposed it, though we hadn't then that perfection of slang, and of
(in especial) going and coming along that interminable and incomparable Seine-side front of the Palace against which young
sensibility felt itself almost rub, for endearment and consecration, as a cat invokes the friction of a protective piece of furniture. Such were at any rate some of the vague processes—I see
for how utterly vague they must show—of picking up an education; and I was, in spite of the vagueness, so far from agreeing with my brother afterwards that we didn't pick one up and
that that never *is* done, in any sense not negligible, and also
that an education might, or should, in particular, have picked
us up, and yet didn't—I was so far dissentient, I say, that I think
I quite came to glorify such passages and see them as part of an
order really fortunate. If we had been little asses, I seem to have
reasoned, a higher intention driving us wouldn't have made us
less so—to any point worth mentioning; and as we extracted
such impressions, to put it at the worst, from redemptive accidents (to call Louvres and Luxembourgs nothing better) why
we weren't little asses, but something wholly other: which appeared all I needed to contend for. Above all it would have been
stupid and ignoble, an attested and lasting dishonour, not, with
our chance, to have followed our straggling clues, as many as

we could and disengaging as we happily did, I felt, the gold and the silver ones, whatever the others might have been—not to have followed them and not to have arrived by them, so far as we were to arrive. Instinctively, for any dim designs we might have nourished, we picked out the silver and the gold, attenuated threads though they must have been, and I positively feel that there were more of these, far more, casually interwoven, than will reward any present patience for my unravelling of the too fine tissue.

An obscure hurt

From Notes of a Son and Brother, 1914. *Imbedded in a lengthy meditation on the Civil War, this passage has raised controversy. Although most critics assume reference to a back injury, it has been suggested that some other grievous damage made sexual activity impossible. James introduces the episode—not even giving it a separate paragraph—by noting that an "infinitely small affair in comparison, was a passage of personal history the most entirely personal, but between which, as a private catastrophe or difficulty, bristling with embarrassments, and the great public convulsion that announced itself in bigger terms each day, I felt from the very first an association of the closest, yet withal, I fear, almost of the least clearly expressible."*

All of which would seem to kick up more dust than need quite have hung about so simple a matter as my setting forth to the Cambridge scene with no design that I could honourably exhibit. A superficial account of the matter would have been that my father had a year or two earlier appeared to think so ill of it as to reduce me, given the "delicacy," the inward, not then the outward, which I have glanced at, to mild renunciation—mild I say because I remember in fact, rather to my mystification now, no great pang of disappointment, no soreness of submission. I didn't want anything so much as I wanted a certain good (or wanted thus supremely *to* want it, if I may say so), with which a conventional going to college wouldn't have so tremendously much to do as for the giving it up to break my heart—or an unconventional not-going so tremendously much either. What I "wanted to want" to be was, all intimately, just *literary;* a decent respect for the standard hadn't yet made my approach so straight that there weren't still difficulties that might seem to meet it, questions it would have to depend on. Passing the Harvard portal positively failed in fact to strike me as the shorter cut to literature; the sounds that rose from the scene as I caught them appeared on the contrary the most detached from any such interest that had ever reached my ear. Merely to open the door of the big square closet, the ample American closet, to the like of which Europe had never treated us, on the shelves and round the walls of which the pink Revues sat with the air, row upon row, of a choir of breathing angels, was to take up that particular, that sacred connection in a way that put the coarser process to shame. The drop of the Harvard question had of a truth really meant, as I recover it, a renewed consecration of the rites of that chapel where the taper always twinkled—which circumstance I mention as not only qualifying my sense of loss, but as symbolising, after a queer fashion, the independence, blest vision (to the extent, that is, of its being a closer compact with the life of the imagination), that I should thus both luckily come in for and designingly cultivate: cultivate in other words under the rich cover of obscurity. I have already noted how the independence was, ever so few months later, by so quaint a turn, another mere shake of the tree, to drop into my lap in the form of a great golden apple— a value not a simple windfall only through the fact that my father's hand had after all just lightly loosened it. This accession pointed the moral that there was no difficulty about anything, no intrinsic difficulty; so that, to re-emphasise the sweet bewilderment, I was to "go" where I liked in the Harvard direction and do what I liked in the Harvard relation. Such was the situation as offered me; though as I had to take it and use it I found in it no little difference. Two things and more had come up— the biggest of which, and very wondrous as bearing on any circumstance of mine, as having a grain of weight to spare for it, was the breaking out of the War. The other, the infinitely small affair in comparison, was a passage of personal history the

most entirely personal, but between which, as a private catastrophe or difficulty, bristling with embarrassments, and the
great public convulsion that announced itself in bigger terms
each day, I felt from the very first an association of the closest,
yet withal, I fear, almost of the least clearly expressible. Scarce
at all to be stated, to begin with, the queer fusion or confusion
established in my consciousness during the soft spring of '61 by
the firing on Fort Sumter, Mr. Lincoln's instant first call for volunteers and a physical mishap, already referred to as having
overtaken me at the same dark hour, and the effects of which
were to draw themselves out incalculably and intolerably. Beyond all present notation the interlaced, undivided way in
which what had happened to me, by a turn of fortune's hand,
in twenty odious minutes, kept company of the most unnatural—I can call it nothing less—with my view of what was
happening, with the question of what might still happen, to
everyone about me, to the country at large: it so made of these
marked disparities a single vast visitation. One had the sense, I
mean, of a huge comprehensive ache, and there were hours at
which one could scarce have told whether it came most from
one's own poor organism, still so young and so meant for better things, but which had suffered particular wrong, or from
the enclosing social body, a body rent with a thousand wounds
and that thus treated one to the honour of a sort of tragic fel-
lowship. The twenty minutes had sufficed, at all events, to establish a relation—a relation to everything occurring round me
not only for the next four years but for long afterward—that
was at once extraordinarily intimate and quite awkwardly irrelevant. I must have felt in some befooled way in presence of a
crisis—the smoke of Charleston Bay still so acrid in the air—at
which the likely young should be up and doing or, as familiarly
put, lend a hand much wanted; the willing youths, all round,
were mostly starting to their feet, and to have trumped up a
lameness at such a juncture could be made to pass in no light
for graceful. Jammed into the acute angle between two high
fences, where the rhythmic play of my arms, in tune with that
of several other pairs, but at a dire disadvantage of position, induced a rural, a rusty, a quasi-extemporised old engine to work
and a saving stream to flow, I had done myself, in face of a

shabby conflagration, a horrid even if an obscure hurt; and what was interesting from the first was my not doubting in the least its duration—though what seemed equally clear was that I needn't as a matter of course adopt and appropriate it, so to speak, or place it for increase of interest on exhibition. The interest of it, I very presently knew, would certainly be of the greatest, would even in conditions kept as simple as I might make them become little less than absorbing. The shortest account of what was to follow for a long time after is therefore to plead that the interest never did fail. It was naturally what is called a painful one, but it consistently declined, as an influence at play, to drop for a single instant. Circumstances, by a wonderful chance, overwhelmingly favoured it—*as* an interest, an inexhaustible, I mean; since I also felt in the whole enveloping tonic atmosphere a force promoting its growth. Interest, the interest of life and of death, of our national existence, of the fate of those, the vastly numerous, whom it closely concerned, the interest of the extending War, in fine, the hurrying troops, the transfigured scene, formed a cover for every sort of intensity, made tension itself in fact contagious—so that almost any tension would do, would serve for one's share.

The death of Minnie Temple

From Notes of a Son and Brother, 1914. *In 1870 the death of James's twenty-four-year-old cousin was a monumental loss, and in both* The Portrait of a Lady *and* The Wings of the Dove *her presence is thought to be significant. In* Notes of a Son and Brother *James recalls her life and death, with many excerpts from her letters. Remarkably intelligent, Minnie Temple could be tough on a cousin she clearly loved; at one point she writes James that, "The trouble is, I think, that to me you have no distinct personality. I don't feel sure to whom I am writing when I say to myself that I will write to you. I see mentally three men, all answering to your name, each liable to read my letters and yet differing so much from each other that if it is proper for one of them it is unsuitable to the others."*

Immediately, at any rate, the Albany cousins, or a particular group of them, began again to be intensely in question for us; coloured in due course with reflections of the War as their lives, not less than our own, were to become—and coloured as well too, for all sorts of notation and appreciation, from irrepressible private founts. Mrs. Edmund Tweedy, bereft of her own young children, had at the time I speak of opened her existence, with the amplest hospitality, to her four orphaned nieces, who were also our father's and among whom the second in age, Mary Temple the younger, about in her seventeenth year when she thus renewed her appearance to our view, shone with vividest lustre, an essence that preserves her still, more than half

a century from the date of her death, in a memory or two
where many a relic once sacred has comparatively yielded to
time. Most of these who knew and loved, I was going to say
adored, her have also yielded—which is a reason the more why
thus much of her, faint echo from too far off though it prove,
should be tenderly saved. If I have spoken of the elements and
presences round about us that "counted," Mary Temple was to
count, and in more lives than can now be named, to an extraordinary degree; count as a young and shining apparition, a
creature who owed to the charm of her every aspect (her aspects were so many!) and the originality, vivacity, audacity,
generosity, of her spirit, an indescribable grace and weight—if
one might impute weight to a being so imponderable in common scales. Whatever other values on our scene might, as I
have hinted, appear to fail, she was one of the first order, in the
sense of the immediacy of the impression she produced, and
produced altogether as by the play of her own light spontaneity and curiosity—not, that is, as through a sense of such a
pressure and such a motive, or through a care for them, in others. "Natural" to an effect of perfect felicity that we were never
to see surpassed is what I have already praised all the Albany
cousinage of those years for being; but in none of the company
was the note so clear as in this rarest, though at the same time
symptomatically or ominously palest, flower of the stem; who
was natural at more points and about more things, with a
greater range of freedom and ease and reach of horizon than
any of the others dreamed of. They had that way, delightfully,
with the small, after all, and the common matters—while she
had it with those too, but with the great and rare ones over and
above; so that she was to remain for us the very figure and image of a felt interest in life, an interest as magnanimously far-
spread, or as familiarly and exquisitely fixed, as her splendid
shifting sensibility, moral, personal, nervous, and having at
once such noble flights and such touchingly discouraged drops,
such graces of indifference and inconsequence, might at any
moment determine. She was really to remain, for our appreciation, the supreme case of a taste for life as life, as personal living; of an endlessly active and yet somehow a careless, an
illusionless, a sublimely forewarned curiosity about it: some-

thing that made her, slim and fair and quick, all straightness and charming tossed head, with long light and yet almost sliding steps and a large light postponing, renouncing laugh, the very muse or amateur priestess of rash speculation. To express her in the mere terms of her restless young mind, one felt from the first, was to place her, by a perversion of the truth, under the shadow of female "earnestness"—for which she was much too unliteral and too ironic; so that, superlatively personal and yet as independent, as "off" into higher spaces, at a touch, as all the breadth of her sympathy and her courage could send her, she made it impossible to say whether she was just the most moving of maidens or a disengaged and dancing flame of thought. No one to come after her could easily seem to show either a quick inward life or a brave, or even a bright, outward, either a consistent contempt for social squalors or a very marked genius for moral reactions. She had in her brief passage the enthusiasm of humanity—more, assuredly, than any charming girl who ever circled, and would fain have continued to circle, round a ballroom. This kept her indeed for a time more interested in the individual, the immediate human, than in the race or the social order at large; but that, on the other hand, made her ever so restlessly, or quite inappeasably, "psychologic." The psychology of others, in her shadow—I mean their general resort to it—could only for a long time seem weak and flat and dim, above all not at all amusing. She burned herself out; she died at twenty-four.

*   *   *   *   *

To the gallantry and beauty of which there is little surely to add. But there came a moment, almost immediately after, when all illusion failed; which it is not good to think of or linger on, and yet not pitiful not to note. One may have wondered rather doubtingly—and I have expressed that—what life would have had for her and how her exquisite faculty of challenge could have "worked in" with what she was likely otherwise to have encountered or been confined to. None the less did she in fact cling to consciousness; death, at the last, was dreadful to her; she would have given anything to live—and the image of this, which was long to remain with me, appeared so of the essence of tragedy that I was in the far-off aftertime to seek to lay the ghost by wrapping it, a particular occasion aiding, in the beauty and dignity of art. The figure that was to hover as the ghost has at any rate been of an extreme pertinence, I feel, to my doubtless too loose and confused general picture, vitiated perhaps by the effort to comprehend more than it contains. Much as this cherished companion's presence among us had represented for William and myself—and it is on *his* behalf I especially speak—her death made a mark that must stand here for a too waiting conclusion. We felt it together as the end of our youth.

At the grave of Alice James

From "The American Journals," 29 March 1905, in The Complete Notebooks, ed. Leon Edel and Lyall H. Powers. While working on the essays for The American Scene, James made the following entry in his journal, although he included no reference to his sister's grave in what he published on his American tour. James's more contemporary Italian changes Dante's exact words and makes one error (esilio would be the correct modern spelling), as he writes that "after long exile and martyrdom [she] comes to this peace." The original text of Paradiso X reads "ed essa da martiro e da essilio venne a questa pace." Of course "Basta, basta!"—enough, enough!—does not appear in the Commedia.

But these are wanton lapses and impossible excursions; irrelevant strayings of the pen, in defiance of every economy. My subject awaits me, all too charged and too bristling with the most artful economy possible. What I seem to feel is that the Cambridge *tendresse* stands in the path like a waiting lion—or, more congruously, like a cooing dove that I shrink from scaring away. I want a little of the *tendresse,* but it trembles away over the whole field—or would if it could. Yet to present these accidents is what it is to be a *master;* that and that only. Isn't the highest deepest note of the whole thing the never-to-be-lost memory of that evening hour at Mount Auburn—at the Cambridge Cemetery when I took my way alone—after much waiting for the favouring hour—to that unspeakable group of graves. It was late, in November; the trees all bare, the dusk to fall early, the air all still (at Cambridge, in general, *so* still), with the western sky more and more turning to that terrible, deadly, pure polar pink that shows behind American winter woods. But I can't go over this—I can only, oh, so gently, so tenderly, brush it and breathe upon it—breathe upon it and brush it. It was the moment; it was the hour, it was the blessed flood of emotion that broke out at the touch of one's sudden *vision* and carried me away. I seemed then to know why I had done this; I seemed then to know why I had *come*—and to feel how not to have come would have been miserably, horribly to miss it. It made everything right—it made everything priceless. The moon was there, early, white and young, and seemed reflected in the white face of the great empty Stadium, forming one of the boundaries of Soldiers' Field, that looked over at me, stared over at me, through the clear twilight, from across the Charles. Everything was there, everything *came;* the recognition, stillness, the strangeness, the pity and the sanctity and the terror, the breath-catching passion and the divine relief of tears. William's inspired transcript, on the exquisite little Florentine urn of Alice's ashes, William's divine gift to us, and to *her,* of the Dantean lines—

> *Dopo lungo exilio e martiro*
> *Viene a questa pace—*

took me so at the throat by its penetrating *rightness,* that it was as if one sank down on one's knees in a kind of anguish of gratitude before something for which one had waited with a long, deep *ache.* But why do I write of the all unutterable and the all abysmal? Why does my pen not drop from my hand on approaching the infinite pity and tragedy of all the past? It does, poor helpless pen, with what it meets of the ineffable, what it meets of the cold Medusa-face of life, of all the life *lived,* on every side. *Basta, basta!* x x x x x

VI

CORRESPONDENCE

A few years before his death, James burned most of the letters he had received from his friends, and he urged his friends to do the same with those he had sent. Not everyone did. Leon Edel's four-volume edition of the correspondence printed 1,092 letters of a then-estimated 15,000 that had survived immolation. More recently, Stephen H. Jobe's scrupulous catalog has brought the figure closer to 10,400. This small selection is mostly addressed to close friends or family members, to whom James could sometimes write several thousand words in a single letter.

A thirteen-year-old in Paris writes
to a young friend

The Van Winkles were New York neighbors on 14th Street. In 1913, in A Small Boy and Others, *James would recall his friend Edgar's family in the voice of his full maturity: "I recover, further, some sense of the high places of the Van Winkles, but I think of them as pervaded for us by the upper air of the proprieties, the proprieties that were so numerous, it would appear, when one had had a glimpse of them, rather than by the crude fruits of young improvisation."*

To Edgar Van Winkle, 1856, from Paris

Dear Eddy
As I heard you were going to try to turn the club into a Theatre
And as I was asked w'ether I wanted to belong here is my an-
swer. I would like very much to belong.

Yours Truly
H. James

On the Grand Tour

This letter was one of many written while James was on tour in Europe—and sometimes mined for his subsequent travel essays—to members of his family (to "My darling Mammy," "My dearest Daddy," "Dear Bill," "Beloved Bill," "Beloved sister," and, writing to his sister from Florence, "Carissima sorella").

To William James, October 30, 1869, from Rome

My dearest William—

Some four days since I despatched to you and Father respectively, from Florence, two very doleful epistles, which you will in course of time receive. No sooner had I posted them, however than my spirits were revived by the arrival of a most blessed brotherly letter from you of October 8th, which had been detained either by my banker or the porter of the hotel and a little scrap from Father of a later date, enclosing your review of Mill and a paper of Howells—as well as a couple of *Nations*. Verily, it is worthwhile pining for letters for three weeks to know the exquisite joy of final relief. I took yours with me to the theatre whither I went to see a comedy of Goldoni most delightfully played and read and re-read it between the acts.—But of this anon.—I went as I proposed down to Pisa and spent two very pleasant days with the Nortons. It is a very fine dull old town—and the great Square with its four big treasures is quite the biggest thing I have seen in Italy—or rather was, until my arrival at this well-known locality.—I went about a whole morning with Charles Norton and profited vastly by his excellent knowledge of Italian history and art. I wish I had a small fraction of it. But my visit wouldn't have been complete unless I had got a ramble *solus,* which I did in perfection. On my return to Florence I determined to start immediately for Rome. The afternoon after I had posted those two letters I took a walk out of Florence to an enchanting old Chartreuse—an ancient monastery, perched up on top of a hill and turreted with little cells like a feudal castle. I attacked it and carried it by storm—i.e. obtained admission and went over it. On coming out I swore to myself that while I had life in my body I wouldn't leave a country where adventures of that complexion are the common incidents of your daily constitutional: but that I would hurl myself upon Rome and fight it out on this line at the peril of my existence. Here I am then in the Eternal City. It was easy to leave Florence; the cold had become intolerable and the rain perpetual. I started last night, and at 10 1/2 o'clock and after a bleak and fatiguing journey of twelve hours found myself here with the morning light. There are several places on the *route* I should have been glad to see; but the weather and my own condition made a direct journey imperative. I rushed to this hotel (a very slow and obstructed rush it was, I confess, thanks to the longueurs and lenteurs of the Papal dispensation) and after a wash and a breakfast let myself loose on the city. From midday to dusk I have been roaming the streets. *Que vous en dirai-je?* At last—for the first time—I live! It beats everything: it leaves the Rome of your fancy—your education—nowhere. It makes Venice—Florence—Oxford—London—seem like little cities of pasteboard. I went reeling and moaning thro' the streets, in a fever of enjoyment. In the course of four or five hours I traversed almost the whole of Rome and got a glimpse of everything—the Forum, the Coliseum (stupendissimo!), the Pantheon, the Capitol, St. Peter's, the Column of Trajan, the Castle of St. Angelo—all the Piazzas and ruins and monuments. The effect is something indescribable. For the first time I know what the picturesque is.—In St. Peter's I stayed some time. It's even beyond its reputation. It was filled with foreign ecclesiastics—great armies encamped in prayer on the marble plains of its pavement—an inexhaustible physiognomical study. To crown my day, on my way home, I met his Holiness in person—driving in prodigious purple state—sitting dim within the shadows of his coach with two uplifted benedictory fingers—like some dusky Hindoo idol in the depths of its shrine. Even if I should leave Rome tonight I should feel that I have caught the keynote of its operation on the senses. I have looked along the grassy vista of the Appian Way and seen the topmost stone-work of the Coliseum sitting shrouded in the light of heaven, like the edge of an Alpine chain. I've trod the Forum and I have scaled the Capitol. I've seen the Tiber hurrying along, as swift and dirty as history! From the high tribune of a great chapel of St. Peter's I have heard in the papal choir a strange old man sing in a shrill unpleasant soprano. I've seen troops of little tonsured neophytes clad in scarlet, marching and countermarching and ducking and flopping, like poor little raw recruits for the heavenly host. In fine I've seen Rome, and I shall go to bed a wiser man than I last rose—yesterday morning.—It was a great relief to me to have you at last give me some news of your health. I thank the Lord it's no worse. With all my heart I rejoice that you're going to try loafing and visiting. I discern the "inexorable logic" of the affair; courage, and you'll work out your redemption. I'm delighted with your good report of John La Farge's pictures. I've seen them all save the sleeping woman. I have given up expecting him here. If he does come, *tant mieux*. Your notice of Mill and Bushnell seemed to me (save the opening lines which savored faintly of Eugene Benson) very well and fluently written. Thank Father for his ten lines: may they increase and multiply!—Of course I don't know how long I shall be here. I would give my head to be able to remain three months: it would be a liberal education. As it is, I shall stay, if possible, simply from week to week. My "condition" remains the same. I am living on some medicine (aloes and sulphuric acid) given me by my Florentine doctor. I shall write again very shortly. Kisses to Alice and Mother. Blessings on yourself. Address me *Spada, Flamine* and Cie. Banquiers, Rome. Heaven grant I may be here when your letters come. Love to Father.

À toi
H.J. jr

Henry James, expatriate

Although no one quite recognized it at the time, James's permanent residency in England had just begun.

To the James family, November 1, 1875, from London

Dear People all—

I take possession of the old world—I inhale it—I appropriate it! I have been in it now these twenty-four hours, having arrived at Liverpool yesterday at noon. It is now two o'clock, and I am sitting, in the livid light of a London November Sunday, before a copious fire, in my own particular sitting-room, at the establishment mentioned above. I took the afternoon train from Liverpool yesterday, and having telegraphed in advance, sat down at 10 P.M. to cold roast beef, bread and cheese and ale in this cosy corner of Britain. I have been walking up Piccadilly this morning, and into Hyde Park, to get my land-legs on; I am duly swathed and smoked and chilled, and feel as if I had been here for ten years.—Of course you got my letter from Sandy Hook, and learned that my voyage began comfortably. I am sorry to say it didn't continue so, and I spent my nights and my days declaring that the sea shouldn't catch me again for at least twenty years. But of course I have already forgotten all that and the watery gulf has closed over my miseries. Our voyage was decently rapid (just 10 days) owing to favoring winds; but the winds were boisterous gales, and after the second day we tumbled and tossed all the way across. I was as usual, but I kept pretty steadily on deck, and with my rugs and my chair, managed to worry thro'. The steamer is a superb one, but she was uncomfortably crowded, and she presumably bounced about more than was needful. I was not conversational and communed but little with my multitudinous passengers. My chief interlocutor was Mrs. Lester Wallack, whose principal merit is that she is the sister of Millais the painter. She offers to take me to his studio if he returns to town before I have— which he won't. We had also Anthony Trollope, who wrote novels in his state room all the morning (he does it literally every morning of his life, no matter where he may be,) and played cards with Mrs. Bronson all the evening. He has a gross and repulsive face and manner, but appears *bon enfant* when you talk with him. But he is the dullest Briton of them all. Nothing happened, but I loathed and despised the sea more than ever. I managed to eat a good deal in one way and another, and found it, when once I got it well under way, the best help to tranquillity. It isn't the eating that hurts one, but the stopping.—I shall remain in this place at most a week. It is the same old big black London, and seems, as always, half delicious, half dismal. I am profoundly comfortable, thanks to Mr. Story, the usual highly respectable retired butler, who gives me a sitting room, a bedroom, attendance, lights and fire, for three guineas a week. Everything is of the best, and it is a very honorable residence. Why didn't Aunt Kate and Alice bring me here in '72? I shall probably start for Paris a week from tomorrow, and hope to find there a line from home. If anything very interesting befalls me here I will write again, but in my unfriended condition this is not probable. I hope the Western journey has been safely and smoothly executed and count upon hearing full particulars. If Aunt Kate has gone to New York let her see this. Each of you hold Dido an hour against your heart for me. The sight of all the pretty genteel dogs in Hyde Park a while since brought tears to my eyes. I think that if I could have had Dido in my berth I would have been quite well. But perhaps *she* would have been sea-sick. I have been haunted since I left home by the recollection of three small unpaid bills, which I pray mother to settle for me.

1. At Dollard's, the cobbler's. About 2 dollars.
2. Schönhof and Moellers. About $3.00
3d. At Smith's, the tailor's, 7$ for that summer coat: not 7.50,

as his bill said, which I left on my bedroom table. Excuse these sordid details. This sitting still to write makes me swim and roll about most damnably. Your all-affectionate

H. James jr.

The literary scene in Paris

The enduring friendship between James and William Dean Howells began in 1866 and was nurtured by many shared interests beyond that of the novel, for Howells also had a passion for travel, and especially for France. During a thirteen-month stay in Paris from 1875 to 1876, James published numerous social and artistic letters for the New York Tribune.

To William Dean Howells, May 28, 1876,
from Paris

Dear Howells—

I have just received (an hour ago) your letter of May 14th. I shall be very glad to do my best to divide my story so that it will make twelve numbers, and I think I shall probably succeed. Of course 26 pp. is an impossible instalment for the magazine. I had no idea the second number would make so much, though I half expected your remonstrance. I shall endeavour to give you about 14 pp., and to keep doing it for seven or eight months more. I sent you the other day a fourth part, a portion of which, I suppose, you will allot to the fifth.

My heart was touched by your regret that I hadn't given you "a great deal of my news"—though my reason suggested that I couldn't have given you what there was not to give. "*La plus belle fille du monde ne peut donner que ce qu'elle a.*" I turn out news in very small quantities—it is impossible to imagine an existence less pervaded with any sort of *chiaroscuro*. I am turning into an old, and very contented, Parisian: I feel as if I had struck roots into the Parisian soil, and were likely to let them grow tangled and tenacious there. It is a very comfortable and profitable place, on the whole—I mean, especially, on its general and cosmopolitan side. Of pure Parisianism I see absolutely nothing. The great merit of the place is that one can arrange one's life here exactly as one pleases—that there are facilities for every kind of habit and taste, and that everything is accepted and understood. Paris itself meanwhile is a sort of painted background which keeps shifting and changing, and which is always there, to be looked at when you please, and to be most easily and comfortably ignored when you don't. All this, if you were only here, you would feel much better than I can tell you—and you would write some happy piece of your prose about it which would make me feel it better, afresh. *Ergo,* come—when you can! I shall probably be here still. Of course every good thing is still better in spring, and in spite of much mean weather I have been liking Paris these last weeks more than ever. In fact I have accepted destiny here, under the vernal influence. If you sometimes read my poor letters in the *Tribune,* you get a notion of some of the things I see and do. I suppose also you get some gossip about me from Quincy Street. Besides this there is not a great deal to tell. I have seen a certain number of people all winter who have helped to pass the time, but I have formed but one or two relations of permanent value, and which I desire to perpetuate. I have seen almost nothing of the literary fraternity, and there are fifty reasons why I should not become intimate with them. I don't like their wares, and they don't like any others; and besides, they are not *accueillants.* Tourguéneff is worth the whole heap of them, and yet he himself swallows them down in a manner that excites my extreme wonder. But he is the most loveable of men and takes all things easily. He is so pure and strong a genius that he doesn't need to be on the defensive as regards his opinions and enjoyments. The mistakes he may make don't hurt him. His modesty and naïveté are simply infantine. I gave him some time since the message you sent him, and he bade me to thank you very kindly and to say that he had the most agreeable memory of your two books. He has just gone to Russia to bury himself for

two or three months on his estate, and try and finish a long
novel he has for three or four years been working upon. I hope
to heaven he may. I suspect he works little here.

I interrupted this a couple of hours since to go out and pay a
visit to Gustave Flaubert, it being his time of receiving, and his
last Sunday in Paris, and I owing him a farewell. *He* is a very
fine old fellow, and the most interesting man and strongest
artist of his circle. I had him for an hour alone, and then came
in his "following," talking much of Émile Zola's catastrophe—
Zola having just had a serial novel for which he was being handsomely paid interrupted on account of protests from provincial
subscribers against its indecency. The opinion apparently was
that it was a bore, but that it could only do the book good on
its appearance in a volume. Among your tribulations as editor,
I take it that this particular one at least is not in store for you.
On my [way] down from Flaubert's I met poor Zola climbing
the staircase, looking very pale and sombre, and I saluted him
with the flourish natural to a contributor who has just been invited to make his novel last longer yet.

Warner has come back to Paris, after an apparently raptur-
ous fortnight in London, and the other morning breakfasted
with me—but I have not seen him since, and I imagine he has
reverted to London. He is conspicuously amiable. I have seen
no other Americans all winter—men at least. There are no men
here to see but horribly effeminate and empty-pated little
crevés. But there are some very nice women.—I went yesterday
to see a lady whom and whose *intérieur* it is a vast pity you
shouldn't behold for professional purposes: a certain Baroness
Blaze de Bury—a (supposed) illegitimate daughter of Lord
Brougham. She lives in a queer old mouldy, musty *rez de
chaussée* in the depths of the Faubourg St. Germain, is the
grossest and most audacious lion-huntress in all creation and
has the two most extraordinary little French, emancipated
daughters. One of these, wearing a Spanish mantilla, and got
up apparently to dance the cachacha, presently asked me what
I thought of *incest* as a subject for a novel—adding that it had
against it that it was getting, in families, so terribly common.
Basta! But both figures and setting are a curious picture.—I rejoice in the dawning of your dramatic day, and wish I might be

at the *première* of your piece at Daly's. I give it my tenderest
good wishes—but I wish you had told me more about it, and
about your comedy. Why (since the dramatic door stands so
wide open to you) do you print the latter before having it
acted? This, from a Parisian point of view, seems quite monstrous.—

Your inquiry "Why I don't go to Spain?" is sublime—is what
Philip Van Artevelde says of the Lake of Como, "softly sublime, profusely fair!" I shall spend my summer in the most
tranquil and frugal hole I can unearth in France, and I have no
prospect of travelling for some time to come. The Waverley
Oaks seem strangely far away—yet I remember them well, and
the day we went there. I am sorry I am not to see your novel
sooner, but I applaud your energy in proposing to change it.
The printed thing always seems to me dead and done with. I
suppose you will write something about Philadelphia—I hope
so, as otherwise I am afraid I shall know nothing about it. I
salute your wife and children a thousand times and wish you
an easy and happy summer and abundant inspiration.

Yours very faithfully,
H. James Jr.

Growing fame

Miss Alger's invitation came when The Portrait of a Lady *was near the end of its serialization in the* Atlantic Monthly, *but James's authority concerning the question of "the American girl" had been well established since the publication of* Daisy Miller: A Study. *For most of his career James was shy of the lecture stage, but during his 1904–1905 American tour he did in fact speak, on "The Question of Our Speech," to young women graduating from Bryn Mawr College.*

To Miss Abbey Alger, November 21, 1881,
from Cambridge, Massachusetts

Dear Madam

I am extremely obliged to you for the honour you do me in inviting me to address an audience of seventy young women at the Saturday morning club; but hasten to assure you that the absence of a topic, the entire want of the habit of public speaking, the formidable character of the assembly, and an extremely personal diffidence, present themselves to me as cogent reasons for refusing myself the distinction you so kindly place within my reach. I remain, with many thanks, regrets and compliments, and the request that you will assure the ladies of the Saturday morning club of my extreme consideration,

Very respectfully yours
Henry James Jr.

The friendship with Robert Louis Stevenson

> James first met Stevenson in 1885. When Stevenson
> died in Samoa of tuberculosis, James wrote to his
> widow that "He lighted up a whole province of the
> globe and was in himself a whole province of one's
> imagination."

To Robert Louis Stevenson, July 31, 1888, from London

My dear Louis.

You are too far away—you are too absent—too invisible, in-
audible, inconceivable. Life is too short a business and friendship too delicate a matter for such tricks—for cutting great
gory masses out of 'em by the year at a time. Therefore come
back. Hang it all—sink it all and come back. A little more and
I shall cease to believe in you: I don't mean (in the usual implied
phrase) in your veracity, but literally and more fatally in your
relevancy—your objective reality. You have become a beautiful
myth—a kind of unnatural uncomfortable unburied *mort*. You
put forth a beautiful monthly voice, with such happy notes in
it—but it comes from too far away, from the other side of the
globe, while I vaguely know that you are crawling like a fly on
the nether surface of my chair. Your adventures, no doubt, are
wonderful, but I don't successfully evoke them, understand
them, believe in them. I do in those you write, heaven knows—
but I don't in those you perform, though the latter, I know, are
to lead to new revelations of the former and your capacity for
them is certainly wonderful enough. This is a selfish personal

cry: I wish you back; for literature is lonely and Bournemouth is barren without you. Your place in my affection has not been usurped by another—for there is not the least little scrap of another to usurp it. If there were I would perversely try to care for him. But there isn't—I repeat, and I literally care for nothing but your return. I haven't even your novel to stay my stomach withal. The wan wet months elapse and I see no sign of it. The beautiful portrait of your wife shimmers at me from my chimney-piece—brought some months ago by the natural McClure—but seems to refer to one as dim and distant and delightful as a "toast" of the last century. I wish I could make you homesick—I wish I could spoil your fun. It is a very featureless time. The summer is rank with rheumatism—a dark, drowned, unprecedented season. The town is empty but I am not going away. I have no money, but I have a little work. I have lately written several short fictions—but you may not see them unless you come home. I have just begun a novel which is to run through the *Atlantic* from January 1st and which I aspire to finish by the end of this year. In reality I suppose I shall not be fully delivered of it before the middle of next. After that, with God's help, I propose, for a longish period, to do nothing but short lengths. I want to leave a multitude of pictures of my time, projecting my small circular frame upon as many different spots as possible and going in for number as well as quality, so that the number may constitute a total having a certain value as observation and testimony. But there isn't so much as a creature here even to whisper such an intention to. Nothing lifts its hand in these islands save blackguard party politics. Criticism is of an object density and puerility—it doesn't exist—it writes the intellect of our race too low. Lang, in the D[aily] N[ews], every morning, and I believe in a hundred other places, uses his beautiful thin facility to write everything down to the lowest level of Philistine twaddle—the view of the old lady round the corner or the clever person at the dinner party. The incorporated society of authors (I belong to it, and so do you, I think, but I don't know what it is) gave a dinner the other night to American literati to thank them for praying for international copyright. I carefully forbore to go, thinking the gratulation premature, and I see by this morning's *Times* that the banquetted boon is further off than ever. Edmund Gosse has sent me his clever little life of Congreve, just out, and I have read it—but it isn't so good as his Raleigh. But no more of the insufferable subject. I see—or have lately seen—Colvin in the mazes of the town—defeated of his friends' hope for him of the headship of the museum—but bearing the scarcely-doubted-of loss with a gallantry which still marks him out for honourable preferment. I believe he has had domestic annoyances of a grave order—some embroilment in the City, of his feckless brother and consequent loss of income to his Mother etc.—Of all this however, I have only vague knowledge—only enough to be struck with the fine way he is not worsted by it. We always talk of you—but more and more as a fact not incontestable. "Some say he is going to such and such a place—there is a legend in another quarter that he was last heard of—or that it is generally supposed—" But it is weak, disheartened stuff. Come, my dear Louis, grow not too thin. I can't question you—because, as I say, I don't conjure you up. You have killed the imagination in me—that part of it which formed your element and in which you sat vivid and near. Your wife and Mother and Mr. Lloyd suffer also—I must confess it—by this failure of breath, of faith. Of course I have your letter—from Manasquan (is that the idiotic name?) of the—ingenuous me, to think there was a date! It was terribly impersonal—it did me little good. A little more and I shan't believe in you enough to bless you. Take this, therefore, as your last chance. I follow all with an aching wing, an inadequate geography and an ineradicable hope. Ever, my dear Louis, yours, to the last snub—

Henry James

The death of Alice James

Judged as a "neurasthenic" invalid from a relatively young age, toward the end of her life Alice James received the diagnosis of breast cancer with some satisfaction ("I have longed and longed for a palpable disease"). Within an hour of Alice's death, Henry James cabled the news to his brother William, and William cabled back with the caution that she might not really be dead, for, as he later explained, "Her neurotic temperament & chronically reduced vitality are just the field for trance-tricks. . . ." The reference to "your Alice" at the end of the letter is to the other Alice James, the wife of William James.

To William James, March 8, 1892, from London

My dear William

Alice died at exactly four o'clock on Sunday afternoon (about the same hour of the same day as mother), and it is now Tuesday morning. But, even now the earliest moment my letter can go, or could have gone, to you is tomorrow P.M.—and there were innumerable things yesterday to do. Yesterday afternoon came your cable. You wouldn't have thought your warning necessary if you had been with us, or were with us now. Of course the event comes to you out of the comparative vague and unexplained, for you won't get our letters of Wednesday last and of Saturday for some days yet, alas. I wrote you as fully as I could on both of these days. On Saturday the end seemed near—yet also as if her strange power to *last* might still, for a few days, assert itself. The great sign of change on Saturday A.M. and, as I wrote you, the inexpressibly touching one, was the sudden cessation of all suffering and distress, which, up to Friday night, had been constant and dreadful. The pleuritic pain, the cough, the fever, all the sudden complications of the previous few days which came, so unmistakably, as *the* determining accident at the mercy of which we had felt her to be (and without which she might still have lived on for some weeks—even possibly,—though this I greatly doubt—some months): all these things which, added to the suffering they already found, were pitiful to see, passed from her in the course of a few hours, fell away blissfully and left her consciously and oh, longingly, close to the end. As I wrote you on Saturday, the deathly look in her poor face, added to this simplification, and which, in its new intensity, had come on all together in the night, made me feel that the end *might* come at any moment. I came away on Saturday afternoon, not to break the intense stillness which Katharine wished to create near in order that she might sleep—for though she was quiet she didn't sleep. Lloyd Tuckey saw her, that evening, for the second time that day, and I was back there for the hours before 10. I wanted to stay the night—but Katharine thought I had better not—and it turned out better. For I couldn't have been in the room or done anything. She became restless again—but without pain—said a few barely audible things—(one of which was that she *couldn't,* oh, she COULDN'T and begged it mightn't be exacted of her, live *another* day), had two or three mouthfuls of nourishment at 1 or 2 and then, towards 6, sank into a perfectly gentle sleep. From that sleep she never woke—but after an hour or two it changed its character and became a loud, deep, breathing— almost stertorous, and this was her condition when I got to the house at 9. From that hour till 4 P.M. Katharine and Nurse and I sat by her bed. The doctor (who had doubted of the need of his returning, and judged that she would *not* live till morning) came at 11.30—but on Katharine's going down to him and describing exactly Alice's then condition, asked leave *not* to come into the room, as he preferred not to, in the last hour before death, when there was nothing to do or to suggest, unless it was insisted on. For about seven hours this deep difficult and almost automatic breathing continued—with *no* look of pain in the face—only more and more utterly the look of death. They were infinitely pathetic and, to me, most unspeakable hours. They would have been intolerable if it had not been so evident that all the hideous burden of suffering consciousness was utterly gone. As it is, they were the most appealing and pitiful thing I ever saw. But I have seen, happily, but little death immediately. Toward the end, for about an hour, the breathing became a constant sort of smothered whistle in the lung. The pulse flickered, came and went, ceased and revived a little again, and then with all perceptible action of the heart, altogether ceased to be sensible for some time before the breathing ceased. At three o'clock a blessed change took place—she seemed to sleep—I mean to breathe—without effort, gently, peacefully and naturally, like a child. This lasted an hour, till the respirations, still distinct, paused, intermitted and became rarer—at the last, for seven or eight minutes, only one a minute, by the watch. Her face then seemed in a strange, dim, touching way, to become clearer. I went to the window to let in a little more of the afternoon light upon it (it was a bright, kind, soundless Sunday), and when I came back to the bed she had drawn the breath that was not succeeded by another.

I went out and cabled you about half an hour later—I knew you would be in great suspense every hour after her cable of the day before. Since then I have sat many hours in the still little room in which so many months of her final suffering were compressed, and in which she lies as the very perfection of the image of what she had longed for years, and at the last with pathetic intensity, to be. She looks most beautiful and noble— with *all* of the august expression that you can imagine—and with less, than before, of the almost ghastly emaciation of those last days. Only last night (I have not yet been at the house today) had a little look of change begun. We have made all the arrangements—they have been on the whole simple and easy— with the Cremation Society, for a service tomorrow afternoon (early) at Woking. Of course you know her absolute decision on this point—and she had gone into all the details. For myself I rejoice, as you doubtless will, and Katharine does, that we are not to lay her, far off from the others, in this damp, black alien English earth. Her ashes shall go home and be placed beside Father's and Mother's. She wished we should be simply four— Katharine and I, her Nurse, and Annie Richards, who, though almost never seeing her, has shown devoted friendship to her ever since she (Annie) has been in England. I will try and send you a line tomorrow after it is over. Katharine is the unbroken reed, in all this, that you can imagine, and I rejoice, unspeakably in the rest and liberation that have come to her. The tension—the strain and wear—of these last months has been more serious than any before—and I hope she won't go back immediately to new claims and responsibilities. She has, practically, a large margin of convenience here, as Alice's lease of that pleasant little house runs on till May 1st. She will probably stay yet a month. She considers that there were almost unmistakable signs, in the last weeks of Alice's life, of the existence of the *internal* tumour (the second one), which Baldwin last summer pronounced probable. The final "accident"—brought on (though at a moment when her strength was at the last ebb and her distress from the tumour in the breast and all her nervous condition and her perpetual gout and rheumatism was absolutely unbearable from day to day, and she was simply living from day to day, and night to night, on the last desperate resources of morphia and hypnotism)—this strange complication which simply *made* a sudden collapse of everything was ostensibly a mysterious cold, communicated by nurse (who had a bad one) and producing all the appearance of pleurisy—with a sharp pain in the side (she lived only in perpetual poultices the last three or four days—up to Saturday night when she wished everything off) and a dreadful cough which shook her to pieces and made impossible the quiet which was the only escape from the ever-present addition of "nervousness." But Katharine thinks that an internal tumour close to the lung, where Baldwin placed it, was accountable for much of this last disorganization. However, she will tell you, later, of all these things—perhaps you will think I try to tell too much. I shall write by this post briefly to Bob, but won't you please immediately send him this. I hope he got a prompt echo of my cable.—Katharine will probably also tell you immediately that Alice very wisely under the circumstances, I think, in an alteration made *lately* in her will, after your plan of coming abroad this summer for a year came home to her, named her (K.P.L.) and J. B. Warner her executors. She had first named you and me—but she came later to think it probable that she would die this summer—live *till* then—during the months you would probably be in Europe— which would be for the execution of the will on your part a burdensome delay. Besides, with all the load upon you, she wished to spare you all trouble. But I *must* close this endlessness—even if I send you more of it by the same post. Ever yours, and your Alice's, and Bob's affectionate

Henry James

The friendship with Hendrik C. Andersen

The friendship with the young Norwegian-American sculptor Hendrik Christian Andersen (1872–1940) has been a focal point of the discussion of James's sexual orientation. Of course these two particularly intense letters are written at a moment of crisis, just after the death of Andersen's brother.

To Hendrik C. Andersen, February 9, 1902, from London

My dear, dear dearest Hendrik

Your news fills me with horror and pity, and how can I express the tenderness with which it makes me think of you and the aching wish to be near you and put my arms round you? My heart fairly bleeds and breaks at the vision of you *alone,* in your wicked and indifferent old far-off Rome, with the haunting, blighting, unbearable sorrow. The sense that I can't *help* you, see you, talk to you, touch you, hold you close and long, or do anything to make you rest on me, and feel my participation—this torments me, dearest boy, makes me ache for you, and for myself; makes me gnash my teeth and groan at the bitterness of things. I can only take refuge in hoping you are *not* utterly alone, that some human tenderness of *some* sort, some kindly voice and hand *are* near you that may make a little the difference. What a dismal winter you must have had, with this staggering blow at the climax! I don't of course know *what* fragment of friendship there may be to draw near to you, and in my uncertainty my image of you is of the darkest, and my pity, as I say, feels so helpless. I wish I could go to Rome and put my hands on you (oh, how lovingly I should lay them!) but that, alas, is odiously impossible. (Not, moreover, that apart from *you*, I should so much as like to be there now.) I find myself thrown back on anxiously and doubtless vainly, wondering if there may not, after a while, [be] some possibility of your coming to England, of the current of your trouble inevitably carrying you here—so that I might take consoling, soothing, infinitely close and tender and affectionately-healing *possession* of you. This is the one thought that relieves me about you a little—and I wish you might fix your eyes on it for the idea, just of the possibility. I am in town for a few weeks but I return to Rye April 1st, and sooner or later to *have* you there and do for you, to put my arm round you and *make* you lean on me as on a brother and a lover, and keep you on and on, slowly comforted or at least relieved of the first bitterness of pain—this I try to imagine as thinkable, attainable, not wholly out of the question. There I am, at any rate, and there is my house and my garden and my table and my studio—such as it is!—and your room, and your welcome, and your place everywhere—and I press them upon you, oh so earnestly, dearest boy, if isolation and grief and the worries you are overdone with become intolerable to you. There they are, I say—to fall upon, to rest upon, to find whatever possible shade of oblivion in. I will *nurse* you through your dark passage. I wish I could do something *more*—something straighter and nearer and more immediate but such as it is please let it sink into you. Let all my tenderness, dearest boy, do *that*. This is all now. I wired you three words an hour ago. I can't *think* of your sister-in-law—I brush her vision away and your history with your father, as I've feared it, has haunted me all winter. I embrace you with almost a passion of pity.

Henry James

To Hendrik C. Andersen, February 28, 1902, from Rye

Dearest, dearest Boy, more tenderly embraced than I can say!—
How woefully you must have wondered at my apparently horrid and heartless silence since your last so beautiful, noble,
exquisite letter! *But,* dearest Boy, I've been dismally *ill*—as I
was even when I wrote to you from town; and it's only within
a day or two that free utterance has—to this poor extent—become possible to me. *Don't waste any pity,* any words, on me
now, for it's, at last, blissfully over, I'm convalescent, on firm
grounds, safe, gaining daily—only weak and "down" and
spent, and above all like a helpless pigmy before my accumulation of the mountain of a month's letters etc. To make a long
story of the shortest, I was taken in London, on January 29th—
two days after getting there, with a malignant sudden attack,
through a chill, of inflammation of the bowels: which threw me
into bed, for a week, howling. Then I had a few days of false
and apparent recuperation—*one* of which was the Sunday I
wrote you from the Athenaeum on receipt of *your* direful letter.
But I felt myself collapsing, *re*lapsing again, and hurried down
here on February 11th just in time to save, as it were, my life
from another wretched siege out of my own house. I tumbled
into bed here and had a dozen wretched days of complicated,
aggravated relapse: but at least nursed, tended, cared for, with
all zeal and needfulness. So I've pulled through—and am out—
and surprisingly soon—of a very deep dark hole. *In* my deep
hole, how I thought yearningly, helplessly, dearest Boy, of *you*
as your last letter gives you to me and as I take you, to my
heart. I determined, deliberately, *not* to *wire* you, for I felt it
would but cruelly worry and alarm you; and each day I reached
out to the hope of some scrawl—I mean toward some possibility of a word to you. But that has come duly now. Now, at
least, my weak arms still can feel you close. Infinitely, deeply, as
deeply as you will have felt, for yourself, was I touched by your
second letter. I respond to every throb of it, I participate in
every pang. I've gone through Death, and Death, enough in my
long life, to know how all that we *are,* all that we *have,* all that
is best of us within, our genius, our imagination, our passion,

our whole personal being, become then but aides and channels and open gates to suffering, to being flooded. But, it is better so. Let yourself go and *live,* even as a lacerated, mutilated lover, with your grief, your loss, your sore, unforgettable consciousness. *Possess* them and let them possess you, and life, so, will still hold you in her arms, and press you to her breast, and keep you, like the great merciless but still *most* enfolding and never disowning mighty Mother, on and on for things to come. Beautiful and unspeakable your account of relation to Andreas. Sacred and beyond tears. How I wish I had known him, admirable, loveable boy—but you make me: I *do.* Well, he is *all* yours now: he lives in you and out of all pain. Wait, and you will see; hold fast, sit tight, *stick hard,* and more things than I can tell you now will come back to you. But you know, in your courage, your genius and your patience, more of these things than I need try thus to stammer to you. And now I am tired and spent. I only, for goodnight, for five minutes, take you to my heart. And I'm better, better, better, dearest Boy; don't think of my having been ill. Think only of my love and that I am yours always and ever

Henry James

The death of William James

In 1910 James found himself in the grip of a "black depression." During the spring, his brother William crossed the ocean with his wife, Alice, partly to raise Henry's spirits, partly to see if the cure at Bad Nauheim in Germany could improve his own failing health. While staying in Switzerland, Henry and William received news of the death of their brother Robertson back in the United States. When William and Alice sailed home in August, Henry went with them. Two weeks later William James died at his New Hampshire home.

To Thomas Sergeant Perry, September 2, 1910,
from Chocorua, New Hampshire

My dear old Thomas.

I sit heavily stricken and in darkness—for from far back in dimmest childhood he had been my ideal Elder Brother, and I still, through all the years, saw in him, even as a small timorous boy yet, my protector, my backer, my authority and my pride. His extinction changes the face of life for me—besides the mere missing of his inexhaustible company and personality, original-ity, the whole unspeakably vivid and beautiful presence of him. And his noble intellectual vitality was still but at its climax—he had two or three ardent purposes and plans. He had cast them away, however, at the end—I mean that, dreadfully suffering, he wanted only to die. Alice and I had a bitter pilgrimage with him from far off—he sank here, on his threshold; and then it went horribly fast. I cling for the present to *them*—and so try to stay here through this month. After that I shall be with them in Cambridge for several more—we shall cleave more together. I should like to come and see you for a couple of days much, but it would have to be after the 20th, or even October 1st, I think; and I fear you may not then be still in *villeggiatura*. *If* so I *will* come. You knew him—among those living now—from furthest back with me. Yours and Lilla's all faithfully,

Henry James

To H. G. Wells, September 11, 1910,
from Chocorua, New Hampshire

My dear Wells.
We greatly value, my sister-in-law and I, your beautiful and tender letter about my beloved Brother and our irreparable loss. Be very gratefully thanked for it, and know we are deeply moved by your admirably-expressed sense of what he *was,* so nobly and magnanimously. He did surely shed light to man, and *gave,* of his own great spirit and beautiful genius, with splendid generosity. Of my personal loss—the extinction of so shining a presence in my own life, and from so far back (really from dimmest childhood) I won't pretend to speak. He had an inexhaustible authority for me, and I feel abandoned and afraid, even as a lost child. But he is a possession, of real magnitude, and I shall find myself still living upon him to the end. My life, thank God, is impregnated with him. My sister-in-law and his children are very interesting and absorbing to me, and I shall stay on here (in America I mean) for some months—so that we may hold and cling together. And I hope in the future never to be without some of them. When I return to England I shall see you promptly—and you have perhaps meanwhile an inadequate idea of the moral and aesthetic greed (enriched by criticism) with which I read you. Yours all faithfully

Henry James

The publication of Boon, and the break with H. G. Wells

Although Henry James and H. G. Wells had been friends since 1898, in 1914 Wells took offense when, in "The Younger Generation" (revised as "The New Novel"), James noted the "robust pitch" of the much younger man's work but included him with those insufficiently artistic writers who produced "affluents turbid and unrestrained." Wells considered himself primarily a novelist of ideas, not forms, and his Boon soon attacked James as "the culmination of the Superficial type" and, stylistically, a "painful hippopotamus."

To H. G. Wells, July 6, 1915, from London

My dear Wells.

I was given yesterday at a club your volume *Boon, etc.*, from a loose leaf in which I learn that you kindly sent it me and which yet appears to have lurked there for a considerable time undelivered. I have just been reading, to acknowledge it intelligently, a considerable number of its pages—though not all; for, to be perfectly frank, I have been in that respect beaten for the first time—or rather for the first time but one—by a book of yours: I haven't found the current of it draw me on and on this time—as unfailingly and irresistibly before (which I have repeatedly let you know). However, I shall try again—I hate to lose any scrap of you that *may* make for light or pleasure; and meanwhile I have more or less mastered your appreciation of H.J., which I have found very curious and interesting, after a fashion—though it has naturally not filled me with a fond elation. It is difficult of course for a writer to put himself *fully* in the place of another writer who finds him extraordinarily futile and void, and who is moved to publish that to the world—and I think the case isn't easier when he happens to have enjoyed the other writer enormously, from far back; because there has then grown up the habit of taking some common meeting-ground between them for granted, and the falling away of this is like the collapse of a bridge which made communication possible. But I am by nature more in dread of any fool's paradise, or at least of any bad misguidedness, than in love with the idea of a security proved and the fact that a mind as brilliant as yours *can* resolve me into such an unmitigated mistake, can't enjoy me in anything like the degree in which I like to think I may be enjoyed, makes me greatly want to fix myself, for as long as my nerves will stand it, with such a pair of eyes. I am aware of certain things I have, and not less conscious, I believe, of various others that I am simply reduced to wish I did or could have; so I try, for possible light, to enter into the feelings of a critic for whom the deficiencies so preponderate. The difficulty about that effort, however, is that one can't keep it up—one *has* to fall back on one's sense of one's good parts—one's own sense; and I at least should have to do that, I think, even if your picture were painted with a more searching brush. For I should otherwise seem to forget what it is that my poetic and my appeal to experience rest upon. They rest upon *my* measure of fulness—fulness of life and of the projection of it, which seems to you such an emptiness of both. I don't mean to say I don't wish I could do twenty things I can't—many of which you do so livingly; but I confess I ask myself what would become in that case of some of those to which I am most addicted and by which interest seems to me most beautifully producible. I hold that interest may be, *must* be, exquisitely made and created, and that if we don't make it, we who undertake to, nobody and nothing will make it for us; though nothing is more possible, nothing may even be more certain, than that my quest of it, my constant wish to run it to earth, may entail the sacrifice of certain things that are not on the straight line of it. However, there are too many things to say, and I don't think your chapter is really inquiring enough to entitle you to expect all of them. The fine thing about the fictional form to me is that it opens such widely different windows of attention; but that is just why I like the window so to frame the play and the process!

Faithfully yours
Henry James

To H. G. Wells, July 10, 1915, from London

My dear Wells.

I am bound to tell you that I don't think your letter makes out any sort of case for the bad manners of *Boon*, so far as your indulgence in them at the expense of your poor old H.J. is concerned—I say "your" simply because he has *been* yours, in the most liberal, continual, sacrificial, the most admiring and abounding critical way, ever since he began to know your writings: as to which you have had copious testimony. Your comparison of the book to a wastebasket strikes me as the reverse of felicitous, for what one throws into that receptacle is exactly what one *doesn't* commit to publicity and make the affirmation of one's estimate of one's contemporaries by, I should liken it much rather to the preservative portfolio or drawer in which what is withheld from the basket is savingly laid away. Nor do I feel it anywhere evident that my "view of life and literature," or what you impute to me as such, is carrying everything before it and becoming a public menace—so unaware do I seem, on the contrary, that my products constitute an example in any measurable degree followed or a cause in any degree successfully pleaded: I can't but think that if this were the case I should find it somewhat attested in their circulation—which, alas, I have reached a very advanced age in the entirely defeated hope of. But I *have* no view of life and literature, I maintain, other than that our form of the latter in especial is admirable exactly by its range and variety, its plasticity and liberality, its fairly living on the sincere and shifting experience of the individual practitioner. That is why I have always so admired your so free and strong application of it, the particular rich receptacle of intelligences and impressions emptied out with an energy of its own, that your genius constitutes; and *that* is in particular why, in my letter of two or three days since, I pronounced it curious and interesting that you should find the case I constitute myself only ridiculous and vacuous to the extent of your having to proclaim your sense of it. The curiosity and the interest, however, in this latter connection are of course for my mind those of the break of perception (perception of the vivacity of *my* variety) on the part of a talent so generally inquiring and apprehensive as yours. Of course for myself I live, live intensely and am fed by life, and my value, whatever it be, is in my own kind of expression of that. Therefore I am pulled up to wonder by the fact that for you my kind (my sort of sense of expression and sort of sense of life alike) doesn't exist; and that wonder is, I admit, a disconcerting comment on my idea of the various appreciability of our addiction to the novel and of all the personal and intellectual history, sympathy and curiosity, behind the given example of it. It is when that history and curiosity have been determined in the way most different from my own that I myself want to get at them—precisely *for* the extension of life, which is the novel's best gift. But that is another matter. Meanwhile I absolutely dissent from the claim that there are any differences whatever in the amenability to art of forms of literature aesthetically determined, and hold your distinction between a form that is (like) painting and a form that is (like) architecture for wholly null and void. There is no sense in which architecture is aesthetically "for use" that doesn't leave any other art whatever exactly as much so; and so far from that of literature being irrelevant to the literary report upon life, and to its being made as interesting as possible, I regard it as relevant in a degree that leaves everything else behind. It is art that *makes* life, makes interest, makes importance, for our consideration and application of these things, and I know of no substitute whatever for the force and beauty of its process. If I were Boon I should say that any pretence of such a substitute is helpless and hopeless humbug; but I wouldn't be Boon for the world, and am only yours faithfully

Henry James

VII

DEFINITION AND DESCRIPTION

Although in 1886 Thomas Hardy judged that Henry James had "a ponderously warm way of saying nothing in infinite sentences," he eventually would consider the mature writer to be the finest living novelist and a master at the "extraordinary complicated texture of subtle thoughts and minute sensations." In fact, at every stage of his career, Henry James produced a prose that was often startling in wit and force—as well as in subtlety—and his syntax was rarely as labyrinthine as some have claimed. The following passages, a number of them taken from long novels that could not be included in this edition, suggest the precision of James's language, as well as the evolution of his matchless cadence.

An American encounters some aristocrats

From The American, *1877. Christopher Newman—*
an American who has made his fortune and now
wants a wife—pays a visit to the home of Comtesse
Claire de Bellegarde de Cintré.

He walked across the Seine, late in the summer afternoon, and
made his way through those gray and silent streets of the
Faubourg St. Germain whose houses present to the outer world
a face as impassive and as suggestive of the concentration of
privacy within as the blank walls of Eastern seraglios. Newman
thought it a queer way for rich people to live; his ideal of
grandeur was a splendid façade, diffusing its brilliancy outward too, irradiating hospitality. The house to which he had
been directed had a dark, dusty, painted portal, which swung
open in answer to his ring. It admitted him into a wide, grav-
eled court, surrounded on three sides with closed windows,
and with a doorway facing the street, approached by three
steps and surmounted by a tin canopy. The place was all in the
shade; it answered to Newman's conception of a convent. The
portress could not tell him whether Madame de Cintré was visible; he would please to apply at the farther door. He crossed
the court; a gentleman was sitting, bareheaded, on the steps of
the portico, playing with a beautiful pointer. He rose as Newman approached, and, as he laid his hand upon the bell, said
with a smile, in English, that he was afraid Newman would be
kept waiting; the servants were scattered, he himself had been
ringing, he didn't know what the deuce was in them. He was a

young man, his English was excellent, and his smile very frank. Newman pronounced the name of Madame de Cintré.

"I think," said the young man, "that my sister is visible. Come in, and if you will give me your card I will carry it to her myself."

Newman had been accompanied on his present errand by a slight sentiment, I will not say of defiance—a readiness for aggression or defense, as they might prove needful—but of reflective, good-humored suspicion. He took from his pocket, while he stood on the portico, a card upon which, under his name, he had written the words "San Francisco," and while he presented it he looked warily at his interlocutor. His glance was singularly reassuring; he liked the young man's face; it strongly resembled that of Madame de Cintré. He was evidently her brother. The young man, on his side, had made a rapid inspection of Newman's person. He had taken the card and was about to enter the house with it when another figure appeared on the threshold—an older man, of a fine presence, wearing evening dress. He looked hard at Newman, and Newman looked at him. "Madame de Cintré," the younger man repeated, as an introduction of the visitor. The other took the card from his hand, read it in a rapid glance, looked again at Newman from head to foot, hesitated a moment, and then said, gravely but urbanely, "Madame de Cintré is not at home."

The younger man made a gesture, and then, turning to Newman, "I am very sorry, sir," he said.

Newman gave him a friendly nod, to show that he bore him no malice, and retraced his steps. At the porter's lodge he stopped; the two men were still standing on the portico.

"Who is the gentleman with the dog?" he asked of the old woman who reappeared. He had begun to learn French.

"That is Monsieur le Comte."

"And the other?"

"That is Monsieur le Marquis."

"A marquis?" said Christopher in English, which the old woman fortunately did not understand. "Oh, then he's not the butler!"

An ambitious young Frenchwoman

From The American, *1877. Newman cautions Claire de Cintré's brother, Count Valentin de Bellegarde, concerning an attractive young social climber.*

"Hanged if I should want to have a greedy little adventuress like that know I was giving myself such pains about her!" said Newman.

"A pretty woman is always worth one's pains," objected Valentin. "Mademoiselle Nioche is welcome to be tickled by my curiosity, and to know that I am tickled that she is tickled. She is not so much tickled, by the way."

"You had better go and tell her," Newman rejoined. "She gave me a message for you of some such drift."

"Bless your quiet imagination," said Valentin, "I have been to see her—three times in five days. She is a charming hostess; we talk of Shakespeare and the musical glasses. She is extremely clever and a very curious type; not at all coarse or wanting to be coarse; determined not to be. She means to take very good care of herself. She is extremely perfect; she is as hard and clear-cut as some little figure of a sea-nymph in an antique intaglio, and I will warrant that she has not a grain more of sentiment or heart than if she were scooped out of a big amethyst. You can't scratch her even with a diamond. Extremely pretty,—really, when you know her, she is wonderfully pretty,—intelligent, determined, ambitious, unscrupulous, capable of looking at a man strangled without changing color, she is, upon my honor, extremely entertaining."

"It's a fine list of attractions," said Newman; "they would

serve as a police-detective's description of a favorite criminal. I should sum them up by another word than 'entertaining.'"

"Why, that is just the word to use. I don't say she is laudable or lovable. I don't want her as my wife or my sister. But she is a very curious and ingenious piece of machinery; I like to see it in operation."

"Well, I have seen some very curious machines, too," said Newman; "and once, in a needle factory, I saw a gentleman from the city, who had stepped too near one of them, picked up as neatly as if he had been prodded by a fork, swallowed down straight, and ground into small pieces."

Sarah Bernhardt,
the muse of the newspaper

From "The Comédie Française in London," 1879. Acclaimed as France's greatest actress, Sarah Bernhardt (1844–1923) received little praise from James, who judged her more as a phenomenon than as an actress. Even after her leg was amputated in 1915, she continued to perform and attract attention.

The Comédie Française has been "taken up," collectively and individually, with a warmth which must have taxed the preconceptions of the French imagination, and which does great honour to English courtesy. How the French imagination may have reconciled all this—especially in some of its phases—with the familiar traditions about English stiffness and coldness, English prudery and false delicacy, it profits not to enquire. It is enough that it must occasionally have been sorely puzzled, and have carried away a considerable store of tough problems, to be solved at leisure. One of these, for instance, will be connected, as we may surmise, with the extraordinary vogue of Mademoiselle Sarah Bernhardt, and will concern itself with enquiring into the sources of the tender interest excited by this lady. I speak of her "vogue" for want of a better word; it would require some ingenuity to give an idea of the intensity, the ecstasy, the insanity as some people would say, of curiosity and enthusiasm provoked by Mlle. Bernhardt. I spoke just now of topics, and what they were worth in the London system. This remarkable actress has filled this function with a completeness that leaves nothing to be desired; her success has been altogether the most striking and curious, although by no means, I think, the most gratifying, incident of the visit of the Comédie. It has not been the most gratifying, because it has been but in a very moderate degree an artistic success. It has been the success of a celebrity, pure and simple, and Mlle. Sarah Bernhardt is not, to my sense, a celebrity because she is an artist. She is a celebrity because, apparently, she desires with an intensity that has rarely been equalled to be one, and because for this end all means are alike to her. She may flatter herself that, as regards the London public, she has compassed her end with a completeness which makes of her a sort of fantastically impertinent *victrix* poised upon a perfect pyramid of ruins—the ruins of a hundred British prejudices and proprieties. Mlle. Sarah Bernhardt has remarkable gifts; her success is something quite apart as the woman herself is something quite apart; but her triumph has little to do with the proper lines of the Comédie Française. She is a child of her age—of her moment—and she has known how to profit by the idiosyncrasies of the time. The trade of a celebrity, pure and simple, had been invented, I think, before she came to London; if it had not been, it is certain she would have discovered it. She has in a supreme degree what the French call the *génie de la réclame*—the advertising genius; she may, indeed, be called the muse of the newspaper. Brilliantly as she had already exercised her genius, her visit to London has apparently been a revelation to her of the great extension it may obtain among the Anglo-Saxon peoples, and the *dénoûment* of this latest chapter in the history of the Comédie Française is that Mlle. Sarah Bernhardt has resigned her place as *sociétaire*. You will, of course, have heard long before this reaches you that she has formed projects, more or less definite, for visiting the United States. I strongly suspect that she will find a triumphant career in the Western world. She is too American not to succeed in America. The people who have brought to the highest development the arts and graces of publicity will recognize a kindred spirit in a figure so admirably adapted for conspicuity. Mlle. Bernhardt will be a loss to the Comédie Française, but she will not be a fatal one.

An American education

From The Portrait of a Lady, *1881. Before being taken to England by her aunt, the independent Isabel Archer is established in the isolation of her grandmother's Albany home. In 1913, in* A Small Boy and Others, *James would record how "the attempt to drag me crying and kicking to the first hour of my education failed on the threshold of the Dutch House in Albany."*

On the other side, across the street, was an old house that was called the Dutch House—a peculiar structure dating from the earliest colonial time, composed of bricks that had been painted yellow, crowned with a gable that was pointed out to strangers, defended by a rickety wooden paling and standing sidewise to the street. It was occupied by a primary school for children of both sexes, kept or rather let go, by a demonstrative lady of whom Isabel's chief recollection was that her hair was fastened with strange bedroomy combs at the temples and that she was the widow of some one of consequence. The little girl had been offered the opportunity of laying a foundation of knowledge in this establishment; but having spent a single day in it, she had protested against its laws and had been allowed to stay at home, where, in the September days, when the windows of the Dutch House were open, she used to hear the hum of childish voices repeating the multiplication-table—an incident in which the elation of liberty and the pain of exclusion were indistinguishably mingled. The foundation of her knowledge was really laid in the idleness of her grandmother's house, where, as most of the other inmates were not reading people, she had uncontrolled use of a library full of books with frontispieces, which she used to climb upon a chair to take down. When she had found one to her taste—she was guided in the selection chiefly by the frontispiece—she carried it into a mysterious apartment which lay beyond the library and which was called, traditionally, no one knew why, the office. Whose office it had been and at what period it had flourished, she never learned; it was enough for her that it contained an echo and a pleasant musty smell and that it was a chamber of disgrace for old pieces of furniture whose infirmities were not always apparent (so that the disgrace seemed unmerited and rendered them victims of injustice) and with which, in the manner of children, she had established relations almost human, certainly dramatic. There was an old haircloth sofa in especial, to which she had confided a hundred childish sorrows. The place owed much of its mysterious melancholy to the fact that it was properly entered from the second door of the house, the door that had been condemned, and that it was secured by bolts which a particularly slender little girl found it impossible to slide. She knew that this silent, motionless portal opened into the street; if the sidelights had not been filled with green paper she might have looked out upon the little brown stoop and the well-worn brick pavement. But she had no wish to look out, for this would have interfered with her theory that there was a strange, unseen place on the other side—a place which became to the child's imagination, according to its different moods, a region of delight or of terror.

An American is corrected on what constitutes "the self"

From The Portrait of a Lady, *1881. Madame Merle, a highly Europeanized American, disputes Isabel Archer's assertion of an essential "self."*

"That is very crude of you. When you have lived as long as I, you will see that every human being has his shell, and that you must take the shell into account. By the shell I mean the whole envelope of circumstances. There is no such thing as an isolated man or woman; we are each of us made up of a cluster of appurtenances. What do you call one's self? Where does it begin? where does it end? It overflows into everything that belongs to us—and then it flows back again. I know that a large part of myself is in the dresses I choose to wear. I have a great respect for *things*! One's self—for other people—is one's expression of one's self; and one's house, one's clothes, the book one reads, the company one keeps—these things are all expressive."

This was very metaphysical; not more so, however, than several observations Madame Merle had already made. Isabel was fond of metaphysics, but she was unable to accompany her friend into this bold analysis of the human personality.

"I don't agree with you," she said. "I think just the other way. I don't know whether I succeed in expressing myself, but I know that nothing else expresses me. Nothing that belongs to me is any measure of me; on the contrary, it's a limit, a barrier, and a perfectly arbitrary one. Certainly, the clothes which, as you say, I choose to wear, don't express me; and heaven forbid they should!"

"You dress very well," interposed Madame Merle, skilfully.

"Possibly; but I don't care to be judged by that. My clothes may express the dressmaker, but they don't express me. To begin with, it's not my own choice that I wear them; they are imposed upon me by society."

"Should you prefer to go without them?" Madame Merle inquired, in a tone which virtually terminated the discussion.

An absolutely unmarried woman

From The Bostonians, *1886. Olive Chancellor—with a smile that "might have been likened to a thin ray of moonlight resting upon the wall of a prison"—is frequently discussed as a Jamesian consideration of lesbian sexuality. In the full development of the novel, she is treated with far more sympathy and sensitivity than this biting early description may suggest.*

. . . what Basil Ransom actually perceived was that Miss Chancellor was a signal old maid. That was her quality, her destiny; nothing could be more distinctly written. There are women who are unmarried by accident, and others who are unmarried by option; but Olive Chancellor was unmarried by every implication of her being. She was a spinster as Shelley was a lyric poet, or as the month of August is sultry. She was so essentially a celibate that Ransom found himself thinking of her as old, though when he came to look at her (as he said to himself) it was apparent that her years were fewer than his own. He did not dislike her, she had been so friendly; but, little by little, she gave him an uneasy feeling—the sense that you could never be safe with a person who took things so hard. It came over him that it was because she took things hard she had sought his acquaintance; it had been because she was strenuous, not because she was genial; she had had in her eye—and what an extraordinary eye it was!—not a pleasure, but a duty. She would expect him to be strenuous in return; but he couldn't—in private life, he couldn't; privacy for Basil Ransom consisted entirely in what he called "laying off." She was not so plain on further acquaintance as she had seemed to him at first; even the young Mississippian had culture enough to see that she was refined. Her white skin had a singular look of being drawn tightly across her face; but her features, though sharp and irregular, were delicate in a fashion that suggested good breeding. Their line was perverse, but it was not poor. The curious tint of her eyes was a living colour; when she turned it upon you, you thought vaguely of the glitter of green ice. She had absolutely no figure, and presented a certain appearance of feeling cold. With all this, there was something very modern and highly developed in her aspect; she had the advantages as well as the drawbacks of a nervous organisation. She smiled constantly at her guest, but from the beginning to the end of dinner, though he made several remarks that he thought might prove amusing, she never once laughed. Later, he saw that she was a woman without laughter; exhilaration, if it ever visited her, was dumb. Once only, in the course of his subsequent acquaintance with her, did it find a voice; and then the sound remained in Ransom's ear as one of the strangest he had heard.

Philistine decor

From The Spoils of Poynton, *1897. At Waterbath, the home of the vulgar Brigstocks, Fleda Vetch encounters Mrs. Gereth, whose own home is the exquisite Poynton.*

What was dreadful now, what was horrible, was the intimate ugliness of Waterbath, and it was of that phenomenon these ladies talked while they sat in the shade and drew refreshment from the great tranquil sky, from which no blue saucers were suspended. It was an ugliness fundamental and systematic, the result of the abnormal nature of the Brigstocks, from whose composition the principle of taste had been extravagantly omitted. In the arrangement of their home some other principle, remarkably active, but uncanny and obscure, had operated instead, with consequences depressing to behold, consequences that took the form of a universal futility. The house was bad in all conscience, but it might have passed if they had only let it alone. This saving mercy was beyond them; they had smothered it with trumpery ornament and scrapbook art, with strange excrescences and bunchy draperies, with gimcracks that might have been keepsakes for maid-servants and nondescript conveniences that might have been prizes for the blind. They had gone wildly astray over carpets and curtains; they had an infallible instinct for disaster, and were so cruelly doom-ridden that it rendered them almost tragic. Their drawing-room, Mrs. Gereth lowered her voice to mention, caused her face to burn, and each of the new friends confided to the other that in her own apartment she had given way to tears. There was in the elder lady's a set of comic water-colors, a family joke by a family genius, and in the younger's a souvenir from some centennial or other Exhibition, that they shudderingly alluded to. The house was perversely full of souvenirs of places even more ugly than itself and of things it would have been a pious duty to forget. The worst horror was the acres of varnish, something advertised and smelly, with which everything was smeared; it was Fleda Vetch's conviction that the application of it, by their own hands and hilariously shoving each other, was the amusement of the Brigstocks on rainy days.

The really rich

From The Wings of the Dove, *1902. The fabulously wealthy Milly Theale is touring Europe with her traveling companion Susan Stringham.*

It came back of course to the question of money, and our observant lady had by this time repeatedly reflected that if one were talking of the "difference," it was just this, this incomparably and nothing else, that when all was said and done most made it. A less vulgarly, a less obviously purchasing or parading person she couldn't have imagined; but it was, all the same, the truth of truths that the girl couldn't get away from her wealth. She might leave her conscientious companion as freely alone with it as possible and never ask a question, scarce even tolerate a reference; but it was in the fine folds of the helplessly expensive little black frock that she drew over the grass as she now strolled vaguely off; it was in the curious and splendid coils of hair, "done" with no eye whatever to the *mode du jour,* that peeped from under the corresponding indifference of her hat, the merely personal tradition that suggested a sort of noble inelegance; it lurked between the leaves of the uncut but antiquated Tauchnitz volume of which, before going out, she had mechanically possessed herself. She couldn't dress it away, nor walk it away, nor read it away, nor think it away; she could neither smile it away in any dreamy absence nor blow it away in any softened sigh. She couldn't have lost it if she had tried—that was what it was to be really rich. It had to be *the* thing you were.

New York identity

From The Wings of the Dove, 1902. *Many years after he had left New York, James began to rethink his native city. After establishing the heroine of* The Wings of the Dove *as an emphatic New Yorker, he revisited the city in 1904–5, provided numerous impressions of the place in* The American Scene, *and then offered it as the setting of his late tale "The Jolly Corner." In 1907–9 he gave it definitive tribute in the title of the* New York Edition *of his fiction.*

Milly Theale had Boston friends, such as they were, and of recent making; and it was understood that her visit to them—a visit that was not to be meagre—had been undertaken, after a series of bereavements, in the interest of the particular peace that New York couldn't give. It was recognised, liberally enough, that there were many things—perhaps even too many—New York *could* give; but this was felt to make no difference in the important truth that what you had most to do, under the discipline of life, or of death, was really to feel your situation as grave. Boston could help you to that as nothing else could, and it had extended to Milly, by every presumption, some such measure of assistance. Mrs. Stringham was never to forget—for the moment had not faded, nor the infinitely fine vibration it set up in any degree ceased—her own first sight of the striking apparition, then unheralded and unexplained: the slim, constantly pale, delicately haggard, anomalously, agreeably angular young person, of not more than two-and-twenty summers, in spite of her marks, whose hair was somehow exceptionally red even for the real thing, which it innocently confessed to being, and whose clothes were remarkably black even for robes of mourning, which was the meaning they expressed. It was New York mourning, it was New York hair, it was a New York history, confused as yet, but multitudinous, of the loss of parents, brothers, sisters, almost every human appendage, all on a scale and with a sweep that had required the greater stage; it was a New York legend of affecting, of romantic isolation, and, beyond everything, it was by most accounts, in respect to the mass of money so piled on the girl's back, a set of New York possibilities. She was alone, she was stricken, she was rich, and in particular was strange—a combination in itself of a nature to engage Mrs. Stringham's attention.

*   *   *   *   *

For such was essentially the point: it was rich, romantic, abysmal, to have, as was evident, thousands and thousands a year, to have youth and intelligence and if not beauty, at least, in equal measure, a high, dim, charming, ambiguous oddity, which was even better, and then on top of all to enjoy boundless freedom, the freedom of the wind in the desert—it was unspeakably touching to be so equipped and yet to have been reduced by fortune to little humble-minded mistakes.

It brought our friend's imagination back again to New York, where aberrations were so possible in the intellectual sphere, and it in fact caused a visit she presently paid there to overflow with interest. As Milly had beautifully invited her, so she would hold out if she could against the strain of so much confidence in her mind; and the remarkable thing was that even at the end of three weeks she *had* held out. But by this time her mind had grown comparatively bold and free; it was dealing with new quantities, a different proportion altogether—and that had made for refreshment: she had accordingly gone home in convenient possession of her subject. New York was vast, New York was startling, with strange histories, with wild cosmopolite backward generations that accounted for anything; and to have got nearer the luxuriant tribe of which the rare creature was the final flower, the immense, extravagant, unregulated cluster, with free-living ancestors, handsome dead cousins, lurid uncles, beautiful vanished aunts, persons all bust and curls, preserved, though so exposed, in the marble of famous French chisels—all this, to say nothing of the effect of closer growths of the stem, was to have had one's small world-space both crowded and enlarged.

A Venetian majordomo

From The Wings of the Dove, 1902. *Eugenio, Milly Theale's majordomo in Venice, has the name of the courier who in 1878 was judged to be on excessively intimate terms with Daisy Miller and her family in Rome.*

The great Eugenio, recommended by grand-dukes and Americans, had entered her service during the last hours of all—had crossed from Paris, after multiplied *pourparlers* with Mrs. Stringham, to whom she had allowed more than ever a free hand, on purpose to escort her to the continent and encompass her there, and had dedicated to her, from the moment of their meeting, all the treasures of his experience. She had judged him in advance, polyglot and universal, very dear and very deep, as probably but a swindler finished to the finger-tips; for he was forever carrying one well-kept Italian hand to his heart and plunging the other straight into her pocket, which, as she had instantly observed him to recognise, fitted it like a glove. The remarkable thing was that these elements of their common consciousness had rapidly gathered into an indestructible link, formed the ground of a happy relation; being by this time, strangely, grotesquely, delightfully, what most kept up confidence between them and what most expressed it.

Like a scene from a Maeterlinck play

From The Wings of the Dove, 1902. *A dying American heiress, and her rival, a formidable English beauty, are presented in aesthetic juxtaposition. The description suggests the dreamlike* symboliste *theater of the Belgian playwright Maurice Maeterlinck, who would be awarded the Nobel Prize in 1911, despite the efforts of Edith Wharton, Edmund Gosse, and William Dean Howells to have that prize go to Henry James.*

Certain aspects of the connection of these young women show for us, such is the twilight that gathers about them, in the likeness of some dim scene in a Maeterlinck play; we have positively the image, in the delicate dusk, of the figures so associated and yet so opposed, so mutually watchful: that of the angular, pale princess, ostrich-plumed, black-robed, hung about with amulets, reminders, relics, mainly seated, mainly still, and that of the upright, restless, slow-circling lady of her court, who exchanges with her, across the black water streaked with evening gleams, fitful questions and answers. The upright lady, with thick, dark braids down her back, drawing over the grass a more embroidered train, makes the whole circuit, and makes it again, and the broken talk, brief and sparingly allusive, seems more to cover than to free their sense. This is because, when it fairly comes to not having others to consider, they meet in an air that appears rather anxiously to wait for their words. Such an impression as that was in fact grave, and might be tragic; so that, plainly enough, systematically at last, they settled to a care of what they said.

A private thought

From The Wings of the Dove, *1902. Just before her death, Milly Theale learns that Merton Densher has been after her for her money, but she still leaves him a stupendous fortune—and a letter which presumably explains her action. Densher's mistress burns the letter before he can read it; the "thought" here considered concerns what Milly Theale might have communicated in that letter.*

The thought was all his own, and his intimate companion was the last person he might have shared it with. He kept it back like a favourite pang; left it behind him, so to say, when he went out, but came home again the sooner for the certainty of finding it there. Then he took it out of its sacred corner and its soft wrappings; he undid them one by one, handling them, handling *it,* as a father, baffled and tender, might handle a maimed child. But so it was before him—in his dread of who else might see it. Then he took to himself at such hours, in other words, that he should never, never know what had been in Milly's letter. The intention announced in it he should but too probably know; but that would have been, for the depths of his spirit, the least part of it. The part of it missed for ever was the turn she would have given her act. That turn had possibilities that, somehow, by wondering about them, his imagination had extraordinarily filled out and refined. It had made of them a revelation the loss of which was like the sight of a priceless pearl cast before his eyes—his pledge given not to save it—into the fathomless sea, or rather even it was like the sacrifice of something sentient and throbbing, something that, for the spiritual ear, might have been audible as a faint, far wail. This was the sound that he cherished, when alone, in the stillness of his rooms. He sought and guarded the stillness, so that it might prevail there till the inevitable sounds of life, once more, comparatively coarse and harsh, should smother and deaden it—doubtless by the same process with which they would officiously heal the ache, in his soul, that was somehow one with it. It deepened moreover the sacred hush that he couldn't complain.

The seduction of Europe

From The Ambassadors, *1903. Back in Europe for the first time in many years, Strether meets Maria Gostrey, who reintroduces him to a way of life he had forgotten in New England. Waymarsh, his grim "old friend" from Massachusetts, dislikes the whole business.*

Was what was happening to himself then, was what already *had* happened, really that a woman of fashion was floating him into society and that an old friend deserted on the brink was watching the force of the current? When the woman of fashion permitted Strether—as she permitted him at the most—the purchase of a pair of gloves, the terms she made about it, the prohibition of neckties and other items till she should be able to guide him through the Burlington Arcade, were such as to fall upon a sensitive ear as a challenge to just imputations. Miss Gostrey was such a woman of fashion as could make without a symptom of vulgar blinking an appointment for the Burlington Arcade. Mere discriminations about a pair of gloves could thus at any rate represent—always for such sensitive ears as were in question—possibilities of something that Strether could make a mark against only as the peril of apparent wantonness. He had quite the consciousness of his new friend, for their companion, that he might have had of a Jesuit in petticoats, a representative of the recruiting interests of the Catholic Church. The Catholic Church, for Waymarsh—that was to say the enemy, the monster of bulging eyes and far-reaching quivering groping tentacles—was exactly society, exactly the multiplication of shibboleths, exactly the discrimination of types and tones, exactly the wicked old Rows of Chester, rank with feudalism; exactly in short Europe.

A *femme du monde*

From The Ambassadors, *1903. At a garden party in Paris, Strether meets the enchanting Comtesse Marie de Vionnet.*

Madame de Vionnet, having meanwhile come in, was at present close to them, and Miss Barrace hereupon, instead of risking a rejoinder, became again with a look that measured her from top to toe all mere long-handled appreciative tortoise-shell. She had struck our friend, from the first of her appearing, as dressed for a great occasion, and she met still more than on either of the others the conception reawakened in him at their garden-party, the idea of the *femme du monde* in her habit as she lived. Her bare shoulders and arms were white and beautiful; the materials of her dress, a mixture, as he supposed, of silk and crape, were of a silvery grey so artfully composed as to give an impression of warm splendour; and round her neck she wore a collar of large old emeralds, the green note of which was more dimly repeated, at other points of her apparel, in embroidery, in enamel, in satin, in substances and textures vaguely rich. Her head, extremely fair and exquisitely festal, was like a happy fancy, a notion of the antique, on an old precious medal, some silver coin of the Renaissance; while her slim lightness and brightness, her gaiety, her expression, her decision, contributed to an effect that might have been felt by a poet as half mythological and half conventional. He could have compared her to a goddess still partly engaged in a morning cloud, or to a sea-nymph waist-high in the summer surge. Above all she suggested to him the reflexion that the *femme du monde*—in these finest developments of the type—was, like Cleopatra in the play, indeed various and multifold. She had aspects, characters, days, nights—or had them at least, showed them by a mysterious law of her own, when in addition to everything she happened also to be a woman of genius. She was an obscure person, a muffled person one day, and a showy person, an uncovered person the next. He thought of Madame de Vionnet to-night as showy and uncovered, though he felt the formula rough, because, thanks to one of the short-cuts of genius, she had taken all his categories by surprise.

An intimate recollection of
a beautiful woman

From The Golden Bowl, *1904. Engaged to the wealthy Maggie Verver, Prince Amerigo encounters his penniless former lover, Charlotte Stant, at the home of a mutual friend.*

Making use then of clumsy terms of excess, the face was too narrow and too long, the eyes not large, and the mouth, on the other hand, by no means small, with substance in its lips and a slight, the very slightest, tendency to protrusion in the solid teeth, otherwise indeed well arrayed and flashingly white. But it was, strangely, as a cluster of possessions of his own that these things, in Charlotte Stant, now affected him; items in a full list, items recognised, each of them, as if, for the long interval, they had been "stored" wrapped up, numbered, put away in a cabinet. While she faced Mrs. Assingham the door of the cabinet had opened of itself; he took the relics out, one by one, and it was more and more, each instant, as if she were giving him time. He saw again that her thick hair was, vulgarly speaking, brown, but that there was a shade of tawny autumn leaf in it, for "appreciation"—a colour indescribable and of which he had known no other case, something that gave her at moments the sylvan head of a huntress. He saw the sleeves of her jacket drawn to her wrists, but he again made out the free arms within them to be of the completely rounded, the polished slimness that Florentine sculptors, in the great time, had loved, and of which the apparent firmness is expressed in their old silver and old bronze. He knew her narrow hands, he knew her long fingers and the shape and colour of her finger-nails, he knew her special beauty of movement and line when she turned her back, and the perfect working of all her main attachments, that of some wonderful finished instrument, something intently made for exhibition, for a prize. He knew above all the extraordinary fineness of her flexible waist, the stem of an expanded flower, which gave her a likeness also to some long, loose silk purse, well filled with gold pieces, but having been passed, empty, through a finger-ring that held it together. It was as if, before she turned to him, he had weighed the whole thing in his open palm and even heard a little the chink of the metal. When she did turn to him it was to recognise with her eyes what he might have been doing. She made no circumstance of thus coming upon him, save so far as the intelligence in her face could at any moment make a circumstance of almost anything. If when she moved off she looked like a huntress, she looked when she came nearer like his notion, perhaps not wholly correct, of a muse.

Colossal immodesty

From "New England: An Autumn Impression," in The American Scene, 1907. *Traveling around New Hampshire, James notes that "here might manners too be happily studied"—and then he comes upon this trio. In his* A Commonplace Book, *W. H. Auden offered this passage as an example of "annihilating prose."*

That curiosity held its breath, in truth, for fear of breaking the spell—the spell of the large liberty with which a pair of summer girls and a summer youth, from the hotel, took all nature and all society (so far as society was present on the top of the coach) into the confidence of their personal relation. Their personal relation—that of the young man was with the two summer girls, whose own was all with *him;* any other, with their mother, for instance, who sat speechless and serene beside me, with the other passengers, with the coachman, the guard, the quick-eared four-in-hand, being for the time completely suspended. The freedoms of the young three—who were, by the way, not in their earliest bloom either—were thus bandied in the void of the gorgeous valley without even a consciousness of its shriller, its recording echoes. The whole phenomenon was documentary; it started, for the restless analyst, innumerable questions, amid which he felt himself sink beyond his depth. The immodesty was too colossal to be anything but innocence—yet the innocence, on the other hand, was too colossal to be anything but inane. And they were alive, the slightly stale three: they talked, they laughed, they sang, they shrieked, they romped, they scaled the pinnacle of publicity and perched on it flapping their wings; whereby they were shown in possession of many of the movements of life.

The individual Jew

From "New York and the Hudson: A Spring Impression," in The American Scene, 1907. Although James's remarks on "the New Jerusalem" of Manhattan's Lower East Side have been judged by some to be anti-Semitic, his praise of Jewish "intensity" has been seen as positive by others; see also James on the Yiddish theater, in "The Bowery and Thereabouts," printed in its entirety in the "Travel" section of this edition.

There is no swarming like that of Israel when once Israel has got a start, and the scene here bristled, at every step, with the signs and sounds, immitigable, unmistakable, of a Jewry that had burst all bounds. That it has burst all bounds in New York, almost any combination of figures or of objects taken at hazard sufficiently proclaims; but I remember how the rising waters, on this summer night, rose, to the imagination, even above the housetops and seemed to sound their murmur to the pale distant stars. It was as if we had been thus, in the crowded hustled roadway, where multiplication, multiplication of everything, was the dominant note, at the bottom of some vast sallow aquarium in which innumerable fish, of overdeveloped proboscis, were to bump together, for ever, amid heaped spoils of the sea.

The children swarmed above all—here was multiplication with a vengeance; and the number of very old persons, of either sex, was almost equally remarkable; the very old persons being in equal vague occupation of the doorstep, pavement, curbstone, gutter, roadway, and every one alike using the street for overflow. As overflow, in the whole quarter, is the main fact of life—I was to learn later on that, with the exception of some shy corner of Asia, no district in the world known to the statistician has so many inhabitants to the yard—the scene hummed with the human presence beyond any I had ever faced in quest even of refreshment; producing part of the impression, moreover, no doubt, as a direct consequence of the intensity of the Jewish aspect. This, I think, makes the individual Jew more of a concentrated person, savingly possessed of everything that is in him, than any other human, noted at random—or is it simply, rather, that the unsurpassed strength of the race permits of the chopping into myriads of fine fragments without loss of race-quality? There are small strange animals, known to natural history, snakes or worms, I believe, who, when cut into pieces, wriggle away contentedly and live in the snippet as completely as in the whole. So the denizens of the New York Ghetto, heaped as thick as the splinters on the table of a glass-blower, had each, like the fine glass particle, his or her individual share of the whole hard glitter of Israel. This diffused intensity, as I have called it, causes any array of Jews to resemble (if I may be allowed another image) some long nocturnal street where every window in every house shows a maintained light. The advanced age of so many of the figures, the ubiquity of the children, carried out in fact this analogy; they were all there for race, and not, as it were, for reason: that excess of lurid meaning, in some of the old men's and old women's faces in particular, would have been absurd, in the conditions, as a really directed attention—it could only be the gathered past of Israel mechanically pushing through. The way, at the same time, this chapter of history did, all that evening, seem to push, was a matter that made the "ethnic" apparition again sit like a skeleton at the feast. It was fairly as if I could see the spectre grin while the talk of the hour gave me, across the board, facts and figures, chapter and verse, for the extent of the Hebrew conquest of New York. With a reverence for intellect, one should doubtless have drunk in tribute to an intellectual people; but I remember being at no time more conscious of that merely portentous element, in the aspects of American growth, which reduces to inanity any marked dismay quite as much as any high elation. The portent is one of too many—you always come back, as I have hinted, with your easier gasp, to *that*: it will be time enough to sigh or to shout when the relation of the particular appearance to all the other relations shall have cleared itself up. Phantasmagoric for me, accordingly, in a high degree, are the interesting hours I here glance at content to remain—setting in this respect, I recognize, an excellent example to all the rest of the New York phantasmagoria. Let me speak of the remainder only as phantasmagoric too, so that I may both the more kindly recall it and the sooner have done with it.

New York City Hall

From "New York Revisited," in The American Scene,
1907. In The American Scene, James often complains
about the thinness of American culture and an "absence of penetralia." Although despairing of the "original sin of the longitudinal avenues perpetually, yet
meanly intersected" in Manhattan, he initially has
some hope for layered mystery in the fine French renaissance palace that is New York's City Hall.

The consistency of this effort, under difficulties, has been the
story that brings tears to the eyes of the hovering kindly critic,
and it is through his tears, no doubt, that such a personage
reads the best passages of the tale and makes out the proportions of the object. Mine, I recognize, didn't prevent my seeing
that the pale yellow marble (or whatever it may be) of the City
Hall has lost, by some late excoriation, the remembered charm
of its old surface, the pleasant promiscuous patina of time; but
the perfect taste and finish, the reduced yet ample scale, the
harmony of parts, the just proportions, the modest classic
grace, the living look of the type aimed at, these things, with
gaiety of detail undiminished and "quaintness" of effect aug-
mented, are all there; and I see them, as I write, in that glow of
appreciation which made it necessary, of a fine June morning,
that I should somehow pay the whole place my respects. The
simplest, in fact the only way, was, obviously, to pass under the
charming portico and brave the consequences: this impunity of
such audacities being, in America, one of the last of the lessons
the repatriated absentee finds himself learning. The crushed spirit

NEW YORK CITY HALL

he brings back from European discipline never quite rises to the height of the native argument, the brave sense that the public, the civic building is his very own, for any honest use, so that he may tread even its most expensive pavements and staircases (and very expensive, for the American citizen, these have lately become,) without a question asked. This further and further unchallenged penetration begets in the perverted person I speak of a really romantic thrill: it is like some assault of the dim seraglio, with the guards bribed, the eunuchs drugged and one's life carried in one's hand. The only drawback to such freedom is that penetralia it is so easy to penetrate fail a little of a due impressiveness, and that if stationed sentinels are bad for the temper of the freeman they are good for the "prestige" of the building.

The absence of penetralia

From "Boston," in The American Scene, 1907. *Visiting the Boston Public Library, James again complains of "the thinness of tone" of so many American cultural institutions.*

The Boston institution then is a great and complete institution, with this reserve of its striking the restored absentee as practically without *penetralia*. A library without *penetralia* may affect him but as a temple without altars; it will at any rate exemplify the distinction between a benefit given and a benefit taken, a borrowed, a lent, and an owned, an appropriated convenience. The British Museum, the Louvre, the Bibliothèque Nationale, the treasures of South Kensington, are assuredly, under forms, at the disposal of the people; but it is to be observed, I think, that the people walk there more or less under the shadow of the right waited for and conceded. It remains as difficult as it is always interesting, however, to trace the detail (much of it obvious enough, but much more indefinable) of the personal port of a democracy that, unlike the English, is social as well as political. One of these denotements is that social democracies are unfriendly to the preservation of *penetralia;* so that when *penetralia* are of the essence, as in a place of study and meditation, they inevitably go to the wall.

New York power

From "New York Revisited," in The American Scene,
1907. Although The American Scene repeatedly
refers to New York as "the terrible town," the apparently harsh adjective may suggest awe as well as revulsion in a place where James finds "all notes scattered
about . . . joyously romping together."

The aspect the power wears then is indescribable; it is the
power of the most extravagant of cities, rejoicing, as with the
voice of the morning, in its might, its fortune, its unsurpassable
conditions, and imparting to every object and element, to the
motion and expression of every floating, hurrying, panting
thing, to the throb of ferries and tugs, to the plash of waves and
the play of winds and the glint of lights and the shrill of whis-
tles and the quality and authority of breeze-borne cries—all,
practically, a diffused, wasted clamour of *detonations*—something of its sharp free accent and, above all, of its sovereign
sense of being "backed" and able to back. The universal *applied* passion struck me as shining unprecedentedly out of the
composition; in the bigness and bravery and insolence, especially, of everything that rushed and shrieked; in the air as of a
great intricate frenzied dance, half merry, half desperate, or at
least half defiant, performed on the huge watery floor. This appearance of the bold lacing-together, across the waters, of the
scattered members of the monstrous organism—lacing as by
the ceaseless play of an enormous system of steam-shuttles or
electric bobbins (I scarce know what to call them), commensu-
rate in form with their infinite work—does perhaps more than

anything else to give the pitch of the vision of energy. One has
the sense that the monster grows and grows, flinging abroad its
loose limbs even as some unmannered young giant at his
"larks," and that the binding stitches must for ever fly further
and faster and draw harder; the future complexity of the web,
all under the sky and over the sea, becoming thus that of some
colossal set of clockworks, some steel-souled machine-room of
brandished arms and hammering fists and opening and closing
jaws. The immeasurable bridges are but as the horizontal
sheaths of pistons working at high pressure, day and night, and
subject, one apprehends with perhaps inconsistent gloom, to
certain, to fantastic, to merciless multiplication. In the light of
this apprehension indeed the breezy brightness of the Bay puts
on the semblance of the vast white page that awaits beyond any
other perhaps the black overscoring of science.

American teeth

From "New York: Social Notes," in The American
Scene, 1907. After long residence in England, James
comprehends the main differences between his adopted
home and his native land.

Why should the general "feeling" for the boot, in the United
States, be so mature, so evolved, and the feeling for the hat lag
at such a distance behind it? The standard as to that article of
dress struck me as, everywhere, of the lowest; governed by no
consensus of view, custom or instinct, no sense of its "vital importance" in the manly aspect. And yet the wearer of any loose
improvisation in the way of a head-cover will testify as frankly,
in his degree, to the extreme consideration given by the community at large, as I have intimated, to the dental question. The
terms in which this evidence is presented are often, among the
people, strikingly artless, but they are a marked advance on
the omnipresent opposite signs, those of a systematic detachment
from the chair of anguish, with which any promiscuous "European" exhibition is apt to bristle. I remember to have heard it
remarked by a French friend, of a young woman who had returned to her native land after some years of domestic service
in America, that she had acquired there, with other advantages,
le sourire Californien, and the "Californian" smile, indeed, expressed, more or less copiously, in undissimulated cubes of the
precious metal, plays between lips that render scant other tribute to civilization. The greater interest, in this connection, however, is that impression of the state and appearance of the teeth
viewed among the "refined" as supremely important, which

the restored absentee, long surrounded elsewhere with the strangest cynicisms of indifference on this article, makes the subject of one of his very first notes. Every one, in "society," has good, handsome, pretty, has above all cherished and tended, teeth; so that the offered spectacle, frequent in other societies, of strange irregularities, protrusions, deficiencies, fangs and tusks and cavities, is quite refreshingly and consolingly absent. The consequences of care and forethought, from an early age, thus write themselves on the facial page distinctly and happily, and it is not too much to say that the total show is, among American aspects, cumulatively charming. One sees it sometimes balance, for charm, against a greater number of less fortunate items, in that totality, than one would quite know how to begin estimating.

A young priest apart from
the Roman carnival

From "A Roman Holiday," in Italian Hours, *1909.
James has just reported that, while observing the noisy
celebration of the Roman carnival, "I stood regardful,
I suppose, but with a peculiarly tempting blankness of
visage, for in a moment I received half a bushel of
flour on my too-philosophic head." With "ears full of
flour," he turns away from the crowd and seeks a quiet
place in the city.*

Beyond these stands a small church with a front so modest that
you hardly recognise it till you see the leather curtain. I never
see a leather curtain without lifting it; it is sure to cover a constituted *scene* of some sort—good, bad or indifferent. The scene
this time was meagre—whitewash and tarnished candlesticks
and mouldy muslin flowers being its principal features. I
shouldn't have remained if I hadn't been struck with the attitude of the single worshipper—a young priest kneeling before
one of the side-altars, who, as I entered, lifted his head and
gave me a sidelong look so charged with the languor of devotion that he immediately became an object of interest. He was
visiting each of the altars in turn and kissing the balustrade beneath them. He was alone in the church, and indeed in the
whole region. There were no beggars even at the door; they
were plying their trade on the skirts of the Carnival. In the entirely deserted place he alone knelt for religion, and as I sat respectfully by it seemed to me I could hear in the perfect silence
the far-away uproar of the maskers. It was my late impression
of these frivolous people, I suppose, joined with the extraordi-

nary gravity of the young priest's face—his pious fatigue, his droning prayer and his isolation—that gave me just then and there a supreme vision of the religious passion, its privations and resignations and exhaustions and its terribly small share of amusement. He was young and strong and evidently of not too refined a fibre to enjoy the Carnival; but, planted there with his face pale with fasting and his knees stiff with praying, he seemed so stern a satire on it and on the crazy thousands who were preferring it to *his* way, that I half expected to see some heavenly portent out of a monastic legend come down and confirm his choice. Yet I confess that though I wasn't enamoured of the Carnival myself, his seemed a grim preference and this forswearing of the world a terrible game—a gaining one only if your zeal never falters; a hard fight when it does. In such an hour, to a stout young fellow like the hero of my anecdote, the smell of incense must seem horribly stale and the muslin flowers and gilt candlesticks to figure no great bribe. And it wouldn't have helped him much to think that not so very far away, just beyond the Forum, in the Corso, there was sport for the million, and for nothing. I doubt on the other hand whether my young priest had thought of this. He had made himself a temple out of the very elements of his innocence, and his prayers followed each other too fast for the tempter to slip in a whisper.

VIII

NAMES

The accustomed Jamesian forgets how strange it can seem that someone named Fleda Vetch is presented as an attractive heroine, or that two remarkable women fall in love with a young man named Merton Densher. If such Jamesian names generally lose their oddity after only a few pages, it is in part because of the magnificent idiosyncrasy of the entire Jamesian universe. Yet behind many of the names James considered or used for characters in his novels and tales, there surely remains a playful and often sly impulse.

FROM THE FICTION

Fleda Vetch in *The Spoils of Poynton*
Beale Farange in *What Maisie Knew*
Booby Manger in *The Awkward Age*
Merton Densher in *The Wings of the Dove*
Urania Lendon and Goodwood Grindon in *The Tragic Muse*
Peregrine Midmore in *The Sense of the Past*
Hyacinth Robinson in *The Princess Casamassima*
Henrietta Stackpole and Caspar Goodwood in *The Portrait of a Lady*
Baroness Eugenia-Camilla-Delores Young Münster of Silberstadt-Schreckenstein in *The Europeans*
Fanny Assingham in *The Golden Bowl*
Fanny Knocker in "The Wheel of Time"
Maggie Mangler in "The Chaperon"
Alfred Bonus in "Collaboration"
Dolcino Ambient in "The Author of Beltraffio"
Paul Overt in "The Lesson of the Master"
Remson Sturch in "The Special Type"
Newton Winch in "A Round of Visits"
Ulick Moreen in "The Pupil"
Cuthbert Frush in "The Third Person"
Lady Beadel-Muffet, the Misses Beadel-Muffet, Miranda Beadel-Muffet, and Sir A.B.C. Beadel-Muffet K.C.B., M.P., in "The Papers"

FROM THE NOTEBOOKS

Dexter Frere, Lucky Da Costa, Peregrine King, Lucy Curd, Oddsley Brasher, Tagus Shout, Wenty Hench, Cridge, Noad, Grunlus, Florimond, Frankenshaw, Olimpino, Lightbody, Busk, Squirl, Secretan, Oriel, Jump, Theory, Lupus, Maplethorpe, Fury, Trist, Croucher, Buttery, Ermelinda, Lonely, Trantum,

Peachey, Pontifex, Suchbury, Gleed, Six, Gamage, Fluid, Quibbler, Chick, Lumb, Yeo, Void, Funnel, Ulic, Fade, Wharton, Bullet, Douce, Twentyman, Runting, Scruby, Keep, Vigors, Film, Jury, Cubit Gole, Yellowley, Farthing, Pudney, Taunt, Punchard, Dunderdale, Bygrave, Zambra, Negretti, Bing, Bing-Bing, Popkiss, Peckover, Alum, Pillow, Gracedew, Bounce, Smout, Daft, Buddle, Parm, Dainty, Slight, Cloak, Vizard, Overend, Balbeck, Maliphant, Sneath, Tocs, Bleat, Thanks, Pilbeam, Husk, Murkle, Mockbeggar, Osprey, Blint, Blay, Podd, Tant, Mant, Budgett, Smallpiece, Grabham, Crapp, Didcock, Putchin, Coxeter, Cockster, Dickwinter, Tester, Player, Hoy, Doy, Boys, and Polycarp.

IX

PARODY

Few of the many parodies of Henry James are successful. The following two are among the best—and James knew them both. Frank Moore Colby's very brief imitation, imbedded as it was in a sly essay, disturbed him; in *A Backward Glance* Edith Wharton notes her regret at having been the one who had shown him the piece: "I shall never forget the misery, the mortification even, which tried to conceal itself behind an air of offended dignity." Of course parody was not Colby's main point, and his essay began with the following: "Some time ago, when Henry James wrote an essay on women that brought to my cheek the hot, rebellious blush, I said nothing about it, thinking that perhaps, after all, the man's style was his sufficient fig leaf and that few would see how shocking he really was." But Edmund Gosse reported that James read Max Beerbohm's *A Christmas Garland* "with the most extraordinary vivacity and appreciation." As to James's reaction to the specific parody itself, Gosse informed Beerbohm that their friend "desired me to let you know at once that no one can have read it with more wonder and delight than he." But the James biographer Leon Edel asserted an unsettling effect: so acute was the little Beerbohm masterpiece that after James read it, he "felt that he was parodying himself."

Frank Moore Colby

from IN DARKEST JAMES

In *Imaginary Obligations*, 1904

"If—" she sparkled.

"If!" he asked. He had lurched from the meaning for a moment.

"I might"—she replied abundantly.

His eye had eaten the meaning—"Me!" he gloriously burst.

"Precisely," she thrilled. "How splendidly you *do* understand."

Max Beerbohm

THE MOTE IN THE MIDDLE DISTANCE
BY H*NRY J*MES

In *A Christmas Garland*, 1912

It was with the sense of a, for him, very memorable something
that he peered now into the immediate future, and tried, not
without compunction, to take that period up where he had,
prospectively, left it. But just where the deuce *had* he left it?
The consciousness of dubiety was, for our friend, not, this
morning, quite yet clean-cut enough to outline the figures on
what she had called his "horizon," between which and himself
the twilight was indeed of a quality somewhat intimidating. He
had run up, in the course of time, against a good number of
"teasers"; and the function of teasing them back—of, as it
were, giving them, every now and then, "what for"—was in
him so much a habit that he would have been at a loss had
there been, on the face of it, nothing to lose. Oh, he always had
offered rewards, of course—had ever so liberally pasted the
windows of his soul with staring appeals, minute descriptions,
promises that knew no bounds. But the actual recovery of the
article—the business of drawing and crossing the cheque,
blotched though this were with tears of joy—had blankly appeared to him rather in the light of a sacrilege, casting, he
sometimes felt, a palpable chill on the fervour of the next quest.
It was just this fervour that was threatened as, raising himself
on his elbow, he stared at the foot of his bed. That his eyes refused to rest there for more than the fraction of an instant, may
be taken—*was*, even then, taken by Keith Tantalus—as a hint
of his recollection that after all the phenomenon wasn't to be
singular. Thus the exact repetition, at the foot of Eva's bed, of

the shape pendulous at the foot of *his* was hardly enough to account for the fixity with which he envisaged it, and for which
he was to find, some years later, a motive in the (as it turned
out) hardly generous fear that Eva had already made the great investigation "on her own." Her very regular breathing presently
reassured him that, if she *had* peeped into "her" stocking, she
must have done so in sleep. Whether he should wake her now,
or wait for their nurse to wake them both in due course, was a
problem presently solved by a new development. It was plain
that his sister was now watching him between her eyelashes.
He had half expected that. She really was—he had often told
her that she really was—magnificent; and her magnificence was
never more obvious than in the pause that elapsed before she
all of a sudden remarked, "They so very indubitably *are,* you
know!"

It occurred to him as befitting Eva's remoteness, which was a
part of Eva's magnificence, that her voice emerged somewhat
muffled by the bedclothes. She was ever, indeed, the most tele-
phonic of her sex. In talking to Eva you always had, as it were,
your lips to the receiver. If you didn't try to meet her fine eyes,
it was that you simply couldn't hope to: there were too many
dark, too many buzzing and bewildering and all frankly not ne-
gotiable leagues in between. Snatches of other voices seemed
often to interlude themselves in the parley; and your loyal effort not to overhear these was complicated by your fear of
missing what Eva might be twittering. "Oh, you certainly
haven't, my dear, the trick of propinquity!" was a thrust she
had once parried by saying that, in that case, *he* hadn't—to
which his unspoken rejoinder that she had caught her tone
from the peevish young women at the Central seemed to him (if
not perhaps in the last, certainly in the last but one, analysis) to
lack finality. With Eva, he had found, it was always safest to
"ring off." It was with a certain sense of his rashness in the
matter, therefore, that he now, with an air of feverishly "holding the line," said, "Oh, as to that!"

Had *she,* he presently asked himself, "rung off"? It was
characteristic of our friend—was indeed "him all over"—that
his fear of what she was going to say was as nothing to his fear
of what she might be going to leave unsaid. He had, in his con-

verse with her, been never so conscious as now of the intervening leagues; they had never so insistently beaten the drum of his ear; and he caught himself in the act of awfully computing, with a certain statistical passion, the distance between Rome and Boston. He has never been able to decide which of these points he was psychically the nearer to at the moment when Eva, replying, "Well, one does, anyhow, leave a margin for the pretex, you know!" made him, for the first time in his life, wonder whether she were not more magnificent than even he had ever given her credit for being. Perhaps it was to test this theory, or perhaps merely to gain time, that he now raised himself to his knees, and, leaning with outstretched arm towards the foot of his bed, made as though to touch the stocking which Santa Claus had, overnight, left dangling there. His posture, as he stared obliquely at Eva, with a sort of beaming defiance, recalled to him something seen in an "illustration." This reminiscence, however—if such it was, save in the scarred, the poor dear old woebegone and so very beguilingly *not* refractive mirror of the moment—took a peculiar twist from Eva's behaviour. She had, with startling suddenness, sat bolt upright, and looked to him as if she were overhearing some tragedy at the other end of the wire, where, in the nature of things, she was unable to arrest it. The gaze she fixed on her extravagant kinsman was of a kind to make him wonder how he contrived to remain, as he beautifully did, rigid. His prop was possibly the reflection that flashed on him that, if *she* abounded in attenuations, well, hang it all, so did *he*! It was simply a difference of plane. Readjust the "values," as painters say, and there you were! He was to feel that he was only too crudely "there" when, leaning further forward, he laid a chubby forefinger on the stocking, causing that receptacle to rock ponderously to and fro. This effect was more expected than the tears which started to Eva's eyes and the intensity with which "Don't you," she exclaimed, "see?"

"The mote in the middle distance?" he asked. "Did you ever, my dear, know me to see anything else? I tell you it blocks out everything. It's a cathedral, it's a herd of elephants, it's the whole habitable globe. Oh, it's, believe me, of an obsessiveness!" But his sense of the one thing it *didn't* block out from his purview enabled him to launch at Eva a speculation as to just how far Santa Claus had, for the particular occasion, gone. The gauge, for both of them, of this seasonable distance seemed almost blatantly suspended in the silhouettes of the two stockings. Over and above the basis of (presumably) sweetmeats in the toes and heels, certain extrusions stood for a very plenary fulfilment of desire. And since Eva *had* set her heart on a doll of ample proportions and practicable eyelids—*had* asked that most admirable of her sex, their mother, for it with not less directness than he himself had put into his demand for a sword and helmet—her coyness now struck Keith as lying near to, at indeed a hardly measurable distance from, the border line of his patience. If she didn't *want* the doll, why the deuce had she made such a point of getting it? He was perhaps on the verge of putting this question to her, when, waving her hand to include both stockings, she said, "Of course, my dear, you *do* see. There they are, and you know I know you know we wouldn't, either of us, dip a finger into them." With a vibrancy of tone that seemed to bring her voice quite close to him, "One doesn't," she added, "violate the shrine—pick the pearl from the shell!"

Even had the answering question "Doesn't one just?" which for an instant hovered on the tip of his tongue, been uttered, it could not have obscured for Keith the change which her magnificence had wrought in him. Something, perhaps, of the bigotry of the convert was already discernible in the way that, averting his eyes, he said, "One doesn't even peer." As to whether, in the years that have elapsed since he said this, either of our friends (now adult) has, in fact, "peered," is a question which, whenever I call at the house, I am tempted to put to one or other of them. But any regret I may feel in my invariable failure to "come up to the scratch" of yielding to this temptation is balanced, for me, by my impression—my sometimes all but throned and anointed certainty—that the answer, if vouchsafed, would be in the negative.

X

LEGACY

The Muses have been notoriously stingy with honorific titles, and of course it took more than a university degree to make Boswell's distinguished friend into the icon known as Dr. Johnson. When Joseph Conrad began addressing his own distinguished friend as *"Cher Maître,"* the appellation took, and soon James was being called "the Master" by many contemporaries, and then by the next generation of writers, and then by the next. Henry James's influence on the twentieth century was widespread and profound, and the following passages merely suggest a range of appreciation by some prominent figures. For consideration of the luminous shadow James cast on literature, film, the visual arts, and even music, see Adeline R. Tintner, *Henry James's Legacy: The Afterlife of His Figure and Fiction.*

W. H. Auden

AT THE GRAVE OF HENRY JAMES

1941

The snow, less intransigeant than their marble,
Has left the defence of whiteness to these tombs;
   For all the pools at my feet
Accommodate blue now, and echo such clouds as occur
To the sky, and whatever bird or mourner the passing
   Moment remarks they repeat

While the rocks, named after singular spaces
Within which images wandered once that caused
   All to tremble and offend,
Stand here in an innocent stillness, each marking the spot
Where one more series of errors lost its uniqueness
   And novelty came to an end.

To whose real advantage were such transactions
When words of reflection were exchanged for trees?
   What living occasion can
Be just to the absent? O noon but reflects on itself,
And the small taciturn stone that is the only witness
   To a great and talkative man

Has no more judgement than my ignorant shadow
Of odious comparisons or distant clocks
   Which challenge and interfere
With the heart's instantaneous reading of time, time that is
A warm enigma no longer in you for whom I
   Surrender my private cheer.

Startling the awkward footsteps of my apprehension,
The flushed assault of your recognition is
   The *donnée* of this doubtful hour:
O stern proconsul of intractable provinces,
O poet of the difficult, dear addicted artist,
   Assent to my soil and flower.

As I stand awake on our solar fabric,
That primary machine, the earth, which gendarmes, banks,
   And aspirin pre-suppose,
On which the clumsy and sad may all sit down,
                                          and any who will
Say their a-ha to the beautiful, the common locus
   Of the master and the rose.

Our theatre, scaffold, and erotic city
Where all the infirm species are partners in the act
   Of encroachment bodies crave,
Though solitude in death is *de rigueur* for their flesh
And the self-denying hermit flies as it approaches
   Like the carnivore to a cave.

That its plural numbers may unite in meaning,
Its vulgar tongues unravel the knotted mass
   Of the improperly conjunct,
Open my eyes now to all its hinted significant forms,
Sharpen my ears to detect amid its brilliant uproar
   The low thud of the defunct.

O dwell, ironic at my living centre,
Half ancestor, half child; because the actual self
   Round whom time revolves so fast
Is so afraid of what its motions might possibly do
That the actor is never there when his really important
   Acts happen. Only the past

Is present, no one about but the dead as,
Equipped with a few inherited odds and ends,
   One after another we are

Fired into life to seek that unseen target where all
Our equivocal judgements are judged and resolved in
    One whole Alas or Hurrah.

And only the unborn remark the disaster
When, though it makes no difference to the pretty airs
    The bird of Appetite sings,
And Amour Propre is his usual amusing self,
Out from the jungle of an undistinguished moment
    The flexible shadow springs.

Now more than ever, when torches and snare-drum
Excite the squat women of the saurian brain
    Till a milling mob of fears
Breaks in insultingly on anywhere, when in our dreams
Pigs play on the organs and the blue sky runs shrieking
    As the Crack of Doom appears,

Are the good ghosts needed with the white magic
Of their subtle loves. War has no ambiguities
    Like a marriage; the result
Required of its *affaire fatale* is simple and sad,
The physical removal of all human objects
    That conceal the Difficult.

Then remember me that I may remember
The test we have to learn to shudder for is not
    An historical event,
That neither the low democracy of a nightmare nor
An army's primitive tidiness may deceive me
    About our predicament,

That catastrophic situation which neither
Victory nor defeat can annul; to be
    Deaf yet determined to sing,
To be lame and blind yet burning for the Great Good Place,
To be radically corrupt yet mournfully attracted
    By the Real Distinguished Thing.

And shall I not specially bless you as, vexed with
My little inferior questions, to-day I stand
    Beside the bed where you rest
Who opened such passionate arms to your *Bon* when It ran
Towards you with Its overwhelming reasons pleading
    All beautifully in Its breast?

O with what innocence your hand submitted
To those formal rules that help a child to play,
    While your heart, fastidious as
A delicate nun, remained true to the rare noblesse
Of your lucid gift and, for its own sake, ignored the
    Resentful muttering Mass,

Whose ruminant hatred of all which cannot
Be simplified or stolen is still at large;
    No death can assuage its lust
To vilify the landscape of Distinction and see
The heart of the Personal brought to a systolic standstill,
    The Tall to diminished dust.

Preserve me, Master, from its vague incitement;
Yours be the disciplinary image that holds
    Me back from agreeable wrong
And the clutch of eddying muddle, lest Proportion shed
The alpine chill of her shrugging editorial shoulder
    On my loose impromptu song.

Suggest; so may I segregate my disorder
Into districts of prospective value: approve;
    Lightly, lightly, then, may I dance
Over the frontier of the obvious and fumble no more
In the old limp pocket of the minor exhibition,
    Nor riot with irrelevance,

And no longer shoe geese or water stakes, but
Bolt in my day my grain of truth to the barn
    Where tribulations may leap
With their long-lost brothers at last in the festival

Of which not one has a dissenting image, and the
   Flushed immediacy sleep.

Into this city from the shining lowlands
Blows a wind that whispers of uncovered skulls
   And fresh ruins under the moon,
Of hopes that will not survive the *secousse* of this spring
Of blood and flames, of the terror that walks by night and
   The sickness that strikes at noon.

All will be judged. Master of nuance and scruple,
Pray for me and for all writers living or dead;
   Because there are many whose works
Are in better taste than their lives; because there is no end
To the vanity of our calling: make intercession
   For the treason of all clerks.

Because the darkness is never so distant,
And there is never much time for the arrogant
   Spirit to flutter its wings,
Or the broken bone to rejoice, or the cruel to cry
For Him whose property is always to have mercy, the author
   And giver of all good things.

Joseph Conrad

from HENRY JAMES: AN APPRECIATION

North American Review, January 1905

In one of his critical studies, published some fifteen years ago, Mr. Henry James claims for the novelist the standing of the historian as the only adequate one, as for himself and before his audience. I think that the claim cannot be contested, and that the position is unassailable. Fiction is history, human history, or it is nothing. But it is also more than that; it stands on firmer ground, being based on the reality of forms and the observation of social phenomena, whereas history is based on documents, and the reading of print and handwriting—on second-hand impression. Thus fiction is nearer truth. But let that pass. A historian may be an artist too, and a novelist is a historian, the preserver, the keeper, the expounder, of human experience. As is meet for a man of his descent and tradition, Mr. Henry James is the historian of fine consciences.

Of course, this is a general statement; but I don't think its truth will be, or can be questioned. Its fault is that it leaves so much out; and, besides, Mr. Henry James is much too considerable to be put into the nutshell of a phrase. The fact remains that he has made his choice, and that his choice is justified up to the hilt by the success of his art. He has taken for himself the greater part. The range of a fine conscience covers more good and evil than the range of conscience which may be called, roughly, not fine; a conscience, less troubled by the nice discrimination of shades of conduct. A fine conscience is more concerned with essentials; its triumphs are more perfect, if less profitable, in a worldly sense. There is, in short, more truth in its working for a historian to detect and to show. It is a thing of infinite complication and suggestion. None of these escapes the

art of Mr. Henry James. He has mastered the country, his domain, not wild indeed, but full of romantic glimpses, of deep
shadows and sunny places. There are no secrets left within his
range. He has disclosed them as they should be disclosed—that
is, beautifully. And, indeed, ugliness has but little place in this
world of his creation. Yet, it is always felt in the truthfulness of
his art; it is there, it surrounds the scene, it presses close upon
it. It is made visible, tangible, in the struggles, in the contacts of
the fine consciences, in their perplexities, in the sophism of
their mistakes. For a fine conscience is naturally a virtuous one.
What is natural about it is just its fineness, an abiding sense of
the intangible, ever-present, right. It is most visible in their ultimate triumph, in their emergence from miracle, through an energetic act of renunciation. Energetic, not violent: the distinction is
wide, enormous, like that between substance and shadow.

Through it all Mr. Henry James keeps a firm hold of the substance, of what is worth having, of what is worth holding. The
contrary opinion has been, if not absolutely affirmed, then at
least implied, with some frequency. To most of us, living will-
ingly in a sort of intellectual moonlight, in the faintly reflected
light of truth, the shadows so firmly renounced by Mr. Henry
James's men and women, stand out endowed with extraordinary value, with a value so extraordinary that their rejection
offends, by its uncalled-for scrupulousness, those business-like
instincts which a careful Providence has implanted in our
breasts. And, apart from that just cause of discontent, it is obvious that a solution by rejection must always present a certain
lack of finality, especially startling when contrasted with the
usual methods of solution by rewards and punishments, by
crowned love, by fortune, by a broken leg or a sudden death.
Why the reading public which, as a body, has never laid upon
a story-teller the command to be an artist, should demand from
him this sham of Divine Omnipotence, is utterly incomprehen-
sible. But so it is; and these solutions are legitimate inasmuch as
they satisfy the desire for finality, for which our hearts yearn
with a longing greater than the longing for the loaves and fishes
of this earth. Perhaps the only true desire of mankind, coming
thus to light in its hours of leisure, is to be set at rest. One is
never set at rest by Mr. Henry James's novels. His books end as

an episode in life ends. You remain with the sense of the life still going on; and even the subtle presence of the dead is felt in that silence that comes upon the artist-creation when the last word has been read. It is eminently satisfying, but it is not final. Mr. Henry James, great artist and faithful historian, never attempts the impossible.

T. S. Eliot

from IN MEMORY

The Little Review, August 1918

He was a critic who preyed not upon ideas, but upon living be-
ings. It is criticism which is in a very high sense creative. The
characters, the best of them, are each a distinct success of creation: Daisy Miller's small brother is one of these. Done in a
clean flat drawing, each is extracted out of a reality of its own,
substantial enough: everything given is true for that individual;
but what is given is chosen with great art for its place in a general scheme. The general scheme is not one character, nor a
group of characters in a plot or merely in a crowd. The focus is
a situation, a relation, an atmosphere, to which the characters
pay tribute, but being allowed to give only what the writer
wants. The real hero, in any of James's stories, is a social entity
of which men and women are constituents. It is, in The Europeans, that particular conjunction of people at the Wentworth
house, a situation in which several memorable scenes are
merely timeless parts, only occurring necessarily in succession.
In this aspect, you can say that James is dramatic; as what
Pinero and Mr. Jones used to do for a large public, James does
for the intelligent. It is the chemistry of these subtle substances,
these curious precipitates and explosive gases which are suddenly formed by the contact of mind with mind, that James is
unequalled. Compared with James's, other novelists' characters
seem to be only accidentally in the same book. Naturally, there
is something terrible, as disconcerting as a quicksand, in this
discovery, though it only becomes absolutely dominant in such
stories as The Turn of the Screw. It is partly foretold in
Hawthorne, but James carried it much farther. And it makes

the reader, as well as the personae, uneasily the victim of a merciless clairvoyance.

James's critical genius comes out most tellingly in his mastery over, his baffling escape from, Ideas; a mastery and an escape which are perhaps the last test of a superior intelligence. He had a mind so fine that no idea could violate it. Englishmen, with their uncritical admiration (in the present age) for France, like to refer to France as the Home of Ideas; a phrase which, if we could twist it into truth, or at least a compliment, ought to mean that in France ideas are very severely looked after; not allowed to stray, but preserved for the inspection of civic pride in a Jardin des Plantes, and frugally dispatched on occasions of public necessity. England, on the other hand, if it is not the Home of Ideas, has at least become infested with them in about the space of time within which Australia has been overrun by rabbits. In England ideas run wild and pasture on the emotions; instead of thinking with our feelings (a very different thing) we corrupt our feelings with ideas; we produce the political, the emotional idea, evading sensation and thought. George Meredith (a disciple of Carlyle) was fertile in ideas; his epigrams are a facile substitute for observation and inference. Mr. Chesterton's brain swarms with ideas; I see no evidence that it thinks. James in his novels is like the best French critics in maintaining a point of view, a view-point untouched by the parasite idea. He is the most intelligent man of his generation.

Graham Greene

from HENRY JAMES:
THE PRIVATE UNIVERSE

The Lost Childhood and Other Essays, 1951

"Art itself," Conrad wrote, "may be defined as a single-minded attempt to render the highest kind of justice to the visible universe," and no definition in his own prefaces better describes the object Henry James so passionately pursued, if the word visible does not exclude the private vision. If there are times when we feel, in *The Sacred Fount,* even in the exquisite *Golden Bowl,* that the judge is taking too much into consideration, that he could have passed his sentence on less evidence, we have always to admit, as the long record of human corruption unrolls, that he has never allowed us to lose sight of the main case; and because his mind is bent on rendering even evil "the highest kind of justice," the symmetry of his thought lends the whole body of his work the importance of a system.

. . . For his father believed, in his own words, that "the evil or hellish element in our nature, even when out of divine order . . . is yet not only no less vigorous than the latter, but on the contrary much more vigorous, sagacious, and productive of eminent earthly uses" (so one might describe the acquisition of Milly Theale's money). The difference, of course, was greater than the resemblance. The son was not an optimist, he didn't share his father's hopes of the hellish element, he only pitied those who were immersed in it; and it is in the final justice of his pity, the completeness of an analysis which enabled him to pity the most shabby, the most corrupt, of his human actors, that he ranks with the greatest of creative writers. He is as solitary in the history of the novel as Shakespeare in the history of poetry.

Ezra Pound

from HENRY JAMES

The Little Review, August 1918

I am tired of hearing pettiness talked about Henry James's style. The subject has been discussed enough in all conscience, along with the minor James. Yet I have heard no word of the major James, of the hater of tyranny; book after early book against oppression, against all the sordid petty personal crushing oppression, the domination of modern life; not worked out in diagrams of Greek tragedy, not labelled "epos" or "Aeschylus." The outbursts in *The Tragic Muse,* the whole of *The Turn of the Screw,* human liberty, personal liberty, the rights of the individual against all sorts of intangible bondage! The passion of it, the continual passion of it in this man who, fools said, didn't "feel." I have never yet found a man of emotion against whom idiots didn't raise this cry.

And the great labour, this labour of translation, of making America intelligible, of making it possible for individuals to meet across national borders. I think half the American idiom is recorded in Henry James' writing, and whole decades of American life that otherwise would have been utterly lost, wasted, rotting in unhermetic jars of bad writing, of inaccurate writing. No English reader will ever know how good are his New York and his New England; no one who does not see his grandmother's friends in the pages of the American books. The whole great assaying and weighing, the research for the significance of nationality, French, English, American.

Edith Wharton

from A BACKWARD GLANCE

1934

Once again—and again unintentionally—I was guilty of a similar blunder. I was naturally much interested in James's technical theories and experiments, though I thought, and still think, that he tended to sacrifice to them that spontaneity which is the life of fiction. Everything, in the latest novels, had to be fitted into a predestined design, and design, in his strict geometrical sense, is to me one of the least important things in fiction. Therefore, though I greatly admired some of the principles he had formulated, such as that of always letting the tale, as it unfolded, be seen through the mind most capable of reaching to its periphery, I thought it was paying too dear even for such a principle to subordinate to it the irregular and irrelevant movements of life. And one result of the application of his theories puzzled and troubled me. His latest novels, for all their profound moral beauty, seemed to me more and more lacking in atmosphere, more and more severed from that thick nourishing human air in which we all live and move. The characters in "The Wings of the Dove" and "The Golden Bowl" seem isolated in a Crookes tube for our inspection: his stage was cleared like that of the Théâtre Français in the good old days when no chair or table was introduced that was not *relevant to the action* (a good rule for the stage, but an unnecessary embarrassment to fiction). Preoccupied by this, I one day said to him: "What was your idea in suspending the four principal characters in 'The Golden Bowl' in the void? What sort of life did they lead when they were not watching each other, and

LEGACY

fencing with each other? Why have you stripped them of all the *human fringes* we necessarily trail after us through life?"

He looked at me in surprise, and I saw at once that the surprise was painful, and wished I had not spoken. I had assumed that his system was a deliberate one, carefully thought out, and had been genuinely anxious to hear his reasons. But after a pause of reflection he answered in a disturbed voice: "My dear—I didn't know I had!"

Virginia Woolf

from REVIEW OF *THE LETTERS OF*
HENRY JAMES

1920

And so on and so on. There, portentous and prodigious, we
hear unmistakably the voice of Henry James. There, to our
thinking, we have exploded in our ears the report of his enormous, sustained, increasing, and overwhelming love for life. It
issues from whatever tortuous channels and dark tunnels like a
flood at its fullest. There is nothing too little, too large, too remote, too queer for it not to flow round, float off, and make its
own. Nothing in the end has chilled or repressed him; everything has fed and filled him; the saturation is complete. The
labours of the morning might be elaborate and austere. There
remained an irrepressible fund of vitality which the flying hand
at midnight addressed fully and affectionately to friend after
friend, each sentence, from the whole fling of his person to the
last snap of his fingers, firmly fashioned and throwing out at its
swiftest well-nigh incredible felicities of phrase.

The only difficulty, perhaps, was to find an envelope that
would contain the bulky product, or any reason, when two
sheets were blackened, for not filling a third. Truly, Lamb
House was not sanctuary, but rather a "small, crammed, and
wholly unlucrative hotel," and the hermit no meagre solitary
but a tough and even stoical man of the world, English in his
humour, Johnsonian in his sanity, who lived every second with
insatiable gusto and in the flux and fury of his impressions
obeyed his own injunction to remain "as solid and fixed and
dense as you can." For to be as subtle as Henry James one must
also be as robust; to enjoy his power of exquisite selection, one

must have "lived and loved and cursed and floundered and enjoyed and suffered," and, with the appetite of a giant, have swallowed the whole.

Yet, if he shared with magnanimity, if he enjoyed hugely, there remained something incommunicable, something reserved, as if in the last resort, it was not to us that he turned, nor from us that he received, nor into our hands that he placed his offerings. There they stand, the many books, products of "an inexhaustible sensibility," all with the final seal upon them of artistic form, which, as it imposes its stamp, sets apart the object thus consecrated and makes it no longer part of ourselves. In this impersonality the maker himself desired to share—"to take it," as he said, "wholly, exclusively with the pen (the style, the genius) and absolutely not at all with the person," to be "the mask without the face," the alien in our midst, the worker who when his work is done turns even from that and reserves his confidence for the solitary hour, like that at midnight when, alone on the threshold of creation, Henry James speaks aloud to himself "and the prospect clears and flushes, and my poor blest old genius pats me so admirably and lovingly on the back that I turn, I screw round, and bend my lips to passionately, in my gratitude, kiss its hands." So that is why, perhaps, as life swings and clangs, booms and reverberates, we have the sense of an altar of service, of sacrifice, to which, as we pass out, we bend the knee.

Suggestions for Further Reading

FICTION

In 1913 Mrs. G. W. Prothero asked James which five of his novels he would recommend to an uninitiated reader. He supplied two lists, the second being the "more 'advanced.'" The first named *Roderick Hudson, The Portrait of a Lady, The Princess Casamassima, The Wings of the Dove,* and *The Golden Bowl.* The second named *The American, The Tragic Muse, The Wings of the Dove, The Ambassadors,* and *The Golden Bowl.* Perhaps James was being playful (he promised to suggest shorter works at a later time, but "you shall have your little tarts when you have eaten your beef and potatoes"). Today *The Portrait of a Lady* would rank at the top of many lists. *The American* might be the novel to read next (or perhaps first, for some readers find it is less challenging than *Portrait,* and, with its emphatic "international theme," it provides a good introduction to representative concerns). Then, if the reader is still willing, *The Bostonians,* with its strange sexual tension, generally stirs excitement. The revolutionaries and anarchists in *The Princess Casamassima* today strike many false notes, and *Roderick Hudson* has sometimes been judged a heavy-handed story of a troubled young artist. Although James himself recognized structural flaws in *The Tragic Muse,* it has many admirers. The short novel *Washington Square* continues to draw interest; it has been the subject of over a dozen film or television productions (see Susan M. Griffin, ed., *Henry James Goes to the Movies*). *The Spoils of Poynton* is witty, fast, and engaging; the great James biographer Leon Edel once noted that *What Maisie Knew* was his favorite James novel.

Those who would enter into deep James will arrive at the great novels of "the major phase," even if good people sometimes admit to being baffled by the extraordinary exercise of consciousness that marks these masterpieces. Even that defender Ezra Pound judged them as "cobwebby," and in *A Backward Glance,* Edith Wharton would concede that the late novels, "for all their profound moral beauty, seemed to me more and more lacking in atmosphere, more and more severed from that thick nourishing air in which we all live and move." With its brilliant fin-de-siècle setting in Paris, *The Ambassadors,* "quite the best, 'all around,' of my productions," is often judged the most accessible. With its aesthetic pitch, high moral ambiguity, and Venetian climax, *The Wings of the Dove* is a favorite of many readers. The magnificent *The Golden Bowl* is the only novel James included on both lists for Mrs. Prothero.

James's twenty-two novels are listed here. Of his 114 tales—some of considerable length and some categorized as "nouvelles"—the sixteen listed here are of particular interest. (Those marked with an asterisk[*] are included in this edition.)

Novels

Watch and Ward (serially published, 1871; book publication, 1878)

Roderick Hudson (1875)

The American (1877)

The Europeans (1878)

Confidence (1879)

Washington Square (1881)

The Portrait of a Lady (1881)

The Bostonians (1886)

The Princess Casamassima (1886)

The Reverberator (1888)

The Other House (1896; first written as a play and then turned into a novel)

The Spoils of Poynton (1897)

What Maisie Knew (1897)

The Awkward Age (1899)

The Tragic Muse (1900)

The Sacred Fount (1901)

The Wings of the Dove (1902)

The Ambassadors (1903)

The Golden Bowl (1904)

The Outcry (1911; first written as a play and then turned into a novel)

The Ivory Tower (1917; posthumous and incomplete)

The Sense of the Past (1917; posthumous and incomplete)

Selected Tales

Daisy Miller: A Study (1879)

"Pandora" (1884)

"The Aspern Papers" (1888)

"The Pupil" (1891)

*"Brooksmith" (1891)

*"The Real Thing" (1892)

*"The Middle Years" (1893)

"The Altar of the Dead" (1895)

"The Figure in the Carpet" (1896)

"In the Cage" (1898)

The Turn of the Screw (1898)

"The Great Good Place" (1900)

"Maud Evelyn" (1900)

*"The Beast in the Jungle" (1903)

*"The Jolly Corner" (1908)

"The Bench of Desolation" (1910)

TRAVEL

James's finest travel book, the 1907 *The American Scene*, provides brilliant impressions of his American tour of 1904–1905. Although *Italian Hours* was published two years after *The American Scene*, it collects essays written from 1872 to 1909; a comparison of the early and late essays on Venice, Rome, and Naples is particularly rewarding. Neither *English Hours* (published 1905 but with most essays from the 1870s), nor *A Little Tour in France* (1884) is as richly analytical as the American and the Italian travel books.

AUTOBIOGRAPHY AND BIOGRAPHY

As noted in the introduction to the Autobiography section of this book (and fully cited in the Selected Bibliography), a one-volume edition collects James's work in this genre. James's 1903 biography, *William Wetmore Story and His Friends: From Letters, Diaries, and Recollections,* was a commissioned work that holds interest mainly for its evocation of life in the Anglo-American community in Rome.

LITERARY CRITICISM

In a fine two-volume edition, the Library of America publishes over 3,000 pages of literary criticism by James; there are helpful notes and an extensive index (edited by Leon Edel, with the assistance of Mark Wilson, *Henry James: Literary Criticism: French Writers, Other European Writers, the Prefaces to the* New York Edition; and *Henry James: Literary Criticism: Essays on Literature, American Writers, English Writers,* New York: Library of America, 1984); the edition offers 120 pages on Balzac alone, 100 on George Sand ("As a man Madame Sand was admirable. . . ."), and, reprinting James's entire 1879 *Hawthorne* volume as well as some additional later commentary, over 150 pages on Nathaniel Hawthorne. In all, James discusses several hundred writers. Among its many features, the edition also reprints the complete prefaces to the *New York Edition.* Judiciously selected and well edited is Roger Gard, ed., *Henry James: The Critical Muse: Selected Literary Criticism,* London and New York: Penguin, 1984.

PLAYS

For James's initially successful but eventually disastrous excursion into the theater, see Leon Edel, ed., *The Complete Plays of Henry James,* Oxford: Oxford University Press, 1949.

THEATRICAL CRITICISM

For James's reviews of the theater, see Allan Wade, ed., *Henry James: The Scenic Art: Notes on Acting and Drama, 1872–1901,* New Brunswick, N.J.: Rutgers University Press, 1948.

ART CRITICISM

A fine selection of his art criticism is presented in Susan M. Griffin and John L. Sweeney, eds., *Henry James: The Painter's Eye: Notes and Essays on the Pictorial Arts,* Madison: University of Wisconsin Press, 1994 (revised from Sweeney's 1956 edition).

Selected Bibliography

In 1930 Vernon Louis Parrington's *Main Currents in American Thought* promised a comprehensive "interpretation of American literature." The influential study dedicated six pages to Peter Cooper, eight to John Fiske, twelve to William Dean Howells, thirteen to Edward Bellamy, and fourteen to Edwin Lawrence Godkin. Henry James was summed up in less than two pages. Today there are more than 220 critical studies listed among the almost one thousand Henry James entries in the catalog of the Library of Congress.

REFERENCE

American Literary Scholarship, Durham, N.C.: Duke University Press, 1963–present. An annual review of the year's publications in James studies; indispensable for serious research.

Nicola Bradbury, *An Annotated Critical Bibliography of Henry James,* New York: St. Martin's, 1987.

Leon Edel and Dan H. Laurence, with James Rambeau, *A Bibliography of Henry James,* 3rd ed., Oxford: Clarendon Press, 1982.

Leon Edel and Adeline R. Tintner, eds., *The Library of Henry James,* Ann Arbor, Mich.: UMI Research Press, 1987. The catalog of James's own library.

Daniel Mark Fogel, ed., *A Companion to Henry James Studies,* Westport, Conn.: Greenwood Press, 1993. The most comprehensive handbook, on the fiction, the nonfiction, and the criticism; with an excellent annotated bibliography.

Jonathan Freedman, ed., *The Cambridge Companion to Henry James,* Cambridge: Cambridge University Press, 1998. Collects twelve fine essays.

Robert Gale, *A Henry James Encyclopedia,* Westport, Conn.: Greenwood Press. 1989. An invaluable reference tool.

S. Gorley Putt, *Henry James: A Reader's Guide,* Ithaca: Cornell University Press, 1966. Ignores the nonfiction, the criticism, and the work for the theater, but provides a basic discussion of every novel and tale.

WEBSITES

The Henry James Scholar's Guide to Web Sites: http://www2.newpaltz. edu/~hathaway/. An excellent website, conceived and maintained by Richard Hathaway at SUNY–New Paltz. E-texts, links to other Henry James items, an e-journal, concordances, articles and reviews, a discussion group.
(See also Jobe and Gunter, under *Correspondence*.)

JOURNALS

The Henry James Review, 1979–present. A distinguished journal founded by Daniel Mark Fogel.

BIOGRAPHY

Leon Edel, *Henry James: The Untried Years 1843–1870: Vol. I; The Conquest of London 1870–1881: Vol. II; The Middle Years 1882–1895: Vol. III; The Treacherous Years 1895–1901: Vol. IV; The Master 1901–1916: Vol. V;* Philadelphia: Lippincott, 1953–72. The standard biography.

————. *Henry James: A Life,* 1985. The one-volume abridgment of the five-volume biography offers more frank treatment of the issue of homoeroticism and homosexuality.

Philip Horne, *Henry James: A Life in Letters,* New York: Viking, 1999. Choice correspondence linked by shrewd editorial commentary.

Henry James, *A Small Boy and Others,* 1913; *Notes of a Son and Brother,* 1914; *The Middle Years,* 1917. Republished in one volume under the title *Autobiography;* edited with an introduction by Frederick Dupee, New York: Criterion Books, 1956.

Fred Kaplan, *Henry James: The Imagination of Genius,* New York: William Morrow, 1992. The first full biography since Edel; a worthy addition.

R. W. B. Lewis, *The Jameses: A Family Narrative,* New York: Farrar, Straus and Giroux, 1991.

Sheldon Novick, *Henry James: The Young Master,* New York: Random House, 1996. Controversial in its assertion of an active homosexual life.

CORRESPONDENCE

The first volume of *The Complete Letters of Henry James,* edited by Greg W. Zacharias and Pierre Walker, will be published by the University of Nebraska Press in 2003. The edition is planned for at least thirty print volumes, and it will also be accessible on the web and in DVD format. The first volume will publish approximately 100 of the over 10,000 letters that have been catalogued.

Leon Edel, ed., *Henry James Letters,* 4 vols., Cambridge: Harvard University Press, 1974–84.

Stephen H. Jobe and Susan Elizabeth Gunter, eds., *A Calendar of the Letters of Henry James & Biographical Register of Henry James's Correspondents.* "This website provides access to a database of all known letters written by Henry James, and brief biographical information on the recipients of these letters." http://jamescalendar.unl.edu/

(See also Philip Horne, under *Biography.*)

Percy Lubbock, ed., *The Letters of Henry James,* 2 vols., New York: Scribner's, 1920.

Ignas K. Skrupskelis and Elizabeth M. Berkeley, with the assistance of Bernice Grohskopf and Wilma Bradbeer, eds., *The Correspondence of William James: William and Henry,* 3 vols., Charlottesville and London: University Press of Virginia, 1992–94. An essential supplement to Edel and Lubbock.

NOTEBOOKS

Leon Edel and Lyall H. Powers, eds., *The Complete Notebooks of Henry James,* New York: Oxford University Press, 1987.

CRITICISM

This highly selective list includes some groundbreaking works, some works of unusually sustained influence, and for the general student some especially helpful titles. A few studies are included because of their relevance to decisions made for the present edition.

Michael Anesko, *"Friction with the Market": Henry James and the Profession of Authorship,* New York: Oxford University Press, 1986.

John Auchard, *Silence in Henry James: The Heritage of Symbolism and Decadence,* University Park: Penn State Press, 1986.

Millicent Bell, *Meaning in Henry James,* Cambridge: Harvard University Press, 1991.

Sara Blair, *Henry James and the Writing of Race and Nation,* Cambridge: Cambridge University Press, 1996.

Peter Buithenhuis, *The Grasping Imagination: The American Writings of Henry James,* Toronto: University of Toronto Press, 1970.

Oscar Cargill, *The Novels of Henry James,* New York: Macmillan, 1961.

Sarah B. Daugherty, *The Literary Criticism of Henry James,* Athens: Ohio University Press, 1981.

Jonathan Freedman, *Professions of Taste: Henry James, British Aestheticism, and Commodity Culture,* Stanford: Stanford University Press, 1990.

Roger Gard, ed., *Henry James: The Critical Heritage,* London: Routledge & Kegan Paul, 1968.

Susan M. Griffin, *The Historical Eye: The Texture of the Visual in Late James,* Boston: Northeastern University Press, 1991.

———, ed., *Henry James Goes to the Movies,* Lexington: University Press of Kentucky, 2002.

Beverly Haviland, *Henry James's Last Romance: Making Sense of the Past and The American Scene,* Cambridge: Cambridge University Press, 1997.

Richard Hocks, *Henry James and Pragmatistic Thought: A Study in the Relationship Between the Philosophy of William James and the Literary Art of Henry James,* Chapel Hill: University of North Carolina Press, 1974.

Philip Horne, *Henry James and Revision,* Oxford: Clarendon Press, 1990.

Roslyn Jolly, *Henry James: History, Narrative, Fiction,* Oxford: Clarendon Press, 1993.

Vivien Jones, *Henry James the Critic,* London: Macmillan, 1984.

Dorothea Krook, *The Ordeal of Consciousness in Henry James,* Cambridge: Cambridge University Press, 1962.

F. O. Matthiessen, *Henry James: The Major Phase,* Oxford: Clarendon Press, 1944.

David McWhirter, ed., *Henry James's New York Edition: The Construction of Authorship,* Stanford: Stanford University Press, 1995.

Sergio Perosa, *Henry James and the Experimental Novel,* Charlottesville: University Press of Virginia, 1978.

Richard Poirier, *The Comic Sense of Henry James: A Study of the Early Novels,* New York: Oxford University Press, 1967.

Ross Posnock, *The Trial of Curiosity: Henry James, William James, and the Challenge of Modernity*, New York: Oxford University Press, 1991.

John Carlos Rowe, *The Theoretical Dimensions of Henry James*, Madison: University of Wisconsin Press, 1984.

Eve Kosofsky Sedgwick, *The Epistemology of the Closet*, Berkeley: University of California Press, 1990.

Mark Seltzer, *Henry James and the Art of Power*, Ithaca: Cornell University Press, 1984.

Hugh Stevens, *Henry James and Sexuality*, Cambridge: Cambridge University Press, 1998.

Adeline R. Tintner, *The Museum World of Henry James*, Ann Arbor, Mich.: UMI Research Press, 1986; *The Book World of Henry James: Appropriating the Classics*, Ann Arbor, Mich.: UMI Research Press, 1987; *The Cosmopolitan World of Henry James*, Baton Rouge: Louisiana State University Press, 1991; *Henry James and the Lust of the Eyes: Thirteen Artists in His Work*, Baton Rouge: Louisiana State University Press, 1993; *Henry James's Legacy: The Afterlife of His Figure and Fiction*, Baton Rouge: Louisiana State University Press, 1998; *The Twentieth-Century World of Henry James: Changes in His Work after 1900*, Baton Rouge: Louisiana State University Press, 2000.

Priscilla Walton, *The Disruption of the Feminine in Henry James*, Toronto: University of Toronto Press, 1992.

Viola Hopkins Winner, *Henry James and the Visual Arts*, Charlottesville: University Press of Virginia, 1970.

Ruth Bernard Yeazell, *Language and Knowledge in the Late Novels of Henry James*, Chicago: University of Chicago Press, 1976.

Permissions